CW00819051

The Seduction of Mary Kelly

WILLIAM J PERRING

THE SEDUCTION
OF
MARY KELLY

D'ARCY COLLECTION

First published in 2005 by D'Arcy Collection

www.darcycollection.co.uk

Copyright © William J Perring

William J Perring asserts the moral right to
be identified as the author of this work

ISBN 0 9549770 0 9
ISBN 978 0 9549770 0 9
A CIP catalogue record for this book is available from the British Library

This novel is a work of fiction. The murdered women: Emma Smith; Martha Tabram;
Polly Nichols; Annie Chapman; Liz Stride; Katherine Eddowes, and Mary Jane Kelly
are real people, as are Michael Kidney; Lizzie Albrook; Joe and Danny Barnett; John
McCarthy; 'Indian' Harry Bowyer; Walter Ringer; Caroline Maxwell; George Hutchinson;
Dr George Bagster Phillips, and Dr Bond. However, except for a few instances of
documented speech, their characters are invented and should under no circumstances be
considered true and faithful representations of their real-life personae.
All other characters are the product of the author's imagination, and any resemblance to
actual persons, living or dead, is entirely coincidental.

Printed and bound in Great Britain by
Antony Rowe Ltd., Chippenham, Wiltshire

D'Arcy Collection
8 Marlpit Lane
Coulsdon, Surrey CR5 2HB

Kelly did not originally belong to the 'gutter' class. She was a woman of respectable parentage and superior breeding, who had gradually sunk into the state of degradation in which she was existing when she met her terrible death.

The Graphic 17th November 1888

What we know, or think we know, of Mary Kelly comes almost entirely from the accounts of her life she gave to friends and acquaintances. All, or none, could be true.

PROLOGUE

California 1968

The television picture was grainy and indistinct, but still the image of jar upon jar of severed body parts made Beth Williams shiver. 'Did they really need to show that?' she murmured half to herself.

The scene changed to an outside shot of a handcuffed young man, his head lowered, almost shyly, as he walked between the two police officers, the camera following them to the waiting squad car, lingering on it until it drove off and disappeared from view.

'But thank God they've caught him at last.' She turned toward the bed. 'They're already talking about him going down in history as the most famous serial killer since Jack the Ripper.'

'Famous?' The old man lay motionless against the hospital pillow. For days he had been drifting in and out of consciousness, barely clinging to life, but now a little of his old spark seemed to return. 'That's an odd choice of word.'

'Serial killers are big news these days, Jimmy.'

James *Jimmy* Hawkins looked up at the TV screen. 'They always were,' he said as the presenter's face was replaced by a series of black and white photographs showing Victorian London; the streets and alleyways of Whitechapel finally dissolving to show a close-up of a dead woman's face, taken from the foot of the plain wooden coffin in which she lay.

Beth followed his gaze. 'I guess so. It's strange – I've always thought the world was a nicer, safer place back in your day.'

The photograph of the dead woman gave way to another, her rounded features relaxed in death, then another, and still another, this one more horrific, the naked body hanging from mortuary hooks in the same way that dead gunslingers had once been displayed, the savage mutilations to the woman's face and torso clearly visible. Then, lastly, a photograph showing the interior of a room. It wasn't a good photograph, too much contrast made it hard to discern the true subject, so it was several seconds before Beth realised she was looking at the grotesquely mutilated body of a young woman. She wanted to look away, but there was something so horribly compelling about the image that she reached for the volume control instead.

'… *And culminating in the murder of Mary Jane Kelly in the early hours of November ninth, 1888.*' The presenter reappeared, looking stern as he stared out of the screen. '*Despite killing five women, Jack the Ripper was never caught – and to this day his identity remains one of the greatest unsolved mysteries. Thankfully, following today's arrest, the same will not be said about …*'

Beth lowered the volume again and crossed to the bed, looking down at her patient. His eyes were closed once more, and he lay so still that she instinctively felt for his pulse. It was weak, but it was there, and she felt a wave of relief.

For two weeks the old actor had clung on, and in that time she had grown closer to him than she should have allowed. It was unprofessional and she knew it – but in a city where yesterday was ancient history, who else would spare the time for a forgotten old man whose hey-day had been in the silent era. 'Sleep well, Jimmy,' she said.

The television news programme had begun showing photographs of the shy-looking young man's victims: colour snapshots of smiling faces, a chilling twenty-seven in total. Beth shook her head. 'I think the world *was* a safer place back in your day, Jimmy,' she sighed. 'Even the *infamous* Jack the Ripper only killed five.'

In the stillness of the room, the murmured reply was barely audible. '*Three*,' he said, before slipping into unconsciousness once more.

*

Frankie Stoweski was mopping the floor in the hospital reception area as Beth came on duty the following morning. 'Hi, Frankie,' she smiled. 'How's it going?'

He grinned. 'Bad. Real, real bad. It's going to end in bloodshed.'

'Doesn't it always?'

'Not *always* – but this guy Nero is really asking for it.' He pulled a heavy book from the cleaning cart and handed it to her. 'Did you know he used to go out at night, dressed as an ordinary Joe, and attack people – just for the heck of it. Wouldn't surprise me if he hadn't killed even more people than this guy they've just arrested.'

Beth looked at the book. 'The Roman Empire?' she said, handing it back to him. 'I thought you were still working through the civil war?'

'No, finished that last week.'

She laughed. 'How on earth do you remember all this stuff you read?'

'Don't know. Just got that kind of brain, I guess.' He shrugged, put the book back on the cart, and picked up the mop. 'So how's it going with that new boyfriend? What was his name? Richard? Still certain he's the one?'

'Uh-uhhh,' she grinned. 'He just needs a little more convincing that *I'm* the one.' She made to leave – then paused. 'Frankie? You ever read anything about Jack the Ripper?'

'Sure. Why?'

'Oh, nothing, really. I was just wondering … do you happen to know how many people he killed?'

'Good question,' he said, looking thoughtful. 'Most people say it was five. The first was a woman called Polly Nichols.' He began counting them off on his fingers. 'Then … let me see … Annie Chapman, Elizabeth Stride, Katherine Eddowes, and Mary Jane Kelly. I'm pretty sure that's the right order.'

'But you say that only *most people* think it was five – so it might have been fewer?'

Frankie looked surprised. 'Fewer? No, I've never heard that. There are some who think it could have been more. There were two other women murdered that same year – a woman called Smith, can't remember her first name, and another called Martha Tabram – but the murder weapon was different in both cases, and they aren't generally considered as Ripper killings. There were also a few women killed in the area a year or two after Mary Kelly's murder, but most people don't connect them. Five is pretty much the accepted number. Why do you ask?'

'Just curious. There was mention of Jack the Ripper on the television yesterday. I was talking to Jimmy about it – and I thought I heard him say there were only three.'

Frankie shook his head. 'No – definitely five.'

*

'So, I suppose you're going to tell me you knew Jack the Ripper?' she smiled as she straightened his pillow.

Jimmy's eyelids fluttered open. 'And why would you suppose that, my dear?'

'Just something you said yesterday.'

'Oh, you shouldn't go taking any notice of me. Nothing more than an old man's ramblings.' For an instant his eyes held a look of secret amusement – the passing ghost of the expression that had once been his trademark. 'Just like when I told you about the film I made with Fairbanks, and he cut me open with his …' He began to cough, deep wracking coughs, and she held his hand, gently stroking the papyrus skin, trying to soothe him.

'Well, how about I read to you?' she asked, once the attack had passed.

Too weak to answer immediately, he lay staring up at the ceiling, until with great effort he said, 'You know I'd love you to – but you shouldn't spend so much time in here with me. You'll lose your job.'

Beth glanced at her watch. 'I've been off duty these last ten minutes – so I guess I can choose for myself who I spend time with, huh?' She settled herself on to the chair by his bed. 'So? What shall it be? The book?'

He gave a tremulous smile. 'How many times have you read that to me, now?'

'This will be the third,' she grinned. 'But it's okay. I know how much you love that story – and I'm getting to like it pretty well myself. Besides, on my salary, I don't get to read too many classics in first edition.'

His hand found hers. 'How old are you, Beth? Nineteen? Twenty?'

'Twenty-five, you old flatterer.'

'Too young to waste your life watching an old man ride off into the sunset. This movie has gone on a reel too long as it is.'

She made to protest, but the words would not pass the sudden constriction in her throat. 'Well,' she said at last, almost achieving a lighter note, 'I was always the type to stay put all through the end credits.'

Barely possessing the strength to smile, he watched her pick up the book. 'Then – if you really don't mind reading to me …' He hesitated. 'There's … there's another story I should like to hear for one last time.'

She squeezed his hand. 'Of course. Is it here?'

'In a box … in my valise.'

He heard her cross to the cupboard and take out the old-fashioned travelling bag – but he could no longer see her. Despite the sunlight that filled the room, his vision had been growing increasingly dark – now it had faded to black.

'It's a diary – or some kind of journal,' she said in surprise. 'Is this the book?'

'Yes.'

She flicked through the pages. 'Such beautiful handwriting.'

'I want you to have it … I want you to have all my books, but … *this one is just for you.*'

'I couldn't, Jimmy. It's wonderfully kind of you, but it's against all the rules.'

'Then … just look after it for me … until I ask for it back?'

She brushed at her eyes. 'We'll see,' she said, coming back to sit by him, squaring her shoulders, hiding behind the caricature of starchy professionalism. 'Now, are we going to read this or not?'

'Yes … please.'

Beth opened the book on her lap.

Beyond the window, the distant hills shimmered in the heat; across town, in a small, run-down movie theatre, a handful of people sat in the dark, watching a young and athletic Jimmy Hawkins battle his way through a horde of costumed extras – and in the quiet of the hospital room, Beth began to read.

There was a hill, just outside our village, where we would play in those distant, happier days – before my father's illness. In fine weather the climb was manageable for a young girl's sturdy legs, and we would clamber to the top, dancing with joy, and feeling such mastery over this part of our world.

But then the rain would come, making the steep sides slippery so that my small feet would slide, unable to gain a purchase on the muddy earth. The older boys and girls, or even my brother Henry, would pull me up, encouraging me to try harder, but no sooner would they let go my hand than I'd lose my footing, sometimes falling so badly that I would slide past my original clinging spot.

Time and time again I would try, determined to join them, only to slip down and out of their reach until, finally, I could fall no further.

I think of this hill often when I look back over my life. My name is Mary Jane Kelly and I was born in 1863 …

BOOK 1

WALES 1876

Chapter One

'In Ireland? You are a liar, Mary Kelly. A damnable liar!'

Sitting primly at her desk, Mary's cheeks flushed as the neatly written pages of her essay were hurled into the air – falling like large white leaves amongst her giggling classmates.

'*Well*?' Mr Griffiths's face was darkly crimson, his breath snorting, bull-like as he loomed over her. 'What do you have to say for yourself?'

'They … they aren't lies, sir, they're …'

'Aren't lies? – *Aren't lies*?' His voice climbed an octave before slipping into menacing sarcasm. 'Born in Ireland? In Limerick, is it? In the family castle, I suppose, eh? Well, you *would* need a castle wouldn't you? With all those brothers and sisters. Six, was it?'

Mary stared into her lap as howls of merriment rang out from a class grateful for the interruption. Behind her, Davy Briggs, a scruffy, gangly boy, leaned forward and gave her a sharp poke in the back, but Griffiths chose to ignore it, unwilling to be distracted from the matter at hand.

'Lot of servants, were there, hmmm? Maids and butlers, no doubt – and surely a governess? Oh yes – but, you know, I'm surprised she didn't explain to you the difference between fact and fiction!' His patronising tone became one of irritation. 'Well, we'll have to remedy that, won't we!'

Seated next to Mary, Gwyneth Davies stiffened, her hand creeping beneath the desk to find Mary's as Griffiths strode to the front of the class to pick up the cane.

'Come out here, girl!'

Frightened, Mary kept a firm grip on Gwyneth, but then a look of defiance crossed her face, and she let go, making her way to the front, her attention fixed on Griffiths's gold watch chain to avoid meeting his eyes or seeing the long stick in his hand.

'I had the misfortune to be teaching your idiot of a brother on the very day you were born – right here in Wales.' Griffiths flexed the cane. 'That's a *fact*, Mary Kelly – and that's what you need in this world! Facts and only facts! Not damn fairytales! Now, put out your …!'

Without waiting Mary raised her left hand, holding it in front of her, palm upwards.

Griffiths noted the small act of defiance and gave another snort. 'Were you born in Ireland?'

Gritting her teeth, Mary gave a small nod, and immediately the thin brown cane sang through the air, searing her palm. It was a harsh stroke that stung her to tears, but she kept her hand outstretched.

'Where?'

'Limerick, sir – in Ireland.'

Griffiths brought the cane down again.

From behind her Mary heard Gwyneth start to cry, and determinedly she forced open her fingers where the stroke had curled them into a fist.

'Where?' Griffiths's voice was loud in her ear, and she could feel his breath against her cheek.

'Lim … Lim …' The sobs she had been trying to suppress burst out, preventing her from speaking, but Griffiths had heard enough. He whipped the stick across her reddened palm yet again. This time the pain was too much, and she snatched her hand away, wedging it under her arm as great tears ran down her cheeks. 'Wales … I … I was born in … in Nant-y-Pridd, in Wales.'

Griffiths gave a snort of satisfaction, and put down the cane. 'Return to your desk. You will re-write the essay and deliver it to me first thing tomorrow morning. And this time I expect it to contain the truth!'

*

It was only the first week of the Michaelmas term, and the early autumn sun was still warm as the two girls started for home, walking in silence for a good part of the way.

At a point where the road curved to skirt the hills, a footpath followed a more direct route along the side of the river, and they took it, walking by the slow moving water and pausing to watch a dragonfly skimming over the surface.

'Do you ever think of doing things, Gwyn?'

'Doing things? Like what?'

'I don't know …' Mary closed her eyes and tilted her face to catch the sun. 'Just something *different*. Maybe even something – *shocking*.'

'No – and you shouldn't be doing *that*,' said Gwyneth, moving into the shade of a tree. 'You'll get all brown, like a gypsy, then no one will want to marry you.'

'Who says I want to get married? And besides, I should like to be a gypsy.'

'Stop being silly.'

16

'What's silly about it? There has to be more to life than getting married. Just think – roaming all over the world in a caravan. Wouldn't you like that? I think it would be *so* romantic!'

'I don't think it would be romantic at all. Very uncomfortable and smelly I shouldn't wonder – probably dangerous, too!'

'Oh, Gwyn!' A desperation filled Mary's voice. 'I just want … Oh, I don't *know* what I want, but …' She looked down at the water, a mischievous glint coming to her eye. 'Actually – *I do*! I want to swim, naked, in this river! Right now!'

Gwyneth's eyes widened. 'You wouldn't?' Then, with an anxious note, '*Would you*?'

'I will if you will.'

'I would *never*!'

For a moment, Mary remained staring at the river, feeling the warmth of the sun on her skin, then with a forlorn sigh she turned back toward the path. 'Come on,' she said with a sad smile. 'Let's go home.'

The Davies' house was one of a row of colliery cottages that lay on the outskirts of the village, and Gwyneth's mother was standing in the doorway as the two girls arrived. 'I'm afraid you can't come in, Mary. The boys are just back from their shift, and our Thomas is in the bath. But if you'd like a bite of something to eat before you go, I can bring it out to you?'

'That's very kind of you, Mrs Davies, but I can't stay. Mother's waiting for me, I expect.'

Meg Davies struggled to maintain her smile. 'Oh, yes – I expect she is. Well, just wait you there a minute. I'll be right back.' She disappeared into the house, and her place in the doorway was taken by Gwyneth's second brother, Alan, still black with coal-dust.

'I hear you got a proper whacking today.'

Gwyneth shot him a harsh look. 'You just leave her alone. And how do you know, anyway?'

'Oh, news travels fast enough, 'specially when it's on them skinny little legs o' Davy Briggs!' He laughed, giving Mary a wink. 'Old Griffiths was it? By, but he's a mean old bugger! You just say the word, Mary, and I'll go up there, and give him a taste of his own medicine.'

Thomas, the eldest of the Davies' offspring, appeared in the doorway, still buttoning his shirt, his wet hair glistening. 'You'll do no such thing, and stop embarrassing the girl.'

'By heck, that's got to be the fastest I've ever seen you out of that bath, boy!' said Alan. He winked again at Mary. 'You'll have to come by more often, my love. Makes a nice change to get the water while it's still hot!'

'Get away off with you,' Thomas growled. 'And mind my clean shirt while you're at it!'

'Don't worry, I'm going.' Alan paused, grinning. 'Here, you've gone a bit red in the face you have. Water *too* hot, was it?'

Thomas glared at him, but remained standing awkwardly in the shadows, and when his mother came back moments later carrying a paper-wrapped package, he was almost grateful to be shooed away.

'I'm sure your mam's got your tea all ready,' said Meg, 'but here's some bread and cheese, just in case you get hungry on the way, like.' With some embarrassment she handed over the parcel, hovering uncertainly for a moment. 'Well, I suppose I should be getting tea ready, myself. Proper gannets my lot are these days.'

Gwyneth waited until her mother had gone, then looked down at Mary's hand where it hung by her side. 'Can I look?' she asked nervously.

'If you want to.' Mary held it out for Gwyneth's examination. 'It didn't hurt you know. I just pretended it did.'

A small crease formed between Gwyneth's eyebrows as she looked at the reddened flesh. 'Oh, Mary …'

'Hey, Kelly! Can I come and stay in your castle?'

The sudden shout startled them both, but Mary quickly recovered, aiming a smack at the boy's head as he ran past.

'I'll do for you at school tomorrow, Davy Briggs, you see if I don't!'

From a safe distance, Briggs affected a pained expression and shook his hand. 'Hurt, did it? Never mind, eh. Get the butler to see to it. I would!' Then, laughing, he turned and disappeared up the road.

Gwyneth watched him go. 'Why do you do it, Mary? You get yourself into such trouble.'

'I don't care. Griffiths doesn't frighten me – and I'll be born where I please.'

'Mary! Listen to me! You've got to stop making up these silly stories. Everyone knows about you and your family – and they just laugh at you.'

'I told you, I don't care.'

'But I do! I can't bear it when …' Gwyneth broke off, biting her lip. 'You don't need to make up stories for them!'

Resentfully, Mary started away, but after just a few paces she stopped and turned. 'I don't do it for *them*,' she said.

*

'Fight. Fight. Fight. Fight. Fight.'

Drawn by the sound of chanting, Nathaniel Abrahams went to his study window and looked beyond the school gates to where a large group of children were gathered around two boys and a girl.

He placed his cup back on to its saucer and took out his watch. Ten minutes to nine; too early to ring the bell. 'Mr Griffiths,' he said, turning his head a fraction. 'There would appear to be several members of your

18

class involved in a fracas. I think you had better step out and put an end to it.'

Griffiths sauntered over, peering with mild interest at the melee. 'Oh, Briggs, is it? And Kelly, of course – can't quite make out the other one. Ah, Harris! I should have known! Nothing for us to worry about. They'll sort it out amongst themselves.'

Abrahams looked at him. 'Possibly, Mr Griffiths. But I should prefer *you* to sort it out.'

'With respect, Headmaster. When you've been here a few years, well, you'll see the wisdom of turning a blind eye to this kind of thing – the odd scrap, like. They're a rough lot of kids around here, and I've always found it better not to get involved in their high spirits when it's off school property.'

Abrahams gave the man a penetrating look. 'I have been in this profession for over forty years, and in all that time I have never thought of two boys fighting one girl as *high spirits*! I very much doubt my opinion will change during the few years that remain to me.'

'It won't do *her* any harm,' Griffiths snorted. 'Might even take her down a peg or two! And if she's anything like the rest of her family she'll probably flatten the two of them. Her mother's quite a brawler when she's …'

'Mr Griffiths! I will not have this! You will go down and stop the fight immediately – then bring the three of them to my study. Is that understood?'

Griffiths's nostrils flared, and the broken veins on his cheeks darkened. 'As you wish, Headmaster,' he said.

Like a solid living thing, the tightly packed ring of spectators moved this way and that, following the progress of the fight as Mary wrestled with the two boys, hitting and kicking for all she was worth. 'Leave her alone! You bloody well leave her alone!' she screamed, grabbing Harris by his hair, wrenching him round and slapping at his head, while Briggs tried to pin her arms from behind.

'Break it up!' boomed Griffiths, striding through the gate, the crowd parting to make way for him.

Harris broke free from Mary's grasp to stand wild-eyed and panting, but Davy Briggs kept his arms around Mary, as though he had a tiger by the tail.

'Stop it! The pair of you!' Griffiths prised Briggs off, pushing him back. 'Now, what's all this about?'

'It was Briggs and Harris, sir,' piped up a small girl from the crowd. 'They threw muck all over Gwyneth Davies, sir.'

'Is that so? Where is she?'

The far end of the circle opened to reveal Gwyneth, huddled against the railings, tears running down her cheeks, and horse dung splattered over her face and clothes.

'God, will you look at you!' Griffiths snorted. 'Making such a fuss! Get inside and clean yourself up, girl!' He watched her start toward the school, then turned his attention back to the three protagonists, looking at each of them in turn. Harris's lip was cut, and both Mary and Davy Briggs had blood running from their noses. 'Right, the Headmaster wants to see you, so you'd better get to his study, sharpish! And he's a bit hot on fighting, see, so I wouldn't go expecting anything less than a good thrashing!'

Standing alone in front of the Headmaster's desk, Mary fretted at her torn cuff. Her face was still flushed from the fight – and the closeness of the room added to her discomfort, for despite the mild autumn weather there was a fire burning in the grate.

'Is it a little warm for you?' Mr Abrahams enquired pleasantly, closing the door. 'I'm afraid that as my years advance so does my susceptibility to the cold.'

'I'm alright, thank you, sir.'

He crossed the room and seated himself behind the heavy teak desk. 'Gwyneth Davies is a friend of yours?'

On the scuffed leather desktop lay the cane that had recently been applied to the backsides of Harris and Briggs, six apiece, the sound of the strokes clearly audible to Mary as she'd waited outside. She stole a nervous glance at it. 'Yes, sir. My best friend, sir.'

'And you thought to avenge this disgusting attack? You didn't think it better to come and report it, rather than take on these two boys yourself?'

'I had to stop them, sir. They were ...' She paused.

'They were what?'

'They were trying to make her eat it.'

A look of horror crossed Abrahams's face. 'Surely not! She has said nothing of this to me!'

'She wouldn't, sir.'

The fingers of his left hand tapped at the desk. 'I see,' he said, then after a few moments, 'How is your nose? It appears to have stopped bleeding.'

'It was nothing, sir – just a scratch.'

'It looks to have been rather more than a scratch from the amount of blood on your pinafore.'

'I ... I don't think it's all mine, sir.'

He resisted the urge to smile. 'I cannot condone fighting, Mary. I want to make that quite clear to you.'

'Yes, sir.'

He nodded, then cleared his throat. 'Now, I see from the punishment book that you feature quite prominently. Indeed, although he has not seen fit to enter it, I believe Mr Griffiths had cause to cane you only yesterday.' Some papers lay on the desk, and he picked them up, sifting through the four pages of beautifully executed copperplate. 'The cause of the trouble was this essay, entitled *My Life*, was it not?'

'Yes, sir. I was just …'

Mr Abrahams raised a silencing hand. 'I can see why Mr Griffiths might take exception to this – but the work is not without merit.' He read for some moments more, then he asked, 'And your father, *is* he a painter?'

'Yes, sir. That is – he *was*. He doesn't have to work now.'

Abrahams steepled his fingers and looked up at her. 'I see,' he said softly. 'A fortunate man. So there would be someone in the house now?'

'Yes, sir.'

'Well, I am sending Gwyneth Davies home since she is in no fit state to sit in class – and as you are in a somewhat similar condition, I think perhaps you should accompany her.'

Mary brightened. 'Thank you, sir. We can walk together.'

'Walk? Goodness, no. That is quite out of the question. I shall take you myself.'

'Oh,' said Mary, suddenly anxious. 'Oh, yes … I see.'

Chapter Two

They rode most of the way to the small mining village of Nant-y-Pridd without speaking. Abrahams made a few attempts at conversation, but though the girls answered politely enough he could tell they were ill at ease, and as the outskirts of Caerphilly gave way to open countryside he fell silent, content to sit quietly and watch the unfolding scenery.

With its mountains and valleys, impressive views and grim little mining towns, Wales was a far cry from the softer, prettier landscape of Surrey where he had spent most of his working life. But children were children wherever one went, and so, he thought, were schoolmasters. For every half-dozen decent ones, there was always a Griffiths – dull, pedantic, bullying, and invariably too lazy to bother with pupils who were troubled in the way the Kelly girl seemed troubled. Abrahams glanced at her, finding it hard to reconcile the few snippets of gossip that had come his way with the girl who appeared at school each morning in the clean white pinafore and brightly polished shoes. In his mind he went back over the pages of the punishment book; so many entries with the name Mary Jane Kelly.

The road swung away from the river, beginning a gentle climb into the distant mountains, and as the gig crested the first rise he reined in the mare. To his left, the sparkling ribbon of water wound its way toward the village with its turning pit wheel and smoking chimneys, and in the misty morning sunshine the scene possessed an austere beauty he found breath-taking.

'It's really quite beautiful,' he mused. 'I shall have to make a point of returning with my camera.'

Mary looked at him with interest. 'You have a camera, sir?'

'Yes, rather a good one, actually. Though I must confess to achieving very mixed results. Are you interested in photography, by any chance?'

'I don't know, sir.' She turned, gazing at the village beneath its haze of chimney smoke. 'I suppose it is sort of beautiful – when you look at it in that way,' she said at last.

Gwyneth followed their eyes, puzzled. 'It looks just the same as always.'

'Well,' he said kindly, 'perhaps the trick is knowing how to look?' Then he flicked the reins, and the gig started the gentle run into the village.

The surprise and confusion Megan Davies exhibited on opening the door had quickly given way to thinly veiled anger toward the two boys responsible. Abrahams had done his best to reassure her that they had been adequately punished, and he'd left feeling confident the matter was closed – at least as far as the Davies' were concerned.

But Mary still worried him. It was obvious she didn't want to be taken all the way home, and now, as they moved beyond the village toward a shamble of jerrybuilt hovels, he began to understand why. Even in the bright sunlight the place looked wretched, and he shuddered to think how it must appear in the depths of winter. He could only see it as an area where all hope had died – and his words to Gwyneth, just twenty minutes earlier, suddenly sounded very hollow indeed.

A little way off from these decaying heaps of brick, wood and slate stood a labourer's cottage that had once seen better days, and it was to this that Mary reluctantly directed him.

'Will you come in, please, sir?' she asked as she climbed from the gig. 'I think my father is at home.'

Abrahams tethered the horse and followed Mary into the house, pausing just inside the doorway to let his eyes adjust to the gloom. He shivered. The place had a damp, unhealthy feel that the few pathetic embers glowing in the grate did nothing to dispel.

'Mr Kelly?' he called.

In a large, wooden-armed chair pulled close to the fireplace sat a man, and Mary ran to him. 'Father!' she chided, kissing him on the forehead. 'You've let the fire go out, now whatever will Mr Abrahams think?' She crouched down, putting pieces of wood and scraps of coal into the grate where they smouldered and smoked. 'Mr Abrahams is the Headmaster of the new school, and he's come all this way to see you.' She straightened, tucking back her hair and brushing at her dress with a quaint primness. 'We're not so used to visitors these days, Mr Abrahams, so you will rather have to take us as you find us. Of course, it hasn't always been this way. We used to have such parties – you couldn't possibly imagine.'

Astonished by the sudden transformation, Abrahams watched her move about the sparsely furnished room, tidying this, rearranging that, all the while keeping up the unnaturally cheerful stream of conversation. 'Mr Kelly?' he tried again.

In the chair, the man moved restlessly, but said nothing.

'Will you take some tea, Mr Abrahams? I shall be making some for father – so it will be no trouble.'

She was standing bright-eyed by the chair, barely recognisable but for the torn, bloodstained apron, and Abrahams felt suddenly very cold. He came forward, looking down at her father. The man's eyes stared fixedly ahead, and his mouth hung loosely open, his body twitched into agitated movement by occasional spasms that would have toppled him from the chair had he not been bound to it with leather straps.

Mary caught Abrahams's fleeting look of horror, but for a few seconds more kept the bright look on her face. 'It's really so nice … so very nice of you to …' Then, as he turned to her, she saw the dreadful reality mirrored in his eyes, and the effort of keeping up the pretence became too much.

Abrahams reached out to her, and in the next moment she was in his arms, sobbing against his chest.

'How long has he been like this, Mary?' Abrahams asked softly, sipping the tea she had prepared for them.

'Not long, not like this, anyway. He's been ill for about three years.' Her voice tailed away, and sitting on the floor by her father's side she rested her head against his thigh. 'But he *will* get better, you know – then it will be just like it was before.'

Abrahams put down the cup. 'Mary …' he began, but lost for words he turned his attention to the fire that now burned brightly with the last of the coal. 'Well, it's a little warmer in here now.'

John Kelly had fallen asleep, his head lolling against his chest, and Mary got quietly to her feet. 'We could sit outside now if you wish? I know it isn't so very grand in here.'

Although the room was bare and badly in need of repair, Abrahams could see the cottage had once been a very respectable household. Along the wooden mantelpiece, pencil sketches had been pinned in an attempt at decoration, and the re-kindled fire had gone some way to dispelling the musty dampness that pervaded the room – but still he found the idea of escaping to the warmth of the sun a temptation. 'Perhaps we might take your father outside? I'm sure the sunlight would be beneficial.'

Mary looked down, embarrassed. 'We can't do that. Mother won't allow it. She doesn't like anyone to see.'

'Then let us sit here – the three of us.' Abrahams turned his face from her, making a show of examining the nearest drawing where it hung from the mantel-shelf.

Mary refilled his cup. 'I am *partly* Irish, you know,' she said, breaking the silence. 'My mother comes from Cardiff, but Father was born in Limerick – a descendent of the Irish Kings of …' she broke off guiltily.

'And are these his sketches?' The drawings were unpolished, even a little

24

crude in places, and Abrahams guessed the man was already ill at the time of their execution. Yet for all that, they showed a natural ability and a good grasp of perspective.

'No, sir. They're mine.'

He turned back in surprise. 'Yours?'

'They're something for him to look at during the day. Mother … well, she has to work, you see.' She unpinned one of the drawings and held it out for Abrahams's inspection. 'This is our family.' A man with a head of fair, curly hair, a woman, and a large group of children were pictured around the door of a splendid cottage. The figures had been drawn only after a great deal of trouble, but the house and background were beautifully rendered. 'I'm not very good at people – but this is Mother and Father, and these are the five boys – Matthew, David and John. The tall one is Huw – he's the eldest and the nicest – and very strong, too! He never lets anyone pick on us. And that's baby Glyn, we all spoil him because he's so little. Father says he'll turn out a little horror, but we just can't help it. And this is me – and *this* …' she pointed proudly, 'is my twin sister, Emma. We do just *everything* together.'

Abrahams studied it for several moments. 'This is very good, Mary, really very good – but I don't understand. You actually do have more than just the one brother?'

She looked into her lap. 'No … not really. They're just stories I make up. I tell them to Father when it's just the two of us here. I know he likes them, and … well, it's how I would *like* things to be.'

Abrahams cleared his throat, giving himself a moment as he looked slowly and thoughtfully along the line of drawings, studying each in turn. 'You've had lessons?' he asked at last.

'No, sir. Mr Griffiths doesn't care for drawing.'

'From your father, then? Before his illness?'

'No, sir. He … well …' She looked down again. 'He's only an artist in our stories. Before he became ill, he was a boot-maker.'

'I see. Well, you have a talent, Mary – and we must see what we can do with it. What I would …' He broke off, rising from his chair as a young man stepped into the house to stand warily just inside the door.

'Henry,' said Mary, running to her brother. 'This is Mr Abrahams. He's the new headmaster.'

Henry Kelly gave a curt nod, eyeing him suspiciously. 'Somethin' we can do for you, is it?' he asked with undisguised hostility. 'Our Mary not been behavin' herself?'

'No, nothing like that, I assure you.'

'Oh, English you are, is it?' Henry regarded him with even greater distrust. 'So, what you here for, then?' His eyes narrowed as he looked from Mary, to the headmaster, then back again. 'Oh,' he said slowly. 'Oh, that's the game, is it? Well, it's nice to see you finally earnin' your keep, Mary. And none too soon, neither, I reckon – wastin' your time at that damned school.'

'Mr Kelly – or may I be permitted to call you Henry?'

'Stow that. We don't go in for fancy manners here.' He grasped Mary by the arm, making her wince as he pulled her close. 'If you want our Mary, then let's see the colour of your money. A nice young 'un like her ought to be worth a fair bit to a dried up old man like you.'

Abrahams tried to conceal his disgust. 'Mr Kelly …'

'Look, do you want her or not?' snapped Henry, shaking his sister roughly. 'She's never been touched to my knowledge – so she's clean.'

'Mr Kelly. Will you please let her go. You're hurting her.'

Henry gave a contemptuous laugh. 'What's that to you? Now either pay up, or get about your business and leave us be!'

'Mr Kelly, I must insist …'

'*Insist*, is it?' Anger flared in Henry's eyes, and he threw Mary from him. 'Listen, you stuck-up old bastard. You're not in your bloody school now, playin' the great lord and master! This is *my* house, where *I* make the rules – and I reckon you just broke 'em.' He moved forward, threateningly, fists raised. 'Mister high and mighty headmaster, eh? Well, this time it's *you* who's for a thrashin'!'

'Please, Mr Kelly. There's no need for …'

Henry feinted with his left, then brought his right up to deliver a hard, open-handed slap to the side of Abrahams's head.

Caught off guard, Abrahams reeled backwards, his hand to his face. 'Mr Kelly, please …'

Mary flew at her brother, tugging ineffectually at him, screaming for him to stop, but Henry thrust her away, sending her crashing against their father's chair, jarring the man into a grotesque wakefulness.

Half-dazed, Abrahams tried to take in the nightmarish scene, but Henry Kelly was advancing upon him, his voice mocking. 'That was just a little smack, like. Now I'll show you what a real beatin' is!' He repeated the feint, this time following up with a hard-fisted right – but Abrahams had no intention of being caught a second time. Shifting on to the balls of his feet, he dropped into a crouch, letting the blow pass just over his head.

For an instant, surprise showed on the youth's face, before Abrahams delivered a straight right to the jaw that sent Henry Kelly sprawling on the floor.

Mary went to her brother, but Henry pushed her away, his eyes fixed on Abrahams, the aggressive bravado of moments before, replaced by a sullen, almost childish petulance. 'I … I'll have the law on you,' he whimpered, dabbing the blood from his broken lip. 'Comin' into a man's house, and …'

'Mr Kelly,' Abrahams was breathing hard, but he kept his voice steady. 'It is not my place to advise you on the matter, but I doubt it would do much for your reputation to have it known you were knocked down by a *dried up old man*, now would it? I am more than happy to forget this unfortunate incident if you are.'

Hesitantly, Henry got to his feet. 'Just a lucky punch,' he muttered, keeping his distance. He dabbed again at his mouth, glancing to where Mary was trying to soothe their father. 'Can't you keep him quiet?' he growled, venting his anger in a safer direction. 'Bloody noise to have to listen to!' He looked furtively back at Abrahams. 'So, what *do* you want?'

'Nothing, I assure you. Just to help if I can.'

'He brought me home,' said Mary. 'There was a fight – at the school.'

Henry Kelly's lips curled into a sneer. 'That's why you're lookin' like somethin' the cat dragged in, is it?' he said, edging away to take down a small gin-trap that hung from a peg on the wall.

Abrahams remained on his guard, but Henry had had quite enough. From the safety of the doorway he spat in the headmaster's direction. 'Well, we don't need your help, see? So don't come crawlin' round here again, or you'll be sorry. And you …' He glared across the room at Mary. 'You'd better have my dinner ready when I get back – or you'll be *more* than sorry.'

With Henry gone, Abrahams took a deep breath and inspected his grazed knuckles. He knew he had grown soft with age, yet still the slowness of his reactions had surprised him. It had been a close thing, but years of coaching boys in the art of boxing had stood him in good stead, and he was not too displeased with his performance. Half way to a smile, he became aware of Mary staring at him. 'Yes, well …' he said, giving an embarrassed cough.

Mary looked equally embarrassed. 'I'm sorry about my brother, sir.'

'He seems a very angry young man.' Abrahams looked at her with concern. 'You will be alright?'

Mary nodded, but the way she kept her eyes lowered, left Abrahams troubled. 'Very well,' he said at last. 'But if you should ever need my help.'

She nodded again, and after a moment more he turned his attention back to the sketches pinned to the mantelpiece. 'Then, as I was saying before we were interrupted, what I should like is to buy one of your drawings from you, if I may?'

'I'm sorry, sir. I couldn't sell any of these.' She put her arm about her father's shoulders.

'Yes. Yes, of course. I do understand.' He gave her a brief smile. 'Well, I really should be getting back. I shall see you at school tomorrow?'

'Yes, sir.'

John Kelly had grown still once more, and Abrahams reached down, taking his hand in his own. 'It's been a pleasure to meet you, sir,' he said into the expressionless face. 'I hope we shall meet again soon.'

Mary walked with Abrahams to the door and stood watching as he climbed up on to the seat of the gig. 'I … I could draw you a picture,' she began uncertainly. 'A special one, just for you – if you wanted me to?'

'A commission?' He considered the idea. 'Yes, a capital suggestion. A landscape perhaps?'

She nodded excitedly. 'The view from the hill – where we stopped?'

'That would be perfect.' He stroked his chin. 'I suppose we should discuss payment? Winter is approaching, and you seem to be low on coal. A bag of the colliery's best, do you think?'

'Oh, no, sir …'

He smiled. 'I see you drive a hard bargain, Mary. Very well, *two* bags. But I shall want a favour from you in return.'

Her forehead creased into a small frown. 'Sir?'

'That business back there with your brother.' He gave the reins a gentle flick, urging the horse into motion. 'I shouldn't like it to become common knowledge. As I said earlier – I really can't condone fighting.'

Chapter Three

From the window of his study, Abrahams watched a group of girls run across the puddled playground, their hands clasped to skirts and shawls against the raging wind.

The morning had started fair, but leaden clouds driving in from the west had made it dark enough by two-thirty for the classroom lamps to be lit, and now a heavy rain was falling.

'I apologise for presuming upon you with yet another meeting,' he said, turning to address the small gathering, 'but I thought it might be time for us to evaluate our progress.'

Perched on a chair, Miss Peebles, stick thin and dressed from head to foot in black, twitched her head in his direction, while behind her, Mr Griffiths sighed as he leaned against the wall, his arms folded.

'I'm pleased to see the changes are being implemented,' Abrahams continued, taking his seat. 'But it seems to me we are not yet *one* school. Rather, we are still a collection of small village schools gathered under one roof.' He noticed Griffiths beginning to fidget, and he went on quickly. 'It is no easy matter to change from running your own establishment, with your own methods and routines, to becoming part of a grander design – and you have both done extremely well under the circumstances. But, unless we can alter our whole way of ...'

Griffiths pushed himself from the wall to stand with his feet apart and his thumbs shoved into the pockets of his waistcoat. 'With respect, Headmaster.'

'Yes, Mr Griffiths?'

'Your ideas may work very well in English public schools, but you have no experience of the people in these parts. They go into the mines, the lucky ones. A few to the factories, else it's on the land. Not much call for drawing and music, whichever way.'

Abrahams kept his voice calm. 'Surely there is always a place for art and music? This country is famous for its choirs, after all.'

'Choirs are one thing, but giving these children aspirations over and above their situation does nothing but harm. There's precious little for them in this life but damned hard work.'

'It doesn't have to be that way.'

'That's how it is! Nothing to be done about it. Filling their heads with fancy ideas won't help them when they're hacking coal in a three foot seam, will it? To read and write and know the word of God is what they need – and enough arithmetic to count their wages.'

Abrahams stared at him. 'You surely cannot believe that?'

'I'm afraid he's quite right, Headmaster.' Miss Peebles gave him an apologetic look. 'They mostly go to the mines. It's a shame, I know, but …'

'Shame be damned!' Griffiths roared. 'The money's better than they'd earn working the land or sweating in a factory. It's the best they can hope for. If you must pity anyone, pity the poor devils who *can't* get into the mines.'

The Headmaster placed his hands on the desk. 'No, Mr Griffiths. That won't do. There are always exceptions. Those with a special talent.'

'Occasionally there are,' conceded Griffiths, 'and I've known one or two. But you only have to look at those we have here at present …'

'I *have* looked, and I see potential – Mary Kelly for instance.'

'Mary Kelly is a damned fool! I've tried my best …'

Abrahams leaped to his feet. 'Your best? Beating her for daring to show a little imagination? Is that your best?'

'And what would you have me do?'

'Encourage her! Help her to make something of herself.'

'Mary Kelly's only talent is for telling lies!'

'*Stories*, Mr Griffiths. She makes up stories. There is a difference.'

'There is indeed a difference, Headmaster. *Stories* are told by those who can afford it. Those who can't are merely liars – ridiculed by their own kind and deemed unemployable by their betters!' He paused, his tone becoming more restrained. 'Mary Kelly's father is a cripple. It's thought he'll not see the spring. Her brother is a bully and a wastrel – but at least he'll poach the odd rabbit to keep them in meat – that is until he gets caught. Her mother is a tuppenny whore who spends the time she's not on her back, drinking herself into a stupor.'

'Mr Griffiths! I have warned you about repeating such gossip.'

Griffiths was unperturbed. 'It is not gossip, Headmaster, it is common knowledge! Everyone knows it – and if you were not an outsider *you* would know it! Oh, I know you've been over to Nant-y-Pridd, but are you also aware that Mary Kelly works for two hours every morning, washing and cleaning, just to pay her school pence and keep herself dressed? She's thirteen, for God's sake. She should be out at work, not wasting her time

30

here in the vain hope of *bettering* herself.' He gave a mirthless laugh. 'If she manages to be better than her mother she'll have achieved a small miracle! She's not a bad looking girl, and in a few years time she'll probably find a husband who'll knock this damn foolishness out of her. But in the meantime she should find a position as a maid, a kitchen skivvy, anything that'll keep her respectable. But she won't! Her head's too full of fanciful ideas – and you want me to encourage them? What Mary Kelly needs is both feet planted firmly on the ground – and for her own sake I'd beat her bloody to achieve that!'

Caught in the crossfire, Miss Peebles studied the floor in embarrassed silence.

'Well,' Mr Abrahams sat down. 'I take your point, Mr Griffiths – but I believe you are wrong. So, from the start of next week, I shall be forming a new class from the most able children – a class which I, myself, shall teach. Now, if we might turn our attention to some of the other matters I have outlined.'

*

The rain was still falling hard the next morning when Mary awoke, stretching her leg across the straw-filled mattress to the chill space where her mother should have lain. Outside it was pitch dark, and a howling wind buffeted the small window, lifting the edges of the board that covered a broken pane.

Her nose and cheeks were cold, and she gave herself a few extra minutes beneath the blankets, listening to the reassuring rhythm of her father's breathing on the far side of the wooden partition. Then, reluctantly, she climbed from bed.

With the fire lit, and some tea stewing in the pot, she went to her father's room. He lay asleep, with no sign that Henry had been there at all that night, and she sighed, knowing that without help she would never get her father out of the bed and into his chair.

She brushed her fingers against his cheek. 'Time to wake up, Da,' she said softly. 'Mother will be having the breakfast on the table in no time at all.'

The man's eyes opened slowly, and for a moment she thought he was smiling up at her, but then his lips drew into a travesty of a grin, as they jerked and snatched in spasm.

'I'll bring you a nice cup of tea in a minute,' she said making her way back to the fire. 'It's a terrible day out there – blowing a gale, it is. And it's such a shame. Mother wanted to take the boys into Caerphilly today. Huw's getting so tall now he's fairly out of that new jacket she bought him, and she says she won't have him going up to university looking anything less than the gentleman.'

From a cupboard on the wall she took the stale remains of a loaf, and holding it against her chest, she sawed off two slices.

'I was hoping to go, too. Poor Emma desperately needs a new piece for her pinafore.' She speared a slice of bread with a long fork and placed it before the smoking coals to toast.

'I really shouldn't be telling you this, Da – but she got in a fight at school the other day. Oh, of course, it wasn't her fault. Some of the boys were being beastly and – well, I don't know *what* I would have done if she hadn't been there. She was very brave – but her pinafore was ruined. It really needs a new frill, and though mother would mend it in a minute, I would so like to do it myself.'

The pinafore, dress and thin coat she had worn the previous day lay drying over the backs of two chairs, and she moved them closer to the fire. 'Would you like to play a game later, Da? You know how much John and David love those guessing games you make up. Do you remember how they laughed last time – and mother was laughing too, and trying so hard to keep a straight face, and calling us all *silly monkeys*?'

She poured some tea into a cup and took it, with the toasted bread, to where her father lay. 'Breakfast, Da,' she said.

Sitting on the edge of the bed she raised his head, helping him to eat the dry toast, giving him sips of tea to wash it down.

'Mother's done us proud this morning,' she said as she worked the last piece of toast between his lips. 'She must have been up ever so early to get all this baking done. I don't think I could eat another bite.'

Lowering him on to the pillow, she kissed him lightly on the forehead, then made her way back to the meagre warmth of the fire, to wash herself from head to toe with the remains of the hot water.

Outside it was beginning to lighten, but only enough to show the trees as silhouettes against a brooding sky and the rain slanting down with a vengeance. 'You know, Da? I do believe the rain is letting up.' She shuddered as she pulled on the wet clothes. 'So I think I might just pop into Caerphilly after all.' Wrapping her dry shift and dress in an oilskin cloth, she put them ready by the door. Her boots were still wet through, but with the long walk ahead of her, it hardly mattered.

'I'm going off now, Da.' She opened the door and scanned the road in both directions, hoping her mother, or even Henry, would come home so that she might leave with a clear conscience, but there was no movement other than the driving rain. For a moment she hesitated, then she closed the door and walked to the room where her father lay. Even from the doorway, Mary could smell the evidence of his incontinence. 'Oh, Da,' she said, a tremor in her voice as she pulled back the blankets, 'Oh, Da …'

*

Hubert Llewellyn, proprietor of the small guesthouse known as The Cross Keys Hotel, Caerphilly, was bristling with indignation. 'What time do you call this, then!' he demanded.

At the back door, half in the shelter of the porch and half in the rain, Mary stood drenched to the skin, her fair hair plastered to her head and across her face. 'I'm sorry, Mr Llewellyn. It was the rain and …'

'Well, I can't help the weather, can I? Half past six we needed you here, not quarter to seven, see?'

Behind him the portly figure of his wife hove into view. 'Oh, for heaven's sake, let her in, Mr Llewellyn. Can't you see the poor girl's wet through?'

'I'd be obliged if you'd let me deal with this, Mrs Llewellyn!'

'I'm sure you would, Mr Llewellyn! And in the meantime she's going to catch her death, and then where will you be? In prison! On a charge of murder I shouldn't wonder! And who's going to have the trouble of coming to visit you? Me, I suppose!' She bustled past him. 'Don't you mind him, Mary, dear. Just you come on in.'

'I have brought some dry clothes.' From beneath her coat Mary produced the oilskin parcel. 'And I'll come early tomorrow – to make up the time.'

Edith Llewellyn put her hands on her ample hips, giving her husband a sharp look. 'There! There you are Mr Llewellyn! You see! She'll make up the time!'

'Well, that's not exactly the point, is it, Mrs Llewellyn? It's very considerate of her, but she's still late today! No good being late in this business! We'd soon be out on the street if I was late paying the bills, now wouldn't we? Out on our ears, we'd be, lock, stock and barrel, we would! Oh yes!'

'Well, then it's a good job *I* pay them, isn't it!' She turned to Mary, 'Now you go upstairs and get yourself dried off. The last room on the second floor isn't being used. Oh, and while you're up there you can tell Alice to come down to me. That girl will idle away half the day if I let her!' She waited until Mary had gone upstairs then glanced sideways at her husband. ' Just like someone else I know!'

In the act of picking up his newspaper, Hubert's eyes widened. 'What? What are you implying?'

She gave him a withering look. 'Just that I have some jobs for you!'

'Oh, jobs, is it, Mrs Llewellyn! I see! And what might these jobs be?'

'Just what I say, Mr Llewellyn. Jobs! I'm not having you slipping off.'

He began to protest, but she cut him short. 'You always were a lazy man, Mr Llewellyn. I remember my dear mother remarking on it! Watch out for lazy, idle men, she said to me! Oh, she should have lived to see how right she was!'

*

'Y'know it's a quarter t' nine?' said Mrs Cartwright, coming to the door of the pantry. 'I'd get a move on with that floor if I was you. Missus won't be 'appy if it ain't finished.'

Kneeling on the cold flagstones, Mary scrubbed, clasping the brush with both hands and using the whole weight of her body to propel it back and forth. 'I'm – nearly – done,' she gasped, her breath clouding in the unheated pantry. 'Just – this last bit.' Beside her a metal bucket held a harsh mixture of water, soap and soda, and with each dip of the brush, she winced as it seeped into her cracked and reddened knuckles. But worse was the agony in her knees when she finally stood up and, almost crying with pain, carried the bucket into the scullery to empty it.

'Come on, cheer up. Worse things 'appen at sea – or so they tell me,' said the cook, looking up from the pastry she was rolling out.

Wiping her cuff across her eyes, Mary gave a half smile.

'That's more like it. Yer can't let it beat yer, y'know. Now, I've ironed yer clothes – though Gawd knows why. It's rainin' cats and dogs out there an' you'll be as wet as when you arrived by the time yer get t' school. Ain't yer got no umbrella?'

Mary shook her head.

'Lawd! I suppose they ain't been invented where you come from! Why, even the littlest mites 'as umbrellas back 'ome!'

Though she'd lived the greater part of her life in Caerphilly, Mrs Cartwright had never lost her Cockney twang nor her love of singing London's praises, something Mary found both amusing and exciting. 'I thought you said it never rained there,' she smiled, changing into her freshly ironed clothes.

'An' no more it don't – least, not like it does 'ere. I remember when …' Mrs Cartwright gave her a sideways glance. ''Ere, you ain't got no time for stories – an' anyway, you've 'eard 'em all afore – an' if yer don't get off soon you'll be late for school. I've put a smidgen o' polish on yer boots, though what's 'oldin' 'em together, I don't know!' She chuckled. 'Now that's one thing yer *don't* get too much of in London – bloomin' miracles!'

Mary laughed. 'Well, I'd best not go there, then,' she said, pulling on her pinafore and slipping her feet into the damp boots.

'Maybe I should go back – afore it's too late.' Mrs Cartwright sprinkled flour on to the pastry in a thoughtful manner. '*See London an' die.* That's what they say, ain't it?'

'I think that was Venice,' said Mary, apologetically.

'Was it? Well, if it was, I expect it was said by one o' them foreigners what never got no further than the channel.' The old woman busied herself cutting out pie cases. 'See yer tomorrow, then?'

'Yes, see you tomorrow,' said Mary, putting the rest of her clothing into the oilskin and making ready to leave.

34

Rain was leaping from the stone steps that led up to street level, and Mrs Cartwright watched the girl hesitate. It was only a brief dash to the school, but she didn't envy her even that short trip. ''Ere, yer can borrow my ol' mushroom, if yer want,' she said, going to a stick stand by the door and bringing out a battered umbrella. 'But I want it back, mind!'

Chapter Four

Owen Davies peered with hungry expectation as his wife placed the steaming crock on the table. 'Mutton stew, is it?'

'You know it is.'

'Always mutton stew on Tuesdays,' chipped in Alan, giving Gwyneth a nudge. 'Better than a calendar, I reckon.'

Owen shot him a warning look. 'Mind your cheek, boy. You're not too old for a damn good hiding yet, you know.' But there was humour in his voice, and Alan grinned as he reached for a slice of bread.

'Now *that* I won't have.' said his father. 'You just wait till your mother is seated. Whatever else a man might have to go without, manners cost nothing, and he should have his full share.'

Meg scowled as Alan replaced the bread. 'Seventeen, is it? You act more like seven sometimes.' She ladled the stew into a bowl and set it in front of her husband.

'By heck, that smells good! Fit for a king, that is!' he said, reaching round to pat her behind.

'Owen!'

He feigned innocence. 'What is it woman? Can't a man pay his wife a compliment, then?'

She filled another bowl and passed it to Thomas. 'Fine example, I must say,' she muttered – but there was a blush to her cheeks, and the trace of a smile on her lips.

Alan watched hungrily as a brimming bowl was passed to him. 'I hear there was an explosion over at Merthyr this morning. Twenty killed, so they're saying – and another fifty or more still under …' He stopped short as Thomas gave him a warning kick. 'Ah … well, that's what I heard,' he finished lamely.

Meg appeared not to notice, but the smile had gone from her face.

'So, Gwyneth, my little petal,' said Owen in the awkward silence that followed. 'How was school today?'

Gwyneth set down the bowl her mother handed her, guiltily licking her thumb where it had slipped over the edge and into the stew. 'We went out to Caerphilly Castle – *drawing*!' she said importantly. She had been waiting for this moment, and now gave the statement its full dignity.

Her father leaned back in his chair. 'Drawing, is it? Well, well! I didn't know we had an artist in the family.' He gave a sly wink as Gwyneth looked proudly about the table. 'Mind you, I'm not surprised. I like a bit o' drawing, myself – 'specially when it's my wages on a Saturday morning.'

Alan laughed. 'You can draw my bath water tomorrow, if you like, Gwyn.'

Blushing, Gwyneth turned sullen. 'I'm no good at it, anyway.'

'Oh, come on, now.' Her father placed his hand on her arm. 'No need to go taking yourself so seriously. You're not thinking of making your living at it, are you? Well, then. What's it matter whether you're good at it or not?'

Gwyneth brightened a little.

'Mary can draw a bit, can't she?' asked Thomas.

'She seems to draw you,' chuckled Alan.

It was Thomas's turn to blush. 'Get away with you! She's just a kid! I was just asking because …'

Meg took her seat at the far end of the table. 'If you are all *quite* finished?' she said pointedly.

They fell silent. Owen waited for them to bend their heads, then did likewise, speaking the words of the short prayer in a low voice.

'I was just asking,' Thomas persisted the moment his father lifted his head, 'because she could teach Gwyn – help her along a bit?'

Alan looked up from his bowl. 'Damn fool idea!'

'We'll not have that kind of language, if you please!' said Owen.

'Sorry, Da. But it sounds a waste o' time if you ask me.'

Meg turned to him. 'Well, no one *did* ask you. So I'd be obliged if you'd mind your own business.'

'She is good, though,' said Gwyneth. 'She gave a drawing to Mr Abrahams at the school. Proper fine it is – he thinks she could be an artist.'

Owen looked puzzled. 'Abrahams? Who's he then? I thought it was Griffiths that taught you.'

'Mr Abrahams is the Headmaster they brought in from England,' said Meg. 'He's the one who drove Gwyn home the other day – in a gig, no less.'

'Oh, England, is it?' said Owen. 'Griffiths not good enough for Gladstone, then?'

Meg looked up. 'My, but you've never had a good word for Mr Griffiths in all these years!'

'True enough. But at least he's a local man. Doesn't seem right, putting an outsider in charge.' He turned to Gwyneth. 'What do you make of this Abrahams, Gwyn?'

'He seems nice enough. Not like Mr Griffiths.'

Alan gave a grunt. 'No one's like Griffiths!'

'Griffiths isn't so bad,' said Thomas. 'Not really.'

'Not bad? Why, he's a devil, man! He's given me more stick than I can remember – and Da had to be stopped from going down there and teaching him a lesson after he laid into *you*!'

'Well,' said Owen. 'I may have been a wee bit hasty there. Schoolmaster's got to be a bit hard, I suppose. This new chap won't last long if he's not.'

Meg shook her head. 'I don't believe you sometimes, Owen. I really don't!'

*

Grabbing her daughter by the hair, Annie Kelly dragged Mary across the room. 'You ... you bloody, *bloody* little cow!' she screamed, slapping at her head and face with all her might. 'The minute I turn my back!'

Mary was close to hysteria, blood and mucus running from her nose to mix with the tears that streamed down her cheeks. 'No, Mam – it's not true!'

'You lying little bitch! Where'd that come from, then?' She shoved Mary, sending her sprawling into the coal from the newly delivered sacks. 'I'll give you a whipping you won't forget, you little *whore*!' She swayed drunkenly toward Henry. 'Give me your bloody belt!'

Standing in the door to block his sister's escape, Henry Kelly unbuckled the thick leather belt, then leaned back to watch with satisfaction as his mother wrapped it around her fist, leaving a two-foot strap.

'I didn't do anything, Mam! I didn't!'

'Don't you lie to me!' Annie lashed the belt across the small of Mary's back, making her scream with pain.

'It ... it was a present, Mam! Don't! It was a ...' she screamed again as the leather snaked across her shoulder.

'She had that old feller from up the school,' goaded Henry. 'I caught 'em here together the other mornin'. I knew they was up to no good.'

'You damned little whore!' Annie Kelly lashed again, then again, but in her gin-soaked anger she missed her mark, and the blows struck the coals, sending small pieces skidding across the floor.

Seizing her chance, Mary flung herself from the fireplace and ran to the far side of the room, staring out from beneath her dishevelled hair like a hunted animal. 'I'm not!' she shrieked. 'It was a present!'

'Present, my arse!' Annie wiped the spittle from the side of her mouth, and advanced on Mary.

'It was a present – a payment – for a drawing. That's all! Go and ...' The leather seared across her left arm, and she dashed into the refuge of the corner. 'Go and ask if you don't believe me!'

'Oh, you'd like that! Make me look a right bloody fool, wouldn't it!' Annie began lashing from left and right, swinging wildly and striking the walls more often than not, but still landing enough strokes to elicit screams of agony.

'You don't think I have enough to contend with!' She jerked her head toward the room where John Kelly lay. 'It's bad enough I've got a useless cripple for a husband – but to think that a daughter of mine would …'

Stung by the reference to her father, Mary's eyes flared angrily, and she drew herself up, as though suddenly impervious to the lashes. 'Would what? Follow your example? Two sacks of coal would be a good price, wouldn't it? How much do *you* charge?'

Taken aback, Annie let her arm drop, the strap dangling by her side. 'What do you mean?' she hissed.

'Do you think I don't know what you do when you go to Cardiff? *Everyone* knows!'

'You know nothing … none of you! How dare you! You ungrateful little *whore.*'

'You are the whore – *you!*' Mary's eyes filled with tears. 'You bring the stink of it into our bed when you come creeping home – when you *bother* to come home!'

'Don't take that from her!' shouted Henry, disappointed at the turn of events – but Annie had lost her momentum. 'You keep out of it!' She turned to Mary, staggering a little, reaching for the wall to steady herself. 'You think I like it? What *else* am I supposed to do?'

No longer sobered by fury, Annie's voice became slurred. 'How else do you think we've managed all these years?' She waved an arm toward the place where her husband lay befouled in his bed. 'He's been no good these past years – useless – a millstone, that's what he's been – a *bloody* millstone round my neck.'

'Don't you dare say that!'

'Oh, don't I dare? He's been a millstone alright – dragging me down – and so have you – both of you – bloody great millstones.' She turned to look at Henry, 'What use have *you* ever been?'

But Henry had heard it all before. Snatching back his belt, he spat on the floor at her feet, then pushed his way through the door, making off to the fields and his snares.

Annie looked down at the spattered ground, trying to focus, her body listing precariously. 'Just you and me, now, eh, Mary?' she said, looking up with mocking affection. 'Dear little Mary – clever little Mary – Da's little pride and joy. Too good to go out to work. Da says little Mary must stay at school.'

'It's what he wanted,' Mary protested bitterly. 'He said I should …'

'Better yourself?' Annie tapped the side of her nose with her finger and leered. 'I wonder what Da would say if he knew what his clever little girl had been up to, eh? Letting old men have her for a few bags of coal.'

'That's a lie – you know it is!'

But her mother was no longer listening. 'Clever, pretty little girl you are, but I shall tell him – he won't think you so bloody perfect then! Oh, dear me, no!' She started towards the bedroom but fell against the table, reeling backwards to slump on to a chair.

For a moment she sat there looking confused, then she gave a lopsided smile. 'I was pretty – once upon a time – had my pick in those days. Dances! Oh, such dances – such strong, handsome boys. Now look at me!' She jerked up her head. 'Well, you take a good long look, pretty little Mary. This is what you'll be seeing in the mirror before too long. And there'll be no presents of coal from gentlemen then!'

Mary's lip quivered. 'I know, Mam,' she said quietly, seeing her mother for the pitiable creature she had become. 'I'm sorry.'

'Sorry? I don't want your sodding pity!' Annie glared, her mood turning belligerent once more. 'I do what I do because I have to, see? To put bread on the table! Because no one else will. Because I'm surrounded by a lot of damned millstones! God knows what I did to deserve this. Stuck with a cripple, and a wastrel – and a daughter that thinks she's too good for the rest of us.'

Fresh tears brimmed in Mary's eyes.

'You? You don't know the half of it!' Annie went on. 'You think I like doing it? Do you? Going out night after night – with all those men? All those … those big, dirty men.' Then she gave a little giggle. 'Well – I'm entitled to a few drinks, aren't I? A few little drinks and a bit of fun?' She gave her daughter a lewd grin. 'And I can *still* give them what they want.'

Horrified, Mary watched the crude accompanying gesture, her lips trembling – then choking back the sobs she ran from the house.

Chapter Five

Nathaniel Abrahams stood by the broad, high window of Taff Lodge and looked out at the gathering gloom of the autumn evening. The soirée of local dignitaries was a humble affair compared to those he had been duty-bound to attend at his previous school – and since he had never cared for those, he was unsurprised to find the time weighing heavily upon him.

'Mr Abrahams,' said his hostess, her hands fluttering nervously as she descended upon him with a swaggering, bewhiskered figure in tow. 'I'd like you to meet Mr Mawden Protheroe. You two have something in common, you know – so I shall expect you to get on famously.'

'I'm pleased to meet you, sir. Pleased to meet you indeed,' said Protheroe, laughing heartily as he grasped Abrahams by the hand. 'Though the devil knows what it is we have in common.'

Mr Abrahams smiled. 'You are a schoolmaster, perhaps?'

'A *schoolmaster*? No, sir, indeed I am not!'

'Oh, Mr Abrahams,' chided the woman in a high, giggly voice. 'You mustn't tease so. Mr Protheroe is our famous local artist.'

Protheroe beamed and made an elaborate bow. 'At your service, sir.'

'Though he does run a very fine painting school as well,' the woman added after a moment's thought.

'An *academy*, madam,' protested Protheroe. 'Some difference, I think!'

'Oh, of course. I didn't mean …' Mrs Lewis simpered, then quickly changing the subject, she said, 'Mr Abrahams is the Headmaster of the new Board School in Caerphilly.' She bestowed an ingratiating look upon him. 'They brought you all the way from Kent, so I believe.'

'From Surrey,' Abrahams corrected, smiling politely.

She frowned. '*Really*? Are you sure?'

'I believe so.' He smiled again. 'But it is of no great consequence.'

Protheroe threw out his chest. 'Well, you have landed on your feet well enough, sir. Mrs Lewis's gatherings are indeed the envy of all Cardiff.'

The woman blushed, uttering small, appreciative sounds, while her hands erupted into another flurry of nervous activity, and Abrahams waited until the gesticulations began to wane before asking, 'So, what do Mr Protheroe and I have in common, Mrs Lewis? I am anxious to learn.'

She eyed him with humorous indulgence, taking his arm and giving it a friendly squeeze. 'Oh, don't think we haven't seen you out and about with that camera of yours. You've caused something of a stir with it, you know. So now we have two artists in our midst.'

Mawden Protheroe went quite crimson. 'A camera?' he boomed. 'A damnable camera?'

Mrs Lewis's face fell, and she looked nervously about. 'Mawden, *really!*'

'I'm sorry, Mrs Lewis,' he said, partially recovering his composure. 'But I cannot countenance the association of a camera with any form of art!'

Seeing the poor woman's discomfort, Abrahams came to her rescue. 'I understand perfectly, Mr Protheroe. I would never consider myself any kind of artist. Indeed, I see the camera merely as a tool for recording the day to day minutiae – as nothing more than a pen in the hands of a diarist.'

Protheroe softened a little. 'Well – yes, I suppose the thing might have certain *artisan* uses. But it makes my blood boil when these … these photographers … No, you are right – *diarists* – start getting above themselves!' He paused, beginning again in a calmer voice. 'I hope you will accept my apologies. But if they think painting is dead – well, they can damn well think again!'

Abrahams nodded. 'Quite so,' he said.

*

A pump stood by the row of cottages where Gwyneth lived, and it was there that Mary washed her face, and tidied her hair as best she could. She had arrived at the Davies' house without any conscious decision, but standing outside in the gathering dusk, bloodied, tear-stained and dirty, she realised she couldn't intrude. Through the window she had watched them at their meal. Their warm, good-natured faces, animated in conversation as they sat around the table, made a picture so perfect she'd had to turn away.

Along the horizon a crimson streak showed above the hills, and the sky had taken on the pale, washed-out hue that meant darkness within the hour. She shivered. It was already growing chilly, and in her haste she had left her coat behind, but there was nothing to be done about it now.

The pump squealed as she gave the handle one final pull, cupping her hand beneath the stream and drinking from it, then straightening her dress and smoothing her hair, she slowly walked away.

*

'So, you don't subscribe to Delaroche's views?'

Abrahams shook his head. 'No. Photography and painting are two very different … forms.' He had been about to say *art forms* but managed to check himself. 'Those words of his are almost forty years old, yet I see no decline in the demand for paintings.'

'And you won't, sir!' said Protheroe, blowing the smoke from his cigar into the night air.

They had taken a turn in the garden: Protheroe to partake of a large Havana; Abrahams to escape the dreary chit-chat of the drawing-room.

'And this academy of yours, is it successful?' Abrahams asked at length.

'Successful?' mused Protheroe. 'How can such things be measured? One merely lays one's talents before the muddy feet of ingrates.'

'Surely the accomplishment of the pupil determines the Master's worth?'

Protheroe blew another cloud of smoke and gave a rumbling laugh. 'If that be so – then I am a pauper, sir, for they are dullards, all!'

'Then why …?'

'Because they pay, my dear fellow, they pay!' He paused to toss the finished cigar into a cluster of rhododendrons, then walked on with his hands thrust deep into his pockets. 'The pursuit of Mammon – and you cannot reproach me more than I reproach myself. A shameful waste of genius! Scandalous!'

Walking beside him, Abrahams nodded understandingly. 'It is a sad fact that talent and wealth seldom go hand in hand.'

Protheroe stopped in his tracks, his eyes glazed with the emotion of several large brandies. 'Wealth? Wealth would not come into it, man! I tell you! Let the Gods bless me with one talented student, and I would lay open the gates of knowledge to him and never think of reward!'

Abrahams raised an eyebrow, then he smiled. 'Well – who knows quite what the Gods may have in store for us, Mr Protheroe.'

*

Retiring to his chair by the fire, Owen Davies lit his pipe, studying the newspaper while Meg and Gwyneth cleared the table. 'You off to see that girl of yours?' he asked as Alan clattered down the tiny, winding stair that gave access to the single room above.

The boy was wearing his best jacket, and he paused to smooth his hair before the mirror that hung above the mantelpiece. 'Thought I might just walk over there,' he said with a grin.

'Well, make sure you're not late back. We're on early shift tomorrow.'

'Right you are, Da.' He gave himself one final look, then made for the door, stepping aside as Thomas returned with a pail of fresh water.

'Cissy Hewlip, is it?'

'Aye, man,' said Alan, giving his brother a wink before dashing off.

Thomas took the pail into the small scullery where Gwyneth was preparing to wash the dishes.

'She's a big girl, that Cissy,' said Owen, with a chuckle. 'Talk about drawing – draw a brewer's dray, she could!'

'I'm not so sure I approve of his seeing her,' said Meg, taking out the last few items of crockery. 'Not sure at all.'

'Oh, let the boy be. It's not serious, is it?'

'Serious or not …' She left the sentence unfinished, bustling back into the room with the remains of the stew in a covered bowl. 'Gwyneth. Leave that, my love. *I'll* finish the dishes. I want you to take this over to Mary's. And maybe you'd go with her, Thomas?'

'By, but the boy's only just got his boots off …' Owen began, falling silent as Meg shot him a meaningful look.

*

Protheroe's cheeks bore the crimson flush of over-indulgence as he took Mr Abrahams by the hand. 'Pleasure to meet you, sir. A pleasure …' he gave a belch, '… and an honour.'

'For me also, Mr Protheroe.'

'You have my card, sir. Look me up when next you are in Cardiff.'

Abrahams gave a slight bow. 'I should be delighted to. I'd be most interested to visit this academy of yours.' With some difficulty he extracted his hand and climbed up on to the seat of the gig, but before he could drive off, Protheroe slapped his palm against the rim of the wheel. 'A pen – in the hand of a diarist!' he roared, as though suddenly remembering a joke. 'Capital description! Capital! A damned pen – in the hand of a damnable diarist!'

Taking the reins in his hands, Abrahams permitted himself a small smile, thinking as he left the laughing figure of Protheroe behind that the self same pen in the hand of a Shakespeare or a Boswell was *quite* a different matter.

*

'So what was all that about, then?' asked Owen, once they were alone.

Meg fussed with the mantelpiece, tidying the already neat ornaments and flicking away imaginary dust. 'It's Annie …' she began.

'Annie Kelly?'

'Yes. I'm worried – about Mary.'

Owen sucked on his pipe, then leaned forward. 'Come and sit you down,' he said, reaching for her hand. 'Now, what is it?'

'There's talk that Annie was in the village this afternoon, so drunk she could hardly stand. You know how she gets when the drink is on her.'

'Well, they do say she's a real scrapper – and a good many other things besides. But it's not as though it's the first time is it. A regular occurrence in Cardiff, or so I'm told.'

'Yes, but never *here*. She's always come home sober.'

'And you think Mary might be in danger?'

'I don't know, Owen – I just have this feeling.'

He patted her hand. 'Well, then you've done the right thing. Thomas will handle it if there is trouble.' He gave a small chuckle as he reached for the poker. 'And there was me, worried that you were matchmaking.'

Meg looked up in surprise. 'Is that what you thought?'

'Well, it crossed my mind, like. She's a nice enough girl – but there's no denying she's daft as a brush!'

'She is not!'

''Course she is. All those daft stories she tells people. And anyway, she's only thirteen.'

'Well, Thomas is only eighteen.'

'That's not the point, Meg. She's far too young for him.'

'Oh, and how old was I the first time you came to Da's farm, looking for work?'

Owen smiled and poked lazily at the coals. 'I don't remember.'

'My, but you've a convenient memory. Fourteen I was, and you a great strapping brute of twenty!'

'Well,' he grinned. 'Things were different in those days.'

'Is that so?'

'Oh, yes.' He reached for her hand again, stroking it gently, then touched her knee. 'But I do remember *something* we used to …'

With a crash the front door flew open, and they turned to see Gwyneth, dishevelled and fighting for breath.

'Come quick, Da,' she gasped, 'You've got to come quick!'

*

The crowd circled the burning building, pressing in as close as the intense heat would allow, so that Thomas had to fight and jostle his way through. 'Did everyone get out?' he shouted over the crackling of the flames, grabbing at one of the bystanders.

The man's eyes stood out, white against his smoke-blackened face. 'No one has come out while I've been here. We tried to get in – but the place went up in an instant!'

'What about Mary?'

'No one, man – no one came out of there!'

Thomas lurched toward the burning building, his arm thrust across his face, shielding it from the blistering heat. 'Mary!'

'Give it up, boy! There's nothing you can do.'

Even as the man spoke there was a huge groan, and the remains of the chimney staggered and dropped into the inferno, flooding the night sky with glowing embers.

Amidst the blizzard of falling ash, a haggard-looking woman jumped from the crowd and began dancing a mad jig, clapping her hands and shrieking with joy. 'See that?' She pointed to the purple bruising on her cheek. 'D'yer see it? Do yer? She did it! That old witch! Ha, ha … but she's got her come-uppance! Oh, she got it, alright! She got it!'

Thomas grabbed her by the arms. 'Did you see who was in there? The girl, Mary? Did you see her?'

'Didn't see no one!' cackled the woman, deliriously. 'Only that old witch! Oh, she thought to have a fine big fire – stoking and stoking she was. Well, she'll be stoking in Hell now!'

But Thomas was no longer listening. He fell to his knees, sobbing into the cindered grass, and was still there when Owen came to fetch him.

*

A chill white mist hung above the river, glowing eerily in the faint starlight and creeping up on to the bank to swirl about Mary's legs, making her shiver. It was the spot where, as a child, she had seen the pale, lifeless body of a young woman pulled from the water.

Afterwards, walking home with her father, her small hand enclosed in his, she had been powerless to understand what might drive someone to take their own life. But now she thought she understood the crushing despair that must have motivated the girl, and there sprang within her a feeling of kinship. For a while she stood looking at the dark, slow moving river, then murmuring a short prayer for the anonymous soul, she turned back along the path, regaining the road and making her way towards home.

A few yards from Gwyneth's house, a group of people were gathered, talking excitedly as they stood in the spill of light from the open doorway.

Curious, Mary was tempted to go and listen, but then thoughts of her mother pushed into her mind, and she lowered her head, intending to slink past in the darkness. But as she drew level with the crowd, a voice broke above the murmur.

'Mary?'

She stopped.

'Mary? Is that …? Oh, my God! It is! Let me through! Please! Let me through!' Meg Davies burst from the group and caught her up, hugging her so tightly she could barely breathe.

'Oh, God! Mary, my love – my poor, poor love!'

*

'She hasn't cried,' Meg whispered as she set the kettle to boil.

'Shock I expect.' Owen pushed off his boots and leaned back in the chair, his face grimy with smoke and ash. 'She will soon enough, poor kid.'

Perching on the settle, Meg wrung her hands. 'What about her family?'

'They found two bodies ...' He turned to poke at the fire, reluctant to be drawn into a description of the charred and blackened remains that had been discovered. 'They're saying it was the chimney. Probably not swept for years – then the thatch went. Annie was seen just before it happened, dead drunk and building a real blaze. Likely she passed out soon after. I doubt she knew a thing about it.'

Meg flicked a glance toward the ceiling, and the room above where Mary had been tucked into bed with Gwyneth. 'And her da?'

Owen tried not to imagine John Kelly lying helpless as the flames consumed him. 'Best out of it,' he said.

In the darkness of the upstairs room, Gwyneth lay awake, listening to the low murmur of voices from below. A curtain screened her bed from the one her brothers shared, and she could hear Alan's slow, steady breathing and the occasional creak as one or the other shifted restlessly.

'Gwyn?' Thomas's voice came softly through the dark.

'Yes?' she whispered back.

'How is she?'

'Sleeping.'

'Oh ... that's good then ... *isn't it?*'

'Yes ... I think so.'

The bed creaked again, and he fell silent. But he did not sleep, and neither did Gwyneth. Lying in the darkness, with Mary nestling against her body in a child-like embrace, she stared into the rafters, shedding the tears that Mary could not.

*

'The cheek of some people, Mr Llewellyn! It quite beggars belief!'

Hubert Llewellyn was in the dining room setting the tables for dinner. 'Cheek, Mrs Llewellyn? Dear me. Those kids from the school again, is it?'

'Not the kids! No! The teachers it is now! They must think we're running some kind of a charity!'

'You look a little flustered, my dear,' said Hubert, beaming with delight. 'You should have let me deal with it. I'm sure it was some trifling matter.'

'Trifling matter? There's nothing trifling about being asked to take in every waif and stray that passes by! Well, I soon put a stop to that idea!' She picked up a knife, looked at it critically, then put it down and moved amongst the other tables, stopping here and there to fuss with the cutlery.

Hubert was quick to follow, undoing the changes she'd made. 'So, what idea was this, then?'

'Well!' she said, full of indignation. 'He came to see us about Mary – Mary Kelly. You know – the cleaning girl?'

'Yes, yes, Mrs Llewellyn, of course I know! What about her?'

'Apparently her parents were killed in that fire over at Nant-y-Pridd, and he wanted us to take her in. Give her a live-in job here! Can you imagine!'

'Well now,' he said, taking a fork from her hand and putting it back on the table. 'I think you may have been a little hasty. Perhaps in future you will see fit to consult me on these matters.'

'Consult you?' She turned to face him. 'Why, only last week you said we couldn't afford to replace Alice when she leaves at the end of the month.' She picked up the fork again, wagging it in his face. 'Now did you or did you not?'

'I may have said that – but that was last week. And that Kelly girl is a good little worker – and cheap! It's hard to find good servants at that price. Oh, I think you've cost us a pretty penny, Mrs Llewellyn – a pretty penny, and no mistake!'

'Oh, I see! That's the way of it, is it?' She said, tossing the fork back on to the table. 'I see your little game, Mr Llewellyn. Well, you shan't lay the blame for this at my door. I shall go and tell him I've changed my mind. Never mind that I shall look a complete fool!' She flounced away. 'If you want her, then you shall have her – and never mind my pride!'

Hubert picked up the fork, studied it for a moment, then took a napkin and began polishing, whistling happily all the while.

Pulling the door closed behind her, Mrs Llewellyn paused to smile to herself, before bustling across the small lobby and into the lounge where the man was sitting, awaiting her return.

'Yes, it's perfectly alright,' she said as he got to his feet. 'My husband totally agrees with me. She can come with her belongings as soon as she likes.'

*

I never did tell Gwyneth of how I had lain awake that night of the fire, cuddling against her as she stroked my hair, wetting it with tears that should have been mine – tears I could not cry then – nor for a long time after.

Henry came to see me the next morning. He had stayed with friends in a neighbouring village, and only learned of the accident on his return. We sat in the window of the Davies' house like two strangers. When he left, I watched from the doorway as he walked off in the direction of Cardiff. He never looked back.

Working at the hotel was hard and the hours were long, but that in itself, was a blessing, for it gave me scant time to think about my parents – and when the floodgates finally opened and the grief bore down on me, Mrs Cartwright was there to cheer me along or comfort me in her huge arms.

I was sorry to leave school, but Gwyneth would often call in on her way home, to tell me the latest news, and on my half-day I would go to see Mr Abrahams who had offered to help me with my drawing.

They were golden hours, those Sunday afternoons. In summer we would sketch in the shade of a tree, or out on a sunny hillside – and in winter, sit before his fire, drawing and studying, with tea and scones the reward for our labours.

Then, in May of 1881, just before my eighteenth birthday, I received two, very different proposals.

Chapter Six

The image swam into view, stayed for a moment in almost perfect clarity, softened into a blur, then sharpened again. 'Hold it there, please, Mary.' Beneath the black cloth, Mr Abrahams studied the upside down image that filled the focusing screen of his camera. 'Now, turn this way a little.'

She had taken to wearing her hair up, highlighting her graceful neck, and as she turned, looking into the lens with a confident tilt of the chin and an easy smile, he found it difficult to remember her as the girl who had run sobbing into his arms just a few years earlier.

He came out from beneath the cloth, blinking at the sunlight. 'Just one moment, please.' Closing the shutter and adjusting the aperture, he carefully placed the plate holder in the back of the camera and removed the dark slide. 'Quite still now…' He paused for a heartbeat then pressed the release. 'There. Now I shall have something to remember you by.'

She furrowed her brow – and he looked away from her, gazing across the valley to where the pit wheel shimmered in the afternoon heat. 'Mary, there's something I've been wanting to talk to you about – with regard to your drawing lessons. My knowledge of the subject has always been limited, and now there's really nothing more I can teach you.' She made to protest, but he lifted his hand. 'It's the truth. As a matter of fact it's been the truth this entire winter – it was only selfishness on my part that prevented me from telling you long ago.' He turned back to her. 'So I would like you to give some thought to attending an art school.'

Mary's eyes widened. 'But how could I?'

'It might be possible. I think you have talent – more, as I am led to believe, than many who attend such schools.' He took a card from his pocket book and passed it to her. 'So I would like you to put together a portfolio of your work and show it to this man.'

Mary took the card. '*Mr Mawden Protheroe, Cardiff Academy of Art,*' she read, then she looked up. 'I could never afford this.'

'I have reason to believe the fees might be surprisingly low,' he smiled. 'Of course, you would need some money to live on should you be successful in your application, but – whilst my salary is not overly large, neither is my expenditure – I think the money could be found.'

'You would do that for me?'

'There is no guarantee he will accept you – so it might be better if we kept this arrangement just between ourselves until we know for certain – but should it prove the case, then – yes.'

Slowly she shook her head. 'It's a wonderful offer, but I could never let you …'

'Mary, listen to me. I have had a good life in many ways, a great many ways, but I've never had a family – never felt the need. But in these last four years …' He looked at her. 'Please, Mary. Let me do this for you.'

For a moment she sat stunned, then she was on her feet, hugging him, sobbing against his shoulder.

'Come, come,' he said, feeling the sudden tightness in his throat. 'You are making something of a habit of this.'

*

'So then Mrs Llewellyn says to the guest, *I don't allow any hanky-panky in this hotel*, and the gentleman turns round to Mr Llewellyn, calm as you like, and says, *bad luck for you, old chap!*'

'By, Mary,' said Owen, laughing, 'you haven't lost your touch for telling stories.'

Embarrassed by the innocent remark, she looked into her lap, then turned to Gwyneth. 'I hear you are going to be a teacher?'

'Aye, going to be worse than old Griffiths, aren't you, Gwyn!' laughed Alan. 'We'll have to mind our P's and Q's now, I suppose.'

Standing by the table, cutting slices of cake, Meg glowed with happiness. 'Right proud of her, we are. Never had a teacher in the family before.'

Mary smiled. 'It's wonderful news, Gwyn. I'm so pleased for you.'

'I don't know how I'm going to get everything ready in time,' said Gwyneth. 'I've got to go into Cardiff next Saturday to buy some new clothes and things.'

'Aye,' grinned Owen. 'Damn fine job it is that costs you an arm and a leg before you even start, eh?'

'Oh, Da!' Gwyneth gave him a light slap on the knee.

'See!' Owen chuckled. 'Already she's giving us a good smack to keep us in line!'

'I was just wondering,' continued Gwyneth, 'if you could change your half-day and come with me. It would be … well, just like old times.'

'Oh, I should love to!'

'But you'll miss your drawing lesson, won't you?' asked Meg, handing her a slice of cake on a plate.

'Yes. But it doesn't matter. I'm going to …' She broke off. 'Well, I … I'm going to have to miss the odd one here and there.'

Sitting opposite her, wearing his best suit and with his shoes buffed to a high gloss, Thomas shifted uncomfortably. 'How is it going? With the drawing, that is …'

'Alright,' she smiled, looking down at her plate as though it had acquired a sudden fascination.

'Well …' he cleared his throat, '… that's good, then.'

'Yes.'

Meg picked up the tea-pot, refilling their cups.

'Oh, not for me,' said Mary. 'I should be getting back.'

Thomas got to his feet. 'I could walk you home … if you'd like?'

'Oh … *yes* … that would be very kind.'

'What, kinder than last time?' laughed Alan. 'Or the time before that?'

Meg shot him a look.

'I'll ask about my half-day the moment I get home,' said Mary, gathering her things. 'I'm sure the Llewellyns won't mind – and it will be *just* like old times.'

Filled with happiness, Gwyneth followed them into the street. 'Go safely.'

'Yes, go safely – the both of you,' called Meg, coming to the door and waving until Mary and Thomas were almost out of view.

'You know?' said Gwyneth, coming back into the house. 'I think I'll fetch my coat and catch them up. I should quite like a walk, myself.'

Meg quietly closed the front-door. 'No,' she said. 'No, you wouldn't.'

Walking side-by-side, Mary and Thomas made their way up on to the Caerphilly road, barely speaking at first, the long silences punctuated by small, self-conscious exchanges. But as they passed the halfway milestone, Mary made as though she had stumbled and caught of hold of Thomas's arm, holding him close for the remainder of the journey.

The summer evening was warm, the landscape tinted with the muted pinks and purples of twilight, and dotted here and there by the lights from distant farms, and though he felt awkward at first, Thomas found himself relaxing into this new intimacy, listening attentively as Mary told him of the Llewellyns and Mrs Cartwright, of Griffiths and Mr Abrahams, and then, finally, of her mother and father.

'You must miss them.' He placed his hand on hers, but feeling her tense he quickly removed it. 'I'm sorry – I didn't mean to be bold.'

'No … it wasn't that.' She tightened her grip on his arm, and for several minutes they walked without speaking. 'Thomas?' she said at last. 'If I tell you something – something I've never told anyone – will you try not to despise me?'

'I could never despise you, Mary.'

She halted, searching his face. '*You might*, Thomas.'

'No – *never*.'

They began to walk again, and with the lights of Caerphilly growing ever nearer, she told him of the night of the fire. This time there was no pretence, no fairytales, and she poured out her heart, holding back nothing as she let each wretched detail flow from her, until in the darkened back streets she stopped, wiping at her eyes. 'I loved them – and I miss them so very much. But … back then … there was some horrible, *horrible* part of me that felt … *relieved*.'

He moved closer, putting his arms around her. 'It's alright, Mary, it's alright. I understand.' Then his cheek was against hers, and the scent of her hair was filling his senses. 'Oh, Mary … I wish …'

She found his lips, silencing him with a kiss, melting against him as he held her, and for long minutes they remained locked in the embrace, pressing against each other as though nothing would tear them apart. Then Thomas let his mouth slide from hers, kissing along her jaw until he came to the soft lobe of her ear. 'Marry me,' he whispered.

*

'Yer love 'im, don't yer?' asked Mrs Cartwright.

'I think so.'

'Well, yer don't sound very sure, I must say!'

Sitting on the bed with her legs drawn up and her chin resting on her knees, Mary looked at the sketches scattered about the floor of the small attic bedroom, then back to where Mrs Cartwright sat sewing. 'I do love him. I'm sure I do. But …'

'Well, but what, then? Yer can't keep 'im waitin' for an answer for ever. He sounds like a nice enough boy – an' they ain't so easy t' come by.'

Mary sighed. 'It's just that – suppose you'd had the chance to do something, become something – maybe an artist?'

'Lawd!' she chuckled. 'Me? – an artist? Now I should think even an imagination like yours might 'ave trouble with that idea!'

'Well, something else then.'

Mrs Cartwright rested the blouse she was sewing on her lap. 'I don't know nothin' about no art – nor no artists, neither – but I do know that nice young fellers like your Thomas don't grow on trees.'

On the shelf behind her the candle began to flicker and die. Mary made to light another, but Mrs Cartwright stopped her. 'There's no need. I shall 'ave t' be off t' my bed soon, anyways,' she said – yet she made no effort to leave, and sat motionless in the darkened corner for some while.

'I 'ad a young man once,' she said at length. 'Oh, I was a slim young thing like yerself in them days – but not pretty, yer see. No, I was never what yer might call pretty. *Plain Peg*, they used to call me at school.'

Mary hugged her knees more tightly. 'That was cruel.'

'Cruel? No! It was the truth, plain an' simple! No point in tryin' t' fool m'self – or anyone else for that matter. I just 'ad t' make the best of it. An' I did! I went t' work as a kitchen maid in a big 'ouse up the West End. Gawd, the cook there was a slave driver if ever there was one – but she knew 'er business right enough. An' I watched 'er like an 'awk, learning everythin' I could. Well, over time I worked my way up, an' in a few more years I could 'ave looked for a position as a cook in my own right.' She leaned back against the chair and turned her head in the direction of the small window that looked out over the rooftops of Caerphilly. 'It's dark, ain't it! Always bloomin' dark 'ere! The room I 'ad in those days, blimey, what a view! All the lights o' London – stretched out as far as the eye could see! I told my Charlie about it once an' 'e used to say to me, *Go on, Peg, let's sneak up there an' 'ave a look* – an' then 'e'd give me a wink! Oh, 'e was a cheeky devil.'

'And he was your young man?'

Peggy nodded. ''E used t' deliver the orders from this big shop up Kensington way. Proper posh 'e looked, in a dark green uniform an' a top 'at – not like yer ordinary delivery men. I don't know what it was 'e saw in me, 'cos I 'adn't got no better lookin' – but there must 'ave been somethin' 'cos 'e asked me out – though I 'ad to be careful an' meet 'im at the end of the road 'cos the lady of that house didn't allow no followers. 'E looked right different out of 'is uniform. So 'andsome, 'e was. We'd go walkin' in the park on my 'alf-days. An' boatin'! We was sittin' in a boat on the Serpentine when 'e asked me t' marry 'im.' She broke off, her hand brushing briefly at her eye. 'I was so 'appy. We 'ad it all planned out. We'd wait a bit – save up our money while I learned all I could – then we'd start a little restaurant of our own. *Peg's Pantry*, Charlie wanted t' call it. Daft name, eh?' She paused again, then sighed.

'Two days later the whole 'ousehold was told the family was movin' up t' this God-forsaken place. I'd never even 'eard of Caerphilly up until then. I didn't 'ave t' go o' course – but I wouldn't 'ave got such a good position anywhere else. Charlie made some enquiries about jobs up 'ere, but there was nothin' for 'im that paid 'alf as well. So we agreed t' wait. Just a couple o' years. It didn't seem so long, really – but it was too long. 'Course, we wrote to each other reg'lar for the first six months. But then 'is letters just stopped. I 'eard later that 'e'd married the girl who served in the grocer's shop. Pretty, she was, as I remember.' Slowly she got up, bundling the sewing in her large hands and moving toward the door. 'I suppose that was my one chance. There weren't no more followers after that. Yer get called *Mrs* when yer reach my age – out of sympathy, I s'pose.' With her hand on the doorknob, she paused. 'You're a pretty girl, Mary. I dare say there'll be plenty more young men for you. But don't let 'em all slip by. It can be a lonely ol' life.'

Mary came from the bed, and putting her hand on the woman's shoulder, kissed her on the cheek.

'Life's full of regrets,' Peggy smiled sadly. 'Maybe me an' Charlie weren't never meant t' be. But I wish … that just once … I'd taken 'im up t' look at the lights.'

Chapter Seven

Beyond the mullioned windows of the milliner's, the wind blew with a vengeance, swirling about the mass of cabs and carriages, tradesmen's vans and crowded omnibuses, while on the pavement people hurried past, heads down, shielding their eyes from the spiralling dust.

'So, what do you think, Gwyn?' Standing in the gloomy interior of the shop, Mary spun around, an old fashioned, but very expensive bonnet on her head.

Gwyneth pretended to consider it. 'A little *young* for you, I think.'

'Oh, really, well then, how about …?'

The shopkeeper gave a disapproving cough. 'Will that be all, ladies? Or is there something else I might show you?'

Gwyneth turned back to him, blushing. 'Oh, yes … that is … no, nothing else, thank you.'

The man wrapped the gloves Gwyneth had chosen, then showed the girls to the door with the solemnity of an undertaker.

'Will that be all, ladies?' mimicked Mary the moment they were back on the street.

'Mary!' Gwyneth chided, taking her arm as they battled their way along the High Street against the buffeting wind. 'Goodness knows what he must have thought.'

'I expect he thought we were two spirited young ladies on a spree.' She pulled Gwyneth closer, smiling. 'And if so, then he would have been quite correct. Now, where to next?'

Gwyneth felt for the list in her pocket. 'Well …'

'Mary! Hey, Mary!' From across the road a shabbily dressed young woman pushed her way toward them to stand with her hands on her hips and a broad smile across her face. 'Mary Jane Kelly! God, I hardly recognised you!'

'Hettie?'

The woman grinned. 'My, but you've grown a bit since the last time I saw you!' Then the smile faded. 'I was sorry to hear about your mam and da. Terrible business. I'd only seen Annie – your mam – the day before. I did mean to get in touch, like, but – well, you know how things get. It was Henry who told us about it.'

'He's here?'

'No. He stayed with us for a while – you know – after the fire. But there was some trouble.' She paused, looking warily at Gwyneth.

'It's alright,' Mary patted Gwyneth's arm. 'This is Gwyn – my best friend.' Then to Gwyneth. 'This is my cousin, Hettie Jones. She lives here in Cardiff – or at least …?' She turned to Hettie with an enquiring look.

'Oh, yes, still here alright! I'm married now, of course. Have been these past two years. I'm Hettie Cruickshank these days – God, what a name, eh?' A strong gust of wind sent her straw hat bowling into a shop doorway, and she went to fetch it, her shawl streaming out in front of her as Mary and Gwyneth clutched at their skirts. 'Come on,' she called to them. 'No point standing here chattering when we can do it out of this wind and have us a drink at the same time.'

The Red Dragon public house stood on a mean corner, close to the docks and a good five-minute walk from the centre of town.

'We're not going in *there*?' murmured Gwyneth, staring wide-eyed at the unsavoury facade.

Mary paused, looking uncertain.

'It's alright,' laughed Hettie, pushing open the door. 'It won't bite you. This was a favourite of your mam's. Might not be much to look at, but it's cheap and cheerful.'

Gwyneth drew back. '*Mary*,' she whispered anxiously, 'I've never been in one of these places before.'

'Neither have I. But … well, it can't do any harm, can it? Oh, come on Gwyn, it'll be an adventure, don't you think?'

Inside the air was thick with tobacco smoke and the heady smell of beer and spirits. 'What'll you have?' called Hettie, pushing her way to the bar.

Mary squeezed through after her. 'What are you having?'

'Penn'orth o' gin, I shouldn't wonder.'

'Well … we'll have a penn'orth of gin, too, won't we, Gwyn?'

Following in Mary's wake, Gwyneth nodded doubtfully.

'Here, Sid,' Hettie called to the barman. 'Give us three penn'orths – and don't go being miserly with it.'

'*Mary*.' This time Gwyneth's urgent whisper was accompanied by a sharp tug at her sleeve.

'What is it?'

'*Look*.' Gwyneth motioned with eyes as wide as saucers to where a man was leaning into a fat woman, laughing and joking – and with his hand up under her skirts. 'Mary – please let's not stay?'

'Here you go then, girls.'

Still blushing, Mary turned to find Hettie holding two small glasses. 'Oh, thank you,' she said, fumbling in her pocket for the tuppence.

Hettie shook her head. 'That's alright. My treat.' She handed them their drinks, then picked up her own, raising it in salute. 'To ruined mothers, eh?'

Sniffing at the colourless liquid, Mary took a tentative sip.

'Not tasted that before, have you?' grinned Hettie as Gwyneth followed Mary's lead. 'Well, it takes a little getting used to, like – but it does you a power of good.'

'It's – *quite* nice,' said Gwyneth, swallowing the rest down in one go and breaking into a fit of coughing.

Hettie let out a burst of laughter. 'Go easy! You're not supposed to swig it like beer – well, not till you're used to it, that is. Here, let me get you another.' She pushed her way back to the bar, returning a few minutes later with the refilled glass.

'You were going to tell me about Henry?' Mary prompted.

'Oh, yes.' Hettie lowered her voice. 'Well, he was here for a couple weeks. But there was some trouble – you know – with the police.'

'What kind of trouble?'

'A fight it was – well, to start with, leastways. Don't know what started it, like – but he has got a bit of a temper on him, that brother of yours.'

'So what happened?'

'Don't know for sure. The other man was off one of the boats. Only a little chap, but he made mincemeat of Henry – that much I do know.' Hettie leaned closer. 'That should have been the end of it, but sometime later that night someone took a knife to the man, cut him real bad, so they say. The police came looking for Henry straight off, but we'd already had the word they were on their way, and he legged it sharpish, like. For what it's worth, I don't think he did it. He just decided it was better not to be there when they arrived. But we haven't seen hide nor hair of him since.'

Mary sighed, then noticing Hettie's glass was empty she felt for the coins in her pocket. 'Would you like another one? My treat this time.'

'I should say so. Another penn'orth all round, is it?' She cocked her head to one side, regarding Gwyneth with amusement. 'But I think your friend might be wanting some fresh air first.'

Gwyneth blinked several times, then, very deliberately, put her empty glass on to the table beside her. 'I'm alright.' She looked from one to the other. 'I *am* – really.'

''Course you are, my love,' laughed Hettie. 'But I think you've had enough just for the moment.'

Faint strains of music reached their ears as they emerged on to the street, the sound growing louder and louder, until from around a corner a procession came into view: a broad column of well-dressed men and women marching four abreast, accompanied by a brass band playing rousing hymn tunes.

'Look at these silly buggers!' chuckled Hettie. 'What they marching for?'

The procession was now only thirty yards away, and several of the banners proclaimed *Abolish Child Slavery* and *Suffer The Little Children* in letters two feet high. 'It's against child labour,' said Mary, suddenly realising her cousin couldn't read.

'Some people! Must be nice having nothing better to do with your time!' As she spoke, a tall, thin man with a drooping moustache approached, handing each of them a printed foolscap sheet before striding off in step with the procession. Hettie tossed the sheet into the road. 'Bloody load of nonsense! It's alright for them lot – but what about the poor sods that needs the money, eh? What's wrong with kids earning their keep, I should like to know!'

Gwyneth studied the leaflet. 'This is disgraceful.'

'You're right there, my love,' said Hettie, turning back toward the pub. 'They want to mind their own bloody business!'

'No, I mean …' Gwyneth looked up, her eyes shimmering. 'We should do something.'

Mary studied her own sheet. 'We should? What?'

'I don't know. But something …' She gazed earnestly at Mary. 'We could join the march.'

'You aren't serious?'

'Yes, yes I am!' She gripped Mary's arm. 'Come on. You were always telling me I shouldn't be so dull.'

'Gwyn! I never did!'

Gwyneth smiled, her eyes moist with emotion. 'It's alright. I *am* dull. I know I am. And I've always wished I could be like you, Mary. But this,' she shook the sheet she was holding. 'This is such a worthwhile cause – and it would be an adventure, wouldn't it? Come on. What do you say? Shall we march with them?'

'But what about your shopping?'

'What about another drink?' said Hettie, coming back to where they were standing – but Gwyneth seemed not to hear her.

'We can easily get the shopping later. Oh, come on Mary – please?'

'Gwyn?' But Gwyneth's excitement was infectious, and Mary felt it surge through her. 'Are you really sure?'

'Oh, yes! Yes!'

Hettie stared at them incredulously. 'Don't be bloody daft! Come back and have another gin.'

'I'm sorry, Hettie.' Mary looked to where Gwyneth was already running toward the procession, and quickly took two pennies from her pocket, pushing them into Hettie's hand. 'It was nice seeing you again.'

'We want to march with you!' Gwyneth shouted jubilantly over the ringing trumpets and the throb of the single bass drum.

Marching toward the rear of the column, a large, bespectacled woman with wiry, grey hair and a thick, fur-trimmed coat, eyed her with relief. She carried one end of a banner, and was red in the face from struggling with the pole as the wind tried to wrench the billowing sheet from its mooring. 'Well then, perhaps you would like to take this? I'm sure your young arms are stronger than mine.'

Gwyneth grasped the long pole, holding it resolutely.

'Well done, you girls!' said the woman moving back a position to make room for Mary.

'We are having an adventure, aren't we?' grinned Gwyneth as she fought to hold the pole steady in the face of a fresh gust.

Mary took her arm, squeezing it with delight. 'Oh yes! Though I never would have believed it.'

'Can you imagine what my da would say if he knew?'

'*What do you think you're up to, Gwyneth Davies!*' said Mary, imitating Owen's deep voice. '*Making a proper spectacle of yourself!*'

Gwyneth laughed delightedly, hiccupped, then laughed again.

'Gwyn! You're drunk!'

'I am not!' Gwyneth tried to look insulted, but then she hiccupped again and they both burst into giggles. They were still laughing as they entered Queen Street, where the music ended raggedly, and the procession came to an unexpected halt.

'Mary?' said Gwyneth, becoming serious as they stood waiting. 'You won't marry Thomas, will you?'

Mary looked at her in surprise.

'I overheard him tell Mam. I wasn't trying to listen – but you know what our house is like. It's hard not to hear things.'

For a moment, Mary made no answer. Then she asked, 'You think I shouldn't?'

Gwyneth leaned closer. 'It's not for me to say. But it was you that always wanted to do something different – something special – and you were right! I can see that now. There *is* more to life.' She looked deeply into Mary's eyes. 'Thomas is the best brother anyone could ever want – and he'll make someone a good, reliable husband – but is that really all you want now?'

Mary chewed at her lip. 'Gwyn … I don't know. I …'

'You, boy!' came the shrill, imperious voice of the bespectacled woman as an earnest young man came running by. 'Why have we stopped?'

60

'The police won't let us go any further. They're insisting we go back toward the docks. It looks as if we'll have to – or abandon the march.' The words had barely left his lips when the band started up again, and to the strains of *I love Jesus, yes I do*, the procession moved off once more, turning sharply left into one of the side roads, shepherded by half a dozen constables.

In a very short time the elegant shops and houses of Queen Street were left behind, and both the surroundings and the people lining the kerb became increasingly mean and forbidding.

From in front of grimy factory gates and dirty, dilapidated houses, unshaven men and lank-haired women hurled taunts and abuse, while ragged and barefoot children looked on – their sallow faces mirroring the hatred that surrounded them.

Mary began to feel uneasy.

They were marching directly into the wind, which gusted so fiercely that several times Gwyneth needed Mary's help to keep the banner from being torn from her hands. Then, from somewhere in front, a brown bowler hat flew from the head of a marcher, and rolled into the gutter – where it was quickly and deliberately crushed beneath the boot of a short, stocky and extremely vicious-looking man.

'Keep looking straight ahead, girls,' commanded the imperious voice from behind. 'We'll soon be past them.'

But the crushing of the hat seemed to serve as a signal to others in the crowd, and despite the police presence, several men left the pavement to knock hats from the heads of marchers, while the rest swore and spat.

The band was already in some disarray, out of time and out of tune, when a lump of brick chimed off the euphonium, bringing the music to a discordant end. Almost immediately, other missiles began to fly into the column. A woman fell to her knees, blood pouring from her forehead, and suddenly there was a breaking of ranks as several of the younger men set about their tormentors while the police waded in, truncheons drawn.

Mary looked about her in terror. 'Run, Gwyn!' she screamed, bolting from the melee to where some of the marchers were rallying by a factory gate.

Violent skirmishes were breaking out everywhere, and amidst it all stood Gwyneth, uncomprehending, holding her pole aloft, the banner stretching down to the cobbled road where the other pole lay abandoned.

'Gwyn! Gwyn!' screamed Mary, but her voice was lost over the shouts and curses and the blasts from police whistles that were already bringing reinforcements running to the scene.

'Just drop it, Gwyn! Drop the banner. Please!' But Gwyneth seemed transfixed. 'Gwyn, please!' Mary thrust herself from the huddled group, fighting off the hands that sought to pull her back to safety. 'Gwyn!'

Twenty yards away two constables were running toward Gwyneth, separating to pass her by on each side, when a great gust came rushing up the road, driving a cloud of dust before it and sending rubbish and pieces of clothing high into the air. It struck Gwyneth with its gritty breath, blinding her and filling the great sail of her banner so that she spun like a top, the heavy pole she still gripped flailing the air to crash with a sickening thud into the face of one of the running policemen.

The wind swept on, and in the calm that followed, Gwyneth rubbed her eyes and looked down in disbelief at the unconscious man at her feet, the blood from his shattered nose pooling where his cheek lay pressed to the cobbles.

Chapter Eight

Thomas became my saviour that terrible day. We met on the road to Nant-y-Pridd, and he held me tightly, listening with infinite patience as I sobbed out the awful story. It was he who broke the news to his parents, while I trembled by his side, and it was he who walked me home afterwards, trying with every step to assure me that I wasn't to blame.

But I was.

I was the one who had always wanted adventures and excitement, without thought to the consequences, and now Gwyneth was paying the price.

I'd searched the faces of Owen and Meg as they learned of their daughter's arrest. If they held me in anyway responsible, they did not show it – but in those terrible days prior to Gwyneth's trial, I never stopped searching.

'All rise!'

With a business-like air, the magistrate, Mr William Fellowes, took his seat, casting an appraising eye over the public box, where well-dressed figures rubbed shoulders with the more usual characters, before turning his attention to the clerk of the court. 'This afternoon's business continues to concern the disturbance in Bute Street?'

The clerk came to a semblance of attention. 'Yes, sir.'

'Very well. Please call the next defendant.'

'Are you waiting for someone?' whispered a woman sitting next to Meg.

Meg shot her a worried glance. 'Yes, my daughter.'

The woman reached out and gave Meg's arm a reassuring squeeze. 'If she was on the march, she'll be alright. Mr Fellowes is an enthusiastic supporter of the temperance movement. You wait and see, it will be exactly as it was this morning. Your girl will get off with a shilling fine, and those ruffians who started the trouble will be lucky to escape a gaol sentence.'

'Gwyneth Alice Davies,' announced the clerk of the court.

Gwyneth's frightened face appeared above the wooden partition screening the stairs to the cells as she was escorted into the dock. She looked neat and tidy in the clean dress Owen had brought for her, but there was a drawn, haggard look about her face, and her eyes were ringed with dark smudges.

Mary cast a quick glance across at Meg, then at Owen. 'Do you think it will be alright?' she whispered.

Sitting stiffly and formally erect, Owen could not bring himself to answer, but instead reached for his wife's hand, squeezing it in his thick, calloused palm.

The magistrate regarded Gwyneth kindly. 'You are charged with causing grievous bodily harm to a Police Constable in the execution of his duty. How do you plead?'

'Guilty, sir,' she said in a tiny voice.

'You'll have to speak up, my dear.'

Gwyneth swallowed hard. 'Guilty, sir. But it was an accident – the wind caught the banner – I didn't mean to …' Her voice quavered and tailed away.

'Hmmm.' Fellowes drummed his fingers on the case notes, then leaned forward to address the clerk. 'Is the injured officer present?'

'No, sir. Still in hospital, sir.'

'I see. Then I suppose we must call Sergeant Wynford.'

The uniformed officer took the stand.

'You were the arresting officer in this case, also?'

Sergeant Wynford smoothed his moustache and drew himself up importantly. 'Yes, sir.'

'What were the injuries sustained by Police Constable Murphy?'

'Broken nose and concussion, sir. I expect he will be off duty for some time. As a matter of fact it's probably the worst …'

'If you would please confine yourself to answering *just* the question, Sergeant. Should I require elaboration, you may rest assured that I will ask.' Fellowes shuffled the papers before him. 'Now it seems to me that you cannot have been the only witness to this attack which was with a … ah, yes, a wooden baton.'

'More of a barge pole, sir. If you don't mind me saying.'

The magistrate eyed him with annoyance. 'And in *your* opinion this *piece of wood* was wielded with intent?'

'Yes, sir. In my opinion it was with the deliberate intention of preventing Police Constable Murphy from answering my summons for assistance.'

Fellowes rubbed thoughtfully at his chin. 'Are there really no other witnesses to corroborate the girl's story? Surely someone participating in the march?'

'Not so far as I have been able to ascertain, sir. But then the defendant is not a member of any of the groups involved, and only joined the march after having become drunk at the Red Dragon public house.'

Fellowes stared at Gwyneth in astonishment. 'Is this true, Miss Davies?'

'No, sir – that is I …' Gwyneth paled as Fellowes' friendly manner disappeared before her eyes.

'Were you or were you not drunk at the time?'

Large tears rolled down Gwyneth's cheeks.

'It would appear the girl did have a female accomplice,' Wynford volunteered. 'But Miss Davies has been uncooperative on that account, and we have not been able to trace her. However, I do have a statement taken from Miss Davies upon arrival at Wood Street Police Station.'

Fellowes gave him an exasperated look. 'Then please do read it.'

'Certainly, sir.' With a self-important flourish, the sergeant took up the sheet of paper. 'On asking Miss Davies how she had come to be part of the march, she replied – *I just wanted to. We'd had some gin, and thought it would be fun.*'

Fellowes studied her over his spectacles, his brows drawn into a condemning frown. 'Miss Davies,' he said severely. 'Do you deny making this statement?'

Gwyneth lowered her head in shame. 'No, sir.'

'I see. Then have you anything else to say in your defence?'

Confused, she cast about for the faces of her parents.

'Miss Davies! You will be so good as to look at *me*. The crime you are charged with is a serious one. Have you anything to say in your defence?'

'It wasn't like that – you're making it sound so horrible. It was an accident. I didn't mean to do it – *I didn't.*'

'Yes, yes,' Fellowes said impatiently. 'But you don't deny you had been drinking, and were still under the influence when this incident occurred?'

Gwyneth dabbed at her eyes with a handkerchief. 'N-No, sir. I'm sorry.'

'Well, in as much that you are sorry, I do believe you.' He removed his spectacles, folded them and placed them purposely into the pocket of his jacket. 'It was my mistaken assumption you had been brought before me as an idealistic young lady caught up in an unfortunate incident perpetrated by ruffians. However, I now see that for you it was nothing more than a drunken lark which culminated in the maiming of a police constable.' He paused, adding a new degree of gravity to his voice. 'I will not tolerate public drunkenness, neither will I tolerate any form of violence toward a police officer – and in view of the slur you might well have cast over the whole temperance movement, I am tempted to increase the severity of your sentence. However, I shall take your age and previous good character into consideration and be lenient.'

She looked up at him with grateful, tear-filled eyes.

'I find you guilty as charged,' he continued, 'and sentence you to one week in gaol with hard labour!'

For a moment Gwyneth didn't seem to hear, then she swayed, her mouth open and her face a deathly white.

'This is an outrage!' Owen shouted, leaping to his feet. 'This is no bloody justice. It was an accident! Just a damned accident!'

Fellowes motioned for Owen to be removed from the court, instantly returning his attention to the dock. 'Take her down.'

'Gwyneth!' Owen half shouted, half cried, staring across the chasm of the court room as she was led away. 'Gwyneth!'

Slowly Gwyneth turned, finding his face and holding it until the moment she disappeared from view.

'Mr and Mrs Davies?'

The sun was dazzlingly bright as Meg, Owen and Mary emerged from the court building to find a portly, bespectacled woman waiting for them.

'I just wanted to express my sympathy – for the sentence your daughter received.'

Meg gave her a tearful smile. 'Thank you,' she began.

But the woman would tolerate no interruption. 'It was harsher than we expected, though I have to say it could have been much worse. He could easily have given her six months, you know! Still, it was something of a shock all the same – such a terrible, terrible accident. I still shudder to think about it.'

Owen stared at her. 'You saw what happened?'

The woman gave him a condescending look. 'Yes, of course. I was on the march myself. In fact, I was the one who gave her the banner. Naturally, we had no way of knowing the girls had been drinking,' she gave Mary a disapproving glance, 'and when we found out – well, of course ...'

'Why the hell didn't you tell them?' Owen's face flushed crimson. 'You saw it was an accident – and yet you said nothing!'

The woman blinked several times then drew herself up, indignantly. 'Mr Davies! I am not used to being spoken to in such a manner – and I would ask you to moderate your language!' Owen made to answer but she continued without pause. 'To begin with, your daughter *was* drunk as charged. Secondly, although many of us witnessed what certainly appeared to be an accident, none of us can be really sure – and our cause is far too important to ...'

Owen would hear no more. 'Your cause? Your cause? Our daughter has just been sent to prison! I think that is a damn sight more important than your cause, don't you?'

The woman regarded him with disdain. 'I can see I am wasting my time,' she said at last. 'I merely wanted to offer my sympathy – and I have done so.' She made to leave, but paused. 'Let me just say this. Can you possibly imagine the scandal had we appeared to be connected in any way to a girl who violently attacked a policeman with a temperance society banner – while she was under the influence of drink? We would have become a laughing stock! In a week she will be out of prison and the matter forgotten, but we see our work as having far greater significance. You cannot conceivably think we would jeopardise that. Now, I bid you good day.'

'And you call yourselves Christians!' said Meg, unable to remain silent a second longer.

The woman eyed her, her face perfectly composed. 'Yes, Mrs Davies, we do. If we are ultimately judged wrong in our actions, then *we* at least can plead that it was for the greater good. However, there is one person who might have spoken up for whom that is not the case!'

Mary felt her cheeks burn as the woman gave her a withering look.

'She's right,' said Mary as they watched the woman stride away down the street. 'I'll go back – tell the police I was there.'

'And that you'd been drinking, too?' Owen's voice was heavy with defeat. 'It's too late. There's nothing you can do – not now – but you *could* have prevented it from happening in the first place.'

In that moment, Mary saw in Owen's eyes the look she had been so desperately hoping not to find.

Chapter Nine

'Damn me!' said Alan, his hands shaking with anger and frustration. 'And damn the bastard magistrate, too! It can't be right, can it, Da?'

Slumped in his chair, Owen stared into the empty fireplace. 'I don't know, boy. I'm not sure I know anything anymore. My poor Gwyn.' His hand went to cover his mouth, and he turned his face further from them.

'There must be something we can do!' persisted Alan.

Sitting stooped and red-eyed, Meg gave the boy a weak smile. 'What, my love? What can we do?'

'There has to be something! Some sort of appeal, like?'

Thomas sighed. 'Don't be daft, man. Chances are it would just make matters worse.'

'Can't get much worse, as I can see!'

'Can't it? You want to try looking in the newspaper now and then!' *The Western Mail* lay on the table in front of Thomas, and he opened it. '*Police Intelligence*,' he read. 'Interesting reading this makes.' His finger traced the lines of small type. 'Cardiff woman found guilty of being drunk and disorderly in St Mary's street – three months in gaol.' He skipped several entries. 'Here's a man found guilty in Carmarthen of knocking over a policeman and then kicking him. He's fined twelve shillings, yet another man from Caerphilly is given six months with hard labour for getting drunk and merely pushing the arresting officer against a wall!' He pushed the paper away. 'No rhyme nor reason to it as I can see. There's nothing to be done. A week isn't so long.'

'Not so long?' Owen turned, his eyes moist. 'It'll break my little Gwyn.'

Thomas saw the pain written on his father's face and he softened his voice. 'It won't be easy, I know that, Da. But she'll be alright – and it's not as if there was anything we could have done to prevent it.'

'*Mary* could have prevented it.'

'How, Da? How could she?'

'She could have left our Gwyneth alone! Gwyn would never have done any of those things if Mary hadn't filled her head with bloody daft ideas!'

'It wasn't Mary's fault!'

'And I say it was!' He slammed his hand on to the arm of the chair. 'A fine friend she turned out to be! She could have stood up in court – but she didn't!'

Meg looked up at him. 'Owen, love. You said yourself it wouldn't have done any good.'

'They would have seen her as an accomplice,' said Thomas. 'Perhaps even sent her to gaol as well. She'd have lost everything, her job, her reputation.'

Owen glared at him. 'And what about your sister's reputation?' His knuckles grew white as he tightened his grip on the chair. 'It's all Mary's fault – all the fault of that damn Kelly girl. If it hadn't been for her …'

'Don't, Da – please.'

Meg tried to take Owen's hand, but he shook her off. 'She's not welcome in this house ever again! You hear me – all of you? Not ever again!'

'Owen, you're upset – we all are. But you can't go blaming Mary.'

'Can't I?' He turned his face from them to gaze once more into the cold ashes.

In the silence that followed, Thomas picked up his jacket and walked from the house.

*

It was just after six o'clock that evening when a flustered Mrs Cartwright answered the light rapping at the kitchen door of the Cross Keys.

'An' about time, too, m'girl! The missus'll be …' She stopped abruptly. 'Oh! You're 'er young man, ain't yer?'

Thomas flushed a little, embarrassed. 'Yes, well … I suppose.'

'Gawd, you two make a right pair! Neither of yer seem t' know what yer about!' She searched past him. 'Well? Ain't she with yer?'

'No. I … I thought she'd be here.'

'Well, she ain't! An' if the Missus finds out there'll be the devil t' pay!'

'There was the court case this afternoon,' he offered.

'Yes, yes, I know all about that,' Mrs Cartwright said in a hushed voice. 'But we don't want the whole bloomin' town knowin', do we! Yer'd better come in.'

Inside the heat was oppressive. The ovens and cooking ranges that kept it warm and inviting on a cold winter's day made it far less welcoming in mid-summer. He moped his brow. 'Have you not seen her?'

'Oh, I seen 'er, alright! Came straight in an' went up to 'er room. I told 'er t' get a move on, 'cos o' the big dinner we got on tonight, but she didn't come down. So, I went up after 'er – only she wasn't there. Must 'ave gone out the front, I s'pose. But these were all over 'er bed.' She gestured to a bundle of papers that lay on the table. 'All 'er lovely drawin's …'

Thomas picked them up. Every one had been torn in half.

*

Why did you undress? Was it easier like that? Just like swimming …

The evening sun was warm on Mary's skin, and the river lay smooth as a millpond.

… and never coming back?

Unbuttoning her boots, she slipped them off, along with her stockings, then stood up, her bare toes on the cool mud.

Or did you long to do something shocking?

She moved to the water's edge.

I thought I wanted that.

Taking off her blouse, she tossed it on to the grass and began unfastening her skirt, dropping it around her ankles along with her petticoat and drawers to stand naked on the riverbank.

As if doing shocking things could change anything.

Her hands moved to unpin her hair, so that it fell about her shoulders.

But children don't see things as they really are …

She moved a few steps past the water's edge, feeling the refreshing coldness swirl about her ankles. The riverbed dropped steeply away and the water was soon lapping at her thighs as she moved forward.

… they think wishes can come true. Dreams can become real.

She smiled sadly, remembering Gwyneth's constant admonitions. She was waist deep now, and she raised her face toward the sun, just as she had on that day, so long ago, when they had walked back from school. 'You were right, Gwyn,' she whispered to her absent friend. 'It *was* all just being silly – and I'm so very sorry.'

As the water reached her chest, she let her feet slip from the bottom – and sank into the green, silent depths.

*

'Mam, can't you have a word with him, like?' Alan was leaning by the scullery window, looking out to where his father was digging over the small vegetable garden, a blue haze of pipe smoke drifting above his head as he worked with a grim determination.

'There's no need.'

'But what if Mary says yes?'

Meg barely paused as she washed the plates. 'I don't know what you're talking about, I'm sure.'

'Oh, come on, Mam. You can't keep a secret in this house.'

She piled more crockery in the sink and straightened up, her hands on her hips. 'If you know so much, then you should also know that whatever else your father is, he is fair! He's upset at the moment, but if he's being unreasonable, he'll know it. He'll need no words from me.'

'But they'll have to live here, won't they? I mean, there's a waiting list for colliery houses, and I can't see our Thomas renting private, even if there was anywhere – not with the ten percent cut in wages that's in the offing.'

Meg wiped her hands on her apron, then rolled her sleeves further up her arms. 'She hasn't given him an answer yet, at least to my knowledge – so we'll cross that bridge when we come to it.'

*

In the depths of the river, Mary heard the frantic splashing as a series of muffled explosions, and kicked out with powerful strokes, breaking the surface twenty feet from where Thomas was standing thigh deep in the water, casting around with a worried expression.

'Mary?' he called, squinting into the sunlight as he spotted her. 'Are you alright?' He started toward her. 'God, Mary, what are you doing? I thought for a minute …'

'I'm alright.'

He took another step toward her.

'No! Don't come any closer!' She felt herself blushing, 'I haven't got any clothes on.'

Thomas's eyes widened. 'I … I couldn't anyway. I can't swim!' Then, filled with relief and a sense of how ridiculous he looked and sounded, he began to laugh. It was the first time she had seen him really laugh, and watching him stand there, fully dressed, with the water lapping about his waist, she laughed with him.

'Do you still want to marry me, Thomas?' she called, suddenly serious.

He stopped laughing. 'Yes,' he said. 'Yes – I do.'

Her feet felt for the bottom, and she began to move toward him. 'Then – I suppose clothes don't matter.'

In the midst of the river he held her, wet, naked and willing, and she smothered him in kisses while his hands explored the contours of her body. But though she felt his desire as she clung to him, he did not press his advantage, and instead led her from the water, gallantly turning his back while she dressed.

'God, Mary, but you gave me a scare. When I came down the path and saw your clothes, I thought …' He faltered, unable to say the words.

'That I'd drowned myself?'

'I'm sorry, Mary. It was stupid of me.'

'I once told Gwyneth I wanted to swim naked in this river. Now I've done it – my one, shocking thing.' She came to him, drawing a finger gently over the puzzled crease that remained between his eyebrows. 'The rest is gone, Thomas – drowned like the poor dead girl. No more stories – and no more adventures. All I ever want now is to be Mrs Thomas Davies.'

*

Nathaniel Abrahams looked at her over his clasped fingers as he sat hunched in his chair, his elbows resting on the padded leather arms. 'You are quite sure, Mary?'

She gave a slow nod. 'Are you very disappointed?'

He made a small dismissive gesture. 'I have only ever wanted your happiness, my dear. I just need to be absolutely certain this is what you want.'

She crossed the cosy, familiar room to kneel by him, taking his hand. 'I am certain – I'm sure I am. I'll always be grateful for what you've done for me, Mr Abrahams, always – but Thomas loves me.'

'I can well understand that, my dear, and if you truly love him, then he is the most fortunate man in the world.'

She pressed his hand to her cheek.

'Come now!' he said, tilting her face to his. 'No tears, eh?'

Nodding, she wiped at her eyes. 'On one condition?'

'Upon my soul, Mary, I see you *still* drive a hard bargain! Very well, what shall it be?'

Still clasping his hand, she looked up. 'On the day of my wedding, I should like you to be by my side – to take the place of my father.'

Abrahams was grateful the room had grown too dark for her to see his face clearly, and it was some time before he could trust himself to answer. When he did, his voice was thick with emotion. 'I should be very honoured,' he said.

*

The grey early morning light gave the room a dreary pallor as Meg bustled about putting food into the three tommy boxes and filling the cans with tea.

'Something nice, I hope,' said Owen, coming from their small bedroom.

'No, just some scraps the cat didn't want.' Her words were sharp, but there was a smile in her voice.

He crossed to the fire, taking a spill from the mantelpiece and bending to light it. 'You're such a hard woman, Megan Davies! Proper sorry for me they are down at the face, when they see the poor bit o' dinner I often has to make do with!'

'Why you old devil! As if you ever had anything to complain about.' She flicked at him with the tea towel, then stood watching as he straightened, using the spill to light his pipe. Almost a week had passed since the trial, and she was pleased to see Owen regaining a little of his old humour, although there was still an uneasy atmosphere between him and Thomas.

'I suppose I've little enough,' he said winking at her through a cloud of tobacco smoke.

Above their heads the ceiling creaked and groaned as the two boys moved about, pulling on their working clothes before clattering down the stairs.

Alan pushed open the stair door. 'Where's my box and jack, Mam?'

'Where it is every morning.' She handed him his food box and can of tea, yet her eyes remained on Owen, hoping for some small sign of recon-ciliation as Thomas came into the room. But there was none, and Owen turned away from the boy.

'Are you ready, Da?' asked Alan, putting on his coat.

From the moment the boys had started work, their father had walked proudly with them to the mine, but since Thomas had announced his intention to wed, Owen had not spoken a word to him, and had taken to walking alone.

'Your da will be along presently. You two get away off with you.' Meg re-opened Owen's box in pretence of some alteration, wanting to avoid words being said that would delay the healing.

Thomas took up his box and jack, and moved toward the door, reach-ing for his coat. 'See you later, Mam.'

She gave him a smile. 'Go safely,' she said. 'Both of you.' From the door-way she watched the two boys set off down the street, waiting until they were almost out of sight before turning back to Owen. 'Gwyn will be back tomorrow,' she said brightly, closing the box once more.

Owen pulled on his jacket. 'God, but I've missed her, Meg. I've never known a week longer.'

'I know, my love.'

'Will you come tomorrow – to bring her home?'

'Of course, you don't think I'd trust you to do it on your own, do you?' She saw the hint of a smile return to his eyes.

'And maybe Alan?' he said. 'Make it a grand, family welcome, eh?'

She struggled to maintain her smile. 'We're already losing one day's wage. Let's just the two of us go, eh?'

'Right you are, then,' he smiled. 'Just the two of us it is.' Knocking out his pipe in the fireplace, he put it into his pocket, then picked up his tea can and box. 'Cat's leavings, is it?' he said, planting a kiss on her lips as he made for the door. 'Damned fussy cat, if you ask me!'

'Go safely,' she called after him.

*

In the lee of the old barn, Mary shivered and drew her shawl about her as she watched the morning shift make their way to the mine.

She had crept from the hotel just after dawn to make the two mile journey to Nant-y-Pridd, arriving at her chosen vantage point a quarter of an hour before the first men started to make their way out of the village and up the hill to where the turning pit wheel dominated the skyline.

Thomas and Alan had passed by, unaware of her presence, but there was still no sign of Owen, and Mary began to grow anxious. Then she saw him, walking alone, and leaving her hiding place she fell into step by his side. 'Mr Davies?'

He turned in surprise, then looked away, his mouth set in a downward curve, increasing his pace as he continued to climb the hill.

'Mr Davies?' Her long skirt made it difficult for her to keep up with him, and she lifted it clear of the ground. 'I know you blame me for what happened to Gwyn – and you are right to blame me. It *was* my fault – I should have looked after her. She didn't want to go drinking that day.'

Owen kept walking.

'But Gwyn is my best friend. Do you really think I'd intentionally do anything to hurt her?'

He stopped and spun round, gripping her by the arm. 'But you did, Mary! Intentionally or not – you did! With your damn silly ideas!'

She lowered her eyes. 'I know … I know, and I am so very sorry, and if there was anything I could do to change it …' She looked up at him. 'How you must hate me.'

Owen's jaw worked as emotion raged inside him. 'Oh, bugger it!' he said at last. 'I *want* to hate you, Mary. God knows I do – but I can't. And I suppose that's just as well since Thomas seems set on marrying you. Though damn me if I know how it's going to work! A man needs a steady wife. Someone who'll have his work clothes clean and mended for when he goes out in the morning, and his dinner on the table when he gets back at night – not some bit of a girl with her head in the bloody clouds!'

She looked steadily into his eyes. 'There will be no more silliness. I want to make Thomas a good wife – and I know I can do that. But there will be no marriage unless it's with your blessing.'

Owen shook his head. 'Thomas has made up his mind. He'll marry you, blessing or no blessing!'

'But *I* won't marry him without it.'

He stood very still, regarding her in silence, then reached into his pocket and took out his pipe, not lighting it, but chewing on the stem. 'I've got to go,' he said. But still he did not move, continuing to look at her, until with a long sigh he clamped his pipe firmly between his teeth, turned, and strode away.

Alan and Thomas were already in the cage when Owen stepped in.

'Thought you weren't coming, Da,' said Alan. 'We waited as long as we could.'

Owen gave him a nod, but said nothing more as the grabs were pulled open and they dropped into the shaft at a stomach-wrenching speed.

At the pit bottom they filed out into the dank road to sit for a few minutes, letting their eyes grow accustomed to the blackness.

Thomas leaned back against the wall, listening in silence to the other men laughing and joking, until something scurried past him and he kicked out, striking Alan's leg.

'Careful, man. It's just a mouse!'

'Sorry,' he murmured, hunching forward. He could just begin to make out the face of Davy Briggs sitting opposite him, and was preparing to rise when he felt a hand on his shoulder. 'Da?' he said, uncertainly.

'I suppose,' said his father slowly, 'if you've found a girl daft enough to marry you, you'd better bring her home quick – before she changes her mind.'

*

The morning was fine and clear, and the fat, frowzy woman stepped out into the needle-sharp sunlight, blinking and hitching up her skirts as she waddled away from the grim facade of Cardiff Prison.

A little way off, Owen and Meg watched her depart, their eyes following her for some way before darting back to the gateway at a sign of movement. Another two women emerged: scrawny, bedraggled harridans, clutching their small bundles and shuffling quickly away as though they feared being grabbed and drawn back in. Then, from deep within the gloomy interior, the slight, timid figure of Gwyneth advanced toward the light, pausing for a moment before stepping out into the warming sun and the welcoming arms of her parents.

Chapter Ten

Gwyneth came to see me on the afternoon of her release – an act of absolution for which I shall always be grateful.

We sat, as we had done on so many occasions, drinking tea at the Cross Keys' kitchen table and talking – mostly about the wedding. The reservations she had voiced in Cardiff seemed forgotten, and she was almost her old self, yet there was something distant and withdrawn about her, and when I asked about her experiences in prison, she would not talk of them.

I took her hand as we said goodbye. She was wearing the gloves she'd bought that fateful day, and it was only after she had left that I realised, in all the time we had been talking, she had never once removed them.

The weeks that followed saw wages at Nant-y-Pridd and several other pits cut by ten percent, and on my Sunday afternoon visits the talk would often turn to the threat of strikes. The Iron and Steel workers were already striking over similar cuts, and miners' wages had never been lower. Closures in other industries had brought an influx of people to the mines, with the result that housing was impossible to find. By any standard it was an inauspicious time to be planning a wedding – but we were undaunted.

When it was proposed we should make our home in the Davies' house, I readily agreed, remembering how, as a child, I had longed to be a part of that family.

In the confined space of the attic bedroom, Mrs Cartwright put a hand into the small of Mary's back and hauled on the corset laces. 'There!' she said, after much grunting and heaving. 'I can't get it no smaller no matter what yer say!'

Mary ran the tape measure around her waist. 'Nineteen inches,' she said, glumly. 'An inch for every year is what they say.' She gave Peggy a hopeful look. 'If I really suck in my breath?'

'No!' Mrs Cartwright wiped the perspiration from her face. 'Damn silly fashion! An inch for every year indeed! London might be full o' daft young things a-faintin' all over the place – but I thought you 'ad more sense! Eighteen inches! T'ain't natural!'

'Another half inch? Please Peg.'

'No! I'm not 'avin' it on my conscience that yer fainted on yer way up the aisle! Gawd, Mary, you're as skinny as a broomstick already!' She gave the laces one final pull then tied them firmly. 'Lots o' men like a bit o' meat on their girls. *Somethin' to 'old on to*, my Charlie used t' say.' She ran her hands over her ample stomach. 'An inch for every year? Blimey! I'm certainly in the fashion!'

'I just want Thomas to be proud of me.'

'Proud of yer? If 'e ain't already the proudest man in the whole country, then 'e don't bloomin' well deserve yer!'

Mary was suddenly aware of how much she would miss the old woman. 'Peg …' she began.

'Come on, come on,' Peggy said quickly, 'We ain't got all day! Your Mr Abrahams'll be 'ere in no time, an' you'll be off t' the chapel in yer drawers if yer don't get a move on!'

*

The Davies' household was in a state of ordered confusion as Meg over-saw the constant stream of neighbours who arrived with food cooked in the adjoining houses.

'Any more hot water, Mam?' shouted Alan from Owen and Meg's bedroom where the bath had been placed to afford some privacy. 'It's getting a bit chilly in here, like!'

With her arms full of borrowed plates, Meg crossed to the kitchen fire. 'The kettle's just starting to boil now, my love. Your da'll bring it to you.' She turned to Owen, who was struggling to fasten his collar. 'Can you take Alan some water when you're done with your preening?'

He looked at her in the mirror. 'Preening, is it? You should have seen me when I used to come a-courting you. Hours I took then.'

'Oh, yes, I can imagine. You were a vain one then, right enough.'

'Before I got old and lost my looks, eh?'

She smiled. 'You look just the same to me.'

Straightening his tie, he put on his jacket, pulling it into place where it didn't quite fit. 'I should do,' he said with a wink. 'It's the same suit!'

'Hurry up with that water, Da!' came Alan's voice from the bedroom.

Owen made for the fireplace, then looked at his hands and down at his clothes. 'Here, Thomas,' he said. 'Take Alan some hot water, will you. Don't want to get m'self dirty from the kettle now that I'm all dressed up.'

Thomas looked up from where he was polishing his best shoes. 'Right, Da. I'll just finish these, like.'

Owen looked at him. 'By, but that's a shine and a half you're putting on them, boyo,' he laughed. 'Y'know – it's not the sparkle on her husband's *shoes* that interests a girl on her wedding night.'

'Owen!' Meg gave him a shocked look.

'Oh, get away with you, woman! He'll be a married man in a couple of hours.'

'I was thinking of Gwyn – and the neighbours!'

He chuckled. 'Well, perhaps we'd better go and have our *rough men's talk* elsewhere, and leave you in peace. Think those shoes might stand a walk to the Quarryman for a pint of Dutch courage, Thomas? It's traditional for the condemned man, you know.'

Thomas grinned up at him. 'I think they might, Da.'

Owen made his way to the door, stepping aside as Mrs Jenkins arrived bringing two freshly baked loaves.

'Going to be a right crush in here, I reckon,' said the woman. 'I wonder you don't hire that room down at the Quarryman. It's bigger – and it don't cost much.'

Meg took the bread. 'Yes, well, it's not the money.'

'Tradition it is, Mrs Jenkins!' said Owen, smiling and taking out his pipe. 'My wife's a stickler for tradition, she is. Her family always has the wedding reception at the house, see. Why, they're never happier than when folks is crammed together like them sardines you get in boxes.' He laughed as Meg threw him a mock glare.

There was a creak on the stairs, and the door opened a fraction as Gwyneth put her head round. 'Oh!' she said, seeing Mrs Jenkins.

'It's alright, dear,' said the woman, 'I'm just off. See you in Chapel.'

'Sardines indeed!' Meg flounced into the scullery. 'I'll give you sardines.'

Gwyneth, dressed only in her shift, kept the door half closed. 'Is Alan out of the bath yet?'

'No, I'm not! And I won't be till someone brings me some hot water!'

Thomas slipped on his jacket and made to leave. 'Gwyn, take him some water, will you. I'm just off with Da.'

'I'm not dressed,' she began, but her protest was directed at an empty room. 'Oh, alright,' she said, gingerly pushing open the door and stepping into the kitchen.

'Gwyneth!' said Meg, coming from the scullery. 'You can't come down here like that. It's open house here today, and you don't know who's going to walk in!'

'But it's Alan's water. I'll never get a bath at this rate!'

Meg shooed her back upstairs. 'I'll do it,' she said, then shaking her head, 'Can't think why I didn't do it myself in the first place!'

*

'Oh, doesn't she look lovely! Come and look, Mr Llewellyn, you must come and look!'

Mary stood at the foot of the stairs with Mrs Cartwright behind her, the old woman's face filled with motherly pride as she worried at the creamy folds falling from Mary's tiny waist.

'Quickly! Hubert, quickly!' Edith Llewellyn insisted.

Hubert came into the hallway, fixing a carnation in the buttonhole of his best suit. 'I'm coming, Mrs Llewellyn, I'm coming. The girl isn't going anywhere just yet, is she?' He stopped, giving Mary an appraising look. 'Oh, yes, very nice.'

Edith gasped. '*Very nice*? Is that all you can say?'

He gave her a patronising smile. 'I do believe your mother said I was a man of few words, didn't she?'

'That she did!' She halted, realising she was being taunted. 'Horrible man!' she hissed under her breath.

Mary moved toward them. 'I just wanted to tell you how very grateful I am to you for taking me in after my parents were ...' she hesitated, unable to say the word. Instead she reached down and took their hands. 'I don't think I could ever repay your kindness.'

Mrs Llewellyn scrabbled for her handkerchief and dabbed at her eyes. 'Oh!' she said, 'Oh, my.'

Mr Llewellyn looked at his wife, then back to Mary. 'Well, it wasn't really our idea, you know. It was that teacher chap's.'

Edith shot him a glance. 'Mr Llewellyn, you know very well that he swore me to secrecy!'

'It's alright. I already knew,' Mary looked down guiltily. 'I overheard you talking about it a few days after I came here. I have so many things to thank Mr Abrahams for.'

Mrs Llewellyn looked at her in surprise. 'Oh, but it wasn't ...' she checked herself. 'Well, I suppose it hardly matters now. It wasn't Mr Abrahams, dear, it was Mr Griffiths.'

The smile vanished from Mary's face. 'Mr Griffiths?'

'Yes,' Mrs Llewellyn angled her head to look into Mary's eyes. 'Why, does it matter, then?'

'No ... it's just that ...' Mary forced a smile. 'No – of course not.'

Mr Llewellyn examined his watch. 'Well, that's alright then. But Mr Abrahams *will* be here soon to drive you over to Nant-y-Pridd – so we'd better get on.'

Fresh tears welled in Mrs Llewellyn's eyes. 'Yes – you don't want to keep your young man waiting.' She turned away, pressing her lips together to keep them from trembling as she bustled toward the door. 'Come on, Mr Llewellyn. We can't be standing around here all day.'

Hubert followed his wife into the dining-room and closed the doors, crossing to the tall window overlooking the street. 'We may have lost business there, Mrs Llewellyn,' he said sourly, watching a small group of well-to-do visitors make their way up the road toward the railway station. 'Nice class of people, too, by the look of them. I really can't see why we have to close for the whole day. The wedding'll be over in an hour.'

Edith turned on him, dabbing at her eyes. 'Business? Is that all you ever think about? Do you know when we last closed this place for a day, Mr Llewellyn? I'll tell you! It was eight years ago – and that was to bury my poor mother!' She dabbed at her eyes again. 'And you even complained about that!'

'I was only saying, like …' He came over, putting his arm around her. 'Come on, now – what's wrong?'

'I'm going to miss her, Hubert.'

'Who? Your mother?'

'No!' she said, blowing her nose noisily and wiping her cheeks. 'Mary. I'll miss Mary.'

'Oh,' he said, 'is that all? Well, don't you worry your head over that. Why, I've already arranged for a new girl to come on Monday.'

She shrugged off his arm. 'You think I'm upset because we haven't got a maid! God, but my mother was right! You *are* heartless, Hubert Llewellyn! *Heartless!* That girl's been like one of the family these past years.'

He adopted a pained expression. 'Oh, I see, I see. Well – let's look on the bright side then, shall we?'

She stopped crying and looked at him with irritation. 'The bright side, Mr Llewellyn? The bright side? Whatever are you talking about?'

'Well, with luck they might not get on, like – her and this chap she's marrying. Then she'll want to come back, see?'

Mrs Llewellyn's face hardened, and she eyed him coldly. 'Oh! You are a horrible man, Mr Llewellyn! Horrible!'

'Am I dear? Well, I'm sure you are right. I expect your mother told you as much, eh?'

Without another word she snatched up her hat and strode from the room.

Hubert waited for her to disappear into the hall, then allowed himself a little smile. 'That's more like it,' he said to himself. 'That's more like my Edith.'

*

Meg eased open the bedroom door. 'There's a letter just come for you, my love,' she said, placing it on the bed, close to where Gwyneth sat hunched over her knees in the tin bath. 'Don't be too long, now. We need to be getting off soon.'

Gwyneth waited for Meg to close the door, then drying her hands, she picked up the envelope and opened it. Inside was a newspaper clipping.

> *Gwyneth Alice Davies, a seventeen-year-old girl, was charged at Cardiff Police Court with a serious assault on a police officer while in a state of drunkenness. According to the evidence, Miss Davies and an unnamed accomplice joined the salvationist procession after drinking heavily. When a disturbance halted the march, Miss Davies was seen to attack Police Constable Murphy with a wooden pole, breaking his nose. The case was conclusively proven against her, and she was committed to gaol for one week with hard labour.*

It wasn't the first time Gwyneth had read it; it had appeared in *The Western Mail* over a month ago, but still she shuddered. Turning it over and finding nothing written on either side, she re-checked the envelope, and a printed card dropped into the bath. Even without picking it up she could see the address of the school at which she was due to start work, and below, in copperplate handwriting already dissolving in the water: *For reasons you will understand, your services will no longer be required.*

*

Left alone in the lobby of the hotel, Mary made her way into the lounge and then to the french doors that overlooked Caerphilly Castle, resting her head against the cool glass. It was a view she had sketched many times, and on this bright summer morning it was especially beautiful – but today it only served to make her feel sad. Wetting her finger, she traced on to the pane the outline of the castle with its familiar leaning tower, then she unlocked the doors and stepped out on to the small terrace.

The air was delightfully warm, yet there was a chill deep inside her. It had been there when she awoke, small, barely noticeable, and easily denied in the hustle and bustle of the preparations, but now, in her solitude, it could not be ignored.

A low gate gave way to the grassy slope that had once edged the moat, and lost in thought she passed through, making her way down the incline, toward the ancient, craggy walls, to stand beneath the south gate. It was a peaceful spot, and her fingers roved over the stone and mortar as she imagined those who had lived there so many years ago. What had their lives been like? How many had ridden out with Red Gilbert de Clare to do battle with the native lords, never to return? How many fortunes had been won or lost? How many marriages entered into and quickly regretted? So many decisions made – rightly or wrongly – but all rendered insignificant by the passage of time. Each life, seemingly so important, proved as inconsequential as that of a mayfly when viewed from the distance of centuries, and deep within her the chill receded until it too seemed inconsequential. She *did* love Thomas. It was not how she had expected love to feel, but still she felt certain. And if she was wrong – then what would it matter in a hundred years.

From somewhere above she heard her name called, and she turned to see Mrs Cartwright standing atop the bank, waving frantically.

'Gawd, what on earth was yer thinkin' of?' asked Peggy as Mary mounted the slope. 'Mr Abrahams is 'ere – an' 'as been for a good ten minutes! We didn't know where yer'd gone to!' She gave Mary a questioning look. 'You ain't 'avin' second thoughts, are yer?'

Mary took hold of her hand. 'No, Peg. Not any more.'

*

The chapel at Nant-y-Pridd was full to bursting as Thomas and Mary stood before the preacher to be made man and wife – so that the man who entered the chapel after the ceremony had begun was hardly noticed, except by those who nodded and shifted to make a space for him by the back wall.

At the front, and with due solemnity, Mr Abrahams gave the bride into Thomas's care, and Alan dutifully carried out his task as best man under the watchful eye of Meg and Owen – then it was over.

At the back of the room the latecomer gave a small nod of contentment and turned to leave.

'My wife loves a good wedding,' said the man next to him, inclining his head toward a group of women seated in the rear pews. 'Not so bothered, m'self, but I comes with her, like. Not bad though, eh?'

The latecomer paused. 'A satisfactory outcome, Mr Briggs. Quite satisfactory.'

Briggs scratched his head. 'Oh, aye, well – as you say, Mr Griffiths. As you say.'

Chapter Eleven

The afternoon was hot and humid, and the press of people filling the Davies' small cottage flowed out into the street in front and the garden behind. The food, which had seemed more than sufficient that morning, was gone long before any of the family found time to eat, forcing Meg to send to the shop for bread and cheese.

'By!' said Owen as she brought him a thick cut sandwich. 'But I was just fancying a bit o' pie, like. Or maybe some ham.'

She pushed the plate toward him. 'Well, you can fancy all you like, Owen Davies – but it's this or nothing.'

He laughed. 'It'll have to do, I suppose – though it comes to something when I eat better underground than I do in my own house.'

Threading her way back toward the scullery, Meg found Alan near the door. 'Have you had something to eat, my love?'

'Not yet,' he said, giving her a wink. 'Door seems to have jammed, like.'

'Jammed?' She made to push it open, but it held fast. 'Oh,' she said, suddenly realising. 'Well, they can have five minutes – then I'm going in, *jam, or no jam*!'

On the far side of the door, Thomas leaned back, his hands around Mary's waist. '*Mrs Thomas Davies*,' he said with a note of disbelief.

'It has a fine sound to it.'

'I never thought, Mary. Never even dared to hope …'

His eyes were wet with emotion, and his words slurred by drink, but there was an openness about him Mary had never seen. 'What, Thomas?' she asked, wanting to hear the words. 'Please – tell me.'

His arms went around her, hard, muscular, almost crushing her. 'I … I just can't believe it. I can't believe you're mine. I've always loved you, Mary – *always*. But I never dared to think that *you'd love me*.'

She nuzzled his chest, his waistcoat rough against her cheek. 'I *do* love you, Thomas, and I want you so much.' She lifted her face to his. 'Let's go, *now* – to Cardiff.'

'What? To the hotel? It's too early. We can't.'

'Yes, we can.'

He leaned to kiss her with an urgency that made her melt into him. 'Yes,' he said, his mouth barely lifting from hers. 'Yes, we can.'

They opened the door, and Thomas took her hand, leading her into the crowded kitchen. 'Have you seen the carrier, Mam?' he asked, swaying just a little.

'Yes, my love. He was just outside – but you're not going yet, are you? Your Aunt Angharad and Uncle Seldon have just arrived. Come all the way from Carmarthen, they have.'

Thomas looked uncertainly from his mother to his wife, but suddenly a balding man was by his side. 'Thomas! Thomas!' said the man, clapping him on the shoulder. 'Is this the bride? Come here m'dear. Come here where I can see you! – Ah!' He slapped Thomas's shoulder again. 'She's too good for you, boy! Too good by half! Now, put her down, and come and have a drink with your old Uncle Seldon!'

'Well, we were just …' Thomas glanced at Mary in mute appeal, but she rested her hand on his arm. 'Of course you must go, Thomas,' she said. 'I'll be in the garden when you're ready.'

A wooden bench stood at the far end of the garden where blackcurrant bushes added to the scent of warm earth and dry grass, and it was here Gwyneth sat in seclusion, staring at the far hills and the dark band of cloud above.

'Gwyn?'

Gwyneth started, looking round to find Mary gazing down at her with concern.

'Are you alright, Gwyn?'

Secreting the newspaper clipping in her pocket, Gwyneth attempted a smile. 'Yes, yes, I'm alright. Just thinking, that's all.'

Mary spread her skirt and sat down. 'Gwyn …' she began uncertainly. 'We haven't really talked, not properly, like – not since that terrible day in Cardiff …' She saw Gwyneth's reluctance to speak of it, and she paused, but the question still nagged at her. 'It's just that … you said back then that I shouldn't marry Thomas. You don't still think that?'

'No – it was just the gin talking.'

'I don't think it was.'

Gwyneth looked into the distance. 'I suppose it was that I could never imagine you marrying someone like Thomas – and just being *ordinary*.'

'I want to be ordinary, Gwyn – I think I shall suit ordinary very well.'

'Yes,' Gwyneth answered, but without conviction.

'So you aren't angry with me?'

Gwyneth reached for Mary's hand, holding it tightly. 'Of course not. I'm very happy for you – for both of you. Really.'

'Oh, Gwyn,' said Mary, leaning forward to kiss her friend's cheek. 'I *am* so very happy.'

Across the fields, small eddies of dust lifted in the freshening breeze, and they sat in silence for several minutes, enjoying the cooling air.

'Was it awful?' Mary asked softly. 'The prison? You've never told me.'

Gwyneth looked down. 'It was worse than awful. You can't imagine, Mary. I was made to do such horrible, *horrible* things.' She turned her hands palm upwards to study her fingertips. 'They bleed, you know – from picking oakum. Your fingers get raw and bleed – but they won't let you stop. I used to beg them.'

'Was that why you wouldn't take off your gloves that day?'

'I didn't want you to see. I didn't want *anyone* to see.' She let her hands drop into her lap. 'Still, it was my own silly fault – and at least that part's behind me.'

'That part?' but Mary got no further, for they were interrupted by the approaching figure of Mrs Cartwright.

At the end of the row of houses, the group of men standing around the water pump grinned or shook their heads at the spectacle before them.

'Get him stripped to the waist,' said Owen, grasping the handle of the pump as Alan and several others struggled to remove Thomas's waistcoat and shirt.

'Drunk, is it? Proper disgrace – and on his wedding day, too!' said old Price, the carrier. 'He's never going to get to Cardiff in that state, is he!'

Owen ignored him and began pumping while Alan held his brother's head under the gushing water.

'He's only had four or five pints, Da,' said Alan, as Thomas began coughing and spluttering. 'But he hasn't had a bite to eat, like.'

'Ah!' said old Price. 'Empty stomach, is it?'

Owen dowsed the boy several more times. 'How you feeling now?' he asked as Thomas stood gasping, water streaming from his hair.

'Alright … I'm … alright. Where's Mary?'

'Never you mind about Mary,' said Owen. 'Better she doesn't know about this. Damn fine impression you'd make. Get yourself dressed – then take a good long walk to sober up. You can stop off at the Quarryman and get some food inside you. There's not a crumb left in the house, of that I'm sure!'

Thomas staggered a little, but managed to pull on his shirt.

'Leave the rest – just in case,' commanded Owen as Thomas made a grab at his waistcoat. 'We can always wash a shirt. Alan, you go with him.

Get him to eat – but only water to drink, mind!'

'Right you are, Da.'

'So, when is it to Cardiff, then, Mr Davies?' asked old Price in exasperation.

'When they get back.'

'But when will that be? I can't be a-waiting all day.'

'Soon,' said Owen. 'Soon!'

*

The first fat spots of rain began to fall as Thomas and Alan returned to the house two hours later, and Thomas lifted his face, enjoying the refreshing sting. Food had given weight to his stomach, and a quantity of water seemed to have cleared his head sufficiently for him to walk steadily for the half-mile home, but he still felt queasy.

The rain began to fall faster, quickly becoming a deluge, while away in the distance, lightning flashed between the hills.

'Come on, man!' shouted Alan, grabbing his arm. 'We'll have to run!'

Water was already running in rivulets down the road, turning it to mud as they crested the hill and made for the house, flinging themselves through the door like two laughing schoolboys.

In his chair by the fire, Owen looked up from watching the simmering kettle that hissed and spat as rain found its way down the chimney.

'Where is everyone?' asked Alan.

'Gone this last half hour!' said Meg, clearing plates from the table. 'What with the coming rain – and no bridegroom!' She put the piled plates back on the table with a crash. 'I've *never* been so ashamed.'

Owen lit his pipe. 'Leave the boy alone, Meg,' he said, quietly. 'I expect he feels bad enough already. How *do* you feel now, boy?'

'Alright, Da.'

'Well, you don't deserve to be!' said Meg, gathering up knives and forks, and clattering them on to the plates. 'It's poor Mary I feel sorry for!'

Thomas looked about the room. 'Where is she?'

'Upstairs, seeing if Gwyn is alright. Your sister wasn't feeling too well either, and has gone to bed. Fine day this has turned out to be!'

'I'm sorry, Mam.'

Meg sighed, and leaned to peer out the window. 'Well, you won't be going anywhere just yet. Old Price won't come out in weather like this, so you might as well have a cup of tea while you're waiting. I'll send round for him as soon as it stops.'

Thomas shuffled his feet. 'I'd better go up,' he said. 'Is she angry?'

'She has every right to be.'

'But *is* she?'

Meg turned to face him. 'Better ask her yourself,' she said, looking over his shoulder to where Mary stood in the stairs' open doorway.

*

'This is in for the night!' said Hubert Llewellyn, standing by the lounge window. 'It's a good job we left when we did.'

Mrs Llewellyn came to stand by him. 'Yes,' she said, watching a solitary figure make his way up the road, battling with an umbrella that was all but useless against such weather. 'I *do* wish they'd accepted the offer to stay here. Heaven knows what they charge at the Royal these days!'

'I know very well what they charge, Mrs Llewellyn.'

She raised her hands to her ears. 'Don't you dare tell me! I don't want to know! But it's scandalous I'm sure!'

'Oh, quite scandalous,' he said with a small grin, then cocking his head to one side, 'It's strange isn't it? Having the hotel so quiet? I can't remember the last time we had the place to ourselves.'

'The day we buried my poor mother, Mr Llewellyn.'

'Ah, yes. How could I forget that?' He yawned and stretched. 'Well, I think I shall turn in early tonight.'

'But it's only half past eight!'

'Yes,' he said.

*

'He doesn't deserve her!' whispered Meg. 'The girl's a saint! Her wedding day ruined, and not a word of complaint! *I'd* have had something to say about it, and that's a fact!'

'Oh, sainthood now, is it?' said Owen, with a quiet chuckle.

The three of them were in the scullery, Meg washing dishes while Owen and Alan set to with cloths, drying the borrowed glasses and crockery.

Alan took a sideways step toward the door to peer through the crack. 'Not acting like any saints I've ever heard of.'

Meg gave him a sharp clout. 'You come away from there!' she hissed.

'Not exactly ruined now, was it?' said Owen. 'It's not like he's the first to get a little drunk on his wedding day, after all.'

'It's the first time in *my* family! That ashamed I am!' Meg said.

Owen put down the plate he had been absent-mindedly wiping, and looked out at the rain. Across the valley the black cloud was unbroken but for the frequent flash and crackle of lightning. 'Well, least said, soonest mended, I reckon.' He took out his watch. 'Nearly nine o'clock. I can't see them getting to Cardiff tonight.'

Meg shot him a harrowed look. 'But they've got to get there. They've already paid for the room.'

'Can't be helped,' said Owen. 'They'll just have to make the best of it.'

*

Hubert was already in bed when Edith entered and stood before the mirror to unpin her hair, inspecting her wrinkled face, and pushing at the extra flesh around her jowls as though seeing it for the first time. 'Do you think they'll be happy?' she sighed, half to herself.

Hubert rolled over to face her. 'Who's that then, dear?'

'Mary and her Thomas, of course.'

'Oh, them. Yes, I expect so.' Through half-closed eyes he watched her undress. 'You know – they reminded me of us, all those years ago.'

'Well, if that's the case, it'll be a dog's life for the poor girl, good and proper!' Edith, dropped her skirt and stepped out of it – but she paused before picking it up. 'Did they?' she asked, suspiciously. 'Did they really?'

He nodded, smiling. 'Yes,' he said, 'they did. And we've been happy, haven't we – in our own way?'

She looked at him. 'Yes,' she said, warily, then allowing a smile, 'Yes, we have. Better than many.' She turned down the lamp, finishing her undressing in the dark before climbing into bed. 'Goodnight, Hubert.'

'Goodnight?' he asked, moving closer.

She turned in surprise, feeling him against her, the almost forgotten touch of his body – and then the touch of something else. 'Oh! Oh, you horrible man!' she said, but there was laughter in her voice.

*

The storm did not move away, but crept along the valley to lay directly over Nant-y-Pridd, where it reached down with jagged tendrils, searing the sky.

'I'm sorry, Mary.' Sitting by the window, Thomas stared through the streaming glass. 'I'm so sorry.'

She squeezed his hand. 'Don't be. It doesn't matter.'

Perched on the wooden settle, Meg looked to Owen, then back to the pair of them. 'Why don't you have our room? Just for tonight? It won't take a minute to change the sheets.'

Thomas brightened, but Mary was already shaking her head. 'It's very kind of you, but there's no need. We'd only booked for one night, and would have been back here tomorrow in any event. Besides, I think I much prefer it this way – starting as we mean to go on.'

Owen leaned forward to tap out his pipe. 'Come on then, Meg. It's time we were leaving them alone and off to bed ourselves.' He stood up. 'Goodnight to the pair of you.'

'Yes, goodnight, my loves.' Meg took a candle from the mantelpiece and moved toward the back bedroom. 'I've given you an extra blanket, Alan,' she said, looking towards the camp bed in the corner of the kitchen.

Owen didn't follow immediately, but remained by the fire, toying with his pipe. 'Mary ...' he began, hesitantly. 'I wasn't always sure about ...

well, about *you*. I was wrong. I hope you can forgive me.'

The sharp, sweet sting of happiness moistened Mary's eyes, and she rose to kiss him on the cheek. 'There's nothing to forgive, Da.'

'Well … goodnight then.' Almost bashfully he turned toward the bedroom door, but then stopped and gave a small chuckle. 'I reckon your mam's right, Thomas,' he said. 'You don't deserve her.'

A candle was burning by the bed, flickering in the draught from the rain battered window. Mary looked about her. The upstairs room seemed smaller than she remembered, but the thick curtain that screened Gwyneth was the same. It stirred as the wind howled in the eaves, and she reached out to touch it, remembering the nights she had lain on its far side, snug against the body of her friend.

Then Thomas was with her, and she was in his arms, his lips against hers, but softly now, as though feeling their way, hovering, just as his hands hovered at her waist.

She moved into him, pressing the length of her body against his and returning his kisses, wanting the passion that had been theirs that afternoon. 'I love you, Thomas. I love you, love you, love you,' she whispered, kissing his face, his chin, his neck, but instead of increasing the strength of his touch, he stood back from her.

'Should we undress?' he asked.

Mary was suddenly conscious of the cold air about her shoulders. 'Yes,' she said, but neither made any move as they stood looking at each other.

On the far side of the curtain, Gwyneth's bed creaked.

'Should I put out the light?' Thomas whispered, still not moving.

'If you want to …'

Grateful for something to do, Thomas made his way to the small table and blew out the candle, then they began to undress, slowly and quietly – the darkness seeming to amplify every small noise.

Just a few feet away, Mary could hear the rustle of Thomas shedding his clothes, and there were other sounds, too: the creak of the boards as he moved – and from below, the soft murmur of Owen's voice, and the sound of Alan in the kitchen. She let down her hair, then untied the laces of her corset, allowing it to fall away before removing the rest of her clothes to stand naked, uncertain, and with goosebumps rising on her flesh.

'Mary?' Thomas's voice came softly. 'Are you ready?'

'Yes.'

'Shall we get into bed?' He pulled back the covers, and she waited, shivering in the chill air, feeling suddenly uncomfortable and vulnerable. Away in the distance lightning flickered, briefly illuminating Thomas as he stood by the bed, dressed in a nightshirt, his eyes on her nakedness – and her hands moved to cover herself. Then it was black once more, and she felt for her shift, pulling it on before climbing into the bed.

Thomas was already there, and she reached for him, moving closer as he ran his hand over her hair, then along the line of her jaw, smoothing her cheek. She shifted closer still, wanting the crushing feel of his arms and the urgency of his flesh. She kissed his throat, the small triangle of chest that remained bare, and he responded, moaning softly and running his hands over her hips, her thighs, gentle, butterfly touches that began the first stirrings of passion, so that she clung to him, feeling his stiffness against her belly, frightening yet arousing. Then his hand was on her shoulder, coaxing her on to her back as he moved over her, his other hand going to the hem of the shift, tugging it upwards, fighting the white cotton up over her knees.

The sound of Owen coughing drifted up from the room below.

'Thomas,' she began, but he was groping between her legs with an urgency she did not yet feel. 'Thomas …'

He raised his head from her shoulder. 'I love you so much, Mary.'

With eyes now accustomed to the darkness, she could just make out the eagerness in his features, and she reached for his face to kiss him, but his head moved back against her shoulder, and his member pressed between her thighs. She spread her legs wider, and he pushed, then pushed again, but the placing was wrong and only caused her to emit a small whimper. He pressed harder, his fingers scrabbling to assist his entry, and again she felt the pain of his thrust. He shifted his weight a little and tried once more. This time the pain was so intense she gave a little cry.

'Am I hurting you?' he asked, his eyes full of concern.

'A little.'

He looked unsure. 'It's supposed to hurt – *a little* – isn't it?'

'Yes … I think so.'

She could feel the muscles of his back bunching as he prepared to try again, and she gritted her teeth. He thrust at her, harder this time, grunting with the effort, and despite the hurt she suddenly felt sick with embarrassment – wondering if Gwyneth were truly asleep, and remembering her own pretence that first night, when she'd lain awake, listening to the small sounds coming from this very bed.

Thomas re-doubled his efforts, pushing harder, and she cried out.

'Are you alright?' he asked, frightened.

'Yes …' She stared up at the rafters in an effort to calm her rising panic, while her body tensed in anticipation of another thrust. When it came, tears squeezed from between her eyelids, flowing faster with the agony of each new onslaught.

'I'm so sorry, my love,' he said, his voice breaking with emotion. 'I … I can't do it – I just don't know what to do.'

She held him, gently rubbing his back as he lay panting, childlike, against her breast, 'It's alright. I think it's supposed to be hard the first time. There wouldn't be blood, otherwise. Why not rest a little.'

For several minutes they lay together, then Thomas roused himself from her arms. 'This time,' he said, kissing her.

She gave him a brave smile. 'This time.'

But it was not to be this time – nor the next. Again and again Thomas tried, until she felt sure she must be bruised, bloodied and torn – and when, in the early hours of the morning, she felt him soften and roll from her for the last time, it was with the greatest relief.

She awoke a little after dawn to find him sitting on the end of the bed. 'Thomas?' she called softly.

He half turned, then reached out to take her hand, his voice a whisper, 'I'm sorry, Mary. I don't understand what's wrong.'

She pushed back the bedclothes and came to him, putting her arms about his shoulders and laying her head against his neck. 'It's alright, my love, it's alright. Come back to bed.'

'It's *not* alright,' he said, his voice still low but with a sharpness he instantly regretted. He reached for her cheek, stroking it. 'I'm sorry. I must be doing something wrong – but I don't know *what*.'

She took his hand, kissing his fingers. 'I'm sure it's nothing. It will be alright next time, I *know* it will. Come back to bed now.'

As he looked at her he felt his confidence returning, and with it came a stirring in his loins. He felt for her breast, fondling it for a moment, then reached between her legs.

Mary gasped in pain – a pain that came not just from the bruised flesh, but from deeper within – and Thomas quickly withdrew his hand. 'Have I hurt you?'

'No ... just a little ... it's nothing.' She watched his manhood dwindle beneath his nightshirt. 'Tonight,' she said. 'I shall be healed by tonight. Can you wait until then?'

He put his head against her breast. 'I'd wait forever, Mary – it's not that.'

'Then what, my love?'

'All I ever wanted was to make you my wife.'

'But you have.'

'No ... I haven't. Not properly. I've shamed us both.'

She lifted his face to hers, looking deeply into his eyes. 'You *did* make me your wife, Thomas. There *was* no problem. You did it.'

He looked at her in confusion. 'We ... we can't?'

'Yes – *we can*. If we want it to have happened – then it *did* happen.'

'What about Mam?' he said, 'She'll know from the sheets.'

Mary held him tightly, soothing him. 'I'll deal with it.'

Chapter Twelve

Meg returned from the shops the next morning, quietly crossing the kitchen so as not to awaken Alan. She smiled. The smell of frying bacon would rouse everyone soon enough – except for Thomas and Mary, she supposed.

She was unpacking her basket in the scullery when her eye was drawn to something large and white fluttering in the sunlight just outside the window, and she walked to the back door. On a line strung across the garden, hung a freshly washed bed sheet, a pair of button boots and the hem of a skirt just visible beneath. 'Mary?'

Mary stepped into view, pushing back a strand of hair. 'Good morning … *Mam*.'

Meg gave her a motherly smile. 'I would have done that for you.'

'I know – but it was no trouble.'

'Oh, my love,' said Meg, putting her arm around Mary's shoulders. 'It's always a bit messy the first time. Nothing to be ashamed of. More reason to be ashamed if there wasn't anything. Come on, I've got a nice bit of steak for your breakfasts.'

*

'No steak for me, then, is it?' asked Owen, looking to his plate where thick rashers of bacon lay snug against two fried eggs.

Meg put the kettle on to boil. 'You had your steak breakfast twenty-four years ago.'

'Aye,' he smiled. 'And very nice it was, too.'

She came to stand by him, stroking the back of his neck as he started in on the bacon. 'Do you want some tea, Gwyneth?' she asked.

At the far end of the table, Gwyneth shook her head.

'Still not feeling well?'

'I'm alright.'

'You want to eat, girl,' laughed Owen. 'Eat whenever you can, it is, in this house. Learned that lesson yesterday.'

'Would you like some of this?' Mary nudged her plate toward Gwyneth. 'It's more than I can manage.'

'*No.*'

Owen raised an eyebrow. 'So,' he said, swallowing his irritation. 'The newly-weds slept well, did they?'

Thomas's knife scraped against the plate. 'Yes, Da,' he said without looking up.

'Good,' said Owen.

Silence reigned for several minutes, then Meg asked, 'Should I make you some toast, Gwyn?'

'No! Just leave me alone, can't you!'

Owen lifted his eyes to her. '*Gwyneth,*' he said sternly.

'I'm sorry – No, *thank you.*'

'Well …' said Alan, breaking the tension. 'How was the honeymoon suite, then? Up to the standard of the Royal, was it?'

'It was *perfectly* satisfactory, thank you, my good man,' said Mary. 'We shall most *certainly* come again.'

Alan laughed heartily. 'Ho, well, jolly good for you, what! Hoi, myself, slept werry, werry badly due to the bed being hawfully hard an' hawfully huncomfortable!'

'Oh. *Awfully* bad luck,' said Mary.

Thomas looked at her. She was smiling and joking, with no hint of their disastrous night, and he loved her more in that moment than ever before. Slowly and very gently, he leaned and kissed her cheek.

Flushed with happiness, Meg cleared her throat. 'Well, his lordship won't have to suffer for too long, because once Gwyneth takes up her new position, he can have her bed.'

'So, just when *are* you going, Gwyn?' asked Owen. 'Have they given you a date yet?'

There was no answer.

'Gwyneth?'

Gwyneth shot to her feet, toppling her chair. 'I'm not going!' she said, her eyes glistening. 'I'm not going anywhere! And I probably never shall!' And running from the table, she fled the room in tears.

*

For a long time it seemed Gwyneth was right. Twice she was successful in gaining a position, only to be dismissed as soon as her employers heard of her past. I offered to approach Mr and Mrs Llewellyn, or even Mr Abrahams, feeling sure they would take her on, but she was so desperately ashamed, she would not hear of it.

The situation in the mines deteriorated, with further wage cuts and the threat of strikes – though the men of Nant-y-Pridd, seeing how little such actions benefited those in other valleys, swallowed their pride, stuck to their jobs, and tightened their belts. With three wage earners in the house we were better off than many, but it was not a time when men could hold their heads high, and I felt for Thomas all the more in the months that followed.

Each night I prayed we would succeed, but no sooner would he try to enter me than my muscles would seize and render his efforts useless. I would lie there, stifling my cries of pain, knowing Gwyneth was awake and listening as Thomas laboured over me. Then one night there was blood – but not the blood we so hoped for. My poor, sweet Thomas was horrified, and after that he stopped trying.

*

The first snow came early that year. At the rear of the Cross Keys Hotel, the steps had been swept clear, and Mary walked down them, enjoying the familiar afternoon aroma of bread, buns and cakes.

'Gawd! I wasn't expectin' you!' said Peggy, opening the door and gathering Mary in her arms. 'Come in, girl. Come an' 'ave a cup o' tea!'

Mary looked over the woman's shoulder, into the warmly lit kitchen where two girls were polishing silverware. 'It's not inconvenient?'

''Course not! It's lovely t' see yer.'

The girls stood up and bobbed small, nervous curtseys. Neither looked to be much older than fourteen, and their maids' uniforms hung on their thin frames.

'This is Bronwyn, an' that's Daisy, though Gawd knows what I done t' deserve 'em – daft as brushes, the pair of 'em.'

Mary gave them a smile. 'I don't expect they are for one minute, and I seem to remember you saying much the same about me.'

'Well if I did then I didn't know when I was well off!' A large fruitcake stood on the dresser, and Peggy cut two enormous wedges, placing them on plates which she shoved in front of the two maids. ''Ere, eat that, then get yerselves upstairs an' see t' them fires.' She indicated a chair at the far end of the table. 'Sit yerself down, Mary. I shan't be a minute.' Taking two biscuits from a tray that was cooling she added them to the girls' plates. 'It's either feed 'em up or take in them uniforms – an' these days my eyes ain't so good for the sewin'.'

Mary sat down. 'So, how are you, Peggy?'

'Oh, right as ninepence,' she gave the two girls a look as they started in on the cake, '*considerin*'.'

'You have two maids now?'

'Well, Mr Llewellyn thought we needed another girl – what with his wife's condition an' all.' Peggy rolled her eyes. 'Though I only gets the same amount o' work out o' the pair of 'em as I did out o' you.'

Mary looked concerned. 'Mrs Llewellyn?' she asked. 'Is there something wrong with her?'

'Lord, no! Didn't yer know? She's fallen for a kid.'

Mary's mouth dropped open. *Mrs Llewellyn?*

'Yes. Pleased as punch they are. Always wanted a kid but never could 'ave one, see? She's a bit old, o'course, but they've been 'avin' the doctor in an' 'e says as long as she takes it easy it ought t' be alright.'

Mary made to rise. 'Perhaps I should just go up and see her.'

'Yer can't. They're not 'ere. Gone off t' Cardiff for the day – for a rest supposedly.' Then she smiled. 'But they'll come back loaded with baby things, you mark my words.' She went to fill the teapot. 'Still, I expect you'll be doin' the same soon, eh?' There was no answer, and seeing Mary's downcast eyes she turned her gaze on Daisy and Bronwyn. 'You two still 'ere? Get yerselves up them stairs an' see t' them bloomin' fires. I'm not 'avin' you sittin' around all day eatin' cake an' earwiggin'.' She watched the two girls scurry away, then brought the teapot over to the table. 'Now,' she said, filling two cups. 'I can see there's somethin' wrong. So – yer goin' t' tell me what it is?'

'An' yer say you ain't *never* done it? Not in all these months?'

Mary shook her head. 'I don't know what to do, Peggy. Everyone thinks we have, but we haven't – and Thomas won't even try now.'

Mrs Cartwright sighed. 'Yer've come to the wrong person, 'ere, Mary. Yer need t' talk t' someone with experience o' such things.'

'I can't, Peg. You're the *only* one I can talk to. No one else must ever know ... *ever!*'

'Well, 'course I shan't tell anyone, but I don't know what else I can do. You sure this 'usband o' yours won't let yer see a doctor?'

'No. He's forbidden it. He says if I do, then it will be all over the valley.'

'What about the doctor 'ere – Rees-Morgan? 'E's lookin' after Mrs Llewellyn. A right pig of a man to my mind, but the missus thinks the world of 'im.'

'I wouldn't dare. Anyway, I couldn't afford him. It's not good at the mines just now.'

They sat in silence for a while, then Peggy said, 'Look, if yer *was* thinkin' t' go against yer 'usband's wishes – an' I'm not sayin' as yer should, mind – but, well, I've got a bit o' money put by. Maybe, if yer was t' go t' Cardiff ...?' she paused. ''Ere! Just 'old on a minute.' She got up and went to the stairs. 'Daisy!' There was no reply, so she climbed half way up. 'Daisy! Come back down 'ere!'

Moments later, a frightened face peered round the door. 'Yes, m'um?'

'Come in 'ere, girl. I ain't goin' t' bite yer! Now, where was that place you was tellin' us about – the place yer went when you was 'avin them belly aches afore yer came 'ere?'

'The free clinic, m'um?'

'If that's where yer went? Yes.'

'Yes, m'um, it was.'

'Well?'

'Well, what, m'um?'

Mrs Cartwright rolled her eyes again. 'Lord, Mary. Yer see what I 'as t' put up with!'

Mary smiled at the girl. 'Could you tell us about it?'

Daisy fiddled with her apron. 'Well, it's this clinic, like … and it's free … in Cardiff, on Wood Street, it is.' Her eyes flitted from Mary to Mrs Cartwright, then back again. 'Supposed to be every Tuesday – but I don't know if it's still going because it'd only just started when I went – but it don't cost nothing, like. Free it is … in the chapel hall … Tuesdays … got a doctor there an' everything.' Daisy smiled, looking very pleased with herself – until Mrs Cartwright frowned at her.

'Alright, alright, yer can get off back t' them fires now.'

Daisy hesitated. 'I've … I've done them, m'um.'

'Well – bloomin' well do 'em again!'

*

The chapel hall lay at the end of an alley that squeezed between a blind factory wall on one side, and the broken, decaying fence of a slaughterer's yard on the other. Austere and utilitarian, the place gave a cold welcome even on a bright morning – and the morning was far from bright; it was wet and miserable, and Mary cringed as she stood amongst the mass of grey, huddled figures – steam rising from their rain-sodden clothes to fill the dimly-lit hall with a foul humidity.

Beside her, a woman with a baby wrapped in a shawl gave her an enquiring glance. 'You been here before?'

Mary shook her head.

'Then make sure you watch who's ahead of you. There's a lot won't think twice about pushin' in if you give them half a chance.'

'Thank you. I'll try. But …' Mary looked around in confusion.

'Oh, don't worry,' said the woman. 'You're after me. I'll watch out for you. I know most of this lot. What you got, anyway? A dose, is it?'

Mary gave her a puzzled look. 'A dose?'

'The clap. The pox.'

'Oh! No!' she blushed.

The woman hefted the baby into a more comfortable position. 'Well, that's lucky, then. It's what I've bloody well got. Soddin' sailors!' She rolled her eyes, sighing at the unfairness of it all, then glanced at the child – then at Mary. 'Here, you couldn't do us a favour, my love?' she asked, holding out the baby. 'Look after him for a minute? It's dyin' for a piss, I am.'

By five-thirty, all was blackness beyond the chapel hall's high windows, and the gas jets cast a sickly light on Mary as she sat alone.

It had been early afternoon before the baby's mother returned, smelling of gin, and full of apologies. 'Well, my love,' she'd said. 'It's a long old wait without a little somethin' inside you.'

Mary hadn't minded. She'd liked holding the baby – and playing with him had kept her from dwelling on Thomas, and the enormity of what she was about to do.

At two o'clock, an old woman in a white apron had locked the main doors, and slowly the hall began to empty. Mary's new friend had been true to her word, tenaciously guarding their places, but no sooner had she gone than those remaining had been quick to take advantage. Unwilling to make a scene, Mary resigned herself to being last.

'Next,' said the aproned woman, opening the door and admitting Mary to the small surgery. 'This is the last one, Doctor.'

'Thank you, Mrs Pope.' The man glanced over his shoulder at Mary as he stood with his back to the room, washing his hands at the sink. 'Please, take a seat. I shan't be a moment.'

Gratefully, she moved to the chair. She'd had nothing to eat or drink since breakfast that morning and was beginning to feel light headed.

'Now,' he turned to her, 'what can I do for you, Miss …?'

'Kelly … It's Mrs Kelly.' She felt her face grow hot, not only at the deception, but because the man before her was not in the least what she had expected. She doubted he could be older than twenty-five, and his dark hair was cut in the new, shorter fashion, giving him the appearance of a London man-about-town rather than a Cardiff doctor.

'I hope you won't mind if I dispense with my jacket?' he said, rolling down his sleeves. 'I have to keep a good fire going, and it can get rather hot in here.' He watched the old woman tut her disapproval as she tidied the room, then he cleared his throat. 'So,' he said, seating himself behind the desk. 'What seems to be the problem, Mrs Kelly?'

Gripped by a sudden and irrational panic, Mary got to her feet, her hand reaching for the edge of the desk as the abrupt movement made her feel faint. 'I … I'm sorry. There is no problem … I've made a mistake. I shouldn't be here.' She swayed, and in a second he was at her side, but she recovered sufficiently to steady herself.

'Please,' he motioned toward the chair. 'You've obviously been waiting a long time. Won't you at least sit until you are feeling a little better?'

'No …' she began, but there was a reassuring quality to his dark and serious eyes, and slowly she sat down again.

'Mrs Pope,' he said. 'Would you mind waiting outside?'

The old woman glanced pointedly at Mary. 'Really, Doctor – do you think that is wise? You being *alone*?'

'If it is alright with Mrs Kelly,' he looked questioningly at Mary, and receiving a hesitant nod he continued, 'then I believe it will be perfectly alright. I shall call you if I need you.'

He waited until Mrs Pope had closed the door behind her, then sat back, studying Mary over his steepled fingers. 'Is it a sexual matter?'

'Yes.'

'A disease?'

Mary's eyes widened. 'No!'

'Forgive me, I meant no offence.' Then more softly, 'Well – perhaps in your own time?'

She looked into her lap, her fingers feeling for the sleeve of her dress. 'It's just that …' She took a deep breath, then glanced up, ashamed and frightened. 'It's just that … I'm not able … I've *never* been able to … to be a *proper* wife,' she began.

'There would appear to be nothing physically wrong,' he said, as Mary emerged hot and embarrassed from behind the modesty screen. 'At least, there are no abnormalities I can detect. I wasn't able to make a very thorough examination, of course, for the same reason your husband has not been able to achieve penetration.'

Mary felt her cheeks burn, and she kept her eyes lowered. 'Then … there's nothing you can do?'

'I don't know. I am sure the problem is caused solely by the muscles going into spasm. You felt the tightening – when I touched you?'

She nodded, colouring even more.

'And there appeared to be considerable pain.'

She nodded again.

'Yes. It *is* an unusual condition – but one I'm fairly certain I've heard of before.' His eyes took on a far away look, and his fingers drummed on the edge of the desk for a moment, then finding Mary looking at him, he shifted in his chair, adopting a more formal attitude. 'The important point is to identify a treatment – and so I'd like to consult a colleague of mine who is better acquainted with these matters. It will mean sending a letter to London, but a week should be more than sufficient for me to receive his reply. Could you return here next Tuesday?'

Mary looked doubtful. 'You really think you could do something?'

'I can make no promises.'

'Yes, I understand. It's just that …' She worried at her sleeve. 'Yes … alright, next Tuesday.'

'Excellent. And it might be useful if you were to bring your husband.'

'No – No, that's impossible.'

He said nothing, but his dark eyes were grave and questioning.

'He has forbidden me to see a doctor,' she said.

'But why on earth …?'

'He doesn't want anyone to know. We've pretended, you see. Pretended that everything is alright between us.'

'I see.' He rose, escorting her to a door that led out into a small court-yard at the far end of the alley. 'Then we shall just have to do what we can.'

'You've been very kind,' she said, extending her hand. 'Doctor …?'

'Rees-Morgan.'

She paled, her voice becoming barely a whisper. 'Rees-Morgan? From Caerphilly?'

'Yes.' He searched her face, alarmed by the sudden change in her manner. 'But you are probably thinking of my father. Why – is something wrong?'

She swayed, her hand going to her temple. 'I'm sorry,' she said, starting away into the darkness. 'I … I can't come again.'

She was half way along the alley when he caught hold of her arm.

'Mrs Kelly …?'

'Please … let me go. It was a mistake to come here – a terrible mistake.'

'But why?'

She shook her head.

'You must tell me. If there is something about my family name that upsets you, then I have a right to know.'

'Please … just let me go.'

Behind him the door to the hall opened and Mrs Pope came out, peer-ing into the darkness. 'What's going on out here?' She took a step closer, her eyes widening with surprise. 'Is that you, Doctor Rees-Morgan?'

'It's alright, Mrs Pope. The lady is just a little upset. Please go back inside.' He turned urgently to Mary, steadying her. 'Mrs Kelly …?'

The old woman advanced toward them. 'Should I fetch a constable?'

'No – everything is under control, thank you, Mrs Pope.'

The woman continued to advance. 'You don't know these street women, Doctor! They're a bad lot. I think I'd better …'

'Will you just leave us be, damn you!'

The force of his words set her back on her heels. 'Well! Indeed I will!' she bristled, pulling her shawl about her shoulders. 'I'll not stay here to be talked to like that! And don't go expecting me back! I always knew you was no gentleman.'

He watched her leave. 'She's right,' he sighed, letting go of Mary's arm. 'I'm sorry, Mrs Kelly. I've acted unforgivably.'

Slowly, Mary drew herself up, taking a steadying breath.

'But, please,' he said, tilting his head to look into her eyes, 'won't you come back inside?'

*

'What time is it now?' Meg called over her shoulder.

Owen opened his pocket watch. 'A quarter past six. Now will you shut the door, woman. There's a draught fit to cut the legs off a man.'

She cast another glance along the deserted road, white now with glistening ice crystals, then came in and closed the door. 'I hope she's alright. She's been gone for hours – and it's getting right slippery underfoot. She can't *still* be looking for a job.'

'Should I go and look?' asked Thomas getting to his feet. 'I could go along the Caerphilly road.'

Owen rustled his newspaper. 'Oh, leave the girl alone. She'll likely have had a poor day of it as far as jobs go. There's not a thing going in Caerphilly, or anywhere else abouts, as I hear. I expect she's cheering herself with talk of babies up at the Cross Keys. Now *that* was a turn up for the books! Still, better a baby there than here as things are.'

Meg shot him a look. 'There's always room for a baby in *this* house.'

He lowered the paper. 'I wasn't saying …'

'Well, I should hope not! It'd be a fine thing to be saying, if you were!'

Owen gave her an exasperated look, then turned to Thomas. 'Your mam's right. Perhaps you'd better take a walk over to Caerphilly.'

'No, no. Your da was right,' she said. 'She'll likely be home soon, and her dinner will keep.' She gave the stew a final stir, then straightening up she called into the scullery, 'Gwyneth. Will you come and lay the table? I'm going to dish up.'

*

'So, you know my father?' he asked, pouring her some tea as they sat in the warmth of the make-shift surgery.

She nodded. 'Only by sight, of course – and I know *you*.'

It was his turn to show surprise, and she went on quickly, 'I knew there was *something* the moment I walked in – but it wasn't until you told me your name …'

He studied her carefully. 'I'm sorry – I don't remember you.'

'Oh, you wouldn't. We've never spoken. But I used to see you riding – with your father.'

'In Caerphilly?'

'Yes. I went to school there – and I was the maid-of-all-work at the Cross Keys Hotel. I live in Nant-y-Pridd now.'

'Nant-y-Pridd? But that's over nine miles from here.'

'I needed somewhere I wasn't known. I didn't dare go to a local doctor.'

'Mrs Kelly,' he said, beginning to understand. 'You must believe that whatever you tell me will always be held in the strictest confidence.'

She looked up into the dark, serious eyes – feeling a strange and almost disquieting sense of trust. 'Yes ...' she said, '*I do.*'

Chapter Thirteen

Ice crackled beneath the wheels of the gig as it rolled to a halt on the deserted road. The incessant rain had finally cleared to leave a clear, moonless sky that was bright with stars, and from the valley below long fingers of smoke stretched upwards from the clustered houses.

Holding the reins in his gloved hands, Dr. Evan Rees-Morgan turned, his breath white in the sharp air. 'Please, Mrs Kelly. It's still a good mile or more to Nant-y-Pridd. At least let me take you a little closer?'

Mary pushed the blanket from her knees. 'No. It's very kind of you, but you mustn't.'

'But you will consider my offer?'

Stepping down on to the road, she cast a nervous glance back toward Caerphilly, then over toward Nant-y-Pridd. 'I … I really don't think I can.'

'But why ever not? You *are* going to keep the appointment next week – and you *are* looking for a job?'

'Yes … but …'

'You would be doing me a very great favour.'

'I don't know,' she said, her heart racing, aware of how people would gossip if she should be seen with him. 'I ought to go before someone comes.'

'Look, why don't I call for you next Tuesday? Would half past eight be too early?'

Her eyes widened in alarm. 'No! You must *never* do that.' She gave another nervous glance up and down the road, but apart from the horse pawing impatiently at the ground, all was still. Looking up at him, she pulled her coat close against the cold. 'I'll meet you … by the station in Caerphilly.'

*

Ivor Rees-Morgan was almost apoplectic. 'Damn you, boy! Surely you must see that this free clinic of yours does more harm than good?'

The fire in the drawing-room was dying down, and Evan leaned from the leather armchair to pitch another log into the ornate fire basket. 'How so?' he asked quietly.

'To start with, *respect* – or rather, the lack of it! People only respect what they have to pay for! The more you charge, the greater they respect you for it! And ring for the damned servants if you want another log on the fire. It's what *they're* paid for!'

Evan touched his hand to his mouth, his forefinger rubbing thoughtfully across his lips to conceal the smile. He had been home barely a month, but it was as if he had never been away. 'And what of self-respect?' he asked.

Sitting a genteel distance from the fire, his mother placed her hands in her lap, eyeing her husband with regal detachment. 'Yes, surely we have a duty?' she said as he poured another brandy. '*Noblesse oblige?*'

Ivor tossed back his head, draining the glass. 'Noblesse bloody nonsense!'

'As you wish.'

Evan looked at her with admiration. She was still a strikingly handsome woman, but it was her ability to counter his father's bluster with the simplest of statements that had always impressed him. He toyed with his glass. 'You don't believe then, sir, that we have a duty to those less fortunate than ourselves?'

'If we have a *duty*, it is to give those *less fortunate* the incentive to improve their lot. It is not our duty to shore them up in their destitution with damned charity!'

'But without charity, many cannot – and do not, survive.'

His mother gave him an encouraging smile, pleased that her son had not inherited *all* his father's traits. 'Without charity we are little different to the beasts of the field, I think,' she said.

Ivor rounded on her. 'Better, then, to be like beasts, madam! Asking no quarter and giving none.'

She raised her eyebrows. 'Ivor, really! You go too far! What if the servants were to overhear!'

The corners of Evan's mouth curled into a smile. 'Father. You don't believe that any more than I do.'

The old man scratched at his side-whiskers for a moment. 'Maybe not,' he conceded. 'But *charity* is a curse. It perpetuates the very thing it tries to alleviate. When you give a man something for nothing you take away his incentive to better himself and his situation. I'm not saying you should charge fancy London fees ... not even *my* fees. But you should charge *something!*'

'But many of these people have nothing at all.'

'They can usually find the price of a drink!'

Evan tapped thoughtfully at the arm of the chair. 'Alright,' he said at last. 'Let us say you are right, and I make a nominal charge of what? Fourpence? Sixpence?'

Ivor roared. '*A whole sixpence*? Getting above yourself, aren't you, boy?'

'Very well,' Evan smiled. 'Let us say that, influenced by my father's *philanthropic* attitude to fees, I charge the princely sum of one penny – the price of a glass of gin. Then what?'

'Then you'd lose half your damn patients I shouldn't wonder.'

'And that is a good thing?'

'It is an excellent thing in as much that, stay or go, they have each taken responsibility for their own condition.'

Evan threw himself back into the chair in exasperation. 'And possibly die because of it!'

'Quite possibly!'

'And that is your argument?'

'A fever must oft get worse before it gets better. You should know that!' Ivor moved closer to the fire, rubbing his hands before the flames. 'Listen,' he said, quietly. 'You remember when the Board School was built in the town a few years ago?' He cast a sideways glance toward his son. 'What did you think of that?'

'I thought it was not before time.'

'And do you know why it was built?'

Evan sighed. 'Because of the new education bill. I do read the newspapers, you know – why, we even have such things in London. But I can't see what this has to do with charity.'

'I'm sure you don't – but bear with me.' He tipped brandy into Evan's glass, then refilled his own. 'The only reason we have that new school is because the previous ones got so bad they could no longer be ignored and there was no choice but to build new ones. I take it you won't argue with me over that?'

'No.'

'Good. Now, let us say that a few years earlier your mother and her charitable ladies had descended upon those self same hovels, and – *in the spirit of compassion* – had spent a few miserable pounds on improving them just sufficiently to pass muster with the inspectors. Would we have that new school? Indeed we would not! Those ramshackle places would have creaked on for year after year, bolstered on damned charity!'

Evan stared at him, unsettled by the logic of the argument, then he violently shook his head. 'No. No. No. That really won't do. Using that hypothesis we should never administer a cure because it might propagate the disease!'

Florence Rees-Morgan took up her embroidery and settled herself to the work. After thirty years of marriage to Ivor she was in no doubt it was going to be a long and quarrelsome evening.

*

Seated next to Thomas in the crowded kitchen, Mary finished the last of her stew.

'Have you had enough, my love? There's a mite more if you could manage it,' said Meg as she took the empty plate.

'No, thank you. I couldn't eat another mouthful.' Mary made to get up. 'But, please, let me do that.'

'You sit back down. You must be half dead from walking around town all day. My, but you picked a terrible day for it – it's barely stopped raining. Still, it all worked out well in the end, didn't it.'

In his chair by the fire, Owen cleared his throat grumpily and retreated behind his newspaper. 'Can't see how this job's going to be worth it – one day a week – and just for a month – *and* all the way to Cardiff.'

Thomas took Mary's hand. 'Come on, Da. Mary wouldn't have taken the job without thinking about that.'

'Oh, for heaven's sake, leave the poor girl alone,' Meg admonished. 'Can't you see she's tired out?'

Mary turned to look at the clock; it was a few minutes before nine. 'Actually, I am tired,' she said, stifling a yawn. 'Would you mind very much if I went up to bed?'

Thomas pushed back his chair and got to his feet. 'You go on up. I'll be along presently.' He watched her climb the stairs, then slowly made his way to stand before the fire. 'Da,' he said, keeping his voice very low, 'I know you don't approve.'

Owen brought the paper down. 'Do *you* approve?'

'Yes ... that is ... no – I'd sooner she stayed at home. But, with Mam and Gwyn here, well, there's little enough for her to do. When things pick up a bit, maybe we could get a house of our own, like, but until then ...'

'You think I should mind my own business?'

Thomas looked uncomfortable.

'And you are right,' said Owen, 'I should. A man should be master of his own affairs.'

'I didn't mean ...' began Thomas, but Owen leaned forward and gripped his arm.

'I don't agree with it. A wife's place is in the home. But she's *your* wife, and it's no one's business but your own – and it's proud I am that you stand up for her.'

'Thank you, Da.'

Owen waved him away. 'Oh, get off to bed with you.'

Having put the kettle on to boil, Meg was about to sit down when she spotted Mary's boots by the door. 'I should put those by the fire,' she said. 'They must be soaked through.'

Thomas turned quickly. 'It's alright, Mam. I'll do it,' he said, picking up the boots and carrying them over to the hearth, setting them a little distance away so as not to crack the leather – even though he'd noticed when she had taken them off that they were not the least bit wet.

Chapter Fourteen

Mary's footsteps echoed in the empty hall as she double locked the doors and turned off the gas jets before returning to the comparative cosiness of the small surgery.

'Should I make some tea, Doctor?'

Evan glanced up briefly from his casebook. 'Yes, please, Mrs Kelly. I was just doing it myself.' He made a vague gesture to where the kettle was beginning to boil.

She went to the sink and emptied the teapot, keeping her back to him as she took a steadying breath. 'My name isn't really Kelly.'

'Hmm?'

'My name – it isn't Kelly. It's Davies. Kelly was my maiden name.' She turned. 'I just wanted you to know.'

'Most people who come here don't bother giving a name at all, so even a false one is a step in the right direction. And I *do* understand.' He put down the pen and leaned back in the chair. 'But I *should* like to know your first name.'

'It's Mary.'

'May I be permitted to call you that?'

She hesitated. 'I suppose that would be alright.'

'But you still cannot bring yourself to call me Evan?' There was a teasing note to his voice.

'I don't think that would be proper.'

'No,' he said quickly, sensing her discomfort. 'I'm sure you're right.' Then in an attempt to lighten the mood he gave a small laugh. 'My father would certainly approve. He's a stickler when it comes to the proper show of respect.'

In spite of her insistence on formality, Mary felt herself chafing at this reminder of their social differences. 'He *is* very respected, I believe,' she said tersely, busying herself with washing the teacups.

Evan got to his feet, coming to stand close behind her. 'Such things are important to *him* – not to *me*.'

She tensed, feeling the warmth of his breath on her neck and the touch of his arm as he reached round to take the cup.

'Here, let me,' he said. 'If I'm deserving of any respect, then it is most certainly for my tea-making.'

'But it's *my* job.'

'We're both off duty now. I think this is *one* convention we might set aside, don't you?'

His grip tightened on the cup, and reluctantly she surrendered it to him, stepping away and moving uncertainly to the desk. Work had conferred a feeling of security, of place, but now she felt adrift, unsure how to conduct herself, and not entirely certain he wasn't mocking her.

'I … I was wondering whether you had heard anything from the man you wrote to?' she said.

'No, I'm so very sorry. I left instructions that if anything should arrive by a later post, it should be brought straight here – but I'm afraid there has been nothing.'

An odd sense of relief swept over her, and she sat down, watching as he warmed the pot then spooned in the dark brown leaves. As on her previous visit, he was in his shirtsleeves, but this time a waistcoat gave shape to his back, and she found herself studying it, noticing how straight and slender it appeared in comparison to Thomas's broad, muscular frame.

'I'm certain I shall have received a reply by next week,' he said, cutting across her thoughts. He glanced over his shoulder. 'You *can* come again?'

She nodded, and he smiled. 'So …' he began in a lighter tone, 'how did you enjoy your first day?'

'I … I liked it very well.'

He turned, brandishing the teapot. 'God, but you are a liar, Mary Davies! You hated it.'

'I didn't.'

He was grinning now. 'Yes you did. On at least two occasions I thought you were going to be sick – but you were marvellous! Absolutely marvellous!' She looked at him, embarrassed – then puzzled – and he gave a small chuckle before growing serious once more. 'Believe me, I know what it's like. When I was twelve years old, my father had me dissect a rabbit. That was *my* first time, and I very nearly passed out. As it was, I cried so much I could barely see what I was doing, and I made a complete mess of it. Father was furious, not because of my inexperience and lack of skill, nor because I was revolted by the whole thing, but because I'd let my revulsion affect what I had to do. I'd let it *show*. The point is – *you* didn't let it show.' He filled the teapot, then turned to her, smiling once more. 'I could tell what you were thinking, but I don't believe any of those people who came today could. And you certainly had a baptism of fire!'

Mary gave a weak smile. 'It *was* awful at times.'

'You'll get used to it. And it isn't always as bad as that.'

'I don't know.' She pursed her lips uncertainly. 'It *was* bad, but I think the most awful thing was that sometimes, well, I …'

'Wanted to laugh?'

'Yes!' she said in astonishment.

The corners of his eyes creased into a smile. 'I know – but you *didn't*, did you.'

'But those poor people. It's awful to even think of doing it.'

'Of course it isn't. We're only human, for God's sake. Sometimes things *are* funny. The man with the boil, for instance?'

'Oh, yes!' she said, starting to laugh. 'And the woman with the bad feet.'

Evan grinned. '*I'm cursed with these feet, Doctor – 'ad 'em for years, I 'ave!*'

'Oh, and the boy with stomach-ache – who'd eaten a *whole jar* of sweets.'

'And his mother, insisting he'd had nothing but half a herring all day.'

'And when she picked him up, he was sick all over her apron.'

Evan placed a finger to his lips, covering his smile. 'Very colourful!' he said wryly. 'Turner could not have done better.'

She looked at him. 'Turner?'

It was Evan's turn to be embarrassed. 'An artist,' he explained, 'but it really doesn't matter.'

'I know who Turner was,' she said, more emphatically than she intended, quickly lowering her eyes in apology.

Evan studied her. 'Do you like Turner's work?'

She met his gaze once more. 'I believe I would adore it.'

'You *believe*?'

'I've only ever seen engravings, never the actual paintings. Have *you* seen them?'

'Yes, in London.'

'Are they as wonderful as they say?'

'They are passionate, certainly, but given the choice I would take a Tadema every time.'

'Alma-Tadema? Yes, I know of him. His draughtsmanship is wonderful of course … but isn't it said he lacks excitement? Energy?'

He stared at her, shaking his head. 'You really are full of surprises, Mary Davies. I think I shall …' An urgent knock at the back door stopped him in mid flow, and he got to his feet. 'The caretaker, I expect,' he said, turning the latch. 'I asked him last week about more chairs for the hall.'

Beyond the open door, all was in darkness, but just enough light spilled from the room to reveal a young woman huddled in a shawl.

Mary stood up, expecting Evan to show the visitor into the surgery, but instead he went out to her, closing the door behind him, and Mary moved closer, trying to overhear the urgent murmurings.

Then, suddenly, he was back, pulling on his jacket and reaching for his coat and bag. 'Mary, I'm sorry. I have to make a house call. It really can't wait.'

'Should I come with you?'

'No, please. Just wait for me here. I should only be half an hour.' A look of uncertainty crossed his face. 'But you should be getting home.' He reached into his jacket, pulling out his pocket book. 'If you would prefer, I can give you some money for the train?'

The door had swung open, and Mary looked past him to where the young woman was standing in the shadows, watching with anxious, almost haunted eyes.

'No,' she said. 'No, it's alright. I'll wait.'

*

Florence Rees-Morgan stood by the drawing-room window of Pendragon, looking out over the rooftops of Caerphilly as the last glimmer of daylight waned. 'You've been with us for such a long time, Mrs Broadwood. Is there nothing I can say to persuade you to stay?'

The housekeeper shifted awkwardly on the sofa. 'No, m'um. I shall be sorry to go, of course.'

'Are you in a great deal of pain?'

'Some days are worse than others, m'um.'

There was a knock at the door, and Lucy, the maid, entered carrying two lighted lamps which she carefully placed in position before crossing to the window and drawing the curtains. 'I'll just see to the fire, m'um.' Under the gimlet eye of the housekeeper, she moved to the fireplace and raked at the coals.

'Would you bring us some sherry,' said Florence as Lucy straightened up – then to the housekeeper, 'You will take a glass with me?'

'Oh … yes, m'um. That is very kind of you, I'm sure.'

'A very capable girl,' observed Florence once the maid had departed.

'Yes, m'um.' Mrs Broadwood set her mouth in a downward curve. 'Though I shall have something to say to her about that hearth.'

Florence followed the woman's gaze to where tiny flecks of coal lay on the polished tiles.

'Of course, I shall be happy to stay until you've found a replacement,' the housekeeper continued, 'if that is your wish, m'um.'

'I shouldn't like to cause you any discomfort, but perhaps, if you could manage until after Christmas?'

'Of course, m'um.'

There was another knock, and Lucy reappeared with a tray bearing a decanter, and two glasses which she filled before silently taking her leave.

'You will be very much missed, Mrs Broadwood,' said Florence.

With no small effort, Mrs Broadwood picked up her glass, holding it in a hand made claw-like by arthritis. 'Thank you, m'um.'

*

Queen Street was bustling with activity as Evan steered the gig into the stream of traffic. He'd been quiet and pensive ever since returning from the house call, and seemed barely to notice the festive atmosphere: the cabs and carriages, their lamps gleaming in the darkness, and the lighted windows of shops already dressed for Christmas.

But for Mary it was a far cry from the quiet, dingy streets from which they had just emerged, and she felt intoxicated by it all.

'And what of Mr Ruskin? Do you like him?' she asked, sitting snug beneath the blanket, her cheeks flushed with cold.

'As a man or as an artist?'

Mary looked at him in surprise. 'You've actually *met* him?'

'Just the once. He wasn't as opinionated as I had been led to believe, but then he was quite ill at the time.'

'I believe he is a great admirer of Mr Turner,' she said.

'He is indeed. As a matter of fact, it was at an exhibition he put on last year that I met him.'

'At the *Gallery of the Fine Art Society*. One hundred and twenty-six of Turner's drawings,' she smiled. 'Yes, I read about it.'

Evan glanced at her. 'You seem incredibly well informed for a ...' he stopped short, '... for someone who has never been further than Cardiff.' It was a lame attempt, and he turned to apologise, only to find her staring after an expensive-looking carriage with two liveried footmen perched high on the driving seat.

'Did you see that?' she said, wide-eyed. 'That lady in the Brougham?'

Evan watched it pull ahead, unsure of exactly what he was meant to be seeing.

'She nodded to me!' Mary said, incredulously. 'She actually smiled and nodded!'

Evan turned his attention back to the road, his good humour gradually returning. 'And why shouldn't she?'

'*Why*?' Mary looked down to where the blanket covered most of her shabby coat, and self-consciously she moved further into the shadow of the raised hood.

'So, how on earth did you know about the Turner exhibition?' he asked.

'Oh, Mr Abrahams, a friend of mine, subscribed to *The Art Journal*, and always gave them to me after he'd read them.' She smiled at the memory. 'Actually, I don't think he *ever* read them himself. But tell me – the exhibition – was it wonderful?'

'Yes, it was, actually,' he said with a fervour that surprised him. He paused. There was an infectious quality to Mary's enthusiasm that he found almost disturbing. 'Yes …' he said again, trying to keep his voice as controlled as possible. 'It was … *quite wonderful.*'

*

The hall clock was just striking eight as Lucy came down the kitchen stairs. 'Master Evan's just back from Cardiff,' she announced, sitting down at the long scullery table.

Seated opposite, Maggie, the young skivvy, looked up from the coppers she was polishing, wiping a dirty hand across her forehead to leave a dark smear. She grinned, then winked. 'He's a bit of alright, he is.'

Lucy gave her a shocked look. '*A bit of alright?*'

'Go on with you,' said Maggie. 'You've been makin' eyes at him ever since he came back from London.' She winked again. 'I wouldn't mind him keepin' me warm at night, that I wouldn't!'

'You don't think he'd look at the likes of you!'

Maggie sniffed as she began polishing once more. 'He might do. Why, you jealous?'

'What, of a scruffy little thing like you? I should think not – and I should get on with them pans if I were you! Mrs Broadwood will be down in a minute.'

'You know what *I* heard?' said Maggie, taking no notice.

Lucy tilted her chin and straightened her apron. 'What?' she said, trying to sound uninterested.

'I heard,' Maggie leaned forward, lowering her voice, 'that the master – old Doctor Rees-Morgan – well, I heard that he ain't no proper gentleman.'

''Course he is.'

'He ain't.'

'You're daft, you are.'

'Maybe,' said Maggie, taking up a small saucepan and setting to with her polishing cloth.

Lucy sat for several moments, tapping her fingers on the scrubbed table-top. 'Alright,' she said at last, 'so why isn't he a proper gentleman?'

'Oh, don't ask me. I'm daft, I am.'

'Oooo – *Maggie!*' said Lucy, gritting her teeth and drumming her feet on the stone floor.

'Well,' said Maggie, pushing one of the copper pans and a cleaning cloth across the table. 'You know this house is called Pendragon.' She watched as Lucy reluctantly picked up the pan and began polishing. 'Well, the master had it built himself.'

'I know that!'

'Ah – but do you know *why* he called it Pendragon?'

Lucy shook her head.

'Because that was the name of the pub his dad used to run in Caernar-von – *The Pendragon Arms*. He ain't no more a gentleman than I am!'

'I don't believe it!'

'It's true.'

'Who told you all this?'

Maggie touched her finger to her nose, leaving another smudge. 'I ain't sayin'. But it's God's truth.' She grinned. 'They say he was a right young buck before he was married. All over the ladies, he was – an' they was all over him, too – an' still are by all accounts. Too old for me, though. But that Master Evan … Ooooh.' She wriggled with pleasure.

Lucy eyed her suspiciously. 'So what about *her*? The mistress?'

'She's proper gentry.'

'Then you *are* daft!' said Lucy, shoving the pan back across the table. 'If she's gentry, then he must be, too. She wouldn't go marrying no common-as-muck son of a publican!'

Maggie pushed the copper back toward Lucy. 'Ah, but her family had lost all their money, see.'

On a board above their heads, the drawing-room bell rang.

'You'll have to tell me later,' said Lucy, jumping up. 'Oh, hell, look at my hands!' She ran to the sink, quickly washing them before hurrying upstairs and across the hall to the drawing-room.

Inside, Ivor was standing with his back to the fireplace, resplendent in evening dress and holding a large whisky glass, the perfect image of a gentleman, and she tried not to stare at him.

'Ah, Lucy,' said Florence. 'My husband and I shall be leaving presently, so would you have the carriage brought round.'

'Yes, m'um.' She bobbed a curtsey and turned to leave, but Evan's voice stopped her.

'I should like a bath made ready in my room, when you have a moment,' he said. 'But please don't hurry, I shall be staying in this evening.'

'Yes, sir. I'll see to it straight away.'

'Oh, and, Lucy?'

'Yes, sir?'

'Something warm in the dining room afterwards?'

'Yes sir, I'll tell cook, sir.' She could feel herself growing red, and she stole a glance at him. 'Will that be all, sir?'

He smiled. 'Yes, thank you.'

Back in the hallway she leaned against the banisters. *Something warm in the dining room, afterwards*, she thought longingly.

*

'You don't have to do this, Mary,' whispered Thomas as they lay together in the blackness of the small upstairs room. 'We can manage.'

She patted his arm. 'It's alright. I don't mind the work, and it brings in a little extra money.'

'But those things you were saying downstairs. *All those sick people.*'

'Oh, I'll get used to it. The thing is not to let it show. If something upsets you, you just have to pretend.'

He moved closer, nuzzling her ear. 'We should both be good at that,' he said sadly, giving her a light kiss.

She reached for his hand, clasping it and drawing it on to her chest, feeling his warmth through the cotton of her chemise. 'I *do* love you, Thomas.'

His grip tightened, but he made no move to touch her more intimately. 'That's all I want. That's all I've ever wanted.'

She pressed his hand to her breast, feeling him stir against her thigh. 'Do you want to try? It's been a long time since we …'

'I couldn't hurt you. Not again. Not like last time.'

She could already feel the first tentative clenching of her muscles, but despite his protestations, Thomas's ardour was pressing against her hip. 'It *might* be alright now,' she whispered.

'Do you really think so?'

On the far side of the curtain, Gwyneth rolled over, coughing, and Mary tensed as she instinctively turned toward the sound. When she turned back, Thomas was still holding her, but his pressing insistence was barely there.

'I love you, Mary,' he said, moving his hand from her breast and holding her about the waist instead. 'You do know that?'

'Yes.'

He sighed, nestling into her. 'Tell me about the clinic again.'

So she told him – cradling his head on her shoulder, she told him about the place, the people and the events. But she did not tell him of Evan: of how they had sat laughing at the end of the day, or of how they had discussed art so fervently. Neither did she tell him of how she had ridden through the streets of Cardiff, feeling like a lady – and sitting so very close to him.

Thomas was on the point of sleep as she finished with the story of the boy and the stolen sweets, and he nuzzled her neck. 'I expect he caught a good hiding when he got home.'

She gave a soft laugh. 'You should have seen it. Turner couldn't have done better.'

'Turner?' he asked drowsily. 'Who's he, then?'

Mary stroked his hair. 'Nobody,' she said, staring up into the darkness. 'Nobody at all.'

Chapter Fifteen

No one could remember a worse year for weather. With a week to go before Christmas, the pattern looked set to continue, and the people in the valleys braced themselves for a long, hard winter, made all the harder by the situation in the mines.

The threatened strikes had not come to Nant-y-Pridd, but the worry showed in every face – even those that surrounded me in the Davies' cosy home – and Gwyneth, already living with the taint of prison, felt it the most, growing increasingly withdrawn.

My heart went out to her – all the more so because I at least had the momentary escape of going to Cardiff each Tuesday – and it was an escape.

The work was often unpleasant, but it never seemed so. The letter we were expecting still had not come, but it didn't matter – the importance of my original purpose had faded with each passing week, and I began to look forward more and more to those hours for reasons I desperately tried to deny.

*

'Go safely,' said Meg as she handed Owen his box and jack in the lamp-lit kitchen.

'Go safely yourself, woman.'

She laughed and gave him a push. 'Go on – get off with you. Some of us have work to do this morning, and can't be doing it while you three great lumps are cluttering the place.'

'Oh, *you* have work to do, is it? Well, come on my boys. We'd best be away underground for another little *holiday*.' He looked out into the dark street. 'You be sure to bring that bathing suit of yours, Alan. Looks like you'll be needing it.'

'No room, I'm h'afraid.' Alan went to the door, grinning. 'H'awfully loaded down with golf clubs and lawn tennis racquets, don't-you-know.'

Mary gave a little curtsey as he passed. 'Would sir like me to reserve him a bathchair at the bottom of the shaft?'

'Now, Mary, don't you go encouraging their silliness,' said Meg, shooing Alan out of the house.

Outside it was beginning to drizzle, and Alan turned up his collar, pulling his cap down over his eyes. 'Well, there's a surprise – it's raining! Come on, Thomas, get a move on.'

Putting her arms about Thomas's neck, Mary kissed him. 'Go safely,' she said as he made for the door.

Owen stood aside, allowing him to pass, then looked meaningfully at Meg, raising his eyes toward the upstairs room. 'Don't go letting her sleep in,' he said. 'It won't help her to be left moping around up there.'

Meg nodded. 'I know,' she said sadly.

With the men gone, Mary and Meg set about clearing the breakfast things.

'You'd better go and wake Gwyneth,' said Meg as they stood side by side in the scullery.

Mary put down the plate she was drying, and made toward the door, but Meg stopped her. 'Mary ...?' she began awkwardly. 'I ... I've never seen Gwyneth like this before. That business ... going to court, losing her job ... *everything*. It seems to have knocked all the wind out of her sails. And you know what people are like around here – there are a good many won't even speak to her because she's been to prison – and no one will employ her. She's tried so hard to ...' she reached out, touching Mary's arm. 'I know it's not your fault, not any of it, but ... well, you finding that job in Cardiff, and making it sound so interesting ... I think that was the final straw for Gwyneth.'

Mary looked at her, ashen-faced. 'Oh, Mam. I'm so sorry. I never intended to ...'

'No – of course you didn't. That's not what I meant. It's just ...' Meg paused, wiping the back of her hand across her eyes. 'I was thinking ... if she had a job – any job – then she might start to pull herself together.'

'But there are no jobs.'

'There's yours.'

'Mine?'

'Yes. You could let Gwyneth go in your place. I know it finishes next week, but I think it would be enough to give Gwyn her confidence back. I'm certain that's all she needs.'

'But how ...?'

'You could tell Gwyn everything she needs to know – about how to do the job, like. Then next Tuesday you could write a note saying you were too ill to come, and that you were sending your sister-in-law in your place. This doctor chap won't be wanting a character reference – not at such short notice. But it would do Gwyneth the world of good to get away from

116

here, to be doing something – even if it is only for one day.'

It was as though a fist had tightened about Mary's stomach. 'I … I suppose it *might* work.' She swallowed hard. 'Yes … of course.'

'Oh, Mary,' said Meg, hugging her tightly. 'Thank you. Thank you so very much.'

*

Ivor grunted as he buttered his toast. 'I'll tell you this,' he began, stabbing the air with his knife. 'If these strikes continue then there's going to be …' He paused as the maid entered bearing the breakfast tray.

Florence turned to Evan. 'You missed a most delightful evening, darling, you really should have come. Young Adele Williams was there. She asked after you.'

'That was kind of her.'

'She has become quite the prettiest thing – and with a fine singing voice.'

Ivor grunted again. 'She's pretty enough – but I've heard a cat make a more palatable noise.'

A rasher of bacon fell from Lucy's serving tongs, landing on the clean white tablecloth, just by Ivor's side. 'Oh, oh, I'm sorry,' she stammered.

Ivor speared it on the point of his knife and dropped it on to his plate before waving her away. 'Still, I expect you found something here to amuse you,' he said, watching as the girl moved to Evan's side.

'Yes, but then almost anything is more amusing than one of Mrs Lewis's gatherings.' Evan raised his hand as Lucy made to place some ham on to his plate. 'No, thank you, Lucy.'

Florence waited until the girl had departed, then she sighed. 'I do wish you'd be a little more charitable.'

'I don't think Mrs Lewis needs my charity, Mother. She is, after all, one of the wealthiest women in South Wales.'

'You *know* what I mean – and whether you like it or not, certain *duties* are expected, Evan. A number of people whose acquaintance you would do well to cultivate remarked on your absence.'

'Wealthy people? Influential people?'

'Yes.'

'But not particularly *interesting* people.'

Florence pursed her lips. 'Of course they are *interesting*.'

'Then I am truly sorry to have missed them,' he said with the hint of a smile, 'for they must surely have wandered in by mistake – and will doubtless be at great pains not to repeat it.'

Ivor chuckled, and Florence shot him a disapproving glance. 'There are people one must *know*, Evan – and a good many introductions might have been effected last evening. You simply cannot shut yourself away here and refuse to call on people.

'The point is,' said Evan, 'I'm more than happy to call on *anyone* who is stimulating or exciting, and it wouldn't matter if she ... *they* lived in the meanest house in the poorest village. Wealth, position or influence should never enter into the equation.'

At the head of the table, Ivor roared with laughter. 'Spoken like a damned fool who's never known a day's poverty in his life!'

There was a soft knock at the door, and Lucy reappeared with another pot of tea. 'Will there be anything else, sir?' she asked.

Ivor studied her. 'Yes,' he said. 'Have my horse saddled.' He leaned toward Evan. 'There's a case I'd like you to see over in the next valley. Will you ride with me this morning?'

'Of course – if you think a damned fool can be of any assistance.'

Ivor grinned and tossed down his napkin. 'Have my son's horse saddled, too. We shall be ready to leave in half an hour.'

*

'No. No! I won't do it!'

'Gwyn, please. It would really be helping me.'

Gwyneth turned away, staring out of the kitchen window. 'You must think I'm stupid! I don't need your help – or your cast off jobs.'

'Thomas doesn't like me going – you know that. Won't you do it? As a favour to me?' Mary reached out to her, but Gwyneth snatched her arm away and continued to stare out of the window in silence.

'Well, at least come with me to Caerphilly. We could do some Christmas shopping.'

Gwyneth slowly turned to look at her. 'And I *don't* need cheering up.'

'I'm not trying to cheer you up. I just want some company, that's all. But if that's too much trouble, then ... then don't bother!' With a rustle of skirts, Mary strode across the kitchen and into the scullery, slamming the door behind her.

Meg looked up anxiously from the potatoes she was peeling, but Mary put a silencing finger to her lips, going to the sink and banging the pots around irritably.

'I didn't know you were planning to go into town,' whispered Meg after a few minutes had passed.

'I wasn't.' Mary gave a sigh. 'But I shall have to go now, or she'll know I was just making it up. Can you manage – just for an hour or two?'

Meg smiled, though her eyes remained sad. 'I've managed all these years,' she said. 'You go on – and don't go rushing back. I'm sorry about Gwyn – but it was good of you to try.'

*

The case was syphilis, and barring one exception, in a more advanced state than Evan had ever witnessed. Covered in lesions, and totally blind, the retired ship's captain lay growling and grumbling in the room that served as his cell, the disease having stripped away all vestiges of humanity to leave a wild and vicious animal trapped in the body of a man.

'It is time,' said Ivor quietly.

The old woman wrung her hands, weeping copiously. 'Oh, no. Please, no. Not yet. It wasn't his fault … he didn't mean it … he sometimes doesn't know me, you see?'

Ivor looked toward the Captain, bound hand and foot, and held by two burly grooms, then back to the woman, reaching out to cup her chin with his hand. 'And the next time?' He gently turned her face, letting the light play on the cut cheek and blackened eye. 'He could very easily kill you. You've done everything a wife can do – God knows I can vouch for that, but he cannot stay here any longer.' He placed his arm about her shoulder, dwarfing the frail old lady. 'I shall leave you something to help you sleep – but now I think we'd better take a closer look at that cut.'

Suddenly childlike in her trusting obedience, she allowed herself to be led from the room. 'Yes,' she said vaguely. 'Whatever you think best, Doctor.'

'The strength of madness,' said Ivor as they rode back along the valley. 'Incredible! The Captain is well over sixty, riddled with disease, yet it takes two strapping great stable lads to subdue him. Such cases defy all the normal laws of physics.' He scratched thoughtfully at his whiskers. 'I remember an accident at the docks several years ago. A hogshead of beer had fallen from the back of a brewer's dray – crushing a small girl. I examined the mother shortly after. She was thin, undernourished, and with less muscular tissue than the average ten year old boy – yet somehow, she had lifted the barrel from her child!'

'Were you able to test her?' asked Evan. 'Could she repeat it?'

'Not even with the barrel empty. I tell you, there is a strength that comes with madness, or in moments of great anguish, that defies all explanation.'

They rode on in silence for several minutes. 'Awful business – the old Captain,' said Ivor. 'The asylum's no place to spend your last days. His own damn fault, I suppose – but a man can't remain celibate.'

'Perhaps not, but he *can* remain faithful.'

'Damn it, you pious young prig! The man was at sea for two years at a time. What was he supposed to do? There are no pretty little parlour maids to tumble on board ship!'

Evan caught the inference, but the protest died on his lips for Ivor had gone very red in the face, and had his hand to his forehead. 'Are you alright?'

'Yes, it's nothing. Damned headache. It's what comes of mixing the grape with the grain. Always a mistake.'

'Physician, heal thyself,' said Evan. 'Surely you have some of your miracle hangover cure in your bag?'

Ivor gave him a sideways glance. 'It won't work for me – I know what's in it.'

'What do you mean? What *is* in it?'

'Water and some colouring.'

'And?'

'And nothing. That's it.'

'But … but it works! I've taken it myself!'

Ivor reined in his horse, chuckling. 'The power of suggestion, my boy! It works because *I* say it will work – and because I charge a great deal for it.'

Evan stared at him, then burst out laughing. 'Why – you old Quack!'

'Quackery has its place. There's a lesson for you in that – *and* I won't charge you so much as a penny for it. Now, I need to make arrangements for the Captain, but first I want to call in on the Llewellyn woman. That baby of her's isn't due for another three months, but she'll worry the thing out of her belly in time for Christmas if she isn't careful.' He looked out over the valley. 'Let's cut across country. It takes ten minutes off the journey – more if we gallop.'

'Gallop?' Evan smiled. 'Don't you think it's time you took Mother's advice and started using the carriage?'

Ivor spurred his horse, setting off across the hillside at a thundering pace. 'No, I damn well don't!' he yelled.

*

The scullery door creaked open a small way. 'Mam?'

Meg quickly wiped her face on her sleeves, then half turned, hiding eyes that were red and puffy from crying. 'What is it, my love?' The door opened a few inches more to reveal Gwyneth, tidily dressed, with her hair combed and braided – and Meg's heart leaped. 'Oh, my love, you look lovely.'

Gwyneth dropped her gaze. 'Do you think … if I were to go after Mary?'

'She'd love you to. You know she would.'

'She seemed angry.'

'Oh, Gwyn, no one is angry with you. Come on.' Drying her hands on her apron, she took Gwyneth by the arm, leading her to the front door. 'Here, put your coat on. If you go now, you'll catch her in town. Have you got some money? Well, look, you'd better take this.' She went to the cupboard and took down an old tin box. 'It's not much, but you buy yourself something.'

'I can't take this, it's yours.'

'And now it's yours.' Meg's smile trembled on her lips as she pressed the money into Gwyneth's hand. 'I've been saving it for a rainy day – and well, I reckon we've had quite enough of those lately.'

'I'm sorry, Mam.'

Meg stepped closer, helping to button her coat. 'Nothing to be sorry about. You just get away off to town or you'll be meeting Mary on her way back.'

'Not if I know Mary,' said Gwyneth, and she gave a small, shy laugh.

It was music to Meg's ears – a sweet music that seemed to have been missing for a lifetime. 'Go safely,' she said.

Chapter Sixteen

The town clock was striking eleven as Mary emerged from the last of the shops and made her way back along the high street toward the Cross Keys. The satisfying feel of coins no longer gave weight to her pocket, but she felt happy, content in the knowledge she'd found a suitable gift for every-one – and with threepence to spare.

She was pondering this small windfall when she came to the bookshop, and she stopped, looking into the quaint old window with its bull's eye glass. It had been a favourite haunt of hers since childhood, and almost guiltily she stepped in, making her way between the tall shelves of books, running her fingers over the bright new bindings.

'I really should be a detective.'

The voice made her jump, and she whirled around to find Evan looking at her. 'Oh, Doctor Rees-Morgan. You startled me.'

Evan smiled. 'Mrs Davies,' he said with a mock bow. 'I deduce there are only two places in the whole of Caerphilly where one might successfully find you – this being the second.'

'You've been trying to find me?'

He gave a small laugh. 'No, I'm afraid my deductive powers work only in hindsight. I saw you enter this shop while I was waiting for my father. He's just examining Mrs Llewellyn, up at the Cross Keys.' He laughed again. 'That would have been my first choice of places to look, by the way.'

'Mrs Llewellyn?' Mary sounded concerned. 'Is something wrong?'

'No, not at all. Everything is perfectly alright.' He took down the book she had been touching. 'Ah, our friend Mr Turner. Are you buying it?'

She thought ruefully of the remaining three copper coins in her pocket. 'No, I don't think so.'

Evan put back the book, searching further along the shelf. 'Well, perhaps we might browse together? I was thinking of …'

'I really should be going.'

'You can stay a few minutes, surely?' He selected another large volume and opened it. 'How about this?' He looked up from the pages, to her face, then closed the book. 'No, I don't think so,' he smiled. 'I can see you and I have remarkably similar tastes.' He continued along the shelf, his finger tapping thoughtfully at his lips. 'Canaletto? Rembrandt …?'

Lured by his voice and the magic of the names, she followed after him.

'Ah, now what about this?' he said, taking down a heavy volume. '*The Romance of the Landscape*?'

She glanced about. In Cardiff, at the clinic, she felt at ease with him, but here, where she was known, it felt wrong – even dangerous. 'I'm sorry,' she said, starting toward the door, 'I really do have to go. But …' She hesitated at the end of the aisle. 'If you like landscapes – then perhaps you like Constable?'

'Very much so.'

'There's a book,' she whispered guiltily. 'Up there in the far corner – behind the pamphlets.'

He watched her leave, then found the book and took it down. It was old, expensive, and not a little dusty, and he smiled with understanding as he thought of her secreting it away in that darkened corner, unable to possess it – but equally unable to give it up.

*

Hubert Llewellyn beamed as he poured the double measure of brandy into the glass. 'So it's alright, then? Really alright?'

'It is perfect,' said Ivor, downing the liquor.

'Nothing to worry about then?'

'Nothing.'

'There! There you see, Mrs Llewellyn! Nothing to worry about at all. Just as I told you.'

Edith Llewellyn, her belly swollen beneath her skirts, eased herself on to a chair. 'No need to go telling *me*, Mr Llewellyn. I was the one being examined, wasn't I?'

Ivor raised an eyebrow in amusement. He had been the Llewellyns' doctor for more years than he could remember, and was well used to their ways, but now he detected a softer note to their continual sniping. 'There is nothing to concern yourselves about in the least,' he assured them. 'I wish I could say the same for all my prospective mothers.'

'Oh, I'm not worried,' said Edith. 'It's Mr Llewellyn, the old goat. He thinks I'm too old to carry a baby without I sit idle all day. As if I *could*, with a hotel to run!'

Ivor towered over her, his back straight and his face stern. 'Now,' he said very deliberately. 'You listen to him and do as he says. I shall be very angry should I hear anything to the contrary on my next visit.' He took her hand, and making a small bow, kissed it. 'As your Doctor, I am allowed the privilege of observing that you are a fine, healthy woman, Mrs Llewellyn – one in the prime of her life …'

Edith's face flushed pink with pleasure.

'… but that should not be taken as an excuse for recklessness. Allow that your husband knows what is best, and do accordingly is my advice to you.' He picked up his overcoat. 'I shall call again next week, though there really is no need other than to partake of your excellent brandy.' At the door he turned. 'They say spring babies are the bonniest.'

Mr Llewellyn showed him out, then made his way back into the lounge. 'I *do* hope you'll take notice of Dr Rees-Morgan, my dear,' he said, adopting a similarly upright stance.

Edith sighed, her cheeks still rosy with delight. 'Yes, Hubert,' she said.

*

Walking back along the street, Mary was uncertain what to do next. If she went to the Cross Keys as planned she would likely meet Evan again, and that would never do – not after the schoolgirlish way she'd acted in the bookshop. Her face grew red at the memory. She was still chiding herself when there was a touch on her shoulder, and she whirled around, her expectant smile dropping away in surprise. 'Gwyn?'

Mistaking the look for reproach, Gwyneth lowered her eyes. 'I'm sorry, Mary.'

'Oh, Gwyn. Don't be silly,' said Mary, recovering her thoughts and taking Gwyneth's arm. 'I'm so very glad you came. It's been lonely shopping without you. Not the least bit like Christmas.'

Gwyneth gave a tentative smile, looking at the small collection of packages Mary was carrying. 'I suppose you've already got everything you wanted?'

'Well, I've spent nearly all my money, if that's what you mean,' laughed Mary.

'Want to come and help me spend mine then?'

'Just you try and stop me. We can start with Meridrew's. There was a lovely little …' Mary paused, as two riders emerged from the rear of the Cross Keys and started up the high street. 'No, I tell you what,' she said quickly, pulling Gwyneth into the nearest shop. 'Let's look in here first.'

Through the window, Mary watched the Rees-Morgans pass by, her eyes lingering on Evan's straight back until it disappeared around the bend of the road.

'There doesn't seem to be much in here,' said Gwyneth puzzling at the brooms and buckets that cluttered the small ironmonger's shop. 'What exactly did you have in mind?'

*

It was two o'clock in the afternoon as Mary crossed the crowded chapel hall to lock the doors, and feeling a tug at her sleeve, she turned to find her former protector looking at her with surprise.

'You *workin'* here now?' asked the woman. 'How'd you manage that, then?'

'I don't know. It just sort of happened.' Mary stroked the baby's cheek, and he gurgled happily, reaching up with a chubby hand to grasp her finger.

'Oh, he likes you, he does,' said the woman. 'And he don't like everyone. Here, I suppose you couldn't …?' Then she laughed, 'No, I don't suppose you could. Oh well, never mind, eh. I'll find someone to look after him in a minute.'

The baby relaxed his grip, and Mary moved away, but the woman followed close on her heels. 'Here,' she said as they reached the door, 'what's the doctor like?'

'He's nice.'

'Oh, I know that,' laughed the woman. 'I'd almost do him for free.'

Mary bent to push home the bolt, hiding her blushes.

'No,' whispered the woman, giving her a nudge. 'I mean what's he like for bein' *accommodatin'*?'

Mary looked at her. 'Accommodating?'

'You know … like if a girl was to find herself *in trouble*, sort of thing?'

'Oh, I'm quite sure he wouldn't do anything like that.'

The woman pulled a long face. 'Pity,' she said, then seeing Mary's concern, she added, 'Oh, don't worry – it's not me.' She touched a finger to the side of her nose. 'But it never hurts to know such things, if you know what I mean?'

Mary nodded uncertainly and made to go.

'Just a minute – there is one other thing.' She pulled Mary back toward the door, standing close and speaking in a low voice. 'I suppose he keeps all manner of medicines and such in that room of his, eh?'

'Yes, some …'

'Arsenic and such stuff?'

'I really don't know. Look, I must get back.'

'Hold on, hold on. He can manage without you for a minute or two. Old mother Gwilliam has just gone in – and it'll take her half an hour to list what's wrong with her.' She lowered her voice again. 'It's just that I has a number of gentleman friends who are partial to a little arsenic.'

Mary's eyes widened. 'But that's poison.'

'Not in small amounts, it's not,' she winked. 'Perks them up good and proper – I can vouch for that. But it's not so easy to come by, these days. So, I was thinkin' maybe you could do me a little favour?'

'No, I couldn't … I wouldn't even know what it looked like.'

'It'll have a bloody label on it, for Christ's sake.'

Mary shook her head. 'No, I'm sorry,' she said, moving quickly away.

The woman watched her go. 'Suit yourself,' she muttered. 'There's more than one way to skin a cat – you stuck-up bloody cow.' She sauntered over to an elderly woman with bloated ankles. 'Ungrateful, some people! Looked after her proper, last time she was here – and that's what thanks I get for it.'

The old woman sniffed. 'Always the same these days – no one got time for no one else. What did you want?'

'Just for her to mind the baby for a couple of minutes, that's all.'

'And she wouldn't? Bloody shameful. Here, give him to me.'

'Oh, would you? You are a darlin'. He's no trouble, and I won't be long. You'll let me back in, won't you? Just dyin' for a piss I am.'

'There was a woman outside – enquiring about arsenic,' said Mary as soon as she was alone with Evan.

He smiled. 'It's not the first time – and I doubt it will be the last.' He got up and stretched. 'I think we could do with a break for some tea, don't you?'

'Yes, of course, I'll see to it.'

She started toward the sink, but he stepped in front of her, furrowing his brow in a look of mock severity. 'Mrs Davies – I really don't expect my assistants to be such slow learners. Now please – *sit down.*'

Mary sat, watching him as he filled the teapot. 'And suppose someone should come in and see this – the master waiting on the maid?'

'I would lay the blame on you. Tell them you had enslaved me. Made me Samson to your Delilah, Herod to your Salome.'

She stared at him, no longer smiling. 'That's blasphemous, isn't it?'

'Is it?' He half turned to look at her. 'I suppose it might well be. Are you shocked?'

Slowly she shook her head.

'I thought not.'

She began to laugh. 'Don't you believe in *anything*?'

'I believe in many things. For instance …' He crossed to the valise he had brought with him that morning. 'I *believe* I have a confession to make.' From inside the bag he brought out a blue and gold, leather-bound volume and handed it to her. 'It's your book – the one on Constable. I couldn't resist it.'

'You bought it?'

'I didn't *steal* it,' he laughed. 'But now I feel guilty. It was *your* book.'

'It was never mine.'

'Then it was your *secret* – and that amounts to much the same thing.' He sat down opposite her, growing serious as he watched her pore over the familiar pages. 'You know I leave for Paris soon?'

She made no immediate answer, and when she did reply she kept her eyes lowered, as if still perusing the book. 'I envy you. Will you visit the galleries while you are there? The Louvre?'

He gave a wry smile. 'I'm away for five years. I should *just* have time.'

'When do you go?'

'The beginning of January. New Year's Day.'

'This really is the last clinic, then.'

'Yes.' He reached out to touch the book. 'Will you take it? A parting gift?'

'I couldn't.'

'Look after it for me then. Give it back to me when I return.'

She stroked the pages longingly. 'I can't.'

'Social convention? Where would we be without it?' He sighed. 'Well, I shall just have to take it with me. Or perhaps I should hide it back on the shelf – so that you might look at it with a clear conscience, knowing you were no longer defrauding the owner?'

She laughed, but the sadness of the moment made it only fleeting, and she stood and went to where the tea was brewing, her fingers toying nervously with the warm china pot. 'There's something I've been wanting to ask you. I hope you don't mind?'

'Of course not.'

'I was wondering if perhaps you knew of any vacant positions? It wouldn't have to be anything grand.'

'I'm afraid I don't. Are things very bad for you at home?'

'It's not for me. It's for my sister-in-law, Gwyneth.' She hesitated. 'The thing is … she's been to prison.'

Evan stared at her in surprise.

'It was all a horrible misunderstanding,' she continued quickly. 'But now she can't get a job, and … well, this is my last chance to ask you. Any job would do – a maid – anything. It's just that without a character no one will take her, and I just thought … perhaps, if you put in a good word?'

He shook his head. 'I doubt my word carries as much weight as you imagine, but I'm not aware of any vacant positions. I'm sorry.'

Mary sighed. 'No, I'm sorry. I shouldn't have troubled you with it.'

There was another silence, then he said. 'Actually, there's something *I* need to discuss with you.'

'The letter?' Mary tensed. 'You've had a reply?'

He looked embarrassed. 'I don't know what to say, Mary. I was so sure I'd hear before this. I've even telegraphed him, but …'

'It's alright.'

'No, it's *not* alright. Look, let me consult my father – maybe he can help.'

'No, please.'

He sighed. 'Very well. But there is still time before I leave. If I should hear anything at all, I'll contact you.'

Mary shook her head. 'You can't.'

'There has to be a way.' He thought for a moment. 'Look, give me your address. I'll write to you.'

'No.'

'Don't worry, I shall merely write you a short note thanking you for your help here at the clinic, no one would think anything of that should they see it, *but* – if you should receive such a note you will know to meet me the following day in the bookshop in Caerphilly – say at midday? We can make arrangements from there.'

'But I might not be able to get away at such short notice.'

'Then I shall be there at the same time the next day – and the next, and the next, if need be.'

She looked at him. 'I couldn't possibly ask you to do all that.'

'You don't have to.' He saw the torment of indecision in her eyes. 'You *can* trust me, Mary.'

For a moment more she wavered, then very deliberately she picked up his pen.

The empty hall had a melancholic feel as Mary double-locked the doors for the final time. She crossed back to the surgery, pausing to take one last look around, then turned off the gas.

'A cup of tea?' she asked, stepping into the warmth of the back room.

Evan looked up from putting his instruments into the valise. 'That would be nice – but I'd rather get packed away early. Everything has to be cleared this evening.'

'Yes … of course.' Aching with disappointment, she went to the large, locking cupboard and began removing the rows of medicine bottles and bandages, placing them on the desk ready for Evan to put away. 'I shall miss all this,' she said.

'I shall, too.'

'It's been … *pleasant.*'

'Yes.' Wrapping each bottle in a cloth, he placed them in the bag. 'You were very good, you know. A great improvement on Mrs Pope.'

She blushed and turned away. 'Well, you were right. It did get easier.' With the cupboard cleared, she went to the stove, looking in at the fire. 'Should I put it out?'

'No, it'll burn itself out in a few hours.'

She hovered awkwardly for a few seconds, then took the cups and saucers from the draining board. They were already dry, but she wiped them anyway. 'Do these belong to the hall?'

'Everything but the teapot. I bought that when I first came here. Still, you may as well leave it. My gift to the next occupant.'

'May *I* have it?'

He glanced at her. 'I should like that,' he said. 'But if you couldn't explain the book, how will you explain the teapot?'

'I could never afford the book,' she said, looking down at the patterned china. 'And besides, this means more to me.' She raised her eyes to his, but he turned from her, busying himself with bottles and jars, and for a long while she stood watching him, feeling the sense of loss – yet still he made no answer, and reluctantly she returned to putting away the cups. 'Well,' she said with a forced lightness. 'It shouldn't take us long to clear away these last few things. Shall I call for your gig?'

'No,' he said, keeping his back to her. 'Actually, I wasn't planning on going home straight away. There's a new exhibition at a gallery I know of, not too far from here. I thought I might walk over and see it.' Finally he turned, looking into her eyes. 'And I was just wondering if … perhaps you would accompany me?'

Chapter Seventeen

'Here we are,' said Evan, coming to a halt before a bow-fronted facade in a quiet, tree-lined street.

Mary looked into the brightly lit gallery, to where an elegantly dressed woman was moving slowly from picture to picture, escorted by the proprietor, a balding man in an immaculate dark suit. 'I can't go in *there*,' she said, almost in a whisper.

'Why ever not?'

'*Why not*?' She looked down at herself – at the clothes she had thought respectable enough back at the surgery, but which suddenly seemed like rags. 'Look at me!'

'You look lovely.'

'Please, don't joke about this.'

'I'm not joking,' he said. 'If you really don't want to go in – then we shan't, but I do think you look lovely.'

She fretted at her hair, pushing at imaginary stray strands. '*You* may think that, but they're just going to laugh at me – I'm not even sure *you* aren't making fun of me. Is that what this is about – something to laugh over later with your friends?'

His eyes grew dark. 'Would you believe that of me?'

'Some gentlemen might find it amusing.'

He continued to hold her gaze. 'But would you believe that of *me*?'

'No …'

'Well then, if clothing is all that stands in our way, the remedy is simple.'

A hansom cab stood some little way off, and Evan walked over to it, calling up to the driver who was beating his hands together as he waited for a fare. 'How warm is your overcoat, cabbie?'

'Warm enough, sir. Thank you, sir.'

'Not as warm as this one, though?'

'No, sir. That does look a fine coat, indeed.'

'Then you would not object to exchanging it for yours?'

The cab driver eyed him with suspicion. 'Some catch, is it?'

'No catch. If it fits, it's yours.'

The man climbed down from his seat and took off his overcoat.

'That's an interesting jacket you are wearing,' said Evan.

'It's a little worn in the elbows, like,' said the man, appraising Evan's perfectly tailored suit. 'But not bad, otherwise. You can have it if you want.'

Evan removed his own jacket and took the faded grey worsted in return.

'That tie o' yours,' said the cabbie, hopefully. 'It looks a wee bit out of place now, if you don't mind me saying.'

Grinning, Evan took off his tie and passed it over, putting on the cabbie's woollen choker instead. 'You won't mind if I keep my waistcoat?'

'As you like,' said the man, offhandedly. 'I can take it or leave it.'

For a moment they eyed each other's trousers, then thinking better of it, pulled on their newly acquired overcoats.

'I've got a few more bits and pieces at home if you was interested, like,' said the man, climbing back on to his cab and adjusting his sleeves to show some cuff.

Evan smiled. 'I'll let you know.' He strolled back to where Mary was standing, astonished. 'Right, Mary Davies. If there is to be amusement at anyone's expense, it will be at *mine*. Shall we go in?'

She stared at him, shaking her head in disbelief – then she burst into laughter.

'Should I take that as a yes?' he asked, pushing open the door.

They had barely stepped inside when the elongated figure in the dark suit came gliding toward them, barring their way. 'Can I help you?' he asked, looking down his nose.

Evan stared back at him. 'No, thank you. We only wish to look.'

The man's face registered surprise at the cultured accent, but he made no attempt to move back, rather he spread his arms a little as though to usher them out. 'I'm sorry but the gallery is ...'

'Oh, look,' Mary intoned aristocratically, pointing to a nearby wall. 'There they are, darling. Oh, I do so *adore* the Dutch school of painting, don't you? They're so ... so ...' she raised a graceful finger to her lips in thought, 'so ... *small*.' She took Evan's arm. 'You *must* come and see the one I picked out yesterday. It's quite delightful.'

'Yes,' said Evan, 'Yes, of course ... *darling*.'

The proprietor was still barring their way, and she gave a small laugh. 'You must forgive the way we look this evening, Mr Gilpin,' she said, conspiratorially. 'We are just on our way to a little soirée. It's a terribly novel idea to have everyone dress up – but I do think my husband might *rather* have overdone the costume, don't you?'

Mr Gilpin's eyes swivelled in their sockets as he looked back and forth from Mary to Evan. 'I ... I,' he began uncertainly, then he caught sight of Evan's highly-polished shoes and the expensive trousers that emerged from beneath the worn cabman's overcoat. 'Oh,' he said, stepping back to let them pass, 'Oh, yes, of course. I *am* sorry.'

With the smallest of nods, Mary led Evan into the gallery.

'How on earth did you know his name?' he whispered as they stood looking at a small canvas of skaters on a frozen millpond.

'It was on a plaque in the window.'

'And that voice – the accent?'

She gave a shrug. 'You hear a lot of that when you work in a hotel.' She glanced over his shoulder to where Mr Gilpin was deep in conversation with the well-dressed woman. 'Well, at least we've given them something to talk about.'

'But I still don't understand,' said Evan, keeping his voice low, and following as Mary moved along the wall, scrutinizing each painting. 'Outside you were frightened to come in – but look at you now.'

She stopped in front of a brooding seascape. On a spuming shore, a boat was putting out to sea in the early dawn, while on the beach the single figure of a girl watched forlornly. 'Out in the street, I was myself,' she said.

Evan continued to stare at her. 'So ... who are you now?'

Wistfully, she gazed at the lone figure in the painting. 'My sister, Emma. She's always been braver than me.'

'Your sister?'

She gave him a sideways glance. 'I'll tell you all about her – *one day*,' then she grinned. 'Come on, we have paintings to view.'

Intrigued, he watched the gentle sway of her body as she went to stand before a loose, sprawling scene rendered in broad strokes and moody colours.

'You like this one?' he asked, coming to her side.

'Yes. Don't you?'

'It's alright, I suppose – but you don't find it too sombre?'

'No, that's *why* I like it. That sky – it's so dark and menacing, and yet there's something ... optimistic?' She looked at him. 'As though the artist wants to show the promise of something – like when you see a tiny patch of blue on the horizon in the middle of a terrible storm. And here – see how the foreground is painted. So full of life. It's really nothing more than a few squidges of dark paint, not a single *real* detail – and yet ... Well, what do *you* see?'

Evan looked. 'A city,' he said after a moment. 'A dark, sprawling city.'

'An evil place, do you think?'

'I think it is.'

'But look here,' she said, pointing. 'That small dab of colour – a light from a window? Someone working late into the night? Perhaps it's an inventor who has made some wonderful discovery?'

'Or perhaps he has merely set his house on fire?' said Evan with a smile.

The life went from Mary's eyes. 'Yes … perhaps.'

'So … what do you see?' he asked, breaking the awkward silence.

She stared at the painting. 'I see a dark forest – and beyond the forest, just here between the sky and the land, a stormy sea. There are people camped amongst the trees – these little flecks are their tents – and *here*,' she pointed to the same dab of colour, smiling wryly, 'where your man's house is alight, that is where *my* people have built their great camp fire.'

Evan looked at her, taking in the clear, bright eyes, the soft swell of her cheek and the full, yet delicate lips. 'Do they live in the forest?'

'No …' She thought for a moment. 'No, they've travelled here from some cold, hard place – and now they are building boats for the next part of their journey. Look, you see? Here – and here,' she pointed excitedly at small squirls of paint. 'Soon the storm will clear, and they'll put to sea – and sail for a warm and wonderful land just over the horizon.'

'And will they find happiness?' he asked, captivated by her voice.

'Oh, yes.'

He wanted to touch her then. To take her arm and draw her to him. To feel her slender body against his. To explore her lips. To taste her and smell her and feel her warmth. Instead he forced himself to walk away, stopping before a painting of a dog posed in a log basket. 'Landseer has a lot to answer for,' he said with a strained laugh.

She came to join him. 'You don't like Mr Landseer's work?'

'Not his *comical* dogs, I don't. And I like imitators of his comical dogs even less!' He moved on, dismissing picture after picture with a joke, until they came to stand in front of a canvas hung discreetly in an alcove.

'Venus and Adonis,' he read from the brass plate.

Mary gazed at it. In a muted wood a naked couple were embracing, holding each other with a tender passion while cherubs played at their feet amidst lush viridian leaves. 'It's wonderful,' she said.

He nodded. 'Though an unpleasant story.'

'Is it?'

'Well, it is if I correctly remember my Greek mythology. As I recall, Uranus was causing his lover, Earth, some distress. So, to spare her suffering, her son, Cronus, castrated him and threw the severed parts into the sea. From this, Venus was born, rising up from the waves.'

Mary looked at him. 'You're making it up.'

'No,' said Evan, 'It's true … or at least as true as any mythology can be. Venus grew to be a beautiful Goddess – and Adonis fell in love with her. But Adonis had a darker passion, for he loved to hunt, and although she pleaded with him to give it up, he refused – and as a consequence, died a terrible and bloody death.'

'That's a horrible story.'

Evan smiled. 'Perhaps we should revise it?'

'If I were to buy this picture, I should insist on it,' she said with mock haughtiness. Across the room, Mr Gilpin's ears pricked up at the word *buy*, and he smiled ingratiatingly in her direction. 'Let me see,' she continued, moving closer to Evan, and lowering her voice to a whisper. 'I think Venus is a noble young woman who has been cast out by her family for falling in love with a man they think unsuitable.'

'Why is he unsuitable?'

She cast him a sideways glance. 'He steals cab drivers' clothes.'

'I see.' He regarded the naked figure. 'He doesn't appear to be very successful at it, does he.'

She laughed. 'I suppose *you* have a better story?'

'I think,' he said, suddenly serious, 'they are so very much in love that whatever they are is of absolutely no consequence. What he feels for her, and she for him, is so pure, so immediate, that it transcends anything and everything. No obstacle can stand in the way of such a love for it negates time itself, and without time there can be no past – and with no past there can be no obstacle.'

Mary looked at him. 'It would be lovely if such things were possible.'

'Perhaps they are.'

She dropped her gaze. 'Perhaps … perhaps Adonis believes that,' she said uncertainly, 'but … I think Venus is unsure.'

Evan slowly shook his head. 'Not in her heart.'

She glanced quickly at him, then lifted her eyes to the picture. 'Look. She arches away from him.'

'But look at her hand, how it cups his cheek. I think she's not pulling back, but rather offering up her lips for a kiss.'

'A kiss of friendship,' she said. 'A harmless token.'

'No,' said Evan, his eyes fixed on the painting. 'See how he holds her – his hand beneath her breast, the fingers pressing so hard with desire they must surely bruise her flesh. There is a violence of passion here.'

'He hurts her?'

'A little, perhaps, but he would sooner die than harm her.'

'Then why?'

'Because he is drowning in his love – and like the drowning man who clings to the one thing that can save him, his fingers are imbued with a strength beyond all consciousness.'

'I think she yearns for such hurt,' said Mary, scarcely breathing.

'I think so, too.'

'Yet her own hands are so tender on him, she strokes his cheek, caresses his thigh.'

'She is coy,' he said. 'You see how she inclines her legs away, as though to hide her secrets from his eyes?'

'Yet longing for him to see …'

Evan moved closer. 'So he responds with loving words and kisses, and gradually she grows bolder, arching her back …'

'Offering herself …'

'To his touch …'

'Yes.'

As they stood, side-by-side, in perfect silence, Mary felt the press of his arm against her own, and almost imperceptibly she too moved closer. 'Will he always love her like this?' she asked.

'Always.'

Their hands brushed, a fleeting touch of skin on skin, yet more electrifying than anything either of them had ever known, and their fingers reached out, like slender, frightened creatures, hardly daring to touch at first, but growing bolder and bolder until soon they were intertwined.

Flushed, Mary let go of his hand and took a step away, avoiding his gaze. 'I think *Mary* should be going home now,' she said.

They walked back to the hall in silence, more ill at ease than they had been on their first meeting, but as they crossed Queen Street Evan took her arm, and she allowed it, letting him guide her through the traffic with no thought to anything other than the wonderful feel of his hand pressing upon her – and the huge sense of loss when he relinquished his grip on reaching the far side.

'I hope you enjoyed this evening,' he said, his voice stilted.

'I did … very much. Thank you.'

They turned into Wood Street and stopped at the entrance to the alley. 'I feel I have made something of a fool of myself,' he said.

'No – no, not at all.'

'Well, we shall see on the ride home.' He felt the shabby coat. 'The weather's growing colder, and I think I've made a poor bargain.'

'Oh … I see,' she blushed, quickly starting down the narrow passage. 'It might not have been the cleverest bargain,' she said quietly, without turning round, 'but it was a wonderful thing to do.'

Evan followed her. 'Well, if ever I give up medicine, at least I shall have the right clothes to be a cab driver.'

She laughed, stepping warily as she felt her way in the darkness. The front of the hall was unlit, but as they approached the tiny courtyard at the rear, a faint light showed through the partly opened door, and she gave Evan a questioning look.

'It's alright,' he said. 'It will be the caretaker, I expect.' He walked over to the door and peered in. 'Hello?'

The light came from a stub of a candle that burned on the desk, but all else was quiet and still.

'Hello?' he tried again, stepping inside. 'Is anyone …?' He got no further for an arm was around his neck, pulling him backwards, choking him, while from in front another figure scurried, rat-like, from the darkened corner to ram a fist into his stomach – followed by another to his face.

Evan tasted blood, and kicked upwards with all his strength, his foot jarring against bone as the man screamed and buckled over, clutching his groin.

But there was no relief from the choking grip, and Evan fell to his knees, bright spots of light dancing in front of his eyes as he struggled in vain. Then, suddenly, he was falling sideways, dragged down by the weight of his assailant crashing to the floor under the ferocity of Mary's attack. She had taken the man completely off guard, gripping his hair, pulling him sideways, using every ounce of her weight and strength.

It was enough for Evan. He twisted free and struggled to his feet, but the man was also rising, a knife glinting in his hand.

'Mary, get away!' yelled Evan, leaping backwards as the intruder lunged, sweeping the knife in a savage arc.

The blade hissed again, then the man was upon him, one hand at his throat, the other stabbing the knife into his ribs, the momentum of the attack bringing their faces within inches of each other. Evan felt the sharp touch of steel, but before the man could stab again Evan swept his arm up, dislodging the grip on his neck – then jerked his head forward to butt the man full in the face.

The ruffian reeled back, clutching his shattered nose, and Evan whirled away, grabbing the poker from beside the stove and swinging it viciously against the man's wrist. The bones cracked like twigs, and in the silence before the ensuing scream, the knife clattered on to the floor. But Evan continued to advance, the poker raised, his eyes predatory in the flickering candlelight.

'Alright, we're goin' … we're goin'.' The man backed away, his face deathly white, stumbling against his accomplice who was already hobbling toward the door.

'Evan!' Mary came from the shelter of the wall. 'Please! Let them go!'

At the sound of his name, he faltered, then slowly he let his arm drop.

The men needed no further encouragement. Nursing their wounds, they fled into the darkness.

'Are you alright, Evan?' asked Mary, rushing over to him.

'I'm not sure,' he said, wincing as she took hold of him, 'I … I think I've been stabbed.'

*

'Will you not have your tea?' asked Meg, as the rest of the family sat down at the table.

Thomas shook his head. 'No, I'll have mine with Mary when she comes in. She can't be too much longer.'

Meg looked at the clock. 'She could be an hour or more yet. That clinic always seems to run so late.'

'Lot of sick people in Cardiff,' chuckled Alan. 'Love sick, I reckon.'

Thomas turned on him. 'What's that supposed to mean?'

'Nothing, man. Just having a joke, I was. With someone pretty like Mary working there – well, I reckon they've probably had a lot more blokes suddenly feeling ill …' his voice trailed away. 'Just a joke, like.'

Owen looked from one to the other, fixing on Thomas. 'Come and sit, boy. I never could settle down to eat without everyone having a plate in front of them – and Mary wouldn't want you waiting, you know that.'

Thomas hesitated, then turned and went to the door, taking his coat and cap from the peg. 'Think I'll take a walk up along the Caerphilly road,' he said. 'I feel like some air – and I'll probably meet her on the way.'

*

There was blood – a good deal of blood – but the cut, high up under his arm and spanning two ribs, proved to be only superficial.

'Good old cabby's coat,' said Evan.

'If you'd kept your own overcoat you wouldn't have been cut at all,' chided Mary as she cleaned the wound. 'It was twice as thick as that rag you have now.' She took a bandage and some squares of padding from his valise. 'What do you think they were after?'

'Arsenic probably. You said someone was asking about it.'

Standing behind him, she ran her fingers over his ribs, to one side of the inch-long wound. 'They might have killed you,' she said, her heart beating very fast.

He gave a small shrug.

Reluctantly she took her fingers away and picked up the pad, gently pressing it into place. 'You don't seem very concerned.'

He raised his arms, allowing her to bandage him, and she caught the warm smell of his flesh – felt the pressure of his hip against her belly as she wound the bandage around and around, her face only inches from his body.

'I'm sorry, Mary …' he murmured, '… for what happened at the gallery. It was unforgivable of me. I promise it will never happen again.'

She stared at his bare shoulders, so smooth and white, and suddenly tears welled in her eyes. 'Please,' she begged. 'Don't *ever* promise that. Never, *ever*.' Then her cheek was against him, her lips pressed to his skin.

Evan gave a low moan, shuddering with the pleasure of her touch, but then he twisted away, gripping her arms, looking in anguish at her. 'No, Mary. We can't do this! You know we can't!'

'I don't know anything … I only know I love you so much I could die from trying to hide it.'

He let her go, and she fell into his arms, her face pressed to his chest. 'Tell me you don't love me.'

'I *don't* love you.'

She held him tighter, sobbing and laughing at the same time. 'God, but you are a *liar*, Evan Rees-Morgan!'

He stroked her hair, then lifted her face to his. 'I know,' he said, kissing her passionately and hungrily. 'Oh, Mary, I've wanted you ever since that first day. You don't know how much.'

She worked her way down his chin, kissing, biting. 'I wanted you, too. I tried so hard not to …'

He covered her mouth with his own, tasting the softness of her tongue, while his hands explored her body with increasing urgency.

'The door,' she said, smothering him in kisses. 'Someone might see the light.'

Still holding her to him, he swung a chair to rest against the broken door, wedging it beneath the handle, then he reached up and turned out the gas, leaving only the candle flickering in the darkness.

For long moments they stayed there, clinging to each other, then using the cabman's overcoat as a blanket he gently laid her down, and in the warmth of the nearby stove, undressed her, slowly, peeling away layer after layer, with soft words and even softer caresses, until she lay before him naked.

'You know I *can't*,' she began, suddenly fearful for his disappointment, but he put his fingers to her lips. 'I love you, Mary. God, I love you so much.'

Slowly he got to his feet, and she watched through half-closed eyes as he undressed, easily and unhurriedly, the soft candlelight playing over the curves of his body. 'Evan,' she said, reaching out for him, wanting him so badly that the pain and frustration she knew must come no longer mattered.

He knelt by her side, putting two fingertips to her cheek, smiling as he drew them up across her nose then down to play at her lips. Hungrily she kissed them, trying to draw first one and then the other into her mouth, but he was already moving on, over the point of her chin and down her neck to linger over her breasts.

She shuddered, wriggling her hips, stretching out her arms to him as he leaned forward to kiss her, his fingers continuing their journey across the soft, flat plain of her belly. 'I love you more than I ever thought it was possible to love,' he whispered.

Mary moaned, lifting her hips, soliciting his touch, and he drew back, placing his hands flat against the insides of her thighs, easing them apart, feeling her tense in anticipation of the gripping agony that would surely follow his touch. 'It's alright,' he breathed. 'Everything is alright.' He increased the pressure of his touch ever so slightly, then feeling her relax, he bowed his head and kissed her just above the knee. She strained toward him, and he kissed her again a few inches higher, then higher still, brushing his lips against her soft inner thigh, until she writhed with desire, and his head swam with the scent of her arousal.

A wave of pleasure unlike anything she had ever experienced coursed through her as she felt his tongue slipping through the sparse curls to alight on her soft, pink opening, and she cried out, pushing herself on to his mouth, desperately wanting more before the terrible pain began – but there was no pain, nothing but wave after wave of sensual delight.

'Oh, God, Evan!' she cried in disbelief.

He moved up her body, covering it with his, while beneath him she writhed, wanting only the feel of his flesh against her own. He was rougher now as he gave full rein to his own desire, his kisses hard and passionate as he made ready to take her. His weight was upon her, and his hand went between her legs, cupping her mound, the middle finger crooking to worm its way between the moist folds, and she gasped – but not with pain.

His manhood was pressing between her legs, and she opened to him, her small, plaintive whimpers becoming choked cries of pleasure.

He pushed harder, inching his way in, feeling the resistance, then with one thrust it was gone, and he sank into her.

A small sob bubbled from her as she felt the sweet sting of her lost virginity, then her hands were entwined in his hair. 'Evan, oh Evan,' she breathed, happiness and disbelief mingling together.

*

Standing by the milestone, in the icy cold of the December night, Thomas peered along the dark and deserted Caerphilly road, stamping his feet and beating his arms across his chest.

Away in the distance lay the lights of Nant-y-Pridd, and his thoughts went once more to the warm fire and hot dinner awaiting him. He breathed deeply, his breath clouding in the frosty air, then with one last look along the road, he turned for home.

*

From that day on I knew what love was. It was not the quiet, comfortable friendship I had allowed myself to believe, but everything I had hoped and dreamed it would be. Thrilling, exhilarating, dizzying in its intensity, yet safe and steadying in its surety.

139

As I lay in Evan's arms I felt whole, complete, as though a part of me had been missing, unrealised until that moment. It was a feeling so wonderful and unmistakable that I wanted to weep at the ignorance that had led me to think I had ever loved Thomas, except as a brother. And weep I did, for though I would not have changed one moment of our lovemaking, it was a bitter revelation. That night, as I lay next to Thomas, dreading his touch, and feeling the walls of the upstairs room pressing in upon me, I cried silently – for the things that were, the things that might have been, and the things I knew must never be again.

Chapter Eighteen

'The hunt would always meet on Christmas morning, when I was a boy. *Damned* fine way to start the day.'

'Ivor, please!'

Ivor Rees-Morgan continued to stare mournfully at the drawing-room ceiling, but Florence would not be ignored. 'You *must* have a word with Evan. I've never seen him like this – so listless and moody. Do you suppose there might be some infection – from that knife wound?'

'That *scratch*? I doubt it. But you are right,' he said, taking up the decanter and pouring himself a brandy. 'The boy is most certainly sick. I've seen the symptoms many times.'

Florence's heart missed a beat. 'It's nothing serious?'

'Nothing a short sea voyage won't cure.' He drained his glass. 'A *one way* sea voyage.'

There was the slightest hint of irritation in Florence's voice. 'Ivor, *please*. Just tell me what is wrong with him.'

'He's *lovesick*, woman!'

Her eyes widened. 'Lovesick? He can't be. With whom?'

'Does it matter? He'll be in Paris in little over a week.'

'Of course it matters. If she's a suitable girl, we shall need to …'

He laughed mirthlessly. 'I very much doubt she's *suitable* – in view of all that poppycock the other day about the poorest girl in the poorest village. Damned lovesick nonsense! I thought for a while he was tumbling Lucy.'

'Lucy? *Our* Lucy?' Florence put her hand to her mouth. 'What are you going to do?'

'Nothing. It's not her, I'm convinced of that now – and it's damned lucky for her – because if it was, she'd have been out of here, bag and baggage, this very morning. Christmas Day or no Christmas Day!'

*

Christmas dinner in the Davies' household was the equal of anything to be had in the grandest of houses, in quality if not quantity – or so Owen declared as he pushed himself back from the table.

In the days before Christmas, Meg had baked and bottled, filling the house with the scent of puddings and pies and wine made from the last of the autumn fruit, while the girls had set about transforming the kitchen with garlands of winter greenery and paper decorations. Now she gave her husband a sideways glance as she cleared the empty dishes. 'Oh, not enough for you, is it?'

'By, Meg,' he laughed, running a hand over his stomach. 'Another mouthful and I'll split like an over-ripe plum.'

'No pudding, then?'

He pursed his lips. 'A temptress you are, Megan Davies. Oh, a temptress indeed. Well, maybe just a little?'

Alan looked across at Mary's plate where two slices of beef lay untouched, all that remained of the mouth-watering fore-rib Meg had taken from the chimney oven just half an hour earlier. 'Are you not wanting that, Mary?'

'Alan!' scolded Meg. 'Where are your manners?'

Thomas put down his knife and fork, and reached for his wife's arm. 'Are you alright, my love? You've hardly touched your dinner again today.'

'Yes, I'm alright. A little off colour, perhaps. But it was a delicious meal, Mam. Thank you.'

Meg placed a comforting hand on Mary's shoulder. 'It's probably being at that clinic. It can't have been healthy – not with all those sick people.' She took the plate. 'Well, waste not, want not,' she said, passing it to Alan. 'Gwyneth, will you fetch the pudding?'

Alan wolfed down the beef and sat back expectantly as Gwyneth brought the cloth-covered basin from the scullery. 'I've been invited over to Mrs Jenkins's this afternoon,' he said casually.

'Mrs Jenkins's is it?' Owen raised an eyebrow. 'Funny I haven't heard of it until now. Any news that woman has is usually all over the village before it's even happened.'

'Owen!' chided Meg. 'A little charity at Christmas.'

'Oh, indeed yes,' he said piously, then he grinned. 'Getting serious with her Lizzie then?'

'Well, I don't know about that, Da.'

'Well, you'd better be quick to find out,' said Meg. 'Young Lizzie Jenkins is a nice girl, and I won't have you messing her about.'

Alan's cheeks coloured. 'You going into Caerphilly this afternoon, Mary?' he asked, changing the subject.

'No …' She shifted uneasily. 'No, I don't think so.'

'Surely you'll visit Mr Abrahams?' asked Meg. 'Christmas must be a lonely time for him.'

'He's gone to London.'

'Oh, that'll be nice. Visiting friends, is it?'

'Business, I think. Something to do with investments.'

'Well, what about the Cross Keys, then?'

Mary shook her head again, 'I thought I'd wait – until after New Year.'

'But that's a week from now!'

'Yes, but …' she chewed at her lip. Since that night with Evan, she'd kept herself cloistered with her resolve, afraid of the temptation that would follow even the briefest encounter.

Thomas stroked her hand. 'Why don't you go? The walk will do you good.'

'He's right,' said Meg. 'Some fresh air might give you back your appetite.'

Mary plucked at her sleeve, then turned to Thomas. 'If I *do* go to see Peggy, will you come with me?'

'Yes … that is … if you *really* want me to?'

She looked at him anxiously. 'Why wouldn't I?'

'It's just that I don't know your friends at the hotel – not very well – and maybe …' he looked embarrassed, 'you might think I was a bit … *out-of-place*, like.'

Gwyneth cut a slice of pudding. 'I have an idea, Mary,' she said brightly. 'Why don't I come, too? After eating so much I'd enjoy a walk, and if you were to let Thomas be *my* beau for the afternoon, we could drop you at the hotel, then call for you on the way back.'

⋆

Evan stared distractedly out of the drawing-room window. It was mid-afternoon and already the light was fading. He tapped at his chin with the folded paper he was holding, and looked over in the direction of Nant-y-Pridd. 'What time is it?' he asked without turning round.

Ivor looked at the clock on the mantelpiece. 'Just after three.'

'Dinner is at five,' Florence reminded him gently. 'I expect you will be wanting to dress soon?'

There was a long silence.

'Is that the letter that came yesterday?' Ivor asked conversationally. 'The one from London?'

Evan walked over to the fireplace. 'Yes. I wrote to a chap I met there – a colleague – about a case of mine.'

'An interesting case?'

'I would say so, yes.' He stroked the paper against his chin one final time, then crumpled it into a ball and tossed it into the flames. 'Though his reply is a trifle late – and somewhat redundant, as it turns out.'

'The patient died?'

'No,' he sighed. 'Far from it.'

There was a soft knock at the door, and Lucy appeared. 'I'm terribly sorry, sir,' she said, addressing Ivor. 'But there's someone asking for you. They need a doctor urgently.'

*

'Oh, Gawd, Mary! Come in, girl. Quickly, quickly.' Mrs Cartwright's face wore a harrowed look as she came to the back door. 'It's the missus! She's bleedin'!'

Mary put her hand to her mouth. 'Not the baby?'

Peggy Cartwright nodded. 'Started twenty minutes ago. We've got 'er up t' bed, an' I've sent Daisy for the doctor but ...' She was cut short as Daisy burst into the kitchen and fell against the wall, panting. 'I ... I ran ... all the way ... Mrs Cartwright ... all the way ... there and back.'

'Yes, yes. But is 'e comin'?'

The girl nodded, clutching her chest and fighting for breath.

'Well, you wait down 'ere an' bring 'im up as soon as 'e arrives.'

Daisy nodded again.

'Right, Mary. We'd best go up. Maybe you can calm 'er a bit – though she's that far up in the air with fright, you'll need a bloomin' ladder.'

Hubert Llewellyn met them at the top of the stairs, wringing his hands. 'Is he coming? The doctor? Can he come?'

'Yes, yes,' said Mrs Cartwright, ''e's comin'. I've told young Daisy t' fetch 'im up as soon as 'e arrives.'

'May I go in and see her?' asked Mary.

Hubert appeared to notice her for the first time. 'Oh, Mary, yes, please do.'

Edith Llewellyn was lying in the big brass bed, the sheet clutched to her face, wet from crying. 'Oh, I'm going to lose it. I know I am. I can feel it. My poor little mite ... my poor little ...' She burst into tears again.

'There, there,' said Hubert, rushing to her side. 'It's alright. The doctor's on his way. He'll soon put things right.' He turned to where Mary and Mrs Cartwright were standing, a pleading look in his eyes. 'Won't he?'

Mary moved to the bedside, taking Edith's hand. 'Yes, of course he will. I'm sure there's nothing to worry about.'

Edith choked back a sob and attempted a brave smile. 'Do you think so? Really?'

'Yes. There were several women at the clinic last week who ...'

Daisy put her head round the door. 'The doctor's here, m'um,' she said, stepping back to allow him to enter.

'I'm sorry,' said Evan, acknowledging the surprised looks. 'My father has only just gone out on another call, but I've left word, and he'll come as soon as he can.' He gave Mrs Llewellyn a reassuring smile. 'I am sure it's nothing to worry about. Though I should like to examine you, if I may?'

Clutching the sheet, Edith gave a small nod.

Hubert looked anxiously at her. 'You don't think we should wait?' he asked, then turning back to Evan, 'No offence intended, Doctor.'

'None taken. We can wait by all means.'

'No, no,' said Edith between sobs. 'I want to know … I *have* to know the worst. Oh, my poor, poor little mite.'

Mary squeezed her hand. 'It'll be alright. You'll see.'

'No.' Edith Llewellyn shook her head. 'My dear mother said this would happen. She told me the day I married. She … she said I'd never …' She turned her face away, sobbing into the sheet.

Evan put down his bag. 'Well, let us see, shall we?' he said softly. 'If I might ask everyone to leave for a few moments.'

Mary got up to go.

'Mrs Davies,' he said. 'Could you stay and assist me?'

She had tried not to look at him, as though by denying his presence she might deny her feelings, but now, as their eyes met across the bed, she knew how impossible that would always be. With the greatest effort she forced herself back into the safe and reassuring routine of past weeks. 'Yes, Doctor,' she said.

'There would seem to be little cause for concern, Mrs Llewellyn,' said Evan as he rinsed his hands at the washstand some ten minutes later.

'I'm *not* losing it? Not losing my baby?' Mrs Llewellyn's voice was incredulous.

Evan smiled. 'Not to the best of my knowledge. It is not uncommon to have a little bleeding at this stage. However, I'm sure my father will want to examine you, and I *do* recommend a long period of bed rest, just to be certain. But I see no reason why you shouldn't be dandling that baby on your lap three months from now.' He looked toward Mary. 'Perhaps you would be so kind as to call Mr Llewellyn back in?'

'Oh, my! Oh, my, my, my!' exclaimed Edith, patting her stomach, half crying, half laughing. 'That silly old goat, Mr Llewellyn. Getting himself all worked up over nothing! That silly, silly old goat.'

Hubert bounded into the room the moment Mary opened the door. 'Is it alright?' he asked, rushing to his wife's side. 'Is it?'

Edith nodded. 'You old goat!'

There was another knock, and Daisy entered, making a small curtsey. 'Begging your pardon, but Mrs Cartwright says to tell you she has some tea made – if the doctor would like to take it in the sitting room?'

'Tell her I should be delighted,' said Evan, pulling on his jacket. He turned to Mary. 'Perhaps you would join me, Mrs Davies? We really should be leaving Mrs Llewellyn in peace.'

'Where have you *been*?' He whispered urgently, as soon as they were out of earshot. 'I've been looking for you every day ...'

Mary stopped half-way down the stairs, looking cautiously up and down before speaking in a hushed voice. 'I couldn't ... *no* ... I *wouldn't* come.' She touched his arm. 'You were right – that night in the surgery. We *mustn't*. It has to stop.'

'No! I was wrong! Mary, I can't imagine a life where you and I aren't together.'

'You have to – and so do I. I'll always love you, Evan – but that has to be enough.' She pressed herself to him, 'God knows, I wish it could be different.'

'It can. Come with me to Paris.'

Slowly, reluctantly, she drew away. 'I can't. I'll never hurt Thomas. *Never.*'

'I won't give you up, Mary.' There were tears in his eyes. 'We were meant for each other ... you *know* it.'

'Is that you, Mary?' The sound of Mrs Cartwright's voice calling up the stairwell jolted them apart.

'Yes ... Yes, just coming, Peggy.' She started down the stairs, but Evan caught her arm. 'Think about it, Mary. *Please*,' he whispered. 'The train leaves at six o'clock on New Year's morning – I shall be waiting for you.'

Chapter Nineteen

The new year was barely four hours old when Mary crept from her bed, silently gathering up her clothes before feeling her way down the narrow stairs.

In the far corner of the kitchen, Alan shifted on the camp bed, and she froze, hardly daring to breathe as she waited for him to speak, but he only turned again, coughed and lay still.

She tiptoed into the scullery and lit a candle. It was bitterly cold: the water she had drawn the previous evening was partly frozen, and the stone floor was icy beneath her bare feet, making her shiver as she washed, dressed, and put up her hair.

Finally, with her boots buttoned, she glanced at herself in the small, tarnished mirror that hung above the sink – took a deep, steadying breath, then blew out the candle and opened the scullery door.

The kitchen was bathed in the warm glow from the dying fire, and as she crossed the room an ember spat noisily in the grate. She turned, pausing to take one last look around. This was her home – the home she had once wanted to be a part of more than anything in the world. She bit her lip. It all seemed such a long, long time ago. Then, taking down her coat, she slipped the front door latch and stepped out into the night.

*

A heavy wagon was pulling from Caerphilly railway yard, its iron-rimmed wheels grinding on the cobbles, and Mary drew back, hiding her face as she waited for it to pass, before gathering up her skirts and hurrying toward the station building.

Above the booking hall door hung a lighted lamp, and as she stood beneath it a figure came from the darkness. 'Evan …?' In the next instant she was in his arms, drowning in kisses which she returned ten fold, delighting in the feel of his body pressing closer and closer.

'I'll never stop loving you, Evan. Never forget that.'

He took her face in his hands, his thumbs softly caressing her nose and cheeks. 'I *want* to forget,' he smiled, 'so that every single day you will have to remind me.'

She held him tightly, burying her face in his chest.

'We're going to be so happy, Mary. You'll love France. I'll take you to the Louvre. I'll take you to *all* the galleries. We'll do *everything* – the only way I ever want to do it – *together*.' He nuzzled her hair. 'And this time you will have *such* clothes …' he chuckled delightedly at the memory, then feeling her tremble he drew her close to warm her – but the trembling gave way to sobbing, and he gently tilted her face to his, searching her eyes and finding them filled with tears.

A dreadful chill washed over him, stealing his breath, so that he could hardly speak. 'You aren't coming with me, are you.'

She shook her head, her lips tightly pressed, her eyes streaming.

'Mary …' he began, pleading against the inevitability he had sensed from the very beginning, but then he sighed, and letting go of her, took a small leather case from his pocket, pressing it into her hand. 'I was saving this – for our first night in Paris,' he said, his voice breaking with emotion.

Barely able to see him through her tears, she took a step back. 'See the Louvre for me?'

'*Never* without you.'

For a moment she faltered. 'I love you, Evan.' Then she turned and walked quickly away, not daring to look back.

*

Dawn was still an hour away as Mary walked back into Nant-y-Pridd, yet already the blackness was pricked here and there by the dull glow from windows as the grinding daily routine got under way once more.

She knew Meg would be up soon, but as she approached the house she was relieved to find the lamps had not been lit, and she hastened across the street, quietly opening the door and slipping off her coat.

On his bed in the corner, Alan still lay sleeping, snoring loudly as she put on her apron, lit the lamps, then set about re-kindling the fire. She was about to pick up the kettle when the door to the upstairs room opened and she looked up to find Thomas standing there.

'You're up early,' he said quietly.

She turned away, taking up the kettle and going through into the scullery. 'I had a headache … I couldn't sleep.'

'Neither could I.'

Her heart missed a beat. 'I didn't wake you, did I?'

'No, you didn't wake me.' He came into the small, dimly lit room and leaned against the sink. 'You look ill, my love. Are you *sure* you're alright?'

'Yes, of course.' Keeping her face from him she filled the kettle, quickly wiping a sleeve across her eyes. 'Just a headache – but it's alright now.'

'Some fresh air, was it?'

'Yes,' she said, 'some fresh air.'

He reached out to touch her, but she flinched and he drew back. 'I'm sorry.'

'No …' She groped blindly for him, taking his hand and pressing it to her cheek. 'No, *I'm* sorry, Thomas. I … I don't know what's the matter with me.'

'Headache,' he said.

'Yes … a headache.'

'But it's over now, eh?'

'Yes,' she could feel the tears welling in her eyes. 'Yes … it's over now.'

'Well, that's alright then, isn't it?' He felt his fingers becoming damp where they were pressed to her face, and he eased his hand away, moving back toward the kitchen. 'Just as long as it's all over,' he said.

*

'Really, Mary, you don't look at all well,' Gwyneth said later that morning as they prepared for the weekly cleaning of the kitchen. 'Why don't you have a little lie down? Mam and me can manage.'

'Yes, do, Mary, love,' said Meg, coming from the scullery with the black-lead and brushes. 'If you haven't been sleeping you'll be all the better for a little rest now.'

'No, I'm alright, honestly.'

Meg looked at her. 'No you're not. You're as pale as a ghost.'

'Well …' Mary felt in the pocket of her skirt for the box Evan had given her. 'Yes, perhaps I will then – if you really don't mind?'

'You go and shut your eyes for a while.'

At the foot of the stairs, Mary paused, feeling guilty.

'Mary Davies,' said Meg firmly, her hands on her hips but a smile in her eyes. 'Get yourself up those stairs this minute or there'll be trouble!'

'Do you think she's alright?' whispered Gwyneth, hearing Mary's tread in the bedroom above.

'Oh, she'll be alright – given time. Thomas said she was up early this morning – a headache he says, but what do men ever know.'

Gwyneth looked puzzled, then she stared. 'You don't think she's …?'

'Oh, yes,' smiled Meg. 'Oh, yes indeed. I can't see what else it can be. But not a word to anyone, mind.'

Mary lay on her bed, curled into a foetal position, listening to the murmur of voices coming from the room below, but all she could think about was Evan. Slipping her hand into her pocket, she withdrew the box, bringing it close to her face, hoping to detect his scent on the dark leather, then she gently lifted the lid.

Inside lay a necklace, a thin gold chain with a heart-shaped pendant. She pressed it hard to her mouth, trying to stem the tears, and as she did so, her fingertips found the inscription on the back. With trembling hands she turned the bright little heart and read: *Ble'r ei di, fe af finnau – Where you go, I will go.*

It was growing dark when Mary opened her eyes to find Gwyneth looking down at her. 'Are you feeling better now?' Gwyneth asked softly.

'Oh … yes.' She blinked sleepily. 'But what time is it?'

'Nearly four o'clock.'

'Four! It can't be.'

Gwyneth smiled. 'It's alright. Thomas won't be back for a while yet. Come down whenever you're ready. There's some tea for you – and …' a worried frown creased her brow, '… and something else.'

'What is it, Gwyn?'

'A telegram has just come for you.'

'A telegram?' Mary sat up, suddenly wide awake. 'It must be a mistake.'

'No, it's not. It has your name on it. We had to sign for it.'

An anxious knot tightened in Mary's stomach. The message could only be from Evan, and she grew cold at the thought of what it might contain.

The unopened telegram was lying on the table as she came down into the kitchen.

'Who do you think it could be from?' asked Gwyneth.

'I don't know.'

'Well,' said Meg coming to look. 'We'll find out soon enough, won't we.'

'Perhaps I shouldn't open it.'

'Of course you should,' said Meg. 'If it's bad news, it won't go away just from being ignored. Come on, my love – it might even be *good* news.'

With trembling fingers, Mary opened the envelope, quickly scanning the message. 'It's from London,' she sighed. 'And it *is* good news.' She held out the telegram, her hand still shaking.

Gwyneth took the paper. 'Dear Mrs Davies,' she read slowly and carefully. 'Should your sister-in-law still require a position, please ask her to report to Pendragon where Mrs Broadwood is expecting her. My sincere gratitude for all your hard work at the clinic. Dr E. Rees-Morgan.'

*

Gwyneth began work at Pendragon the following week, and just as she had envied me my job at the clinic, so I now envied her, for she was working and sleeping in his house, walking in rooms where he had walked, touching the things he had touched.

I felt ill all the time. Meg was kind and supportive, always urging me to rest, but with Gwyneth gone I couldn't allow myself to impose, and so threw myself into the daily household chores, trying to deaden my grief with work – just as I had done once before.

Alan was quick to take Gwyneth's bed, and I was secretly glad, seeing his presence on the other side of the curtain as a safeguard against Thomas's advances. My poor Thomas, yet still he was patient and undemanding – and as the days became weeks and the weeks, months, so the sadness began to lift, and I could once again see him for the kind, wonderful man he was: sweet, loving and gentle – but incapable of reaching the great, desolate space in my heart that only Evan could fill.

Chapter Twenty

'March. Comes in like a lion and goes out like a lamb.' Meg stared out at the dark, scudding clouds. 'That's what they say, is it? Well! Fat lot they know!' She crossed to the fire and gave the pot a stir. 'So, how was Mr Abrahams?'

Sitting by the fireside, wearing her best clothes, Mary gave a worried shrug. 'Better – I think. He's hoping to be back in school by the end of the month.'

'Well, I'm sure he will be. But I'm not surprised he was taken poorly in London. Unhealthy place, I hear. Now that he's home, he'll soon get back on his feet.'

'They say it's his heart.'

'Oh, it's *they* again, is it? *They* say a lot of things – usually a lot of nonsense in my experience.' She patted Mary's knee. 'You mark my words, that old gentleman will outlive us all.'

'Yes – yes, I'm sure you're right.'

'And what about the Llewellyn's baby?'

Mary brightened a little. 'He's a darling. They'll have him completely spoiled by the time he's a year old – but it's wonderful to see them so happy.'

'There's nothing like having a baby in the house,' said Meg, moving over to the table and spreading the cloth. 'I remember when I told Owen the first time. He was *that* pleased – like a dog with two tails, he was. And each time after that was the same.' She laid out the spoons. 'The thing is, my love, I was worried how he would take it. Some men can be a bit funny, like. But I needn't have been afraid.' She returned to the fire and gave the pot another stir. 'And neither should you be.'

Mary looked up suddenly. 'You … you know?'

Meg nodded, continuing to stir the pot. 'It's not a secret you can easily keep from another woman – especially not in a small house like this.' She sat in Owen's chair and took Mary's hands. 'But it's wonderful news.

Thomas will be so thrilled when you tell him.'

'No, please, Mam – It might be a false alarm.'

'It's been three months, hasn't it?'

Mary looked guiltily away.

'Well,' said Meg. 'You must tell him in your own time. I shan't say a word. But you see if I'm not right. I know Thomas better than anyone.' She got up and crossed to the scullery door. 'And this will make him happier than you can ever imagine.'

*

Standing atop the step-ladder, Gwyneth reached up gingerly, wiping the crystal pendants that hung from the dining room chandelier. 'You *are* holding it, Maggie?' she called nervously.

'Yes, I'm holdin' it alright.' Maggie yawned, one hand resting limply on the steps while she flicked at her hair with the other.

Gwyneth wobbled a little. 'I … I don't like heights.'

'Don't you? Well, reckon you'll have to get used to them, won't you?' Maggie glanced quickly about, making sure they were alone, then gave the steps a nudge.

'Oh!' Gwyneth made a grab for the chandelier. 'Maggie! You're not keeping them still!'

'I am too! But I ain't bloomin' Hercules! It's you – you're wobblin' too much.'

'Am I?' Gwyneth steadied herself. 'I'm sorry.'

'An' I wouldn't go hangin' on to them chandeliers, neither. *Better you should fall and break your neck than break one of the chandeliers, my girl* – that's what Mrs Broadwood used to say – silly old cow.'

Gwyneth chanced a look down. 'You shouldn't talk like that.'

'Oh, shouldn't I just?' She waited until Gwyneth was on tip-toe then nudged the steps again. 'Careful, clumsy! You'll be havin' the whole lot down in a minute!'

'I can't help it.'

'I take it there weren't no ladders in prison, then?'

Gwyneth stiffened. 'How did you know about that?'

'What? About you bein' a *gaolbird*, like? An' comin' here an' gettin' a job what you didn't have no right to, on account of you havin' no character an' no experience neither?'

Gwyneth remained silent.

'I don't know – must have heard it somewhere I suppose.'

'But where?' Gwyneth took a step down, then another. 'No one was supposed to know.'

'What – you mean you never told the mistress?' said Maggie, feigning outrage.

'Yes – yes of course I did – but Mrs Rees-Morgan promised no one else would find out.'

'Ah,' said Maggie, clicking her fingers. 'Now *that's* just where I heard it. From the mistress, herself.'

Gwyneth's face dropped. 'You didn't? I don't believe you.'

'Oh yes, it's true. I remember it well. *Maggie*, she says to me, I'm afraid we've got to give that job what's rightfully yours to this here useless article what's been in prison – an' who'll probably murder us all in our beds afore long. An' I wants to give *you*, Maggie, the special privilege of followin' round after her, to make sure she don't go breakin' her silly neck before she gets the chance to do it.'

'To do *what*, Maggie?' Wearing a plain black dress, and with her hair pulled back more severely than had been her previous custom, Lucy stood stiffly in the open doorway.

Maggie sniffed. 'Just havin' a bit of joke, Lucy. That's all.'

'Well don't! Just get on with your work.' She made to go, then paused. 'And how many times do I have to tell you – it's *Lawrence* now.'

'She's worse than old Broadwood since she got made Housekeeper,' said Maggie as soon as they were alone once more.

Gwyneth started back up the steps. 'She didn't really tell you, did she? The mistress?'

'No, well not directly, like. I overheard them talkin' one night. I couldn't help it,' she gave a wink, 'seein' as how I was listenin' at the door. Anyway, dead concerned the old doctor was. I'll tell you what they said if you like?'

'I'm not sure … it wouldn't be right.'

'Suit yourself.'

Gwyneth chewed at her lip. 'Oh, go on then.'

'Ho,' laughed Maggie. 'I ain't so green as I am cabbage lookin'! You want to know, then *you* do the boots an' shoes tomorrow. Alright?'

'Oh, yes, alright. Now tell me.'

'Well – the old doctor, he was a bit worried that you wasn't really no charity case just out of clink – but some trollop that young Master Evan was havin' a bit of a fling with – an' that was why he got you the job.'

'But I've never even seen him – well, only in that photograph Mrs Rees-Morgan showed me.'

'That wasn't him,' chuckled Maggie. 'She was testin' you. Anyway she quickly put the old man's mind at rest – so that's alright, ain't it. The Doctor, well he had a good old laugh over it afterwards. Said he should have known it wasn't you, because Master Evan would never go for such a plain, mousy little thing. There, now has that put the smile back on your face?'

'Yes …' said Gwyneth uncertainly.

'I hope so,' Maggie grinned, 'because doin' all them boots an' shoes tomorrow will soon wipe it off again!'

*

Mary was in the scullery when Thomas came to her, fresh from his bath, and smelling of soap and clean linen. 'Fancy a walk, my love?' he asked, putting his hands about her waist as she stood chopping vegetables.

'It looks like rain.'

'No, no rain today.'

There was an odd note to his voice, and she put down the knife, looking toward the small window and the threatening clouds beyond. 'Well, I see you are right. But the sun is shining so brightly I'm afraid I might get heatstroke.' She picked up the knife and continued chopping.

'Come on, Mary. Just a little walk? Before it gets too dark?'

She looked at him for the first time. 'Now?'

He nodded.

'But ...'

'Dinner will keep.' He untied the strings of her apron. 'Just a short walk?'

She let herself be drawn into the kitchen where Meg and Alan were starting to empty the bath. Alan winked, but Meg merely gave a bemused look. 'Don't ask me, my love,' she said. 'Gone proper daft that husband of yours, coming home late, then wanting to go walking about in this weather! Well, mind you wrap up warm.'

Rain was beginning to spot the ground as they stepped out a few minutes later and made their way down the hill.

Thomas, his hands deep in his pockets, extended his elbow a little. 'Will you take my arm, Mary?'

She took it, and they walked in silence down the mean little streets of Nant-y-Pridd, the small, unassuming houses squeezed shoulder to shoulder beneath the leaden sky, and everywhere the smell of coal smoke that hung heavy in the evening air.

Thomas stopped in front of a house. From outside it was not much different to their own, but it stood in a more squalid and low-lying part of the village, bordered on two sides by colliery yards that constantly spread a film of black dust over sills and steps.

'Shall we go in?' he asked, pushing open the door. 'Come on, come and look.'

The kitchen was deserted but for a single broken-backed chair; the papered walls, patchy where furniture or pictures had once protected them, and the stone floor, greasy and stained.

'It's ours – if we want it,' he said.

'Ours?'

'We need a house of our own, Mary.'

She looked about. 'Can we afford it?'

'It will be tight, there's no denying it. But others manage.'

'But we'll need furniture, crockery.'

'Da has a little money put by.'

'We can't ask him.'

'He *wants* to help.'

The door to the upstairs room hung askew, the lower hinge broken, and she eased it open, peering up the narrow staircase. 'Is it the same upstairs? Just like at home?'

He nodded. 'But we won't need that.' He nudged open the door to the back bedroom. '*This* will be ours.'

She stood staring at the empty room, imagining it as the cosy place Owen and Meg shared, with its thick curtains, mahogany dresser and large, solid bed. So warm and private.

'Shall we take it?' he asked softly.

She went to the window and looked out into the darkening street. 'Thomas, I ...'

'It's alright. There's no need.'

He made to come to her, but she turned quickly, hands raised, arms tight to her body, fending him off – unable to meet his eyes. 'No, Thomas, no, please. You have to listen ...'

'You don't need to tell me *anything*.'

She looked up at him.

'I watched you go that morning, Mary. I watched you go ... and I thought you weren't coming back – but you *did*.'

'You ... you knew?'

He reached out a hand to touch hers. 'He asked you to go with him that day, didn't he?'

She nodded, looking away.

'But you didn't go, Mary – you *didn't*. That's all that matters.' He grasped her hand, holding it in his two great, calloused fists and pressing it to his face. 'I wish I had the words ... I wish I could tell you ...'

She wrenched free, pressing herself against the wall as tears filled her eyes. 'No, please ... don't! You *don't* know it all. I've shamed you.'

'It doesn't matter.'

'It *does*! I'm having his baby, Thomas.'

He stiffened, his eyes dropping to her belly, then he took a step toward her, and she braced herself, closing her eyes and tilting her face to receive the blow she felt sure must come. But instead he only touched her cheek. 'Is it *really* all over between the two of you?'

She nodded again, sobbing now.

'Then it doesn't matter. None of it matters. Not as long as I still have you.' He gathered her in his arms, stroking her hair as she wept against him. 'It's alright. It's alright, my love,' he soothed. 'No need to cry.'

Her fingers clutched at his shoulders. 'I'm sorry, Thomas. I'm so sorry.'

Tenderly, he kissed her forehead. 'Things will be different once we have a house of our own, you'll see. And as for the baby … well, we always said we'd have a family, didn't we my love?'

*

We moved in the following day. While Meg and I scrubbed and cleaned, Thomas, Owen and Alan bought what furniture they could find at a reasonable price, and by evening we were sitting by our own fire, on our own chairs, eating off our own plates, and finally, when everyone had gone home, closing the door to our own bedroom.

Thomas made love to me that night for the first time. It was quick and painless, and made him wonderfully happy – and for that I was glad.

And Thomas was right – things were different. I had long since realised I could never love him the way he loved me, and never a day passed when I did not think of Evan – but the quiet, forgiving dignity of the man I had married so shamed me in my own eyes that I swore to do all I could to repay the debt and make him content. So, just as I had woven a story around my childhood, I began to construct one around the two of us – and a fine story it was. A story where we were in love – where each evening we would sit by the fire talking, discussing, laughing, or merely sitting in contented silence, happy just to be in each other's company. A story where each night I took him into my body, eagerly and passionately, feeling the same intoxicating excitement I had known that one magical evening in Cardiff.

Then, in the autumn, a new character entered the fairy-tale. We named the baby Owen, after Thomas's father, and he arrived on a warm September afternoon with less bother than a washing day. But my darling little boy was no invention, and with his arrival I found fact and fiction becoming so entwined that when Thomas came home and sat with Little Owen in his arms, playing happily while I prepared supper, I could easily believe that all the rest was true – and I think those days, before Owen became ill, were almost the happiest I had ever known.

*

'There, my little one. What's Dada got for you then?'

The baby gurgled and reached for the knitted rabbit Thomas was holding over the cot.

'Well, you'll have to come and get it if you want it, won't you. No?' Thomas reached in and lifted little Owen, cradling him with one arm and offering the toy with the other. 'You really think he's a bit better this week, Mary?'

Mary closed the lid of the tommy box. She looked pale and tired, but so did Thomas. 'Yes,' she said attempting a smile. 'He hardly coughed at all yesterday. It's the spring weather. Dry and warm.'

'No need to take him off to Switzerland after all, then.'

'No.' She watched as Thomas turned his head and gave one of the deep, chesty coughs that kept her awake night after night. 'But yours isn't getting any better – maybe we should get the doctor again?'

Thomas passed Owen to her. 'No, no need for that,' he said, wiping his mouth with the back of his hand. He picked up his box and jack, then tickled the baby under the chin. 'We'll all be better now summer's on the way, eh? Kiss for your da?'

Mary lifted Owen for Thomas to kiss. 'And one for his mam?' she asked.

He grinned. 'Oh yes. Maybe even two?'

'Greedy, you are! One now, one when you come home.'

He leaned forward and brushed his lips against hers. 'Half now, *one and a half* when I come home, eh?'

The baby reached for his face, and he smiled. 'No time to play now, boyo. Your dada's got to go to work.'

Mary followed him to the door. '*Two* later,' she said.

He gave a great wracking cough, then smiled. 'Two it is.'

'Go safely,' she said.

Owen and Alan were waiting at the crossroads as usual, and the three of them joined the straggling line as it made its way up the hill to the pit-head.

'How's that grandson of mine?' asked Owen.

'He seems a bit better, like.' Thomas coughed. 'He sleeps right through some nights.'

'Well, that'll be more than Mary does if that's the noise you make when you're in bed,' said Alan, giving him a sideways glance.

Owen chewed on his pipe. 'You'll let me know – if it's a question of money?'

'It's not a matter of money, Da. Well, not the sort of money any of us will ever have.'

'Poor little mite. Damn me, but it's unfair!' Owen's hands were bunched into fists, his knuckles white. 'Well, if there's anything to be done you just let me know, alright?'

They walked without speaking for the rest of the way, filing into the cage and dropping into the damp darkness of the mine. With the lighter mornings the customary *stae weld* had become necessary once more, and they sat, squatting in the darkness, letting their eyes adjust before moving off.

Thomas coughed.

158

'God. We goin' to be havin' that noise every mornin', like?'

'That you, Davy Briggs?' said Owen steadily. 'Because if it is, I would recommend a few manners and a bit of respect.'

Briggs chuckled. 'No offence, Mr Davies. No offence.'

Minutes passed, and they got to their feet, eyes blinking as they made their way along the road, deeper and deeper, following the steel tracks. A heavily-laden truck passed, the confined space filling with the smell of horse as the straining pony evacuated its bowels, and Thomas broke into deep, rattling coughs.

'Oh, hell,' said Briggs from somewhere just in front. 'Here we go again. It's no wonder that baby of yours is always coughin'. The poor bugger probably thinks it's how you talk.' He laughed loudly. 'Most people teach their kids to say *dada.*'

Alan lashed out, catching Briggs a hard clout across the side of the head. 'You take that back or I'll flatten you, so help me I will!'

'It's alright,' Thomas coughed again. 'It doesn't matter.'

But Briggs was already moving away up the tunnel. 'It'll take more than you!' he shouted defiantly. 'Come and try it – see what you get!'

Alan started forward, fists raised, moving toward the shadowy figure of Davy Briggs. 'You've had this coming for a long time, you little bugger.'

There was a scraping sound.

'Careful man!' someone shouted, 'He's got a shovel!'

Alan stopped abruptly, then flung himself sideways as the steel blade shot from the darkness, tearing a piece from his ear as it hissed past.

Standing ten feet behind, Thomas observed the approaching shovel, as though time had slowed. Clearly it was going to fall short of where he was standing, and he watched, mesmerised, following in the dim light of his lamp the long, graceful curve of its trajectory as it sliced past Alan to strike the steel rail just a few yards ahead. In the low, vaulted tunnel it rang like a church bell – and raised one bright, solitary spark.

*

Meg looked embarrassed as she stood on the doorstep. 'I know it's a bit early, Mary, but I walked down with Owen and Alan as far as the bakery, and I thought I'd just call in. But I won't stay if you're busy.'

Mary smiled, wiping her hands on her apron and pushing her hair into place. 'No, please, come in, though you'll have to forgive the house. Thomas has only just left, and I haven't had time to finish clearing breakfast yet.'

'I could do that for you.'

'No, I wouldn't dream of it – but you could look after little Owen for me while I just pop down to the shop for some eggs. He takes one in his milk, and there's none in the house. Would you mind?'

'Mind?' Meg bustled into the kitchen, stooping to lift the baby from the cot. 'And how's my little boy, then, eh?' She rubbed his nose with her own, then settled him in her arms, rocking him gently. 'You know,' she said as she watched Mary clearing the table, 'when I was first married it was a real treat to have the house to myself. Big family I came from, you see – and a house no bigger than what we have now – but now that I'm on my own again most of the day, well … it doesn't seem quite the same.'

'You're always welcome to come here, you know that, Mam.'

'You don't want me cluttering up the place. You've got your work to be getting on with.'

'Yes, and I can do it better if I haven't got to keep one eye on that little gentleman the whole time.'

Meg laughed. 'Well, there's truth in that. I remember when Alan was born. Thomas was never any trouble – but Alan! Never stayed still for a minute. Always into one thing or another. It's a wonder he didn't do himself a mischief, and that's a fact.' She looked at the baby in her arms. 'How's the little one's cough? He seems quieter.'

'Thomas thinks I'm imagining it, but I'm sure he's improving.'

'Have you had the doctor to him again?'

Mary took the plates into the scullery. 'No. He's already said there's nothing more he can do. Well, we'll just have to see about that, won't we? We'll build him up, and he'll be right as ninepence, you see if he isn't.'

'Yes.' Meg looked at the baby, the smile trembling on her lips. 'Yes, I'm sure he will be.'

'Well, I won't be a minute.' Mary went to the front door and took down her coat. 'I'll make us some tea when I get back.'

Meg watched her go, then turned back to survey the room, hefting little Owen on to her hip. 'Come on. Let's have these breakfast things put away by the time your mam gets back. Are you going to come and give Nana some help?' Owen reached out to stroke her face, and she smiled. 'No? Well perhaps we'll pop you back in your cot where I can keep an eye on you while I just wash these few things.' She laid him down and went into the scullery, filling the sink from the kettle Mary had already prepared. 'Your mam's right,' she called through. 'Doctors don't know everything. You're going to grow up to be just like your dada. He wasn't so very big when he was your age, but look at him now – and your uncle Alan. Hardly fit them both into one house, you can!'

She began to wash the plates and cups, 'Mind, they ate like horses, they did. Never a crumb left on their plates and still wanting more, it was.' She smiled at the memory. 'And that's how it's going to have to be with you, see? You'll never go short when it comes to food. Your nana and gran'da will see to that.'

The dishes finished, she brought them through to the kitchen, piling them on the dresser, standing them carefully, side by side, on the shelf.

'And anyway – what's so special about being big and strong? Not so very much I don't suppose.' She hung the cups from their hooks. 'Maybe it's better not to be. If you aren't so strong, then perhaps you won't have to go down that horrible …'

As she reached up to put the final saucer in place she felt the briefest of tremors beneath her feet, so tiny it might have gone unnoticed had it not been for the faint tinkling of the plates, and the cups swinging almost imperceptibly on their hooks. Meg stared at them, then slowly lowered her hand. 'Oh no,' she said. 'Oh dear God, please, no …'

The shrill scream of the alarm began to sound from the pit-head as Mary was making her way back from the shop. She stopped, staring up toward the turning wheel, then she began to run, the eggs she'd bought falling to smash, unheeded, on the road.

People were flooding out of their houses, pulling on clothes as they came, faces grey and anxious. On every side, windows began to fly open as men from the night shift craned out, bleary-eyed but suddenly alert.

'What is it? Please … someone tell me,' shrieked a frail old woman staggering to her door, fear etched deeply into her face, but Mary was already past her, racing toward home.

With skirts flying, she turned into her street, clutching her breast against the searing pain. The front door was standing open. 'Mam?' she gasped, 'Mam, where are you?'

Little Owen was sitting in his cot, crying, but Mary rushed past him, pushing open the scullery door. 'Mam?' The room was deserted, so she tried the bedroom, then, finding that empty, she ran up the narrow wooden stairs to the bare room above, but Meg was nowhere to be seen.

Outside the alarm shrieked on. 'Please, please,' she said as she rushed back down the stairs, gathering Owen in her arms, holding him tightly and kissing him again and again. '*Please* don't let it be Thomas.'

Chapter Twenty-One

Alan opened his eyes, closed them again, then opened them wider – but there was nothing except thick, sooty blackness, darker even than when his eyes were closed, for then he could see distant, dancing lights, while reality held nothing at all.

From somewhere to his right he heard a faint cough. 'Thomas? Is that you, man?' He laughed with relief, 'Damn me but it sounds like that cough o' yours is finally getting better, not half so loud now, it is. Is Da with you?'

There was no answer so he tried again. 'Alright, don't worry, *I'll* come to find *you*.'

He tried to stand, but couldn't. A small outcrop of rock was pressing painfully into his back, so he tried to edge sideways, but could only manage to lean a little to the right or left – positions that quickly became even more uncomfortable.

'Can anyone else hear me?' He reached out, exploring blindly. There was nothing within touching distance above or immediately in front of him, but as he lowered his hands he found the huge mound of loose rubble and dust that covered him to the tops of his thighs. 'Bugger it,' he said to himself, then he shouted, 'I've just got to dig myself out, Thomas. Then I'll come to find you and Da.'

He began scraping away at the heap, pushing the dirt and rock to either side, piling it as far away as he could manage. 'Got a couple of pretty poor heaps going here, alright, Da,' he said after a quarter of an hour. 'Proper ashamed of them you'd be.' He leaned back against the wall, panting for breath, then he laughed, 'Reckon they'll be sliding down around my arse at the first drop of rain.'

It was hot and airless, and as he sat resting he drew his arm across his forehead, catching his bloodied ear with his sleeve. 'Bloody hell!' he said through clenched teeth. 'Briggs, I'll get you for this, you hear! I'll bloody well murder you. Here, Thomas, that little bugger nearly took my lug off!'

The faint cough came again.

'You can bloody well laugh, man! I'm going to see Old Mrs Jenkins tonight – about me and Lizzie. Fine bloody picture I'd make – going up the aisle with only one ear!' Using the back of his hand he wiped his nose, then took it between his thumb and forefinger, moving it from side to side thoughtfully. 'Look like a bloody teapot – with the spout stuck round the side, wouldn't I!' He leaned back, chuckling, then rubbed his hands together, spitting into the darkness to take the dust from his mouth. 'Right, boyo,' he said. 'Shan't be long now. Second shift's just coming on!'

*

Meg walked slowly back up the hill, oblivious to the hustle and bustle going on all around. Several times she was almost knocked from her feet by people rushing in the opposite direction, but neither the buffeting nor the constant scream of the siren managed to break in upon her thoughts.

She was confused, unsure of exactly why she was there. Well, she thought, it would come back to her, and then she'd feel fool enough. *A proper fool.* She smiled, hearing the first words she'd ever spoken to Owen.

'A proper fool you are to be gawping at me like that!'
'Fool, am I? Don't they teach manners at school these days, then?'
'I would have thought even you could tell that I'm all finished with school. What are you doing here, anyway?'
'Well, I was looking for work, see? And your dada said he had this shrew of a daughter, like – and as how he'd pay me to put her over my knee and teach her some common courtesy. You haven't seen such a person about, I suppose?'
'You're a bit full of yourself, aren't you?'
'I could say the same for you – if you wasn't blushing so much.'
'I am not!'
'It's alright – pretty it is.'
'I am not blushing! I'm hot, that's all.'
'Oh, aye. Hot work, is it – collecting eggs?'
'Shouldn't you be getting on with your work?'
'Well, I works when I please and go where I please, see? Man of the road, I am.'
'Oh, that right, is it? You got a name, then?'
'Owen. Owen Davies.'
'Well, Mr Owen Davies. My da shall hear about how you waste time in idle chit-chat – and I expect you'll be a man of the road again sooner than you was thinking.'

Meg paused in the middle of the street. She'd had a fleeting fancy she'd been on her way to the shops – yet that surely couldn't be right for she had no basket.

'Don't bang the basket down like that, Megan, my love, you'll break the eggs if you aren't more careful.'
'I am being careful, Mam!'
'No need to go biting my head off. What's the matter? You're looking all flushed.'
'I am not!'
'Oh – oh, I see.'
'What? What do you see? And why are you smiling like that?'
'Oh – nothing. Fetch me over that large copper, will you? That young chap's staying for dinner – so you'll need to make another place at table.'
'I don't want to make a place for him. Why should I?'
'There's nothing wrong in making the poor boy feel like part of the family.'
'But he's not! He's nothing to do with us! He's no part of this family – and never will be!'
'Sshhh, Megan.'
'He's just a cuckoo in the nest, that's what he is – and I don't care who hears me.'

Unaware of the furore all around her, Meg moved on, walking with slow, measured steps.

'So, Mr Owen Davies. You just going to walk about the whole of your life, then? Never settling down?'
'I might – or I might not. Why should you care?'
'I don't.'
'Well then! Here, pass me up that new tile. Actually, I was thinking of going to sea.'
'What ... on a ship?'
'No, on this here ladder! What do you think, girl! There, that's the roof fixed. No more leaks now, eh? – I suppose if I was to go you'd miss me, would you?'
'I can't say I would.'
'Oh, but you can't say you wouldn't?'
'Well ...'

A boy came tearing out of a house, crashing into Meg, sending her sprawling in the road.

'Come and lie yourself down here by me, my little Megan. There's nothing like the smell of new mown hay.'

'As long as that's all you have in mind.'

'Did I tell you? I met a chap in town the other day. He said there are some jobs going – over toward Caerphilly.'

'But that's over the mountain!'

'It's not so far.'

'What sort of jobs?'

'Regular jobs – settling down sort of jobs.'

'I thought you were a man of the road.'

'Perhaps I'm not anymore – perhaps I never really was.'

'Perhaps.'

'By, Meg, but it really is hot.'

'Yes.'

'Not a cloud in the sky.'

'No, not a cloud.'

'No …'

'You … you could put your arm around me … if you wanted to?'

'What – like this, you mean?'

'Yes …'

'That's cosy, it is, Meg.'

'Yes.'

'And, well … I suppose you could put your head just here, like – on my chest … if you wanted to?'

'Alright.'

'Oh, that's nice, that is.'

'I can hear your heart.'

'Can you? You'll tell me if it stops, won't you? I wouldn't want to be walking about and not knowing I was dead, like.'

'Owen!'

'What? What you laughing at girl. I knew a man once and that very thing happened to him.'

'It did not!'

'Well – maybe you're right.'

'It's nice here, Owen.'

'Yes.'

'Very quiet.'

'Yes.'

'If … if you wanted to … you could kiss me – but only if you wanted to, mind.'

'What – like this?'

'Yes – or maybe …?'

'Like this?'

'Oh – yes.'

Faces swam before her as she got to her feet, their mouths opening, hands gesturing, but she couldn't hear them, and they quickly moved on, joining the stream of people making their way toward the pit.

'Oh, not down the pit! Say it's not down the pit!'
'It's good regular money, Meg.'
'But it's dangerous.'
'No. No, I hear it's a good mine. Very safe, it is.'
'There's no such thing. Please, Owen. Please don't go.'
'Frightened a big old rock will fall on me and spoil my good looks, are you?'
'Please, please don't joke about it. Stay here. I'm sure Da will need help through the winter.'
'I want a proper job, Meg. I want a house of my own and …'
'And what?'
'Nothing. But it's well into autumn, and I can't sleep out in that barn much longer. I have to be moving on.'
'No, Owen – I'll talk to Da. You could stay in the house …'
'I have to be my own man.'
'Not in the mines – promise me it won't be in the mines.'
'Well, we'll see.'

She turned the corner and the neat little house that had been her home for twenty-five years stood before her.

'This is the house, Meg. So what do you think?'
'It looks alright from the outside, I suppose. Which room is yours, then?'
'All of them.'
'All of them?'
'All four! No more single rooms for me from now on. Come on, I'll show you. There's no furniture yet, of course – but there's an oven, and a sink in the scullery, oh, and a garden at the back for growing vegetables and such. This is the kitchen, see?'
'It has a nice feel to it. Cosy, like.'
'Do you think so?'
'Yes. Very cosy. We … you … could make it lovely. It would make a nice home … for a family.'
'You know, my little Megan. It's very odd, but I was thinking that exact same thing.'

She opened the door and went inside. It *was* a cosy little house, and Owen would be home soon. All she had to do was sit quietly and wait.

*

Alan continued to dig.

'You remember that time, don't you, Thomas? When old Griffiths was laid up with the pneumonia? Damn me but that was a holiday, wasn't it! Me and Billy Unwin used to go by his house at night and make as much noise as we could outside his window, hoping to keep him awake so's he'd get worse and never come back.' Alan laughed to himself as he dug. 'By, but getting even with that miserable old bugger was well worth the whacking he gave us when he did finally come back to school.'

He no longer needed to rest now. For a while, before he had uncovered his knees, it seemed as if he would never have the strength to dig himself out. It had grown unbearably hot, and his back hurt so badly he needed to rest every few minutes – and when he did he could barely breathe. Then he'd caught the unmistakable sound of Thomas's voice. Faint, barely audible at first, but then increasingly clear. Thomas was alright. He was pinned just like himself, but their father had been blown clear and was a part of the team digging toward them. Now it was only a matter of time, and it gave Alan the strength he needed.

Trapped as he was, he could not easily reach to clear his lower legs, but with perseverance he'd found he could strain forward just enough to move a handful or two before having to straighten to ease his screaming muscles. Back and forth he went, and gradually he'd found the rhythm. Forward, scoop two handfuls, sometimes three, then back. Forward again, another two, then back, over and over, and the more he did it, the easier it became; now it didn't hurt at all – and it seemed cooler, too. *Air*. It had to be air getting into the tunnel. That meant they were getting close, and he knew he'd never live it down if he was found sitting there like some slip of a girl when his father finally broke through. Back and forth he went, smiling as he scooped away the debris. But he was worried, too. He hadn't heard Thomas's voice for some time, not even the cough. 'Hey, Thomas,' he called loudly, 'I don't know what I'm going to tell, Mam. I think my damned jack has burst and spilt tea all over the place, I'm digging into mud here. I could just have fancied a nice drop o' tea, too. God, but I've a thirst on me. Mouth like next morning's grate, I've got!' The earth was so thick and cloying that he had to shake it from his fingers. 'Mam'll give me a right telling off. That jack was brand new just last year – or was it the year before? God, but I'm thirsty now. What I wouldn't give for a quart down at the Quarryman.' His fingers continued to claw at the increasingly wet earth, back and forth, back and forth, scooping the clinging mud. 'Nearly there. Nearly there.' He was half way toward his ankles now and elation filled him. 'God, this stuff is wet. It's like being at the bloody seaside, Thomas! That's what it is – I'm at the bloody seaside, man, making bloody sandcastles. You remember that time when we were kids? You and me … making bloody sandcastles weren't we! By, but that was a time, eh? And those crabs … remember we caught those crabs? … and Mam made us throw them back … and Gwyn …' He paused. 'Oh, poor Gwyn … I just remembered … she'll be starting school soon. But just let that bastard Griffiths start on her … I'll fix him …' He began to laugh as he dug into the rubble. 'I'll fix him alright. I'll get some of those bloody crabs … those bloody great big …' His fingers struck something hard, and he scrabbled at it, then he leaned back against the wall. 'Queerest thing, Thomas. Queerest bloody thing, man. There's this big lump of rock … *a bloody great big lump of rock* … right where my legs should be!' He forced a little laugh, 'That can't be right, can it?' He stared blindly toward his feet, then slowly began to cry. 'I … I only wanted to make sandcastles, like. Just sandcastles … but now the tide's coming in! It's coming in fast, Thomas. Too fast. I can feel it all around me …'

There was a movement in the darkness, and he looked up. 'Da …? Is that you, Da …?'

Owen was standing a little way off, looking down at him.

'I'm sorry, Da,' he said, crying freely now, 'I'm so sorry. I tried … I *did* … I tried my best … but now the tide's coming in … and … and …' He wiped at his eyes. 'I just want to go home … I'm *frightened*, Dada …' His head fell back against the rock. It didn't hurt – nothing hurt anymore. Through half-closed lids he looked up into the face of his father. 'Time to go home, Dada?' he said in a small voice. 'Time to go home, is it?'

Owen smiled and nodded. 'Yes, my boyo. Time to go home.'

Alan closed his eyes. He was tired now, so very, very tired. 'Right you are, then, Dada. Right you are ….' And as he drifted away he thought, proudly, how young and strong his father looked – just as he had that day so many years ago when they'd gathered up their things and made their way back across the deserted sands, Thomas on one side, himself on the other, holding their father's great thick hands while their mother followed, carrying a sleeping Gwyneth in her arms. 'Right you are then, Dada …' he said one final time.

It was ten hours later that the scorched but still breathing body of little Willy Price was uncovered. Trapped in a pocket formed by fallen props and slabs of rock, he had fallen asleep, only to be awakened into renewed bouts of coughing by his jubilant rescuers.

But it was a brief moment of joy. Four more hours of careful digging and clearing brought the discovery of three lifeless bodies. Owen Davies, the clothes burned from his back, lay sprawled across the body of Thomas – as though to shelter him from the massive weight that had instantly crushed them both. And, almost within arm's reach, propped against the wall, his lower legs severed by a great slab of rock, Alan sat amidst his own blood, a strangely tranquil smile upon his face.

168

Chapter Twenty-Two

'Oh God, Mary. I came the moment I heard, but I don't know what to do.' Gwyneth's eyes were raw and her face streaked from crying. 'She won't say *anything* … she just sits there.'

'Does she know?'

'We're not sure.'

Mrs Jenkins's sparse frame appeared behind Gwyneth. 'I came straight up and told her – but I don't know if she heard me or not. She was just sitting here – just like she is now.' The old woman came to the door. 'Here, let me hold the little one for you,' she said, taking Owen from Mary's arms.

'I've tried talking to her,' said Gwyneth, between sobs. 'But I don't think she even recognises me. What are we going to do, Mary? Oh, God, what are we going to *do*?'

'Come on, Gwyn,' Mary guided Gwyneth back into the room. 'Let me try talking to her.'

'It won't do any good.'

'It might. We have to do *something*.'

Gwyneth crumpled on to a chair. 'All of them, Mary. Da … Alan … Thomas,' she gazed up with pleading eyes. 'How could it happen? How could God let it happen?'

'I don't know.' Mary took out a handkerchief and wiped Gwyneth's cheeks, then her own, but it was a futile gesture. 'I don't believe there can be a god.'

Mrs Jenkins's eyes narrowed, but she said nothing, looking closely at Owen instead.

'We mustn't think about it, Gwyn. Not just yet, anyway. We need to be strong – to help Mam.'

Mrs Jenkins rocked Owen to and fro. 'I saw a woman go like this once before. Over at Tredegar, it was. Never recovered as far as I know.'

'Mam?' said Mary, sitting opposite Meg and reaching for her hand. 'Mam? Can you hear me? It's me, Mary.' She fought to control the trembling of her lips. 'We're here now ... Gwyneth, myself ... and Owen.'

There was the tiniest spark of life in Meg's eyes. 'Owen?' she murmured vaguely, 'My Owen?'

'Oh, God,' whimpered Gwyneth. 'She *doesn't* know.'

Mary gripped Meg's hands tightly. 'Listen, Mam, please. There's been an accident ... at the pit.'

'Oh, not the pit.' Meg's eyes wandered over the room without focusing. 'Say you won't go down the pit.'

Gwyneth came to kneel at her side. 'They're not coming home, Mam. Alan, Thomas ... Da. They're *not* coming back.'

'No,' said Meg, absently. 'Not just now ...'

'Not *ever*,' sobbed Gwyneth.

'You *do* understand?' asked Mary, gazing into Meg's eyes and seeing only a far away look.

'Not till next summer ... Da will want him again next summer.'

Mrs Jenkins came forward. 'Here, give her the boy. There's no woman alive that won't perk up when she's got a little one to hold – though it's a pity he don't look more like his dada,' she said pointedly. 'Might have helped her to remember, like.'

Mary took him on her lap. 'Will you hold Owen for me, Mam?' Meg continued to stare vacantly, making no move to take the boy, so Mary gently moved Meg's hands from her lap. 'Here, let me make a place for him.'

'No!' Meg jerked her head up, glaring petulantly. 'I don't want to make a place for *him*.'

'Mam?'

'I don't want to! Why should I?'

'Mam, please ...'

Meg's eyes narrowed, and there was anger in her voice. 'He's nothing to do with us!'

The colour drained from Mary's face, and she glanced uneasily about. 'I ... I don't understand. He's Thomas's ... mine and Thomas's.'

'He's no part of this family – and never will be!'

'Mam, please don't ...'

'He's just a cuckoo in the nest, that's what he is ... and I don't care who hears me!'

Mrs Jenkins's expression became pinched and mean. '*Well!*' she hissed. 'I bloody well knew it all along!'

'She ... she doesn't know what she's saying.' Mary stood up, clutching the baby to her. 'He *is* Thomas's ... of course he is.'

But Meg kept her eyes fixed firmly ahead. 'Just a cuckoo!'

Mary stared down at her in horror, then looked anxiously toward

Gwyneth. 'It's … it's not true, Gwyn.'

Triumph gleamed in Mrs Jenkins's eyes. 'Oh, it's true, alright. Just look at your face – guilt written all over it!'

Mary rounded on her. 'Shut up! Just *shut up* you bloody old gossip!' She turned back to Gwyneth. 'Don't listen to her.'

Disgusted, Mrs Jenkins moved to the door. 'She doesn't have to listen to me – she heard it from her own mother!'

'Gwyn … *please …*'

But Gwyneth was on her feet, backing away, her hand going to her throat as her mind struggled with the awful possibility.

'Well,' said Mrs Jenkins, drawing herself up self-righteously. 'It won't come as any great surprise around here – that I can tell you!'

Mary ignored her. 'Gwyn …?' she began, pleading, ashen-faced, clutching Owen to her. 'You don't believe …?' She took a step toward her, but Gwyneth shrank back, a terrible look in her eyes.

For a moment they stared at each other, then Mary lowered her gaze, and without another word, pushed past the old woman and walked from the house.

In the silence of the room, Meg continued to stare vacantly ahead. 'Such a nice home … for a family,' she muttered.

*

'She admitted it, did she?'

'As good as.' Mrs Jenkins watched the scales as the shopkeeper scooped in the sugar. ''Course, I've suspected as much for a long time. I said the same to Mrs Briggs only the other week – and it's as plain as a pikestaff when you look at the boy.'

'Just over the half pound?'

'Well, I don't mind as long as I don't have to pay for the extra.'

The man carefully removed half an ounce. 'So whose is it, then?'

'I've got some ideas about that, too – but not her husband's, that's for sure. Still,' she said, 'I suppose it was only to be expected. Her mother was a bad lot – and *that's* being charitable. I could tell you things, Mr Jones – things as would make your hair stand on end.'

'Yes, I'm sure.' He tipped the sugar into a brown paper bag. 'But how's your Lizzie taking it – the accident, I mean? She was a bit fond of that Davies boy, wasn't she?'

'Oh, she's in a terrible bad way, crying all day and all night it is with her.'

The shopkeeper shook his head sadly. 'Bad business, Mrs Jenkins. Bad business.'

'Yes indeed.'

'Terrible for old Mrs Davies,' he went on. 'Losing her husband and sons like that.'

'Yes! And then to find out that her grandson is a … Well, scandalous, it is! 'Course, you have to feel sorry for her, but you also have to wonder if some folk aren't quite as decent and respectable as they might like to make out. Take that daughter of hers. Been to *prison*, she has!'

'Yes, I know, but …' The bell over the shop door rang and he gave a cautionary cough as Mary entered and made her way toward them.

Mrs Jenkins eyed her, then the child in her arms. 'Perhaps I'll just leave those few things if you don't mind, Mr Jones? For collection later?' She sniffed, looking down her nose at Mary. 'I feel the need for some *fresh* air. There's a funny smell in here all of a sudden.'

'Right you are, Mrs Jenkins,' he said uncomfortably, placing the groceries on the rear counter, then moving away to re-arrange the shelves at the far end of the shop.

Mary walked down to him. 'I should like four ounces of tea, please.'

Without speaking, he returned to the scales, weighed out the loose brown leaves and poured them into a twist of paper.

'And half a dozen eggs and a quarter of butter.'

He took six eggs from the shelf and placed them in a bag, then patted out a generous portion of butter, wrapping it without weighing, and placed it next to the eggs and tea. 'Anything else?'

'No,' she said, matching the chill in his voice. 'Nothing else. How much is that?'

He shook his head. 'No charge. Your husband was a good man. Well respected.' He looked meaningfully at her. 'He deserved better.'

She eyed him coldly. 'What do you mean by that?'

'News travels fast in a small community.'

'*Rumour* travels faster.'

He glanced at the baby in her arms. 'Perhaps.'

For a few seconds they stood staring at each other, then Mary felt for her purse. 'I should prefer to *pay* for my goods, if you don't mind.'

'Please.' He pushed the parcels toward her. 'Just take them – but in future I'd prefer it if you did your shopping elsewhere.'

*

Gwyneth eased open the curtains just enough to allow a sliver of sunlight to brighten the gloom of the kitchen. She felt dirty and tired from sitting up all night with her mother, and the face that looked back at her from the mirror was pinched and drawn, with dark circles around the eyes, and framed with loose strands of lank, untidy hair. She yawned and stretched. 'Would you like a cup of tea, Mam?'

Meg did not answer – just as she had not answered the thousand other questions Gwyneth had put to her.

'Some breakfast, then? No? Well, let's wait a little.' She glanced toward the upstairs room. 'Aunt Angharad and Uncle Seldon will be out of bed soon, and you might feel more like it then, eh?'

She walked into the scullery. Convention did not require the back curtains to be drawn, and she crossed to the window, leaning her forehead against the cool glass as she stared toward the distant hills. Shock, the doctor had said, and that it would wear off in time, but Gwyneth wasn't so sure. When her aunt and uncle had heard of the tragedy, they had rushed over from Carmarthen, and Meg *had* acknowledged them – vaguely and in a way Gwyneth was only now beginning to understand. It was as if her mother had mentally turned back the clock: as if the past twenty-five years had never happened.

Gwyneth was still turning it over in her mind when there came a knock at the door, and she made her way back through the kitchen, straightening her dress and tidying her hair as she went.

Mary was standing in the street, Owen fast asleep against her breast. 'I wanted to see how Mam was,' she said. 'If I'm still welcome?'

Sullenly, Gwyneth moved back into the house.

'Is she any better?' asked Mary, coming to stand just inside the doorway, all too aware of the unspoken hostility.

'No, of course she isn't. What did you expect – that everything would be alright – just like in one of your stupid stories?'

'I shouldn't have come – I'm sorry.' Mary turned to leave.

'Tell me, Mary. Tell me it isn't true. Tell me Owen really *is* Thomas's.'

'Would you believe me?'

'*Make me* believe you. You were always able to do that when we were children.'

'We're not children anymore, Gwyn.'

Gwyneth raised her face, the dark circles giving her eyes a frightening intensity. 'I hate you! I hate you for what you did to Thomas. He loved you *so* much. But I hate you even more for letting the whole world know. For shaming his memory! For shaming us! Why couldn't you have lied? You've always been good at that! For God's sake, why couldn't you have made us believe you?'

'How could I? Mam knew the truth.'

'She didn't! She doesn't know anything that's happened these past twenty-five years. Whatever was going through her mind yesterday, it had nothing to do with you. It was your own guilt that found you out!'

Mary reached for the wall, steadying herself as the enormity of the words sank in.

But Gwyneth was unsympathetic. 'Did Thomas know?'

The memory of Thomas's gentle smile filled Mary's head, and she looked up, meeting Gwyneth's accusing stare. 'Yes, he did. But he forgave me, Gwyn. He *forgave* me.'

173

'He would. He loved you.'

Tears sprang in Mary's eyes, and she turned away.

'What will you do now?' asked Gwyneth, the question cold and emotionless.

'I don't know. Go away somewhere. I can't stay here in Nant-y-Pridd.'

'No.'

'What about you – and Mam? Will you come back and stay with her?'

'And live on what? The five shillings a week widow's money from the Association? Besides, what would be the point? She doesn't remember me anymore than she remembers you or ...' she gave a curt nod toward Owen, '*him*. I shall go back to my job. Mam's going to stay with my uncle and aunt over in Carmarthen.' She went to her mother's side, putting a hand on her shoulder, but there was only the tiniest reaction to the touch.

'Did Thomas pay into the Association?' Gwyneth asked.

'No. He started to – but then we needed furniture.'

'So you won't even get the five shillings.'

Owen began to stir, and Mary made ready to leave. 'Will you walk with me, Gwyn? At the funeral? For old-time's sake?'

Gwyneth eyed her. 'What do *you* think?' she said.

*

'They spit at me, Peggy. They spit on the pavement where I walk.'

'Well, what d'yer expect? Bunch of po-faced, hypocritical bible thumpers! But you've only yerself t' blame.' Peggy Cartwright gave the beef tea a stir, then brought it to the table where Mary was sitting. 'Still,' she sighed, 'you've made me ashamed, Mary, an' that's a fact.'

Mary looked into her lap. 'Don't, Peg. Please ... don't *you* turn against me.'

'I'm not turnin' against yer – yer great turnip.' Peggy sat down on the bench and put her arm about Mary's shoulders, pulling her close. 'What's done is done, an' no amount of cryin' over spilt milk's goin' t' change that – though I'm not sayin' yer shouldn't 'ave a belt taken t' yer for what yer did. But, well, these things 'appen – or so they tell me. What makes me ashamed is that I didn't stop yer from marryin' when I knew yer 'eart wasn't in it.'

'But my heart was in it – I did love Thomas.'

'No yer didn't. I might not know a lot o' things – but I do know that whatever yer was feelin' that mornin' yer got married, it wasn't love. I should 'ave stopped yer – should 'ave said somethin' – but I didn't 'cos I *wanted* yer t' love 'im. I didn't want yer endin' up old and lonely.'

Mary buried her head in the old woman's shoulder, sobbing. 'Oh, Peg. What am I going to do?'

'Well,' said Peggy, giving her a squeeze. 'Firstly yer goin' t' 'ave a good

174

ol' cry. Get it out of yer system, 'ere with me – so as not t' give them miserable psalm-singers the satisfaction of knowin' they've 'urt yer. *Then* you're goin' t' put on yer brave face an' do whatever yer *'ave t'* do. Brazen it out. Yer can't let it beat yer, Mary. I told yer that when yer first came 'ere, didn't I? An' it's as true about life as it is about scrubbin' a bloomin' floor.' She pulled Mary closer, and in the silence of the kitchen they sat together, the old woman gently rocking as she stroked Mary's hair, feeling the warm tears soaking through her blouse.

'Yer tea's gone cold,' Peggy said at last, as the sun dipped below the horizon. 'I'll fetch yer some more.' She got up and went to the stove. 'Now listen, I've been thinkin'. When's the funeral?'

Mary dried her eyes. 'Tomorrow morning at eleven o'clock.'

'Well, we're closed for two weeks. The Llewellyns 'ave shut up shop an' gone on bloomin' 'oliday, if yer don't mind! First time ever as I can recall. Daisy an' Bronwyn 'ave been given time off t' go an' see their families. There's only me 'ere – so why don't yer stay for a few days? I could look after the little 'un for yer – while yer go back t' Nant-y-Pridd tomorrow. Yer can have the best room if yer want.' She winked. 'Ain't no one goin' t' know.'

Mary looked uncertain. 'I'm not sure, Peg. It wouldn't be right.'

''Course it would. The Llewellyns would want yer t' stay if they knew you was in trouble – an' anyway, they owe it t' yer. Blimey, they've 'ad more'n their fair share out of you over the years.'

'It *is* getting dark.'

Peggy Cartwright grinned. 'Yes, it is.'

'If I did stay ... could I have my old room?'

'What, that little box in the attic? Well, if yer want. I can soon put clean sheets on the bed – an' there's a cot I can bring up for the little 'un.'

Mary stood up and threw her arms around the old woman. 'Thank you, Peggy.'

'There, there. T'aint nothin'. Anyway, you don't want t' be goin' 'ome. I've got yer favourite for tea tonight.'

'What?' Mary stepped back, smiling and brushing at her eyes.

Peggy took out the pantry key and dangled it between her fingers. 'Anythin' yer bloomin' well want.'

*

The funeral procession was already forming beneath the stationary pit wheel as Mary entered the colliery yard the next morning. On every side, hostile eyes stared as she walked to where seven coffins lay, adorned with wreaths and supported on wooden trestles draped with black velvet.

Slowly she moved between them, reading the brass plaques: David Arthur Briggs; Samuel William Tindall; Gwilliam Jones; James Percival

Jones; Alan Morgan Davies; Owen Dafyd Davies; and finally, Thomas Alfred Davies. She ran her hand tenderly over the polished lid. 'Go safely, my love,' she whispered, her lips barely moving. 'Go safely.'

Gwyneth was standing amongst a group of weeping mourners, but Mary did not approach, remaining apart as the coffins were lifted on to the shoulders of the men who would carry the bodies to their final shift below ground.

Quietly and solemnly the procession began to move, winding its way out of the yard and into the streets beyond, the widows and children, mothers and fathers following in the wake of each casket.

Mary waited, head bowed, stepping into the empty space behind Thomas's coffin as it passed.

For long minutes she walked alone, feeling exposed and vulnerable to the condemning looks of those who lined the roadside, then Gwyneth was by her side, reaching for her hand.

With overwhelming gratitude, Mary grasped it, just as she had done so many times before, but Gwyneth's face was like stone, her eyes fixed firmly ahead. '*Just* for old time's sake,' she said.

Chapter Twenty-Three

'It's just like it used to be, ain't it?' said Peggy as they sat in the small attic bedroom late one evening.

Curled on the bed, Mary glanced toward the cot containing her son. 'Well – not quite.'

'No, I s'pose not,' Peggy chuckled. 'An' I can't see well enough to sew no more, neither.' She made to rise, but a frown creased her brow, and she sat back. 'I 'aven't asked – an' you've no need t' tell me if yer don't want to – but the little un's dad – 'is *real* dad. Did yer love 'im?'

'Oh, yes.'

'Does 'e know about the boy?'

'No.'

'Married was 'e?'

'No, it wasn't like that. He asked me to go with him, to Paris. But I *couldn't*.'

'Conscience?'

'Yes …' She thought for a moment. 'But more than that. I *did* love Thomas. Not in the same way I love Evan, but …'

'That 'is name? Evan?'

Mary put her hand to her mouth.

'Nice name,' mused Peggy. 'The doctor's son is called …' She stopped and looked searchingly at Mary. 'Gawd. It was '*im*, wasn't it?'

'Please, Peg, you mustn't tell a living soul.'

'Oh, don't worry. T'aint none o' my business – so it certainly ain't no one else's.' She sighed heavily. 'Blimey, I must be gettin' dull in my old age. I should 'ave seen it that Christmas Day when yer were both 'idin' up them stairs like a couple o' bloomin' school kids.'

'That was just before he went away. I didn't even know about the baby myself then.'

'But yer could tell 'im now, couldn't yer?'

Mary looked uncertain.

'Yer still love 'im, don't yer?'

'Oh Peg, I haven't thought of anything else these past days. I must be heartless.'

''Course you ain't. Don't be daft.'

Mary leaned her head against the wall. 'It's not right. Thomas was so good to me.'

'Yes, 'e was. An' you'll always carry a little part of 'im in yer 'eart. But life 'as t' go on – an' denyin' yer feelin's ain't goin' to 'elp no one. It certainly ain't goin' to 'elp that poor little mite not to 'ave no father.'

'But how will I find him – after all this time? I can't just walk up to the Rees-Morgans and ask them.'

'Well, it ain't goin' t' be easy. That's for certain. But I can't see what else yer can do, Mary, my girl.'

*

'Thank you – for coming to see her off,' said Gwyneth a short while after the cart bearing the forlorn figure of Megan Davies had crested the hill and disappeared from view.

There was no friendship in the words, they were just words – a formality requiring no response, and Mary bit her lip, fighting the urge to cry.

She had found it hard to watch Meg's pitifully few possessions being loaded on to the carrier's wagon, and yet Meg herself had seemed oblivious to it all, as though her once cherished belongings were merely someone else's bric-a-brac.

Gwyneth too seemed dulled to what was happening. Drained by grief and lack of sleep, she had helped Meg out of the house and up on to the high seat, only breaking down into tears as the cart moved away and out of sight without her mother giving so much as a backward glance.

'Gwyn?' Mary said softly, following Gwyneth back into the empty house.

Gwyneth looked wearily at her.

'Gwyn, I'm not coming back to Nant-y-Pridd. I'm selling the furniture, and I'd like you to have the money – it was mostly your da's anyway.'

Gwyneth shook her head. 'Keep it. You'll need it.' She looked distractedly about the barren room. 'Funny, isn't it? How little it took to make a home.'

'Are you going to be alright, Gwyn?'

'Does it matter?'

Mary made to answer, but it was as if Gwyneth had built a wall between them, and she could only stand there, searching for the words to break it down, knowing there were none. 'I'm staying at the Cross Keys, Gwyn. If you should …?'

'I shan't.' Gwyneth said flatly.

178

Mary went to the door, wanting to leave, quietly, saying nothing that would add to the pain of this final parting, but she knew she could not. 'Gwyn?' she said, not looking at her. 'The Rees-Morgans …?'

Gwyneth eyed her suspiciously. 'There's no job there if that's what you're after.'

'No, it's not that. I just wondered … if perhaps you'd ever mentioned me to them?'

'You?' Gwyneth's eyes grew angry. 'What – are you looking for gratitude for getting me a job when I couldn't get one for myself?'

'That's not what I meant, Gwyn …'

'Poor Gwyneth should be thankful when anyone takes an interest in her, is it?'

'*Gwyn.*'

'Poor little Gwyneth who no one wants. Who no man would think to look at twice. Poor, dull, *mousy* little Gwyneth …' She stopped abruptly, then stared. 'Oh, God! It was *you*, wasn't it! All that business about Master Evan and his *trollop* … it was *you*! Little Owen is *his* child.'

Mary felt suddenly cold. 'Who called me that?'

'Oh, I *am* a fool. I never even suspected. All those questions they asked me, and *still* I never suspected.'

'Gwyn, tell me. What questions? Who said I was a trollop?'

'What do you care?'

'I care! I'm going to find him again, Gwyn. I'm going to find Evan. You must know where he is. You must see letters?'

'I don't.'

'Then I have to ask his parents.'

Gwyneth looked at her, first in surprise, then with cruel amusement. 'You really *are* mad, aren't you!'

'I'll do whatever it takes.'

'Oh, I'm sure you will. I just hope I'm there to see it. This isn't one of your stories, Mary. This is real life! I nearly lost my job because they thought *I* might be the *trollop*. Can you possibly think they'll welcome you with open arms? You? Of all people? What are you? *Nothing*! You're homeless, destitute – and with a bastard child hanging from your apron strings. You are the Rees-Morgans' worst nightmare!'

Mary felt her lip begin to tremble, but she fought to quell it. 'I don't care. *Evan* loved me. He would have taken me with him.'

'Then you should have gone when you had the chance – and spared Thomas the shame you've heaped upon his memory! Who knows, without you he might not even be dead.'

'That's a *horrible* thing to say, Gwyn.'

Gwyneth slouched against the fireplace, looking sullenly out from beneath her unkempt hair. 'But it's true. Perhaps if he hadn't had to support you and that … that *child*.'

Mary turned away. 'I *am* going to see the Rees-Morgans, but I shan't cause trouble for you, Gwyn. I'm going back to my maiden name. There's no reason to admit you ever knew me.'

Gwyneth looked straight through her. 'I *don't* know you, Mary – I don't think I ever did.'

*

Later that evening Gwyneth closed the door of the little terraced house for the last time. She had been born in that house, as had Thomas and Alan before her, and it felt strange to think a new family would soon be calling it home.

Walking briskly, she made her way out of the village and up on to the Caerphilly road – and suddenly Nant-y-Pridd was below and behind her. She stopped. The dying sun was soft on her face, and as she stood there she cried. For the first time in her life, she was completely alone, and the realisation was frightening. She swallowed hard. *Poor mousy Gwyneth,* she thought. *Who will keep watch for you now?*

*

Mary sighed as she sat hunched over the remains of Owen's dinner, idly pushing at it with the spoon while the baby fretted uncomfortably on the seat beside her.

'Lord, Mary!' said Peggy, coming over to her. 'You're goin' to 'ave t' do better than that or the poor little beggar will never get any stronger.'

'He won't take any more, Peg. I've tried. He never eats very much.'

'Stuff an' nonsense! 'Ere, give us that spoon.'

Mary passed it to her without protest. 'Gwyneth's right,' she said once Peggy had pulled up a chair. 'The Rees-Morgans will never accept me.'

'Well, I never said it would be easy.' Peggy put the spoon to Owen's lips, but he pulled his head away, making small whimpering sounds. 'An' that ol' Doctor Rees-Morgan is a right pig of man if ever there was one. *Woman* he called me once. Bloomin' cheek! *Out of my way, woman,* he says. Just like that! I'd 'ave given 'im a piece o' my mind if …' From the corner of her eye she saw Mary's shoulders droop a little more. ''Course – 'e 'ad been called to an accident what 'ad 'appened just outside – so maybe 'e ain't quite as bad as what I'm makin' out.'

Mary shook her head.

'Alright,' said Peggy, finally getting the spoon into Owen's mouth. 'So what if Gwyneth *is* right? What are yer goin' t' do about it?'

'What can I do?'

'Well, yer can sit around 'ere mopin' – or yer can get up off yer backside an' make somethin' of yerself – somethin' them Rees-Morgans *will* accept.'

She stopped and stared at the baby. 'Gawd, Mary. I swear there's more comin' out of 'is mouth than I put in!'

Mary gave the child a cursory glance before staring back at the table. 'Well, I shall have to find a job. But that won't help.'

'No, it won't. But who's talkin' about a job? I seem t' remember you was all set on becomin' an artist afore yer went off an' got married.'

'It's too late for that now.'

'Is it? *It ain't never too late* my ol' dad used t' say. 'Ad a sayin' for everythin', 'e did.' She dropped the spoon back on to the plate in frustration. 'Though Gawd knows what 'e'd 'ave said about tryin' t' feed this little tyke. Oh, I give up!'

Mary brightened a little. 'Let me try again.'

'I won't stop yer,' said Peggy, getting to her feet, pleased to see a little of the old spark back. 'I'll make us a nice cup o' tea.'

Mary took the spoon and held it out. 'Come on, Owen. One for the Queen, is it?' She looked up. 'I *could* do it, couldn't I, Peg?'

'Yer can do *anythin'* if yer puts yer mind to it.'

'Perhaps … if I went to see Mr Abrahams tomorrow? He always said he'd help.'

'No 'arm in askin'. I only wish *I* could be more 'elp t' yer with that side o' things. Mind you, I do 'ave a *little* money put by.'

'No, Peg. I couldn't.' Mary's face suddenly dropped. 'But I haven't anything to show – any drawings – it would take months to get enough.'

Peggy frowned. 'Yes, I did think you were a bit 'asty in tearin' up them pictures o' yours.' She crossed to the dresser and opened the door, taking out a thick roll of papers. 'Lucky you only tore 'em in 'alf,' she said, laying them on the table, 'or it'd 'ave cost me a month's wages in paste an' paper t' put 'em all back together again.'

*

Maggie was already in bed when Gwyneth entered the narrow bedroom they shared on the top floor of Pendragon. 'You're back then?' she said, half beneath the covers.

'Yes.'

'Well don't go thinkin' I've forgotten about you agreein' to fetch up the bath water – because I ain't.'

Gwyneth sighed. 'I haven't forgotten.'

'I should bloomin' hope not! A bargain's a bargain, y'know.'

'I said I'd do it, didn't I!'

The harsh edge to Gwyneth's voice brought Maggie up sharply, and she rolled over to face the wall. 'I hear you had a bit of bad luck,' she said after a pause.

Gwyneth began to unbutton her dress, keeping her back turned. 'You could say that.'

'Well, at least …' Maggie broke off, turning her head to listen, then she pushed back the bedclothes and sat up. 'Here, you ain't cryin' are you?'

'No … of course not.'

'You are.' Maggie came from her bed, her dark, frizzy hair loose and tangled. 'Look, you don't want to go upsettin' yourself like that.' She put a tentative hand on Gwyneth's shoulder. 'Tell you what. You can forget about the bath water if you like – I'll do it.'

Gwyneth turned to her, tears starting down her cheeks. 'Oh, Maggie … I've lost *everyone*.'

Maggie put her arms about her, awkwardly at first, then with a little more confidence as Gwyneth sobbed against her. 'It's alright …' she said, incapable of finding the right words.

'*Everyone*, Maggie.'

'I know,' said Maggie, softly. 'Lucy told us all about it. But maybe your mam'll get better?'

Gwyneth shook her head. 'I don't think she ever will.' She began to cry freely. 'She doesn't even know me, Maggie. Why did she have to go like that? Why?'

'Don't know. Must be a bit of a shock, I suppose – losin' all her family like that?'

'But she *didn't*, Maggie. She didn't lose *all* her family. She still had *me*, didn't she? She *still* had *me*.'

Chapter Twenty-Four

There was a greyish pallor about Mr Abrahams that disturbed Mary. Although he was dressed as immaculately as always, when he smiled, his expression was weary, and the hand he raised in welcome, trembled.

'It's good to see you, Mary,' he said, then letting go of the smile, 'I was so sorry to hear about your loss. A dreadful, dreadful thing. I didn't really know your husband, but he seemed a good man.'

'He was better than I deserved.'

Abrahams gave her a glance but did not pursue the matter, and minutes ticked by as the etiquette of bereavement was observed. Finally he said, 'If there is anything I can do.'

Almost guiltily she looked up, uncertain how to begin. 'You once said you would help me – to study, to carry on with my drawing?'

Abrahams lowered his gaze, his frail body seeming to crumple into his chair. 'Yes. But it's too late, Mary. I'm sorry.'

'No, it's not. I'm sure I can do it. Mrs Cartwright has kept all my sketches.'

He smiled briefly, seeing the spark of passion in her eyes, then the smile faded. 'It's too late for *me*, my dear.'

'For you?' she said, alarmed.

He looked toward the fire, avoiding her eyes. 'I'm penniless, Mary – or at least, I shall be very soon. It would appear I made some rather foolish investments. I've lost *everything*, and … well, that was the beginning of my heart trouble. The doctors have advised me to retire. My replacement arrives next week.'

Mary went to him, kneeling by his chair and holding his hands tightly in her own. 'I'm sorry. I would never have asked if I'd known.'

'It means everything to me that you *did* ask. I only wish …' he broke off, 'I only wish my circumstances were such that I could help.'

She reached up, touching her fingers to his lips. 'Don't, please. You've already done so much.'

'I feel I've let you down, Mary.'

'No, of course you haven't. I *shall* go to Cardiff – to that school.'

'But how?'

'I don't know. But I *shall* do it. I'm going to make you proud of me.'

'Mary, I've *always* been proud of you. But you have a child now, responsibilities. It's too late to go chasing dreams.'

'They say it's never too late.'

'Then they are terribly wrong. Even if the tuition fees were waived, you'd never survive without patronage of some kind.'

'I shall find a way.' She leaned forward to kiss his cheek. 'A long time ago you opened my eyes to things I'd thought impossible. Now it's up to me to make them happen.'

*

The Red Dragon public house was just as Mary remembered it: the sawdust floor sticky and wet; the air thick with tobacco smoke that lay like a fog above the heads of the rough-looking customers.

'I'm looking for Hettie Cruickshank,' she said, catching the eye of a thin-faced man who was polishing beer mugs with a filthy cloth.

'Are yer? What makes yer think we might know 'er?'

'I came here with her once ...'

'Oh, been 'ere before, 'ave yer?' He looked Mary up and down, 'Nah! You ain't been 'ere before. I'd 'ave remembered a looker like you, I would.'

'It was a long time ago. Two, no, nearly three years.'

'Get off with yer!' he chortled, 'Three years ago? What, suckin' on yer ol' mum's titties, were yer?'

'Oh, leave the girl alone, Sid,' chortled a fat woman propping up the bar, her chins wobbling with mirth. 'Can't you see she's straight out o' the convent and not used to your rough ways.'

'She'll soon learn 'em,' laughed her male companion, reaching round and giving Mary's right buttock a squeeze.

Mary leaped back, crashing into another woman.

'Now, look what yer've done, yer silly cow!' said Sid, the barman, leaning on the counter. 'Yer've gone an' spilled Ethel's drink.'

'What you playin' at, eh?' glared the woman named Ethel.

Mary backed away. 'I'm sorry. It was an accident. That man ... he touched me!'

'*That man ... he touched me!*' mimicked Ethel, putting her hand on her hip in a caricature of outraged virtue – then more dangerously, 'Listen, Miss Hoighty-toighty, you'd better buy me another gin or there'll be trouble, see.'

'Tell yer what,' said Sid, giving Mary a wink. 'You get them skirts up an' show us the drawers you *ain't* wearing, an' I'll buy yer both a drink.'

Mary continued to back away, eyes wide with fright, but her hands bunching into fists.

'Blimey, she's only goin' t' fight yer, Ethel!' laughed Sid. 'Now that's a turn up fer the books.'

'Please, I don't want to fight,' said Mary. 'I was just looking for someone.'

'Looking for a good hiding, more like,' laughed the fat woman.

'How about givin' me another squeeze of your bum, my love?' called the fat woman's companion as the other customers pulled back to form a ring. 'Before Ethel kicks it black and blue, like?'

Mary raised her open hands. 'Alright, alright. I'll buy you another drink.'

'Too bloody late!' said Ethel, pushing up her sleeves to reveal great, thick forearms. 'I'm goin' to rip your bloody hair out an' shove it right up your arse, see!'

'Atta girl, Ethel,' laughed Sid, perching himself on the bar.

Mary took another step back, but an unseen hand thrust her forward, sending her staggering toward Ethel who had begun to advance menacingly.

Regaining her balance, Mary backed away again. 'Please, don't …'

Another shove sent her forward again – then another – but this time she didn't retreat, but stood ready, her fists raised and a wild look in her eyes. 'Why can't you just leave me alone?' she hissed.

Ethel walked slowly forward, hitching up her skirts and spitting on to the sawdust. 'Come on then.'

Someone made a grab for Mary's arm, but she shrugged it off, keeping her eyes fixed defiantly on her opponent, her knuckles standing out white as she braced herself for the attack. There was another attempt to grab her, and this time a voice rose above the din, 'Here, what the bloody hell's going on?'

'Someone lookin' fer a *'Ettie Cruickshank*,' Sid called across the room. ''Course, we told 'er we don't know nothin' about no such person – but she wouldn't take no fer an answer.'

'Well, she wouldn't, would she, you daft bugger,' shouted Hettie. 'She's my bloody cousin!'

'No hard feelin's, I hope,' said Ethel, squeezing her bulk on to the bench next to Mary.

Wedged between Ethel and the fat woman from the bar, Mary shook her head, 'No,' she said, uncertainly, 'No, of course not.'

'It's just that we looks after our own around here, see, an' you never know how it is with strangers askin' questions.' She touched the side of her nose and winked.

'I've got to hand it to you,' said the fat woman, wobbling with laughter,

'Standing up to Ethel, like that.'

Hettie returned carrying four glasses of gin.

'I was just saying, Hettie,' called the fat woman. 'You've got to hand it to the girl – standing up for herself like that.'

Hettie bent forward, placing the drinks on the stained wooden table, then straightened up with an air of exasperation. 'Take your hand off my arse, Jim – I'm dying to sit down.'

The fat woman's companion grinned. 'How can a bloke resist such a lovely big handful?' He looked over to Mary. 'You want to put a bit o' meat on, girl. A bloke needs something to hang on to.'

'Oh, for Christ's sake, do something with him, Marge,' said Hettie, seeing Mary blush. 'He gets worse every day.'

Fat Marge leaned forward and took the man by the sleeve. 'Sit down and shut up, will you?'

'Here,' smiled Hettie, taking a seat and pushing one of the glasses toward Mary. 'Have a little loosener.'

Jim gave Mary another wink. 'No offence, my love. If I'd known you and Hettie was cousins, well – I wouldn't have grabbed you like that.' He gave a short laugh, 'I'd have waited until after we'd been introduced, like.'

Ethel tipped back her head and emptied her glass. 'One o' these days I'm goin' to catch your hand between the cheeks of my arse – an' crack it like a walnut,' she said darkly.

'I bet you would. That's why I never give you the pleasure of a little …' he grinned, making a grabbing motion in the air, '… *visitation.*'

Ethel looked at him. 'Get another round in, an' maybe I'll show you what you've been missin'.'

'What? *Fivepence* – for a *fumble!*' Jim looked shocked. 'Hettie'll do the whole works for a shillin' – Ow!' He reached down, rubbing his shin. 'What you go and do that for?'

'Don't know what you're talking about,' said Hettie, primly. 'So, Mary. What are you doing here? I heard you'd got yourself married.'

Mary shifted in her seat, trying to regain some of the self-assurance she'd felt on leaving Mr Abrahams that morning. 'I did,' she said. 'But there was an explosion – at the mine.'

'Killed was he?' asked Marge.

'Yes.'

Ethel looked into her empty glass. 'My husband died young.'

'Yes,' laughed Jim, 'but that was because *you* killed him.' He leaned toward Mary. '*Black Ethel* we call her – and it ain't on account of her hair colour, neither.'

'So what are you going to do now, my love?' asked Hettie.

Mary looked uncomfortable. 'I don't really know, but I need some-where to stay – in Cardiff – and I was wondering if you might have a room. I don't have very much, but I'd be willing to pay something. The thing is …'

'You come and stay with me,' grinned Jim. 'I've got a nice little room. You'll be very comfortable.'

'Don't you go listening to him,' laughed Hettie. 'He'd throw a fit if you was to take him up on the offer. Still lives with his old mam.' She pinched his cheek. '*Don't you, diddums.*'

Jim blushed, and Ethel and Marge roared with laughter, squeezing Mary between them in the process.

'The thing is …' Mary took a steadying sip of her gin. 'I've got a …'

Sid pushed into view. 'Oi,' he called cheerily, putting a hand on Hettie's shoulder. 'If you lot ain't drinkin' then you ain't stayin'! Yer can sling yer 'ooks an' let some payin' customers 'ave a seat.'

'It's alright,' laughed Hettie, 'Jimmy's just about to get a round in.' She turned to him. 'Off you go, there's a good boy.'

Still a little red in the face, he got to his feet. 'Same again, is it?' he asked, making his way to the bar without waiting for an answer.

'No, please, not for me,' Mary called after him, but he was already lost amongst the crowd.

Fat Marge gave her a nudge. 'You have it, my love. He's felt your goods, so he might as well pay for 'em.'

'An' tasty goods they are, too,' said Sid, chuckling at the blush that spread over Mary's cheeks.

Hettie rolled her eyes. 'Men! What can you do with them!'

'Well, if you lot don't know – then no bugger does.' Sid grinned, fixing his gaze on Mary. ''Ettie tells me you're Annie Kelly's girl.'

Marge's mouth fell open. 'Annie Kelly? You're Annie Kelly's kid?'

'Yes – did you know her?'

'Know her? Christ, everyone in here knew Annie Kelly.' She slapped a hand down on the table. 'Well, if that don't take the biscuit! Annie Kelly's kid coming in here and squaring up to Black Ethel – just like her old mam!'

'She was a scrapper, your ol' lady,' said Sid. ''Specially when the drink was on 'er. She blacked Ethel's eye once.'

'She did,' said Ethel. 'But it cost her a fistful of hair!'

'Didn't shove it up her arse, though, did you!' chuckled Marge. 'Lord, the things you come out with sometimes!'

'They say your mam was a looker in 'er younger days,' said Sid, eyeing Mary over. 'Never believed it m'self – well, not up until now, that is. That offer's still on, by the way.' He gave a leering smile. 'Drawers or no drawers.'

Hettie elbowed him roughly. 'Show a bit of respect, for Christ's sake. She's just lost her husband, hasn't she.'

'Actually … I'm not feeling very well,' said Mary, getting to her feet. 'Do you think we might go outside?'

'Yes, of course,' Hettie rose just as Jim arrived back with five glasses clutched precariously in his hands.

'Where you two goin'?'

'None of your business, *mama's boy*,' she giggled. 'But I'll have this before I go.' Taking a glass, she downed the contents in a single swallow, then smacked her lips. 'You sure you don't want yours, Mary?'

Already squeezing out from behind the table, Mary shook her head.

'Well, waste not, want not,' declared Hettie, taking a second glass and downing it just as quickly. 'See you, girls. Cheers, Jimmy. See you tomorrow, eh?' He nodded, and she leaned against him, whispering into his ear, quickly skipping away as he frantically tried to put the glasses on the table. 'You'll have to be quicker on the uptake than that,' she laughed, flicking her skirt up behind her as she went out into the street.

Mary was waiting for her, leaning unhappily against the wall. 'I ... I feel a bit sick.'

'Something you ate, was it, my love?'

'No ... well, I don't know – I suppose so.'

'They're a laugh, that lot, ain't they. You sure you don't want to go back in? It might buck you up a bit, like.'

'No,' Mary said quickly. Then, 'Maybe ... if we were to walk a little?'

Hettie pulled her shawl about her shoulders. 'As you like. Here, come on, we might as well go back to my place. Get you settled in, like.'

'You mean I can stay?'

''Course you can. We've got a spare room that we let out – but there's no one in it at the moment – and your mam would never have forgiven me if I let family go sleeping on the streets.'

'The thing is ... I've got a child.'

'What, here, now?'

'No, he's being looked after – by a friend in Caerphilly – but I've got to bring him with me.'

Hettie looked doubtful. 'Oh,' she said – then she brightened. 'Oh, that'll be alright. 'Course it will.'

It was Mary's turn to look doubtful. 'Perhaps you should ask your husband first?'

'No, he'll be sweet as pie. I know he likes you.'

Mary looked at her in surprise. 'But I've never met him.'

''Course you have,' laughed Hettie, putting her arm around Mary's shoulders and guiding her down the street. 'My husband's Sid – Sid Cruickshank – the barman.'

Chapter Twenty-Five

Mrs Cartwright was already in the kitchen when Mary came down, bleary-eyed, the next morning. 'Why didn't you wake me, Peggy?' she yawned. 'It's nearly nine o'clock.'

'You were back so late last night I thought I'd better let yer sleep.'

'But Owen?'

'Oh, 'e's right as ninepence.' Peggy nodded to where the boy was sitting amidst a pile of cushions, happily sucking on a biscuit. 'Me an' 'im 'as come to an *understandin'*, as it were.' She laughed. 'Been as good as gold, 'e 'as.'

Mary walked gingerly over to him. 'He looks so much better today, don't you think, Peg?'

''Course 'e does. 'E's not 'avin' t' breathe in all that bloomin' coal dust, is 'e.' Peggy filled the teapot then brought it over to the table. 'But what about you?'

'Me?'

'Yes, *you*. You ain't exactly lookin' fresh as a daisy this mornin', if yer don't mind me sayin' so.'

'Oh, I'm alright – just a bit tired, that's all.'

'I should think you are. It was gone midnight afore yer got back.' She poured two cups of tea, then went to the stove. 'Anyway, now you are up an' about – would yer like a bit o' bacon for yer breakfast?'

'Maybe a little later?'

Peggy gave a small shrug. 'So 'ow did it go in Cardiff yesterday? Did yer find this cousin o' yours?'

'Yes …'

'And?'

'And … it's alright.'

'So yer can stay there?'

Mary nodded.

'The two of yer?'

'Yes.'

'Blimey, Mary! This is worse than drawin' teeth! What's the place like, for 'eaven's sake?'

Mary looked uncomfortable. 'Well … it's very nice. It's quite a small house – but in a nice area. We shall have a room of our own – quite pretty, and it's at the back, so it looks out over the garden.'

'Oh, they got roses, 'ave they?'

'Yes … and sunflowers and … well, some other things.'

'Sounds very nice. So what line o' business is 'er 'usband in?'

'He's a barman … at a hotel.'

'Posh place, I bet.'

'Yes, it is quite. He says there might even be a job for me there – just in the evenings.'

'Oh, I see. Well, all you've got t' do is get yerself accepted at this 'ere drawin' school an' yer all set, eh?'

'Yes.'

Peggy walked slowly over and put a hand on Mary's shoulder. 'Now, why don't yer tell me what it's *really* like?'

Mary looked up at her, moist eyed. 'It's *awful*, Peg. *Horrible.* There are only two rooms and the place is filthy.'

'I take it the 'usband don't work at no 'otel, neither?'

'He *is* a barman … but at this dreadful pub.'

'That's where you 'ad a bit too much t' drink, was it?'

Mary blushed guiltily. 'How did you know about that?'

'I 'eard yer stumblin' about when yer came in, so I looked in on yer, just t' make sure you was alright.'

'I don't remember.'

'That don't surprise me. You was fast asleep by the time I got there – still in yer clothes – an' reekin' of gin.'

'It wasn't my fault, Peggy. I wanted to come straight home after I'd seen the room, but Hettie said it would be better if we went back and told her husband right away about me coming to stay – because he'd be more likely to agree – what with Owen and everything. So we did – but then when we got there …'

'Alright, alright,' said Peggy, making a quietening gesture. 'Blimey, one minute I can't get a word out of yer – an' the next …' She shook her head sadly, then sat down. 'What bothers me is that you left 'ere yesterday brimmin' with confidence – but now, this mornin', yer look like a whipped dog – an' I think it's more than just an 'angover.'

'I can't go back there, Peg. I can't.'

'So where else can yer afford t' stay in Cardiff?'

'Nowhere.'

'Then it seems to me you either make the best of it – or give up afore yer've even started.' She reached for Mary's hand. 'Alright, so the place is dirty – that's what soap an' water was put on this earth for. If they won't clean it, then you'll 'ave to. Gawd knows, yer've 'ad practice enough.'

'But the people, Peg. They're …'

'They're just *people*. Some yer like, some yer don't. That's the same the world over – 'ceptin' in London, o' course.'

Mary gave half a smile. '*Where even the littlest mites 'as umbrellas?*'

'Yes,' chuckled Peggy. 'An' everyone's got a smile on their face an' a pound in their pocket.'

'I wish *I* was going to London.'

'You an' me, both. But we ain't. I'm stayin' 'ere – an' you're goin' t' Cardiff t' make somethin' of yourself.' She fixed Mary with a firm look. 'An' yer goin' t' do whatever yer 'ave t' do – am I right?'

Mary felt the confidence trickling back. 'Yes, I *will*,' she said, looking over to where Owen was still engrossed with his biscuit, 'I owe *him* that much.'

'Yer do.' Peggy got to her feet. 'But yer also owe it to yerself. Yer only get one life, Mary. Now – do yer want that bacon yet?'

Suddenly hungry, Mary nodded.

'Good,' said Peggy. 'An' when yer done, we'll take a little walk along the 'igh street. There's a dress I saw yesterday – it's second 'and, but it looks as if it won't 'ardly need no alteration t' fit yer – an' if it don't impress this chap at the school – then I don't know what will!'

*

Number fourteen Cutler Street was a two up and two down house in a grimy terrace, hemmed in on all sides by dozens of equally grimy terraces. In good weather the smell from the nearby tanneries pervaded every nook and cranny, while in bad weather the changing winds brought the odour of tar, coal and rank estuary mud from the docks.

In the back room, Sid Cruickshank rolled over in bed, his right hand sleepily exploring the vacant space next to him. He opened one eye, squinting at the light. 'What bleedin' time is it?'

'Ten o'clock,' said Hettie, buttoning the neck of her blouse.

'Ten o' bleedin' clock? In the *mornin'*?'

''Course I mean in the morning.'

'Well what the bloody 'ell are yer doin' up this early?'

'I was going to clean the place up a bit, that's all. Mary's coming this afternoon, remember?'

He lay back, a slow grin spreading across his face. 'Oh, yes I remember 'er, all right. 'Ere, 'ow much did yer tell 'er? Fer the room?'

Hettie glanced at him uneasily. 'Two shillings.'

'Two bob! What, a week?'

'She can't afford much, Sid.'

'So what! This ain't the bleedin' poor-'ouse! Bloody 'ell, I must 'ave been 'alf cut last night or I'd never 'ave agreed to it.' He sat up in the bed, scratching his head. 'An' another thing. That business – about 'er 'avin a kid – it *was* a bleedin' joke, wasn't it?'

'No ... no, she's got a baby. About nine months it is now, I reckon.'

'I don't care if it's two years with bleedin' 'ard labour! We ain't 'avin it 'ere. What the 'ell was yer thinkin' of, 'Ettie?'

'She's *family!*'

Groaning, he let his head fall back against the wall. 'Bloody 'ell!' Then he smirked. 'She is a looker, though. I s'pose I could always let 'er work off the rest of the rent money – know what I mean?'

'Don't you dare even think of it.'

'What? Don't fancy a nice, cosy threesome, then?'

'Sid!'

'It'd be a sort of family get-together?' He gave a laugh, 'We could 'ave Bert bring 'is piano round an' give us some musical accompaniment.'

Hettie began to giggle. 'You're a dirty sod!'

'I think yer might be right,' he grinned, lifting the blanket and peering beneath. 'Well – *someone's* goin' to 'ave t' take care of this stiff little bugger.' He gave her a wink. 'So it's either you – or that stuck-up cousin o' yours.'

Hettie's fingers went to the buttons at her waist. 'Reckon it's going to have to be me, then.'

'So what about the bleedin' cleanin'?'

The skirt fell about her ankles. 'Sod that,' she laughed.

*

Peggy Cartwright looked along the track at the distant finger of smoke that heralded the arrival of the Cardiff train. 'What time's the next one?' she asked anxiously – then without waiting for a reply, 'Look, why don't we go 'ome an' 'ave a nice cup o' tea before yer go? I've made some cake – an' yer could get the train after this. It wouldn't matter if yer went that bit later, would it?'

Mary touched the old woman's arm. 'I don't think I'd ever leave if I went home with you now.'

Peggy nodded, sighing heavily. 'Yes, yes, 'course you're right.' She leaned to kiss Owen on the cheek. 'You be a good boy, now. I don't want to 'ear about you not eatin' again – or I shall be comin' down t' Cardiff an' givin' yer what-for, m'lad.'

The train arrived in a welter of steam and noise, the harsh hiss and pant of the engine giving way to the banging of doors as passengers disembarked.

''Ere, you be careful with that!' Peggy called to the porter as he shoved the trunk containing Mary's worldly possessions into the guard's van.

He shot her a sideways glance, gave the trunk another hard shove and slammed the door. 'You'll have to board now, miss,' he said.

With Owen in her arms, Mary climbed into the train. 'Thank you, Peggy. Thank you so very much.'

'Never mind about all that. You just remember what I told yer, y'hear?'

Mary nodded. '*Whatever it takes.*'

'Oh, an' it might be best if yer didn't go mentionin' yer little stay at the 'otel t' the Llewellyns.' She tapped the side of her nose. '*What the eye don't see, the 'eart don't grieve over*, my ol' dad used to say.'

'It'll be our secret.'

Peggy's smile trembled on her lips. 'Look after yerself, Mary.'

The train jolted into movement, and Mary watched the waving figure of Mrs Cartwright grow smaller and smaller, becoming little more than a speck before vanishing completely into the distance. 'I think,' she whispered into Owen's ear, 'the heart grieves *most* for what the eye doesn't see.'

*

In the heat of mid-afternoon, the four-wheeled growler pulled into Cutler Street and came to a halt outside number fourteen.

'That'll be sixpence,' called the driver without looking round.

Holding on to Owen, Mary squeezed from the musty interior and stepped down on to the pavement. It was a hot, airless day, and she had to shield her eyes from the sun as she looked up to where the man was sitting. 'Would you help me in with my trunk, please?'

The cabbie tutted irritably, climbed down, retrieved the box and dropped it on to the road. 'Sixpence,' he said again.

Mary's fingers tightened about the shilling she'd taken from her purse. 'Please – keep the change,' she said stiffly, handing him the coin.

The cabbie glanced at it in the palm of his hand, then he pushed it into his waistcoat pocket as a smile lifted the corners of his thin lips. 'Oh, thank you very much. Very kind, it is. Take your trunk in for you shall I?'

'Yes … please,' she said, surprised by his sudden change of attitude.

With difficulty he lifted the box up on to the pavement, then dragged it to the front door. 'Just moving in, is it?' He lifted his face to the sky and sniffed. 'Doesn't always smell so bad as this. Pretty strong it is today, like, but then there's no wind, see? Mind, I've known it worse.'

'Yes, I'm sure,' said Mary, a little brusquely, finding the ingratiating friendliness almost as unpleasant as his previously sullen manner.

'Ah, here we are,' he smiled as the front door swung open, and Hettie came out into the street. 'Just take it through shall I?'

'In the front room,' said Hettie. 'And mind you don't break anything.' She watched him struggle along the narrow passageway, then turned to Mary. 'This your kid then? Well, he's not so very big, is he. Sid won't hardly know he's here.' She gave Owen's cheek a little squeeze. 'Come on, I'll put the kettle on – unless you'd rather go down the pub?'

'No … tea would be nice.'

The cabbie emerged, red-faced and panting. 'There you are, all safe and sound – and nothing broken.'

'A good thing, too,' said Hettie.

'Well, I'll just be on my way then, shall I?' He stood expectantly, his fingers working in anticipation of another tip, but Hettie was already ushering Mary inside. 'We can manage on our own now,' she said over her shoulder.

The man looked disappointed. 'Oh, you're certain, are you?'

'Yes, quite certain. Thank you very much,' she said, slamming the front door with a backward kick. 'Christ, Mary. How much did you tip him?'

'Sixpence.'

Hettie laughed. 'Thought as much. You don't get that kind of civility for under a tanner, these days.' She made her way into the front room and stood looking at the trunk. 'There aren't no more boxes coming, are there? Because I don't know where we'll put them if there are.'

'No, there's just this one.'

'Well, that's alright then.' Hettie looked about the room. 'I was going to have a bit of a clear up, but – well, you know how it is. Cosy, though, eh?'

Mary looked about her. In the lamplight of the previous evening the room had seemed dank and depressing with its stained, dirty wall paper, grimy boards and rusting iron bedstead, but now, with the sunlight filtering through the dusty glass, it looked a hundred times worse. Slowly she nodded.

'There's the lavvy out the back. Make sure you get in there of a morning before old misery guts upstairs.' Hettie motioned with her eyes toward the ceiling. 'Spends hours in there, she does – and stinks the place out something chronic.' She laughed, wafting her hand under her nose. 'Anyway, I expect you must be gasping. Come on, I'll make that tea.'

They moved into the back room. 'Sod it, the fire's gone out,' said Hettie, slumping on the unmade bed. 'You sure you wouldn't rather go to the pub? Sid's down there.'

'No, really. Actually, I'm a little tired – and Owen could probably do with a nap. But you go, if you like.'

Hettie brightened and got to her feet. 'Well, if you're sure you don't mind.' She crossed to where Mary was standing just inside the door and ruffled Owen's hair. 'He's a quiet little mite.'

'He's not been well – but he's getting better now.'

'That's nice. Well, make yourself at home, eh? I'll bring something in for tea. Fancy a bloater?'

'Please, there's no need to bother. I can buy something.'

Hettie was already half way to the front door. 'Oh, it's no bother. See you later then, eh?'

'Yes, alright.'

'There's a key on the mantelpiece,' she called – then she was gone.

Holding Owen to her chest, Mary looked about the empty room. Apart from the muddle of personal effects – clothes, empty bottles, dirty plates and rumpled bed clothes – it was little different to the one next door.

She went to the fire, raking it over in the hope of finding a few embers that could be re-kindled, and was rewarded with a dull red glow from deep inside the pile of ash. 'We'll soon get this going again, won't we, my love,' she said, straightening up. 'Come on, let's find you somewhere to sit, eh?'

Going to the bed she pulled the blanket up, covering the stained sheets, then sat Owen on top of it. 'Comfy, my little one? Good. So! Tea first – then it's set to with hot water and soap.' She put some kindling on to the embers, added some coal, then searched for the kettle, finding it half beneath the bed. 'And we'd better make a good job of it or we'll have Mrs Cartwright to answer to.'

*

It was early evening before Hettie returned, pushing open the front door and weaving down the passageway, coming to an uncertain halt outside Mary's room. 'Blimey,' she said, nudging open the door and staggering against the frame. 'You've been a busy little bee, haven't you!' She hiccupped, grinning foolishly. 'All nice and clean, eh?'

Mary got to her feet, wiping her sleeve across her forehead, the scrubbing brush still in her hand. 'Just tidying up,' she said with a tired smile.

''Course you are.' With some effort, Hettie managed to find her nose with her finger, giving it a sideways tap. 'I didn't forget, you know. Come on, I got something nice for tea. Sid's just bringing it.' She turned to look at the bed where Owen lay asleep. 'And bring the little 'un with you. Plenty to go round.'

'I won't wake him just now,' said Mary, coming to the door. 'I went to the shop earlier, so he won't be hungry just yet.'

Hettie pushed herself erect. 'Suit yourself. Come on then.' She turned, swayed uncertainly, then fell flat on her face in the passage.

'Silly cow!' laughed Sid, lounging on the bed next to the semi-conscious Hettie. He gave her a hard nudge. ''Ere, get a whiff o' that bloater! Lovely, eh?'

Hettie groaned, her cheeks puffing out as she made to vomit. 'Take it away!' She waved a hand blindly. 'For God's sake, take it away.'

'Alright, alright,' Sid chuckled, wafting the plate in front of her face one final time. 'I'll give it an 'ome. Come t' me, m'beauty.' He broke away a portion of the fish with his fingers and pushed it into his mouth, chewing noisily. 'Silly cow never could 'old 'er drink. Not like your mum. Now *she* could drink all night an' *still* turn a trick!'

Mary looked down at her plate, picking at her food to cover her embarrassment. 'Do you have any knives and forks?' she asked.

'Somewhere,' said Sid. He belched loudly, then shoved another wedge in his mouth, eyeing her as he chewed. 'She did alright, your mum. She weren't no looker – not by a long chalk – not like you. But she did alright.'

'She wasn't always like that.'

'Who is, eh?' He gave a laugh. 'An' who bloody cares? It's 'ow yer end up s'all that matters in this life, gel. Your mum did alright fer 'erself. She made money.' He stopped chewing. 'But with my 'elp, *you* could make a lot more.'

Mary stared at him.

'Oh, don't give me that wide-eyed look,' he sneered. 'You're Annie Kelly's kid, ain't yer? Got 'er blood in yer veins – an' yer can't go against that, no matter 'ow 'ard yer try.'

On the bed, Hettie groaned, bubbles of spittle foaming on her dry lips, and Sid gave her a shove. 'Shut up, fer Chris' sake. Can't yer see I'm 'avin a conversation.'

'Sid,' Hettie groaned again, her face the colour of putty. Weakly, she made to get up, her arms trembling with the effort, then her mouth opened and a gush of thick, ginny liquid spewed forth.

'Jesus bloody Christ!' yelled Sid, tossing his plate aside – then he was on his feet, dragging Hettie toward the door. 'Not in 'ere yer don't, yer dirty bitch!'

He'd barely taken three steps when there came a sharp rapping from the room above. 'An' *you* can shut yer bloody noise, yer dried up ol' bag!' he shouted fiercely, but the rapping continued with renewed fervour, and he raised his eyes to the ceiling, pulling on Hettie's arm all the while. 'Shut up! Shut up or I'll ram that stick down yer bleedin' throat! See if I don't!' Hettie stumbled, on the point of passing out, and he wrapped his arm around her waist, hauling her from the room. 'Don't you faint on me, gel, or I'll bleedin' well swing fer yer!' He jerked his head toward the room above. 'I'll swing fer the bleedin' pair o' yer!'

Appalled, Mary jumped up and ran to the door, watching as Sid hustled Hettie down the unlit passage, their bodies swaying back and forth like two macabre dancers, while in the room above the old woman continued to beat her tattoo.

She put her hands to her ears, trying to shut out the incessant banging, the smell of vomit filling her senses, then in despair she ran to her room and locked the door.

Owen was stirring fitfully on the bed, roused by the noise, and she went to him, curling up by his side, holding him and nuzzling him gently as she wept silently into her pillow.

*

I cried that night, and for several nights after. Not because of Sid, or Hettie, or the foul conditions in which we lived, nor for myself and everything I had lost. I cried for Owen. I cried because I had brought him to a life of squalor, ugliness and violence – a life of mean pleasures and mean spirits – a life that would surely be his if I were to fail in the task I'd set myself.

But if I feared for his future, I feared even more in the days that followed for his increasingly terrifying present.

*

Mary awoke with a start. 'Owen? Owen, are you alright?'

It was past midnight, but a street lamp cast its glow through the window, and by its light she could just make out the tortured features of her son.

'Owen?' There was panic in her voice as she caught the small, choking gasps. 'Owen, my love?'

With shaking hands she found a match and lit the candle that stood on the dresser, then she picked the boy up, hugging him to her as he fought for breath, his arms writhing, pushing against her in frantic torment. 'It's alright, it's alright,' she soothed, walking up and down the tiny room. 'Please, my love, don't keep frightening your mama, like this. *Please.*' But his breathing only became more laboured, and clutching him tightly to her she pulled open the door and felt her way along the pitch-dark passage toward the back room.

'I have to have a doctor,' she said as Hettie answered the urgent knock, her face a sickly grey in the light from the candle she was holding.

'What, now?'

'Yes. Right away. It's Owen.'

Hettie looked doubtful. 'I don't know … it's the middle of the night.'

'There has to be one around here somewhere.'

'Yes, but,' she caught the sound of Owen's distressed breathing. 'Can't you give him a drop of gin or something? Keep him quiet till the morning?'

'I need a doctor *now,* Hettie.'

'Alright, alright, I'm trying to think.'

A board creaked in the room above.

'Oh, hell,' whispered Hettie, looking nervously over her shoulder. 'Sid'll go bonkers if that old cow wakes him up.' Gingerly, she put a hand to her bruised cheekbone, running her fingers over it as she tried to think. 'There's a doctor up toward the High Street. Between the knacker's yard and the Lord Napier – on the corner of Monmouth Street. Think you can find it?' She saw Mary's uncertain look, and ducked back into the room, 'Hang on a minute – I'll come with you.'

*

'That will be two shillings and sixpence – and please be good enough to wait until the usual hours in future.'

Sitting in the dingy surgery, Mary took the half-crown from her purse. 'I'm sorry, but I was so worried. He's never been as bad as this. I thought he was going to die.'

The doctor turned a morose eye upon her as he washed his hands at the sink. 'We are all going to die sooner or later.'

'But he will he be alright now?'

'The medicine I've given him will ease the condition – but no, he won't.'

Mary's arms tightened about the boy, making him stir restlessly against her breast. 'There must be something you can do?'

'Do you have any money?' He rinsed his hands, then dried them. 'Because if you do, then I would advise you to move away from Cardiff and take him somewhere the air is clean, and preferably dry and warm. Once you are there, you must ensure he has a rich diet – lots of red meat, eggs, cream, a little wine, perhaps. Can you afford to do that?'

Slowly, Mary shook her head.

'In that case I stand by my original prognosis, and suggest you do not get too attached to the child.'

'He's my son, for God's sake!' Angrily, she got to her feet. 'How can you be so … so callous?'

'Necessity – and years of practice.'

She looked at him in disbelief – then with contempt. 'I'm sorry you've been troubled,' she said, snatching up the medicine bottle and making to leave.

'So am I,' he replied, his voice empty of emotion. 'When the symptoms return, my advice is to stay at home. It will be cheaper in the long run and save the child a deal of …' The slamming of the door cut him short.

For a few moments he stood looking around the dilapidated surgery, then he turned off the gas and made his way wearily up the stairs. At the second landing he paused, looking into the room that had once been his wife's – untouched these past months and growing dusty in the absence of a maid. Then he began to climb again, up to the nursery where his daughter lay coughing – fresh spots of blood staining her sheets.

He leaned forward and mopped her brow, wiping away the beads of perspiration for the thousandth time, then he put aside the towel and picked up the pillow he'd brought from his own bed. 'I'm sorry my angel,' he said. 'I'm so very sorry.'

'So what did he say?' asked Hettie as they made their way home through the dark and empty streets.

Holding Owen tight to her chest, Mary made no answer. Anger was fast giving way to tears, and she did not trust herself to speak.

'Only it's about looking after him, like,' continued Hettie. The night air had brought back something of her old colour, but now fresh worries were sallowing her complexion. 'I mean, I wouldn't mind looking after the kid during the day – if he was well, like – but if he's going to be ill all the time, well … Sid don't like the arrangement as it is, and …'

'It's alright,' said Mary, staring straight ahead. 'I know what I have to do.'

Chapter Twenty-Six

A photograph of Evan stood on the morning-room table, expensively framed in worked silver. He was looking straight into the camera lens, his formal expression softened by a tiny creasing at the corners of his eyes and an almost imperceptible smile. It was the same look of secret amusement Mary had grown to know so well, and she felt an ache of longing as she looked at it.

'So, Mrs Kelly?' said Florence, seating herself on the couch opposite, 'My housekeeper tells me you wish to see me on a personal matter?'

Wearing the dress Mrs Cartwright had bought her, Mary nodded nervously, patting Owen's back as he lay against her breast. 'It's very good of you to see me, Mrs Rees-Morgan. I know how very busy you must be and …' Annoyed with herself, she bit her lip. 'It's about my son, Owen,' she began again in a less diffident tone. 'He's been ill for a long time – but he seems to be getting worse, and I'm afraid that if he doesn't get help soon, he'll die.'

Florence looked with sympathy, first at the boy, then at Mary. 'I do understand, but it's my husband you need to consult, and unfortunately he is unavailable at present.' She made to rise. 'However, I could arrange an appointment for you, if you wish?'

'I should like the doctor to examine him, of course, but …'

Florence settled on to the couch once more, leaning forward slightly. 'Is it a matter of money?' she asked quietly.

'In a way … yes.' Mary looked down at her lap.

'Peut–être vous préféreriez le français?' prompted Florence, giving the briefest glance toward the door. 'S'il s'agit d'une question délicate?'

Embarrassment coloured Mary's cheeks. 'I'm sorry, I don't speak French.'

'Well, it is of no consequence,' Florence smiled reassuringly. 'We shall not be overheard, and I promise that whatever you tell me will go no further than these four walls.'

Mary looked into the woman's eyes. 'You're very kind,' she said, suddenly sorry for the news she was about to unleash. 'I only wish …' she paused, mustering her resolve, then turned Owen about, positioning him on her lap so that Florence might gaze fully upon him. 'He looks very much like his father,' she said softly, 'don't you think?'

Surprise rippled the calm surface of Florence's countenance. 'I'm sorry, but I don't believe we are acquainted with your husband.'

'No,' said Mary. 'But my husband wasn't Owen's father.'

'I see.' There was neither criticism nor condemnation in Florence's voice, but then as she looked into Owen's face there came an awful glimmer of understanding. 'So … what exactly are you saying?'

'He's Evan's baby – your grandchild.'

'Nonsense! That's preposterous!'

'Surely you can see it?'

Florence tore her eyes from the boy, and quickly stood. 'I can see nothing of the sort – and I should like you to leave now.'

'You only have to look at him to …'

'I can have you put from the house if you would prefer,' Florence said brusquely, reaching for the bell.

Mary got to her feet. 'No, it's alright. I'll go. I don't wish to make this difficult for you.' She paused, looking searchingly at Florence. 'I didn't want to come here today – I was terrified to come. I knew how unwelcome this news would be – but I had no choice. Without help, Owen is going to die, and I must find Evan – even if it means searching every street in Paris.' She made to leave. 'Thank you for seeing me, Mrs Rees-Morgan. I'm very sorry to have troubled you.'

'Wait.' Florence crossed to the window, standing in silence, her hands clasped tightly in front of her. 'Perhaps …' she said at last, 'perhaps you'll tell me under what circumstances you met my son?'

'I was his assistant at the clinic in Cardiff.'

'I see,' she stared out through the tall windows. 'But that was more than eighteen months ago – why is it only now you choose to come to us?'

'I was married, and at the time there was no need for anyone to know – not even Evan. But now Owen needs more than I can give him. If he doesn't get it, he's going to die – and I have no one else I can turn to.'

'What about your husband?'

'He's dead.'

'Oh,' said Florence, more softly, 'I'm sorry.' She left the window and came to stand in front of Mary. 'So, what is it you want? Is it money?'

'No – I don't want your money! Not for me!'

'Then what?'

'I want Owen to *live*. I still love Evan, and I believe he still loves me – and I'll wait for all eternity to be with him if that's what it takes. But it will be too late for our son. All I ask is that you contact Evan for me. *Please.*'

'And what if he denies all knowledge of you?'

'He won't.'

'You seem very sure.'

Mary felt for the chain about her neck, holding up the small gold heart for Florence to see. 'The man who gave me this won't deny me.'

'*Ble'r ei di, fe af finnau,*' read Florence. '*Where you go – I will go.* A pretty sentiment.' She sighed, letting the pendant fall back against Mary's dress, then looked long and hard at the child. 'He does look so very much like Evan.'

'Then you *do* believe me?'

'I'm not sure what I believe.' She continued to gaze down at Owen. 'But perhaps there are, after all, sufficient grounds to warrant writing to my son.'

'That's all I ask. Thank you. Thank you so *very* much.'

'But you must realise it is not my decision. I shall have to discuss this with Dr Rees-Morgan, and it is he who will decide.'

'Yes. Of course.'

'My husband will be back this evening, and I shall talk to him the moment he returns. Could you come back tomorrow morning? Shall we say at eleven?' Florence reached out, taking Mary's arm and leading her to the door. 'And rest assured that I shall do whatever I can to persuade him.'

*

Ivor bent to warm his hands by the evening fire. 'She actually came here? To this house?'

Sitting in perfect calm upon the chaise-longue, Florence watched him. She had long since learned to gauge his mood, and knew he was profoundly displeased. 'Yes,' she said.

'The damned hussy! What was she after? Money I suppose!' He crossed to the table and poured himself a large brandy. 'I hope you sent her off with a flea in her ear!'

'I said I would discuss the matter with you.'

'Did you, by God! Well consider the matter *discussed*, madam!' He took a deep draught, then banged the glass back on to the polished mahogany. 'Damn me, but it comes to a pretty state of affairs when a fourpenny whore can come to a man's front door and demand payment for a two year old tumble!'

Having anticipated her husband's reaction, Florence let the torrent of abuse pass unheeded.

'When she comes back tomorrow,' Ivor continued, jamming his hand into his trouser pocket and withdrawing a few pennies, 'you can give her this!' He tossed the coins on to the seat by his wife's side. 'And tell her to get the money *first*, next time!'

'I'm afraid it is a little more complicated than that.' Florence looked calmly up at him. 'There is a child.'

Ivor's eyes widened, then he raised them to the ceiling, exhaling in a great, noisy sigh. 'Evan's?'

'Yes, I believe so.'

'God damn the boy! God damn him to hell and back again!' He returned to the fire, hands clasped behind his back as he stared into the flames – then he half turned. 'How can we be sure it's actually his?'

'He gave her a pendant,' said Florence. 'An *inscribed* pendant.' On her lap lay the family bible, and she ran her fingers over the leather binding with its tooled crest. '*Ble'r ei di, fe af finnau*,' she said. 'It has been my family's motto for nearly two hundred years.'

'It proves nothing!'

'No,' she said quietly, 'It doesn't.'

Ivor scratched at his side-whiskers. 'What's she like – this girl? Pretty is she?'

'She is *attractive* – but poor. Quite possibly destitute. I recognised the dress she was wearing as a cast-off I donated to a charity for the homeless.'

'Hell and damnation!' He slammed the flat of his hand on to the mantel-shelf. 'Well, I suppose I had better see her. If it *is* Evan's child, then he must come back and face the consequences.'

Florence looked up. 'You would actually write to him about this?'

'Of course.'

'But … surely we must consider his position?'

'Position be damned! He should have thought about that before he went dipping his wick. It would serve the damned fool right if he had to marry her.' He gave a mirthless laugh. 'But it won't come to that. She'll settle for money, and Evan can be back in Paris inside the week.'

'But what if she *won't*?' said Florence, losing her last ounce of composure. 'Do we *have* to write to Evan at all?'

Ivor's brows drew into a frown. 'Yes, damn it, we do! I'd have happily horsewhipped the pair of them to prevent this – *fiasco*! But it's too late. The deed is done, and I'll not have him hiding from his responsibilities like some wheedling, spineless fop! By God, I won't! He'll come back here and pay her off himself!'

'Ivor, please,' Florence went a ghostly white. 'There must be another way?'

He gave her an inquiring look. 'What exactly is it you want from me, madam? You've pleaded the girl's case – and I've agreed to see her. What *more* do you want?'

She put a hand to her head. 'I … I don't know.'

Ivor's eyes narrowed in suspicion. 'Or were you supposing I'd devise some underhand scheme to get rid of her without causing a scandal – and without Evan ever needing to know? Is that it? Have *me* deal with it so you can continue to play the charitable lady with a clear conscience?' He saw the guilt in her eyes. 'By God, that's it, isn't it! You care less about this … this *doxy* than I do – and you've played me like a fish, thinking to keep your hands clean of the matter.' He thrust his thumbs deep into the pockets of his waistcoat. 'Well, Evan *will* face up to his responsibilities. When the girl comes tomorrow, you'll keep her here until I return. If the child is what she claims, we will then decide on the best course of action. Is that clear?'

Shaken, Florence nodded, refusing to meet his eyes.

'*Charity*!' he snorted, pouring himself another brandy. 'Damned hypocrisy! Look after the poor and needy, is it?' He took a long draught, then turned to look at her. 'But be damned sure to keep them below stairs, eh?'

*

Florence had lain awake most of the night, and by mid-morning was beginning to feel the effect. She looked at her reflection in the huge gilt-framed mirror, noting the dark smudges beneath her eyes. It was not a flattering picture – but there was consolation in that it was, at least, more suited to the task in hand.

The morning-room clock struck the quarter, and she sighed. The girl was fifteen minutes late, but it was too early to hope she would not come at all, and the idea was dashed from her mind as there came a knock at the door.

'The lady is here, ma'am,' Gwyneth announced, an almost apologetic look on her face.

Florence gave her a weak smile, noting the imperceptible emphasis on the word *lady*. Under any other circumstance, she would have quietly remonstrated with her, but now she felt oddly reassured by it. 'Please show her in, Gwyneth,' she said.

'I'm sorry I'm late,' said Mary the moment she entered. 'The train was delayed and …' She stopped, conscious of both the poor image she was presenting, and Gwyneth's silent criticism.

Florence smiled politely. 'It is a lady's prerogative. Won't you please sit down?'

Mary sat, settling Owen on her shoulder, drawing back her feet and adjusting her skirt to cover her worn boots.

'Might I offer you some tea?'

'No … thank you.'

Florence seated herself. 'Gwyneth, will you please see to it that we aren't disturbed.'

'Yes, ma'am. Of course, ma'am.'

'It's a beautiful morning,' said Florence, as soon as Gwyneth had withdrawn. 'So very warm for the time of year, don't you think?'

'Yes.'

'And your journey? Not too tiresome, I trust?'

'No, not really.'

With the greatest reluctance, Florence gave up the small pleasantries and prepared herself for the unpalatable task ahead. 'Well,' she began, her hands tightening their grip on each other as they lay in her lap. 'I have spoken to my husband and ...' she paused, steeling herself, '... and, it *isn't* good news I'm afraid. He refuses even to see you.'

Hope faded from Mary's eyes. 'He won't write to Evan?'

'No. I'm so *terribly* sorry.'

'Couldn't *you* write to him?' Mary clutched Owen to her, desperation creeping into her voice.

'He has forbidden me to ever mention so much as your name to my son – and I cannot possibly go against his instructions. You must understand that?'

For a moment, Mary seemed to crumple, then anger stiffened her resolve. 'What about *my* son?'

'I wish I could do more.'

'Then give me Evan's address. *I'll* write to him.'

Florence looked uncomfortable. 'Oh dear – this is very awkward. The thing of it is, you see – he's *married*.'

It was as though Mary had been struck. 'Married?'

'Yes. In Paris last year. I'm sorry, I should have mentioned it yesterday, but after the way you talked of Evan – well, I just didn't know how to tell you.'

'I ... I see.'

'It must be a great shock to you.'

Mary looked about the expensively furnished room as if for the first time, tears blurring her vision. Evan was married, and the beautiful, impossible dreams she had harboured were exposed for what they were: fanciful lies that floated about her like the thrown pages of an essay. *Facts! Mary Kelly. Facts and only facts! That's what you need in this world! Not damn fairytales.* She shivered. Griffiths's words were true – starkly and undeniably – and with the realisation came a clear, cold calm. Slowly she took Owen from her shoulder. 'Take my son,' she said very deliberately. 'Please.'

Florence stared at her. 'Take him?'

'If he stays with me, he *will* die.'

'I couldn't possibly.' Florence got to her feet.

'He's Evan's child. Your grandson. He has a chance with you.'

'It's completely out of the question. My husband would never hear of such a thing.'

'It's *me* he doesn't want – and I can understand that. But Owen is his own flesh and blood. You could convince him – tell him I abandoned the boy, and you had no choice.'

Florence wrung her hands in agitation. Throughout the long night she had meticulously thought through her plan, but such a development had never entered her head. 'It's quite impossible,' she protested weakly. 'Evan? How could I keep it from him?'

'It could be done. Evan need never know. You could adopt Owen as a foundling – as an act of charity. No one else need ever know the truth.'

Florence looked down at the boy's familiar features and felt the first small pang of longing. 'But the likeness?'

'A coincidence – the very thing that brought him to your attention.'

Florence stared at her. 'How can you possibly do this – *so calmly*?'

'What choice do I have?'

'But you're giving away your only child.'

'I'm not giving him away – I'm giving him a chance to live.'

There was an intensity to Mary's eyes that chilled Florence – lifting the hairs on the back of her neck. 'And what about you?' she asked nervously.

'I'd go away. Back to Cardiff. You'd never see me again.'

Beyond the tall morning-room windows, the sun crept above the elms, flooding the room with light. '*A coincidence*,' she mused, warmed by more than the sun's rosy glow. 'We could make that work.'

*

'God, it makes your toes curl, it does.' Fat Marge shivered despite the stifling heat of the Red Dragon's smoky, airless bar. 'Fancy doing a thing like that!'

Seated next to her on the bench, her thick forearms resting on the beer stained table, Black Ethel nodded. 'Killin' yourself is one thing, but that? Well, it takes some guts, that does.'

'Takes somethin', alright,' grinned Jim, looking up from the newspaper. 'Just imagine?' He placed the back of his thumb against the side of his neck then drew it across his throat. 'One great big slice! Ear to ear!'

Marge gave another shudder 'Oh, give it over. It don't bear thinking about!'

'Just as well he did, though. He'd have hanged for sure after smotherin' that kid of his.'

'But she was dying anyway, wasn't she?'

'Don't matter,' said Jim, 'Not in the eyes o' the law, like. Don't you remember all that hullabaloo in the papers a while back? The girl from down by the docks that cut her own mother's throat?'

'Ooh, proper sinful that was,' said Marge. 'Her own blooming mother! I don't know how you could live with yourself after doing such a thing, that I don't.'

'She might have killed her mam,' said Ethel, 'but she didn't kill herself, did she.'

Jim put down the paper. 'I never said she did, did I?'

'She was a sight more clever than this doctor chap o' yours. She was off an' away right sharpish.'

'The point I'm tryin' to make is that her old mam was riddled with the pox and …'

'Raving she was,' said Marge. 'I remember hearing about it.'

'Yes, anyway, the old girl only had a few weeks to …'

'And violent,' said Marge.

Ethel nodded solemnly. 'Takes you like that sometimes, the pox does.'

'Look, are you two bloody listenin' or not? The point I'm tryin' to make is that in this here country it's against the law to go killin' people – whether they're on death's door or not. If this here doctor hadn't topped himself, then the law would have done it for him, see?'

Marge thought about it. 'So what happened to her, then?'

'Who?'

'The girl that killed her mother.'

'I don't bloody know, do I.'

'Oh,' said Marge, picking up her drink.

Jim began to read again, his lips moving soundlessly, then he gave a great roar of laughter. 'Well, that settles it, that does! He was as mad as a hatter!'

'Who we talking about now?' asked Marge, with a frown.

'The bloke who killed his own kid. He's a doctor, right? Only he can't be a very good one because he's losin' money hand over fist. Then two months ago his old lady ups and leaves him for another bloke!'

Marge finished the last of her gin. 'Poor sod.'

'Oh, it gets better,' chuckled Jim. 'So now he's got creditors knockin' on the door, not a penny in the bank, and a kid what's on her last legs with consumption. So what does he do? He smothers the kid with a pillow, then cuts his own throat.'

'Both better off out of it, I reckon,' said Ethel.

'Ah, but here's the thing of it.' He began to laugh. 'Before he sets to hackin' his own bloody head off, he only goes and leaves half-a-crown on the table to pay the arrears on his soddin' rent!'

Marge shook her head. 'Now that *is* daft!'

'Wouldn't catch me doin' that.' He tossed the paper on to the table. 'I'd have taken the half-crown, had a bloody good drink – and got my leg over while I was at it.'

'You promise to cut your own throat an' I'll buy you a drink – *an'* give you a leg over,' said Ethel.

Marge shivered again. 'Can we stop all this talk? It's fair making my skin crawl.'

'What surprises me,' grinned Jim, 'is that he didn't drop the razor before he was half way through. I'm bloody sure I wouldn't have been able to finish the job.' He lurched forward as Hettie pushed through the crowd and half fell against him.

'That's always been your trouble, Jimmy,' she hiccupped, then giggled, dangling one finger. 'You never could go the whole voyage!'

He blushed. 'Go easy, Hettie,' he said, wiping away the gin she'd spilt on his jacket.

'You've had a skinful by the look o' you,' laughed Marge, watching Hettie manoeuvre herself uncertainly on to a chair. 'Been having a celebration, have you?'

'I've been comise … comisering … commiserating – with my dear cousin.' She searched the crowd. 'Now where's the silly cow gone? Oh, here she comes!'

Mary weaved toward them, two fresh glasses in her hands, and came to halt by the table, swaying dangerously. 'On the house,' she announced in a grand, if slurred manner. 'Courtesy of Mr Sidney Cruickshank, *Esquire.*'

'You'd better sit down before you fall down,' laughed Jim, taking the glasses from her, putting one on the table and passing the other to Hettie.

Mary looked about her. 'One doesn't seem to have a chair.'

Marge roared with laughter. 'Don't she do that well. She should go on the boards.'

'The Duchess of Dock Town,' grinned Jim, reaching for her arm and pulling her on to his lap. 'Come on Duchess, here's a nice comfy seat for you.'

Mary giggled. 'Thank you, my man. You are most, *most* kind.'

'So, what are you commi–what's-itin' about?' asked Ethel.

'*Commiserating*,' said Hettie, managing the word in one go and looking pleased with herself. Then she frowned crossly and put a finger to her lips. 'Shsssh,' she said in a loud whisper, 'Her kid – but we don't want to talk about it – alright?' She hiccupped. 'Not a word. Got to cheer her up, see?'

Ethel looked across to where Jim had his arms around Mary's waist and was jiggling her up and down on his lap, the pair of them laughing. 'Looks as if you've cheered her legless.'

'No, she's alright.' Hettie turned to look at them. 'Here, Jimmy. I thought you liked a bit more meat?'

'Changed my mind, haven't I.'

Hettie wagged a finger at him, her eyes trying to follow it without success. 'You treat her nice, now, you … you dirty little bugger.'

208

'You can trust me,' he winked, stroking a hand along Mary's thigh.

Oblivious to his touch, Mary picked up her gin and drained it, a sad, far-away look coming to her eyes. 'Would you like to hear a song?' she asked of no one in particular, cradling the empty glass against her chest,

'A song, is it?' Marge's ruddy cheeks plumped into a grin. 'I said she should go on the boards, didn't I?' She turned to Hettie, 'Didn't I say that?'

'You haven't heard her yet,' laughed Jim.

Hettie made to slap his arm but missed. 'You go on, Mary, m'darling. You sing if you want to.'

Mary's lips parted in readiness, but no sound emerged.

'Sing up,' chuckled Jim. 'We can't hear you at the back.'

This time Hettie struck him full on the shoulder. 'Shut up and give her a chance, can't you? Go on, Mary, my love. Give us a nice song. A right good belter, eh?'

Mary tried again, drawing herself up, her voice, at last, coming soft and clear.

> 'Sleep my child and peace attend thee,
> All through the night.
> Guardian angels God will send thee,
> All through the night.
> Soft the drowsy hours are creeping,
> Hill and vale in slumber sleeping,
> I my loving vigil keeping,
> All through the night.
>
> 'Love, to thee my thoughts are turning,
> All through the night.
> All for thee my heart is yearning,
> All through the night.
> Though sad fate our lives may sever,
> Parting will not last forever,
> There's a hope that leaves me never,
> All through the night.'

There was silence from the small group gathered about the table, then Hettie reached out, touching Mary's hand. 'There, there, don't cry, my love, don't cry. Everything's alright. Here, I'll get us some more drinks. Another couple of gins? That'll do the trick, eh?' Holding on to the table, she got unsteadily to her feet, then launched herself toward the bar.

When she returned a few minutes later, Mary was fast asleep, curled up on Jim's lap, her head resting on his shoulder.

Chapter Twenty-Seven

Evan came to her that night, slipping into the bed, his warm body against hers, softly, tenderly, touching and kissing until she ached for that once-tasted passion – yet at the very height of her excitement he withdrew, moving from her, drifting away …

She awoke, bleary eyed, to a cold and cloudy afternoon.

'Thought you were going to sleep all day,' said Hettie, leaning in the doorway. She put her hand to her forehead. 'God, I feel like death warmed up. How about you?'

Mary made to rise, but feeling sick she fell back against the pillow.

'What a night, eh?' Hettie gave a tentative laugh, 'What a bloody *day and a night.*' She came to sit on the edge of the bed. 'A hair o' the dog is what we need. Maybe even …' She caught sight of the two-shilling piece on the nearby table. 'Bloody hell! Is that what he gave you? Two bob?'

Mary opened one eye. 'What do you mean? Who?'

'Jim, of course.'

'Jim?'

Hettie laughed, then winced, putting a soothing hand to her temple. 'Don't worry, my love. There's a good many nights I can't remember either.'

Jolted into wakefulness, Mary forced herself up on one arm. 'Jim? From the Red Dragon? He was here?'

'Well, it wasn't Old Nick. Though from the noise you two was making it bloody well could have been.' She glanced up at the ceiling. 'It's a wonder you didn't set old misery guts off.'

Mary grew whiter still. 'You don't mean it? No! I don't believe you. I would never have …' then feeling beneath the sheet, she shuddered with revulsion. 'Oh God, Hettie, how could you let him?'

'*I* never let him. *You* let him,' said Hettie indignantly, then she softened. 'But it's alright. Where's the harm? He's not a bad sort,' she tossed the coin again, 'and it's not as if he hasn't paid you right handsomely. Two bleeding bob, mind!'

Mary's skin began to crawl, and she drew her legs together, curling into a ball. 'I don't want his bloody money!'

'Oh, don't you, then? Got private means, have you? Because if you have, you might like to think about paying the rent – and I mean the proper rent, not the piddling amount we're charging you.'

'I'll get what I owe you,' Mary snapped, quickly lowering her voice as the throbbing in her head flared into a searing pain. 'But never *that* way. It's disgusting!'

'Disgusting? What's disgusting about it? Natural is what it is! What do you think you've got down there, the bread of heaven, is it? No, my love. It's just goods – same as your eyes and hands! You'd be happy enough to sell them to some sweater for a few pence an hour, I suppose?'

'It's not the same.'

''Course it is – just easier work, and better paid than sewing or making bloody matchboxes.' She held out the coin, but Mary pushed it away. 'God, but you're an ungrateful cow, Mary Kelly.' Hettie stood up, slipping the coin into her pocket. 'Well, if you don't want this, I'll take it as the week's rent. Now, I've just put the kettle on. You want anything?'

Mary glowered at her. 'Yes – a bath.'

'A bath? What do you think this is, the Royal Hotel?'

'Well, some hot water, then – and a bowl.'

Hettie shrugged. 'Please yourself – the bowl's out the back.' She shuffled into the passage – then poked her head back into the room. 'Look, how about we go to the pub? Sid's working there this afternoon, so it won't cost us.'

'I can't. I'm going out.'

'Going out? Where?'

'To the Art School. To do what I came here to do!'

*

Maggie pulled a long face. 'This is daft, this is!'

'No it isn't.'

'It is!'

Seated at a table in the Caerphilly tea-rooms, Gwyneth sighed. 'So, what do you *normally* do with your half day?'

'Lots of things.'

'Such as?'

'None o' your business.'

Gwyneth poured milk into their cups. 'Sugar?'

'Four.' Maggie's brows drew into a frown. '*Maybe* I'm wantin' to go an' meet my young man.'

'Are you?'

'I might be …' she watched Gwyneth pour the tea, '… or I might not be. What you want to go bringin' me in here for, anyway? It ain't like we're friends or anythin'.'

'We could be, couldn't we?'

'Ho,' scoffed Maggie. 'So that's the game, is it? I ain't just fallen off the tree, y'know. We get all friendly an' then I suppose it'll be, *Oh, Maggie, dear. Won't you just go up an' clean them chandeliers – an' anythin' else what's a bit high, on account of me bein' your friend an' scared of ladders an' all.*'

'There's no need to worry about that,' Gwyneth said calmly. 'I shan't be going up the ladder anymore.'

'Oh, won't you, now!'

'No.'

Maggie gave her a suspicious glance. 'How's that then?'

'Because it's *your* job. According to Lawrence, it was always *your* job. You just forgot to tell me, I suppose.'

'Well,' Maggie smiled grudgingly, 'Maybe it did just slip my mind.'

'Hmmm,' said Gwyneth.

A waitress arrived with a selection of cakes, and Maggie eyed them greedily. 'You still goin' to pay for all this?'

'Yes.'

'Well, then I'll have that big one with the jam an' cream.'

Wiping the sticky crumbs from her mouth a few minutes later, Maggie leaned forward excitedly. 'Here, what about this baby, then? You ever heard the like of it? Gawd, but there was a to-do about it when the old doctor came home. I was layin' the fire in the bedroom – an' I could hear him up through the floor. Rantin' an' ravin' he was.' She affected an offended expression, 'I heard language what no young girl should hear – an' that's a fact.'

'What were they saying?' Gwyneth asked, toying with her teaspoon.

Maggie looked pointedly about for the waitress. 'Y'know, I wouldn't mind another one o' them cakes, as it happens.'

'You couldn't manage *another* one?'

'Oh, couldn't I just? Growin' girl, I am.'

Gwyneth rolled her eyes.

'Well,' said Maggie, as soon as the waitress had departed, leaving another large pastry. 'I couldn't hear properly, not everythin' like – not even with my ear stuck to the floor boards – but it seems that woman what called again yesterday, she only went an' dumped her kid on the mistress! Just like that! Can you imagine? The old doctor was callin' her – the woman that is – every kind of trollop from here to Christmas!' She leaned forward, whispering. 'Well, you know what I reckon?'

Gwyneth shook her head.

'I reckon it's *his*.'

'Whose?'

'The old doctor's, o' course. Wouldn't make no sense them keepin' it otherwise, would it?'

'They're keeping the baby?'

Maggie nodded. 'Advertisin' for a nanny, they are. 'Course, you can guess who's goin' to get stuck with wipin' its bum till they find one!'

'I see.' Gwyneth sipped at her tea. 'And what about ... the woman?'

'Gone – an' not comin' back, neither. The mistress was sayin' as how she'd begged her to stay until the old doctor got home – but she wouldn't have none of it. Well, she wouldn't, would she. Too frightened, I reckon – an' I can't say's I blame her.'

'Well, I'm sure it's all for the best.' Gwyneth carefully placed the cup into its saucer. 'After all, we wouldn't want *that* class of woman in the house, would we?'

*

Mawden Protheroe leaned back in his chair and studied the carefully repaired drawings that covered his desk. 'You were dissatisfied with them, I see, Miss Kelly!'

'They were torn accidentally. I ...'

'No, no!' He raised a cautionary finger. 'You were *not* pleased with them, and you were quite right! Immature work! Ill-conceived and poorly executed! A dozen immediately apparent faults – and doubtless another dozen should I care to look more closely – which I do not! But I see your little plan, and I applaud it! Yes, yes my dear, I do indeed!'

Mary stared at him, uncomprehending.

'Come, come,' he smiled. 'We must not overplay the coquette. You have very cleverly whetted my appetite, and as you can see, I am all a-quiver to see your most recent work.'

'This *is* my most recent work, Mr Protheroe.'

'But these are dated over three years ago!'

'I've been ... ill ... for some considerable time.'

'Ah!' He spread his hands. '*La fragilité de l'esprit artistique*! Well, well, well. This puts a different light on it. A very different light indeed! I must reconsider!' He pulled the nearest sheet toward him. 'Despite their faults I see promise here! Yes, promise indeed! With work? Yes! Yes, I think with work ...' Leaning forward he pinched the bridge of his nose, holding the theatrical pose for several seconds before bringing his hand down flat on to the table. 'My mind is made up! I shall take you on! My fees are twenty-five guineas a term – in advance – and you will supply all your own requirements, *viz*, materials. My congratulations to you, Miss Kelly!'

Mary took a steadying breath. 'I believe you know a friend of mine – a Mr Abrahams?'

'Abrahams? Abrahams?' He tapped thoughtfully at his lip. 'No, can't say I do. But then in my profession one meets a great many people.'

'He is – or rather he *was* – the Headmaster at the Caerphilly Board School.'

'A pedagogue? A chalk eater? Ah, now I have him! An oldish chap – with one of those damned *cameras*?'

'Yes, he does have a ...'

Protheroe grew red in the face. '*Photographers!*' he sneered. 'Can't stomach them in the normal course of events – but I do seem to recall he was amiable company. So, he's a friend of yours, is he?'

'Yes. Well, the thing is ...' She forced her hand from where it was picking at her sleeve. 'He suggested you might ... if you thought I had *promise* ... that you might ... forgo the fees?'

Protheroe's head jerked up. 'Forgo the fees?' he boomed. 'Is this some kind of joke? Some foolish jape? For if it is, then I am not in the least amused! No, indeed not! Come, tell me! Who put you up to this? Was it that young jackanapes Smethwick? By God, if it was, then ...!'

Mary got swiftly to her feet, snatching up her drawings. 'I'm sorry, I've obviously wasted your time.'

'Indeed you have, madam!' He glared at her for a moment, his brows drawn thunderously, then he exhaled noisily 'Very well – *twenty* guineas a term – and that is my final offer.'

She bundled the papers under her arm. 'I don't have twenty guineas.'

'How much *do* you have?'

'Nothing.'

Protheroe noticed for the first time the underlying shabbiness of her clothes, and he let forth a great peal of laughter. 'Damn me!' he said. 'If your artistic ability was equal to one half of your brass neck, I damn well *would* teach you for nothing!' He pushed back his chair and stood up. 'But this is no charitable institution.'

'I wasn't looking for *charity*. I was led to believe ... well, it doesn't matter now. I have no money – so I'm sorry for taking up your afternoon.'

Protheroe stabbed a finger toward the studio. 'I have fifteen *paying* students out there. Dull as yesterday's dishwater they are! But any one of them could do better than those scribblings you're clutching. Why on earth would this ... this *Abrahams* believe I would teach you for free? The man must have been drunk – or mad – or both!'

Tears pricked Mary's eyes. 'He thought I had talent.'

'He's a damned schoolmaster! Worse! A damnable *photographer*! What in heaven's name would he know? Do I have the impudence to go into *his* classroom and ...'

'I believe you've made your point, Mr Protheroe,' she said, gathering her dignity. 'I shan't waste any more of your time.'

He stopped abruptly, looking at her with renewed interest. 'A moment,' he said cocking his head to one side, running an appraising eye over her, then, 'Please. I should like you to put down those drawings.'

'I don't think we have anything more to discuss.'

'We may not have exhausted *all* possibilities.'

Mary hesitated, then set the sketches down on the desk.

'Now, go and stand by the window.'

'Why?'

'Because I have asked you to.'

She moved warily into the light. 'Here?'

'It will do. Now turn this way a little – no, too far – back a fraction. Hmmm … good. Now the other way.' He circled her, then stood back. 'You have poise. Good bone structure. Have you ever *posed* before?'

'No.'

'Good models are not easily come by. Wrinkled harridans are plentiful, indeed my cup runneth over! But finding someone to give flesh to Venus! To stand succedaneum for Aphrodite! Ah that is a different matter entirely!'

The image of Venus and Adonis came back to her, and she blushed. 'I didn't come here to model,' she said.

'No. You came here to learn. I am offering you the opportunity.'

'But you said I had no talent.'

'I merely stated that your talent was less remarkable than your *photographer* friend would have you believe – but you *can* draw. The rest might possibly be achieved by hard work.'

'So … what would I have to do?'

'Pose for my students. Then, allowing those skirts do not conceal some abnormality of the lower torso, I should *allow* you to pose for me – as well as performing any small domestic duties that might be required. In return, you would receive whatever tuition you might glean from keeping your eyes and ears open – and possibly *some* private tuition whenever it might prove convenient. Do we have a bargain?'

'The posing?' She could feel her cheeks growing hot.

'Oft times gilded – but just as often *as nature intended*.'

'I couldn't.'

'Then I must bid you good day.'

She wavered, glancing at the drawings on the desk. 'Do I really have *some* talent?'

'Some.' He returned to his chair and reached for a cigar. 'Enough to make the effort worthwhile, certainly.'

'And would I be paid – for the modelling?'

Protheroe threw up his hands in mute appeal. 'I cast open the doors to wisdom – and you muddy the steps with requests for money?'

'I have to live.'

'If I had taken you as a student and forgone the fees – how would you have lived then?'

'I don't know. I would have found work – at night.'

'Then find it.'

She crossed to the desk and picked up the drawings. 'No. If I'm to model during the day, I shall need time to study, to practise.'

His eyes traced the line of her jaw, the sweep of her neck and the curve of her waist. 'Very well,' he said pursing his lips. 'Come tomorrow morning. If Venus is truly concealed beneath that faded frippery, *then* we shall discuss terms.'

Chapter Twenty-Eight

Standing on a small platform, her back to the class, her arms raised and her fingers resting on her head, Mary sneezed, then quickly resumed the pose. A few feet in front of her a glowing coal fire warmed her belly and legs, flushing them a deep pink, while her back and bottom remained pale and chilled. She sneezed again.

'No. No. *No!*' Protheroe's voice boomed behind her. 'Do you see the model *at all*, Mr Smethwick? Look, sir! *Look!* Use your eyes! A rare and singular idea to you, no doubt – but one that has more than stood the test of time!'

Mary heard him tear the drawing from the board, followed by the sound of his footsteps as he strode to the podium to stand close behind her.

'Here we have the graceful line of a neck – not, as you have drawn, a gnarled trunk, suitable only for the seating of leprechauns!' He stroked along the underside of her arm. 'Here I behold the slender sweep of a limb – where you, Smethwick, *apparently*, see the connecting rods of a Great Western express! And here …' his fingers moved to the small of her back, travelling down, tracing the contour of her right buttock, 'where nature has conspired to produce a posterior, exquisite in both tone and form, you have conspired to represent …' he shook the drawing in disgust, 'sacks of cauliflowers! If your leaning is toward horticulture, sir, might I suggest you take up market gardening and leave the arts to those of us with an eye for the sublime – rather than the ridiculous!'

The footsteps receded, and Mary relaxed a little. In the five months since she had first climbed upon the podium she had all but lost her embarrassment, yet she could never quite overcome her dread of his touch.

Her arms began to ache, and she glanced toward the clock that hung above the door. It was then she noticed the smartly dressed man who had arrived unannounced and was regarding her with interest.

'Rest!' announced Protheroe from the back of the room.

Mary lowered her arms, shaking the life back into them, then reached for the loose gown, slipping into it.

'Mr Morganstone,' Protheroe beamed, striding the length of the room. 'How very good to see you, my dear sir. Please, come through to my study.' He turned to look around the studio. 'We shall break for lunch, gentlemen. Oh, and for Mr Smethwick's benefit we shall resume this afternoon with a still-life. *Winter vegetables*, I think.'

'Will I be required again today, Mr Protheroe?' asked Mary.

He waved her away with a sweep of his hand. 'No, no. I have cast sufficient pearls before these progeny of Circe.' Then as an afterthought, 'You may find yourself a space at the back this afternoon, if you wish.'

*

Sitting close to the fire, Mary half closed her eyes as she looked from the drawing propped on the easel in front of her, to the plaster bust that was her model. She sneezed, the sound echoing around the empty studio.

'Bless you.'

She gave a small start, and turned to find the man she'd heard addressed as Morganstone standing by her shoulder.

'I do apologise. I didn't mean to startle you.'

'No,' she said, bundling her handkerchief into her lap, 'It's perfectly alright. I didn't hear you come in.' She made to get up. 'Should I fetch Mr Protheroe?'

'Not at all. I have just this moment left him to his lunch.' He leaned forward, examining the sketch. 'You draw well. Are you both student *and* model?'

'Yes.' She waited for the inevitable proposition, the sly suggestion, or the blatant offer of money for favours – but it didn't come, and so she said, 'It's how I pay for my lessons.'

'I see,' he straightened up. 'That is wonderfully dedicated of you. I am very impressed.' He stopped and looked embarrassed. 'I say, I do hope that doesn't sound condescending.'

Mary studied him, uncertain whether he was making fun of her, but his face gave no hint, and his precise English accent was difficult for her to read. 'No,' she said, 'not if you mean it.'

'Oh, I most certainly do.'

She wiped her nose, then smiled. 'Well, then – thank you.'

'You have a cold,' he said, as though noticing for the first time her reddened nose and sodden handkerchief. 'An occupational hazard at this time of year, I expect.' He reached into his pocket and withdrew a square of clean white linen, handing it to her. 'Please, take mine.'

Mary took it gratefully.

'Well,' he said, 'I suppose I should leave you to your studies, but ...' he gave her a querying look, 'I don't suppose you would be hungry, by any chance?'

Logs burned in the inglenook, filling the old-fashioned chop house with the drowsy scent of apple wood.

'And do you work there, alone, every day?' Morganstone asked as he sat across the table from Mary in the corner booth.

'It's often the only time I can study.'

He looked up. 'Ah, now you have made me feel guilty for dragging you away.'

Mary sipped at the hot brandy and water. 'It wasn't going very well.' She dabbed at her nose. 'As you could probably see.'

'On the contrary. As a matter of fact, I *would* say that your talent is wasted on the podium – but then, that wouldn't be *entirely* true.'

'Mr Morganstone,' Mary put down her glass. 'I'm sure you mean it kindly, but – well, often men assume ...'

'That because you pose naked you would be willing to do *other things*?'

She met his eyes. 'Yes.'

'It is a common assumption.'

'It may be, but ...'

'It is a common assumption amongst *non-professionals*.'

Mary regarded him. 'And you are a professional?'

'I like to think so.' He raised an eyebrow. 'But you are not convinced. Would it help if I told you what I do?'

'It's really none of my business.'

'It's no great secret, I assure you. I am simply an agent. The market for art has never been better, with a great deal of new money chasing relatively few pictures. I suppose you could say I am rather like a prospector, looking for new seams.'

'I see. And you are going to buy Mr Protheroe's work?'

'I may. I am currently searching for a *particular* style of painting, and so it rather depends on Mr Protheroe.'

The waiter arrived, placing before them two plates of mutton chops and steaming vegetables. Mary waited until he had left, then looked apologetically across the table. 'I'm sorry about what I said. I didn't mean to presume.'

'Not at all. You are quite right, it *is* a common assumption, and I'm very glad we've cleared the matter between us, because it *is* your modelling I should like to discuss.' He picked up his knife and fork, cutting at the fatty meat. 'How much does Protheroe pay you?'

'Eight shillings a week.'

Morganstone's knife chimed against his plate. 'Eight shillings?'

'Plus my tuition.'

'Tuition? Sitting alone in an empty studio?'

'Sometimes he teaches me privately.'

'Oh, really?' He gave the barest hint of a smile. 'You know – what I said earlier about paintings is equally true about good models. Do you have any idea what someone with your attributes might earn in London?' Taking a card from his pocket he scribbled a figure on the back, pushing it toward her.

'That much?' said Mary, staring at it. 'A week?'

'A week? Absolutely not. A *day*.'

'It doesn't seem possible.' She fumbled the handkerchief out of her pocket and dabbed at her nose. 'But I couldn't go to London.'

'No, of course not. I wasn't suggesting you should. I just thought you might want to renegotiate your fees in light of what I've just said.'

Mary studied the card. 'Really that much? A day?'

Morganstone nodded, cutting into his chop. 'Take my advice and tackle the old skinflint. He'll never match that figure, but I'll be surprised if he can't do better than eight shillings.'

'Thank you.' She pushed the card back to him.

'No, no. You keep it. There's an address on the other side. If ever you *should* find yourself in London, just go there and mention my name.' He glanced at her untouched plate. 'Now, come on. Eat up. *Feed a cold and starve a fever*, nanny used to say.'

*

Two days of blustery gales had given way to a bright, crisp morning, but now the light was fading, and Mawden Protheroe stood back, squinting through half-closed lids at the canvas – then across to where Mary stood facing him on the small dais.

'How the devil is a man supposed to work on these confounded winter days?' He put down his palette – but continued to look at her.

'Should I get down?' asked Mary, still holding the pose.

'No. Indeed, no - stay as you are. I should like to make a few corrections to the drawing. There's light enough for that, at least.' Distractedly he took up a brush, dipping it into the thinned umber and redrawing the sensuous line of her hip and thigh, his gaze constantly returning to the model, mentally caressing the soft curves, gentle slopes and beguiling valleys until the woman, not the painting, became the whole focus of his attention, and he put down the brush.

On the raised podium, Mary saw the first movement toward her, and tensed.

'You are as elusive to capture as ever,' he said, coming to stand before her, his voice husky, his face level with her breasts. 'As elusive as Venus herself.' He eased her arms from her side, then reached out with both hands, running the tips of his fingers along the outline of her thighs. 'No. Surely more elusive, yet.'

Mary held the pose, standing with quiet resignation as he stroked up over the swell of her flanks, his palms warm against her chilled skin.

'Such a perfect sweep.' He continued upwards, flowing out over her hips, dipping into the slender waist, then upwards and outwards again, coming to rest high on her ribs, his thumbs lightly touching the swell of her breasts.

'Please, Mr Protheroe?'

He took a step back, his bushy brows drawn into a frown. 'Yes?'

Mary faltered, embarrassed, not by her nudity, but by what she had been steeling herself to say. 'I'm sorry, Mr Protheroe, but … I'd rather you didn't touch me.'

'Touch you?' Protheroe's eyes widened for a moment, then his brows drew even closer. '*Touch* you? Do you mistake me for some lubricious-fingered stage-door Johnny? Some lecherous roué?'

'No …'

'Some concupiscent fumbler?'

Mary began to blush. 'No. Of course not.'

'I am not *touching* you, dear girl. I am *experiencing* you – and there is some small difference, I think!' Indignantly, he strode back to the canvas, regarding it, his head thrown back in an imperial fashion. 'How are we to capture the very essence of that which we have not experienced to the fullest capacity?' He fixed his gaze upon her. 'Answer me that!'

'I …'

'You can't! It's impossible! Why, even that damned charlatan, Turner, knew as much.' He raised a trembling finger toward the main studio, as though the man himself waited there. 'When he decided to paint a storm at sea, did he merely peer through the window of some tawdry sea-side lodging house? No, indeed he did not! He took ship! Lashed himself to the mast and *experienced* the wrath of the heavens for himself!'

'I … I can see that, it's just …' Apologetically, she made to resume the pose.

'No,' said Protheroe, waving his hand dismissively before bringing it to his face, pinching the bridge of his nose. 'No. Please. Get dressed. My muse has left me for today.'

*

'Why?' said Ivor, matter-of-factly. 'Because there was no reason to tell you – that's why. What would it have achieved – other than to disrupt your studies? We seriously considered not telling you at all!'

Evan stared at him across the luncheon table, then at his mother. 'But he's my child!'

'And is he any less your child for you remaining in ignorance these past months?'

'We did what we thought was best,' said Florence.

'Best? Best for whom?'

'For you, you damned ungrateful whelp!' Ivor's face glowed like an ember amidst the snow of his whiskers. 'Have you any concept of what this business might have done to our standing?' He put a hand on his wife's shoulder. 'It was only the quick thinking of your mother that saved us from disgrace.'

'The boy is our ward,' explained Florence. 'As far as everyone else is concerned we have taken him in as an act of charity – and it *must* stay that way, Evan.'

'No! He's my son. I won't have him as some … some half-brother.'

Florence pursed her lips. 'You are being unreasonable.'

'Am I?' He began to pace up and down. 'Where's Mary? I don't understand any of this.'

'She's gone.'

'Gone? Gone where for God's sake?'

'We don't know.'

'Then I'll go and find her. She'd never abandon her own child and go away like that. Never!'

Ivor stepped in front of him. 'I forbid it. She had her chance. We would have written to you, kept her here until you returned, but all she wanted was to be rid of the boy – to get him out from under her skirts – no doubt to make room for paying customers.'

Evan's fists clenched, the knuckles standing out white. 'Don't *ever* say anything like that again.'

'I'm sorry, Evan,' said Florence, coming between them, 'but it's probably very close to the truth. I did everything I could to persuade her to stay. *Everything.*'

Evan turned away, going to the window.

'And anyway,' added Ivor. 'It's been five months … she could be anywhere by now.'

Evan looked out over the frosted trees, his eyes darting this way and that, scanning the line of the horizon. 'I don't care. I *will* find her.'

*

Mawden Protheroe sat squarely behind his office desk. 'Miss Kelly,' he said from behind a cloud of cigar smoke. 'Be so kind as to come in and close the door.'

He waited until she was seated, then leaned back in his chair. 'I've been considering this morning's solicitation of a wage increase – and I'm afraid it will not do. It will not do at all. Do you realise it is an extra *fifty percent*?'

'But I'm only asking for another four shillings.'

He blew another cloud of smoke. 'Pennies, shillings, pounds? The coinage is inconsequential. Percentages, my dear girl! That is what the modern world works on!'

Mary studied him. 'I should tell you,' she said, 'I *have* been offered another job – at better money.'

'Have you, indeed?' Protheroe came forward a little, but catching himself he leaned back once more. 'Ah, but will they also teach you, hmmm? Will they tap the font of knowledge and let you drink?'

'Yes,' she lied.

This time Protheroe started forward and remained there, eyeing her suspiciously. 'And where might this *Eldorado*, be?'

'In London.'

'Ah!' He smiled, waving the cigar. 'The promised land!' He leaned back once more. 'I thought for a moment you were serious.'

'I *am* serious.'

'Of course. Doubtless you have numerous friends in London? Somewhere to stay? Not to mention the means of getting there!' He looked at her along the length of his nose. 'You *do* have those things?'

'I have what I need.'

His mouth curled at the corners for a moment, then he stubbed out the cigar. 'Let us set aside this *theatre* and be frank with each other, shall we?'

Mary shifted uneasily. 'I should like that.'

He regarded her for a moment. 'The fact is, you will *never* make an artist.' He saw the colour drain from her face, and went on quickly. 'Oh, you make passable enough drawings of the inanimate, no question of that, but even then there is nothing to raise them above the mundane. There is no …' He raised his hand, as though grasping at some invisible object that hung before him. 'No *passion*. No *spirit*. No – *inspiration*.'

A well of emptiness opened in Mary's stomach. 'I don't understand. When I first came to you, you said you saw promise.'

'I saw twenty-five guineas a term.'

'But you still took me, even when you knew I had nothing.' A look of awful realisation crossed her face. 'It can't have been *just* to have me model?'

Protheroe remained impassive. 'Shall we just say the promise was never fulfilled.'

She got unsteadily to her feet, holding back her tears. 'I should collect my things.'

'Now, now,' he said, waving her back into her seat. 'Let us not be too hasty. I have *another* proposition.'

Trying to control her emotions, Mary settled herself back on the chair. 'I'm listening.'

'I have agreed to undertake a number of new commissions. Classical studies – after a fashion – for which I will require a model of the very highest calibre.' He blew a cloud of smoke. 'I should like *you* to be that model.'

'And *then* you would continue to teach me?'

'No. These paintings will be time consuming, so I shall be handing over the running of the school to an ex-student of mine. Of course, what you do in your own time is your own affair, though, believe me, you would be wasting your efforts.'

'But …?'

'There are no buts. I don't know what inflated ideas this Mr Abrahams has been feeding you, but I suspect his viewpoint has been somewhat *coloured* – like many of the doting fathers I have to deal with. Though, please, seek a second opinion if you wish.'

Slowly, Mary shook her head. 'It's funny,' she said, half to herself. 'It's as if I've known it all along.' She sat quietly, staring into her lap. *Facts, Mary Kelly, that's what you need in this world.* 'Alright,' she said, meeting his eyes. 'Then what about the increase in wages?'

'Under the circumstances I will agree to the twelve shillings.'

'I want eighteen.'

Protheroe's eyes widened. '*Eighteen*? Are you mad?'

The blood was flooding back into Mary's cheeks and with it a new resolve. 'If I'm to be a professional model, then I should be paid as such.'

'No model of mine has ever earned eighteen shillings!'

'Then I shall be the first.'

'Never.'

She got to her feet once more. 'Then we have nothing more to say to each other.'

Protheroe bit through the end of his cigar in surprise. 'Wait,' he called to her, picking the wet end from his mouth. 'Fourteen shillings.'

'*Eighteen*.'

'It's highway robbery!' He dropped the cigar into the ashtray, watching it smoulder while Mary waited, her hand on the doorknob. 'Very well,' he said at last. 'Eighteen shillings. But I *must* be free to work as I see fit – without any of your *petty prudery*!'

She hesitated for the briefest of moments, then let her hand drop from the door. 'Yes, alright.'

For the first time that afternoon Protheroe truly relaxed. 'Very well,' he said, rising from his chair. 'Then, if you have no objections, I should like to begin immediately.'

*

'More fireworks!' announced Maggie, grinning gleefully as she came down into the kitchen. 'Never a dull minute here these days.' She dropped on to one of the chairs that stood about the scrubbed deal table. 'Been nothin' but fireworks since Master Evan came home!'

Gwyneth looked up from her mending. 'You shouldn't go listening, Maggie. You'll get yourself into trouble one of these days.'

'Can't help it if I happen to overhear, can I? I mean, I can't shut my ears off.'

'No, but you don't have to press them to the wall.'

Maggie chuckled, rubbing her hands together. 'Ooh, I love a good row, I do.'

'So, what were they arguing about?'

'Oh,' said Maggie, looking down her nose. 'You shouldn't go askin' them sort of questions. You'll get yourself in trouble one of these days.'

Gwyneth half smiled. 'Yes – you're quite right. Thank you, Maggie.' She returned to her sewing, working in silence for several minutes until Maggie, growing restless, said, 'The old doctor's gone out. *Slammed the door* he did.'

'Mmmm?'

'An' the mistress, too. Sent for the carriage – an' took Nanny Reeves an' the baby as well.'

Gwyneth made no reply, but held up the carefully repaired linen. 'What do you think?'

'Here!' said Maggie, indignantly. 'I ain't interested in your bloomin' drawers. Do you want to know what they was sayin', or don't you?'

'Oh – were you going to tell me?'

Maggie chewed peevishly at her lip. 'Well …' she began, then sat back in her chair, folding her arms. 'No. No, *actually*, I don't think I was.'

'Well, suit yourself.' Gwyneth got to her feet. 'It's getting dark. I'd better go up and light the lamps and see to the fires.'

She was almost at the top of the stairs when Maggie came to stand in the pool of light at the bottom. 'I'll tell you when you get back, if you like,' she called quietly.

Above stairs, the house was unnaturally quiet, the rooms gloomy in the winter twilight, so that the oil lamp Gwyneth took into the drawing-room and set upon the table served only to darken the reaches beyond the immediate spill of light.

On the mantelshelf the clock chimed the half hour, loud in the silence, and she crossed to the fireplace, stooping to poke the glowing coals into life, and raising a few flickering flames.

'Where's Mary?'

Gwyneth dropped the poker and jerked upright, clutching her chest.

'Oh, I – I'm sorry, sir. You frightened me. I didn't know you were there.'

'Where is she, Gwyneth? Where did she go?' Evan's eyes gleamed in the firelight, the pupils, black, penetrating. 'You must know.'

'She went away. That's *all* I know.'

'You must have *some* idea?' He took a step toward her, dropping his voice even further. 'What *happened*, Gwyneth?'

She steadied herself. 'There was an explosion … at the mine.'

'Yes, yes, I know.' He reached for her arm. 'I'm sorry. It must have been terrible.'

'Yes – it was.' Gwyneth stooped to pick up the poker and place it back on the stand. 'I should be about my duties, sir.'

'Please, wait.' He advanced on her again. 'Did … did Mary ever speak to you …' he began uncertainly, searching her face, '… about me?'

Gwyneth clasped her hands, holding them stiffly against her apron. 'Only that she worked for you in Cardiff.'

'Yes … yes, she did. It's just that … I can't believe she'd abandon her son and run away without good reason. What was it, Gwyneth? What happened?'

'I don't know, sir.'

'But you must.'

'I don't *want* to know.'

Evan stared at her. 'She's your friend.'

'No!' Gwyneth stared back. 'A friend wouldn't do what she did!'

The accusing look in her eyes made an absurdity of further pretence. 'I'm sorry,' he said. 'I can understand how you must feel, but you can't possibly know how it was. Neither of us wanted it to happen – certainly not Mary – but it did happen, and I can *never* be sorry for that.'

'I can't help you, sir.'

'*Please*, Gwyneth. *I love her.*'

'So did my brother! But what difference did that make?' Gwyneth knew she should leave, but months of suppressed hatred welled within her. 'She didn't even love her own son enough to stand by him – so why on earth would you think she'd treat *you* any differently? You're well rid of her!'

Evan held her gaze a moment longer, then looked away. 'I appreciate your candour,' he said quietly.

'There's only one person Mary loves – herself!'

'No. Think of me what you will, but Mary was always a true friend to you.'

Gwyneth's jaw tightened. 'You mean I owe my position to her?'

'I mean she always cared about you.'

'No! Whatever she did for me had to be for her own benefit.'

'You can't honestly believe that.'

'Can't I?' She checked herself, her lips compressing into a thin line. 'I should be seeing to the fire in the nursery, sir, if you'll excuse me?'

Evan watched her cross the room. 'Gwyneth – *please*.'

She stopped, her shoulders stiff, her face fixed firmly away from him.

'Gwyneth, if you have the least idea where she might be …?'

Her hands tensed, the knuckles becoming white.

'I'm *begging* you, Gwyneth.'

'I don't know where she's gone – and I don't care.' She willed herself to leave, to just walk away, but found that she couldn't. 'She … she has a cousin,' she said, haltingly, begrudging every word. 'In Cardiff. Cutler Street. I don't know the number.'

'Is that where she is?'

'She has no one else.'

'Thank you, Gwyneth.'

'Don't thank me.' She opened the door. 'Now we're even. I couldn't bear to be in debt to either of you.'

Chapter Twenty-Nine

'We can't go in.' Hettie was leaning against the passage wall, a bleary look about her face.

'It's my bleedin' 'ouse an' I'll go where I soddin' well please.' Holding a candle in front of him, Sid turned the spare key in the lock and shoved open the door to Mary's room. 'She's 'oldin' out on us, 'Ettie. I bloody well know she is.'

Hettie came to stand in the doorway, pulling her shawl about her. 'She isn't. She just hasn't got the money, that's all.'

'Yeah, an' I'm the Prince o' bloody Wales.' He set the candle on the table and looked about him. 'Blimey! 'Ow come yer don't keep our place as tidy as this?'

'I do my best. It's not easy, you know.'

'Not if yer a bloody lazy cow, it ain't!' Mary's trunk stood in the corner, and he crouched down, lifting the lid and rifling through the contents. 'She's got some money 'ere somewhere or I'm a bleedin' Dutchman.'

'Where would she get it? She only earns eight bob a week at that school.'

'Oh, do leave off! Yer don't believe all that nonsense, d'yer? Modellin'? Must be bloody dirty work, this modellin'!' He spat into the grate. 'Always washin' 'erself, ain't she? An' anyone what washes as often as she does must 'ave somethin' to 'ide.'

Hettie pushed sleepily at her hair. 'What? What are you talking about?'

'Use yer loaf, 'Ettie! She's turnin' tricks an' keepin' quiet about it, ain't she! Good payin' tricks, too, I reckon, what with 'er looks an' 'er bloody la-di-da ways.' He pulled out a handful of clean linen and threw it aside. 'An' *that's* all just a bloody show! Didn't seem so posh that night she came into the Dragon an' squared up to Ethel, did she? Pure bloody Annie, that was!'

Hettie chuckled. 'That was a laugh, that was. I nearly …' Her eye fell on the white blouse Sid had just pulled from the trunk. 'Oh, quick, give it here, Sid. I've always liked that one.'

Sid flung it across to her, and she held it to herself, tucking the collar beneath her chin. 'Here, what do you reckon? Fancy me in this, could you?'

He looked her over. 'Yeah,' he grinned, 'but I'd fancy yer more if you was 'alf in an' 'alf out – if yer get my drift?'

'Dirty sod,' she giggled, teasing it aside to expose her covered breast.

'Why don't yer keep it?'

'I couldn't!' Hettie looked shocked, but continued to stroke the blouse. 'She'd know.'

'So what? She owes us, don't she?'

'Well, I suppose,' she began – but there was a knock at the front door. 'Oh shit. It's her!' she whispered, flinging the blouse into the trunk. 'Quick, put it all back!'

'Too late!' Sid blew out the candle then crept to the window, peering out. 'It's alright. Just some bloke. Blimey, come in a bleedin' 'ansom, 'e 'as!' He pushed past her, into the passage. 'I'll go an' see what 'e wants. You 'ave another look through 'er stuff.'

Though the man standing just beyond the doorstep was silhouetted against the street lamp, Sid could tell he was a gentleman, and adopted a cautiously defensive tone. 'Yes?'

'I'm sorry to trouble you – but I believe a Miss Mary Kelly lives here?'

'Maybe. What d'yer want 'er for?'

'It's a personal matter,' said Evan, trying to remain affable. 'She's a friend of mine.'

Sid sucked at his teeth. 'Friend, eh? 'Ere, 'Ettie,' he called over his shoulder, 'got a *friend* of Mary's 'ere. Now there's a turn up fer the books, ain't it?' He turned back to Evan. 'Been a *friend* of 'ers fer long, 'ave yer?'

'If I could just see her?'

'All in good time, Clarence. All in good time.' He flashed his stained teeth in a sly grin. 'Nice gel, ain't she?'

'Yes,' said Evan, cautiously. 'Yes, she is.'

'So, 'ow much did yer pay 'er?'

Evan stared at him. 'I don't see that is any of your business. Now is she here, or isn't she?'

'Easy, Clarence, easy.'

Hettie came to the door, twisting a lock of hair around her finger as she leaned against her husband. 'You meet her up at this here art school, did you?' she said, trying not to laugh.

'Art school?'

She giggled drunkenly. 'Like a bit of *drawing* do you?'

'Where? Where is this school?'

'You don't want t' go traipsin' all the way over there,' interrupted Sid in a more friendly tone. 'I'm sure we can accommodate a discernin' gen'leman like yerself. Why don't yer nip in an' warm yerself by the fire?' He gave a wink. 'I'm just on my way out, like – but 'Ettie'll look after yer. Yer can draw 'er, if yer like.' He winked again. 'Yer could say 'er an' Mary was fillies from the same stable – if yer catch my drift?'

Evan looked at him, then at Hettie, unable to disguise his disgust.

'Here, don't you bloody well look at me like that!' shouted Hettie, her eyes bloodshot and staring. 'Who the hell do you think you are?'

Sid shot her a warning look. 'Shut it, 'Ettie.'

'I've had better men than you, I have!' She lunged forward, claws drawn, but Sid grabbed her by the collar, holding her back so that she strained like a dog on a leash, kicking and spitting. 'I've *shit* better men than you!'

Stunned, Evan backed toward the waiting cab.

'I can do anything Mary can bloody well do! *And* I can do it better!'

Along the street small patches of light sprang in the darkness as curtains were pulled back.

'Looks like yer drawin' lesson's off,' laughed Sid. 'Yer'd better 'op it, Clarence – afore she snaps yer pencil in 'alf.'

Hettie continued shouting and swearing, even after the cab had disappeared around the corner, and Sid raised his free hand, giving her a sharp cuff about the ear. 'I said cut it out,' he snapped, dragging her inside and slamming the door. 'I knew it,' he muttered. 'I knew that stuck-up cow was 'oldin' out on us. *I bloody knew it!*'

*

Evan was still shaking with anger and disgust as the cab rolled to a halt outside the gallery. 'Wait for me,' he called up to the driver as he leaped from the metal step.

High on his perch, the driver nodded, stifling the grin that had been fixed to his face ever since they'd left Cutler Street.

The bell above the gallery door summoned a far more obsequious Mr Gilpin than the one who had greeted Evan on his previous visit. 'Can I be of assistance, sir?'

Evan was breathing hard. 'I'm looking for an art school. Somewhere here in Cardiff.'

The abrupt tone, far from upsetting the man, served only to make him all the more eager to please. 'Perhaps you are thinking of Mr Protheroe's establishment, sir?' He drew back a little, his hands wafting toward a large canvas. 'We are frequently honoured to represent Mr Protheroe. If you would care to …'

'You have the address?'

'Yes, yes, of course.' Gilpin withdrew to his desk and opened a ledger, running his finger down the page. 'Ah, yes, here we are, sir. The Cardiff Academy of Art, 22 Wellington Road. But, please – if there is anything I might …?' The bell tinkled again, and Gilpin looked up to find himself quite alone.

*

Protheroe put down his palette and stood back from the canvas. It was three hours since he had laid in the first sweeping brushstrokes, and already the painting was coming to life. He stepped closer, blending an edge with the tip of his little finger, then stood back again, repeating the process until the undulating line of the hip flowed seamlessly into the rich brown background to give an illusion of soft, sensual flesh.

He looked past the canvas to where Mary lay, her arms and legs painstakingly arranged into an impression of careless, even wanton abandon. She was lying very still, with only the gentle rise and fall of her breasts to show that she lived, and for a long time he watched her – then he returned to the easel, wiping the colour from the tip of his finger before putting it to the wet paint with a touch as light as an angel's kiss, softening the triangle of ochres and siennas that fanned from between the pinks, whites and delicate blues of her thighs.

His hand began to shake, and he snatched it away, fearful of spoiling the effect he had created. How much closer to God could a man get, he wondered: to take nothing more than a handful of powdered colour, some oil, a pinch of animal hair and the bristles from a pig – and create an object with the power to delight the senses and inflame the passions. And yet it was all artifice, a sham, untouchable with anything but the imagination.

His eyes went back to Mary, a sculpture of warm flesh and blood instead of flat, cold pigment, and he felt himself stiffen, wanting to touch her once again, to have beneath his fingers that which his mind had explored a thousand times. 'There is a problem … with the angle of the leg,' he said, crossing the small area of floor that separated them. 'Please keep still, it will only take a moment.' He knelt, his hand going to explore the shallow dip where thigh liquesced into hip, a transition as subtle as anything the finest sable might accomplish, yet despite the beauty of this small perfection, his eyes were drawn to one infinitely more seductive. Almost as if in a dream, he watched his hand reach out for it.

'No!' At the first touch, Mary snapped from the pose, clambering to sit upright, drawing her legs tightly together. 'Don't!'

Horrified, Protheroe reached to reassure her, his fingers outstretched, hands shaking, but she pushed them away.

'Please, Miss Kelly, I didn't mean to …' his voice rasped dryly. 'The painting … you must understand … it was for the painting, that's all, it was *just* for the painting.'

Pulling the sheet she had been lying on close about her, Mary glared at him. 'It wasn't! You *know* it wasn't!'

He drew back from her, looking for refuge in the elaborate phrase, the eloquent explanation, but only the basest of terms for his action would come to him, and even unvoiced they made him ashamed. He got slowly to his feet and walked back to the canvas, his shoulders hunched and head lowered, until finally he turned to her, a confused, lost look in his eyes. 'Is it really such a terrible thing to do? Just to touch?'

Mary stared at him. 'Of course it is! How could you possibly think otherwise?'

He nodded, slowly, as if coming to a long-suspected, yet ultimately terrible conclusion, 'I would never have … *harmed* you. You *do* know that? I just wanted to touch – to *experience* you.' He caught her sceptical look, and gave a brief, sad sigh. 'No – you are right, of course. It was *never* for the painting.' He paused, shaking his head in regret. 'I suppose, if one were charitable, one might describe it as the *white lie* which allowed the consummation of a very one-sided love affair?'

'You don't love me. You've lied to me – used me.'

'Love often makes cheats and liars of us.'

Mary lowered her eyes, guiltily – then raised them again. 'No – because this isn't *love.*'

'You don't think so?' Protheroe gazed at the unfinished painting. 'Have you never seen a picture – or a sculpture, perhaps – so perfect it made you tremble with the desire to own it?' His eyes seemed to fix on a point well beyond the canvas. 'When I was a young man – a boy, I suppose – I saw such a picture – and I *trembled*. One thousand pounds was the asking price! No great sum for a piece of pure perfection, but to me it might as well have been one million – one hundred million. Yet I *ached* to own it. Ached in my heart – and in my loins.' He glanced toward Mary. 'Don't look so surprised. If you think great art stimulates only the mind, then you have never experienced great art. I lusted for that painting like any red-blooded swain – would have lied for it, even stolen it – and when it sold I felt all the murderous jealousy of a star-crossed lover. Can you imagine that? Desiring something so badly you hurt?'

'Yes,' she said.

The sincerity in her voice made him look at her, but then shame made him turn way. 'Well … that is how badly I wanted you. I don't love you, Mary Kelly.' Protheroe looked down at his feet. 'As a matter of fact, I've never loved any woman – not for herself.' He tapped a finger to his temple. 'Not for what lies in here. But I *worship* the female form – its perfection, the pure, sensual art that is woman – I don't love *you*, but I love your perfection. You are a masterpiece. An erotic *tour de force* that I would give Heaven and Earth to possess.'

Mary got to her feet, pulling the sheet about her. 'Just by *touching*?'

'I would not expect you to understand.' He looked at her, embarrassed. 'The truth is – I am incapable of doing more. To resort to the actions of sweating, grunting beasts is to sully the very perfection I worship.' Very deliberately, he picked up a piece of rag and dragged it across the wet paint, leaving nothing of the naked figure but a muddy smear. 'The gods will have their fun with us, won't they, my dear?'

Mary moved quietly to stand beside Protheroe, looking past him to the ruin of his painting, placing her hand gently on his shoulder.

He turned abruptly from her. 'For God's sake, Mary, don't! All I have is my self-respect. Don't take that from me with pity.'

'I wouldn't,' she said, letting the sheet fall from her.

*

The wheel of the Hansom grated against the kerbstones and came to a juddering halt. 'Will I wait again, sir?'

Evan climbed from the cab. Since leaving Cutler Street, he'd urged the driver to make haste, first to the gallery, then here, to the address Gilpin had given him, but now, standing in front of the seemingly deserted building, he felt nervous, unsure of what he might discover. 'No,' he said, pushing open the wrought iron gate, then he hesitated. 'Yes. Yes, wait for me.'

The Cardiff Academy of Art lay in darkness, with no break in the monotony of black and lifeless windows, but as he approached the heavy front door a sliver of light showed where a careless student had left it ajar. Evan paused, his hand half way to the bell-pull, then on an impulse he gave the door a push and it opened into a long, empty hall, the gloom broken only by light falling through a series of stained glass panels at the far end.

Hesitantly, he stepped in. To his right lay a large studio, the ranks of abandoned easels discernable in the dying glow of the fire, and to his left a broad staircase climbed out of view. But both were deserted, and he moved instinctively to the source of the light, crossing the marble hall to stand before the windows bearing the ludicrously ornamented initials of Mawden Protheroe.

He leaned forward, trying to make out the low murmurs coming from inside, and as he did so he noticed a small circle of light on the front of his coat. He ran his hand over it, catching the glimmer on the backs of his fingers, then went down on one knee to examine its source.

At the bottom of the nearest pane, a tiny piece of emerald glass was missing, allowing a thin, bright shaft to burst through, and he put his eye to it. The hole was smaller than a farthing, but it showed enough for his stomach to twist into a queasy knot of disgust.

In the churchlike glow of the stained glass he bowed his head, then got to his feet, feeling the bile rise in his throat. It was all true – the disgusting suggestions of the drunken woman screaming her filthy abuse: *fillies from the same stable*. He felt cold – a deep, penetrating cold that settled in his heart to leave him empty and emotionless – and as quietly as he had entered, so he left.

*

A hard, biting frost cut Mary to the bone as she slipped and slid her way back to Cutler Street. She could still feel Protheroe's touch upon her, but she no longer had the urge to scrub every last vestige of the man from her skin.

'Hettie?' she called, closing the front door behind her. At the far end of the passage, a chink of light showed from Sid and Hettie's room, but there was no other sign of life, and she unlocked her own door, crossing to the candle and lighting it. As the flame lengthened, her eyes fell upon a white frill poking from her trunk. She stared at it, feeling a shiver of misgiving, then she slowly reached down and lifted the lid. Inside, the usually neat piles of clothing lay in tangled disarray, strewn with broken pieces of the teapot Evan had given her. She backed away, looking anxiously about the room before moving quickly into the passageway. '*Hettie?*' she called, lowering her voice to just above a whisper. '*Sid?*'

The door to the back room opened and Sid appeared. 'What's up, gel?'

'Someone's been in my room.'

'Blimey!' He stepped aside. ''Ere, you'd better come in. They might still be lurkin' about.'

Gratefully she stepped inside. 'I don't think there's anyone there now, but I ...' Her eyes widened as she caught sight of Hettie, propped against the fireplace, a glass of gin in her hand and a half-empty bottle at her elbow.

'Hello, Mary, m'love. How's the toast of the *arty-farty* set, then?' She raised the glass in salute. 'You should have been here earlier. Sid and me, well, we had what you might call *a little windfall.*'

'You're wearing my blouse!'

Hettie pulled in her chin, squinting down her nose, trying to focus on the frills at her chest. 'Nice, ain't it? Makes me look the proper lady.'

'Didn't think you'd mind,' smiled Sid, affably.

Mary looked from Hettie to Sid, then back at Hettie. 'Keep it,' she said through clenched teeth.

'Oh, don't worry, I intend to. And these!' Hettie lifted her skirts to show the leg of a pair of drawers. 'I haven't had a pair of these for years.'

'Fetchin' ain't they?' laughed Sid – then, as Mary started for the door, ''Ere, don't go. At least 'ave a drink first. After all, you've paid for it.'

She spun round, eyeing him with suspicion. 'What do you mean?'

'Slow on the up-take, ain't she?' he called across to Hettie. 'Must run in the family.'

Hettie began to laugh, then stopped. 'Here! You watch it!'

'What do you mean I've paid for it?' Mary insisted, taking a step closer to Sid.

'Easy, gel. You'll 'ave me pissin' down my leg in a minute.'

Mary turned on Hettie. 'What *else* have you taken?'

'Nothing much.'

'Nah,' said Sid. 'Nothin' much. Just that little necklace with the Welsh twaddle on it. Gold, it was. Did yer know that?'

Mary flew at him. 'Where is it? What have you done with it?'

He thrust her away, sending her crashing against the door. 'It's gone. Sold.'

'Get it back! Get it back, *now!*'

'Or *what?*'

Pushing away from the door, Mary launched herself at him, her fingers raking his cheek, drawing blood, and Sid fell back against the wall, his hands raised to ward off the blows until Hettie came to his aid, grabbing Mary by the hair and swinging her round. 'You bloody cow!' she screamed. 'I stuck up for you all these bloody months – and you had *that* all the time!' She let go, and Mary went sprawling at the foot of the bed, the unemptied chamber pot spilling about her.

'Oh, shit!' said Sid. 'As if it don't stink bad enough in 'ere already.' He dabbed at the blood on his cheek. 'Fer Chris'sake sit on 'er, 'Ettie.'

But Mary was already rising, her teeth bared. '*Get it back!*'

Hettie faced her, weaving drunkenly. 'No!' In the next instant she reeled against Sid as Mary's fist caught her square on the jaw.

For a moment Sid looked down at the woman lolling in his arms, then he casually dropped her on to the floor. 'Now yer've gone an' done it,' he said, stepping over Hettie's body.

Mary remained half crouched, watching his approach, but no sooner was he within striking distance than he stopped and grinned, putting a hand to his torn face. '*Look,*' he said, 'we shouldn't be arguin' like this. We're family, ain't we? 'Ow about I get the necklace back, an' we let bygones be bygones?'

'Just get it back,' she panted, unclenching her fists. 'I don't care about the rest – just the …'

From out of nowhere, Sid's fist swept up, catching her on the side of the head, sending her spinning into the wall. But no sooner had her face struck the greasy paper than she was wrenched away, dragged across the room and slammed against the far side.

'Like t' play rough, do yer?' He twisted his fingers in her hair, wrenching her head back, lifting her face to his and back-handing her repeatedly across the mouth.

Blood splattered Mary's cheeks, and she sagged like a rag doll, but Sid shoved his knee between her thighs, pinning her to the wall. 'Oh, 'ere we bloody go!' he said, as from above came the sharp, insistent rapping. 'A little musical accompaniment, eh?' He put a hand about Mary's throat, squeezing, and she strained upwards, blood bubbling from between her smashed lips. 'Fancy a song, do yer?' He began to sing. 'Good-night *ladies*! Good-night *ladies*!' driving his fist into her face in time with the tune. Blood streamed from her nose, and he shifted his stance, punching into her stiff, corseted midriff, then lower, into her unprotected belly, his voice soaring over the hammering from above. 'Good-night *ladies* … it's time to say *goodnight*!' He released his grip and took a step back, letting her slide to the floor. 'Come on, sing up! I seem t' remember yer like singin' – or is the stink of that piss pot puttin' yer off?' He put his boot on her head, grinding her face into the wet boards, then leaned down, tousling her hair with mock affection. 'Don't reckon Clarence'd be so keen on yer now, eh? But never mind, 'cos *I* still fancy yer.'

Dazed, Mary began to push herself up, coughing and retching, blood dribbling from her mouth.

Sid backed off a little to watch her. 'So 'ow much yer goin' t' charge me, then? Gotta be less than Clarence, 'cos I 'ave t' say yer've lost yer looks a bit – an' yer smell somethin' chronic!' He cocked his head to one side in a parody of listening. 'Eh? What's that? Yer want me to 'ave it fer free? Now that's insultin' my professional pride, that is.' In one stride he covered the distance between them, lifting her several inches from the floor with a vicious kick to the ribs. 'Ain't yer gonna scream? I could do with some-thin' to drown out that racket from upstairs. Go on,' he kicked her again. 'Scream, yer stuck-up cow!'

In silence, Mary began to claw her way across the floor, dragging herself toward the door.

'Now, there's an idea,' said Sid, standing over her, catching his breath. ''Ow about we 'ave a bit of a wager? You make it t' the street, an' I'll let yer go. Can't be fairer than that, can I?'

With bloodstained and trembling fingers she reached out, trying to find a purchase on the broken boards.

'Oops,' said Sid, stepping on to her hand. He stepped back and kicked her again, then again, lifting her on to her side, sinking his iron nailed boots into her soft belly until she finally lay motionless against the wall. 'Looks like you lose, gel.' He bent down, roughly taking hold of the hem of her skirt and dragging it upwards to expose her white drawers – only they were no longer white. A dark red stain was spreading from between her legs. He hesitated, his nose turning up in disgust, then he spat on to her.

236

'Sod it. Probably got the pox, anyway.'

It was as he tossed back her skirt that a bank note fell from her pocket, and he snatched it up. 'Ten quid! *Ten bleedin' quid!*' He looked across at the still unconscious Hettie. 'Told yer she was 'oldin' out on us, didn't I, my ol' darlin',' then he chuckled. 'Who'd 'ave thought it! Two bleedin' windfalls in one day!'

In the early hours of the morning, Hettie awoke from her drunken sleep and groped about the unlit room.

'Leave me on the bloody floor, why don't you?' she called toward the bed as she got groggily to her feet. There was no answer, and she felt her way along the wall, kicking angrily at the ragged bundle that snared her feet and almost sent her sprawling. 'Bloody hell! Now what have you brought back?'

On the bed, Sid turned noisily in his sleep.

'Oh, don't let me wake you,' muttered Hettie. Feeling ill, she leaned down, one hand pressed to the wall, supporting herself as she bent to examine the bundle – snatching back her hand and jerking upright as she encountered matted, blood encrusted hair. 'Oh shit!' Panic stricken she looked into the blackness where Sid lay. 'Sid? *Sid!*'

He grunted and she made to call again, but thinking better of it she felt her way to the mantelpiece instead, lighting a candle, holding it out with trembling hands. The sight revealed by the feeble light brought her heart into her mouth.

'Oh, no,' she said. 'Oh, Christ, no.'

Chapter Thirty

A deathly hush presided over the breakfast table.

'You were home late last night, Evan,' said Florence, breaking the monopoly of tinkling china.

'I went to Cardiff.'

'Cardiff?' Ivor eyed him. 'Chasing after that … *girl*?' he said, deciding on tact.

Evan wiped his mouth with his napkin. 'I did make some enquires – but mostly I walked. As a matter of fact I walked home.'

'Did you, by God?'

Florence looked at him in surprise, then with concern. 'But it was dreadfully cold last night – and it's nearly seven miles.'

'Do him good. Get some of that soft French living off his bones.' Ivor pushed his plate away and leaned back in his chair. 'So – did you find her?'

'No. The person I was looking for wasn't there.'

Ivor lifted an eyebrow. 'The *person*? We're very formal all of a sudden.'

'Well, I've been criticised often enough in the past for being too informal. Perhaps I've seen the error of my ways. It seems I have been wrong about a good many things.'

Surprise registered on Ivor's face, and he opened his mouth to speak, but Florence shot him a meaningful glance and he fell silent.

'Well,' she said brightly, changing the subject. 'I understand that Adele Williams has just returned from Switzerland and is spending some time with Mrs Lewis. I thought perhaps we might …'

'I'm afraid not,' said Evan.

Ivor sucked at his teeth. 'You can't stay single forever, you know.'

'I appreciate your advice.' Evan got to his feet. 'But, I intend to return to Paris this afternoon.'

'But, damn it, you've only just arrived. What about Christmas?'

Florence's face lost its colour. 'What about Owen?' she asked in almost a whisper.

'Christmas will take place with or without me.' He turned to his mother. 'As for Owen – if you are content to keep him, then I am content to let you. I shall be financially responsible for him, of course, but otherwise …' He left the sentence unfinished.

*

It must have been toward evening on the first or second day that I briefly opened my eyes to find the setting sun lighting the high whitewashed ceiling, and I thought how beautiful it was – so warm and soothing.

When next I opened my eyes it was to the cold, blue-white of morning and such pain as I'd never imagined.

*

'She don't look so bad today,' said Hettie, hanging her shawl behind the door. 'Still all puffy, like, 'specially her face – but she can talk a bit.'

Sitting on the edge of the bed, his hands held out to the fire, Sid looked askance at her. 'Talkin' t' who, though, eh?'

'*Me* you daft bugger.' She crossed to the fireplace, putting the kettle on, before slumping down on to the bed beside him. 'God, my feet are killing me. It's bloody miles to that infirmary.'

Sid twisted to look at her. 'But *who else* she been talkin' to, eh?'

'No one. And she's not going to – as long as we get the necklace back.'

'I've told yer, I *can't* get it back. I sold it t' daft Sammy, an' 'e flogged it t' some sailor. It's probably 'alf way t' bleedin' Australia by now.'

Hettie sighed, her mouth drawing down at the corners, and she slapped angrily at his head. '*Why* did you do it, Sid? *Why*? For God's sake, she might have been due a beating – but not like that!'

He let her rain blows on him. 'I'd 'ad too much t' drink. I didn't know what I was doin.' Yer know 'ow my temper is, 'Ettie.'

'You nearly killed her.'

'She shouldn't 'ave gone fer my face.' He ran his fingers over his scabbed cheek. 'It was that what did it.'

'I don't know why. You're no bloody oil painting.'

He smiled sheepishly and reached for her knee. 'Yer really think yer can keep 'er sweet?'

Hettie began stroking his neck. 'Yes. She'll keep quiet for my sake. I laid it on pretty thick. Bloody nuisance about that necklace, though. How much of the money we got left?'

'Seven quid.'

'What, including the tenner you got out of her pocket?'

He nodded. 'We've 'ad a few binges since that night.'

'Well, it'll have to do.' She began pulling off her boots, wriggling her bare toes. 'You know, the doctor's told her she probably won't have no more kids. Reckons something's mucked up inside.'

'Yeah?' Sid shook his head. 'No kids, eh?' he sucked thoughtfully at his teeth. 'S'pose every cloud's got a silver linin', then, ain't it, gel?'

*

Hettie came to visit me often, always promising the return of the pendant, and seldom leaving without shedding tears over the fate of Sid and herself should I inform the police – an idea I had long since abandoned. I didn't care anymore. I saw the ugliness of my life as clearly as if it were a beetle, speared to a card and exhibited under glass. I hated Cardiff. I hated the dirty little streets and the coarse people. I hated Sid for what he'd done to me – for the babies I would never carry – and I hated them both for taking from me my precious keepsake.

But I had one last treasure – a card bearing an address, and, on the reverse side, a figure that promised things far removed from Cutler Street.

The weeks turned into months. I could walk with minimum discomfort, and the bruising began to fade. To fill the hours I began to help in the wards – just light work to begin with, but enough to make me useful and so postpone my leaving until I had fully recovered – for I had no intention of returning to Hettie's.

*

The wards were quiet and peaceful as Mary made a final round. It had been a beautifully warm day, and now the dusky light cast an orange glow along the tops of the walls, allowing even those patients who found sleep elusive to become drowsy.

A vase of flowers stood on a table in the centre of the room, and she stopped to rearrange them, looking over to where a man lay emaciated, eaten from inside by a cancer. It was over two weeks since he had been admitted, yet still he held on, and in all that time there had been not a single visitor. She gave the flowers one last tidy, then started toward the door, but as she passed his bed, she paused.

'Mr Griffiths.' she whispered, going to his side.

Lying on his back, his face grey and sunken, Griffiths opened his eyes, trying to focus on the shadowy figure standing over him. 'Who is it?' he asked with some effort.

'It's Mary. Mary Kelly.'

He snorted, but it came merely as a soft rush of air. 'Ah, *Mary Kelly.*'

The old resentment rose within her, yet the pitiable figure lying on the bed was so far removed from the bullying Griffiths she had known that she could not walk away. 'I just wanted to say … *thank you.*' The words almost stuck in her throat. 'Mrs Llewellyn told me it was you that went to see her after the fire. I know you never liked me, and – well, it was a kind thing to do.'

'I liked you well enough.' Griffiths turned his head imperceptibly. 'You think I didn't?'

'I *know* you didn't.'

'Because I was hard on you?'

'You were cruel.'

'Ah … cruel.' He stared up at the ceiling. '*Life* is cruel, Mary Kelly. You, above all, should know that.'

'That's no excuse. Mr Abrahams was never cruel.'

'Abrahams?' Griffiths gazed at her with watery eyes. '*His* cruelty will stay with you the rest of your life.'

She shook her head angrily. 'That's nonsense, and you know it.'

'Abrahams poured a poison into your ear – one for which there is no antidote.'

'No! He made me happy.'

'Happy? No, I don't think so.' For a moment his eyes blazed with a suggestion of his old fervour, then it faded and he sank back on to the pillow. 'Search your heart, Mary Kelly. Tell me you don't yearn for things you know you can never have.'

'Everyone does.'

'No, not everyone. They may grumble – wanting a few shillings more in their pay – or an hour off the working day, but otherwise they are happy enough with their lot. But *you*? You want far, *far* more.'

'I … I don't.'

Griffiths gave the ghost of a smile, the outline of his teeth showing through the thin, almost transparent lips. 'You're a liar … you always were.'

She felt her cheeks redden, but she refused to look away.

'I could have helped you,' he went on, 'but for Abrahams – that silver-tongued seducer!' He closed his eyes, summoning his remaining strength. 'You are a briar rose, Mary. A common weed. We're mostly all weeds in this Godforsaken place – clinging to life in conditions where garden plants would shrivel and die. But weeds are strong – they have to be – and the harder you cut them back the stronger they grow! I had to make you strong, Mary Kelly. I had to make you all strong – each and every one of you.'

She stared at him.

'*I* was never cruel to you, girl. A briar is happy enough with its stony patch until someone shows it a garden. Abrahams showed you *such* a garden – but he could *never* give you the key. *That* is cruelty.'

'He only wanted to help.'

'The road to hell …' he sighed, turning his face to the wall.

The sun was down behind the hills now, and she shivered in the grey twilight of the room.

'Thank you,' he said, so softly she could barely hear. 'For coming – and I pray you find that key, Mary. For without it your life is truly cursed.'

*

On the day before I was discharged, Hettie brought my one good set of clothes and four pounds, ten shillings. The remainder of my things I gave to her. I could not bear to return to the house to collect them – but more than that, they were tainted goods – soured by failure, a stink that no amount of washing could eradicate. I would start again.

The sun was shining the day I left the infirmary. A bright, fresh spring day, perfectly suited to new beginnings, and I walked to the railway station without a backward look.

At Portskewett we had to disembark and take the boat across the river Severn before boarding the London train. It was cold out on the water, but I'd bought myself a warm coat before leaving Cardiff, and I pulled it about me, imagining Evan making this same journey two years before. Then I put him and everything else behind me as I looked toward England.

BOOK 2

LONDON 1884

Chapter Thirty-One

The hansom drew to a halt in front of the imposing five-storey house. ''Ere we are. Forty-three Gloucester Gardens, Knightsbridge. That'll be three bob, sweet'eart.'

'Three shillings?' Mary tried to hide her surprise.

'Nah, I'm only raggin' yer,' grinned the perky young cabbie. 'It's only a bob – but yer can tip me if yer like. Sixpence is usual.' He took the money, touching a finger to the brim of his cap. 'First time in London, is it?'

'Yes.'

'Thought so.' He winked. 'Maybe I could show yer around on yer 'alf-day? Like that, would yer?'

Mary drew herself up. 'What makes you think I *work* here?'

'Well, yer certainly ain't the lady of the 'ouse, are yer,' he laughed, flicking the reins. 'You think about it, Taffy, darlin'. I'm round this way a fair bit, so I'll look out for yer, alright?'

Unsettled, Mary watched him drive away, then looked down at her clothes, but whatever their shortcomings, there was nothing she could do about them now, so she turned instead to the house, feeling for the card and checking the address in the fading light, before pushing open the gate and climbing the stone steps to the front entrance.

'I would like to see Mr Morganstone,' she said when the door was opened by a timorous-looking maid.

'Mr Morganstone, ma'am?' The young woman's brow creased, and she pushed nervously at a loose strand of hair. 'Oh … yes. Won't you come in, ma'am.'

The interior of the house was even more impressive than the outside. Richly decorated, the grand, oak-panelled hallway was crowned by a sweeping staircase, while overhead and around the walls, crystal gleamed in the gaslight.

'Will you wait in here, ma'am?' said the maid, showing Mary into a drawing-room of similar opulence. 'If you are cold, ma'am, I can make up the fire?'

'No … Please don't trouble.'

'Then I shall tell Madame you are here. May I take your name, ma'am?'

'It's Kelly.' Mary hesitated, collecting herself. '*Miss* Mary Kelly.'

'Very good, ma'am.'

Alone in the room, Mary looked about her. The wine-red walls were hung with paintings, whilst on every polished surface stood something to capture the eye or delight the senses. Fresh flowers scented the air, and amidst the vases and cut glass, bronze nymphs flirted and played while bronze heroes looked on, their bearded countenances fixed forever in stern disapproval.

From the street came the sound of children's voices, and she crossed to the window, edging aside the lace curtain to look out. In the distance the stark trees of Hyde Park stood misty in the evening twilight, the lamps of cabs and carriages glimmering between them like will-o'-the-wisps, while on the other side of the road a nanny, half scolding, half laughing, shepherded her two young charges home. It was another world, and Mary watched entranced, feeling a flutter of excitement – until from behind her came a discreet cough, and she spun round.

The tall middle-aged woman standing just inside the doorway was dressed in a black riding habit that accentuated her figure, and perfectly complemented her look of haughty disdain – a look that disappeared the moment she smiled. 'You wish to see me, *Miss* …?'

'Kelly.' Mary prompted.

'Miss Kelly. Please forgive me. My maid, Emily, is quite terrible with names.' The woman unpinned her hat, placing it on the table, then looked up, her strong face and patrician nose softened by a pair of bright, good-humoured eyes. 'Now, I understand you wish to see Mr Morganstone. But I'm afraid he does not reside here.'

'But I have his card.'

The woman removed a glove and took Mary's hand. 'I am Madame Bennaire,' she said, the hint of a French accent colouring her otherwise flawless English.

'I am very pleased to meet you. But, I don't understand. He gave me the card himself.'

'There is no need for alarm, my dear. Mr Morganstone is …' The woman broke off, letting go of Mary's hand and reaching for her face instead, touching her fingers to the faint pink scar near her jaw. 'But you have recently been in an accident,' she said with concern.

Startled, Mary drew back a little. 'No … well, that is, *yes*, but …'

'You must be more careful, my dear,' said Mme Bennaire softly, her scented hand lingering close to Mary's face. 'Such delicate, expressive features should *never* be allowed to become spoiled. It would be quite unforgivable.'

Seduced by the soothing, almost mesmeric tone, Mary let her cheek brush against the woman's fingers once more, then she stepped back, blushing.

'Well,' Mme Bennaire smiled, moving away to pat the back of an arm-chair. 'Why don't you come and sit down and tell me what our dear friend, Mr Morganstone, has been up to.' She reached for the bell-pull. 'Will you take sherry? I usually do at this hour.'

'Yes … please.' Mary followed her to the chair, sitting self-consciously. 'He … Mr Morganstone, said that if ever I was in London, I should call on him here. That he could find me modelling work.'

'You have worked as a model before?'

'Yes, in Cardiff.'

'In Cardiff?' Mme Bennaire's face lit up. 'What a delightful coincidence! I must introduce you to one of my other young ladies. She too comes from Cardiff.'

'So you *do* employ models?'

'Oh yes. Mr Morganstone has, on occasion, sent me young women he finds exceptional – and he is *most* discerning. Tell me …'

There was a tap at the door and the maid appeared. 'You rang, ma'am?'

'Yes, Emily. You may pour the sherry.'

'Yes, ma'am.'

'And Emily?'

'Yes, ma'am?'

'Why is the fire not lit?'

'I'm sorry, ma'am. I did ask the lady …'

'Silence!' snapped Mme Bennaire. 'How dare you try to implicate a guest!' A hard glint came to her eyes. 'I shall most certainly speak to you about this later.'

'Yes, ma'am.'

Emily brought the sherry, bobbing a curtsey as she handed each of them a glass, but Mme Bennaire continued to eye her coldly. 'Now, you will ask Miss Julia to come downstairs – then you will come back and attend to this fire. Is that quite understood?'

'Yes, ma'am. Thank you, ma'am.'

Mary watched the wretched woman scurry away, anxious to say something in her defence, but the sudden change in Mme Bennaire was unnerving, and she remained silent.

'So, Miss Kelly,' said Mme Bennaire, instantly regaining her good humour. 'What are your plans now that you are in London?'

'I don't really have any.'

'And where may I contact you?'

'I don't know,' said Mary, beginning to feel foolish. 'I came here straight from the railway station.'

Mme Bennaire's eyebrows arched upwards. 'But what of your luggage?'

'I haven't any.'

The woman glanced again at the faint traces of violence on Mary's face, and sighed. 'I suspect you have a story to tell, my dear, hmm? But I can see you are tired and in no condition for confidences at present, so why don't I have Emily fetch a cab to take you straight to a hotel. There is an excellent one quite close by.'

Mary hesitated. 'It won't be too expensive? I do have money, but …'

'There is no need to concern yourself. I'm sure we can find you a most suitable accommodation for less than fifteen shillings a night.'

Mary blanched, shaking her head. 'I couldn't possibly afford that.'

'Oh, stuff and nonsense. I shall have it put on my account – and, if and when we have you working, you can reimburse me.'

'Then, it *is* possible you might have a job for me?'

Mme Bennaire smiled serenely. 'We must wait and see, mustn't we. But I have *every* reason to hope. Mr Morganstone has seldom let me down.'

A timid knock at the door presaged the reappearance of Emily. 'Please, ma'am,' she said. 'Miss Julia says she cannot come down at present.'

'Ah, yes, of course,' said Mme Bennaire with a glance toward the clock. 'How *very* vexing.' She smiled at Mary. 'Well, you will meet her tomorrow. I shall send her to call on you. Would eleven o'clock be too early?' Then, turning to the maid, 'Come, come! Don't stand gawping, Emily! I want a cab. A hansom, mind – not an old growler. And I want it *now*!'

*

The young woman standing in the foyer of the Alexandra Hotel the next morning was a picture of sophistication. In her early twenties, with her slender figure displayed to perfection in an expensive chocolate brown suit, and her hair pulled up beneath a matching hat, she seemed to Mary completely unapproachable – until she turned, and her face creased into a broad smile. 'You must be Mary Kelly. I'm Julia – Julia Devereaux.'

'I'm very pleased to meet you,' said Mary, tentatively extending her hand.

Julia clasped it, lifting an eyebrow in amusement. 'Likewise. You've had breakfast?'

'Yes.'

She ran a critical eye over Mary's clothes. 'In your room, would be my guess. Well, never mind. We'll soon sort you out. Come on, I've got a cab waiting.'

'Where are we going?'

'Shopping. But don't worry, Madame is paying, so all you have to do is sit back and enjoy yourself.' She took Mary's arm, leading her out into the spring sunshine and toward the waiting hansom. 'Up you go,' she said, helping Mary to mount the iron step. She stepped back, shading her eyes from the sun. 'Regent Street, cabbie. But don't go straight there. Give us a bit of a tour, alright?' The haggard old driver gave her a bored nod, and she followed Mary into the cab, settling herself on to the seat as they pulled from the kerb. 'So, I hear you're from Cardiff. Bit different here, eh?'

'Yes, a bit.'

The hansom turned into the park, moving briskly and easily along the tree-lined roads. 'It's too early for the carriage trade,' said Julia. 'But come the season, you can't move for them along here. Landaus, Victorias and all manner of others – and the pavements filled with people who've come just to watch you ride up and down. How do you fancy that for a lark?'

'I should think it's wonderful.'

'Oh, it is. I love it.'

'You have a carriage?'

'Madame does.'

Mary sat back, picking at her sleeve, watching the passing scenery with increasing anxiety, until finally she threw up her hands. 'This is madness! I have absolutely no idea what I'm doing here. And the *cost* of it all! That hotel! I couldn't sleep for worrying about it – five shillings and sixpence a night – *just for the room*! Dinner, another five shillings! Even breakfast costs a half-crown! It all comes to more than I'd earn in a fortnight. And everyone looking at me, thinking I shouldn't be there. And they're right – I shouldn't.' She shifted in her seat, turning to look squarely at the other woman. 'I don't belong. Even the cabbie yesterday could see it.'

'Who cares what a bloody cabbie thinks. And besides, by the time we're finished today, he won't be able to tell you from the Princess Royal.'

Mary lowered her head, staring into her lap. 'I'm terrified. I've already spent more money than I've got. And now we're going shopping? I could never begin to pay any of this back.'

'You needn't worry – truly.' Julia leaned forward, trying to recapture Mary's gaze. 'Madame *will* take care of it.'

'But why? I don't even know her. Why would she do all this for me?'

'She's a very special person.'

'Yes, but …' Mary chewed at her lip. 'Oh, I don't know – none of it makes any sense.' She gave a sideways glance. 'And besides … don't you find her a bit … *frightening*?'

'Who? *Madame*?'

'Yesterday, she seemed so kind, but then, suddenly – with the maid …'

Julia's puzzled frown melted away. '*Emily*?' she chuckled. 'Is that who you're worried about? Listen, whatever happens to that silly girl – she brings it on herself.'

'But …?' Mary gave an exasperated look, then a deep sigh. '*Please* – I have to know. Is this all genuine?'

Julia smiled. 'Oh, it's genuine. But I do understand. When I first arrived, I wouldn't even have breakfast for fear of running up a bill I couldn't pay.' She looked searchingly at Mary. 'You *did* have breakfast, didn't you?'

Mary shook her head. 'I haven't eaten since yesterday morning.'

'I should have guessed,' laughed Julia, taking Mary's hand and squeezing it. 'Well, I think an early lunch is called for, don't you?' She pushed open the small hatch above her head. 'Driver! Never mind Regent Street. Take us to Epitaux's in the Haymarket.'

*

'It might have been made for you,' exclaimed Julia three hours later as Mary emerged from the fitting room. 'Black suits you very well – and in my opinion it's not a colour everyone can wear.'

Mary ran her hands adoringly over the tight bodice and full skirt. 'It's *lovely*. But perhaps I should try something else? Something less expensive?'

Standing a little way off, Madame Coubret looked suitably offended.

'There isn't anything else,' laughed Julia. 'Madame Coubret only makes to order. This isn't some Bute Street pawn shop, you know.'

'Then how …?' Mary looked down at the dress.

'It's mine – or it would have been. Now it's yours.' She got to her feet. 'It's perfect, as always, Madame. She'll wear it now.'

Mme Coubret motioned disdainfully toward the dressing room. 'Should I dispose of Mademoiselle's other clothes?'

'No,' said Julia. 'I have a use for those. Would you have them delivered?'

'Of course, Mademoiselle.'

Mary was still admiring herself in the mirror, turning this way and that, lifting her skirt to show the sleek new button boots – and Julia stood watching her. 'My but don't you fancy yourself now,' she grinned.

'I don't.'

'Don't you just! You're standing a good two inches taller.'

Mary laughed with embarrassment, turning her head to catch her reflection. 'I'm sorry, but it's just so gorgeous.'

'Don't be sorry. It's what it's all about – clothes, and how to wear them. Just be sure to keep your head up, do everything slowly, never look higher than the bridge of your nose – and you'll be the perfect lady.'

'Like this?' Mary laughed, looking down her nose, her eyes crossing.

'Well – not *exactly*.'

'Then how about this?' She walked slowly to the door, her head tilted regally, looking back at Julia with an expression of perfect serenity. 'Shall we go, Julia, *dear*?'

Julia nodded, smiling in appreciation. 'Oh, yes,' she said. '*Exactly* like that.'

*

'And now, may I present – fresh from the unspoiled fields of Wales – Mary, *The Flower of Nant-y-Pridd.*' Julia stepped theatrically into the drawing-room to reveal Mary, transformed in black velvet, standing stiffly, and not a little self-consciously, in the doorway.

'Oh, merveilleux, ma chérie!' Mme Bennaire rose from her chair, turning enthusiastically to the two young women seated about her in the lamplight. 'Such presence! Such bearing, don't you think?' She crossed to the door taking Mary by the hand. 'Do come and join us. We are just taking a late tea. Do you like muffins? Maud has only this moment fetched them from the dear little man in the street.' She led Mary to the sofa. 'Maudie, darling, be an angel and toast another, would you? And Elspeth? Perhaps you would play for us?'

Elspeth rose, her high cheekbones and severely parted hair adding to her stern appearance. 'Of course, Madame,' she said, giving a stiff little nod. 'Does Madame have a request?'

'Something soothing, dear. Nothing too *Germanic.*'

'Ja, mein mistress!' She clicked her heels, giving Mary a wink.

'You are from Germany?' asked Mary, settling herself carefully on to the chair, the fullness of the new skirt with its elaborate bustle still feeling strange.

Mme Bennaire smiled. 'Not *quite* yet – but soon, hmm, Elspeth?'

Sitting at the piano, Elspeth struck four violent chords, causing a ripple of laughter from the others, before switching to a softer, more haunting melody.

Mme Bennaire rested her head against the back of the sofa, briefly closing her eyes as she listened to the opening bars, then she reached out and patted the empty seat by her side. 'Julia, come and sit. I want to hear all about your day. Did you have a wonderful time?' She waved her hand dismissively. 'Of course you did. You are two *perfect* Welsh lilies. How could you fail to get along other than famously?'

Maud handed Mary a plate with the halves of a buttered muffin. 'Tea? Or would you prefer sherry?'

'Tea, please.'

'It was a *perfect* day,' said Julia, sitting down.

Mme Bennaire beamed. 'I never doubted it. And you see? I was right. The dress you commissioned last month fits her perfectly.' She turned to Mary, stroking the folds of the rich fabric. 'Madame Coubret makes such wonderful clothes. One must be patient, of course, but it is *always* worth the wait.'

Mary looked at her. 'I haven't thanked you, Madame. You've been so incredibly kind.'

'Oh, nonsense.' Taking Mary's hand, she pressed it between her own. 'As I explained yesterday, Mr Morganstone has a flair for spotting hidden talents, and I am becoming ever more convinced that you and I are going to be *very* good for each other.' Her eyes fell to Mary's fingers, and she gently stroked them. 'Do you play?'

'Play?'

'The piano, my dear.'

'Oh – no. I'm sorry.'

'No matter – but if you should care to learn, perhaps Elspeth might teach you? Would you do that, Elspeth?'

'Of course, Madame.'

Mme Bennaire looked about her, sighing with pleasure. 'Well, this *is* nice, don't you think? I do so love these cosy evenings. Lamplight is so flattering – and with a good fire and pleasant company …' She spread her hands. 'What more might one ask for?'

At the piano, Elspeth stopped playing and gently closed the lid. 'One might ask for a play?'

'Oh, yes, yes!' smiled Mme Bennaire. 'Quite perfect.' She gripped Mary's arm. 'Do you like the theatre? I *adore* it. Elspeth and Maud are both accomplished actresses, but Julia is our star performer. Would you like to see her act?'

Mary met Julia's eyes. 'Yes, very much.'

'Then what is your pleasure, ladies?' asked Julia with a mock bow, holding Mary's gaze.

Mme Bennaire thought for a moment. 'Something light and amusing, perhaps?'

'Very well.' Julia went to stand beside the piano, her hands on her hips and her chest thrown out. 'Ladies and *absent* gentlemen. I should like to present, for your edification and delight, a scene from *Captain Jolly's Come-uppance, or, The Bold Young Pirate!*'

There was a ripple of applause.

'Since you have come late to this performance,' boomed Julia, in a deep, throaty voice. 'You have missed both the first and second acts …'

'Shame!' called Maud and Elspeth in unison.

'… as well as the interval for drinks.'

'Even greater shame!' they cried, with Mme Bennaire adding support.

'So I shall give a brief précis of the plot.'

There was a weak *hooray* from Maud and Elspeth.

Julia struck up an heroic pose. 'Cowardly and cruel Captain Jolly of His Majesty's Ship *Lillyliver* – this demanding part to be played by Miss Elspeth …'

Elspeth came from behind the piano and made an elaborate bow.

'… and his faithful, if *misguided,* cabin boy Little Dick – shortly to be played, *or* – to be played, *shortly,* by Miss Maud …'

Maud went to join Elspeth, spreading her skirts in a curtsey before going down on to her knees to gaze up longingly at Captain Jolly.

'… have been confronted on the poop deck by the dashing and, dare I say …' Julia twiddled the end of an imaginary moustache, '… *damnably handsome* pirate, Captain Ironrod.'

'Hooray!' called Mary, entering into the spirit.

Julia bowed to her. 'Thank you, madam. We seldom get patrons of your exquisite taste at the afternoon performance. Please do come again – and be sure to bring your friends.'

'Enough of this, you insolent cur,' cried Elspeth, taking a step forward and flicking at Julia with her handkerchief. 'Do you know who you are dealing with, sir?'

'That's the way to treat 'im, Cap'n,' squeaked Maud, her hands clasped in devotion.

'Indeed I do, sir!' boomed Julia. 'Why, 'tis the scurviest knave that ever sailed the seven seas! The very popinjay I have been seeking out these past two acts – and interminable intermission – and without so much as a drop of grog to wet my whistle!'

'Oh, sir, we are doomed!' squeaked Maud, clutching at Elspeth's leg.

'The Devil we are!' cried Elspeth, drawing an imaginary sword. 'I shall skewer you, sir! Cut you from stem to stern and spread your innards for the gulls!'

'Ooh, sir!' fawned Maud. 'You're *so* brave!'

Elspeth took up a fencing stance and held it.

'The management,' Julia announced with an obsequious bow, 'regrets it is unable to present to you the splendour of thundering cannons, gushing blood – and displays of manly courage, both stout and upright, and humbly requests you use your imagination.' She bowed again, then turned to Elspeth, who groaned and fell against the piano, the back of her hand pressed to her forehead. 'Damn you, Ironrod, I surrender. Strike our colours, Dick!'

'So, Jolly! Finally, I have my revenge!' Julia twiddled the imaginary moustache once more. 'Yet still you do not know me?'

'Know you? All the world knows *you!*' Then Elspeth looked again, raising her hand and pointing at Julia with a trembling finger. 'But wait, *so-called* Captain Ironrod! Now I see through your cunning disguise. Why, you are nothing more than Roger, my former cabin boy – grown to a fine, and *damnably handsome,* young man!'

'Yes, I am indeed Roger the cabin boy! The poor lad who served under you so tirelessly, and whom you would beat and flog in return!'

Maud clung to Elspeth's skirt, looking up with pleading eyes. 'Oh, sir. You can beat and flog *me*. I don't mind.'

'The very same poor boy you would keel-haul and hang by the thumbs from the top-mast!' continued Julia.

'Keel haul *me*!' chirruped Maud, 'I don't mind.'

Elspeth turned on her, lifting an eyebrow. 'And what about hanging you by the thumbs from the top-mast?'

'I … I don't like heights,' whimpered Maud.

Picking up a paper-knife, Julia held the point to Elspeth's throat. 'Your thumb-hanging days are jolly well over, Jolly. I'm going to give you a taste of your own medicine!' She towered over Maud. 'Fetch me a stick, Dick!'

Maud shuffled behind the piano and returned with a stem of bamboo from an arrangement that stood in a vase.

'W-What are you going to do?' quailed Elspeth.

Julia cut the air with the bamboo. 'I'm going to beat you, Jolly. Six good strokes – then six more for good measure. Don't that make you a-tremble, sir?'

'I'm not frightened of you, Ironrod,' said Elspeth, setting her jaw.

'Is that so? Well drop those breeches and we'll soon see the cut of your jib!'

Tears of laughter were coursing down Mary's cheeks, while beside her Mme Bennaire chuckled merrily. Julia glanced at them, grinning, then suddenly began to cough. 'I said …' She coughed again. 'Drop those …' The coughing became continuous and Mme Bennaire rushed to her, gently patting her on the back. 'Elspeth, bring her a little sherry, quickly, there's a dear.'

'I'm alright,' gasped Julia, taking the glass that Elspeth offered and sipping in between bouts of coughing. 'Just give me a minute.'

'No, no,' said Mme Bennaire firmly. 'You must come and sit down.'

'But we haven't finished the play.'

'Well, never mind. We shall just have to wait until another evening. That is, unless …' she looked across to Mary, 'perhaps, *you* would take Julia's part?'

Mary's eyes widened, and she shook her head. 'Oh, but I couldn't. I don't know the words, and …'

'Just make them up,' said Julia, coming to sit by her side. 'You could do it easily, and …' She coughed again. 'We can't have Captain Jolly getting away without his come-uppance, can we?'

'Well,' Mary hesitated, then got slowly to her feet. 'I *could* try, if you'd like?'

'That's the spirit!' cried Mme Bennaire delightedly, taking her by the shoulders and kissing her on both cheeks. 'Now, give us a performance that would do credit to the great Ellen Terry herself.'

Mary picked up the stick, holding it uncertainly.

'Think yourself into the part,' smiled Mme Bennaire. 'That's the secret.' She drew herself up, her hands moving expressively. 'You are in charge. Show it in your every movement.'

Copying her, Mary took a firmer grip on the bamboo.

'Head up and never look higher than the bridge of your nose,' called Julia from the sofa.

Mary grinned and lifted her head, adopting a disdainful look.

'Perfect!'

'You know?' said Mme Bennaire thoughtfully. 'I've just had the most marvellous idea. Don't you think it would be wonderfully novel if the pirate were a woman?'

'A *lady* pirate?' said Julia.

Elspeth scoffed. 'Captain Jolly – bested by a feeble woman? I think not!'

'Ah,' said Mme Bennaire, 'I believe you may be wrong. I think *Mistress* Ironrod might well prove more than a match for Captain Jolly. But let us see.' She threw Mary a smile of encouragement. 'Prove me right, my dear. Show us how a pirate *queen* would do it, hmm?'

'Let's take it from my line,' said Elspeth, hunching her shoulders and gazing fearfully at Mary. 'W-What are you going to do, *Mistress* Ironrod?'

Mary hesitated, looking dubiously at the cane in her hands. 'I think this is going to be rather difficult …'

Sitting on the sofa, Julia glanced nervously at Madame Bennaire.

'… because it seems we have *several* options.' With growing confidence, Mary began to circle the cringing Elspeth. 'Perhaps we should have you judged by a jury of your peers, hmm?' Deliberately, she lifted the bamboo cane, pointing with it toward the sofa. 'You, my *dear* Madame,' she smiled, nodding graciously. 'And you, dear, *sweet* girl. How would *you* have me deal with this blaggard, this ne'er-do-well, this *grovelling* jackanapes?'

A huge smile illuminated Julia's face, then she lowered her eyes demurely, clasping her hands in her lap. 'Oh, madam! I am but a young and innocent gel – freshly come from the country. What can I know of your rough, piratical ways?'

'What indeed?' Mary raised an empirical eyebrow. 'Ah, but I see your little plan, my dear. Oh, indeed I do! For I think you have rather *over-played* the coquette!'

Julia looked up from beneath her lashes. 'Whatever can you mean, madam?'

Taking hold of Elspeth's collar, Mary drew her toward the sofa. 'Do you take me for a simpleton, my dear? A damnable dullard who would not recognise her old captain's daughter, *Miss Julia Jolly*, come to rescue her reprobate father?'

'Oh, lummie!' cried Maud.

'Madam,' said Julia with wide-eyed innocence. ''Tis true I am your wretched captive's daughter – but I have not come to rescue him, but rather to see him flogged to within an inch of his life – for he was very cruel to me when I was a child, and would not buy me a dolly!'

Mary's nostrils flared as she looked down at the hapless Elspeth. 'No dolly! God's blood! Is there no end to your villainy! Bend over, sir! I am going to beat you here and now! In front of these good people.'

The look on Elspeth's face, for all the world like a startled cod, made Mary want to laugh, but she forced her lips into a sardonic smile. 'Six of the very, *very* best.'

'I … I'm not frightened of you,' quavered Elspeth, then looking sternly at Julia. 'You just wait till I get you home, miss!'

Mary kept her head raised, looking at Elspeth along the length of her nose, her chin tilted authoritatively. 'Not frightened, eh?' She gripped the stick at each end, flexing it just as Griffiths had so often done. 'Well, we shall see. Bend over, Captain Jolly.'

Elspeth sneered. 'You can't make me.'

'Can't I? – *Can't I indeed*?' Mary moved her feet apart, swishing the bamboo through the air. 'Perhaps you would prefer twelve? I have all day, you know!'

'Oh, Gawd!' said Maud.

'No, no, Mistress Ironrod. I *will* obey.' Meekly, Elspeth bent forward, her hands on her knees. 'Be gentle with me, *good* Mistress Ironrod.'

Mary raised the cane in readiness – then hesitated.

'Strike!' said Mme Bennaire, beaming. 'Her skirts will protect her.'

In the next second the stick thudded into the dove-grey silk.

'Mercy!'

'Take your punishment like a man!'

Dust flew from Elspeth's skirt as the cane struck again.

'Oh, no, please.'

'Silence!' commanded Mary, delivering yet another stroke.

'Oh, God have mercy. I am undone …' Elspeth threw herself at Mary's feet, grovelling. 'Undone, for all to see!'

There was a deathly hush, then Mme Bennaire was on her feet, clapping delightedly, quickly joined by Julia, then Maud and finally Elspeth. 'Bravo! Bravo! A superb performance! Quite outstanding!'

Flushed with happiness, Mary took their applause, bowing and curt-seying to shouts of *encore* and *author,* until they all broke into laughter and Mme Bennaire came and took hold of her two hands. 'You have the theatre in your blood, my dear. No question of it. That was undoubtedly what Mr Morganstone saw.'

Julia drew to her side. 'Shall we do another?'

'No,' said Madame Bennaire. 'It's time for dinner.' She looked to Mary.

'You *will* join us?'

'I should love to.'

'Wonderful!' She turned to Elspeth. 'Will you escort our guest?'

Elspeth extended her arm, and Mary made a show of taking it, allowing herself to be led from the room.

'Ladies?' said Mme Bennaire.

Maud and Julia came to her, one on each side, and she took their arms, lowering her voice to a whisper. 'You girls may have to look to your laurels,' she said. 'Oh, *indeed* you may.'

Chapter Thirty-Two

Mme Bennaire, Maud and Elspeth were already seated as Julia swept in and took her place for breakfast the following morning.

'I'm sorry I'm late. I was almost dressed when a button came away in my hand. I hope you haven't waited.'

At the head of the table, Mme Bennaire waved dismissively. 'No matter, my dear. A few minutes will not kill us, I think.'

Elspeth looked across the sparkling silverware. 'If you're putting on a little weight – perhaps you might ask Mme Coubret to stitch with twine rather than thread?'

'Thank you, Elspeth,' Julia smiled, nodding politely. 'And it's very nice to see you this morning, too.'

'So,' said Mme Bennaire as Maud removed the covers from the breakfast. 'Now that we have had time to sleep on the matter, I am anxious to know how we all feel about our new prospect. Maudie, darling?'

'I think she'll do very well,' said Maud without looking up.

'Elspeth?'

'Yes – with certain reservations.'

Julia looked across at her. 'Reservations?'

'Naturally. We know nothing about her. She has a flair for parlour games, and seems personable enough – but reputations are at stake, and I would need to know a great deal more before being certain.'

'Quite right,' said Mme Bennaire, smiling. 'You must be patient with us, Julia. You've spent a whole day with Mary – and have a good deal more in common with her.' She poured herself a cup of tea. 'Tell me, does she have any inkling about us?'

'No. I've managed to answer most of her questions without really telling her anything, but she *is* suspicious – mostly, I think, because she believes it's all too good to be true, and she'll end up owing money she can't repay.'

Mme Bennaire sighed. 'The poor girl. You have reassured her?'

'Yes, of course, but …' Julia gave a small shrug.

'Hmm,' Mme Bennaire looked to Maud. 'What is our investment so far?'

Maud thought for a moment. 'Not more than thirty pounds – a little more if we include cab fares.'

'Well, I would not have her fretting over such trifles, but I can't see how it can be avoided, unless …' She looked to Julia. 'Do you think, if we were to make her a gift of some money – possibly as a retainer?'

'And what if she runs off with it?' asked Elspeth.

'Then, my dear, she will have saved us a good deal of time and energy.'

Julia shook her head. 'I'm not sure that giving her money will help, Madame. She'd only feel more indebted.'

'Then there really is nothing to be done, and you must try your best to placate her. Now, what else have you to tell us?'

'Not very much. Her story is true to the best of my knowledge – but since Elspeth has doubts, perhaps we should confirm it with Mr Morganstone, just to be sure?'

'I have already done so,' said Mme Bennaire. 'And he is in no doubt she is genuine. The only question in my mind is whether she is suitable.' She sipped at her tea. 'Perhaps I shall telegraph those dear old reprobates, Drumcanon and Makepiece. Have you any particularly important engagements this evening, Julia? Anything that Maud or Elspeth cannot accommodate?'

'No. But even if I had …' Julia smiled mischievously. 'As you've told us many times, Madame – *disappointment can often be its own reward.*'

Mme Bennaire's eyes twinkled with merriment, then she said, 'But Mary will need some preparation.'

'Leave it to me, Madame.'

'Excellent. Then let us pass on to other business. Tomorrow is the last Friday of the month. *Maud?*'

Maud gave a glum look, and Mme Bennaire shifted her gaze. 'Elspeth?'

'If you wish, Madame.'

'I'll go,' said Julia, looking about the table. 'I quite enjoy it.'

'Of course,' sighed Elspeth, smiling sweetly. '*Nostalgia.*'

Julia returned the smile. 'Perhaps I'll take Mary. Show her the delights of Whitechapel.'

'Oh, and I'm sure she will be *delighted,*' said Elspeth.

'Then that is settled.' Mme Bennaire unfolded her napkin and laid it in her lap. 'Now, one last thing. I understand we are to receive Mr Bull today.' She looked searchingly at Julia. 'I take it the arrangement continues to be satisfactory?'

'Archie?' Julia gave a casual nod. 'Yes, of course.'

'You *will* tell me the moment it becomes *unsatisfactory*?'

'Is there anything we could do about it if it did?' asked Elspeth.

'There is *always* something one can do,' said Mme Bennaire. 'I will not tolerate my girls being treated …' There was a knock at the door. 'Ah, Mattie,' she smiled. 'I was just about to ring. Do you think you could bring us some more tea? This pot has gone quite cold.'

'Yes, ma'am, of course.' The plump, rosy-cheeked housekeeper picked up the teapot. 'Is there anything else I can get you ladies?'

'No, thank you, Mattie.' Mme Bennaire looked up at the clock. 'Has Emily arrived?'

'She's here, ma'am, but she was late again. I've set her cleaning the boots and shoes.'

Mme Bennaire nodded her approval. 'Well, have her do them *twice* – and make sure she pays particular attention to my riding boots – then send her to me.'

'Of course, ma'am.'

Julia waited until the housekeeper had left, then began to laugh.

'What's so funny?' asked an amused Elspeth.

'It's Mary,' Julia looked about her, grinning broadly. 'I forgot to tell you, she's *terribly* concerned for Emily.'

*

The Julia who took her seat in the plush, candlelit restaurant that evening was neither the self-assured young woman Mary remembered from the shopping trip, nor the giggling girl she'd experienced just a few hours ago as they'd teased and preened each other in the privacy of Julia's room. She had become once more the unapproachable Julia – elegant and aloof – only this time Mary felt the thrill of knowing it was all a game – one in which she intended to match her new friend, move for move.

'May I say you look as delightful as always, my dear?' said Captain Makepiece, his gaunt, clean-shaven face still bearing the trace of a tropical tan.

Julia took the compliment as if bestowing a favour. 'Gentlemen, might I introduce you to Miss Mary Kelly?'

'*Enchanté*, Miss Kelly.'

'A pleasure, madam,' beamed Drumcanon, stepping forward.

Mary regarded them both. They were not old, but neither were they young, and immaculate in evening dress they gave off an air of privilege that would have intimidated her had she encountered them under any other circumstance. Even now, transformed as she was by pearls, cream silk and Julia's patient ministrations, her heart beat faster. 'The pleasure is all mine, Gentlemen,' she said, then surprised by her audacity she offered her gloved hand.

260

'Captain William Makepiece, ma'am.' The captain bent low, taking her fingers and kissing her hand.

'And Mr Augustus Drumcanon, ma'am.' Not to be outdone, Drumcanon bowed lower and lingered longer.

'Some wine, ladies?' asked Makepiece, as soon as they were seated.

Julia gave the tiniest nod.

'Miss Kelly, perhaps you have a preference?'

'You are most kind, Captain, but I'm certain that whatever you choose will be quite delightful.'

'No, please, we would deem it a great honour if *you* were to choose.'

Mary caught the look of wicked merriment in Julia's eyes. 'I should hate to presume upon your generosity, Gentlemen.'

'Oh, presume away, dear lady,' said Drumcanon, his stouter, jollier features puckering into a broad smile. 'Hang the expense, eh, Makepiece?'

'Well …' began Mary.

'Champagne,' suggested Julia, finally coming to her rescue.

Mary smiled sweetly. 'Yes, of course. Champagne is always acceptable, don't you think?'

'Oh, it's fine enough, I suppose,' said the Captain, looking disappointed. 'But I get dashed tired of it. Come now, Miss Kelly, why not share with us your favourite tipple, eh?'

'Captain?' Julia reprimanded him quietly.

Makepiece raised his hands. 'My apologies, ma'am.' He nodded to the waiter. 'Bring us two bottles of champagne.'

On the far side of the table, Julia maintained an expression of perfect innocence, even as her foot kicked playfully at Mary's ankle.

Mary gazed at her, discreetly raising an eyebrow before turning to Makepiece. 'Captain,' she said. 'I fear Miss Julia is being a little unfair – and I totally agree with you. Champagne is all very fine, but – if you really don't mind the expense – then might we have a bottle of the Lafite '47? I would, of course, suggest the 1811 – but so few places have it.'

Julia let slip a look of surprise.

'Lafite, you say?' Makepiece called back the waiter. 'Do you have a Lafite 1811?'

The waiter bent forward, speaking close to his ear.

'Is it, by God?' he exclaimed, looking at Mary with a new respect. 'Well, forget the champagne and bring two bottles of the '47.'

'Yes, sir. Of course, sir.'

'You seem to know your wines, dear lady,' said Drumcanon, beaming.

'No, not really.' She smiled sweetly at Julia. 'But one knows what one likes.'

*

A fine rain hung in the afternoon air, cloaking the streets in a dull, yellowish mist as the hansom made its way down Fleet Street and up Ludgate Hill toward St Paul's.

'*But one knows what one likes.*' Julia leaned back against the seat of the cab and laughed. 'You're a card, Mary. How on earth did you manage it?'

'When you work in a hotel you learn all manner of things. There was always someone trying to be all grand and clever, ordering something they knew we wouldn't have. Mrs Cartwright used to say we should order a bottle in – just to spite them.'

'It was priceless. Madame really laughed when I told her. You made a good impression last night, Mary, a *very* good impression.'

Mary sat back happily, looking through the tightly closed windows with all the excitement of an inquisitive child. 'So where are we going today?'

'Somewhere *different.*'

'And we're taking my old clothes?' She looked down at the brown paper parcel resting on the floor by their feet.

'Umm-hmm.'

'But you won't tell me where or what for?'

'You'll see soon enough.'

Mary snuggled down inside the thick winter coat Julia had given her. 'Well, alright. I'll go anywhere, and do anything you want,' she sighed. 'Just don't wake me up because I seem to be having the most lovely dream.'

'So, you're enjoying yourself?'

'You can't imagine.'

'Oh, I don't have to imagine.'

Mary looked at her askance. 'So – what brought you here from Cardiff? Was it Mr Morganstone?'

'No, I met him here in London, about two and a half years ago. I was working as a waitress. Terrible bloody job! Fourteen hours a day – and six of us sleeping in a smelly, pokey little room above the restaurant.' She gave a wry smile. 'I pop in for lunch occasionally, just for old time's sake, but I don't think they recognise me.'

'And Mr Morganstone was a customer?'

'Yes. He came in with a big fat elephant of a man. A right pompous *bastard!*' She laughed at Mary's look of shocked surprise. 'There you are, swearing I am now. See what a bad influence you are on me?'

'So what happened? At the restaurant?'

'Oh, nothing much.' A smile curled the corners of Julia's mouth, then she began to laugh. 'They came in one evening – Morganstone and this other man. I'd been working since lunchtime and my feet were killing me – and it wasn't my best time, either. Then Jumbo starts his antics. *This wine isn't chilled, girl! This soup isn't warm enough, girl! Stand up straight and pay attention when I'm speaking to you, girl!* And of course he's playing to the gallery the whole time. Well, I could see he was looking for special attention, so I saw that he got it. When he ordered pudding and custard I served it up right away, nice and hot – straight in his lap.'

'You didn't?'

'I remember standing there, watching him leap about – and I don't know what possessed me, but all of a sudden I started prodding him with the serving spoon, and calling out, *Hup, Jumbo, hup!*'

'I don't believe you.'

'It's true. Absolutely true.'

'So what did Mr Morganstone do?'

'Well, that was the strange thing. Instead of being angry, he slips his card into my hand. *You may find yourself needing another job*, he says.' She smiled. 'Well, he certainly wasn't wrong about that.'

'And that was when you began modelling for Madame?'

Julia regarded her for a moment, then leaned forward to peer through the misted window. 'Oh, look,' she said as the hansom drew to a halt. 'We're here. Let me be the first to welcome you to hell on earth.'

The rain had stopped, but looking about her as she stepped from the cab, Mary felt the cold splash of reality as sharply as any downpour. It was as though she had awakened from her dream to find herself back in Cutler Street – but a Cutler Street grown a thousand times more awful.

'Should I wait for you?' asked the cabbie, without enthusiasm.

Julia lifted the parcel from the cab. 'No, we'll be alright.'

'Right you are, ma'am – if you're sure.' Giving her no time to reconsider, he flicked the reins, moving off at a rattling pace and scattering a group of ragged youngsters who had already begun to assemble about the unfamiliar sight.

'Providence Row,' announced Julia, looking up at the long yellow brick building. 'It's a night shelter, for the homeless – or at least for the fortunate few who get here early enough for a bed.' She hefted the brown paper parcel. 'Come on, we'll drop this, then I might as well give you a tour of Whitechapel.'

'You mean we've come all this way just to give them my old clothes?'

'Well, not quite.' She handed Mary the package, then pulled on the bell. 'Your bits and pieces are something of a bonus.'

'Perhaps we should have worn them,' said Mary, eyeing the group of children who were edging ever closer. 'We seem to be creating a bit of a stir dressed like this.'

Julia glanced behind her, then spun around, growling like a tiger, her hands raised, claw-like, and her teeth bared.

With startled shrieks, the children fled, except for a barefoot and grimy-faced little boy who viewed her stoically. 'Ain't 'fraid of you,' he said.

'Ain't you, now?' said Julia, aping his accent. 'Well, good for you,

'Orace. Here,' she brought out a penny and tossed it to him. 'And don't go spending it on drink.'

'Will if I like.'

'Go on, bugger off, you little sod!' she laughed, shooing him away as the door behind her opened and a small, wiry nun appeared.

'Oh, it's you, Miss Julia!' the woman beamed, opening the door wider. 'Won't you come in now? You shouldn't be standing out in the street, just there. That's right, come in, come in.' She fussed them inside, closing the heavy door behind them. 'I'm afraid Sister Ignatius isn't here just at present.' She cast an eye over the parcel in Mary's arms. 'Is that from Madame Bennaire? Goodness me, but that woman is a saint if ever there was one. I only wish she'd come here herself – so's I could tell her to her face, that I do. Shall I be taking it from you? It looks awful heavy.'

'This is a little extra donation from my good friend, Miss Mary Kelly.'

'Oh,' said the nun. 'Well, that's very kind of you.' She cocked her head to one side. 'Kelly? Mary Kelly? That wouldn't be the Mary Kelly who was Sister Dorothea's sister's niece from Dublin, would it?'

Mary began to shake her head.

'No, no, wait, I've got it all wrong as usual. It wasn't Sister Dorothea's sister's niece, at all – but her sister's daughter's niece – her with the withered arm, but still as bonny a girl as you could imagine – given the circumstances being what they are and nothing to be done about it.' She jerked the parcel from Mary's hands. 'Will I be taking that from you?'

Julia brought out an envelope. '*This* is from Madame Bennaire.'

'Oh, saints alive, the woman is an angel! Wasn't I only saying to Sister Bernice just the other day, that if it wasn't for people like yourselves and Madame Bennaire, well I don't know what – but it would be a terrible shame and that's the truth of it.' She took the envelope, slipping it into her habit.

'You *will* make sure that Sister Ignatius gets it?' asked Julia.

'Oh, it's as good as done – if not better. Now, can I be offering you some tea?'

'Poor old girl's got a marble loose,' laughed Julia as they emerged on to the street fifteen minutes later. 'But she's alright. You should see her when she's been at the communion wine.'

Mary looked about, taking in the squalor of her surroundings. Across the road a nameless pub stood on the corner, and beyond lay a street: a narrow brick canyon running toward Spitalfields Church, the road and pavement littered with rubbish, whilst in doorways and against walls lay debris of a human kind: bedraggled figures, whether half drunk, half asleep or half dead, Mary could not tell. It was poverty beyond anything she had ever experienced, and it appalled her.

Some way down the street two women were fighting, brutally and viciously, screeching obscenities at each other – until one of them tumbled into the gutter, whereupon the other began trampling her with a pair of heavy boots. The sight brought back memories that made Mary pale.

'Dorset Street,' said Julia, shaking her head. 'Well, I've been to Dorset, and I can tell you – whoever named this place had a sense of humour.' She took Mary's arm. 'Come on.'

'Where to?'

Julia shrugged. 'Nowhere particular. Just to walk. We won't get a cab around here, anyway.' She side-stepped abruptly. 'Oh, and mind where you're stepping.'

Cringing, Mary lifted her skirt a little higher to keep it clear of the foul pavement. 'Why didn't we just ask the cabbie to wait?'

'Because I like to walk here.'

On the far side of the road an old woman was hobbling toward them, stopping every few moments to steady herself against the wall. Suddenly she sank down on to her haunches, a stream of steaming liquid running from beneath her skirts and into the gutter.

'You *like* it?' Mary asked in amazement.

Julia nodded. 'It's reassuring.' She saw Mary's confusion, and smiled. 'When I first came to London I was just like you – had nothing but the clothes I stood up in, no character and no prospects. I was *lucky* to get that waitressing job – and if I'd managed to live to forty I'd have been like the poor cow who's place I'd taken – thrown out after twenty years of slaving, with veins on her legs like ropes, and too short of breath to climb the stairs to that stinking attic.' She glanced toward the old woman who had slid down the wall to sit in her own filth. 'Maybe that's her over there – and in time that would have been me. Yet for all that, I *was* lucky because I *had* a job.' She turned to look at Mary, squeezing her arm. 'Well, now I have a different one – and it's *wonderful*. And if ever I have doubts – then I just take a walk around here.'

Mary came to a halt, looking Julia in the eye. 'This job, with Madame, it *isn't* modelling, is it.'

'Isn't it?'

'I'm not a fool, Julia. I've said nothing these past days because I've *so* wanted it to be true – but it can't be. Even if you trebled the amount Mr Morganstone wrote on that card it wouldn't pay for the way you live – the house, the dresses, everything! I'm not sure what it is you do – or what part I'm expected to play in it. But I have to know now – before I get too used to this life. Before I can't go back.'

Julia looked at her. 'Back to Cardiff?' Then she sighed, looking along the street. 'No, I know *exactly* what you mean. Alright,' she said, taking Mary's arm once more. 'It's time you had a talk with Madame.'

Chapter Thirty-Three

'I understand you are concerned about my maid, Emily,' said Mme Bennaire with frosty indifference.

'Well …' Mary shifted uncomfortably in her seat. From the moment Julia had left them alone in the drawing-room she had been aware of yet another side of Mme Bennaire. Gone was the warm, eccentric friendliness, replaced, not by the sharp, critical manner bestowed upon poor Emily, but by a darker, more sinister mood that made Mary feel increasingly uneasy. 'It … It was partly my fault she got into trouble the other day – and I haven't seen her since.'

'And you feel guilty – believing I have dismissed her?'

'I suppose so, yes.'

Mme Bennaire continued with her cold, hawk-like stare. 'If I *had* dismissed her, would it be any concern of yours? I think not! And be so good as to look at me when I am speaking to you!'

Mary looked up quickly, feeling stupidly childish.

'That's better!' said Mme Bennaire, with no hint of a smile, her tone harsh and insistent. 'But I appear to be frightening you. Am I?'

'No, no, of course not. But … you do seem different today.'

'Is that so? And you find that unsettling, do you?'

'No … not exactly.'

'Then why are you fretting with your cuff?'

Mary snatched her hand away. 'Alright, this isn't what I expected – and yes, I find it … *unsettling*.'

'Good.' The word rang in the stillness of the room as Mme Bennaire's face softened into a smile, her eyes growing warm and friendly once more. 'You have been wanting to know what it is we do. *That* is one of the things we do.'

'I … I'm not sure I understand.'

'We are *actresses*, my dear. And *this*,' Mme Bennaire waved her hand, indicating the four walls, 'is our theatre – where we entertain a select and, as I like to think, rather *privileged* audience.'

Confusion continued to cloud Mary's face, and Mme Bennaire came to sit by her, patting her knee. 'You were concerned about Emily, and I respect you all the more for that – but you must understand that I love Emily dearly and was no more angry with her the other day than I was with you just now.'

'So it was all just pretence?'

'Of course.'

'But why?'

'Why?' Mme Bennaire gave her rich, warm laugh, and put her arm about Mary's shoulder. 'Because, my dear, the naughtier Emily is – the harsher I am with her. And the harsher I am, the happier Emily is. And when she finally drives me to distraction and I take her upstairs and whip her, well – then she is happiest of all.'

'You *whip* her?'

'Regularly. It is, after all, why she pays to come here.'

Mary's face was a picture of incredulity. 'She *pays* to work as a maid?'

'No, of course not. She pays to *play* at being a maid. The reason you haven't seen her recently is because her real-life role is that of the devoted wife and mother – and she can only come here when her husband is away on business.'

'I've never heard of such a thing.'

'Oh, believe me, such yearnings are far more common than you might imagine.' Madame Bennaire smiled. 'Though *not* something people tend to discuss over dinner.'

Mary slowly shook her head. 'It's not at all what I imagined.'

'Possibly not, but now that you know, what are your feelings on the matter?'

'I'm not sure. I'm not sure I even understand what you want from me.'

'It is quite simple. We wish you to join us – to come and live here. We have a great many clients with a diversity of requirements. Maud, Elspeth and Julia have a talent for fulfilling those requirements. I believe you too possess such a talent.'

'I couldn't *beat* anyone.'

'Not maliciously, perhaps. But you did beat Captain Jolly the other evening.'

'That was only play-acting.'

Mme Bennaire smiled wryly. 'As is everything we do here, my dear.'

'But, I would never have *hurt* Elspeth.'

'Ah, but what if Elspeth's greatest pleasure was to be hurt? If the greatest cruelty you could do her was to *refuse* to beat her?'

Mary breathed deeply, looking about the room, confused; a hungry child with her nose pressed to the sweetshop window. 'I don't know … I just don't know.'

Mme Bennaire leaned forward, brushing the backs of her fingers against Mary's cheek. 'Of course you don't. This must seem so very strange to you, and I expect your head is filled with questions. But perhaps I should let Julia answer them. Just promise me you will give careful consideration to our offer.' She patted Mary's shoulder, then stood up. 'Now, I'm afraid I must go and make myself ready. I have an appointment presently.' She gave a small laugh. 'With a rather disobedient Guards Officer.' At the door, she paused. 'But before I go, there is a favour I would ask of you.'

'Of course, Madame.'

'You came here seeking work as a model – I have such a job for you this evening.'

Mary eyed her uncertainly. 'Posing? For a painter?'

'Well, I believe he does paint occasionally,' Mme Bennaire laughed again. 'But no, I shan't lie to you – no one will be painting you.' She cocked her head slightly to one side. 'Will you do this one thing for me?'

'If it *is* just posing.'

'You have my promise. And should you decide not to stay with us after all – then you will owe me nothing.'

'I'll have paid you back? Just from this one job?'

'Oh yes,' said Mme Bennaire.

*

'So, which ones are we doing?' asked Maud as she helped Mattie draw the heavy velvet curtains in the upstairs room.

Elspeth glanced at Mme Bennaire's hand-written note. 'Katy, Bridie, and,' she grinned at Maud, 'Little Maudie et La Belle Dame.'

Mattie lifted an eyebrow. 'That means you'll be wanting me. It would be better if you did that one first, if you don't mind. I'm going to be up and down stairs all evening, and I don't want to be keeping one ear open for a cue.'

'Yes, that's alright,' said Elspeth. 'We'll do La Dame first, then Bridie, and finish with good old Catherine.' She looked across at Mary. 'Madame wants you to take second lead in that one, so we'd better rehearse you. The rest you can pick up as you go.'

Confused, Mary looked about her. The room was twice the length of the downstairs drawing-room, though just as plushly furnished, with the last third divided off by curtains which Elspeth opened to reveal a low stage with a painted backdrop of dimly lit arches and realistic stone walls.

'That's the one for Bridie,' said Julia, coming to stand by Mary. 'Bridewell? You know – the prison?'

'Oh – yes. I think so.'

'It's good, isn't it,' said Elspeth. 'You'd be very surprised to hear who painted it.' She grinned. 'And under what circumstances.' To illustrate the point, she took a cane from a darkened corner and gave it a flick.

'Oddly, he didn't sign it,' laughed Maud.

'Who was it?' asked Mary, stepping on to the stage to study the back-drop.

Julia shook her head. 'We can't tell you – not yet anyway. Madame's rules. Come on, I'll show you where we get dressed.'

To one side of the stage, a door led into a dressing room of generous proportions, brightly lit and with a fire burning in the grate.

'These are our costumes,' said Julia. 'Nice, don't you think?'

Mary walked between the rows of clothing and accessories: elegant, old fashioned gowns; plain shifts and dresses; uniforms; men's suits; assorted hats, wigs and shoes – it was a theatrical outfitters in miniature.

Elspeth came to the door. 'Overture and beginners, if you please.'

'There's no rush, is there?' asked Julia protectively.

'Not particularly – but is there any reason why we shouldn't do it now?'

Mary noted the hint of tension in the exchange. 'It's alright, what do you want me to do?'

'I suppose we'd better have your clothes off,' said Elspeth, coming into the room and seating herself at one of the two dressing tables.

'Very well.'

'*Everything*,' said Elspeth.

'Yes, I'd assumed that.'

Julia crossed to the rack of costumes. 'We'd better get togged up, too.'

'*We* don't need to,' said Elspeth. '*We've* done this dozens of times.'

'Well, then let's go and help Maud set the stage.'

'She can manage on her own.'

Under the watchful eye of Elspeth, Mary began to undress. It was obviously a test, and she felt touched by Julia's efforts to save her blushes, but she had long since grown accustomed to being naked. With a quiet confidence she slipped out of her top clothes, then her undergarments, discarding petticoats and corset until only her drawers and bodice remained.

Maud came to the door, her face shiny with perspiration. 'The frame is ready. Oh, and thank you both *so* much for helping.'

Unbuttoning her bodice, Mary shrugged it from her shoulders, then felt for the ribbon at her waist and untied it, letting her drawers fall about her ankles. 'And what would you like me to do now?' she asked, looking matter-of-factly at Elspeth.

A broad grin spread across Julia's face, and she snatched a chemise from the costume rack, tossing it at Elspeth's head. 'And what of your *reservations* now, meine frau?'

'Satisfied,' said Elspeth, smiling as she disentangled herself. 'For the moment.'

*

Mary found it the strangest feeling. She was sitting primly at her desk, her hair falling across the shoulders of her clean white pinafore, and her eyes wide with fear, while next to her, dressed in similar fashion and reaching beneath the desk to give her hand a reassuring squeeze, sat Gwyneth. Only it wasn't Gwyneth, it was Julia. And it wasn't Griffiths at the front, wielding his cane, but Elspeth, frumpily dressed, with spectacles and a grey wig, and holding aloft a bunch of birch twigs as though in the very act of sweeping them down on the bare girlish buttocks of Maud who lay horsed across Mattie's broad back.

In the darkened room, beyond the brightly lit stage, the anonymous man began to clap, slowly, but with an enthusiastic heaviness, continuing until the curtain closed and the tableau of the Dame School was hidden from his view.

Immediately the frozen image burst into life.

Mattie straightened, lowering Maud to the floor, but not before Elspeth had given her bared backside a playful flick with the birch twigs.

'Sod you!' hissed Maud, rubbing away the sting.

'Shssh!' whispered Julia, sliding off the bench. 'Come on, Mary, the desk goes back here.'

Mattie straightened her uniform. 'I'll bring you some refreshments after the next scene,' she said as calmly as if they'd just been polishing the silver. 'Any preferences?'

'Champagne, of course.' Elspeth laughed softly, pulling the Bridewell backdrop down over Dame's cottage. 'I hear that just *everyone* is drinking it in prison these days.'

With the desk cleared away, Mary and Julia brought on a low, padded whipping bench while Maud brought a steel bucket and various other props from the dressing room.

Elspeth cast a critical eye over the set. 'That looks alright. Come on. Last one changed is an old maid.'

'Catherine The Great,' murmured Madame Bennaire as the curtains opened for the final time.

Sitting close by her side, one hand holding a large cigar, the other resting comfortably on her thigh, the man nodded approvingly. 'Wonderful, quite wonderful – as always, dear lady.'

'You are very kind, sir.'

He leaned toward her, keeping his voice low. 'You know, Julia makes quite the best Catherine I've ever seen. So thoroughly wicked. Quite, quite exquisite.' His hand stroked along Mme Bennaire's leg. 'Of course, the *real* Catherine was also very partial to whipping her servant *boys*.'

Mme Bennaire smiled. 'That scene can be arranged if you wish,' she said, patting his hand. 'But I suspect you have a boy of your own in mind, hmm? One who only very occasionally sees the light of day?'

He chuckled. 'You know me too well, Madame. And if mama wasn't expecting me ...' He sighed. 'But, duty before pleasure, eh?'

'As it should be with all good boys.'

The man laughed heartily and turned his attention back to the tableau. 'I don't recognise the girl spread-eagled on the frame. Is she new?'

'She's making her debut this evening. We are hoping she will stay.'

He drew on his cigar. 'She was the wardress in the Bridewell scene, was she not?'

Mme Bennaire nodded.

'Fine sparkle in her eyes. Just the right mixture of cruelty and lust.' He studied Mary's body. 'Fine legs, too. I should like to meet her.'

'I'm not sure that would be wise. It is possible she may yet leave us.' She opened her hands in a gesture of helplessness.

'Yes – yes I suppose so.' He sighed once again and took out his watch, holding it to catch the light, then looked back to where Julia was standing resplendent in a shimmering gown, her arm drawn back, gripping the lash. 'Damn it, I must go. One dare not keep mama waiting these days.'

'Of course.'

'Naturally, I should like to leave the young ladies a token of my appreciation.'

Mme Bennaire rose and made a slow and elegant curtsey. 'If that is your pleasure, sir.'

'It is – and perhaps a little extra for the new girl? By way of encouragement?' He smiled. 'We should very much like her to stay.'

*

'We are *not* prostitutes,' said Elspeth, pouring herself some more champagne. 'Prostitutes sell the use of their bodies to anyone who will pay. *No one* can buy us.'

Mary looked unconvinced. 'But they just have. That man earlier ...'

'He paid to see some tableaux vivants, some living pictures, that's all. Were you a prostitute when you modelled in Cardiff?'

'Of course not.'

'Then what's the difference? It's just that our clients seldom feel the need to bring their paints and brushes.'

'But that isn't all you do, is it.'

'No. It isn't.' Elspeth levelled her gaze. 'This afternoon, for instance, I had an hour's appointment with a young man whose greatest desire is to be fastened to a whipping bench and severely birched – a desire he was desperate to fulfil and I was happy to accommodate. But does that make me a prostitute?'

'Doesn't it?'

Julia laughed. 'Well, if it does then there are a lot of schoolmasters, policemen and prison warders who are in for a surprise.'

'But that isn't the same thing. You know it isn't.'

'Isn't it? The *act* is exactly the same. The only difference is that my young man *wanted* to be beaten.'

In the small drawing-room the clock chimed two, and Maud yawned and stretched. 'Well, I don't care whether we are or not, quite frankly. I'm tired, and I'm going to bed. Say goodnight to Madame for me.' She got up. 'I hope you decide to stay, Mary – but if you don't, then – goodbye and good luck.'

With Maud gone, Julia poked at the coals, then stretched out on the sofa. 'You've seen the alternatives, Mary. And you said yourself this is the kind of life you've always dreamed of.'

'Yes – but not like this. Because it isn't just living pictures and play-acting, is it?'

'You're worried about having to sleep with the clients?' asked Elspeth.

'That *is* what you do, isn't it?'

Elspeth smiled disarmingly. 'Yes – but only with those I'm genuinely fond of. And it's always *my* decision. I don't see it as so very different to the way a good many society women behave. But if you prefer to offer only theatrical skills – accompanied by some rather vigorous massage – then so be it.'

'And Madame would be content with that?'

'Madame,' said Julia, sleepily, 'would be delighted. She much prefers it that way.'

'She's very protective,' explained Elspeth. 'Rather like an extremely broad-minded mother.'

'Why not stay for a while?' said Julia. 'You know you enjoyed yourself this evening. You did, didn't you?'

'Yes …' Mary began to smile. 'Yes, I did – though I didn't realise you were going to fasten my legs *quite* so far apart.'

Julia giggled into her champagne. 'It gave you such a lovely startled look. Quite in character. Oh, go on, Mary – do stay. At least for a couple of days?'

'We'd have to find you a professional name,' said Elspeth, 'Kelly sounds a little – *common*. How would you like to be Mary Hardwick?'

'No! That makes her sound like some dried up old spinster,' laughed Julia. 'What about Mary Fetherington?'

Elspeth shook her head. 'Too fancy. Almost as bad as Devereaux.'

272

'I like Devereaux,' said Julia indignantly. 'It's aristocratic.'

'It sounds like a pub I know of,' said Elspeth.

Mary looked from one to the other, finally fixing on Julia. 'Devereaux isn't your real name?'

'Let's just say it wasn't always,' grinned Julia.

'Mary Carstairs?' suggested Elspeth.

'Mary Christmas?' said Julia, giggling again.

'Wait, wait!' said Mary. 'If I'm going to change my name, I want to change it all. I want to be *Emma*.'

'Emma?' Elspeth considered it. 'Yes – that has a nice sound to it. But Emma what?'

Julia propped herself up, looking at Mary over the rim of her glass. 'Something to conjure up the way you looked in that dress from Mme Coubret's. Elegant, but in a stark, severe sort of way.' She thought for a moment, then her eyes sparkled in the firelight. '*Black*,' she said. 'Emma Black.'

*

And so I stayed, and became Emma Black.

Changing my name made it easier – but it was Julia who made it feel right. In her I'd found the sister I'd always dreamed of – the sister of my stories, who always knew the right thing to do. She told me everything would be alright – and it was, for no sooner had the decision to stay been made than my doubts began to vanish, and I settled into the life at Gloucester Gardens as naturally as if I had been born to it – and perhaps, as Sid once suggested, I had.

It was a brothel – of a sort, but it was also the most wonderful place in which our working hours were pure theatre, and our leisure times equal to those in the grandest of houses.

Breakfast was at ten, with appointments beginning at twelve and finishing promptly at four when we would meet in the downstairs drawing-room for tea – with muffins and home-made entertainments in winter – strolls or carriage rides in the park in summer. Dinner was between seven and eight – always the most elegant affair – after which we would 'entertain' once more until the early hours.

And over all of this, Madame Bennaire ruled with a motherly beneficence, strictly vetting the clients and dividing the spoils fairly and generously – so generously that, even though I stuck to my principles and received no gifts for 'special favours', I very soon had a wardrobe that would have put many a duchess to shame. It was truly a dream come true.

Of our staff, only Mattie lived in, the other domestic girls arriving in the early morning and working under her direction until midday when they were sent home in order that our clientele might enjoy complete discretion in their coming and going – each appointment carefully tailored to avoid embarrassing meetings. Absolutely no one was permitted to call without prior arrangement – or at least that was the rule.

*

In his mid-forties, Archie Bull was not a tall man, but what he lacked in stature he made up for in presence. With his broad, pointed nose and jutting chin, between which his mouth curved in a thin downward line, he reminded Mary of a shark she had once seen in a book. In Archie's case a somewhat tastelessly-dressed shark.

'Julia, *sweet'eart*,' he said, walking unannounced into the drawing-room, the gash of his mouth lifting into a parody of a smile. 'I don't suppose yer was expectin' t' see me again so soon.'

'*Archie*.' Julia got to her feet, her face fixed in a polite smile. 'This *is* a surprise. Madame didn't tell me you'd made an appointment.'

'I didn't.' He widened his predatory grin. 'Been a bit of a naughty boy in that respect – but a little dicky-bird told me you 'ad a new girl, an' as I was passin' I thought I'd just sneak in an' pay my compliments.' He turned his eyes expectantly in Mary's direction.

'Of course,' Julia took a step toward Mary. 'This is Miss Emma Black. Emma, allow me to introduce you to …'

'Bull's the name,' he said, shoving out his hand.

Mary put down her teacup and slowly rose to meet him, not shaking his hand, but extending her own so that it rested lightly upon his. 'I'm delighted to meet you, Mr Bull.'

'Now *that's* style,' chuckled Archie, bending to brush his lips to her fingers. 'An' it's *Archie* to my friends.'

She arched an eyebrow. 'I see. Well, perhaps, in the fullness of time, we shall come to consider one another as friends.'

He chuckled again, looking across at Julia. 'Gawd, but she's a caution, ain't she?' He turned back, meeting Mary's eyes. 'Let's 'ope that day comes soon, eh?'

'Well,' said Julia, coming between them and taking his arm. 'As it happens I have no engagements this afternoon – so, if you wish, we might attend to this little matter of you arriving uninvited.'

Archie's eyes twinkled. 'Ah, I thought I might 'ave t' pay for that little bit o' cheek. Well, whatever yer think fit, *ma'am*.'

'Oh, I have a tried and tested remedy that is quite perfect for such rude little boys.'

He glanced quickly at Mary. 'An' will Miss Emma be joinin' us?'

'I don't think we need trouble her.'

'An' if I was to insist?'

'Insist?' Julia stiffened, and she turned to glare at him with an expression

274

of the utmost severity. 'I really don't think you want to *insist*, Archibald. *Rude* boys are made to suffer. *Precocious* boys are made to suffer *terribly*. I do hope I make myself understood?'

Archie lowered his eyes, looking almost bashful. 'Yes, ma'am.' Then he glanced at Mary and grinned. 'Well – I suppose I shall just 'ave t' suffer *terribly*, ma'am.'

Chapter Thirty-Four

Standing half-way along Villiers Street, the Princess Alice was a smart, if unassuming public house in a Georgian terrace that ran between the Strand and the newly built Embankment.

On the ground floor the long bar was the chosen watering hole of clerks, shop assistants, and those who lacked the income to frequent the nearby hotel bars and clubs. It was a clean, respectable place for decent, respectable people who had no idea of the much darker empire that was controlled from the plush rooms above.

Standing by the first floor window, Connie Bull looked down into the street, watching the progress of a bedraggled young girl as she hawked her pathetic bunches of flowers. 'You can tell him yourself,' she said, turning back into the room.

The conservatively dressed young man nodded, and a few moments later Archie Bull walked in, a bunch of wilting violets in his hand.

'Enjoy yourself?' asked Connie, stiffly.

'It was alright. 'Ere, I got yer these.' He tossed the flowers to her, then turned his attention to the visitor. 'So what's the news then, Vince?'

Vincent Eastman adjusted his cuffs. 'They *were* at it.'

'That don't surprise me. You taken care of it?'

Eastman nodded.

'Good boy.' Archie studied him with grudging admiration. 'You might come off like some public school nancy – but yer don't mind gettin' yer 'ands dirty. I *like* that.'

The muscle in Eastman's jaw flickered briefly, then he said, 'The French *are* involved.'

'All of 'em?'

'No, only Gerard and Reinhardt.'

'You sure?'

'Yes. I had it from Mr Petersen himself – and I'm inclined to believe him. He was fairly anxious to co-operate just before his demise.'

Archie eyed him, then he laughed. 'I *also* like a man who likes 'is work. You want a whisky?'

'No, thank you. What would you like me to do about the Frenchmen?'

'I dunno – that's a bit more tricky.'

'We can't let them get away with it,' said Connie, laying the violets on the table. 'It's never been our way. You let one lot take liberties and …'

'Yeah, yeah, I know. But we've got t' be careful. We could go upsettin' some very unpleasant people.'

Connie looked at him, her cold grey eyes and strong, lined features unsmiling. '*We* can be very unpleasant people – and *we're* already upset.'

The shark grin split Archie's face. 'Yeah, alright. Well, let's think on it awhile, eh?' He turned to Eastman. 'In the meantime I want you an' Baines t' go over an' 'ave a quiet word with that slimy pratt-prodder in Cleveland Street.'

*

It was a glorious afternoon and the water of the Serpentine shimmered in the summer heat.

'God, it's hot,' said Julia as they sat on a bench in the shade of a weeping willow. 'I envy Maud. Must be lovely in Ramsgate just now. It's been ages since I've been taken anywhere.'

Mary looked up casually from her book. 'When's she due back?'

'Saturday – if he doesn't ask her to marry him, of course.'

'But it was just business, wasn't it?'

'Yes, but he's a keen one – and Maud could do a lot worse.' Out on the lake a model yacht lay becalmed, moving listlessly on the slight swell, and Julia watched it idly. 'So, what are you reading?'

'One of Madame's books – on mythology.'

'*Mythology*?'

'I was told a story once – about the birth of Venus. I just wanted to see if it was true.'

'And is it?'

Mary sighed, closing the book and handing it across. 'Yes.'

'Oh, good,' said Julia, thumbing idly through the volume. 'That's a *huge* weight off my mind. You can't imagine!'

'Julia, *dear*. I'm going to give you *ever* such a hard pinch.'

'Oh, really?' Julia grinned. 'One should like to see one try.' She found the relevant page and read for several minutes. 'Sounds rather gruesome. I think I should prefer to stick with more *conventional* methods.' She leaned back, tilting her parasol a little more. 'God, it *is* hot. Shall we walk for a while? I'm sweating sitting here.'

'Yes, if you like.' Mary got to her feet. 'But may I remind you that ladies don't sweat, they *glow*.'

'Thank you – then I'm *glowing* like a carthorse.' She opened her parasol. 'You know what I'd *really* like to do? Take off every stitch and go for a swim in that lake.'

'What, right now?'

Julia giggled. 'Might take the old boys' minds off their sailing boats, don't you think? Wouldn't be too many flags at half-mast then, eh?' She took Mary's arm and they began to walk, their summer dresses blindingly white in the sunshine. 'No, if we *were* to do it, we'd have to come back later – after it gets dark.'

Mary looked at her askance. 'You aren't serious?'

'You think I wouldn't?'

'I don't know. Would you?'

'I will if you will.'

Mary felt the thrill of the dare run through her, and for an instant she was back with Gwyneth, standing on the riverbank outside Nant-y-Pridd. 'Alright,' she said, nodding serenely to an old gentleman who doffed his hat to them. 'Tonight?'

Julia also acknowledged the man, a placid smile upon her face. 'Quite perfect. And how do you propose we get back into the park?'

'That, my dear, is *your* department. *I* shall be responsible for the bathing suits.'

'Really? How very odd. I didn't think we'd be wearing any.'

'Quite so,' said Mary.

*

Holding the oil lamp before her in one hand, and a jug of hot water in the other, Gwyneth trudged up the final flight of stairs to the attic bedroom and pushed open the door.

She was tired. Her legs ached and so did her back. It had been eighteen hours since she'd crawled unwillingly from her bed, and she felt dirty and smelly, on top of which, her monthly cramps were particularly bad, causing her to double over several times during the course of the heavy spring cleaning.

'God, I hate spring cleanin',' said Maggie, lying sprawled, fully dressed, on her bed. 'I hate the summer. I hate Christmas. An' *I bloody well hate the spring!*'

'It isn't spring,' said Gwyneth wearily, filling the china bowl that stood on the washstand.

'I know that, don't I? That's why it's so bloomin' hot! Spring cleanin' in the spring is bad enough, but spring cleanin' in the summer is downright criminal! An' we've got at least another week of this!'

'It'll soon be over. And it's only once a year.'

'Oh no it ain't! We'll be doin' this all again in three months time – I heard them talkin' about it this mornin'. The old doctor's got this daft idea in his head that it's dust what makes young Master Owen ill.'

'But he's much better than he was when he first came here.'

'Well, whether he is or he ain't, it's not good enough for the doctor, an' he wants the place cleaned from top to bottom four times a year! Have you ever heard such rubbish? God, if a bit of dust was bad for you, I'd have been dead years ago!'

'Well, if we have to, we have to, I suppose.' Almost too tired to move, Gwyneth began to undress. 'Would you mind, Maggie?' she asked, when she stood in only her underwear.

With a grumpy sigh, Maggie turned on to her side, putting her face to the wall. 'You ain't got nothin' I ain't got, you know,' she said, staring absently at the faded whitewash. Then she brightened a little. 'I see there was another of them letters from London for you this morning.'

Reaching under her petticoat, Gwyneth untied her drawers and re-moved the bloodied cloth, quickly slipping it out of sight beneath her bed.

'Well, ain't you goin' to tell me who it was from, then?' persisted Maggie.

'It wasn't from anyone.'

'Don't be daft. It has to be from someone – an' someone with a bit of money, too, by the look of the envelope – proper posh lookin' – smelled nice, too.'

Gwyneth glanced over her shoulder. 'Maggie! You shouldn't go touch-ing other people's letters.'

'I didn't mean to,' protested Maggie, indignantly. 'Thought it might have been for me, that's all. You ain't the only one to get letters, y'know.'

'Oh, yes, that's right. I forgot. I've lost count of the times I've seen the postman come up the drive, staggering under the weight of letters for *you*.' In awkward silence, Gwyneth removed the rest of her clothes and began to wash herself. 'I'm sorry,' she said at last. 'I shouldn't have said that.'

'It's alright,' said Maggie offhandedly. 'So what did it say, then – this letter?'

'I've no idea,' said Gwyneth. 'I threw it on the fire.'

*

There was a light rap at the door, and Mary looked up from her tall desk to find Julia peering in through the slight opening. Immediately she turned back to where the thirty-five year old stockbroker was perched behind a much smaller desk, copying out the verses of an endless and exceptionally tedious poem. 'Did I tell you to stop work?'

The man looked embarrassed. 'No, miss,' he said quickly.

'Very well. Then please continue.' She waited until he had bent to his copying once more, then turned to Julia, raising a quizzical eyebrow.

'*How much longer?*' Julia mouthed silently.

Mary looked up at the clock. It was almost one o'clock in the morning. '*Fifteen minutes,*' she mouthed back.

Julia rolled her eyes impatiently, went to withdraw, then changed her mind and stepped in. 'You, boy!' she said sharply, startling him.

'Yes, miss?' He stared at her in genuine confusion.

'Miss Black tells me you are something of a slacker. Is that correct?'

'I … I try to do my best, miss.'

'Do you? Do you *indeed*?' She came to stand close by him, her skirt brushing his arm, and an icy glint in her eyes. 'Well, as the *Headmistress* of this school, I must tell you that your best is not good enough – not good enough by half.' She reached out, pinching the lobe of his ear between her thumb and forefinger, lifting him from his seat. 'Stand up, boy!'

No sooner was he standing than she turned to Mary, her brows drawn into a frown. 'Miss Black. It seems to me you are being somewhat lenient in your dealings with young …' She snapped her head round to glare at the cringing stockbroker. 'What *is* your name, boy?'

'F-Fanshawe, miss.'

'I *do* apologise, Miss Devereaux,' said Mary, coming out from behind her desk. 'I know I should be stricter with him, but he's *such* a sweet boy, don't you think?'

'Sweet? Nonsense! I'll have no *sentiment* in my establishment. Now you will cane him most severely – and I shall stay to see it is done properly.'

'Yes, of course, if you insist, Miss Devereaux.' Mary made a suggestion of a curtsey and picked up the cane that lay across the front of her desk.

'Fanshawe!' Julia's voice crackled like an electric spark. 'You have ten seconds to bare your behind and bend over the desk.'

Fanshawe made it with two seconds to spare.

'Good,' said Julia. 'I see we are learning.' She moved behind him, flicking up his shirt tails, then lifted her eyes to Mary, her lips silently forming the question, '*How many?*'

Tucking the cane beneath her arm, Mary held up six fingers.

Julia nodded, stepping back to leave a clear field. 'I think *six* strokes will suffice on this occasion, Miss Black.'

'Oh, surely not?' said Mary. 'It seems so *very* severe.'

'I *intend* to be severe, Miss Black. One must be severe with boys like young Fanshawe. Now please begin. My patience is being sorely tried.'

'Yes, of course. As you wish, Headmistress.'

With measured deliberation, Mary gave the six strokes, spacing them evenly and allowing the pain of one to ebb before delivering the next – just as Julia had shown her – then, as Fanshawe lay quietly sobbing, she

280

put down the cane and moved around the desk, gently stroking his hair. 'There, there. That's my brave, brave boy.'

'Stay where you are, Fanshawe!' ordered Julia, standing behind him and running her fingertips over the raised welts. 'I'm not entirely convinced you've been sufficiently punished.' She continued to linger over the cane marks, watching him tense in fearful anticipation, then she slid her hand beneath him to brush against his engorged manhood. 'Well, perhaps *on this occasion* I shall be lenient, hmm?'

Fanshawe sank back on to the desk with a great, satisfied sigh.

'Stay and rest,' said Julia, quietly and kindly now. 'Take as long as you need, then see yourself out when you are ready.'

*

It was half an hour later that the figures of two men made their way along the road, keeping to the shadows wherever possible. Their clothes had seen much better days and hung loosely on their thin frames, and their rough caps were pulled down, shielding their faces, as though they were ashamed to be seen, making them almost indistinguishable from the great mass of homeless men who, night after night, wandered the streets in search of a place to sleep.

By a secluded section of the fence they stopped. 'Here's a good place,' whispered Julia, pushing back her cap, her teeth flashing white in the moonlight.

Mary glanced up at the tall iron railings. 'I can see why we needed to wear trousers.'

'You can climb it can't you?'

'I can if you can.'

'Well, come on then.' With surprising ease, Julia swarmed up and over the fence, dropping on to the grass below. 'Don't take all night about it,' she called in a hushed voice as Mary reached the top and began to clamber down. 'And watch where you're stepping, you sometimes get dossers breaking in here for a sleep.'

Mary landed softly on the grass. 'What do you mean? We can't do this if the park is full of people sleeping.'

'It's alright. There probably aren't any – and even if there are one or two, they're not going to shout about seeing us because if the keepers catch them in here they'll get six months.'

Julia started away, but Mary took a firm grip on her arm. '*In prison?*'

'No – in Buckingham Palace. Of course in prison. But don't worry, they won't catch *us* because we'll be keeping our eyes peeled, won't we?'

'Yes,' said Mary, 'we bloody well will!'

Keeping to the shadows beneath the trees, they moved stealthily through the deserted park, encountering neither officials nor those they were employed to keep out, until at last they came to the edge of the lake.

'That'll do,' whispered Julia, pointing to a cluster of bushes right by the water's edge. 'We can hide our clothes in there.'

Mary felt another twinge of nervousness. 'What if there *are* tramps in here and they steal our things?'

Julia's teeth flashed again. 'Then it'll make getting home even more of an adventure, won't it?'

'Doesn't *anything* frighten you?'

'Of course – but that's what makes it so delicious. Come on,' she pulled at Mary's battered jacket. 'Last one in is an *old bachelor.*'

Undressing as quickly and as quietly as they could, they bundled their clothes together and pushed them into the bushes.

'God, Mary,' giggled Julia, as they stood naked at the water's edge. 'I'm *really* glad you didn't leave. I can't think of one other person who'd do this with me.'

Mary tucked up a few loose strands of hair. 'There are lots – but they're all locked up.' She grinned, reaching for Julia's hand. 'Come on – we'll have to wade right in or someone will hear the splash.'

Stepping into the cool water, they moved away from the bank, eyes fixed on the dark surface as it inched up their legs, until Mary caught sight of a round blotch near the top of Julia's thigh, and came to a dead stop. 'What's that, on your leg?' she asked in an urgent whisper.

Julia looked down. 'A tattoo,' she said proudly. 'Don't you like it?'

'Christ, it gave me a scare. I thought it was an insect or something. What's it meant to be? It's too dark to see it properly.'

'A rose. I'm thinking of having a whole line of them – going all the way round – like a garter.'

'You're mad.'

Julia pulled suddenly on Mary's arm. 'Quick, get down,' she hissed.

On the far side of the lake a speck of light from a bulls-eye lantern was moving between the trees, flashing as it was moved from side to side in search of the sleeping destitute.

'We'll be alright once we start swimming,' whispered Julia. 'They won't think to look out here.'

Keeping quite still, they crouched in the water until the lamp disappeared from sight and they could breathe easily once more. 'It's a bit late to ask,' said Julia, 'but you *can* swim, can't you?'

In lieu of an answer, Mary slipped effortlessly into deeper water, gliding away with barely a ripple.

Julia watched for a moment, enjoying the warm night air on her body, then she too slid into the cool, green depths. 'Isn't this heaven?'

Mary turned on to her back, floating in the moonlight. 'I don't think I've ever been so happy.'

'I don't mean just tonight.'

'I know.'

'No second thoughts, then?'

'No, not really. You were absolutely right. It *is* a wonderful life – but …' She sighed. 'Well, it doesn't matter.'

'No, go on, tell me.'

It was a perfect night, and Mary stared up at a sky bright with stars. 'I just can't help wondering what my Thomas would think. He used to work so hard, and yet we had *nothing*. Nothing to show for all the years of drudgery but a few sticks of worthless furniture. The whole lot wouldn't have paid for my new parasol. But if he could see me now – would he be proud of me? I don't think so.'

Julia swam closer. 'Is what we're doing really so bad?'

'It's immoral. I couldn't tell anyone at home what I'm doing here – not even Peggy. She thinks I'm working in a hotel.'

'Then let her keep thinking that, but it doesn't make what we're doing immoral. I'll tell you what *is* immoral – you told me you left your only child with a family in Caerphilly – why did you do that?'

'You know why.'

'Because you couldn't afford the boy's treatment?'

'He would have died without it. I had no choice …'

Julia lifted her hand from the water, stroking Mary's cheek. 'It's alright, I'm not blaming you, Mary. But don't you see? There are doctors – highly respected people – who have it in their power to save lives – your son's life – and yet many won't do a damn thing unless you pay them. *That's* immoral. And they're not alone, there are dozens of other examples. Take Emily. She's a very wealthy woman, yet she'd rather keep men like your husband in poverty than pay more for the coal to warm her backside – though she'll happily pay us a damn sight more to warm it another way. It's all hypocrisy – all of it. All we do is give a few people a little pleasure now and then. Is that so dreadful?'

'*I* don't think so.'

'And neither do I. So who cares what anyone else thinks?'

Mary looked at her for a few moments. 'You're right,' she said. 'Who cares.' Then, slowly, she started to grin. 'So – will you be bringing your soap box into the park this Sunday?'

'What was that you said earlier?' said Julia, swimming ominously close. 'About someone getting a very hard pinch?'

'Don't you dare!' Mary laughed, pushing her away.

'Shhhsh, you'll get us arrested.'

'Well, that will make getting home even more of an adventure, won't it?'

Julia shook her head, chuckling. 'You're worse than I am. Come on, let's swim up to the bridge – but *quietly*, alright?'

Barely stirring the water they moved into the centre of the lake, swimming side by side to within sight of the bridge. 'We'd better not go any closer,' said Julia, taking hold of Mary's arm. 'Just in case someone comes across.'

'I could do with a rest, anyway.' Mary turned to float on her back once more, her skin gleaming, pearl-like, where it broke the surface. 'It's hard to believe we're in the middle of London.'

'That's half the fun of it, don't you think?'

Mary thought about it. 'We wouldn't *really* go to prison if we were caught?'

'No, I don't think so. We'd plead *high-spirits*. You only get sent to gaol in this country for the things you do in desperation.' She paused, then laughed. 'You know, maybe you're right – perhaps I *will* buy a soapbox.'

'Julia Devereaux – crusader for the common people?'

'It has a nice to ring to it, don't you think?'

'Hmmm? I think I prefer you as Julia – mad, bad and dangerous to know,' laughed Mary, heading to where a tree was growing out from the bank, and catching hold of it.

Julia followed, hoisting herself on to a low branch. 'Madame is very pleased with you, you know.'

'That's because I'm a good girl and don't do *favours*,' said Mary sweetly.

'No, it's not just that. She would prefer we didn't, but she doesn't really mind as long as we're careful. No, she's pleased because you are very, very good at what you do.'

'I've had a good teacher.'

'It can't be taught. You have to have it to begin with. And you *are* very good …'

Mary caught the slight hesitation and glanced up at her. 'But?'

'I just want you to promise me you'll be careful with Archie. He seems to have taken quite a shine to you – but he's not like our other clients.'

'I don't see any difference – apart from his awful taste in clothes.'

Julia laughed softly, making the branch tremble, then she became serious again. 'Don't misjudge him, Mary. And *never* stay in character once he's finished. There are some men who resent the whole business the moment they've spent – and Archie is one of them. Elspeth learned that the hard way, and I've come very close to it. I don't want you getting hurt.'

'But he's always been alright.'

'He is alright – as long as you know how to handle him.'

'Well, I promise I'll be careful. But anyway, I'm only the spear carrier in your little scenarios, so you'll always be there to look after me, won't you?'

Julia made a chivalrous gesture. 'With my life, m'lady.' Then she grinned. 'Come on, let's go home. My bum's cold and I'm ready for some hot tea and toast.'

Chapter Thirty-Five

The Christmas of 1884 was like no Christmas I'd ever experienced, and by Christmas 1885 I was so established in my new life that I was almost able to look back on past events with detachment – as though they were just stories I had invented. Yet, I was never able to quell the ache in my heart for my son, Owen, or stop hoping for word from Gwyneth. And in the early hours of each New Year's Day I would wake crying – over the memory of Evan's leaving – and all that might have been.

*

In the close confines of the back room, the Chinaman's forehead glistened as he bent to his work, his long, bony fingers moving agitatedly, making blood flow as he drove the needle in and out of the smooth lily-white flesh. He paused, squinting upwards. 'You kip still. *Very* still, okay?'

Planted squarely on the rickety chair, her skirts and petticoats bunched about her waist, and her legs parted to give him access to the soft inner thigh, Mary gritted her teeth and nodded.

'Christ, Julia, it *hurts.*'

'Come on. Don't be a baby.' Standing close behind the chair, Julia held Mary's head, her fingers gently stroking at her temple. 'It's nearly done. Here, grip my hand.'

Mary took it, squeezing hard as the tiny black butterfly was completed and the man sat back, wiping away the blood and inspecting his work. 'Okay now. No kip still no more. All finish.'

With a great sigh of relief, Mary looked apprehensively at the design. 'It's still bleeding.'

'It will for a bit,' said Julia. 'But it'll soon scab over, and a few weeks from now it will look delightful. Delightfully *small*,' she grinned, 'but delightful all the same.'

Mary continued to look at it. 'God, that hurt. How could you stand to have all those roses done? It must have been agony.'

'It was, but that's the challenge, isn't it?' She smiled. 'Now, we ought to get you bandaged.'

The Chinaman brought over a strip of grubby-looking cloth, but Julia politely declined it, taking a clean piece of linen from her pocket and kneeling between Mary's thighs. 'There you are,' she said, gently tying the bandage. 'Though I shouldn't put your drawers back on just yet – better to wait until you're sure it's finished bleeding.'

Rising gingerly from the chair, Mary let her skirts fall back into place, then pulled on her plain coat, feeling in the pocket for her purse. 'How much do I owe him?'

'Nothing. I've already paid. This is my Christmas present to you.'

'Well – thank you, my dear. How on earth did you guess that my heart's desire was half an hour of pure torture?'

'Now, don't be ungrateful – or I shan't treat you to the tooth extraction I have planned for next Christmas.'

It was a very bemused Mr Fook who watched them push through the beaded curtain and leave his small shop.

Outside, the Whitechapel streets were wet with recent rain, and Julia pulled her worn coat tightly about her as she emerged into the gathering dusk. 'God, I'd forgotten how cold you get in these thin clothes – still, it's nice not to have everyone gawping at you, I suppose.'

Mary looked down at herself. 'You know, it wasn't so long ago that I'd have thought this suit quite smart.'

'Oh, it *is*! You look *quite* the lady's maid on her half-day.'

'More than I can say for you, I'm afraid,' laughed Mary. 'I'd take you for a kitchen skivvy – at best.'

Julia put her hands on her hips, her head cocked. 'And at worst?'

'You really don't want to know.'

'Hmmm, well, next time *I'll* have first pick from the wardrobe.'

'Yes, well, as you once told me …' Mary smiled serenely as she picked at a loose button. 'That's what it's all about – *clothes, and how to wear them.*'

Julia chuckled. 'So – fancy a bit of Christmas Eve shopping? I know just the place – but I could murder a drink first. How about we blow the rent money on a few penn'orth of mother's ruin?'

Half an hour later, flushed with cheap gin and chewing on ginger biscuits of dubious origin, they were pushing their way through the heaving mass that was Petticoat Lane market, their ears ringing to the shouts of stall-holders, and their noses besieged by the reek of old clothes and unwashed bodies, pickled fish and pickled cucumbers, sarsaparilla, hot chestnuts, and hot potatoes.

'Just like bloomin' Regent Street, ain't it?' said Julia, mimicking the prevailing accent.

On a nearby fish stall, a man with a peppering of grey whiskers about his chin stuck his thumbs into the pockets of his waistcoat. 'Yer won't get nuffink in Regent Street what yer can't get 'ere fer a quarter o' the price, gel. 'Ere, come an' look at this.' He picked up a large mackerel, holding it level with his face and looking into its dead eyes. 'Lovely ain't it? If it was a woman, I'd tickle it under the chin an' give it a kiss, that I would. It's yours for thrupence. Yer old man'll think 'is ship's come in when yer serve 'im this for 'is supper!'

Julia held up her left hand, fingers splayed to show the absence of a ring. 'Ain't got no old man, 'ave I!'

The man remained unflustered. 'Well, you buy this 'ere fish an' yer soon will 'ave! It's the best way to a bloke's 'eart.' Then, seeing them pushing on, he called, ''Ere, what about yer friend? Can't I tempt *you*, luv?'

'I don't think so,' laughed Mary as she followed Julia through the milling throng. 'I'd rather 'ave the fish.'

A little further on there was a stall selling old jewellery, and Mary stopped to look. It was mostly cheap stuff, but amongst the jumbled boxes were a few pendants of varying shapes and sizes. Tentatively she began picking through the tangled mass of chains.

'Oh, don't bother with that,' said Julia, pushing back through the crowd and grabbing hold of her sleeve. 'Come and watch this, it's really funny.'

Reluctantly, Mary let herself be drawn away to where a small crowd was gathered about the light from a flaring naphtha lamp, beneath which a stout, middle-aged Jewish woman was standing on a trestle placed in front of a stall laden with all manner of goods.

'So what you want? You want money back?' The woman struck her forehead with the heel of her hand. 'Well, I don't argue. I give you back money. But first you tell me. How long you have this sheet?'

At the front of the crowd, a sour-faced woman in a shawl hesitantly raised a clean white sheet, a threadbare hole in the centre. 'Five years only!'

'Five years? *Five years*? I don't believe it! You buy from me five years? How many children you got?'

'Children? You ask me about children?'

'Sure, I ask you. That sheet. It guaranteed last ten years – maybe more! I think your husband must make lot of children on that sheet, huh? I think you have fifteen, *at least*, for so much wear!'

The complaining woman looked perplexed, unsure of how to answer. 'I want my money back.'

'Okay. Okay. Mrs Kapinskya no argue. I give you back money – no, wait. I give better! I give *two* new sheets. Then you can go home and make *thirty* more children!' She picked up two folded sheets from the stall and tossed them to the woman. 'Now, anyone else want *personal* guaranteed linen? Finest in London. Two shillings, only.'

Two or three hands went up from the crowd, and the woman handed them out, shoving the money into the pocket of her skirt before turning back to the sour-faced woman. 'What? You here, still? What you want? To bleed Mrs Kapinskya dry? Well, I no sell to you. Next I got something special – for people who see bargain when they hear it!'

Standing at the back of the crowd, Julia leaned close to Mary. 'The woman at the front isn't really complaining. I've seen this before. She's just the stooge – you know, to draw people in?'

Mary nodded. 'Well, she's not very good, is she.' Then, with the bravado of four penn'orth of gin, she said, 'Shall *we* have a go?'

A gleam came to Julia's eyes. 'Alright. You lead, I'll follow.'

Taking her drawers from her pocket, Mary pushed her way to the front of the crowd. ''Ere,' she said, holding out the white, frilled underwear. 'I 'ave a complaint, too.'

Mrs Kapinskya eyed her suspiciously. 'Oh yes?'

'Yes. I bought these 'ere drawers from you *six* years ago.'

'Six years?' Mrs Kapinskya turned to the crowd. 'You see! Six years! Up and down like fiddler's elbow – and still good like new!' Then, studiously ignoring Mary, she picked up some towels. 'Now, here I got ...'

But Mary had aroused the interest of the crowd. 'Who you tryin' t' kid?' shouted an old woman at the back. 'They ain't six years old.'

'Oh, ain't they?' said Mary, looking tearful. 'Well a lot you know. I bought 'em to go on my 'oneymoon, I did – and that was six years ago this very week.'

'What, just come back, 'ave yer?'

Mary pretended to be upset, 'No. No, I ain't – but it feels as though I 'ave.'

'So what's yer complaint?' asked the old woman.

'They won't wear out,' wailed Mary, burying her face in her hands, her body heaving with great sobs.

'There, there,' said Julia squeezing into the small clearing and putting her arm about Mary's shoulder. 'No good upsettin' yerself, darlin'.' She turned to confront the crowd. 'Leave 'er be, won't yer. Yer don't know the trouble she's had since she bought these 'ere drawers from this woman.'

Angrily, Mrs Kapinskya reached down and took the garment from Mary's hand. 'What game you play with me, huh?'

Julia met the woman's accusing stare. 'Ain't no game,' she said, giving her a sly wink. 'Why, this poor girl's 'ad a miserable life since yer sold 'em to 'er.' She turned back to the crowd. 'Yer wouldn't believe the 'orrible tale she 'as to tell. Why, yer wouldn't find the like of it in no penny-dreadful, an' that's a fact! 'Orrible to contemplate, it is. Enough to make yer 'air turn white.'

288

'Well, I'm 'alf way there already,' called the old woman at the back. '*So* – are yer goin' t' tell us about it or not? I can't stand about 'ere all day. I got my old man's tea t' get on.'

'Well, it's like this,' began Julia, pretending to comfort Mary. 'But 'ere – why don't *she* tell yer, 'erself?' she said, quickly stepping back to join the crowd.

Mary lowered her hands from her face to find herself the sole centre of attention. 'W-ell,' she began hesitantly. 'It's my 'usband, see …'

''E's taken to wearin' 'em, 'as 'e?' called a skinny youth.

'No, I wish 'e would. But it's me what's got to wear 'em. 'E likes me in 'em so much, 'e won't let me wear nothin' else.'

'Nothin' else?' laughed the lad. 'Blimey, must be interestin' comin' to tea at your 'ouse.'

Warming to her role, Mary lowered her head, as though hiding a blush. 'Oh, I'm sure you wouldn't think it so funny if 'e was to come kissin' and cuddlin' *you* all day – much as you might like it to begin with.'

The crowd roared with laughter, and the boy went a deep crimson.

'I just wish they'd wear out, and I could be done with 'em,' continued Mary. 'I'm sure I should be left in peace then.'

'Your 'usband sounds a right dirty bugger!' chortled the old woman. 'Still, wait till yer get t' my age an' yer'll be left in peace alright. My old man wouldn't care if my arse was 'angin' in diamonds!'

Towards the back of the crowd a couple of soberly dressed people walked away in disgust, but the mood of the remainder had brightened considerably. Picking up on it, Mrs Kapinskya pulled several new though inferior pairs from her stock, tugging forcibly at the stitching. 'You don't never wear them out,' she said, proudly. 'Made to last! Only very best material. Strong as two horses couldn't tear. My guarantee!' She shrugged and rolled her eyes. 'But effect on your husband nothing to do with me.'

'You got some in my size?' shouted the old woman.

'I got all size, all shape. Ten shilling in West End shop – but I sell for only eighteen pence!'

'Go on then, give us a pair.'

'No, please …' Mary's eyes widened in horror, and she looked imploringly at the crowd. 'You mustn't. You don't know what you're doin'. These ain't just pairs of drawers …'

Mrs Kapinskya tapped a finger to her head. 'Don't listen to crazy girl! She mad – from too much love. Now, I busy woman and only have few left. Who want them? Eighteen pence and I make myself pauper!'

The crowd had grown to double the size and a forest of hands shot up.

'Miriam,' Mrs Kapinskya called to where the sour-faced woman still clutched her sheets. 'Don't stand doing nothing. Take money from these good people.'

Mary continued to beseech them with all the fervour of a fire and brimstone preacher, warning of the awful consequences, and pleading as if their very souls were at stake, while garment after garment flew over her head and into the eager hands of customers – and the more she pleaded, so the more they laughed and reached for their purses and pocket books. 'Well,' she said at last as Mrs Kapinskya's stock of underwear came to an end. 'I've *tried* to warn you. Lord knows I 'ave!' She caught sight of Julia who was clutching her sides with laughter, 'So on your own 'eads be it. I only 'ope you are of great 'eart – *and of even greater stamina* – and I shall pray for the souls of those who aren't. Good evenin' – and a *very merry Christmas.*'

No one in the crowd had been taken in by the performance, it had merely put them in good humour and the mood to spend, and both Mary and Julia received hearty slaps on the back as they pushed their way through. Then, suddenly, Mrs Kapinskya was standing squarely in front of them. 'What for you do that?' she asked suspiciously.

'It was a dare,' said Julia.

'A dare? What is dare?'

'It was just for fun,' explained Mary. 'I'm sorry if it annoyed you.' She saw the woman's uncomprehending look. 'If it made you upset – *angry*?'

Mrs Kapinskya flapped her hands dismissively. 'Ach, I know annoyed. I know annoyed better than no one. My sister, Miriam, always for her I am annoyed. *Never* can she do it right – but *you*, you do it *very* right. You have *chutzpah*. You come back with me now. I give you job.'

'She has a job, thank you,' smiled Julia.

'Hah, what job? All day on knees?' She wagged her head from side to side. '*Yes, ma'am. No, ma'am*? You come with me. I give you *good* job. We make good business, good money.'

Mary caught Julia's look of amusement and tried not to laugh. 'Can I think about it?' she asked.

'Yes, think – think, all you want.' She watched them go, 'But think quick – before Miriam make me crazy – like you!'

Chapter Thirty-Six

The ring was nothing more than two thick ship's ropes tightly encircling the four pillars of the dingy Shoreditch cellar. The floor – unyielding flagstones that extended beyond the enclosure to where the press of spectators sat or stood in the semi-darkness, their feral faces illuminated by excitement and the spill of light from the central gasolier.

Inside the ring, two men were circling: one, heavily built and with a shock of red hair, the other smaller, wiry but strong, both men's faces and naked chests bloodied, their iron-nailed boots grating on the stones.

Murray Baines blinked, then blinked again, letting his eyes adjust after the brightness of the early summer streets.

'Watch out, Carrots!' a woman yelled close to Baines's ear as the wiry man made a frenzied attack, his bare fists driving his opponent into a corner and keeping him there with a barrage of steam-hammer blows. 'Bash the little bugger!'

Unmoved by the encouragement, Carrots stayed against the ropes, arms raised to protect his face as the wiry man punched savagely at his ribs.

'Fight me, you fat bastard.' The smaller man continued to pummel away to little obvious effect until, in frustration, he took a step back and aimed a kick, catching the redhead just below the knee, ripping open the patched corduroy and the flesh below.

He instantly realised his mistake.

With a great bellow of rage, Carrots lurched from the ropes, throwing his opponent back against the brick pillar where they clung to each other, their heads locked together, until the red-head reared back, bloodied flesh clenched in his teeth.

Dazed and clutching at the ragged remains of his ear, the smaller man staggered from the pillar and straight into a bone-shattering punch that dropped him like a pistolled horse.

Immediately, the cellar erupted with cheers and curses as people leaped to their feet, obstructing Baines's way as he pushed through to where Vincent Eastman was seated at the ringside. 'Archie wants us,' he said, over the noise of the crowd.

Eastman regarded him. '*Now*, I suppose?' He looked across to the far side of the ring where two lean young men were pulling off their shirts in readiness, then he sighed and got to his feet. 'Well, it's not before time.'

'Not goin' are yer, Vincey?'

The muscle in Eastman's jaw flickered. 'Yes, I'm afraid so, Mr Farrel.'

'What a shame. These next two boys look promisin', don't yer think?'

'They would seem to promise a little more finesse than the previous bout, certainly.'

A grin creased Farrel's simian features. 'Maybe – but yer don't often lose money on Carroty Ned. 'E's a bit past it, but 'e does the business when 'e's riled up. The Geordie shouldn't 'ave kicked 'im. Not sportin' that. But I'm fuckin' glad 'e did – I was getting worried fer my 'a'pence.' He glanced across at the two young fighters, then back at Eastman. 'But 'e ain't so much to look at, no more, I suppose.' He jerked a thumb toward Baines. 'This young feller your new partner?'

Baines stuck out his hand. 'Pleased to meet you, Mr Farrel. It's a real honour.'

''Eard of me, 'ave yer?' said Farrel, taking a firm grip.

'Of course. Everyone's heard of Harry Farrel and the Hoxton High Rips.'

'Perhaps you could say it a little *louder*?' suggested Eastman.

Baines let go of the man's hand, looking guilty, but Farrel only chuckled. 'It's alright. Everyone knows me 'round 'ere – an' we're all friends.' He nodded toward four men sitting a little way off. 'Even got a few sportin' gentlemen from H division with us today.' He cast another glance toward the ring. 'Sure yer won't stay? Nice pair o' *young boys*, these two.'

Eastman glanced down to where a waifish girl of eight or nine had come to stand quietly by Farrel's side. To the uninitiated, she might have been his granddaughter. 'Is this *your* new partner?' he asked.

Harry Farrel laughed. 'Nah, not my cup o' tea, Vincey. I like 'em *fledged*, if yer know what I mean? I bought 'er for my Sadie.' Seated a little way off, the blowzy figure of Sadie Farrel was scratching herself, laughing with a group of other women, and he pushed the girl in her direction. 'She's always 'ad a likin' fer the young 'un's.' He made to return to his seat. 'Well, give my best to Archie – tell 'im bygones is bygones, an' 'e's always welcome down this way.'

'I'll be sure to convey your message.'

Farrel paused. 'Oh, an' between you an' me, Vincey, I do 'ope 'e ain't losin' 'is grip.' He grinned maliciously. ''Cos I 'ear some Froggies 'ave been takin' the rise out of 'im somethin' chronic.'

*

Mme Bennaire looked grave. 'I'm not sure I approve. I'm really not sure at all.' She leaned back into the sofa, tossing her head in vexation. 'Oh, why did it have to be that *beastly* man!'

'It'll be alright,' said Julia, 'I promise. Besides, Mary's never been further than Brighton – and this is a whole week in Paris.'

'But with Archie Bull?'

'Why not? He's been no trouble recently – and Mary knows how to deal with him just as well as I do.'

Mme Bennaire turned wearily to Mary, taking her hand. 'Please, my dear. Tell me you don't wish to go and I shall be delighted to refuse him.'

Torn between the two of them, wanting to please them both, Mary caught Julia's eye and saw the gleam of excitement. 'I'm sure it will be alright, Madame. Archie's always been the perfect gentleman with me. Besides, Julia will be there, too. And I *would* love to see Paris.'

'Ah, yes, *Paris*,' sighed Mme Bennaire. 'It is a wonderful city. Quite, *quite* wonderful. The Bois de Boulogne will be lovely at this time of year – and there is the most delightful little café …' Catching herself, she smiled. 'Yes, you are right, you *must* experience Paris.' She leaned forward taking hold of each of them by the hand and squeezing. 'Just promise me you will be very, very careful?'

*

'Damn, but it's hot.' Ivor Rees-Morgan leaned back in his chair and let out a long, heavy sigh. He felt uncomfortable and irritable, and the second large brandy that lay warming in his palm was having as little effect as its predecessor. He turned grumpily to Florence. 'Aren't you hot?'

'Not really,' said Florence.

'Well ring for the maid anyway, and have her open the windows.'

'Her name is Gwyneth.'

'What?'

'Her name is *Gwyneth*. She *has* been with us for some time now, Ivor. It would only be courteous to remember her name.'

He looked at her, his face the colour of watered claret. 'Very well, damn it – then ring for *Gwyneth,* and have her open the damned windows!'

Florence reached down, stroking the hair of the boy who was playing at her feet, engrossed in pushing a pair of painted horses across the patterned rug. 'It's getting toward dusk, and I'm not sure the night air is good for Owen's chest.'

'Good God, woman!' Ivor rolled his eyes. 'He hasn't had a serious attack in over a year!'

'But that doesn't mean …'

'The boy *needs* fresh air – and so do I.'

Florence hesitated. 'Well, it's practically his bedtime. I'll have Nanny take him up.' She rose and went to the bell-pull, giving it a gentle tug. 'I'm sure you know best, Ivor – and I know I'm being silly, but I just couldn't stand it if – after all this time, all this progress …' She left the sentence unfinished and crossed to the tall windows, looking into the evening sky. 'He grows more like Evan every day and …' From behind her came the sound of glass breaking on the wooden floor, and she turned. 'Ivor?' she said, then with increasing alarm, '*Ivor*?'

*

In the drawing-room above the Princess Alice, Connie Bull stood perfectly still, her figure so mercilessly corseted she appeared as rigid and immovable as any ship's figure-head. 'Why a *week*?'

Archie studied himself in the mirror, adjusting the lapels of his boldly chequered suit. 'Because that's 'ow long it'll take.' He glanced to where Eastman and Baines stood ready. 'We all ready for the off?'

'Everything's been taken care of, sir,' said Baines, his eyes bright and eager to please.

Archie laughed. ''Ear that, Con? 'E's a caution, ain't 'e?' He turned back to Baines. 'I ain't been knighted, son – not *yet* anyways – so leave out the *sir* stuff. *I* don't call no one *sir* – so don't you do it neither, alright?' His gash of a mouth spread outwards and upwards. ''Ere, nice pair o' bags yer've got on – just right for a stroll up the Shondy-whatsit.' He flicked at his own trousers, then looked across at Eastman. 'You ought t' get yerself some decent clobber, Vince. Yer look like a bleedin' stockbroker or some-thin'. Yer need t' get yerself in the 'oliday mood.'

'This isn't meant to be no holiday,' warned Connie.

Archie gave her a sideways glance. 'I don't expect it will be.'

'We should've taken care of this eighteen months ago.'

'We should 'ave, but we didn't. Now we are, an' it's just goin' t' be that much 'arder, that's all.' He motioned toward the two waiting men. ''Ere, wait for me outside. I'll be down in a minute.'

With Eastman and Baines gone, Connie softened a fraction. 'You be careful, alright?'

Archie grinned. 'If yer that worried maybe yer should go an' 'andle it yerself. It wouldn't be the first time, now would it?'

In a small gesture of tenderness, she reached out, taking the handker-chief from his breast pocket and dabbing at a smut on the side of his nose. 'Still wanting me to fight your battles for you?'

'Why not?' He leaned forward and kissed her. 'Yer *still* wiping my snotty nose, ain't yer?'

*

'Is Archie *really* a criminal, do you think?' asked Mary as they made their way back to their hotel at dusk.

'Madame seems to think so. He's certainly been very secretive over his travel arrangements. God knows if he's even here yet.' Julia gripped Mary's arm, grinning. 'Perhaps he won't come. Wouldn't that be wonderful?'

A light drizzle began to fall, and along the Boulevard des Batignolles the pavements gleamed with the lights from street lamps and shop windows. It was the first rain for many weeks and the roads, coated with summer grime, quickly became slick and treacherous.

'Watch your step,' said Julia, as they crossed the busy thoroughfare, pausing half-way to wait for a gap in the stream of vehicles.

It had been a splendid day, and Mary was giggling like a schoolgirl. 'Come on, I'll race you!' she laughed as a break in the traffic appeared, and they both ran for the far kerb, mounting the pavement in a flurry of skirts.

'Do you really want to go back to the hotel?' asked Julia, catching her breath.

'No – no, I never want this day to end.' Mary whirled around, arms outstretched. 'See Paris and die!'

'A drop more bubbly first, though, eh?'

Mary nodded eagerly, and arm in arm they made their way along the crowded boulevard. 'I don't think I'd ever tire of this,' she said, shaking her head and grinning with delight. 'It's all so different.'

At the corner of Boulevard Malesherbes they were about to cross the street when a sudden shout and clatter of hooves caused them to leap back. A hansom cab was flying up the road, making for a break in the traffic, but moving too fast for the sharp right turn. For a moment the horse's hooves flailed at the wet cobbles as it struggled to regain its footing – but in vain. Wide-eyed and whinnying in terror, it crashed to the ground, stopping the progress of the cab so abruptly that the huge wheels lifted into the air, hurling the driver into the road and its passenger headlong through the glass window that had been closed tight against the rain.

There was a stunned silence, then, eerily, like a thing possessed, the cab began to lurch as the crippled horse kicked and struggled in the shafts.

'Oh, my God!' said Mary, clutching at Julia's arm. 'Look!'

Trapped in a pillory of jagged shards and splintered wood, the sole occupant of the cab slowly raised her head to reveal a bloody mask from which dazed, uncomprehending eyes stared about in disbelief.

Julia's hands went to her throat, and she took a step back, but Mary was already darting from the crowd and calling for her to follow. Stumbling, she started forward.

With every kick of the frightened beast, the cab rocked violently, threatening to rip open the woman's throat on the shattered window.

'Someone get the horse, for Christ's sake!' Julia shouted, suddenly galvanised into action. 'Le cheval! See to the bloody cheval!'

A crowd was forming, and several men were already running to calm the fallen animal as Mary approached the cab. 'It's alright,' she said, trying to soothe the woman. 'Everything's alright.'

Blood was oozing from a huge gash on the woman's forehead, filling her eyes and dribbling from her chin in a thin stream, yet she seemed strangely detached, as though unaware of the true horror of her injuries. She turned blindly in Mary's direction.

'Just keep still, and it will be alright.'

But the woman's fingers were already working at the loose splinters of glass, picking them away before creeping over the frame to explore the gaping rents in her face and the shards still embedded in her cheeks. Her mouth opened, a red, ragged hole laced with sticky strands. 'Mon visage!' she screamed, 'Non! *Non!*'

From the far side of the cab the driver appeared, dazed but seemingly unhurt. 'Ce n'était pas ma faut. Ah, Dieu, ce n'était pas ma faut!'

'I don't know what you're saying!' Julia snapped, pushing him from her so hard he nearly lost his footing. 'Do something useful and stop another cab. We've got to get her to the hospital! *A l'hôpital?*' But the man was uncomprehending. He slumped on to the kerb, his head in his hands. 'Ce n'était pas ma faut …'

The woman was losing a great deal of blood. 'You *have* to be still. Ne bougez pas. Nous …' Mary gritted her teeth in frustration. The smattering of French Madame had taught her, totally inadequate for the situation. 'You're alright,' she said, slowly and deliberately, 'but you're making it worse than it needs to be. Stay still and we'll have you out of there soon.'

For a moment the woman seemed to understand, then without warning there came the sound of a pistol shot, driving her to new fits of hysteria as she struggled frantically to break free.

'Oh, my God!' shouted Mary, startling at the sound, craning to look over her shoulder to where a man was standing by the head of the lifeless horse, a gun in his hand. She turned to Julia. 'She'll bleed to death if we don't quieten her! You'll have to help me hold her!' But Julia was already climbing up on to the hansom, trying to reach into the cab.

Daggers of glass projected from the broken frame, and it took all of Mary's strength to prevent the woman from impaling herself. 'You *must* try to stay calm,' she said as a policeman pushed through the crowd. 'There's help here now.'

The gendarme took in the frightful spectacle. 'Oh, *Mon Dieu!*' he said, going white.

Mary turned away from him, aware that the woman had gone limp in her hands. She looked to Julia. 'Is she …?'

'She's out. Best thing for her at present.'

More policemen pushed into the clearing as Julia jumped down, and with a little help they managed to extract the woman and carry her to the pavement where she was soon lost from sight behind a wall of onlookers.

Shaking, Mary looked at her blood-stained coat and hands, then across at Julia who had grown alarmingly pale. 'Are you alright?' she asked quietly, taking her arm.

Julia nodded, but her face was drawn, and she too was shaking. 'Did you see her face, Mary? Did you see it?'

Mary nodded.

'Could you bear that?' There was a terrible look in Julia's eyes. 'I couldn't – I know I couldn't. I'd rather *die* than be disfigured.'

'Oh, my poor love,' Mary drew Julia into her arms. 'It's all over now.'

'No – no, it's not.' Julia pulled away, her hand going to her face, fingers trembling. 'Do you … do you believe in premonitions?'

Mary stared at her.

'That woman's face … all disfigured … cut to pieces …' Julia looked into Mary's eyes. 'It's going to happen, Mary. I saw it – as clearly as I see you now. *I saw myself like that.*'

Chapter Thirty-Seven

'Yer don't look too good, gel,' said Archie as a waiter brought another two bottles of champagne to the table and set them in the silver ice buckets.

'She's been sick,' said Mary, beginning to slur her words. 'There was an *awful* accident this afternoon just by the hotel.'

Julia fixed a smile on her colourless face. 'But I'm *perfectly* alright now.'

'Well yer don't look it.'

'Well I *am*.'

Archie held up his hands. 'Alright, alright,' he said, then with a sly grin, 'You're the *governess*, eh?'

'I'm glad you remember. We've been here two whole days and not had a single word from you.'

He chuckled. 'Well, I 'ad business to attend to – but it's taken care of now, so what say we 'ave a drop more champers to put the colour back in yer cheeks? Think that might be the ticket?'

Julia nodded, but her indifference was thinly veiled. In the aftermath of the accident she had tried to lighten their spirits by having a bottle of Lafite '47 brought to their rooms, but while Mary had quickly succumbed to its mellowing powers, the alcohol had only served to deepen Julia's sombre mood.

'Yer 'otel alright?' he asked, filling their glasses.

'It's lovely,' gushed Mary. 'And yours?'

'Not bad. I've been in worse places.'

'So where *are* you staying?' asked Julia, sipping her champagne.

He looked at her askance. 'A place over by that big arch-thingy. Can't remember the name of it.'

'The arch – or the hotel?'

'Neither,' he said, irked by her tone, then he grinned and picked up the bottle. ''Ere, 'ave some more of this. It might loosen yer corsets a bit – yer look like yer've been suckin' on a lemon all afternoon.'

Julia eyed him coldly but said nothing.

'Well, I'm ready for somethin' to eat,' he said, topping up Mary's glass. ''Ow about you?'

Mary was beginning to feel very drunk. 'I think something to eat would be *just the ticket*,' she giggled.

Archie grinned at her. 'Yer know, I ain't never seen you drunk, before.'

'*I am not drunk!*' she said with comic indignance.

'It's alright, gel. I like it.' He looked pointedly at Julia, 'Makes a bit of a change t' see a smilin' face. Still, maybe we'd better get yer some fodder, all the same, eh? Seein' as 'ow I'm anticipatin' a long night for the three of us.' He clicked his fingers at a passing waiter. 'Oi! Gas-on! Noos voolong le dinner – *savvy?*'

Perplexed, the waiter shrugged apologetically.

'La carte, s'il vous plaît,' said Julia.

'Ah, oui, Madame.'

'Bloody Froggies,' growled Archie. 'Don't understand their own soddin' language!'

Mary spluttered into her glass. 'That's just like the cartoon in *Punch*,' she chortled, wiping the splashes of champagne from her face. 'You remember, Julia?'

Julia looked meaningfully at her. 'No.'

'Of course you do. You showed it to me. The one where a man and his wife are sitting in a restaurant in France – and the man says just that very same thing.' She pulled a face, not unlike Archie's. '*Bloody Froggies! Don't understand their own soddin' language* – only he didn't swear, of course – and the wife, she says …'

'No, I *don't* remember it,' said Julia, emptying her glass and placing it purposefully on the table. '*So* what are your plans for the remainder of the week, Archie?'

'Oh, you must remember!' persisted Mary. 'It was ever so funny. The wife says, well, *not the way you speak it, dear,* and then – and this is the really funny bit – she says, *actually, if you have anything of a personal nature you wish to tell me, it would be better if you said it in French, as some of these waiters know a little English.*'

Archie's face was like stone. 'Is that supposed t' be aimed at me?' he said quietly as Mary began to rock with laughter.

Apprehension flickered in Julia's eyes. 'She's drunk. I should get her back to the hotel.' She began to rise, but Archie closed his thick fingers about her wrist, making her wince.

'You just stay where you are,' he said, darkly. 'No need t' go breakin' up the party, is there? I can take a joke, can't I?'

Oblivious to the exchange, Mary emptied her glass. 'Anymore?' she asked happily.

Julia gave her a tight-lipped look. 'I think you've had enough, don't you?'

'Let 'er be,' said Archie, reaching for the bottle. 'She's 'avin' a good time.'

'I am,' grinned Mary, watching with studied concentration as he filled her glass once more. 'I'm having a wonderful time – but then, I haven't had any premon …' she hiccupped, ' … itiony, things.'

'What's that when it's at 'ome?'

Julia kicked her sharply under the table, but Mary was too drunk to notice. 'Julia … my best friend … *she* has them,' she looked sadly across the table at Julia, as though to confirm the truth of her statement, then she leaned toward Archie, her expression becoming grave. 'She thinks you're going to cut her up into little pieces – just like that lady in the cab – all cut up into teensy-weensy little bits.'

'Shut up!' said Julia.

Archie raised an eyebrow. 'What's all this about?'

'It's true,' said Mary.

'She's talking nonsense,' said Julia.

'I suppose it's because you're a criminal.'

'Archie. I need to take her home.'

'Are you a *naughty* criminal, Archie?'

Julia grabbed hold of her arm, shaking her. 'Mary, for God's sake!'

'Mary? Who the bleedin' 'ell's Mary? I thought 'er name was Emma.'

'Please, m'sieur,' murmured the head waiter, hurrying to their table. 'You are disturbing the other diners. If the lady is *unwell*, perhaps I could call you a cab?'

Archie looked up angrily, and the man took an involuntary step back, raising his hands. '*Please*, m'sieur …?'

'Alright, alright,' said Archie. 'Keep yer 'air on.' He paused, looking thoughtfully at Mary, then he grinned. 'Yer know,' he said, getting to his feet and patting the man on the shoulder. 'That ain't such a bad idea. In fact I think it's just the ticket. You go an' call us that cab, there's a good lad.'

'I'm sorry, Archie,' whispered Julia as she helped Mary to stand. 'She's never been like this before.'

'No, she ain't, 'as she.'

'She'll be alright tomorrow.'

'Oh, I think she's goin' t' be just perfect tonight.'

Julia looked at him in alarm. 'Look, let me take her back to the hotel and put her to bed – then I'll come back.'

He shook his head. 'No offence, m'darlin', but you ain't exactly scintilla-tin' company this evenin'. I think it's *you* as should go an' 'ave a nice lie down – get some of that old sparkle back. *Alright*?'

'I *really* don't think …' she began, trying for an authoritative tone, but the veiled threat in his eyes cut her short.

'Don't you worry about us,' he said as they moved toward the door. 'Me an' Miss Black are goin' t' be just fine on our own.'

Outside, the warm evening air served only to invigorate Mary, making her even more playful, forcing Julia to hold on to her as they waited for the cab to arrive. 'For God's sake, Mary. Pretend to be ill,' she whispered as a four-wheeler came to a halt at the kerb and Archie went to speak to the driver. 'Faint or something – *anything*.'

Mary looked at her with eyes bright with merriment. 'I will if you will,' she giggled.

'*Please* …' Julia pleaded. '*This isn't a lark!*' Archie was coming toward them, his gash of a grin even more predatory than usual, and she half turned from him, pretending to fasten a button on Mary's dress. 'It wasn't *me*,' she whispered urgently, bending close to her ear. 'I lied. It wasn't *me* I saw this afternoon – it was *you*. Do you understand, Mary? It was *you*.'

Mary stared at her uncomprehendingly, then she giggled again.

'Right,' said Archie, taking Julia by the arm and escorting her to the waiting cab. 'This chap'll take yer back t' yer 'otel. Get yerself some grub, a good night's kip, an' we'll see yer tomorrer, alright?' He helped her in, shutting the door behind her. 'Don't you worry. I'll be a good boy.' He winked. 'Well, a *reasonably* good boy.'

With a jolt, the cab pulled away, and Julia watched helplessly as the figures of Archie and Mary faded into the Parisian twilight.

*

Charpentier's was a place full of verve and excitement, loud voices and even louder laughter. Waiters in stained aprons bustled back and forth between tables set in haphazard fashion on the sawdust-strewn floor, and had it not been for the boiled pig's foot that lay untouched on his plate, Archie would have felt far more at home than in the restaurant they'd been asked to leave two hours earlier.

'It's a bit of alright 'ere, ain't it,' he said.

'Ain't it a *right* bit of alright,' mimicked Mary, giggling into her glass.

He shook his head. 'You're a *right* comical cow.'

'Is that like a pantomime horse?' she said, shaking with laughter.

Mellowed by several quarts of beer, he chuckled. 'You're a bloody caution, that's what you are.' Then poking at the pig's foot, 'Bloody Froggie language. Ought to have the soddin' menu in English. Still, s'pose I was lucky not t' get its bleedin' arse'ole!' Disgustedly he gave the pig's foot a final prod and pushed the plate away. 'Poxy foreigners! I'll be glad t' get back 'ome so's I can get some decent grub inside me.'

'So why'd you come here, then?' she asked, looking distractedly about the room.

'None o' your business.' He took another swig of beer. 'A little bit of de-lousing, if yer must know. A couple of fleas that was in need of squashin', as it were.'

Mary pulled a face and shuddered.

He laughed. 'Well, there's fleas an' then there's *fleas,* ain't there. Some need stampin' on – others can be left alone as long as they stay put an' don't get no funny ideas about nippin' out an' bitin' yer.' He poured some more wine into their glasses. 'But that's enough of that. I want t' know who Mary is. Your name's Emma, ain't it?'

Mary slurped a mouthful of wine, giggled at the noise she'd made, then drew herself up, trying to look serious. 'She's my sister,' she said.

'Who? This 'ere Mary?'

'Yes. She's a timid little thing. I love her dearly – but she *is* a trial. I always have to look after her, you see? If it wasn't for me, well, I don't know how she'd manage. She'd still be scrubbing floors in Caerphilly, I expect.'

Archie sensed she was playing with him, but couldn't quite grasp the joke. 'So what about Julia? I suppose that's '*er* real name, is it?'

'Sort of,' said Mary, her words becoming slurred once more as the wine began to take over from the waning champagne. She smiled happily. 'She's my sister, too.'

'Julia's yer sister?' said Archie in surprise.

Mary nodded. 'She's my twin sister, Emma.'

'But *your* name's Emma.'

'Ah,' said Mary holding up a wavering finger, as if he had chanced upon a brilliant deduction. 'That's right …'

'Must 'ave been a bit confusin' at 'ome.'

'No, because you see, her mother was a midwife and … well, she died … but *mine* died and she was …' She shook her head as though ridding herself of an unpleasant thought. 'Well, that doesn't matter.'

'Well, if yer 'ad different mothers 'ow the 'ell can she be yer twin sister, yer daft 'a'penceworth.'

Mary shook her head again. 'I don't know,' she said looking genuinely puzzled. 'But she is! It just took me a while to find her.'

'You're a bloody silly cow,' he said getting a unsteadily to his feet. 'An' *that* ain't the same as no pantomime 'orse, neither.' He leaned heavily on the table, smiling as he watched her laugh. 'Come on. I don't care what yer name is – or who yer bleedin' sister is, come t' that. But I *do* know,' his face split wide, 'it's time for *Miss Black* t' come out t' play.'

*

'You must come and see this!' The young man leaned forward in the wicker chair, his forearms resting on the wrought iron railings of the balcony as he looked down into the darkened street. 'Quickly, man, or you'll miss it!'

'What is it?'

'A couple down in the avenue. She's as drunk as a lord – and he's not much better.'

'I've seen drunks before.'

'Not like these!' James Spencer laughed, drawing on a thin cheroot and blowing a cloud of smoke into the night sky. 'It's a damn music hall act! She's taken a whip from one of the carriages, and now she's playing the lion-tamer and cracking it at everyone who passes by.'

The man in the room began to pace up and down in the yellow lamp-light, a piece of paper gripped firmly between his fingers.

'Oh, my hat! It's getting better and better!'

'Hmmm?'

'The coachman's just come after her, but she won't give it back! And now she's cracking it at *him,* and he's hopping about like a scalded cat! For God's sake, Evan, you must come and watch. You won't see a show as good as this for two hundred francs.'

Evan came slowly to the open door but did not venture out on to the balcony. 'I've just received a telegram,' he said gravely. 'I shall have to return home tomorrow morning. It seems my father has been taken ill.'

*

Scattered about the plush lounge of the hotel, sedate groups in evening dress sat beneath the potted palms, their voices seldom rising above the background murmur, just as their conversation seldom rose above the banalities of the drawing-room. Sport, politics, and the theatre were all well represented, along with the fashions and gossip of several nations. Only at one table was the subject of murder under discussion.

'I can't sleep for thinking about it,' whispered Murray Baines, leaning forward, his face drawn with fatigue. 'They screamed like bloody women, Vincent. Like bloody women!'

Vincent Eastman crushed a cashew nut between his perfectly white teeth, chewed for a moment, then swallowed. 'That bothers you?'

Baines looked almost embarrassed. 'No, of course not.'

'Well then?'

'Well, I just don't understand why it had to be like *that.* We could have done them without all that … that other business. They'd be just as dead, wouldn't they?'

Eastman levelled his gaze on Baines's face. 'But would it have sent *quite* the same message?'

Murray Baines looked down at his hands, remembering the blood. 'Alright, but we could have done the other stuff *after* they were dead, couldn't we?'

'We could have, but then …' Eastman paused, a second nut half way to his mouth, as a loud and familiar voice rose above the hum of conversation.

'It's Mr Bull,' said Baines, turning to look along the length of the lounge.

'So I see.' Eastman got to his feet, and with Baines following, went to meet Archie, drawing him tactfully back into the foyer. 'Is this wise?' he asked, glancing briefly at Mary. 'I was given to understand that *no one* was to know where you were staying.'

Archie's expression became belligerent. 'Don't come it with me, Vince. *I* pay the wages, *alright*.'

Eastman inclined his head a fraction and gave a courteous nod that was neither impudent nor subservient.

'Good boy,' said Archie, taking it as an apology. 'Now I should like t' introduce yer to a young lady friend o' mine. This 'ere's the fair Emma.'

'Pleased to meet you, gentlemen,' said Mary, executing an unsteady curtsey.

'An' this,' he said, taking hold of the carriage whip she was holding, '*this 'ere* is the most expensive bleedin' whip in the whole of France.' He chuckled drunkenly, 'Do yer know 'ow much this cost me, Vince. Do yer? Go on, 'ave a guess.'

Eastman lifted an eyebrow in a gesture of polite disinterest.

'Five 'undred francs,' said Archie. 'That's what I had t' give the stuck-up arse-wipe to call off the police. Five 'undred bleedin' francs.' He puzzled for a moment. ''Ow much *is* that?'

'Approximately twenty-five pounds.'

'Christ! Bloody sight dearer than I thought.' He chuckled, taking Mary's arm and giving it a playful squeeze. 'Still, I reckon it's goin' t' be worth …' He stopped abruptly, blinking several times before massaging his eyelids with thumb and forefinger.

'What is it?' asked Eastman.

Archie shrugged. 'Nothin'. Must 'ave 'ad one too many.'

Mary began to giggle and he tightened his grip on her arm, giving Eastman a sly wink. 'Time we was goin' upstairs. See you boys in the mornin'.'

Eastman watched them weave their way across the foyer. 'Wonderful,' he said, as they staggered into the lift. 'Just *wonderful*.'

'What are we going to do?' Baines asked anxiously. 'If any of the Froggies have seen him in that state …'

'They'd have to be blind to miss him, wouldn't they?' He breathed deeply as he surveyed the lounge. 'Well, we must presume the damage is done. Go upstairs and put an armchair outside his door. You can take first turn at standing guard.'

In the drawing-room of the seventh floor suite overlooking the Arc de Triomphe, Archie poured himself a whisky. 'Want one?'

Mary shook her head, moving to the window and looking down at the twinkling lights on the boulevard. They made her think of Peggy, and that in turn made her sad. 'Yes, perhaps I will,' she said, wanting to regain the warm, happy drunkenness that was ebbing away to leave her feeling a little sick.

Archie poured a tumbler of the amber liquid and handed it to her. 'Bottoms up,' he said with a twinkle in his eye.

She smiled, but it was forced. She wanted Julia to be there. She couldn't even remember why Julia wasn't there. She took a long pull at the whisky, coughing as it burned her throat.

'Ready?' asked Archie.

She downed the rest of her drink. 'I need the lavatory, first.' Walking unsteadily into the bedroom where Archie had already lit the gas, she went into the bathroom, turning the catch.

'Can I come in an' watch?' he called, coming to sit on the bed.

'No.' The single word a dull statement of fact. She pulled up her skirts, opened her drawers then sat down on the wooden seat. From the bedroom came the clink of glass as Archie poured another whisky, and uncomfortably self-conscious she shifted her position, trying to minimize the sound of her stream into the porcelain bowl.

'Yer goin' t' be much longer?'

'No, I … I'll be out in a moment.' She shrank from the sound of her voice. It wasn't what he was paying for. She should be stern – or lasciviously arrogant, but she felt none of these, only tired, ill and pathetic. She got up, replaced her clothes, then went to the basin, splashing cold water on to her face.

When she came back into the bedroom, Archie was already naked, his squat, hairy body sprawled in an armchair by the bed. 'What do you think you are doing?' she asked, grasping in vain for the mantle of authority.

He got to his feet, standing submissively. 'Waitin' for you, ma'am.'

'Indeed? Didn't I tell you to make yourself ready for a thrashing?'

Archie shuffled his feet. 'I don't believe yer did, ma'am.'

'Well …' There was a moment's hesitation. 'Well … do it now.'

He came forward, his penis hanging flaccidly where it should have been rigidly erect. 'Yes, ma'am.'

'Face down. On the bed.' Mary picked up the carriage whip, waving it vaguely. Her face felt cold and clammy, and she needed to continually swallow to keep down the rising tide in her throat. 'And we'll have you spread-eagled.'

Archie started to climb on to the bed, then he stopped. 'This ain't goin' t' work, is it, gel.'

'Don't argue.'

'I *mean* it.'

'Do as I say! This instant! Or …' the tide in her throat rose to a new height, filling her mouth with the sharp, sour taste of garlic and whisky. She swallowed hard. '… or you'll be sorry!'

'I told yer – give it up,' said Archie. 'It ain't no good. An' anyway, I've got a better idea.' He started toward her, his manhood filling and lifting. 'Look,' he grinned, 'Old Nelson wants 'is fair Emma. Ain't yer got a nice warm berth for a one-eyed Admiral?'

Mary began to back away. 'How dare you!' she said, fear undermining the authority she was so desperately striving for. 'Do as you are told, you … you little *guttersnipe!*'

For the stockbroker Fanshawe and several other of her clients, such derisory words had a pronounced aphrodisiacal quality, but they had barely fallen from her lips before she realised her mistake in using them on Archie. His face went a deathly white, and he glared at her, his mouth opening like a slash in the pale underbelly of a fish. Then his hand was at her throat as he thrust her up against the fireplace, almost lifting her from her feet, only the constricting fingers about her neck preventing her from vomiting in terror as the memory of Sid came flooding back.

Veins were standing out like cords on Archie's temples. 'You tart!' He drew back his fist, a thick, hairy battering ram that must surely crush her skull as easily as an egg shell.

Mary fixed on it with wild, staring eyes, her hand frantically reaching out, scattering ornaments from the mantelshelf as she sought a weapon, but her fingers scrabbled in vain, finding only the empty shelf and the smooth glass of the mirror that hung above it. She began to kick, lashing out with her feet, striking his ankles and knees but he seemed impervious.

'You *fuckin'* tart!'

She saw the fist hurtle toward her, and closed her eyes, bracing herself, the sound of the impact filling her senses so completely she was spared all other sensations – yet she remained conscious, aware of the fingers loosening about her throat, then withdrawing.

Keeping her eyes closed, she remained paralysed against the fireplace, wanting to sink into unconsciousness and death before the agonising pain began, but the merciful oblivion did not come and slowly, fearfully, she opened her eyes.

Archie was standing a few feet away, his bare barrel chest rising and falling as he fought to control his anger, his hand streaming blood from where he'd punched into the polished glass of the mirror.

Half in terror, half in disbelief, Mary felt for her face, the movement of her arm dislodging shards of glass from the mantelpiece, sending them smashing on to the hearth, but her trembling fingers found nothing. She was untouched. Then the contents of her stomach were in her mouth, and she darted into the bathroom, frantically fastening the lock before dropping on to her knees beside the gleaming white lavatory bowl.

Hearing her retch, Archie looked about him, peering at the broken glass as though he had just happened upon the scene. A thin shard was embedded between his knuckles and he drew it out, watching dispassionately as more blood oozed between his fingers.

Sucking at the wound, he crossed to the bathroom door. From inside the sound of retching continued. 'You alright?' he called softly. 'I didn't 'urt yer did I?' There was no answer, so he tried the handle, but it was locked. 'Nah, I know I didn't – I wouldn't. You an' Julia – you're my special gels. I'd never 'urt the pair o' you.' He stood listening for a few moments, but there was still no answer, so he went to fetch the decanter and a glass and sat down on the floor, his back to the door, his legs splayed out in front of him.

'I know yer didn't mean what yer said. Yer couldn't 'ave known.' He poured himself a large measure. 'Funny ain't it – 'ow words can 'urt? They shouldn't. Don't make no sense – they're *just* bleedin' words ...' He lifted the glass to his lips. 'Still, I've done my share of 'urtin' people, too – but then, some people yer 'ave to 'urt.' He drank deeply, smiling to himself. 'Know who told me that?'

Inside the bathroom, Mary slowly lifted her head from the bowl, saliva and mucus hanging in delicate threads from her nose and mouth. Her stomach gave one final heave and she retched dryly, then she groaned, resting her cheek against the wood of the seat. From far off she could hear a voice, though she could not make out the words. She didn't care. She wanted to sleep. She wanted to feel the plump pillow and clean sheets of her bed at Gloucester Gardens. She wanted Julia. She wanted ... She slipped from the lavatory bowl and did not even feel her head strike the floor.

'My Connie. She told me that.' Archie swallowed the last mouthful of whisky and poured another. 'Told me that the first time ever I met 'er. *Some people yer 'ave to 'urt – before they 'urt you,* s'what she said. An' she was bloody right.' He looked at his hand; it was beginning to crust over, but it was still bleeding. 'I reckon this might need stitchin' yer know. Perhaps I'll 'ave Vince fetch a doctor over.' He started to rise, but then another thought made him smile, and he sat back down. ''Ere, you know where I met 'er? My Con? Go on – 'ave a guess. Bet yer can't. No? Well, I'll tell yer. Bermondsey steps! Right down by the stinkin', poxy river. Talk about romantic, eh? I was only a nipper – eight, maybe nine – with a runny nose an' the arse 'angin' out of my trousers. She was older – said she was sixteen, but I don't reckon she was – thirteen'd be more like it. I slept with 'er that first night.' He chuckled. 'Nah, not like that – just cuddled up together, t' keep warm, like. Didn't 'ave a farthin' between us, we didn't. Not a bleedin' farthin'. Don't s'pose yer can imagine that, can yer, gel? Nah, course yer can't. An' cold? Christ, yer've got no idea! When that mist comes up off the water – gets right into yer bones.' He studied the cut glass tumbler in his hand, 'Two raggedy-arsed kids – that was us.' He looked up, letting his eyes rove about the richly furnished room. 'Who'd 'ave thought, back then, eh?' he said, 'Who'd 'ave bloody well thought?'

Chapter Thirty-Eight

The first thing Mary noticed was the soft, insistent roar of the gas lamp, incongruous in the sunlight that flooded the room. The second was the stomach-churning smell of vomit.

She started to rise, but blanching as the pain in her head intensified, she fell back, drawing up her knees to lie wretchedly on the bathroom floor. For a long time she lay still, trying to hold the nausea at bay, until the smell from the lavatory bowl drove her from the uncertain calm, and she hauled herself to the sink, splashing water on to her face and drinking greedily.

The noise of the gas jet continued to nag at her ears, and she reached up to turn it off before creeping to the door, resting her head against it, listening for the smallest sound from the bedroom.

Her palms were damp, and she ran them down her skirt, then with shaking hands she felt for the door catch, trying to turn it, but it was stiff, partially jammed, the wood surrounding it splintered where an attempt had been made to force open the door.

In dread, she cast about for a weapon. There had to be something. In her mind she saw Thomas, standing at the scullery sink, running a gleaming blade up and down the leather strop, honing it to a terrifying sharpness. Archie had to have a razor.

A small leather travelling case stood on a cupboard by the sink and she hurried to it, searching through the contents, but the razor wasn't there. Then her eyes fell upon an empty whisky bottle lying half hidden where it had rolled beneath the cast-iron bath, and she got down on her hands and knees to retrieve it, holding it by the neck like a club as she returned to the door and eased open the lock.

The bedroom curtains were closed, and the sun filtering through the red velvet bathed the room in a crimson twilight, making it hard to see after the brightness of the bathroom. Mary paused, letting her eyes adjust.

Ten feet away she could make out the naked figure of Archie, sprawled face down on the bed, his hairy back and buttocks catching the feeble light, and she felt a wave of relief wash over her. Steadying herself, she edged past the foot of the bed, gripping the bottle tightly, hardly daring to look in his direction lest the weight of a single glance should waken him.

The door to the sitting room was almost within reach when a piece of broken glass crunched beneath her foot, the sound impossibly loud in the silence, and she froze, her heart racing. Archie wasn't a young man, but she knew he could move fast when he wanted to. Half paralysed with fear, she stole a glance toward the bed. He remained motionless, his arms and legs spread wide – unnaturally wide – almost as if ...

In spite of her every instinct, she looked at him, straining to see. It was then she noticed the cords about his thick, colourless ankles, then the ones at his wrists, and then, between his widely spread thighs, she saw the razor, lying on the blood-saturated coverlet.

Sitting in the armchair they'd taken from Baines's room, Vincent Eastman stretched out his legs and looked down at his highly polished shoes. The boy had made a good job of them – a thorough job – and he half smiled, remembering the look of happy astonishment on the lad's face as he'd caught the bright silver coin, four times the value of the shine. A good-looking boy, too, Eastman mused, picturing himself returning from an afternoon on the playing field to find the youngster toasting bread by his study fire, the lad's youthful exuberance tempered only by the proper show of deference. He found it an endearing image.

Taking the watch from his waistcoat pocket, he stood up. Six-thirty. He stifled a yawn, resisting even in the deserted hotel corridor the temptation to indulge this small display of weakness. Baines was always yawning, his broad bruiser's face opening like a cave. It was disgustingly coarse, and Eastman was coming to realise that Baines was never going to be anything other than a sow's ear.

He was still musing on Murray Baines's shortcomings when the porcelain handle to Archie's room began to turn, and he became instantly alert, his slender figure moving into the easy, authoritative stance it wore so well. 'Good morning,' he said, startling the young woman who was quietly letting herself out. She spun around, her untidy hair falling about her ghostly white face – and he caught the smell of vomit. *Not quite the fair Emma this morning*, he thought.

Eyes wide with fright, Mary backed away, her shoulders hunching and her hand going to cover her mouth as she fought the urge to retch.

Eastman smiled. 'A pleasant night?' Then raising an eyebrow, 'Will Mr Bull be out presently?'

'No ...' She continued to back away. 'I ... I have to go ...'

He watched her turn, her hand clamped to her mouth as she ran for the stairs. 'Quite *enchanting*,' he said as he began to laugh.

*

The door to Julia's room stood slightly ajar. 'Julia?' Mary whimpered. 'Are you awake?'

Julia jerked her head from the pillow. 'Oh, thank God, Mary, you're back!' She threw off the covers and leaped from the bed, quickly covering the small distance that lay between them. 'I've been so worried. Did he hurt you?'

'No … not really … I …'

'Let me see.'

'I'm alright … honestly.'

'You look terrible.' Julia reached up, gently taking Mary's face in her hands, her eyes darting back and forth, searching for the signs of violence she felt certain were there. 'I should never have left you with him.'

Mary began to shake, her eyes filling with tears. 'He's dead, Julia. *Archie's dead.*' Unable to support herself any longer, she sank to her knees, cradling her head in her hands. 'There was blood everywhere … and the razor … I couldn't find it, you see … and there was just this horrible red hole where his … Oh, God, Julia, it was *horrible.*'

Julia dropped down beside her, wrapping her arms about Mary's trembling shoulders, pulling her close. 'Shshhh, Mary – I'm here.'

Mary began to heave again, and Julia held her closer, smoothing her hair. 'Come on. It's alright. Everything's alright. You're safe now.'

'I thought he was going to kill me …'

Julia's eyes flared angrily. 'So he *did* hit you.'

'No, he didn't … I ran away, into the bathroom, and then … when I came out he was tied to the bed with the curtain cords and …' she looked up, her eyes wide with terror, 'he'd been *castrated* – no, more than that – everything. *Everything was cut away!*'

Gripping Mary by the shoulders, Julia looked anxiously at her. 'Did anyone see you leave this morning?'

'There was a man outside the door … he spoke to me.'

'Could he have followed you here?'

'I … I don't know … I never thought to …'

'Alright,' said Julia, taking charge. 'Then we need to act – *very* quickly.'

*

Murray Baines was drinking champagne. He normally preferred a plain, honest English beer, but this was exceptionally expensive and exceptionally good champagne, and it seemed fitting to the occasion.

A little way off, Harry Farrel of the Hoxton High Rips was standing,

311

smiling at him. 'Congratulations, Mr Baines.'

'Ah, come on, Harry. No need to stand on ceremony. It's *Murray* to my friends.'

Happiness gleamed in Harry's eyes. 'I always knew you 'ad what it takes to get to the top, Murray. Takes one t' know one, if yer gets my drift? Like two peas in a pod, me an' you – an' with you an' our Gussie gettin' spliced, well – that's the icin' on the cake, ain't it!'

Gussie Farrel pressed her ripe young body against Baines's hip, her hand stroking over the front of his trousers, cooing delightedly at the feel of his rigid flesh.

'Easy, girl,' he chuckled, feeling her fingers tighten about his shaft.

'That's my Gussie,' grinned Farrel. 'Ain't never been touched, an' fair pantin' for it.' He punched playfully at Baines's arm. 'An' from what I 'ear, I *know* you ain't gonna disappoint 'er.'

'You're not wrong there, Harry,' he laughed.

Harry winked and punched at him again, spilling champagne over Murray's suit. 'Easy, easy!' But Harry wouldn't stop, and Murray began to get angry. 'What the bloody …?'

He opened one eye to find Vincent Eastman leaning over the bed, shaking him by the shoulder.

'Get dressed,' said Eastman. 'It seems we have a little problem.'

*

'I could go back and explain.'

'Don't be stupid.' Julia moved agitatedly about the room. 'We have to leave – *now*. I'll go and pack – no, no, there isn't time. We'll just have to abandon everything.' She cast about, wild-eyed. 'Where are the tickets?'

'In my purse.'

Snatching up the bag, Julia tore it open, scattering the contents over the table and seizing upon the tickets. 'Sod it! The bloody things are dated! Quick, how much money do you have on you?'

'I don't know, not much … Oh, Julia … I'm sorry.'

Julia looked at her, seeing how close she was to tears. 'It's alright,' she said, trying to keep the urgency from her voice. 'Look, don't worry. Everything is going to be alright. Go and change your clothes – something suitable for travelling – then I want you to go down to the station and change these tickets. Take a cab.' She went to her own purse and took out some money. 'But don't come back. Wait for me there, alright?'

Like a child being entrusted with an errand, Mary nodded solemnly, and Julia continued, 'I'll make sure there's nothing left here that could lead them to us, then collect the rest of our money from the hotel safe. If we hurry we can catch this morning's train and be back in London before supper. We can decide what to do from there.' She gave Mary's arm a reassuring squeeze. 'It's going to be alright.'

Mary shook her head. 'I should go to the police.'

'No.'

'But …'

'Listen to me, Mary. No good will come of it. Once we're back in London, then *maybe* – but not here. You don't speak the language, for a start – and anyway, it's almost certain Archie's *friends* won't wait for the police to investigate.' She looked deep into Mary's eyes. 'Trust me. I know more about Archie than I've told you. We have to go – and we have to go quickly.'

*

'Shall we walk?' asked Eastman as they came out on to the hotel steps.

Murray Baines, his face grey and haggard from worry and lack of sleep, stared at him as if he were mad. '*Walk*?'

Eastman smiled, tilting his face to the sky, savouring the morning air as though it were fine wine. 'You *do* walk, don't you?'

'Mr Bull is dead, for Chris' sake! Don't you think we've wasted enough time, already?'

'A good breakfast is *never* a waste of time.' Eastman tripped lightly down the steps and into the broad, sunlit street. 'Now, I think the park would be pleasant, don't you?'

Baines followed, drawing a hand over his tired, reddened eyes. 'What are we going to do about the body?'

'What would you like to do with it?'

'Look, stop pissing about, Vincent. We can't just leave it there.'

'But that's exactly what we *can* do.' Eastman took out his watch and contemplated it. 'I expect it's been discovered by now – and the French authorities are far better equipped to send it home.'

'But the police?'

'I made our hotel reservations separately. Doubtless we'll have a few questions to answer when we return – but then we didn't really know the deceased so terribly well, did we? Rather boorish character, actually. Not our type at all.'

'That'll never wash.'

'Oh, believe me, it will.'

In his dulled state, Baines was disinclined to argue, finding comfort in his partner's quiet confidence. 'So what about this … what was her name, Emmy?'

'*Emma*.'

'Right, Emma. How do we know it was her?'

'Well, we don't.' Eastman put a contemplative finger to his lips. 'After all, the mere fact that one of us was sitting outside the door all night …'

'Yeah, yeah, alright. So how are we going to find her?'

'Ah, now that is going to be a little more tricky. As I see it, we have to make a difficult choice – the south gate on to Boulevard Haussmann, or the east gate on to Boulevard Malesherbes.' He shrugged. 'But it's a matter of six of one, half a dozen of the other, as it's just a short stroll to her hotel from either place.'

Stunned, Baines faltered in his step, then quickly stumbled forward to catch up. 'You mean you know where to find her?'

'Well, I am hardly taking you to visit my tailor.'

'But how …?'

'Because I made it my business to know. I make it my business to know a great many things.'

*

'And how much does mademoiselle require?'

Julia met the hotel manager's eyes. 'All of it. S'il vous plait.'

The dapper little man lifted an eyebrow fractionally, and cast the briefest glance toward the carpetbag Julia had placed discreetly by an armchair. 'Mademoiselle is leaving?'

'A small trip, but we shall be returning tomorrow. My friend is …'

The man spread his hands and smiled, confident in the knowledge the room had already been paid for. 'Whatever you wish, mademoiselle.'

Julia managed an uneasy smile, feeling the sweat begin to prick between her shoulders as she watched him disappear into the back office. From inside came the sound of voices, one of them the hotel manager's. It sounded like casual chit-chat, then some laughter, and she began to drum on the counter with her fingers, her eyes constantly going to the clock on the wall as she willed him to return.

'The French,' commiserated the smartly dressed young man who suddenly appeared at her elbow, rolling his eyes to the heavens. 'Little wonder they haven't won a war since before the flood.'

Julia ignored him.

'You must forgive my impertinence,' he persisted. 'I know we haven't been introduced, but a mutual friend of ours asked me to call on you.'

'A mutual friend?' she asked, giving him a nervous glance.

'Mr Bull.'

Julia felt the blood drain from her face. 'Mr Bull? *Archie*?'

The man smiled. 'Yes, *Archie*.' He put out his hand. 'My name's East-man, by the way.'

As if in a nightmare, Julia took it. 'Julia Devereaux,' she said, then pulling her hand from his. 'How is Archie?'

'Oh, you know Archie,' said Eastman with a small, confidential grin. 'Same as always. He's quite desperate to see you, you know. He's had to go out of town for the day and he thought it would be pleasant if you were to join him.' He made the suggestion of a bow. 'I'm here to escort you.'

Julia ran her tongue over lips that had become suddenly dry. 'I'm afraid I have a prior engagement.'

'Oh dear.' Eastman looked disappointed – then thoughtful. 'And does *Miss Emma* also have a prior engagement, I wonder?'

'She isn't here,' she said a little too emphatically.

'Of course not.'

'She *isn't*.'

'Oh, please, I do believe you.' His eyes went to the carpetbag lying in the otherwise deserted foyer. 'Indeed, it would seem we were fortunate to find *you* at home.'

Julia turned in desperation toward the manager's office, but in the next instant Eastman placed his arm about her waist, bringing his mouth close to her ear. 'If you're a silly girl,' he cooed, drawing her to him and smiling, 'I'll gut you where you stand. Now, I have a four-wheeler waiting outside, so let's not keep Archie waiting, eh?'

They were almost at the door when the manager reappeared. 'Oh, pardon, monsieur, mademoiselle. The lady's money – and her bag?'

Keeping Julia close to him, Eastman half turned. 'I shall send my man for them,' he said casually.

'Of course, monsieur.'

Baines was waiting by the cab. 'That's not her.'

'How perceptive you are.' Eastman jerked his head toward the hotel. 'Go in and fetch her money and her bag – and make some excuse to go up to their room. I'm fairly certain our *fair Emma* has flown the coop, but it never hurts to check.'

*

The shrine to smoke and steam that was Gare du Nord seemed far busier and more claustrophobic than Mary remembered, and she fussed with her hair as she paced this way and that, trying to find relief from the wretchedness she was feeling.

Changing the tickets had been a simple matter once an English-speaking ticket clerk had been found – it was the waiting that strained her nerves and fragile constitution.

For almost two hours she'd stood in the arranged spot, growing weaker and more ill, the dull pain in her head becoming an agony. The station concourse was hot and smelly, and she desperately wanted to lie down.

Please, Julia. Please come now.

With a sinking heart she'd watched the departure of almost all the morning boat trains, but still there was no sign of Julia. Now only one remained.

She began to move listlessly about, though never venturing far from the meeting place, running through invented litanies in her head.

Walk to the wall, turn, then back again, and Julia will be here.

A family hurried past, the red-faced mother dragging a protesting child by the arm, his small feet skimming over the pavement.

Go to the main entrance and back, and Julia will be here.

Hungry, sick and feeling faint, she walked with her head down, watching the flow of flagstones disappearing beneath the hem of her sweeping skirt, certain it would break the charm if she looked too early.

Another twenty paces, then I'll look and she'll be here.

Though sweat was breaking beneath her armpits, she felt dreadfully cold, and she paused, shivering – but the pavement continued to move, wavering from side to side for a moment before suddenly rushing up to meet her.

*

'Do you have to smoke those foul things in here?' Evan leaned forward in the cab bringing his face closer to the window.

'Not at all.' Spencer pitched the cheroot into the street. 'Look, don't worry. I'm sure your father is going to be alright. From what you've told me he sounds as strong as a horse.'

Evan continued to stare out of the window. 'Tell LeFranc I'll be back by Sunday.'

'Oh, for heaven's sake, man. There's more to work than life ...' He laughed. 'What I meant to say was ... but no, in your case I think that's perfectly correct.'

'And you will stand in for me at the clinic?'

'Yes, of course. My capacity for self-sacrifice is quite legendary – hadn't you heard?'

The cab pulled into the station, and Evan leaped down. 'You may as well keep the cab and go straight back. I can manage.'

'Wouldn't hear of it. In all the time we've been acquainted, I've never known you to go anywhere. I need to witness this for myself.' He drew himself up, peering past Evan's shoulder. 'Hullo, what's going on over there?'

Evan took his case from the growler, then turned to look. 'An accident?'

'Could be. Big enough crowd.'

'Perhaps we should go over?'

'Don't be a fool. Your train leaves in ten minutes.'

'But someone might be hurt.'

'Probably just a drunk. Listen, you get on that damned train. *I'll* go and take a look if it'll make you feel better.' Spencer started toward the gathering, but quickly drew up. 'Ha! We are saved!' he cried, pointing to a man of enormous girth who was puffing across the concourse toward the pressing throng. 'The redoubtable Doctor Gaston has come to the rescue!' He grinned. 'Though more to *our* rescue than our drunken friend's, I suspect.'

*

Maggie was fidgeting with excitement as she sat at the scrubbed kitchen table. 'Nice day off?' she asked, wanting to dispense with pleasantries as quickly as possible.

Gwyneth looked at the empty table, then about the darkened kitchen. 'You might have made some tea.'

'Oh, never mind that. I've got a whole load of stuff to …'

'I'll make it,' Gwyneth sighed wearily. 'Do you want some?'

'Yes, go on then, if you must. *Anyway*, as I was sayin' …'

'Maggie! You haven't even put the water on to boil!'

Fizzing with impatience, Maggie watched Gwyneth fill the kettle. 'So, how was your mam?' she asked, unwilling to waste any of the good stuff on someone who was only half listening.

'The same.'

'Still don't know you, then?'

Gwyneth shook her head.

'Well, I reckon you was right all along,' said Maggie encouragingly. 'Reckon she won't never do, now.'

Gwyneth stared at her with a mixture of exasperation and disbelief.

'Anyway,' Maggie continued blithely, 'As I was sayin' – there's been a telegram from Master Evan. He's on his way back here right this very minute. Gettin' the night train from London.' She wriggled in her seat. 'I love it when he comes home. It's always fireworks an' more fireworks!'

Gwyneth came to sit across the table from her. 'Is that all?'

'I should bloomin' well say not! Mind, it is goin' to be funny though, ain't it – I mean them all arguin' up there – an' the old doctor not bein' able to talk proper an' makin' them funny noises, an' all.' She pulled a monkeyish face, making strange grunting sounds, then fell about giggling.

'Maggie!'

'What?' said Maggie, jolted from her mirth.

'That's … *terrible*.'

'Just havin' a bit of fun.' She started to pull the face again, but caught Gwyneth's look and thought better of it. 'Anyway,' she said defensively, 'what's wrong with it? He can't hear me, can he.'

'That's not the point. How would you like it if it were the other way about?'

'What – if it was me up there, gettin' ready to push up the daisies, an' him down here havin' himself a good laugh? Well, I should think I'd like it very much, as a matter of fact.'

'You're just being silly.'

'No I'm not. If I was him up there, I'd be thinkin' I'd had a bloomin' good old time of it, lordin' it about all these years – an' if endin' up soundin' like a monkey was all the price I had to pay, well, then I'd reckon I'd had it cheap. An' if *him* – bein' *me* down here – wanted to have himself a bit of jollification over it, then I shouldn't begrudge it him – 'cos I'd know he wasn't goin' to get much else in this life to laugh about!'

The kettle began to boil, and Gwyneth got up to tend to it. 'Well, I still think it's disrespectful.'

'Suit yourself,' said Maggie, huffily. 'All I know is, he's had sixty-odd years of good livin' – with the likes of us waitin' on him hand an' foot. *I'd* settle for livin' like that for the next six months, an' go happy into the ground at Christmas.'

Gwyneth whirled on her, the water splashing from the kettle. 'Don't ever say that – not *ever*! It's …' She turned away, embarrassed by her outburst. 'It's tempting fate, Maggie.'

'I don't care.'

'But *I* do.'

Maggie cocked her head to one side, giving her a puzzled look, then she shrugged. 'Here,' she said, 'let's not go gettin' all soppy – an' anyway, I haven't told you the best bit of news yet.' The gleam of excitement came back to her eyes. 'We're goin' to have a servants' ball!'

'A what?'

'A servants' ball. I heard that Mrs Lewis talkin' about it to the mistress this afternoon. Goin' to be music an' everythin'.'

Gwyneth filled the teapot. 'Oh,' she said without enthusiasm. 'That *does* sound delightful. Can I book a dance now, or has your card already been filled by Lawrence and Cook?'

'No,' said Maggie, 'I don't mean just *us*. I mean a *real* ball. All the big houses are givin' their servants the night off. There'll be loads an' loads of men – an' here, listen to this, you know, the mistress and the others? *They're* goin' to wait on *us*!'

'You must have misunderstood.'

'I knows what I heard,' said Maggie indignantly. She jumped up. 'Oooh, I'm that excited. Can you imagine, a *dance* – an' not some old jiggin' about in a smelly barn, neither, but proper, *modern* dancin' – to an *orchestra*.'

Catching herself in the mirror, Gwyneth pushed nervously at her hair. 'A *real* dance?'

'Heard it plain as I'm hearin' you, didn't I?' Maggie spun around, coming to a giddy halt before leaping away to clomp about the room in a clumsy polka, her arms embracing an invisible partner while her voice rose tunelessly. 'Pom, tiddly-pom-pom. Pom, tiddly-pom.'

Gwyneth watched her for a moment, then looked back into the mirror, her fingers moving tentatively to her cheek.

'Come on,' panted Maggie, whirling to a halt in front of her. 'You need to get some practice – I ain't havin' you showin' me up on the night by fallin' over an' givin' everyone an eyeful of next week's washin'.'

'Don't be silly.'

'You *can* dance, can't you?'

'Of course I can.'

Maggie grabbed hold of her hands. 'Well come on then! Ready?' She stuck her foot out to one side, holding it poised for a moment, then stomped off, yanking Gwyneth after her. 'Pom, tiddly-pom-pom, Pom, tiddly-pom. Pom, tiddly-pom-pom …'

A broad grin spread across Gwyneth's face as she was caught up in the exuberance of the moment, adding her voice to Maggie's as they cavorted about the dimly-lit kitchen, bumping into walls and knocking over chairs. 'Pom, tiddly-pom-pom. Pom, tiddly-pom …'

*

At the far end of the avenue a church bell chimed seven, lifting a flock of pigeons into the early evening sky where they wheeled about the treetops before setting off in the direction of Notre Dame.

Two hundred yards away a couple emerged from the hotel entrance to climb into a cab, and Mary instinctively drew back into the shadows, waiting until they had disappeared before starting forward again, quickly mounting the steps and pushing through the doors into the small foyer.

Standing behind the reception desk, the manager eyed her with surprise. 'Good evening, mademoiselle. We were not expecting you back until tomorrow.'

'I'm looking for my companion – Miss Devereaux?'

'Oh, but Mademoiselle Devereaux left this morning with her gentleman friend. She gave me to understand you would be travelling with her – no?'

Mary felt her stomach tighten. 'Her *gentleman friend*?'

'Oui.'

'Did she say where they were going?'

'I'm sorry, mademoiselle.' The manager spread his hands in apology, regarding her with a small sideways inclination of the head. 'Is everything quite alright, mademoiselle?'

'Yes, of course.'

'But your face?'

Instinctively she put her fingers to the small graze on her cheekbone. 'It's nothing – I fainted, but I'm alright now.' She steadied herself against the polished counter. 'We had some money – in your safe?'

'Mademoiselle Devereaux withdrew it all this morning.' He watched her shoulders sag despondently and added quietly. 'Dinner *is* being served, mademoiselle – and if you prefer I could have it served in your room?'

Mary wavered, weak from hunger, but then from the corner of her eye she saw two men come striding in through the front door, and she froze.

'Mademoiselle?' The manager inclined his head a little more, seeing the look of terror on Mary's face. 'Mademoiselle, are you …?' He paused, dutifully turning his attention to the two portly men as they crossed the foyer. 'Bonsoir, messieurs.'

The men grunted in reply before going through into the dining room.

'Mademoiselle?' The manager tried again.

Struggling to prevent her hands from shaking, Mary reached into her pocket. 'When Miss Devereaux returns would you see that she gets this?' she said, passing one of the railway tickets across the counter.

Then she was gone.

*

The sun was low in the sky as the little boy and girl came back along the lane, kicking up the dust with their scuffed shoes, and stopping every now and then to throw stones into the tall dry grass that sprang from the surrounding fields.

'I wish we didn't have to go back to England tomorrow,' he said. 'Why do holidays always go so quickly – while school seems to drag on forever?'

'I *want* to go home.'

'Then you're stupid!'

She shrugged, turning petulantly away, and they walked on in silence, crossing the stream by the wooden bridge and skirting the stand of neglected bushes and trees.

The boy stopped, looking up to where a crooked chimneystack rose above the branches, and a mischievous grin crossed his face. 'They say a monster lives in that old farmhouse,' he said in a whisper.

The girl eyed him suspiciously. 'There are no such things!'

'Of course there are.' He darted away into the undergrowth. 'Come and see if you don't believe me.'

For a moment she hesitated, pursing her lips, then she ran to catch her brother. 'It's just an old house,' she whispered as they crept through the bushes and approached the ramshackle building.

The boy grinned, making a gobbling motion with his hand. 'Yes, the house of a monster – who eats little girls!'

'Stop it! You don't frighten me.'

'Then go inside.'

She looked uncertainly at the broken door with its flaking paint and split panels. 'No!'

320

'Cowardy custard!'

'I am not.'

'Well, go on then – I dare you.'

Chewing nervously at her lip, she approached the house, climbing the rotting steps then coming to halt, looking back over her shoulder. 'You come with me.'

'Why? It's just an old house, isn't it?' He affected a superior air. 'And it's not as if you believe in monsters. So what's there to be frightened of?'

'Nothing! Because there aren't any monsters. There aren't!'

'So – go inside.'

Tentatively, she pushed open the front door.

The sun had dipped below the trees, and the hazy summer twilight fell softly through the dusty windows, illuminating the wings of the insects swarming about the thing suspended from the blackened ceiling beam.

The girl's lips began to tremble as she stood frozen to the spot, staring up at the grotesque and bloody figure of the naked woman who hung, crucified, before her startled eyes. 'There … there *is* a monster,' she murmured, too frightened to run or to cry. 'There *is* a monster!'

Chapter Thirty-Nine

The lamplighter was making his rounds as Mary came to the corner of Gloucester Gardens, and she paused, looking nervously about. Seventy yards away, on the far side of the road, a four-wheeler stood outside the house, the hunched driver and his tired old horse looking as forlorn as the unnaturally dark and lifeless windows that towered above them.

She drew back, pretending to look for someone amongst the handful of people strolling along Kensington Road, the minutes seeming to stretch into hours as she agonised over what to do next. Then a movement caught her eye, and she watched the shadowy figure of Elspeth descend the steps and enter the waiting cab.

Mary started forward, but had barely covered any distance when the driver whipped up his horse, and the cab pulled from the kerb, coming toward her at a steady pace. It looked as if it wasn't going to slow before turning into the main road, but at the very last minute a passing carriage forced the driver to rein in sharply, and breathless she rushed to the open passenger window. 'Elspeth?'

Inside the unlit interior, Elspeth startled like a frightened rabbit. '*Mary?*'

The driver turned his head, cursing under his breath as he hauled on the brake. ''Ere, what's goin' on?' But Elspeth was already pushing open the door. 'Quick – get in,' she said, barely giving Mary time to clamber inside before shutting the door behind her and pulling down the blinds. 'Drive on!' she called.

The cab lurched into the main road, and Elspeth leaned forward, her eyes white in the half-light. 'What are *you* doing here?'

'Have you heard from Julia?' Mary asked urgently.

'Julia?'

'She missed the train ... I waited all night, but ...'

Elspeth stared at her. 'Missed the train? *She's dead!*'

Mary froze. 'No.'

'She's dead, Mary. They killed her. Have you no idea of what you've done?'

'I left her the ticket – she's coming back.'

'She's *not* coming back,' snapped Elspeth. 'Besides, what would there be to come back to? It's all gone, finished! You've ruined it all!'

Mary closed her eyes, her body growing numb, the sound of Elspeth's voice fading into the background of her own thoughts.

'God, Mary, how could you think you'd get away with it? *Archie* – of all people?' Elspeth shook her head in disbelief. 'None of us liked him, but … Well, it doesn't matter now. Those two men will keep coming back until they find you. You know that, don't you? Maud's already left – and now I'm going.'

Tears squeezed from beneath Mary's lashes, running down her cheeks. '*Julia*,' she murmured.

'Listen,' said Elspeth gripping Mary's arm. 'Forget Julia. Forget *everything*. Get away – go somewhere – *anywhere*.' There was a vacant look to Mary's eyes, and Elspeth shook her. 'Do you understand? *Anywhere*! But for God's sake *don't* go back to the house.'

'I *have* to. My money … my clothes … everything I have is there.'

'Don't! They'll be sure to have someone watching for you, and if you aren't worried for yourself then at least think of Madame.'

'But …' Mary crumpled, dropping her face into her hands. 'I don't know what to do, Elspeth. Tell me. Please … tell me what to do.'

Elspeth softened her grip. 'You'll have to hide. They're looking for an Emma Black, so you must bury her and hide.' She began pulling off her rings, pressing them into Mary's hand. 'Take these, they're all I have on me that's of any value. Sell them and go into hiding – maybe in the East End. Archie once told me he'd never go there – so perhaps neither will his *associates*.'

'But *where*?'

'I don't know – and you mustn't tell me. What I don't know I can't tell – and believe me, Mary, if they ever came looking for me – I *would* tell them.' The cab came to an unexpected halt, and Elspeth inched open the blind. 'The horse has stopped for water,' she said, then more pointedly, 'You can get out here.'

*

Eastman was impressed. Archie Bull had been considered a hard man – as hard as they came – but he doubted whether even Archie would have taken the murder of his spouse with the cold detachment Connie was exhibiting.

'When do you expect to have her?' she asked.

'Soon.' He felt her eyes bore into him. 'We only narrowly missed her in Knightsbridge. I left Baines watching the house, and she turned up as expected, but she got into a cab with one of the other whores before he could reach her.'

'Why didn't he follow them?'

'By the time he found another cab it was too late, but fortunately he recognised their driver. We have the address he drove to – however, I'm afraid our Miss Black got out somewhere in Oxford Street and disappeared.'

'What about the one that remained in the cab?'

'I shall pay her a visit tomorrow.'

'And this *Madame Bennaire*?' She spat out the words as though they contained a foul taste.

'Our tethered goat.'

Connie looked past him, her eyes fixed on some distant point. 'I want this girl, Vincent. You *will* get her for me.' She turned the full force of her stare back on to him. 'Understand?'

He nodded. 'She'll surface soon enough. After all, where can she go? Our people in France have been back to the hotel, and the manager seems quite certain she was in financial difficulties. In London, with no money, she'll be like a fish out of water. She'll have to risk going back to Gloucester Gardens – and when she does …' He left the sentence unfinished and merely smiled his thin smile.

*

I walked for hours that night, down side streets and alleyways, keeping to the shadows, drifting eastwards, and as I walked I thought of Julia, saw her face, her smile, the look of wicked humour in her eyes. She had been my sister in ways blood alone could never achieve – but more than that, she had been my soulmate. I wanted to cry, but the enormity of my grief put me beyond tears. I walked without seeing, without noticing – and when a drunken couple staggered from a pub doorway and sent me sprawling in the filthy street – without even feeling.

I was frightened, lonely and so very tired – and as I walked on I grew light-headed, imagining myself as a piece of driftwood floating on the tide, at the mercy of The Almighty, who, if I would only stop fighting and trust in Him, would surely see me washed safely upon the shore.

*

The sign in the lighted pawnshop window read *Jewellery Bought and Sold*, and Mary stared at it, overwhelming hunger twisting and tightening her stomach.

Along the street, several other shops were open, filling the night air with the smell of hot pies and roasted meats, of coffee, and from a corner pub, the mellow scent of beer. She looked again at the sign, her hand reaching into her pocket for the rings – but they weren't there. She felt in the other pocket, but that too was empty.

She searched again, this time patting at the lining. Then she remembered the drunken couple, the rough hands helping her to her feet, and a cold dread seized her. 'No! Please. Please God – don't do this to me – not now. *Please!*' In desperation she began pulling at her clothes, tugging and straining as if to torment them into giving up the missing items – but they remained adamant, yielding nothing. She bunched her fists and lifted her face to the inky blackness of the sky, her voice rising hysterically. '*Why?* Why do You do it? Can't You *ever* let me have *anything?*'

In answer, a window above the shop flew open and an unshaven face thrust out. 'I'll let yer 'ave a clip roun' the bleedin' ear'ole, if yer don't piss off an' let me get some kip!'

Up and down the street people were stopping to look, stepping out of houses to see the cause of the commotion. Mary whirled on them, self-pity giving way to black fury. 'Go on, look, why don't you?' she raged. 'You might as well! Go on then!' But the anger was short-lived. Starting to cry, she fell back against the window, her fists beating impotently at the glass panes. 'Oh, why don't you all just … just …' Then gathering up her skirts, she began to run, wildly and blindly toward the river.

The Thames lay black beneath the quarter moon as Mary stood gasping at the bottom of the steps, the murky water lapping at her boots. She clenched her teeth, her hands drawing into fists, her whole body shaking as she steeled herself for the jump that would solve everything.

'Oi, wotcha doin'?' The woman's voice with its sing-song quality came from high above.

Mary ignored it. *Do it now*, she said to herself, her knees trembling in readiness, while her feet remained rooted to the spot, so that she swayed precariously above the filthy water.

'I *said*, wotcha doin'?'

'Go away!'

'I will not! It's a free country, ain't it?'

Mary jerked her head up to find the faded pixie features of an older woman looking over the embankment wall. 'Look,' she snarled, 'Just … just *piss off*!'

'Oh, that's nice that is!'

Mary turned back to the river, retreating a step in readiness.

''Ere, 'ang on, 'ang on!' The face disappeared from above the wall and reappeared atop a motley collection of old clothes as the woman hurried down the steps. 'You goin' to throw yerself in, darlin'?'

Mary readied herself to make the leap. 'Don't try to stop me.'

'Let's 'ave yer dress an' coat, then?'

Almost overcoming the reluctance of her feet to leave dry land, Mary teetered on the brink. '*What?*'

'Go on, be a sport. Let's 'ave yer clothes? I mean – you ain't goin' to want 'em, are yer – not if yer goin' to do away with yerself – an' that's quality stuff you're wearin'. If yer don't give 'em to me, the bloke what drags you out in a day or two'll 'ave 'em for sure – an' that don't 'ardly seem fair – not seein' as 'ow I saw yer first.'

Mary moved back from the edge. 'You want my clothes?' she asked incredulously.

The woman grinned. 'Now yer gettin' it. Just the coat an' dress'll do. 'Course, it would be nice to 'ave the other stuff – but a posh girl like you'd probably be a bit embarrassed, I suppose – tossin' 'erself in with nothin' on, like?' She thought for a moment, her grin widening. ''Course, if yer *was* to be feelin' generous, I *could* turn my back. You could leave everythin' just 'ere – an' I wouldn't look until yer'd gone under. 'Ow about that?'

Mary glared at her. 'Are you completely stupid? I'm going to *kill* myself. Don't you understand?'

'Ye-es,' the woman began doubtfully, her brow creasing with child-like concentration as she ticked off the points on her fingers. 'You're goin' to kill yerself – I ain't got no money, an' a thirst on me that'd kill a cactus – that coat of yours alone would keep me in gin till Christmas – an' you ain't goin' to need it about four minutes from now.' She looked up, smiling proudly. 'Yes, that seems about the shape of things to me.'

In a fury, Mary began tearing at her buttons, fresh tears of anger and misery wetting her cheeks. 'Here, take it – take everything! It's all I've got left in the world – so of course you must have it! God forbid I should be allowed to keep *anything!*' She threw the coat on to the steps, then began ripping at the dress, her face turned to the heavens. 'Are You happy now? Well – *are You?*'

''Ere, don't tear it. I won't get 'alf as much if yer tear it. Come 'ere, let me 'elp yer.' The woman moved closer, pushing Mary's hands away and unfastening the small round buttons. 'This won't take a tick. I expect yer anxious to be on yer way – an' I know I am.' She followed Mary's gaze up to where the moon lay veiled by thin cloud. 'I don't know if yer've made '*im* 'appy, m'darlin' – but yer've certainly made my night.'

*

As out of place as a pearl in a piss-pot, the gleaming black Victoria rolled to a halt.

The place stank just as Connie remembered – possibly worse. The river Thames, filled with the excrement of millions, ran like a broad, overflowing gutter through the heart of the city, its fetid vapours seeping into the night air to mingle with the smell of the bordering slums. She remembered it well – the smell of decay, of hopelessness, and ultimately of death.

'Wait for me.'

The coachman turned in his seat. 'Shouldn't I come with you?'

'I *said* wait for me.' Connie climbed down. 'It might look deserted, but I know the people round here – they're like rats, waiting for any opportunity. We'll come back to empty shafts if you're not here to stop them.'

'But what about you?'

'I can look after myself.'

A shop stood on the corner, the darkened interior full of old furniture, but beneath the flaking brown paint, the red of Otto's chandlery still showed. Old German Otto – his big, cheery face came back to her as clear as day, and she paused for the briefest moment before moving on, putting the memory behind her.

Across the cobbled street, the postie was just as she remembered it, too, the scarred iron bollard still leaning at its rakish angle, and she ran her hand over the top, lingering for a few seconds before moving into the alley beyond, and the steps that lead down to the water.

Remember this place, Archie? She walked down to stand on the cobbled slipway, and looked out over the river: the lights of the far bank reflected in the oily swell. *You stand in shit, and you look at the stars – and it never occurs to you just to reach up and grab them – you just keep looking and wishing – until you sink without a trace. Well, we grabbed them alright, didn't we? We grabbed them by the throat and shook them right out of the sky.*

A boat chugged past, the smoke a ghostly white in the darkness.

I'm going to miss you, Archie. I want you to know that. In all the years we were together I never told you how much I … She turned to look at the worn steps. *No, that's not true – I did tell you once. I whispered it while you were sleeping, just here. You never knew, but I did tell you – just that once.*

On the far bank a woman's voice rose briefly and hysterically, the sound carrying clearly in the night air, and Connie glanced over the water, irritated by the interruption.

Do you remember those days, Archie? Do you? You and me, on these steps? Long time ago, that was. What a pair, eh? A snotty-nosed little boy, crying from the cold, and a … She pushed the memory away, lifting her face defiantly to stare up river. *You saved me, Archie. You always thought it was the other way round – but it wasn't. If I hadn't met you that night …* She sniffed. There were no tears, but she sniffed all the same. *But it's going to be alright. I'll get her. I'll do this one last thing for you, Archie. I'll have her heart.*

Across the water the shouting had stopped without her even noticing, and she turned to make the climb back to the street. *Goodbye, Archie – I … * Even in her thoughts the words would not come, and she tightened her jaw – but half way up the steps she paused, looking back and seeing for a brief instant the grubby-faced urchin that had been Archie Bull, curled in sleep upon the steps. 'I … I *love* you,' she whispered.

*

'What's all this then, Katie? You come into some money?'

The woman laughed, hitched up her skirts, and picked up the two white china plates the sweaty-faced man had placed on the counter, fat and meat juice running from steaks fresh from the frying pan. 'Yer know that story about the ugly ducklin' what turns into a swan, Moishe?'

'Yes.' The man scratched at the grey stubble on his chin. 'I seems to recall something of the nature. What of it?'

'Well, I just found myself a swan that turns out to be a bleedin' ducklin', ain't I?'

The man looked across the crowded eating-house to where the girl was sitting hunched over the table. 'Well, at least she ain't no ugly one, eh?' he grinned, tossing the shilling piece into the air. 'You want to find a few more such ducklings – then maybe you'd eat more reg'lar.'

She gave him a wink and started back through the press of tables where porters from the early morning markets sat over greasy plates and steaming mugs.

'All right, Kate?' called a great, bull-necked man with a shock of red hair.

'Oh, wotcha, Carrots. Didn't see yer 'idin' there. 'Ere, yer couldn't let us 'ave a shillin', could yer? Or a even tanner would do.'

The man eyed the two thick steaks. 'A bit hard up are yer?'

She looked down at the plates in her hands. 'Oops,' she giggled, 'Force of 'abit. Well, I'll catch yer another time, alright?' She grinned, moving on to where Mary sat morosely at the small corner table. ''Ere yer go, ducklin',' she said, handing over the plate with the smaller of the two steaks, changing it for the larger one as her conscience pricked.

'Duckling?'

'Just a little joke between me an' Moishe. 'E'll bring us over some tea in a minute – 'e's just brewin' some fresh.' She picked up her knife and fork. 'Well, go on – get stuck in.'

Mary pulled irritably at the collar of the ill-fitting dress, then gingerly took up the knife and fork.

'So, 'ow's the new clobber? Don't fit too bad, eh?'

'It itches.'

Kate laughed and scratched at her own bodice. 'Yes, well that's the benefit of second 'and clothes, ain't it. Yer can't never complain about bein' lonely.'

*

The bed creaked and groaned as Maggie rolled over for the umpteenth time, letting out a long sigh and lying still in the total darkness for a minute or two before pushing back the bedclothes and kicking at them until they disappeared over the bottom of the bed. She sighed again, long and forlornly. 'Are you awake, Gwyn?'

'I am now.'

'I can't sleep neither,' said Maggie. 'Not with it bein' so hot – an' thinkin' about this bloomin' dance, an' all.'

'Try.'

'I am tryin'.'

'Yes,' said Gwyneth with feeling.

'I mean it *is* sort of excitin', ain't it – but ...'

'But what?'

'Well,' Maggie began tentatively, 'supposin' – *just supposin'*, mind – that we was at this here ball, all dressed up an' everythin', an' ... well ... nobody asked us to dance.'

Gwyneth raised herself on one elbow. 'That won't happen.'

'Oh, I know that,' said Maggie, a little too quickly. 'But *just supposin'* it did. I mean, supposin' a girl was sittin' there, all night, stuck in the same rotten chair – *for hours an' bloomin' hours* – watchin' everyone else dancin' an' havin' a good time – but no one ever took no notice of her, or asked her to dance.' She curled up, hugging her knees. 'An' supposin' everyone was lookin' at her, an' makin' jokes.' Maggie's voice grew very small. 'Just *supposin'* such a thing was to happen.'

Gwyneth didn't answer, but lay back, looking up into the blackness until the first light crept over the horizon to chase it away.

*

'Blimey, you *was* 'ungry,' Kate grinned as Mary wiped the plate clean with a slice of bread and butter. 'Feelin' better?'

'No.'

'Well, yer look better.'

'Well, I'm not.' Mary began tugging irritably at her dress. 'And I can't wear this ... this rag!'

'What's the matter with it?'

'What's the matter with it? It smells, it itches ... and ... and it doesn't even fit!'

Kate shrugged. 'Oh, is that all.' She looked up as Moishe brought over two mugs full of a soupy brown liquid.

'Two nice cups of tea. Fresh made,' he said, wiping his nose on his apron.

''Ere, what d'yer think of 'er dress?' asked Kate.

He looked it over. 'Very nice.'

'There you are,' said Kate. ''E thinks yer look a proper picture – an' the smell'll go away with a bit o' wearin' – or maybe yer just won't notice it after a while – but either way it won't bother yer, will it. So that's alright.'

'I won't wear it. I won't!'

Moishe gave Kate a sideways glance, raising his eyebrows. 'Well, I got customers waiting. Take care now, you hear, Katie.'

''Course I will. Ever known me not to?' She waited until he had gone, then leaned forward. 'Now *you* listen 'ere, little Miss Precious. When I plucked you off them steps a few hours ago you 'ad some fancy clothes on yer back – an' nothin' in yer belly but fresh air. Now yer've got a good dinner inside yer *an'* some money in yer pocket. Alright, that dress ain't gonna make no impression at Ascot – but it's as good as anyone's Sunday Best around 'ere – so what are yer mopin' about?'

Mary eyed her resentfully. 'So where *is* the money?'

''Ere.' Thrusting her hand into her pocket, Kate took out a handful of coins and pushed them across the table.

'Is that all?'

'No, 'course not. There was the shillin' we've just scoffed.'

'But …' Mary looked at her aghast. 'I paid twenty-five guineas – just for the dress!'

'Did yer? Blimey, they must 'ave seen you comin'. No wonder yer was all set to chuck yerself in the river – I would too if I'd let m'self be taken for a ride like that!'

Mary's lips began to tremble. 'Just shut up. You don't know anything.'

'Don't I? Well perhaps yer want to tell me – like why yer were goin' to top yerself, maybe?'

'You don't really care.'

Kate laughed. 'No, ducklin'. I don't as a matter of fact. I've 'eard it all before. All the 'ard luck stories in the world – enough to break yer 'eart if yer let 'em. But I don't let 'em. I get on – an' that's what I've got to be doin' now – *gettin' on*.' She pushed back her chair and got to her feet. 'Thanks for the dinner, ducklin'. See yer around.' Mary had her face turned to the wall, and Kate gave her one last look. 'Or maybe *not*, eh?' she said, turning away.

Behind the counter, Moishe gave an enquiring glance as she passed – and she was about to answer with a shrug when a plaintive, tearful voice stopped her in her tracks.

'Please, Kate … *please. Don't leave me.*'

Chapter Forty

The fat woman waddled into the lodging house kitchen, a herring gripped in the podgy fingers of one hand.

'Goin' to cook that for yer breakfast, darlin'?' asked Kate, propped in the corner of the wooden settle, her nose wrinkling at the sudden, over-powering smell that had nothing to do with the fish.

The woman cast about with bleary, suspicious eyes. 'Wha's it t' ye?'

'Oh, nothin' darlin'. Just that the smell of a bit o' fried fish fills a room so nice, don't it – so get it on quick, eh?' She leaned back, putting her feet on the seat opposite, and took out a short clay pipe. 'In the meantime,' she said with a wink to the man sitting across the table from her, 'I think I'll 'ave me a little smoke.'

The man grinned. 'Blow some of it this way.'

'It'll cost yer.'

He gave a quick laugh before turning serious once more. 'So why didn't yer come back to Cooney's last night? I was worried for yer. Lookin' all over the place, I was – till I bumped into Annie an' she told me where to find yer.'

'Cooney's was full up, so I came round 'ere.'

'But I'd already paid for our double.'

'I know, Jack, but … well, I wasn't on my own.' He shot her a glance, and she quickly shook her head. 'No, I don't mean like *that*. I picked up with this girl. Right old state she was in – makin' to chuck 'erself in the river. Reckon she would 'ave an' all, if I 'adn't jollied 'er along – but then I couldn't get rid of 'er. Poor cow didn't seem to know what to do. Dead on 'er feet, she was. 'Ad to practically carry 'er down Commercial Street – an' 'er in floods of tears all the way!' Kate rolled her eyes. 'Reckon I won't need another wash for weeks. Anyway, I couldn't very well leave 'er, could I? So I got us a couple o' beds an' we dossed down 'ere.'

'An' wasted fourpence.'

'No I 'aven't. She paid – though she don't know it yet.' Kate leaned forward, lowering her voice. 'Blimey, yer should 'ear the way she talks. Sounds like a right toff most o' the time – but didn't 'ave a penny to bless 'erself with. An' as for the dress she was wearin' – talk about posh? Says she bought it!' She laughed again. 'Can yer imagine? Must think I've just fallen off the bleedin' turnip cart!'

'So where is she now?'

'Still upstairs, kippin'.'

He got to his feet. 'Well, best leave 'er to it. We need to get crackin' if we're goin' to get down to Kent.'

'I can't just leave 'er, Jack. Not till she wakes up, at least.'

'Why not? She ain't nothin' to you.'

'I dunno – but I can't. It don't feel right. It'd be like …' She broke off as Mary appeared in the doorway, hollow-eyed and frightened. 'Oh, there yer are, ducklin'. Did yer 'ave a good sleep?'

Jack eyed the newcomer. 'Blimey,' he said, beginning to cough. 'I thought yer said she was a *girl*.'

'Well, she's a funny lookin' *bloke*.'

Mary stepped tentatively into the room. 'I … I thought perhaps you'd gone,' she said anxiously. 'My money … someone's stolen my money. What am I going to *do*? I haven't got anything else to sell … and …'

'It's alright, calm yerself down. I've got it.' Kate took the handful of coins from her pocket. 'I took if off yer last night. Thought it best if I looked after it – seein' as 'ow you was dead to the world the minute yer 'ead touched the pillow. It's all there – minus the eightpence for the beds. Now, come an' 'ave a sit down.' She took her boots from the seat and leaned forward. 'This 'ere's Jack. 'E's what passes for my 'usband these days.'

'Pleased to meet yer, I'm sure,' said Jack, putting out his hand.

Mary took it. 'It's a great pleasure,' she said, a slight quaver to her voice.

'See what I mean?' chuckled Kate – then to Mary. 'Oh, don't mind me, ducklin', just a little joke we was 'avin' before yer came in. Feelin' better this mornin', are yer?'

Perching on the edge of the sticky wooden settle, Mary looked nervously about the awful surroundings. 'What is this place?'

'Crossingham's,' said Kate.

'We usually doss at Cooney's, in Flowery Dean,' added Jack, 'I reckon yer get a better class of people over there.'

'Oh yes,' laughed Kate, ''Ad the Prince o' Wales in bed with us one night, didn't we Jack.'

'Yer know what I mean,' he said with a pointed glance toward the fire.

Mary swallowed hard, feeling sick, then put her hand to her mouth. 'I'm sorry, I don't think I can stay in here …'

'Fair takes the skin off yer nose, don't it,' laughed Kate. ''Ere, m' darlin',' she called across to where the fat woman had fallen asleep, the fish curled in a pan upon her lap. 'I thought you was goin' to cook it – not nurse it.'

The woman opened one bloated eyelid. 'Why don' ye fuck off.'

'Goin' to do just that, my old cock.' Kate got up. 'Come on, ducklin', time we was goin'.'

With her hand still covering her nose and mouth, Mary followed them out of the kitchen and along a dark, narrow passageway, its walls stained black to shoulder height by the continual scuffing of dirty clothes.

'Gettin' that autumn feel, already,' said Jack, stepping out into the hazy sunshine and sniffing the air.

'Autumn my arse! We ain't even into September yet.'

'Well, we'd better get crackin' all the same, or we'll be too late.'

Mary stood a little apart from them, thankful to be out of the awful lodging house, but feeling awkward and vulnerable. She felt for her sleeve. 'Do you think, that … maybe tonight … we might be able to get into that other place you mentioned?'

Jack shifted uncomfortably.

'The thing is, ducklin',' said Kate, 'Yer goin' to 'ave to be on yer own from now on.'

Mary's face lost any remaining colour.

'See, me an' Jack are 'oofin' it down to the 'op fields, an' we should 'ave been on our way hours ago. I'd really like to stay an' 'elp yer, but …'

'No … I understand. Of course I do …'

'You'll be alright,' said Kate, attempting a cheery grin. 'Right as ninepence now, eh?'

'Yes.' The smile trembled on Mary's lips. 'Right as … ninepence.'

Kate stood looking at her, wanting to leave, but reluctant to just walk away. 'Look, why don't yer run round to Cooney's, right now, an' book yer bed for tonight? Flower an' Dean Street, can yer remember that? Tell Freddie, the deputy, that Katie Conway sent yer, an' 'e'll fix you up.'

'Yes, alright.'

'Right then. You take good care of that money, now.' Kate gave her a last smile. 'Well, see yer then, ducklin'. Good luck, eh?'

Mary nodded. 'Yes … and good luck to you.'

'Oh, I makes my own luck,' laughed Kate, taking Jack's arm as they started away down the street.

Timidly, Mary looked about her. She had been here before, but that had been with Julia, with money in her pocket and a comfortable home to return to after their slumming. Now the narrow streets pressed in on her, the houses rising on either side, dull, depressing, even threatening, blotting out all but a thin strip of smoky blue sky.

A little way off, a group of hard-faced women eyed her with belligerent curiosity, and despite the warmth of the morning Mary shivered, her hands rising shakily to cover her ears against the noise that was all around: doors banging, women yelling, children playing in the rubbish-strewn gutters, their shrieks and calls swelling the din that was the music of Whitechapel – a music that jarred upon her with all the menace of a cell door slamming. In despair, she leaned against the wall, feeling lost and helpless, and worst of all – so utterly, terrifyingly alone.

''Ere,' said Kate, reappearing in front of her, panting for breath. 'You ever picked 'ops, ducklin'?'

*

Theatrical types, partaking of a mid-day libation prior to the matinee performances, filled the Strand public house, making Murray Baines uncomfortable as he stood amongst them, shoulder to lavender-scented shoulder, trying to catch the barman's eye.

'Bleeding nancies,' he muttered as he returned to the corner table, clutching a pint of frothy beer and a double gin. 'Don't know why Vince likes this place. Gives me the bloody creeps.'

Gussie Farrel ran her hands over the swell of her hips and flashed him a saucy smile. 'That's 'cos you ain't *sophisticated*, like 'im.'

Ignoring the remark, Baines sat down. 'You'd better drink up quick. I don't want him catching you here, or he'll twig about this morning.'

She grinned. 'Better than watchin' that stupid old 'ouse, wasn't it?'

'What do you think? But we've got to be careful, Gussie.'

'Yer not frightened of 'im, are yer?'

'No ... no, of course I'm not.'

'I wouldn't blame yer. 'E gives me right goose pimples at times.' She took a sip of gin, then reached beneath the table, stroking along his thigh. 'So – yer goin' to tell me what yer did to that tart in Paris, then?'

'I told you. We did her. That's all.'

'But what? What did yer do?'

He shifted uncomfortably as her hand slid higher. 'It don't matter. You don't want to know.'

'But I do,' she said, drawing a finger over the bulge in his trousers. 'An' it seems to matter to you, 'cos every time I mention it, this little gentleman down 'ere ...'

'It was just a job! That's all. Just a job. Now leave it alone, can't you?'

She snatched her hand away. 'Alright,' she said huffily. 'If you won't tell me, perhaps I'll ask Vince.'

'Ask me what, Miss Farrel?'

Gussie gave a small start. 'Oh, Vince. I was just askin' yer friend 'ere about this woman that killed Archie. Yer found 'er yet?'

'Not *just* yet.' He drew up a chair and sat down, eyeing Baines. 'I didn't know you two were acquainted.'

Baines toyed nervously with his glass. 'We're not.'

'I was lookin' fer you, Vince,' said Gussie. 'An' I come across yer friend, 'ere. Recognised 'im from the fight the other week.' She smiled. 'Thing is, that young bloke you 'ad money on wasn't as good with 'is maulers as 'e was good lookin' – an' my dad would like the money yer owe 'im.'

'Of course. I'm afraid I've been rather preoccupied of late.' He glanced at Baines. 'I take it our Miss Black didn't show up at Gloucester Gardens this morning?'

'No. Pierce is watching the place this afternoon. How did you get on in Islington? I wasn't expecting you for another hour or more.'

'The lady was as helpful as could be expected, but …' he shrugged dismissively.

'Did yer do fer 'er?' Gussie asked bluntly.

Eastman looked hurt. 'Of course not. What *do* you take me for, Miss Farrel?'

*

'How long are you planning to be away?' asked Evan, looking at the boxes and packing cases that filled every corner of the nursery.

With her arms full of Owen's clothes, Florence crossed to where Nanny Reeves was dressing the boy. 'I'm not sure. Perhaps six months? Your father will benefit from a change of scenery, and more importantly the mountain air will be good for Owen.'

'Father has always said there's nothing seriously wrong with the boy.'

'Yes, well …' She left the sentence unfinished and knelt down by Owen, holding up two small garments. 'What do you think, Nanny? Wool or cotton?'

Miss Reeves glanced toward the sunlit window. 'The wool, I think. Far better to be safe than sorry where this little mite is concerned.'

'Yes, you're absolutely right.' Florence carefully brushed a lock of hair from the boy's forehead. '*Much* better safe than sorry. After all, we can't have anything happening to you, can we, Owen.'

'What about the house? The practice? I shall have to return to Paris soon and …'

'Oh, but you can't. You're needed here.'

'I can't just …'

'It's your duty, Evan. You owe it to your father.' She rose, looking meaningfully at him. 'You must have known it was always his dearest wish that you would take over from him one day?'

'Yes, of course I did, but …'

'Well, then,' she said with finality, giving him a warm smile. 'Your father's been rather depressed of late – and it's going to make him so happy when you tell him.' She touched his arm. 'Why don't you do it now.'

Evan stewed silently for several moments, then finally he sighed. 'Oh, very well.'

Sitting with Owen on her lap, Nanny Reeves wet two fingers and smoothed the child's hair into place. 'I think we're ready for our petticoats now, m'um, if you please?' she said, giving his cheek a little squeeze.

Evan seemed to notice the boy for the first time. 'Do you have to dress him like a girl?'

'It is customary,' said Florence. 'In all the better houses.'

'I was never put into petticoats.'

'Only because your father didn't approve. But *we* intend that Owen should have a *traditional* upbringing.' She handed Miss Reeves the small dress. 'Don't we, Nanny?'

Nanny Reeves slipped it over Owen's head, pulling it into place. 'It's how I've always dressed young gentlemen, sir.'

'And she's been nanny to some very important families.' Florence watched as the pearl buttons were fastened and Owen was set upon his feet in a mass of white frills. 'And besides – doesn't it make him look *so* adorable?'

*

The funeral cortège stretched along Villiers Street, the black plumed horses shaking their heads and pawing impatiently at the ground as they waited to take the emasculated body of Archie Bull to its final resting place.

'Everything is ready,' said Eastman, coming to the top of the stairs and making for Connie's private rooms.

The squat, pugnacious little man placed himself between Eastman and the door. 'Sorry, Mr Eastman, but I can't let you in.'

Vincent looked down at him.

'I … I got instructions … from Connie,' said the man, uneasily.

'That's alright, William.' Eastman raised his eyes, contemplating the closed door.

'She's got the black dog on 'er again,' the man offered, leaning forward and lowering his voice.

'How badly?'

The man shook his head. 'Dunno. Pretty bad. Been talkin' to 'erself in there.' He leaned even closer. 'Mad sort o' stuff. Gives me the willies, if yer want the truth of it.'

'Has she called a doctor?'

'Won't 'ave one. Won't see *no one*.'

Eastman shifted his gaze toward the window, his hands clasped beneath the tails of his coat. 'Well,' he said at last. 'We can't keep Archie waiting.'

Chapter Forty-One

The earth was dry and crumbly, the small ragged clods disintegrating under the pressure of Mary's fingers as she sat on the edge of the hill, watching the sun drop lower and lower in the sky.

She picked up another clump of the light brown earth. It smelled of summer, just as the dry grass, the hedgerows and even her own skin smelled of summer – the warm, rich, roasted smell of the countryside in the dog days of September.

'Wotcha doin'?'

'Piss off.'

Kate gave a throaty chuckle and dropped down on to the grass beside her. 'So what *are* yer doin'?' she asked, feeling for her pipe.

'Just thinking.'

'I mean tomorrow.'

'Oh, I don't know.' Mary watched a thin plume of blue-white smoke rise from a bonfire somewhere down in the valley. 'I'd like to stay here.'

'What? In the sticks? For the winter? Sod that for a game of soldiers!'

'I've lived in the country before.'

''Ave yer? Well, you'll know 'ow bleedin' miserable it is, then, won't yer.' She struck a match and put it to the short clay pipe. 'Me an' my Tommy – 'e was my first 'usband – we 'ad a couple of winters in the sticks. Thought it was goin' to be like summer, only a bit colder. Never again. I'd sooner go to the Bastille – an' that's sayin' somethin' 'cos I'd sooner die than go there.'

'The Bastille?'

'The work'ouse. Blimey, ain't yer learned nothin' this past month?'

Mary smiled. '*Piss off*?'

'Apart from that, I mean.' Kate grinned, stretching herself out and sucking in a lungful of tobacco smoke. 'It's all nice an' jolly 'ere now, 'cos yer've got proper people around yer – but once we all leave what 'ave yer got? A bunch o' carrot-crunchers wadin' around in the mud an' talkin' funny – that's what yer've got! An' it gets bleedin' wearin'.' She closed her eyes. 'Still, it's up to you, ducklin'.'

'*Duckling*? You haven't called me that in a long time.'

'No? Well, I s'pose you 'aven't been lookin' so lost for a long time.'

Mary prised up another piece of dried earth, starting to crumble it. 'I don't know what to do, Kate. I can't go back to that horrible … what was it called … Crossingham's?'

'Yer don't 'ave to. Yer can come to Cooney's with Jack an' me.'

'Is it *really* that different?'

Kate laughed. 'No – not really. But then, yer see, *you're* different now. Blimey, you've been dossin' down with the rest of us this past month, as 'appy as can be, so what's the difference – 'ere or back in London?'

'It's not the same in London.' The last grains of earth slipped from between Mary's fingers, and she sighed. 'But I suppose I'll go back,' she said, rubbing her hands together to remove the last traces of the Kent dust.

Beyond the misty hills, a crimson streak showed above the horizon, and they sat quietly, watching it grow smaller and smaller.

'If you could wish for one thing, Kate, what would it be?'

Kate took the pipe from her mouth, looking across the darkening field to where a rabbit had hopped from the hedge to sit perfectly still in the purple twilight, ears alert, face turned to the glory of the setting sun. 'A gun,' said Kate. 'Love a bit o' rabbit, I do.'

*

Mrs Lewis's hands fluttered excitedly, the rings on her fingers sparkling in the candlelit ballroom. 'Oh, I'm so delighted by the way everyone has entered into the spirit of things.' She gave a simpering sideways glance. 'And especially you, Mrs Rees-Morgan. I know how terribly difficult it must be for you at present. Your dear husband …' She flapped her hands once more. 'Oh, I can hardly bear to think of the poor, poor man being so … and he was such a … still, it must be a comfort to you to have your son … ah … er …?'

'Evan,' said Florence.

'Oh, yes, of course, Ivan. I'm so sorry.' She turned to Evan. 'You must forgive me, Ivan, but we do see so little of you, you know.' She clutched his arm. 'But now that you are coming home for good, you simply must promise me you'll attend more of my little soirées. Will you promise me that?'

Evan gave his mother a fleeting glance. '*Nothing* would give me greater pleasure, Mrs Lewis.'

She simpered again, holding his arm more tightly as she surveyed the long room. In one corner a string quartet was scraping away, while grouped at opposite ends, like warring factions under an uneasy truce, servants and employers regarded each other in awkward silence. 'It seems to be going very well, don't you think?' she asked.

'Actually …' began Evan.

'I think it is going *very* well,' said Florence. 'You are to be congratulated, Mrs Lewis.'

Mrs Lewis smiled happily, then her eye fell on the untouched food. 'Oh,' she said. 'But it seems no one has any appetite. Well, perhaps you'll help me to serve some punch?' She gave Evan's arm another playful squeeze. 'After all, it is *we* who are the servants today, you know.'

The three little kitchen maids looked awkwardly from one to the other.

'Begging your pardon, ladies,' Mrs Lewis attempted a curtsey, 'but could I offer you some refreshment?'

The girls, not one of them older than fourteen, returned the curtsey. 'Er, no, ma'am. Thank you, ma'am.'

'A sandwich, perhaps?'

'No, ma'am, thank you, ma'am. But … if *you* would like one, ma'am?' The eldest girl bobbed another curtsey and started toward the table.

'No, no! You don't understand. Please come back here.'

The girl returned, looking chastened. 'Sorry, ma'am.'

'Look. You mustn't call *me* ma'am. I must call *you* ma'am, because today I am the servant. Do you see?'

The girl looked dubiously at her two friends. 'Yes, ma'am. So … what *should* we call you, ma'am?'

'Well, I suppose you should … that is …'

'Gertrude,' suggested Evan.

Mrs Lewis flushed a bright pink. 'Oh, now really, I don't think that …'

'My dear Mrs Lewis,' said Evan. 'As you said yourself, we *must* enter into the spirit of things.' He smiled and made a small bow to the girls. 'Allow me to present your maids, Gertrude and Florence, and your boot-boy *Ivan*. Now, may we bring you ladies some punch?'

*

The huge bonfire roared and crackled, sparks drifting on the warm breeze.

'We always 'as the biggest bonnie on the last night,' said Kate, with a look of pride. 'Better'n any of the other places. See ours for miles around, yer can – an' long after the others 'ave all gone out.' They walked over to where a man was sitting on an empty beer crate. 'So, wotcha drinkin' then, Mary?'

'Is there any lemonade?'

'Lemonade?' Kate roared with laughter. 'What d'yer take this for – a vicar's tea party?'

'Ginger beer, then.'

'We got any ginger beer, Charlie, or 'ave the kids drunk it all?'

The man sitting on the crate pulled a bottle from the shadows near his feet. 'Bleedin' kids 'ave been 'alf inchin' the ale. If we ain't careful we'll *all* be on ginger beer before the night's out.'

'Well, you guard it good an' proper. I ain't goin' to bed sober tonight – not if I knows anythin' about it.' Kate twisted out the stone stopper and passed the bottle over to Mary. 'Y'know, I ain't never seen yer take a proper drink. Don't yer like it?'

Mary shook her head. 'It was all because of drinking ...' She stopped, and smiled. 'But, that's just another sob story – an' we don't want none o' them, now do we.'

'Now yer learnin'.' Kate paused in the process of opening a bottle of porter, and gave a sideways glance. ''Ere – you takin' the rise out o' me?'

'What, me? Now would I do such a bleedin' thing?'

'Yes,' laughed Kate, 'yer bleedin' well would, yer cheeky young cow. Gawd, an' to think I stopped yer from drownin' yerself. I should 'ave bloody well let yer go swimmin', that I should.'

Mary lowered the bottle and looked meaningfully at her. 'I've never said thank you, Kate.'

'Oh, give it a rest.'

'No, I mean it.'

'I was only after yer bleedin' frock.'

'No you weren't.'

'That's all you know.'

Behind them a concertina squeaked into life, and people began to dance, linking arms and kicking up their heels in the firelight. Mary watched them for a while, sipping from the bottle. 'I don't know what you must have thought of me that first night we met.'

'I've got to say,' laughed Kate, 'you were a right royal pain in the arse – but yer got over it. An' at least yer didn't go swimmin', eh?'

'I would have done it, you know.'

'Well, yer didn't, an' that's all that matters.'

'It's just how you end up in this life, eh?'

'I s'pose,' said Kate with a shrug.

'It was just ... well, I thought I'd hit absolute bottom and there was no way out.'

'An' now yer don't?'

'No, not now.'

Kate looked over the top of her bottle. 'Then you ain't really learned nothin', ducklin' – an' that worries me. This *is* the bottom, yer can't go kiddin' yerself any different. The only place down from 'ere is the Bastille, or the 'ole in the ground they lay you in – an' if yer given the choice, my advice is to take the 'ole.'

'But there's always *up*.'

'Up? I don't know what rung of the bleedin' ladder you'd fallen off that night I found yer, but there ain't no climbin' back on from 'ere. Blimey, what d'yer think? That all it takes is a bit of 'ard work? Try it. Go an' join the silly buggers in the factories – like old Gimpy with 'er mangled-up leg, an' deaf as a post – or Phossie Flo from the match factory. She can't take a drink these days without 'er teeth fallin' into 'er beer.'

'There's domestic service.'

'Not without a character, there ain't. Look about yer. 'Alf the people 'ere live in doss 'ouses or on the street. Don't yer think they'd prefer a nice, warm crib in some toff's house, with as much to eat as they can lay their sticky fingers on – an' the odd trip to the pawnshop with a teaspoon or two?'

'There has to be a way, Kate. There *has* to be.'

Kate shook her head. 'There ain't. I thought you'd learned that much, at least.'

'Learned what? That there's no hope?'

'That yer don't fight it. That yer take each day as it comes, enjoy it, an' let tomorrow take care of itself.'

'I have learned that, Kate, honestly I have. But I won't go back to Crossingham's. Even the Bastille can't be any worse than that.'

Kate shook her head sadly, 'Yer don't know the 'alf of it, ducklin'.'

'Well, it doesn't matter, because I've decided what to do.' Mary smiled. 'I'm going back to Wales – and not with my tail between my legs – but with money in my pocket. I can do it, Kate. I *know* I can. I'm going to make my own luck, too.'

'Yer know?' Kate gave a wry grin, 'I '*alf* believes yer.'

From out of the shadows, Jack approached, a lanky, nervous young man following in his wake. 'G'd evenin' ladies.' He made a mock bow. 'So nice o' you t' attend our li'll gatherin'.'

Kate chuckled. 'Gawd. You drunk already?'

'Not so much as I often 'as been – an' not so much as I *intends* to be.' He bowed again. 'I should like to introduce my werry good friend, Mr 'Utchinson …' He waved a hand toward the embarrassed young man, 'A young gen'leman what's wantin' the pleasure of partakin' of a dance with our Mary – if'n the young lady would be consentin'?'

Mary gave them a broad smile, feeling the thrill of renewed confidence. 'I should be *delighted*,' she said.

*

Out on the polished floor a few couples swirled elegantly, others galloped clumsily, and a few, including Maggie and her partner, cannoned about, spinning like frantically whipped tops.

Gwyneth watched enviously. From the moment the ladies and gentle-men had withdrawn, things had quickly brightened, and Maggie had been approached by a tousle-haired stable boy who proceeded to claim her for dance after dance.

To begin with, only the prettiest girls had been led to the floor as the orchestra launched into the opening strains of *The Jenny Lind*. Then, in a spirit of fairness, a few of the men had mopped their brows, removed their jackets and solicited the company of those of slightly less pleasing appearance.

Gwyneth continued to wait, smiling encouragingly each time Maggie flashed past, held in the arms of her snub-nosed swain and wearing a grin as wide as her face.

When the orchestra slowed into waltz time, a kindly-looking old coachman had asked Gwyneth to dance, and she'd consented, moving and smiling with equal stiffness as he held her at arms' length and told her how much she reminded him of his daughter, who, he said with some pride, was in service in London – and doing very well.

Another polka was followed by a gallop, then two country dances that all the younger girls pooh-poohed as old fashioned, but which they couldn't help enjoying, then more polkas, fast and furious – and through them all Gwyneth sat alone. Several times one of the younger men seemed about to approach, but none did, and she remained sitting by the wall, a bright and cheerful look pinned to the fragile veil of her pride.

*

The night was dry and warm, and lying in the open air close to Kate and Jack, Mary looked up at the sky, dusty with stars. 'If you really had *one* wish – just one. What would it be?'

Kate shifted sleepily, her arm falling across Jack's chest as he lay already dreaming. 'Dunno, m'darlin', she yawned. 'But since we ain't likely to get one, it don't 'ardly matter, do it?'

'But just supposing?'

'Then I'd wish you was asleep.'

Mary laughed softly. 'I'm serious.'

'So am I. We've got a bleedin' long walk 'ome tomorrow.' Reluctantly Kate opened her eyes and sighed. 'Look, I know. Why don't yer tell me what *you'd* wish for – an' I'll just agree with yer.'

'That's just it, I don't know. It seems whatever you wish for, there's always a catch – a price to pay – so that you end up regretting you'd ever wished it.'

'Best to wish to always have nothin', then. That way yer won't be disappointed.'

Mary laughed again. 'Or,' she said, her eyes brightening as the idea came to her, 'you could wish just to be happy – that way no matter what happened, it would always be alright, wouldn't it?'

'Well,' said Kate, sliding her leg over Jack's, and laying her head against his chest. 'If that's the case, then I don't need no wish.'

For a few minutes Mary lay still, looking up at the stars. *I wish I could always be happy,* she said to herself, then she turned her head. 'Goodnight, Kate.'

Kate chuckled drowsily, clinging closer to Jack. 'Does this mean I'm gettin' my first wish after all?' she asked.

*

The bed creaked and groaned as Maggie rolled over and gave a long, lingering sigh. 'You still awake, Gwyn?'

'Yes.'

'Wasn't tonight just the best time you ever had?'

'It was alright.'

Maggie rolled quickly on to her side. 'Here, who were those two old battle-axes you was talkin' to when we came back in? They had faces that'd turn milk!'

'They were very nice, and …' Gwyneth turned her head, looking through the blackness to where the faint silhouette of Maggie lay curled. 'Came back from where?'

Maggie giggled, hugging herself. 'Went for a walk round the back of the house, didn't we. Got too bloomin' hot, what with all that dancin', an' all.' She giggled again, 'So that Bertie, he got a cigar out of this box in the next room, an' we had a go at bein' nobs. Right laugh it was – till he started feelin' sick.'

'You shouldn't have!'

'It's alright. Nobody saw us.'

'That's not the point!'

Maggie turned huffily toward the wall. 'Just a bit of fun. Wish I hadn't told you now.'

'So do I!' snapped Gwyneth.

'You're a right misery sometimes! Do you know that? No wonder no one wants to dance with you …' Maggie broke off, biting her lip. 'I … I didn't mean it, Gwyn. It just sort of … popped out, like.' She waited for a long time, hearing only the sound of Gwyneth's breathing, then looked guiltily over her shoulder. 'Ain't you goin' to answer me, Gwyn?'

Chapter Forty-Two

In late summer, Connie had been all icy composure. With autumn had come a change to a dark and withdrawn malevolence, and now, with winter frost on the London streets, she was a maelstrom of fire and fury. Eastman enjoyed the theatricality of it. 'I've done everything I can,' he said calmly. 'She *will* surface, but we must be patient.'

'It's taking too long, you hear me! Too fucking long!' Connie moved up and down the room, her skirts swishing at each turn with reptilian menace. 'I want her Vincent – and I want her *now*!'

'With respect, I've already got people all over the West End. If I put any more on to searching for her, our other interests will suffer.'

'I don't care. The whole lot can go down the shit-hole. I just want that … that *whore*. You bring her to me, Vince, and I promise you – *I'll* show *you* how to cut! I'll cut her fucking heart out! I'm not pissing about anymore. I haven't got the time.' She began to scratch at her sleeves, the black bombazine of mourning shifting to give a glimpse of the bandages beneath. 'I've been thinking – about something you said the other day. Something's not right about this whole bloody business, not right at all. Archie had been going to that place for years.' She caught Eastman's small look. 'What? Did you think I didn't know?' Connie's lip curled into a sneer. 'I knew all about him and his fucking tarts? The thing is, he'd been seeing this Emma Black for over two years – the other one even longer – why the hell would they kill him? It don't make any sense, unless …' She stopped pacing, her eyes unnaturally bright in their dark rimmed sockets. 'Unless somebody paid them to do it.'

'Our Froggie friends?' Eastman shook his head. 'Unlikely. There was no time to arrange it. They couldn't have known our intentions regarding M'sieurs Gerard and Reinhardt until after we'd dealt with them – and Archie went to see the two *ladies* immediately afterwards.' He paused, thoughtfully. 'But, perhaps – if the Frenchmen somehow had prior knowledge?'

'From someone here? A fucking traitor?' Connie scratched more agitatedly at her wrists. 'Yes, that's got to be it! Good boy, Vince. Good boy.' She began to pace again. 'Right, I want you to go back to Paris – just you and Baines. We can't trust anyone else. Find out who's behind this. Get me names. If this Emma Black is the head of the snake, we'll start with the fucking tail!'

*

'Stockings!' exclaimed the mousy-looking young woman, 'Are the spawn of the devil!' She lowered her head, peering at the crowd over the rims of her spectacles. 'Oh, you may mock, you may chortle – but behold!' With an extravagant sweep of her arm she thrust out the offending article for their inspection. 'Satan himself makes every pair – and why? To inflame men's passions! You sir …' She fixed on a stoutish man at the front. 'You don't seem the sort to be inflamed very easily. Now, can you look me in the eye and tell me that such a pair of stockings – on the undoubtedly well-turned ankle of your wife – would not tempt even you?'

'We ain't married yet,' laughed the woman standing beside him.

'Then take him away this instant! An unmarried man should not even *gaze* upon such an item!' She looked purposefully over the crowd, wagging her finger, her lips pinched and drawn. 'And as for the rest of you – well, I should like to think you'd tell me to burn these lures of the devil – that you'd have me send them back whence they came.' She slowly shook her head. 'But I can see you are set on indulging the sins of pride and lust, so – it's a shilling a pair, first come first served, and you'd better be quick 'cos I've only got four dozen.'

The first few flakes of snow were falling as Bukina Kapinskya turned off the naphtha lamps and came round to where Miriam was counting the money. 'So? How much we make today?'

Miriam shrugged carelessly. 'Not so much. We done better before.'

'Before what?'

'Just before.' She glanced toward the far end of the stall. 'That's all I say. *Before.*'

Mary came toward them, polishing the clear glass lenses of the spectacles with her handkerchief. 'Is something wrong, Buki?'

'Wrong? No, nothing wrong. Only Miriam – *in the head.* You do really good today, Mary. Good crowd. They like this lady with eye glasses, I think.'

'I think the other one is better,' said Miriam, sourly. 'This I can't understand! Not one word.'

'Well, I don't understand so well, too. But –' Bukina waved a hand toward the emptying street, 'they do! So we should care?'

'I can go back to doing the other character,' offered Mary.

'No. Don't listen to Miriam. We do good business today. Best yet.' The snow was beginning to fall harder, and she rubbed her hands, looking across to where steam was rising from the doorway of a brightly lit coffee shop. 'We clear up, then I buy us cake and tea.' She laughed. 'Early Christmas treat, eh?'

*

'Now, when I was a girl,' said Cook, sweating as she mixed the pudding, 'Christmas wasn't nothing so special. Weren't none of this tree business, neither. Proper heathen that is, if you ask me.'

Lucy straightened her dress. 'Well, I like a nice tree. Wouldn't seem like Christmas without one, I don't think.'

'Load of foreign muck!' Cook paused in her mixing, looking pointedly at Maggie. 'And *you* can get off your backside, you lazy good-for-nothing. Go and wash your hands, then come and give this pudding a mix while *I* puts my feet up.'

Maggie slid out from her seat and went to the sink.

'We used to put sixpences in our pudding,' said Lucy.

'Oh, did you, now?' The sour-faced cook prised off one of her shoes and massaged her foot.

Sitting next to her, Lucy wrinkled her nose, then looked across the table to where Gwyneth was sewing. 'What sort of Christmases did you have?'

Gwyneth put down the stocking she was darning. 'Lovely ones.'

'Didn't have none of that tree business, I bet. Not up the valley there,' said Cook.

'No, we didn't. But we always decorated the house.' Gwyneth smiled at the memory. 'We'd put greenery all round the kitchen, and make paper chains.'

'We used to make those,' grinned Lucy. 'Proper tedious job that was, wasn't it.'

'No. No, I used to love it. Me and Thomas and Alan, sitting at the kitchen table, fighting over the paste-pot, and mam …' She looked down at her sewing. 'Well, it was *lovely*.'

'So, what about you, Maggie?' asked Lucy, turning to where Maggie was standing in front of the huge mixing bowl, rolling up her sleeves.

Maggie shrugged sullenly.

'Well?' persisted Lucy. 'Did you have a tree?'

'No.' She gripped the wooden spoon, dragging it through the heavy, cloying mixture.

'What about paper chains?'

'No.'

'Well, what did you have? You must have done something.'

346

Cook prised off her other shoe, flexing her toes until the joints cracked. 'She wouldn't have had none o' that nonsense. She's workhouse,' she said matter-of-factly, then looked up. 'Didn't you know?'

Gwyneth put down her work. 'Oh, Maggie,' she murmured.

Keeping her face lowered, Maggie looked guiltily about the table. 'So what?' she said, 'There's a lot worse places – so don't you go actin' all high an' mighty. We had some good times, we did. Some *right* good times. Probably better than you ever had, I shouldn't wonder.'

'Yes, of course,' said Gwyneth gently.

'An' anyway …' Maggie's bottom lip began to quiver. 'What's so special about Christmas? Nothing. It ain't special at all. It's just a lot of …' She dragged the spoon from the pudding mix and flung it to the far side of the kitchen. '… a lot of *bloody nonsense!*'

Cook stared, her face black as thunder. 'Why you … you little madam! I'll put that spoon across your backside!' She jerked round, making a grab for Maggie as the girl bolted for the door. 'You come back here and …'

Lucy made to go after her, but Gwyneth was already on her feet. 'Let me go? Please?' she said, looking from one to the other.

After a moment's thought, Lucy gave a nod and sat back down. 'But you tell her she's to come down now and clear this mess up – and I mean *now.*'

'Yes, of course. Thank you.'

The echoing sound of a door slamming came from the top of the house as Gwyneth hurried into the hall, and she sprang for the stairs.

'Gwyneth?' said Evan, coming from the drawing-room, a concerned look on his face. 'What was that noise?'

Gwyneth stopped, breathing hard. 'I don't know, sir. I'm just going to find out.' She took a deep breath. 'I think I might have left a window open.'

'I see. Well, as long as everything is alright?'

'Yes, sir.' She waited until he withdrew, then raced up the remaining flights to the attic bedroom.

Inside Maggie sat huddled on her bed, her back to the wall, hugging her knees.

'Maggie?'

'Go away.'

'I can't go away. They want you downstairs.' Gwyneth came closer, sitting on the edge of the bed. 'What is it, Maggie? You've not been yourself for days.'

'Bloody Christmas,' muttered Maggie.

'It's never bothered you before.'

'Well, I ain't never …' she broke off, hugging her knees more tightly.

'Haven't what?'

'Nothin'.' She looked up accusingly. 'Do you know what Christmas is like in the workhouse? Do you? No, 'course you don't. You had a *family*, didn't you. You had a *home*, with paper chains, an' sixpences in the puddin'.' She sank her head on to her knees. 'You had times you *want* to remember.'

'Oh, Maggie,' Gwyneth reached out for her, feeling the tremors running through the slight body. 'That's all behind you now. And I promise, we'll make *this* Christmas one you'll want to remember.'

'I don't care about *me*.'

'Then what?'

Maggie looked at her with reddened eyes. 'I'm goin' to have a baby, Gwyn. I'm goin' to have a baby, an' then I'll have to leave here ... an' then where can I go but back there? I won't be able to do anythin' better for my kid than my mum did for me!'

*

The cramped confines of the coffee shop felt hot and humid after the winter chill of the streets, and Mary shrugged off her coat, laying it over the back of an empty chair.

'What you want?' asked Mrs Kapinskya, turning sideways to edge her way through the crowded cafe. 'Tea or coffee?'

Miriam sat down heavily. 'Why ask? It all taste same here.'

'Then I get tea. It cheaper.'

'No. I take coffee.' Miriam Fleming watched with sullen eyes as Mary followed Buki to the counter, then cast around the steamy interior, nodding to a woman at a nearby table.

'Had a good day?' asked the woman.

The corners of Miriam's mouth drew even further down, and she gave a dismissive grunt.

'Well, Mary seemed to be pulling a good crowd as I came past.'

'Ach, crowd, yes. But money?' she shrugged dolefully. 'Listen, Hilda. You know what I think?'

'No, what?'

'I think this Mary is someone you must watch for.'

'Watch for?'

'I say nothing more.'

Her interest aroused, Hilda leaned closer. 'No, go on – tell me. She's living in my house – so I've a right to know.'

'Well, she live in my house, too – for a little while. But now she don't, eh? I don't like to say why.' Miriam gave a meaningful look. 'I just say you watch for her.'

'You're saying there was a problem?'

'I say nothing. But, sometimes – like today – you no can understand

348

a word she say.' Idly, Miriam ran her fingers over the old coat Mary had taken off. 'My sister, Buki, she pay her good money. I say no, it too much. My son Joseph say the same – but Buki don't listen. Well, that her business. But I ask you – where that money go, eh? You see nice clothes? Pretty dresses? No.' Miriam touched a finger to the side of her nose. 'So I wonder where it go, eh?'

'Drink?' The woman shook her head. 'No. I've never smelled that on her.'

'Well, you listen or no listen. I just tell you what I know. You watch for her. I say nothing more.'

'She knows I run a temperance house.'

'A pig knows its own sty – but you don't leave garden gate open, eh?'

The woman looked uncertainly at Miriam, then across to where Mary was taking cups from the counter. 'Well, I don't know,' she said. 'But I've got to be on my way before all the shops are shut. Tell her I'll see her when she comes home – oh, and can you remind her this week's rent is due?'

'Oh. She don't pay always?'

'No, no there's never been any trouble of that sort.'

'But of other sort, eh?'

'No, no trouble at all. It's just I'm bit short myself this week, that's all.' Hilda cast another glance across the room. 'Well, I can't stay. Say goodbye to Buki for me.'

'You just take my warning, eh? Watch for Mary. I say nothing more.'

With a thoughtful backward glance the woman departed, and Miriam leaned back in the rickety chair, her sagging cheeks settling into heavy immobility as she surveyed the room, finally fixing on an unremarkable looking man sitting two tables away. 'He here again,' she said carelessly as Mary and Buki returned with the watery coffee and three large, doughy cakes.

'Who?' asked Buki, craning to look.

'Him!' Miriam shoved a finger in the direction of the man. 'The one who always come and stand in back of crowd – *but never buy*!'

Mary cast a brief glance over her shoulder, turning quickly back as the man offered a tentative smile. 'Please, don't embarrass him. He doesn't do any harm.'

'I think he like you, Mary,' Buki laughed. 'But you don't worry over him. I make better match for you. Very soon, eh?'

Mary took a sip of coffee, keeping the cup raised and looking at Miriam over the rim. 'Was that Hilda you were talking to just now?'

'Yes. She say you are behind with rent and must pay today.'

Very deliberately, Mary put the cup back into the saucer. 'The rent *is* due today, and I have it ready – but I'm *not* behind with it. You must have misheard.'

Miriam shrugged. 'I hear what I hear.'

'You hear what you want hear,' said Buki.

'I just tell you what she tell me. I can't help whether she don't like you.'

Buki frowned with concern. 'Don't like? What is this? You no get on at you lodging, Mary?'

'Yes, of course I do.' She looked with growing irritation at Miriam. 'What *exactly* did she say?'

'Oh, she ask me questions, that's all.'

'What sort of questions?'

'Just questions – about you. But don't worry – I tell her nothing.'

'But there's nothing to tell,' said Mary trying to control her anger.

'That just what I tell her. I say, don't ask, because I tell you *nothing*.'

*

'But how?' Gwyneth suddenly felt very cold.

'It was at that bloomin' dance,' said Maggie, dragging the backs of her hands across her cheeks, smearing the tears.

'When you went outside? With that boy?'

Maggie nodded sullenly. 'Wish I'd never bloomin' well gone, now.' She sniffed, then started to cry again. 'Oh, Gwyn, what am I goin' to do?'

'Have you told him?'

'I went over there on my last half-day.'

'And he'll stand by you?'

Maggie shook her head. 'He just laughed, an' said it was my own fault – an' called me a silly sod for lettin' him do it.' She looked up. 'An' I am, ain't I?'

'Oh, Maggie ...'

'I'm *stupid*, just like everyone says!' She began pummelling the mattress with her fists. 'Stupid, stupid, *stupid!*'

'Stop it.' Gwyneth grabbed hold of her wrists. 'You're *not* stupid. You've made a mistake, but it will be alright.'

'It won't. 'Course it won't. I'll be out on the bloomin' street soon as anyone gets to know about it.'

'No, I'm sure you won't ...'

'I *will*. You know I will.' Maggie's eyes darted about in desperation. 'But it ain't goin' to show for a while. Maybe ... maybe I could find another man? You know, make him think it was his? I wouldn't mind if he was old – or ugly – or both, just so long as he'd look after us.' She looked up imploringly. 'That's what some girls do, don't they?'

Gwyneth drew Maggie close, taking the girl's head on her breast and gently rocking her, until from far below there came the sound of the hall clock striking the hour. 'Lawrence will be coming to see what's the matter if we don't go down soon,' she said softly.

'Gwyn. You won't tell them? Please, don't tell *anyone*.'

'They'll have to know sooner or later.'

'*Please.*'

Gwyneth sighed. 'Listen. You get undressed and into bed. I'll go down and tell them you're not well – at least that will give Cook time to calm down.' She got up and went to the door. 'If anyone should come to see you, pretend to be asleep.'

'Gwyn. Promise me?'

'Oh, *Maggie*. I don't know … I can't see how I can.' She felt for the knob of the door.

'*Please*, Gwyn.'

Gwyneth looked back at the pathetic little figure in her ill fitting dress, and gave another long sigh. 'Yes. Yes, alright … *I promise*.'

Chapter Forty-Three

A keen January wind, sharp as a razor and infinitely colder, was ripping along Middlesex Street, extinguishing lamps and scattering the wares of the few stallholders who remained.

Mary watched through the misted coffee shop window as an awning was ripped free and sent flapping along the road like an enormous, bedraggled ghost. She shivered, feeling the cold deep in her bones despite the steamy heat of the cafe. 'Another bad day,' she sighed, noticing Buki's worried look as the old woman pored over the sheet of laboriously formed writing.

'Ach,' she said, flapping a podgy hand. 'January always bad. February too. Sometimes March, even.'

On the far side of the table, Miriam grunted. 'Not so bad as this – but then you no get quart into pint pot – so you no get quart *out of* pint pot, eh?'

Mary gave her a hard look. 'What do you mean?'

'Nothing. I say all I have to say.'

'You don't think I'm earning my keep?'

Miriam looked about with baleful eyes. 'We have old saying: When two eat from same spoon – both go hungry.'

Buki looked up from her reading. 'I never hear that. Who say it?'

'Me, I say it – because it true.'

'You getting crazy old woman.' Buki turned to Mary. 'You don't pay her no attention. I think she must drop on head when she born.'

'No. I'm sorry, Buki,' Mary closed her hands about her cup. 'I've put up with this *carping*, for months.' She looked straight at Miriam. 'I don't know what you've been saying about me to Hilda, but there's something different about her – almost as if she didn't want me staying there. So let's have it out now. Do you want me to go?'

Buki's eyes widened. 'No, Mary. You make us good business.' She turned to Miriam. 'You – you crazy woman. You tell her!'

Miriam shrugged. 'I say nothing.'

'Ach!' Buki turned back to Mary. 'Listen, Mary. We need you.' Miriam pulled a sour face, but Buki ignored her. 'Your lady with eyeglasses, your old woman with shawl, they bring in money.' She looked beyond Miriam to the dirt and paper blowing past the window. 'These cold, wet days, no one make money. Never. Not this year, not last year, not any years. But soon, eh? Soon it be like before Christmas.' She rubbed her fingers together as though feeling the coins. 'So you no listen to my sister – because she need you, too.'

Miriam gave a contemptuous grunt.

'You no think?' Angrily, Buki pushed the square of paper across the table. 'Is from my husband – in Poland.' She watched as Miriam held the letter close to her face. 'Every year he say *I come, I come* – but he never come. Now he get sick, and ask for me to go home.' She sighed and shook her head. 'I don't know how soon I come back. So you see, we need you, Mary.'

Miriam finished reading the letter. 'You no see him for ten years – so what you care? You don't go. Simple, eh?'

The two women regarded each other icily.

'I'll get us some more tea,' said Mary, suddenly feeling in the way. She got to her feet, putting her hand on Mrs Kapinskya's shoulder. 'I'm sorry about the news, Buki.'

'I take coffee,' called Miriam, shifting her gaze to avoid her sister's stare and catching sight of the lone man sitting a few tables away. 'And watch out for that one,' she stabbed a finger in his direction. 'The one who makes at you the eyes of the horse.'

'*Cow*,' said Buki. 'Eyes of the cow! How long you been here – and *still* you not know nothing?'

The man was staring into his tea as Mary edged past his table, and she paused. 'I'm sorry about my friend,' she said quietly.

'Your friend?' he looked up, startled. 'Oh … b-but that's … that's perfectly alright …' His voice tailed into an awkward silence.

'Well, I *am* sorry.' She started to move away.

'Sorry? Yes, well, I was just …that is, I m-mean …' He was half way to his feet when the door opened, and a gust of icy air rushed in.

''Ere, wotcha, ducklin',' laughed Kate, her hands on her hips. 'So this is where yer've been 'idin' yerself, is it?'

*

The two men sitting with Murray Baines in the lounge of the Notre Dame hotel looked less like businessmen than well-to-do costermongers on a pub outing.

Eastman fixed a smile on his face as he approached them. 'Drinks, Gentlemen?'

'Werry kind o' you, Mister Eastman.' The older of the two men, leaned forward, extending his hand. ''Orace Suggett,' he grinned broadly, his broken-veined cheeks plumping out to give him the appearance of a villainous gnome. 'An' this 'ere's my boy Tom.'

Pretending not to see the outstretched hand, Eastman seated himself in the leather armchair, casually turning to snap his fingers at the waiter. 'I'm afraid I can't offer you an English beer or porter.' He gave the two newcomers a brief, condescending smile.

'That's alright.' Suggett turned to the boy. 'Wine will do us, won't it, Tom?'

The muscular young man gave a guarded nod.

'Well,' said Eastman, with a hint of surprise. 'Then wine it shall be. I expect my associate, Mr Baines, has brought you up to date with our progress over the past month?'

'Yes, sir. An' me an' Tom will do what we can.'

'Of course you will. And let's hope we don't have to keep you from England for too long, hmm?'

'T' be 'onest with yer, Mr Eastman, we're glad o' the chance t' get away. Things ain't so easy back 'ome these days.'

'Is that so?' Eastman cast an impatient glance in the direction of the waiter.

'It's Connie.' Murray Baines hunched forward in his seat, dropping his voice. 'They say she's starting to crack.'

Suggett looked uncomfortable. 'It's true enough. Reckon she's goin' the way of 'er old mum – Archie was always worried she would.' He looked from Eastman to Baines. 'Yer *did* know 'er old lady died in the loony-bin?'

Baines cast a nervous glance toward Eastman, unsure of the wisdom of the topic, but Eastman seemed unperturbed.

'Anyway,' continued Suggett, 'I've 'eard tell she's taken t' cuttin' 'erself.' He rubbed unconsciously at his forearms, shivering at the idea. 'But that ain't the worst of it. Not by a long chalk. She's started lockin' 'erself away in 'er rooms – won't see no one for days on end – then when she does come out she starts accusin' people, right an' left. People she's known an' trusted for years.'

'She's done for Lanky Bill,' whispered Baines.

'An' there weren't no one more loyal than 'im. Blimey, 'e was with 'er an' Archie way back in the fifties.'

Eastman remembered the squat, pugnacious little man standing guard outside Connie's room on the day of the funeral. 'Perhaps she had good reason. People can become untrustworthy.'

'I dunno, Mr Eastman. All I do know is there's some good blokes that suddenly ain't around no more – an' no one knows who's goin' t' be next.'

The waiter arrived, and Eastman ordered cognac for himself, whisky for Baines, and was in the process of asking for a bottle of the house wine when Suggett gave an apologetic cough.

'Beggin' yer pardon, Mr Eastman, but 'e'll be givin' us the slops if 'e thinks 'e can get away with it.'

Eastman raised an eyebrow in amusement. 'Then, please – feel free.'

Horace Suggett eyed the bored looking Frenchman. 'Quelle est la cuvée du patron?' he asked in a perfect Parisian accent.

'Un Bourgogne, monsieur.'

'Bien, on va voir. Je peux faire la différence. *Comprenez?*'

The waiter bowed and withdrew.

Suggett gave an embarrassed grin. 'My mum was French, born an' bred.'

'Indeed? You are a man of hidden talents, Mr Suggett. I *like* that. And your son? He also speaks French?'

'Yes, sir. Though 'is accent's a little bit more Bethnal Green than Bois de Boulogne, if yer know what I mean.'

Eastman leaned back, studying the young man through narrowed lids. 'Well,' he began at last, but he got no further for the waiter re-appeared at his elbow.

'Un telegraph, monsieur.'

With a small sigh, Eastman took it, flicked open the envelope and read the message. 'Well, it would seem Archie's fears were well founded,' he said quietly, looking about the gathered group. 'For her own safety, Mrs Bull has been committed to an asylum for the insane.'

*

'So you really are going?'

'What can I do, Mary? He send – I must go.'

In the dim light of the winter morning, Hilda paused, standing quietly at the foot of the stairs as she strained to hear the voices coming from Mary's room.

'Listen, Buki, I've been thinking …'

'That good. That *very* good. So, you have new person for crowd to laugh at, eh?'

'No, well, that is, I have – but that's not what I wanted to …'

Mrs Kapinskya's voice took on a worried note. 'You don't tell me you save enough money for Welsh already, and now you go, too?'

'No – the fact is, the way things are, I don't think I'm ever going to save enough for what I want to do.'

'Listen, Mary. I tell you, business be very good soon. *Very good.* You make lots of money. Lots of money for Welsh. But something I no understand. Why you no fetch dresses what your friend Kate say you have? I know people – I get you good price – *best*.'

Hilda leaned closer to the door, trying in vain to catch the murmured reply, then suddenly and without warning the brass doorknob turned, sending her bustling away down the narrow passage as Mary came out, buttoning her coat.

'Well, I come with you, if you want. I afraid of nothing,' said Buki, following behind. 'And I give you more advice. You listen or no – all same to me – but I tell you anyway. I don't like this Kate Conway. I think she no good for you.'

'Kate? She's a good friend.'

'Good friends no keep you out late at night – spending you money.'

'It was only a few shillings.'

'Few shillings today – more shillings tomorrow. I know. I see it lots of time. Then you never get to Welsh!'

Mary opened the front door and looked up into the dull grey sky. 'At least it's dry,' she smiled, changing the subject.

'Dry is good.' Buki waddled after her. 'We do good business today. I feel it – and I never wrong. And after, we go fetch nice dresses from this Night-Bridge, eh?'

Standing in the dark at the end of the passage, Hilda waited several minutes before venturing from her hiding place, then she walked purposefully up to Mary's door and turned the handle. There was no lock, and the door opened to reveal the modest little room with its meagre furniture and neatly made bed.

She looked suspiciously about the four walls, carefully studying the pictures cut from weekly periodicals, but finding little untoward in their content, she turned her attention to the few personal items that lay neatly ordered about the place: a shawl, a dark green skirt, some toiletry items and a few pieces of clean linen. The austerity of it reassured Hilda, and she was on the point of withdrawing when she became aware of something nagging at the periphery of her senses, and she paused, her neck stretching forward like a dog on point, nostrils twitching as she sniffed the air.

*

'Is cold!' said Miriam, rubbing her hands together, her lugubrious face so engulfed by her shawl that only the bright red peaks of her nose and cheeks protruded. 'You want tea, Mary? Nice cup of tea, eh? Keep out cold? I go fetch.'

'I take some tea, too.' Buki watched her sister cross the street to the coffee shop, then came round to where Mary was unpacking bundles of petticoats. 'So, we go to this Night-Bridge tonight, eh? You and me. If you have dresses, then we get them. Whatever trouble you have there, I fix. I talk to lady of house. Make everything okay. You see, eh?'

'The thing is, Buki … ' Mary paused. 'There *aren't* any dresses. It was just a story I made up – the first time I met Kate. She should never have mentioned it.'

Buki shrugged. 'So what is it that give you trouble to think about?'

'It's just that you're going, and …'

Buki followed Mary's gaze across to the coffee shop. 'Miriam? You worry about my sister? Listen, you no worry no more. Miriam, she make me crazy – she make everyone crazy! She make her husband so crazy he run off and no come back! But Miriam? – *she* not crazy. She know what side of bread to put butter – and she know she need you. You wait and see. When I go, she need you even more – and she *know* she need you. When I am gone I think Miriam will be as sweet as the little sheep, eh?'

*

And for a while Buki was right. The change in Miriam was so sudden and dramatic that in the weeks that followed I hardly recognised her. Then came spring, and as business improved along with the weather, so my little nest egg, my 'Going Home Money', began to grow once more. It wasn't a large amount, just twenty pounds, nothing compared to what I'd earned in Knightsbridge, but it was a beginning, and when I banked it that April morning, I felt such confidence and certainty – as if nothing could stand in my way.

Chapter Forty-Four

'What do you think you're doing?' demanded Mary.

The weaselly little man with unshaven cheeks continued to throw boxes on to the stall. 'What's it look like?'

'But this is our stall.'

'Not any more it ain't.' He pushed past her. 'Now, run along, darlin'. Some of us 'as work to do – an' you're gettin' in the way.'

Mary chased after him. 'Get all this stuff off. Do you hear me? Get it off now! *I mean it!*'

He looked at her in amusement. 'Blimey,' he said, cocking his head to one side and sniffing the air, 'can you smell that?' He sniffed again. 'I reckon that must be me – *shittin' myself.*'

'If you don't get your stuff off our stall, I'll call the police.'

'You can call who yer bleedin' well like, darlin'. This stall is bought an' paid for – an' the bleedin' Light Brigade ain't gonna shift me off it, see?'

*

'Miriam!' Mary knocked sharply at the door of the little terraced house. '*Miriam!*'

The curtain moved imperceptibly at the downstairs window, and Mary pressed her nose to the glass, her hands raised, shielding her eyes from the light as she peered into the darkened room. 'Miriam! I know you're in there!'

'Go away!'

'There's a man on our stall!' She banged her fist on the window. 'Why is there a man on our stall?' Up and down the street, people were stepping out to look, but Mary took no notice. 'Open the door, Miriam, or so help me, I'll break this bloody window!' She banged again, rattling the loose fitting frame, then again and again until finally the front door opened and Miriam grudgingly appeared, her features as dour as ever.

'What you want?'

'*What I want,*' hissed Mary, in spiteful imitation, 'is to know what the bloody hell is going on.'

'It nothing to do with you what go on. You nothing! No one! Just a *vantz!*' She turned sharply as behind her the hulking figure of her son came from the back room. 'Go back in, Joseph! It nothing to do with you.'

The sturdily built young man hesitated, then came closer. 'No, I won't,' he said, slowly and with careful deliberation. 'It's not right. It's not right for you to talk to her like that.'

Miriam rounded on him, slapping viciously at his head. 'Shut up. Idiot! You know nothing!'

'Leave him alone!'

Joseph cowered back. 'It's not right,' he whimpered, retreating along the passage.

Mary grabbed Miriam's arm, pulling her round so they were face to face once more. 'You horrible woman! You've sold the stall, haven't you? You had no right! It's Buki's, not yours!'

'Buki? Pah! What she do with it now she don't come back?'

Mary faltered. 'What? What do you mean? Have you heard from her?'

'Sure, I hear. She write, three – maybe four week ago.'

'And you didn't tell me?'

'Tell *you*? Why I tell you? You only hired help. I tell you nothing.'

'You *cow!*' Mary began to shake with anger. 'You … *you bloody cow!*'

Miriam folded her arms, gloating. 'Buki no come back, so I do what I like. You *don't* like?' She gave a careless shrug. 'Too bad!'

*

'It's quiet, ain't it,' said Maggie, holding one side of the pair of wooden steps while Gwyneth took the other, setting them in place beneath the drawing-room chandelier. 'I mean, it's nice not havin' so much work to do – but nothin' happens no more. Ain't had no fireworks since I can't remember when!' She took a firm hold of the ladder and began to climb.

'No, Maggie,' Gwyneth whispered urgently. 'You come back down. *I'll* do it.'

'I can do it.' Maggie paused, putting her hand to her belly. 'Anyway, I've *got* to do it. If Lucy catches you doin' my work one more time, we'll both be out on the street.' She climbed unsteadily to the top, reaching out to flick the dust from the crystal pendants. 'You just hold these bloomin' steps steady – an' don't go givin' them a nudge when I'm on tip-toe, alright?'

Using all her weight to steady the ladder, Gwyneth shook her head in amazement. 'You say the daftest things.'

'Ain't so daft. *Some people* would do *just* that.'

'Of course they wouldn't.'

'Well, a lot you know.' Maggie wiped the sweat from her forehead, breathing deeply as she stared out at the lawns gleaming in the spring sunshine. 'God, I *hate* spring.'

'Then come down and let me do it – please, Maggie.'

'I'll be alright.' She gave the chandelier a few more desultory flicks.

Gwyneth watched her, anxiously. 'I can't believe we've got away with it for this long.'

'Don't suppose we would have if the old doctor an' the mistress was here – but with just Master Evan – well, it's do as you please these days, ain't it.'

'Lawrence is bound to notice soon – and Cook said just the other day that you were getting fat.'

Slowly, Maggie made her way down. 'Oh, I ain't worried about them. They ain't as clever as they think they are. Now, old Broadside, she was a different kettle o' fish. She'd have had my guts for corset strings long before this – *silly old cow*.' She stepped off the ladder and turned around, running her hand over her belly once more. 'An' besides, it ain't very big, is it? Not like some women you see. Bloomin' enormous some of them! You'll just have to lace me up tighter as time goes on.'

Gwyneth closed the steps with a bang. 'No, I'm not going to, Maggie. It's *dangerous*. You shouldn't be wearing a corset at all, let alone ...' She broke off in exasperation, and gave a deep sigh. 'Look, why don't you let me tell Lawrence?'

'No!'

'But, Maggie ...'

'No! You promised me.'

'I know I did – but perhaps if she knew, then ...'

'Then I'd be out – bag an' baggage.'

'You don't know that.'

'An' I don't *not* know it, neither. I ain't goin' to risk it, Gwyn. I *can't*. What would I do if I was turned out? Where could I go – except *there*?'

Gwyneth felt the lump come to her throat, and she took hold of the steps, carrying them to the far end of the room and setting them beneath the second chandelier.

'So you won't tell no one?' asked Maggie, waddling after her.

'No, I won't tell anyone if you don't want me to.'

''Cos a promise is a promise, ain't it?'

'Yes.' Gwyneth looked up at the mass of hanging crystal, then with concern at the constrained swell of Maggie's belly. 'So, how are the pains?'

'Oh, they're alright. Got so used to them I don't even notice no more.' She gently smoothed the swell of her skirt. 'I expect she's a bit cramped, like, but at least she ain't goin' to end up in no workhouse – an' that's all that matters.'

'She?'

'I checked last week,' said Maggie with a self-satisfied grin. 'I saw this gypsy do it at a fair. You hold somethin' over your belly, see? This gypsy woman, she used a crystal on the end of a silver chain – only I didn't have no silver chain, so I had to use string, but I don't suppose it matters none. Anyway, you watch to see which way it starts to swing, an' that tells you whether you're goin' to have a boy or a girl, see?'

'I see,' said Gwyneth, indulgently. 'And have you thought about what you're going to do after *she* is born?'

Maggie touched her finger to the side of her nose. 'Oh, I got a plan, I have. So don't you go worryin' about that.' She made to climb the steps, but something caught her eye, and she crossed to the window instead. 'There goes Lucy on her half-day. I overheard her askin' Master Evan if she could take it today – on account of her old dad bein' in trouble again.'

'Trouble? What sort of trouble?'

'Oh, shameful stuff. I can understand her not wantin' no one to know.' She wandered back to the ladder, looking up at the chandelier. 'Tell you what. Now that she's gone, why don't *you* go up an' clean this one – an' *I'll* stand down here an' tell you all about it. Oh, an' while you're up there,' she rummaged in her pocket and pulled out a long, crystal pendant, 'you can put this back.'

*

Standing at the bar of the Britannia, Kate took the two glasses from the counter, thought for a moment, then put down the one containing ginger beer. ''Ere, Wally?' she whispered to the landlord. 'Shove a penn'orth of gin in that one, will yer? I don't think it's quite *medicinal* enough.'

Walter Ringer's expression remained deadpan. 'You know full well I don't have no licence for spirits,' he said, reaching under the counter for the bottle, and pouring a measure into Mary's drink.

'Yes, I know,' she pushed another penny toward him. 'So 'ere's a little present – to 'elp yer save up for one, alright old cock?'

Ringer's, or The Britannia as it was officially known, was only just beginning to empty after the lunchtime rush, and it took Kate some time to squeeze her way through to where Mary was sitting, staring out at the densely packed carts and barrows lining Commercial Street.

'Bleedin' full in 'ere,' chuckled Kate, settling herself on to the bench.

'I can't believe it. I just can't believe it.'

'Oh, this ain't nothin'. I've stood in 'ere when it's been so packed my feet 'aven't touched the floor all bleedin' night.'

'It makes me so bloody angry!'

'Oh, it wasn't so bad. We'd just 'oofed it back from Stratford Market, so they needed the rest.'

Mary turned from the window. 'I'm sorry, what?'

'Oh, nothin',' Kate smiled. ''Ere, get that inside yer, an' then yer can tell me all about it.'

'I just can't believe it, Kate. That … that *cow* Miriam sold the business – and never even told me.' Mary eyed the glass of ginger beer and sighed.

'I can get yer somethin' stronger if yer want, ducklin'?'

Mary picked up the glass. 'No, I'd better not.'

'Well, I'm sure that'll do the job.'

'It tastes different.'

'Does it? 'Spect, old Wally's found some mug to make the stuff cheaper. 'E'd poison 'is own gran'mother if it'd put a farthin' on the profits. Anyway, I reckon yer should lay off this temperance lark – terrible bad for the features it is.' She laughed. 'An' if yer don't believe me, take a look at that vinegary-faced lot from the Sally Army next time they come round with their bloody collectin' tins.'

Mary's jaw tightened angrily. 'I just can't believe she'd do it to me. I know we didn't get on, but …'

'Oh, for Chris' sake, Mary. It was 'er bleedin' stall, wasn't it?'

'No! Well … *yes* … I suppose … but I worked hard – *bloody hard*, and just when I was getting somewhere …' Mary picked up her drink, calming herself with a long, steady draught.

'Well, I do know what yer mean, ducklin'. Hours I'll spend in 'ere – an' just when I'm startin' to get really, really drunk – wallop, I'm tossed out on my ear … *or worse!* Life just ain't fair.'

Mary glared at her. 'Look, if the best you can do is sit there making fun of me, then … well, you can just piss off!' She caught Kate's look of mock outrage, and slowly, grudgingly, she began to chuckle. 'Sod you, Kate. You're making me laugh – and I don't want to laugh. I want to be angry.'

'No yer don't.'

'Yes I bloody well do – and I've got every right to be.'

'No you ain't.' Kate reached out, touching Mary's arm, feeling the angry tension. 'Come on, ducklin'. Don't go gettin' yerself all worked up. I did tell yer it wasn't goin' to be easy. An' anyway,' she brightened, 'it ain't all gloom an' doom. It'll be 'op-pickin' time again before yer know it. You are comin' with us again this year, ain't yer?'

'*Hopping*? What's the good of going *hopping*? It hardly pays anything – and besides, it's months away yet.'

'Yer know, I reckon it's bein' so optimistic as keeps you goin', ducklin',' Kate chuckled, nudging the glass in Mary's direction. 'Come on. Finish yer drink an' we'll 'ave us another one.'

*

Vincent Eastman stood looking out over Villiers Street, listening to the muffled coughs and shuffling feet of the men gathered in the room behind him. Finally he turned, giving them a benign smile. 'I shall come straight to the point, gentlemen. I visited Mrs Bull again this morning, and, while the doctors remain hopeful of an eventual cure, it would seem unlikely that she will be returning to us in the very near future.'

There were some uneasy glances and more shuffling of feet. 'Beggin' your pardon, Mr Eastman, but some of us 'ave been wonderin' if we might not visit 'er ourselves? Just to pay our respects, like?'

'I'm afraid not. It appears callers are not good for someone in her delicate state of mind – even my own brief visits have caused some regrettable consequences.' He gave a resigned shrug. 'I'm sure you understand.'

A tall, coffin-faced man raised his head. 'What about the 'ouse up in Knightsbridge. No one's been watchin' it for weeks.'

'I think we've wasted enough time on that.'

'But Connie wanted …'

'*Mrs Bull*,' said Eastman, 'wants her husband's killer – as do I.' He began walking slowly up and down in front of them, his hands held behind his back. 'It is my opinion that our Miss Black has fled back to France, and that she will be found via the investigations that continue in Paris even as we speak.'

Several of the men looked uneasy.

'Indeed,' continued Eastman. 'I received a telegram this morning from Mr Suggett who believes he has uncovered yet one more strand of that treacherous rot – the tendrils of which may still have root this side of the channel.' He looked purposefully around the room. 'I sincerely hope he is wrong – but we shall just have to wait and see, won't we?'

*

''Ave you tried the other stalls?'

'I went round the whole market this morning.'

'Well, yer must 'ave enough for a train ticket home by now, ain't yer? P'raps yer should go back an' look for a job there.'

'No. I've already told you, Kate. I'm not going back like a whipped dog. I won't.'

'Alright, alright, keep yer 'air on. Look, why don't yer let me get yer a nice glass of beer? Much more mellowin', beer is.'

Mary stared despondently into her nearly empty glass. 'Oh, why not?'

'That's the spirit!' Kate giggled, 'Or rather – *it ain't.*' She made to get up, but the bar-room had emptied a little more, and her eye fell upon a short, plump, middle-aged woman struggling to quell the tremors in her hands as she lifted a small glass of rum. 'You alright, Annie, my love?'

'I will be.' The haggard looking woman finally managed to lift the glass to her lips and drink down the dark, oily liquid. 'Just had another of my turns.'

Kate gave her a sympathetic smile. 'You're gettin' to be a regular music 'all lately. Maybe yer should take yerself down to the infirmary?'

'I'll be alright in a bit.' Annie Chapman let the rum warm her chest, then straightened a little, her thick features trembling into a smile.

*

A soft rain had begun to fall, drawing a veil about the houses and misting the windows of the lamp-lit drawing-room.

At the piano sat Mme Bennaire, eyes half closed, lips curved into a sensuous smile, while her hands moved effortlessly, seducing the ivory keys into merry laughter. Then she stopped, looking across the deserted room to the valise that stood just inside the door. 'Well, mes chéries,' she said sadly, addressing the empty chairs, the French affectation dropping away to reveal a hint of a Dublin brogue. 'Nothing lasts forever. But wasn't it damn fine while it did?'

Chapter Forty-Five

It was after midnight when Mary turned the corner into Pennington Street. The walk home had been cold and lonely after the warmth and good humour of Ringer's, and as her sobriety returned so did her seething anger. She kicked angrily at a sheet of newspaper that swirled about her feet. '*Bloody Miriam!*'

There were few street lamps in this part of London, and what little light they gave created wells of darkness in the spaces between. It was from out of one of these that the towering figure of a man emerged and came toward her.

'Mary?'

Mary stopped dead in her tracks, her hand to her chest. 'Joseph? Christ, you frightened the life out of me. What are you doing here?'

'Been waiting for you.' He took a few more tentative steps and the light fell upon the face of a young man, his strong, handsome features at odds with the wide-set childlike eyes. 'I know what she did – my mum – and I come to make it better, Mary.'

'How long have you been waiting here?'

'Don't know.'

She felt his coat. 'You're soaked through.'

'It rained,' he said simply.

'But that was hours ago. Oh, Joseph, does Miriam know where you are?'

He looked at her with infantile guile. 'She don't know everything I do. I don't tell her – not always.'

'You'd better go home. You'll get into trouble.'

'Don't want to. Don't want to live with her no more.' He drew himself up, standing head and shoulders above her. 'I want to live with you, Mary. I can look after you. Look.' He fumbled in his pockets and brought out two meagre handfuls of copper coins. 'See? I got money.'

'Joseph, you *can't* come and live with me.'

'Why not? You like me, don't you?'

'Of course I do.'

'Well then? That's what people do when they like each other – they live together – in the same house.' His eyes clouded with doubt. 'Don't they?'

Mary sighed. '*Sometimes.*' She reached up, fastening the top three buttons of his coat. 'Look, you'd better get off home. Your mam will be worried, and you'll catch your death if you don't get out of these wet things.'

'I'm strong, I am.'

'I know.'

He made to speak, but instead pushed his hands deep into his pockets and reluctantly, almost petulantly, started away. He'd taken just a few steps when he turned back. 'I'll come and see you again, won't I?'

'I should like that.'

'Well …' He thought for a moment. 'Then I *will*,' he said resolutely, his mouth widening into a huge, boyish grin. 'And I *will* get it all back for you, Mary – promise.'

A chill wind swept along the street, and Mary shivered, swaying slightly. 'Get what, my love?'

But the child in a man's body was already moving away.

Mary watched him disappear. Poor Joseph, she thought – for all his height and strength she could imagine the trouble in store for him when he got home to Miriam. She clenched her teeth. *Bloody Miriam.*

She was still muttering to herself, standing on the step, fumbling for her key, when the door flew open to reveal Hilda standing squarely in the doorway.

'Oh, hello, Hilda.' Mary straightened, feeling uncomfortable under the woman's cold scrutiny. 'You're up late.'

'I could say the same for you.'

'I met an old friend.' She made to enter, but Hilda remained in the way. 'You're not coming in.'

'What are you talking about? I live here.'

'Not anymore. I told you when you first came – this is a temperance house, and I'll not have you bringing the devil's stink into it.' She leaned forward, sniffing, her face screwing into agonies of disgust. 'You reek of it. And it's not the first time, is it? I should have listened to Miriam long ago.'

'Miriam?' Blood pounded at Mary's temples. '*Miriam?*' She tried to push past into the passageway, but the normally genial Hilda had the fire of righteousness burning in her veins, and would not yield.

'Let me in, Hilda. It's my room. I've paid for it!'

'Get out!'

'*You* get out – out of my *fucking* way!'

The word took on an almost tangible presence, striking Hilda like a blow and rebounding on Mary so that they both recoiled in surprise.

Hilda recovered first, her lips drawing back into a contemptuous sneer. 'Oh, now we see just what sort you are.' She slowly withdrew into the house. 'You can collect your things tomorrow morning – and you'd better come early or they'll be on the doorstep.'

*

'I want to see Kate Conway.'

'We're full up.'

'I just need to see her.'

'See 'er tomorrer.'

'That's too late.'

'Well, I can't go wakin' folks up in the middle of the night. T'ain't right.'

'But it's urgent. Tell her it's Mary Kelly.'

'You tell 'er – *tomorrer*.'

Mary glared at the hard-eyed lodging house deputy, then she forced a smile. 'It's Freddie, isn't it?'

'That's my name.'

'Look, Freddie, I have to talk to Kate. I've been locked out of my room, and I've got no money and nowhere to stay.'

'Well, it costs fourpence a night for a bed 'ere.'

'I can get it for you in the morning.'

'Huh, 'eard that one before. No fourpence – no bed.'

'Then get Kate. She'll lend it to me.'

He laughed. 'Kate Conway? Ain't never known 'er to 'ave more than the price of 'er own bed in all the years she's lived 'ere.'

It was beginning to rain again, and Mary looked miserably up at the sky. 'Just ask her – *please*.'

'Ain't no point,' he said, retreating inside.

'Why not?' She flew at him, her hands scrabbling desperately at the door to stop it closing. 'You miserable sod. Why won't you just do it?'

Enraged, the deputy jerked the door open again, and coming out on to the step, shoved her hard in the chest, sending her sprawling in the gutter. ''Cos we're *full up*,' he hissed. 'Now bugger off!'

*

It was to be a night of cold charity and even colder realisation. I had twenty pounds in the bank, but in the early hours of that April morning it meant nothing. It was out of reach – as distant as the stars and as useless as dreams. I was tired, wet and homeless, and without a single penny in my pocket – the exact price of admission to the harsh and often vicious world of the destitute.

*

By two o'clock in the morning the rain was lashing down, hitting the deserted streets and leaping up again, turning the road into a hissing, boiling lake. Water cascaded from the portico above Mary's head, and she huddled closer to the wall, her face wet against the smooth stone. She was so tired that, despite the misery of it all, her eyelids were beginning to flicker when a policeman appeared in the distance, head lowered, his cape drawn tightly about him.

Through half-closed eyes she watched his approach. He was walking steadily, braced against the storm, but every few yards he'd pause, and each time he paused it seemed that fragments of the grey, lifeless buildings would break free, to scatter before the wind. He came closer, and suddenly the street which had seemed so deserted came alive with huddled figures that scurried from doorways and gateways, like pathetic ragged spectres, conjured forth by this uniformed magician.

'Come on now, get out of there!'

'But I'm not doing anything.'

'Don't you give me any of your lip.' Taking hold of Mary's arm, he dragged her from the doorway into the rain. 'If I've got to walk about in this, so can you – and if I catch you sleeping round here again, I'll run you in. Got it?'

'I wasn't sleeping!' she screamed through the torrent.

'Not now you're not.'

She wanted to cry. 'Where can I go? I haven't got any money, and …'

'That's your problem.' He turned away. 'Me? I'm off for a nice cup of tea – but I'll be back soon, so don't say you haven't been warned.'

I had only been taking shelter, and such senseless cruelty and lack of compassion was beyond my understanding – but the night was still young.

'Fuck off!' The woman's sharp, crudely chiselled features glowered from the dark recess. It was a deep recess, yet she and her clutch of stony-faced children stood barely out of the rain, and Mary sensed rather than saw the steaming mass crammed in the shadows behind them. The stink from the hole was abominable, but it was shelter, and Mary tried to edge her way in.

'I said, fuck off,' growled the woman. 'There's no fucking room.'

In wretched silence, Mary tried again, but a tiny hand clutched at her skirt, and she looked down into the eyes of the youngest child. Then the little girl gave a furious push, kicking and hitting with all her might. 'There's no fucking room!' she screamed in her small, high voice.

I moved on, no longer seeking refuge, for by now I was wet through, and to stop was to feel the sodden clothes, cold against my skin, to know the wretchedness and utter despondency of having nowhere to go, no one to whom I could turn.

I walked, mindlessly, no longer daring to think, for to think was to feel and to care – and I could no longer afford the luxury of such weaknesses. I needed to be strong – in the way that Griffiths had tried to make me strong – and so I walked, becoming increasingly hardened to the sights and to the sounds – and to the rain that fell from the heavens in performance of this savage and most unholy baptism.

The old man was half squatting, his back against the wall and his soaked trousers around his ankles. He was shitting in a doorway, his reddened face screwed into an expression of carnal gratification. 'Let 'em move that on!' he called drunkenly as Mary passed by.

Near Aldgate pump I passed two women fighting like tigresses over a loaf of sodden bread. I saw wretched couples mating in foul alleys, making grotesque caricatures of love as they snatched their few minutes' distraction from the misery of the night – and most terrible of all, by St Botolph's church, I saw a man.

He was sitting huddled against a wall. A father, or perhaps a brother – I had no way of knowing. But clutched in his arms lay a small child, shielded, half hidden beneath his threadbare coat so that only one limp, unnaturally white arm hung free.

Had she been the victim of some terrible accident or ghastly murder, people would have flocked to the site. They would have wept and beaten their breasts over the tragedy of this little girl. They would have shouted, demanding action, incensed by the outrage of her death. But she had merely died of the commonplace – of cold and of hunger – and those same people passed by with barely a thought – and so, to my utmost shame, did I.

*

'I love this fucking weather.' Michael Kidney pressed his face to the window, watching a group of scarecrow women battle their way up the road in desperate search of a dry corner. 'That's what I call it – *fucking weather.*' He laughed, '*Free* fucking weather. Any one of them drabs'll do it on a night like this – just for half an hour in the dry.'

Behind him, seated at the table, Harry Farrel, head of the Hoxton High Rips, shuffled the pack of cards. 'You want to fuck – go an' fuck.'

'Nah, I'll play.'

Farrel began to deal.

'Know what I done once?' grinned Kidney, taking his seat and looking about at the half a dozen other players.

'It didn't involve shuttin' that big flappin' mouth of yours, did it?' asked

Sadie Farrel, scooping up her cards.

Harry chuckled, and Kidney followed suit, though reluctantly. 'Nah, it was a night like this, it was. Pissing down – only freezing cold as well. Real brass monkey weather.' He looked about, but no one laughed, so he carried on, 'Anyway, I looks out my window an' sees this here family huddled under this little lean-to what was right opposite. Had these bleeding kids, didn't they – an' not a pair of shoes between 'em – an' soaking fucking wet the lot of 'em. My guess was they weren't going to last the night – not in that cold. But the wife, well she's a bit of a looker.' He shrugged. 'Well, in a quiet sort of way.'

'Bit like your Lizzie, eh?' suggested Sadie.

Harry filled his wife's glass, then leaned back, eyeing Kidney. 'I don't know what yer see in 'er, Mickey – fuckin' mouthy cow.'

'I only run her – I don't fuck her.'

'I 'ear it's 'er what's been fuckin' you just lately,' chuckled the man to Sadie's right.

'What the fuck's that supposed to mean?' demanded Kidney.

'Easy,' said Harry. 'We're all friends 'ere.' He studied his cards, then put them down. 'So what about this poxy family, then?'

Kidney chewed sullenly at his lip. 'Well,' he said, warming to his subject once more. 'I goes out to 'em, don't I – an' I says as how I'll let 'em come into the house for the night if I can fuck the wife. Well, the husband, he goes barmy, but I ain't too worried about him because he's already knocking on death's door with consumption or something. Still, he rants an' raves a bit, but what with the kids crying an' whimpering, an' the husband coughing his guts up, the wife finally says she will.'

'Must have fancied yer right from the start,' smiled Sadie.

'Yeah, I suppose. Anyway – an' here's the bit that'll make you laugh. I tells her she can come in, but that I ain't going to fuck her with her husband an' kids watching – so they'll have to stay where they are until we're done.' He rubbed his hands together, chuckling. 'So we gets upstairs an' she wants to get it over with quick, like – but I ain't having none of that. She's soaking fucking wet for a start. So I makes her take her clothes off, every fucking stitch, then I pulls her over to the window an' I gives it to her – with her fucking arse pressed up against the glass an' me looking over her shoulder at the silly buggers standing down there in the rain, watching us.'

'You're a cunt,' said Harry, without malice.

Sadie laughed. 'An' did yer let 'em in afterwards?'

He looked about, grinning. 'What do you think?'

Further down the table one of the players folded his cards and stood up.

'What's this, Joe? You goin'?' asked Harry in mild surprise.

'Going? Yes, I b-believe I've had enough.'

Harry shrugged, casually rifling through the slips of paper that lay on the table in front of him. 'Bad time for yer to be callin' it a night, my old son. Still, suit yerself.' He raised an eyebrow. 'Yer *will* be settlin' up soon, I 'ope?'

It was still dark when Joe Barnett left by the side door and made his way in short, erratic sprints along Commercial Street.

Up and down the road his few fellow travellers were either huddled beneath umbrellas, or like him, running from doorway to doorway, stopping only long enough to catch their breath before making the next frantic dash.

He had no need to hurry – Billingsgate market would not open for another hour, but the conversation over the card table had left him with a bitter taste in his mouth and an empty feeling in his stomach that he hoped a breakfast of fried eggs and bacon might remedy.

The wind began to pick up, roaring between the buildings. Women clutched at their skirts and men at their jackets as they bolted for cover, while all around, the ground seethed beneath the scourging rain.

'Jesus!' Joe pressed himself into the lee of a shop doorway. Now the only movement along the road was that of a horse-drawn vehicle that passed in ghostly silence, all sound of its progress drowned by the raging of the storm. He wiped a hand across his face, looking up at the sky. 'Jesus!' he said again.

An unaccompanied umbrella sailed by, jolting and skidding along the road, and as he followed its passage, his eye was led to the vague, wraith-like figure walking slowly and steadily up the street. The woman was making no effort to get out of the rain, nor, he realised as she drew nearer, even acknowledging it. He guessed she was drunk, and he would have been on his way, but a sudden flash of lightning drove him deeper into the doorway.

The woman came closer and was within a few yards of him when he recognised her. 'Excuse m-me,' he yelled against the howling of the wind.

She stopped and looked at him.

'Excuse m-me, b-but aren't you the young lady from the m-market? We spoke once. In the coffee shop it was.'

Bracing herself against the full force of the storm, her hair plastered to her head and the rain streaming from her waterlogged clothes, Mary nodded. 'Yes, I remember.'

'Remember? Oh … Oh, yes … *Good.*' He groped for something to say, his face growing hot despite the weather. 'Look, I'm sorry to have b-bothered you … it's just that …' he looked apprehensively at the sky, then back at Mary, '… it's *raining.*'

'I know.'

In an agony of embarrassment, he squeezed himself further into the corner. 'I just m-meant that you m-might like to stand in here?'

'I have to keep walking. If I don't, I'll freeze.'

She turned away, but he darted after her, pulling his coat up over his head. 'Well ... that is ... I m-mean ... have you got a long way to go?'

Mary looked up at the church clock. 'About five more hours,' she said.

The sparsely furnished room that Joe Barnett called home lay at the back of a three-storey house in Brick Lane. It was small, but neat: comfortable enough for a bachelor whose domestic arrangements were catered for by the nearby coffee shops and cheap eating houses.

'It's no hotel, b-but here we are,' said Joe, emphasising his H's in a way that suggested concentrated effort. 'B-but then I'm not one for b-being at home a great deal.'

Mary looked about her without really noticing. 'It's nice.'

'Nice? Well, it does m-me. Here, let m-me take your coat.' Water pooled about the hem of her skirt and he cast about. 'I wonder ... if you wouldn't m-mind?' A pile of newspapers lay by the hearth, and he seized upon them, laying them on the floor by her feet.

Mary stepped on to them.

'I'll get us a good b-blaze going,' he said quickly. 'Fortunately I've just taken a fresh delivery of Old King.' He gave a little laugh, glancing at her expectantly, but seeing she was starting to shiver he abandoned the joke and set about laying the fire.

'There, that'll quickly have you dried out,' he said as soon as the paper and kindling were sending up long tongues of flame. 'Now we'd b-best get you out of those wet clothes.' He stopped in the act of adding a piece of coal to the small pyre, and leaped to his feet. 'Oh. Oh, I didn't m-mean ... that is, you m-mustn't think ...' But Mary was staring into the flames, seemingly unaware even of his presence, and his eyes fell to the swell of her bodice and the sweep of her waist, the wet clothes clinging to them.

I made her take her clothes off. Every fucking stitch.

Unbidden, the words returned to him, making him deeply ashamed: ashamed of his thoughts, but more immediately, of the rising treachery of his own flesh. He hurried across the room, half turning away as he pulled on his coat. 'I m-meant in a m-moment, of course – once I've left the room.' He glanced nervously over his shoulder. 'I shan't be returning till quite late this afternoon, so there's no need for concern about ... well, about *anything*.' His eyes went to the neatly made bed. 'Perhaps, when you've ...' He swallowed dryly, 'Well, that's to say, while your clothes are drying – if you should want to sleep?'

Mary slowly turned her head to look at him. 'I *would* like to. Thank you.'

'Thank you? Oh …' He gave a bashful smile. 'Oh, that's alright. Think nothing of it.' There was another awkward silence. 'Well, you'll b-be wanting a towel I expect …' He gestured toward the wash-stand, but Mary's fingers were already feeling for the buttons at her neck and he quickly averted his gaze. 'Yes, yes, well, I'd b-better b-be off. M-mustn't b-be late for work – it isn't good for the *soul*, as it were.' Again there was no response, and keeping his face turned from her he gave a self-deprecating laugh. '*Sole*? I work at the fish m-market, you see? Yes, well … anyway,' Joe edged his way through the partially opened door. 'Time and tide, and all that, eh?'

*

I awoke just before midday. My clothes were still wet, but I didn't care. The rain had finally ceased, dry clothing and my few other belongings were waiting for me at my old lodgings – and most important of all, twenty pounds was mine for the asking.

At Pennington Street, Hilda met me with hard, unforgiving eyes and a sharp, if restrained, tongue – but at least she'd not carried out her threat to put my things on the doorstep. In the spirit of true Christian charity, she even allowed me inside long enough to change my dress.

From there I went directly to the bank, where my balance, duly checked and approvingly noted, finally earned me the right to the civility of strangers.

I already had in my pocket the eight shillings I'd kept in my room, and I'd asked to withdraw just two pounds – enough for what I considered were my immediate needs – but as I held it in my hand it suddenly seemed a fortune, a huge amount that, once spent, might never be regained. So I re-deposited it.

Twenty pounds wasn't enough to take me back to Wales, but it was more than a start, and I was going to be damned if I'd let it all just trickle away.

Chapter Forty-Six

Wakened by the strange, animal-like sounds, Gwyneth opened her eyes and looked across to where Maggie lay hidden by darkness. 'Maggie?' There was no answer, but the strange snuffling and groaning continued. 'Maggie, what is it? Are you alright?' She pushed back the bedclothes and reached for the matches, lighting the stub of candle. 'Maggie? Oh, my God!'

Maggie lay on her back, her legs drawn up, knees wide, her hands clawed into the sodden bed sheet.

'The baby?' Gwyneth came to kneel by her, raising the candle to reveal Maggie's agonised face, a wad of cloth clenched between her teeth, permitting nothing more than muted primal noises. 'How long have you been like this?' She reached out with a trembling hand, but a great spasm of pain gripped the girl, making her arch from the bed, and Gwyneth leaped to her feet, snatching up her dress and pulling it on. 'Don't worry, Maggie …'

With a stifled groan, Maggie sank back on to the bed as the wave passed.

'… I'm going to fetch the doctor.'

Maggie spat out the wadding. 'No!'

'I must.'

'Don't! You'll ruin everything! It'll come soon, I know it will.' A fresh contraction began to build and Maggie braced herself, frantically stuffing the wadding back in her mouth, clamping her jaws on it as the pain ripped through her.

The candlelight lent the scene a nightmarish quality, and Gwyneth watched, horrified – her fingers, numb with terror, fumbling uselessly at the fastenings of her dress, until finally the spasm passed and Maggie lay panting for breath.

'Oh, Gwyn,' Maggie sobbed, taking the cloth from between her teeth. 'It *won't* bloody come. I've tried an' tried all night, but it won't come out. *You help me, Gwyn … please.*'

'I can't. I don't know what to do. Maggie – I'm *so* sorry – but I *have* to fetch the doctor.'

'No! You promised me … *you bloody well promised.*'

Another contraction seized Maggie, and Gwyneth wrung her hands, watching, helpless, as the small body arched in torment – then she was out of the door and racing down the stairs.

⋆

'Cooley's in Thrawl Street?' said Joe Barnett in surprise. 'B-but that's just a common lodging house. Someone like you shouldn't b-be in a place like that.'

Mary shrugged. 'Why not? It's cheap. When I find another job, then I'll look for somewhere better.'

'Somewhere b-better – yes, b-but …' Joe took a deep breath. 'Look, why don't …?' He stopped, feeling the blood rush to his face, then losing his nerve he snatched up his glass. 'That is … why don't we have another drink? Same again is it?'

'It's kind of you, but I should be going – but I'm glad I bumped into you again. I never really said thank you for your help.'

'Help? All I did was throw a few handfuls of Old King on the fire.'

Mary smiled. 'Coal,' she said.

'You've got it!' he beamed. 'I always call it that. Don't know why, really. Old King Cole was a m-merry old soul, eh?' There was an awkward silence, and seeing Mary making to rise he said quickly. 'Oh, b-by the way, I was just wondering … that is, whether you ever attend the lectures over at the Working Lads Institute? I go every week … well, m-mostly every week. Sometimes the subject isn't quite as interesting as at other times, b-but I generally find it … well … *interesting.*'

'No, I've never been.'

'I only ask b-because I couldn't help noticing your accent – and it put me in m-mind of a chap who gave an illustrated talk on the history of Caernarvon Castle … or was it Carmarthen?' He stared at the ceiling in thought. 'It'll come to m-me in a m-minute.'

'It was probably Caernarvon. That's the famous one.'

'Famous one? Is it? Yes, yes, now you m-mention it, I'm sure it was Caernarvon. Have you b-been there?'

'No.'

'I should like to. I have hopes of travelling one day – I've m-made a list of places.' Feeling in his pocket he took out a carefully folded sheet. 'Here we are, look, right at the top of the list – Caernarvon Castle. Then there's the Great Pyramid – that's in Egypt. The B-Brunel Suspension B-Bridge.

The B-Battlefield of ...' He looked up excitedly to find Mary staring out through the rain-spotted window. '... of Waterloo,' he finished quietly, his voice trailing away as he re-folded the paper. 'There ... there are a lot of other places, too, b-but ...'

Mary turned back. 'I'm sorry, what did you say?'

'Say? Oh, nothing important.' He followed her gaze back to the window as more rain spattered the glass. 'I'm sorry, I shouldn't be keeping you.'

'No, no, it's alright. You were saying something about Caernarvon?'

'Caernarvon?' he said, brightening a little, the paper trembling between his fingers. 'Well ... well if you're sure?' He stood up. 'B-But, here. Let m-me get you another drink first, eh?'

Feeling just a little light headed, Mary stared at him. 'A leaning tower?'

'Yes, quite a m-miracle it stays up, so this chap said. Everyone talks about the one in Italy, b-but ...'

'That isn't Caernarvon – it's *Caerphilly.*'

'Caerphilly?' Joe pondered the idea. 'Well, you m-might b-be right.'

'I *am* right. I come from there.' She picked up her glass, toying with it. 'And one day, I shall go back.'

'Go b-back?' Nervously, he cleared his throat. 'Have you ... have you got someone b-back there? A husband?'

'Not any more.' She sighed, leaning back and looking sadly into her drink.

'Family then?'

Mary began to shake her head, but then the warm, mellowing effect of the drink washed over her, and she smiled wistfully. 'Yes. Yes, I have. I could tell you about them if you'd like?'

'Huw's the eldest and the nicest ... and very strong, too! He never let any-one pick on us. And lastly there was Glyn, we all used to spoil him because he was so small. Father always said he'd turn out a little horror, but we just couldn't help it.'

'I can see why you'd want to go b-back,' said Joe. He too was feeling mellow, and his eyes were just a little moist as he looked at her.

'Oh, they aren't all there now.' Mary put her head back, resting it against the wall. 'We've mostly gone our different ways. Henry ...' she furrowed her brow. 'Did I say Henry? I meant Huw. My lovely, lovely Huw. He's gone for a soldier, writes to me from all over the world, he does.'

'And what about your sister?'

'Oh, you'd like her. She was an actress, up in the West End. Though more recently,' Mary started to giggle, 'she's been treading the boards at the Middlesex Street Theatre.'

'The M-Middlesex Street Theatre? Where's that, then? I don't b-believe

I've ever heard of it.'

'Gone,' said Mary, 'All gone – just like our drinks.' She rose unsteadily to her feet. 'My round, I think.'

Joe stood up. 'No, please. I'll get them.'

'Can't let you pay all night.'

'I don't m-mind. Please, allow m-me.'

With a shrug, Mary dropped back on to her chair.

'Do you *really* want another drink?' murmured Joe. 'I think we've b-both had enough, don't you?'

Mary shook her head. 'Got to have a last one to help you sleep. My friend Kate says, *a quick 'un 'fore they close the doors, keeps away the bleedin' snores.*'

'Snores?'

'The woman in the bed next to mine – and the one next to that! Snore like pigs they do, see?' She began to laugh drunkenly. 'Though I don't know how much you've got to drink before you stop noticing the smell of feet and farts.' She caught his horrified look, and embarrassment coloured her cheeks. 'Oh, I'm sorry. I didn't mean to …'

'It's alright.' Joe looked nervously about the bar-room. 'Look, I don't like the thought of you sleeping there, with all those …' He bit his lip, ashamed of his lack of charity, then cleared his throat once again. 'Why … that is … why don't you come and stay with m-me?'

*

The sun had risen and long since set when Evan straightened, drawing a hand across his unshaven face. 'It isn't good,' he said quietly.

Kneeling by the bed, Gwyneth continued to cradle Maggie's head, her fingers moving agitatedly as she brushed the damp hair from the girl's forehead. 'But it will be alright?' There was no answer, and she watched him anxiously as he went to the door, opening it a little and talking in a low murmur to Lucy who was waiting outside.

'It *will* be alright?' persisted Gwyneth.

Evan pushed the door closed, leaning back against it, suddenly very tired. 'No, I'm afraid it won't.'

On the bed, Maggie groaned, turning toward the sound of the voice, looking through lids heavy with sedation. 'Why … why won't she come?'

Gwyneth mopped the beads of perspiration from Maggie's pallid face. With four lamps burning, the confines of the attic had become stifling, yet Maggie's skin was clammy to the touch. 'Oh, Maggie …' Gwyneth looked up at Evan, pleading. 'She can't stand anymore of this. It's been over twenty-two hours. There must be something more you can do?'

He did not meet her eyes. 'There is,' he said, the words coming only reluctantly, 'but *she* has to make the decision.'

Another great spasm of pain gripped Maggie, and she writhed. 'Help me! Oh, please, God, help me!'

'You have to give her more morphine!' demanded Gwyneth, her lips trembling.

'Not yet.' Evan went down on one knee by the side of the bed. 'Listen, Maggie,' he said as the screams died away and she sank back into a feverish restlessness. 'The baby's not going to come – not without help.'

Maggie shook her head in confusion, her tongue darting out to wet her dry lips.

'You *must* try to understand what I'm saying to you.'

She began to whimper as the build up to the next contraction began, then slowly and with what seemed a great effort, she nodded.

'If I operate now, the baby will be alright. I'm certain I can save your baby, Maggie – but …' he reached for her hand, squeezing it, 'I can't save you both.'

Gwyneth stared at him in horror.

'Listen to me, Maggie,' he said, keeping his eyes fixed firmly on her. 'We *can* wait, but the baby will most certainly die.' He paused, swallowing hard. 'And I can't offer you any guarantee that you …' He left the sentence unfinished. 'You must tell me what you want me to do.'

With tears coursing down her cheeks, Gwyneth rounded on him. 'You can't ask her to make that choice.'

'She *has* to. She's the only one who can.'

'No.'

He looked into Gwyneth's eyes. 'Then who will? You?' For a moment he recognised the small, bright flame of hatred behind the glassy stare – until a fresh flood of tears welled up, drowning it. He turned back. 'You *must* decide now, Maggie.'

Maggie's breath was coming very fast, her hands clenching and un-clenching about the small black bible she held.

'Maggie?' he tried again.

She pressed her head back into the pillow, lifting her chin, her lips parting in readiness, her words timed to fall between the agonising waves. 'I … I'll wait.'

Gwyneth held her close. 'Oh, Maggie …'

'I won't leave her, Gwyn.' Maggie began to pant, sucking in air, deeply and noisily. 'I won't *never* leave her … *not never!*' Another contraction started to build, and she whimpered. 'An' if I can't be here to keep her safe … an' out of *that* place …' Great sobs began to vie with the spasms wrack-ing her body. '… then … then she'll just have to come with me.'

Evan threw Gwyneth a desperate glance. 'What's she talking about? What place?'

'The workhouse. She was brought up in the workhouse.'

378

The light of understanding showed in Evan's eyes. 'Maggie, you have to let me save the child.'

'No!'

'You can't let her die.'

'Better she should die, than …' Maggie pressed back into the pillow, the sinews of her neck like cords.

'I promise you, she won't go to the workhouse.'

'No, she won't! I'll see to that!' The spasm passed, and she lay quivering, drained of energy, then she began to cry. 'Oh God, please, give me somethin'. I can't take anymore of this. Gwyn, *please*, make him give me somethin'.'

Gwyneth looked pleadingly at him, her hair wild, her eyes red-rimmed, watching as he took the bottle from his bag and drew a small amount into the syringe.

'This will ease the pain,' he said, looking past the shiny needle to where the pathetic bundle that was Maggie lay. Then his eyes went back to the syringe, and with shaking hands he drew in a little more, then more still, until the cylinder was quite full.

From inside their dark rimmed sockets, Maggie's once bright little eyes watched the process, and she began to cry again, this time not with pain, but with a great, overwhelming sorrow.

'Maggie?' He touched her bare arm, fingers stroking over the vein. 'Are you sure? Absolutely sure?'

She nodded dumbly, gritting her teeth and turning her face to the wall.

Evan steeled himself, the needle poised above her arm, then he put down the syringe and took her hands, placing them palms down on her swollen belly. 'Feel her, Maggie. Feel her. She's alive in there. She doesn't have to die. She has a chance. You can still give her life.'

'No!' She started to pant again as the cycle of pain began to build once more, but her hands remained on her belly, lovingly feeling for the movements, even as the next contraction began to build.

'The child won't go to the workhouse.' Evan rested his hands on hers. 'I promise you.'

With the greatest effort she turned to look at him.

'You can't let your baby die, Maggie.'

In desperation she sought Gwyneth's face. 'Gwyn?' she sobbed, 'Oh, God, Gwyn, what do I do?'

Gwyneth held her tightly, shaking her head, unable to speak.

'You always know …' Maggie's lips drew back in a tortured grimace as she fought the rising agony. 'You … you always know what's best … Tell me.'

'I don't know. *I don't know*. Oh, Maggie, I don't want to lose you.' Frantic with grief, Gwyneth lifted her eyes to the square of midnight blue that filled the small attic window, fighting back the tears.

'Tell me, Gwyn. Tell me what to do.'

Gwyneth looked to Evan, seeing the inevitability etched on his face, then down to Maggie. 'Let him save her,' she said, barely able to say the words. 'You have to save your baby.'

The contraction started to bite, but Maggie reached for Evan's arm, seizing it with a vice-like grip. 'Swear it to me.'

'I promise you …'

'No! Swear it. Swear it on this.' She thrust the bible into his hand. 'Swear it on this book …' Another wave of pain lifted her from the bed, and she screamed.

'Give her the morphine,' Gwyneth begged, but Maggie violently shook her head. 'Not till I hear him swear.'

The pain subsided, and Maggie lifted her head, looking into Evan's eyes with a fierce determination. 'Swear to me that you'll never, *ever* let her go to *that place*.'

Evan closed his hand over hers. 'I swear it,' he said.

*

'I daresay a lot of people would look at me and think to themselves, *why, he's just a fish porter, he can't know very m-much about the world* – b-but I don't see any reason why ordinary people can't try to b-better themselves, do you? I *like* to learn about different places and things – even if I haven't been there or seen them.'

Lying in the bed, screened by the blanket Joe had rigged across one end of the room, Mary watched his shadow through increasingly heavy lids as he undressed by the light of the single candle.

'You see, I often liken it to a circus. That probably sounds a b-bit silly to you, b-but it isn't really. I m-mean, in a circus you have the clowns and such at the b-bottom end of the scale – and at the other end you have the b-brave-hearted types, lion-tamers – and those that do rope walking and flying acts – m-making up the aristocracy. Then, in the m-middle there are the dancers and jugglers, and those chaps who walk around on large b-balls.' He thought for a moment. 'I would say knife throwers, b-but I should imagine you'd need pretty steady nerves to do that – even allowing that the knife isn't going to hit you if you get it wrong.' He gave a little laugh. 'No, I'd say you'd need to b-be a *cut above the rest* to b-be a knife thrower, eh?'

Standing in his shirt tails he considered undressing further, but in the small room the hanging blanket felt very close and it did not seem quite the right thing to do.

'Anyway,' he said, getting down on the floor and making a pillow of his folded trousers. 'At the centre of it all you've got the ringmaster. Now he's the M-Master of Ceremonies – so you'd likely say he's the m-most important m-man there – yet he can't tame lions or rope-walk, he can't juggle, and he probably wouldn't even m-make a very good clown. Do you see what I m-mean, M-Mary?' It was the first time he'd used her name, and it caused him to pause. 'You don't m-mind m-me calling you that, do you?'

On the far side of the blanket all was still but for the gentle sound of her breathing, and he stayed for a long time, propped up on one elbow, listening. Then finally he blew out the candle, covered himself with his overcoat, and lay down. 'This is nice,' he said into the darkness. 'This is very, *very* nice.'

Chapter Forty-Seven

'A pot of tea, please.'

The waitress wrote on her pad. 'Yes, m'um. Anything else, m'um?'

Gwyneth looked sadly at the pastry trolley with its selection of Maggie's favourite cream cakes. 'No, thank you. Just the tea.'

'Very good, m'um.'

Only when the waitress had gone did Gwyneth remove her black shawl, then reach for her handkerchief, dabbing eyes and wiping her nose.

Maggie's funeral had been like Maggie herself – small and insignificant, and attended only by those who had surrounded her in life: Evan and Lucy, Cook, as complaining and bad tempered as always, and Gwyneth herself, the four of them lost in the emptiness of the damp smelling church as they listened to the whey-faced old parson disinterestedly eulogising the girl he had never known.

In the church, and later at the side of the grave, Gwyneth hadn't shed a tear – but here, in the place they'd visited together so many times, she felt Maggie's presence, could see her sitting in the chair opposite, eyes bright with the excitement of cakes and gossip and not knowing which was best, and Gwyneth found herself sobbing.

'Are you alright, m'um?' asked the waitress, returning, looking at her with concern.

'Yes,' Gwyneth dabbed again at her eyes, trying to smile reassuringly. 'Yes, thank you.'

'Well, I'll bring you your tea right away, m'um.'

Alone once more, Gwyneth gave her cheeks a final wipe, put away her handkerchief, then took a deep, sighing breath before taking the small black book from her pocket. The dog-eared bible had been Maggie's only possession, and Gwyneth traced her fingers over the sparsely tooled leatherwork. Inside on the fly-leaf a pasted label proclaimed in an overly ornate script: Wolverhampton and District Workhouse. Given on behalf of the Board of Guardians to:–. Underneath, written in a childish scrawl, was the name Margaret Katherine Mullins, and below that, in a very different hand: *God makes no river so weary that it does not wind somewhere safely to sea.*

Gwyneth felt the tears begin to fall again. 'Oh, Maggie,' she murmured.

*

Evan was still in his mourning clothes, gazing out of the drawing-room window as Gwyneth entered, closing the door quietly behind her. He half turned, giving her a sympathetic smile. 'She'll be missed.'

Gwyneth made no response, she had heard enough empty platitudes. 'I should like to give a month's notice,' she said.

He looked at her in surprise, trying to see past the carefully maintained composure. 'You've found another position?'

'Not yet.'

'Then may I ask why?'

'There's nothing here for me now, and ...' she straightened her shoulders, 'and what I have come to ask cannot be asked by a servant.'

'We have been candid with each other in the past.' He gave a tentative smile and took a step toward her, but seeing her stiffen he halted. 'You've never stopped hating me, have you, Gwyneth?'

'It hasn't been my place to like or to hate.'

'*Please*, Gwyneth. Can't you find at least *some* forgiveness?' He read the answer in her eyes, and sighed. 'But then, why should you?' A photograph of Owen stood on a table, and he lingered over it. 'I ask forgiveness – yet I give none.'

Gwyneth noticed the wearied slope of his shoulders, but it did nothing to soften her resolve. 'I came to ask if you intend to honour your promise.'

He glanced at her. 'My promise?'

'To Maggie.'

Genuinely hurt, he said, 'You think I *wouldn't*?'

'I don't know. That's why I have to ask.'

He searched for the smallest flaw in her mask, but finding none he turned back to stare out into the early evening light. 'You needn't worry. I shall find a suitable family for the child, and make provision for her.' He gave Gwyneth the briefest look. 'I *will* ensure she has a good home.'

'But will you ensure she is loved?'

'*That* cannot be bought.'

'Then give her to me.'

He turned once more, searching her face. 'No, Gwyneth. I know how much Maggie meant to you, but ...'

'She was my friend – my *only* friend. Let *me* take her baby. *I'll* look after her. *I'll* love her.'

'You don't know what you're saying. You're still young. One day you'll have a husband, children of your own. If you take Maggie's baby ...'

'It doesn't matter. I want her. *I'll* make sure she never ends up like Maggie. *Never.*'

'But how will you live?'

'I'll manage.'

'But how?'

Gwyneth clasped her hands together to prevent them from betraying her. 'I'll find work.'

'Here, in Caerphilly?' He shook his head. 'Not with a baby. In Cardiff perhaps, as an outworker – that is until you become too ill to work, which sooner or later you will – and when that happens, what option will you have but to break my promise for me?' He saw the tears running down Gwyneth's cheeks, and he stepped a little closer. 'I don't mean to be cruel, Gwyneth. But if you *truly* love this baby, then you'll give her up. You'll give her up and let someone better able to ...' He stopped, feeling an icy chill as the implications of his words came home to him.

*

The asylum was never completely still. During the day, and even more so at night, it rang with an ambient noise: a reverberating clamour of emotions, voiced in tongues both known and unknown, muted and indistinct, contained by stone and steel, so that only the echo of the woman's footsteps in the corridor held sway.

She came into the office. 'Any problems?'

A man in an unbuttoned uniform was sitting with his feet propped upon the cold radiator, a large bunch of keys hanging from his belt and a half eaten sandwich in his hand. 'Nah,' he said, spitting crumbs.

She eyed him. 'What about my pet?'

'Nothin' much.' He gave a careless shrug. 'She's been talkin' to that there Jemmy again.'

'Oh, yes? You've given her back her clothes?'

'You said not to.'

Her mouth flickered. 'So I did. Well, you'd better get off. That little wife of yours will be waiting.'

Clumsily he got to his feet, unclipping the keys from his belt. 'It's goin' to be a cold night,' he said, glancing toward somewhere beyond the dismal confines of the office.

'Yes,' she said. 'Yes, I expect it is.'

*

The door to the nursery stood slightly ajar, giving a glimpse of the figure inside, and Gwyneth paused, then knocked. 'You sent for me, sir?'

384

Evan continued to look down to where the baby lay sleeping, content after her breakfast encounter with the wet-nurse. 'I understand she has a voracious appetite,' he said softly.

An unguarded smile momentarily softened Gwyneth's expression. 'She would have,' she said, before setting her face once more.

He reached in to stroke a finger over the child's wispy, already unruly hair, then looked up. 'There is something I need to discuss with you, Gwyneth.' He saw the look of suspicion in her eyes, and he straightened, resting his hand on the side of the cot. 'My mother wrote to me some time ago. It seems the Swiss climate agrees with my father and she has decided not to return here – therefore it is my intention to sell the practice and the house along with it. I already have a buyer.'

Gwyneth's eyes widened. 'Does Lawrence know – or Cook?'

'Not yet. But there is no need for concern. The new owners are very keen to retain as many of the household as wish to stay.'

She looked uncertain. 'I see.'

'But in the meantime, until I finalise the arrangements, the baby will require a nanny. I should like you to take the position.'

'No. I'm sorry, but no.'

'But why ever not? The other day you said ...'

'How can you even *think* to ask me?' she said angrily. 'You want me to look after her, grow to love her more than I already do – only to give her up when you *finalise your arrangements*?'

'Gwyneth, the other day I said that love couldn't be bought, but I was wrong.' He saw the protest on her lips and quickly held up his hand. 'Please, hear me out. A house has become available – just on the edge of town – and since I am to have a share of the proceeds of Pendragon, I have made a preliminary offer.'

Gwyneth felt her heart quicken.

'I expect you know the house,' said Evan. 'Wild Briar?'

'Wild Briar? But ... but that's *tiny*.'

'It is small, I grant you, but there are three reasonably sized rooms plus a small scullery – and once I have them painted and furnished ...'

Gwyneth looked toward the cot, trying not to let disappointment colour her words. 'Yes, I'm sure you're right.'

'But?'

'But nothing, sir,' she said, the formal facade slipping into place once more. 'Will that be all, sir?'

'No, Gwyneth. You've not answered my question.'

'Your question, sir?'

'Will you stay on here as nanny until the house is ready?'

'I thought I'd made myself clear, sir.'

'But Gwyneth ...?'

She rounded on him. 'Why do you torture me? *Why*? You must hate me more than I ever hated you. Don't you know how much I want Maggie's child? Can't you understand what she means to me? You can't possibly, or you could never be so cruel as to dangle her in front of me, like … like …' Her eyes were red, but she did not cry, instead she fixed him with a cold stare. 'For one moment, just now, I dared hope that you actually meant to keep her. That I might be given the position, not for a month, or for six months, but for as long as she needed me. I would have settled for that. But I can see that was all just stupid, *stupid* dreaming.' She turned away. 'I think it best if I were to leave, now – right away. I wish you happiness in your new home.'

'Gwyneth, I'm sorry. I'm not making myself clear. Once Pendragon is sold, I shall be moving to London. Owen is to be sent to school there, and I shall be taking up a hospital teaching post in order to be near him.' He lowered his eyes. 'I think it's time *I* started to forgive.'

'Then I don't understand.'

'Wild Briar is for you. For you and the baby. I can make you an allowance, not a great amount, but enough, and …'

Gwyneth felt her heart quicken once more, but she steeled herself. 'No. No, I won't take your charity.'

'I felt quite sure you wouldn't, so I am giving you none. The house will be held in trust for …' He looked down at the sleeping girl. 'Have you considered a name for her?'

Gwyneth met his gaze. 'Katherine,' she said.

Evan nodded. 'Then the house will be held in trust for Katherine until she comes of age. The money will be paid to you neither as charity nor as a gift, but as a wage for the one duty I require of you – which is to love her.'

Chapter Forty-Eight

I never returned to the lodging house, but stayed with Joe instead, sleeping in his bed while he slept on the floor.

Each new day I promised myself I'd find work, and then a room of my own, but the few jobs I could find paid a pittance, and as the weeks became months I found it increasingly easy to give in to his insistence that he earned enough for us both.

So I kept house, such as it was, and the months turned into a year. I didn't love Joe, I didn't sleep with him, and I didn't tell him about my twenty pounds – and there is no period in my life of which I am more ashamed.

*

Beyond the dank, narrow archway that led from Dorset Street into the squalid little backwater that was Miller's Court, lay number thirteen, a room so unfortunately placed that no finger of sunlight ever touched its damp and dirty walls.

'It's five shillings a week, as seen, but if you need a washstand, I've got a spare one I can let you have for no extra charge. The pump's right outside your window, so you haven't far to go for that, and the closets are down the end of the court. It's a bit of a walk,' John McCarthy's face creased into a good humoured smile, 'but at least you've got three to choose from once you get there.'

Joe looked uncertainly about the gloomy, twelve-foot square room. 'What do you think, M-Mary?'

'It smells damp.'

The landlord shrugged. 'Well anywhere's going to be a bit damp this early in the year. But once you get a fire going it'll soon be cosy enough. Tell you what, if you take the place, I'll send my man, Harry, over with a bucket of coal – as a house warming present.'

'House warming present?' said Joe. 'I don't know. Five shillings seems a lot for such a small room.'

Mary went to the bed, lifted back the blanket to feel the mattress, then opened the door to the cupboard by the fireplace and peered in. She straightened. 'Four shillings?'

McCarthy shook his head. 'I can't say I wouldn't like to have a more respectable couple living here for a change, but I can't go less than four and sixpence.'

'Four and sixpence?' Joe looked at Mary. 'What do you think?'

'We have to find somewhere by tomorrow.'

McCarthy looked at them askance. 'Not been any trouble, has there? Because the rent's got to be paid – and regularly.'

'Trouble? No, no trouble. Just a b-bit of b-bad luck,' said Joe.

McCarthy deliberated for a moment. 'Well, there's a lot of that about,' he said finally, handing over the key.

*

'Plush. Very plush.' James Spencer reached into the pocket of his coat and withdrew a silver cigarette case. 'Not in the least like our old rooms.'

'When in Bloomsbury …'

'Indeed. And you seem to have done like the Bloomsburyians exceedingly well.' He took out a thin black cheroot. 'I suppose you still object to these foul things?'

Evan passed him an ashtray. 'Of course.'

'You've heard about Gaston?'

'No.'

'Going to be something of a neighbour of yours. He's following your example and coming back here to start up in private practice. Harley Street, I believe.'

'That hardly makes him a neighbour.'

Spencer laughed, blowing a cloud of smoke toward the ceiling.

'And what about you?' asked Evan.

'What? Come back and live here? Are you mad?' He crossed to the rain-spattered window, looking down into the square with its well-ordered gardens. 'Where's the life? Where are the drunks and the whores? And more to the point, where's the damn sun? It's meant to be spring, isn't it?' He shook his head. 'No, I prefer warmer, more congenial surroundings – and *should* I ever feel nostalgic for London, I can always close my shutters, sit in an ice cold bath, and smoke these infernal cheroots until I can't see across the room.'

Evan came to join him, looking out at the rain. 'I do miss Paris.'

'Then come back with me.'

'I can't. My son is returning from Switzerland at the end of the month. He's to go to school here in London.'

'Ah! Hence this unexpected display of domesticity?' Spencer regarded the glowing end of his cheroot. 'It must feel a little strange to be suddenly playing the doting father?'

'That's rather an understatement.' Evan fixed his eyes on the distant houses. 'Except, I don't want to *play* at it. I want to be the father I should have been – it's just that I'm not sure I know how.'

'Daunting.'

'No, not daunting. *Terrifying.*'

*

'Coo, it stinks of piss in that archway,' said Lizzie Albrook, walking through the covered entrance to Miller's Court, and coming to a halt in the small, stone flagged yard.

Mary looked up from the apron she was washing, the enamelled wash-bowl standing upon a chair. 'I'll throw this water down there when I'm done.'

Half perched upon the window-sill, Kate laughed. 'It's not the piss yer need to worry about.'

'Yes,' said Lizzie, her round, country girl's face taking on an earnest expression. 'You got to watch your step – 'specially in the dark. I reckon it's them bloomin' dogs down at number eleven.'

'I reckon it's not,' grinned Kate.

Lizzie looked blankly at her, then came a few steps closer. 'Wotcha doin', Mary?'

'What does it look like?'

'No, I mean what else you got to wash? Only I see you're doin' your aprons, and I was just wonderin' …?'

Mary looked at the girl's stained pinafore. 'Yes, alright. Give it to me.'

'Thanks, Mary. I'll just go and get the rest.'

'*The rest?*'

''Ere,' chuckled Kate as Lizzie ran down the court and disappeared into a doorway. 'You're gettin' to sound just like Joe.'

'Like Joe?'

Kate roared with laughter. 'There yer go again!' She began turning her head from side to side in imitation of a ventriloquist's dummy. ''Ere, Joe, fancy a beer? – *A beer?* – Yes, a beer. It's alright I'm payin' – *I'm payin'*? – Oh, well if yer insist, Joe, thanks very much.' She stopped and looked at Mary. 'Don't tell me yer 'aven't noticed?'

'It's not his fault.'

'I ain't sayin' it is – but it don't 'alf get on yer nerves. I don't know 'ow yer stand it. What with that, an' the stutterin' – must be like livin' with a b-b-b-bleedin' parrot.'

Mary let the apron she'd been wringing fall back into the water. '*I can't* stand it, Kate. Not because of how he talks, that's nothing. It's … *everything else*. It's getting so I can't stand to be with him – but even worse, I can't stand myself for feeling that way. He's a good man … in so many ways, but …'

'Then move out.'

'How can I? He doesn't even realise anything's wrong. He tells me I'm the best thing that ever happened to him. That he wouldn't know how he'd cope if I was ever to leave him. How can I turn round and tell him I can't stand to be in the same room with him? What do I say?'

''Ow about *b-b-bugger off, Joe*?'

Lizzie reappeared with her arms full of linen. 'What you two laughin' about?'

'Grown-up's talk,' said Kate.

'I'm grown right enough.'

''Ow old are yer?'

'Twenty – gettin' on for, anyway.'

'Well, yer've got to be twenty-one before yer proper grown, see?'

Mary took the bundle of washing, adding it to her own few things. 'Don't mind her, Lizzie. She's just teasing you.' She sighed, taking the apron from the soapy water and wringing it out. 'Oh, I don't know what to do, Kate. I'm just so sick of this life.'

'Then come to the pub, ducklin'.'

'That won't help tomorrow, and the day after, and the day after that, will it.'

'It will if yer go again tomorrow, an' the day after, an' the day after that.'

Lizzie's face was a picture of confusion, and Mary gave the apron one last, savage turn, then looked into her eyes. 'You take good notice of me, Lizzie. Mark what I do – then be sure *not* to do it, and I reckon you won't go too far wrong in this life.'

'Yes,' said Kate. 'Yer don't want to turn out like our Mary. Regular bad 'un she is. Why, what she ain't done ain't worth doin'. An' what she '*as* done yer couldn't write a book about without bein' locked up. Ain't that right, ducklin'?'

Lizzie's eyes widened. 'You don't go out on the streets, do you, Mary?'

'Ooh, I should say so,' laughed Kate. 'Blimey, she ain't so much an *unfortunate* as a *downright bloody unlucky*, if yer want the truth of it.'

'You're a silly cow,' said Mary with a grudging laugh.

Kate's face split into a grin. 'Oh, come on. Leave the bloody washin' an' come down the pub. I can't go without yer,' she laughed again, ''cos I'm soddin' well skint.'

'I can't. I've got Joe's shirt to do.'

'And my few bits,' prompted Lizzie.

'Look, I'll see about coming out tonight. I'll talk to Joe when he comes home.'

'Oh, for Chris' sake don't bring ''im!' pleaded Kate. 'I already knows everythin' I wants to know about the ins an' outs of a c-c-cow's arse.'

*

Joe took up his pipe and ran the lighted match over the bowl. 'I do hope the ladies won't m-mind if the gentlemen smoke?' he asked, leaning back, one elbow resting on the table.

'Of course not,' replied Mary, just as she did every evening.

He let the smoke trickle from between his lips. 'Disturbing item in the newspaper today. A woman attacked in B-Brick Lane.'

'Not anyone we know?' asked Mary.

'Anyone we know? No. No, a woman called Emma. *Emma* …' He lifted his eyes to the ceiling. 'Hang on, it'll come to m-me in a m-minute.'

The newspaper lay folded by Joe's elbow, and suddenly apprehensive, Mary crossed to it. 'Is it in here?'

'In here? Yes, that's the one, alright.'

She made to pick it up, but catching his disapproving look, she withdrew her hand. 'Why don't you read it to me.'

Wearing an expression of satisfied propriety, he took up the newspaper, his lips moving imperceptibly as he read in silence for a moment or two. 'Ah, here it is. There's a lot of rather gruesome details, I'm afraid – well, we won't b-bother with those, b-but here we are. Her name was Smith. Emma Smith.'

'Does it say why?'

'Why?'

'Yes, *why*?' said Mary, more sharply than she intended. 'Does it say why she was attacked?'

'There's no need for raised voices, M-Mary.'

She turned away, going to the fire and raking it over. 'I'm sorry. It's just … upsetting news.'

'Upsetting news? Yes, I should certainly say so. It's fortunate I spared you the details. Not very nice reading.' He turned the page. 'Oh, look, here's something a little m-more interesting. Let m-me read you this b-bit about a chap who's done a survey on how m-much m-manure the average horse produces every day. Heavens! Can you imagine, M-Mary? The gross tonnage that has to b-be cleared from the London streets every day is …'

'Actually, I was thinking I might go out this evening – just for a short while. I've been in all day and …'

He looked up. 'Do you know, I b-believe you m-must be a m-mind reader.'

'A mind reader?' Finding herself repeating him, she drove her nails deep into her palms in irritation. 'I mean – you were thinking of going out, too?'

'There's a lecture over at the Working Lads Institute tonight. *From Strolling Players to the B-Barrel Organ – A History of Itinerant Street M-Musicians.*' He gave a little laugh. 'I thought we m-might *stroll* along.'

'The thing is ...' Mary turned to face him. '... I said I'd meet Kate.'

'Now you know I don't approve of her, M-Mary.'

'I know, but she's my friend. If you just got to know her better ...'

'No, M-Mary. No. I absolutely forbid you to go.'

'Forbid?' She stared at him. 'You *forbid* me to go? Look, Joe, I don't know who you think you are, but you *stroll* along to your lecture.' She snatched her shawl from the back of the door. 'I'm going to meet Kate – whether you bloody well like it or not!'

*

The intimidating desk, the dark stained panelling, and the dust motes floating with lethargic grace through the weak sunlight felt uncomfortably familiar to Evan as he sat opposite the Headmaster.

'You do not wish your son to board?' The old man's voice was bluff, and he peered at Evan, then at Owen, with a detached curiosity.

'He's only six.'

'Hmmm.' The Headmaster inclined his head toward the House Master waiting in the shadows. 'Your examination of the boy was satisfactory?'

'Very much so, Headmaster. He is quite proficient for his age, and has a rudimentary knowledge of both the French and the German languages. He is, however, a little weak on ...'

'Yes, yes.' The Headmaster waved his hand in dismissal. 'You attended this school yourself, I believe, Dr Rees-Morgan. That would have been in Dr Brown's time, of course.'

'Yes.'

'A great man – sorely missed.'

'I always found him to be a ...' Evan paused. 'A *fair* man.'

The Headmaster sucked in his lips forming something that might have been a smile. 'Well,' he said, peering at the boy over his spectacles once more. 'Well indeed, Master Owen Rees-Morgan. We shall see if we cannot do for you what Dr Brown did for your father, eh?' He leaned back, returning his attention to Evan. 'Bring him in September for the commencement of the Michaelmas term.'

Outside, the air – redolent as it was with the odours of horse and Thames – felt crisp and fresh after the closeness of the study.

Evan looked down at the boy. 'Well, congratulations. Are you pleased?'

'I don't know, sir.'

'It's not as bad as it looks, you know.'

Owen kept his eyes fixed firmly on the ground.

'You *do* want to attend the school, don't you?'

'I should like to do whatever you want me to do.'

Putting a finger beneath the boy's chin, Evan lifted his face until their eyes met. 'Your Grandmother schooled you in that little speech, did she?' Then, seeing the guilty look on his son's face, he forced a smile. 'It's alright. *Really.*' He paused, looking about the street, unsure of what else to say. 'I know. How about some ice-cream? There must be somewhere near here that serves it. Would you like that?'

'I'm not allowed it. Grandmamma says it's not good for my chest.'

'What? *Ice-cream*? I've never heard such nonsense.'

Owen's lip began to tremble, and Evan quickly went down on one knee. 'I'm sorry. I didn't mean to … I'm not angry with you, you know – it's … it's just that I …' He drew a hand across his face. 'Look, perhaps we should just go straight home?'

Owen raised his eyes a little. 'I should like to if …'

'Yes,' said Evan with a sigh. 'Yes, I know.'

Chapter Forty-Nine

The summer breeze whispered amongst the leaves, swaying the stately hollyhocks and lifting a corner of the linen that lay untroubled by needle and thread upon Gwyneth's lap. It came again, loosing a strand of hair to dance at her cheek, and she awoke, blinking at the brightness of the sun which shone down on her from out of an azure sky. Lazily, she stretched, tilting back her head, allowing the warmth to play upon her already tanned features, then she set aside her sewing and stood up.

A few feet away, on the small square of lawn, Katherine lay sleeping in the shade of an old umbrella, her chubby legs poking from the blanket in which she was wrapped, and Gwyneth went to her, gently covering her before moving into the cool of the house.

The jug of lemonade she'd made that morning stood cooling in a bowl of water, and she filled a glass for herself and a small china cup for Katherine, placing them on a tray along with a few biscuits – then, almost guiltily, she glanced over her shoulder.

The redirected letter stood on the kitchen table, propped against a vase of meadowsweet, Mary's familiar hand partially overwritten by the new owners of Pendragon.

For the twentieth time that day, Gwyneth's eyes wandered to it, then to the range where the fire flickered temptingly – but when she returned to the garden moments later, the letter remained unopened upon the table.

*

Spitalfields church clock was just striking nine as Harry Farrel crossed Commercial Street, walking briskly toward the Ten Bells. 'Wotcha Lumpy,' he called to the figure squatting beneath the street lamp.

'G'd evenin' Mr Farrel, sir.' The old shoe-black got quickly to his feet, bringing a finger to the brim of his frayed hat, his body bent more than was dictated by the hump on his back. 'Can I give you a brush up, sir?'

Farrel glanced down at his shoes, then up at the clock. 'Yeah, alright, go on then.' He lifted his foot on to the box, watching with satisfaction as the misshapen figure went down on his knees, his hands moving in a frenzy of activity over the chestnut brown brogue.

Harry liked the East End, and here, in the poorest part of it, he liked it best. Seeing the poverty of others always made him feel good about himself – and as he looked up and down the darkening street, he felt very good indeed.

''Ere,' he said, growing impatient with the pains the man was taking over the expensive leather. 'Yer can leave 'em be now. I'm late as it is. What's the damage?'

The man shook his head. 'No charge to you, Mr Farrel.'

Harry grinned. 'That's nice of yer, Lumpy.' He took a shilling from the pocket of his waistcoat and tossed it to the man. 'But I'd better pay yer.' He began to laugh. 'Don't want yer gettin' the 'ump, do we?'

The shoe-black caught the coin. 'No, Mr Farrel.' He laughed ingratiatingly. 'No, we wouldn't want that. Thank you, Mr Farrel.'

Harry was still chuckling as he went through the bar of the Ten Bells and up the stairs to the private parlour where Eastman was waiting. 'Sorry I'm late Vince. Got a bit 'eld up.' He poured himself a drink from the decanter that stood on the table, then dropped heavily into one of the plush armchairs, stretching his legs out in front of him as he eyed Eastman with amusement. 'You want to be a bit more trustin', Vince. I couldn't 'elp noticin' yer little friend downstairs. What's 'is name? Baines?'

Unperturbed, Eastman nodded. 'It's a rough area, Mr Farrel. One is naturally concerned about travelling alone.'

Farrel chuckled. 'Well, I tend to agree with yer, Vince. That's why I've got Carroty Ned an' a couple of off duty coppers down there – just keepin' 'im company, as it were.' He took another pull at his drink. 'So, 'ow is dear old Connie, these days? Must be over a year since they carted 'er off, ain't it?'

Eastman gave a slight inclination of the head.

'Rough on the old girl. Still, she always was a bit of a loose cannon in the upstairs department – an' I suppose that Archie gettin' done in that fashion – well, it'd be enough to send a *normal* woman round the bend.' He sucked on his teeth. 'Blimey! Fancy losin' yer weddin' tackle to a razor, eh? Fair makes yer eyes water, don't it?'

'Yes,' said Eastman with a hint of impatience.

Farrel smiled. 'Not found the woman that done it, then?'

'We're still looking.'

''Course yer are, Vince. 'Course yer are. That's what I like about you. Yer *loyal*.' Farrel leaned closer. 'A lot o' blokes in your position, seein' poor old Con go stark ravin' bonkers, well, they might think *fuck 'er,* an' look to jump ship. But not you, Vince. No, you keep 'er little empire goin' fer 'er, don't yer. Go an' visit 'er … even keep up the search for this soddin' mystery woman what carved off Archie's bollocks. Now *that's* loyal.'

'It's nice to be appreciated.'

'Ain't it just,' Farrel laughed. 'An' I do appreciate yer, Vince. Always 'ave. There was a time when …' He smiled to himself, 'Well, that don't matter. Point is – old Con ain't comin' back, is she.'

'The doctors have hopes …'

'Fuck *them*.' Farrel put down the glass and grew serious, looking across the small space that divided them. 'I ain't talkin' about no saw-bones's 'opes. I'm talkin' about *business* – yer get my drift? What I'm askin' you is – you ain't *lettin'* 'er come back, are yer?'

Eastman toyed thoughtfully with his glass. 'No,' he said at last.

A triumphant smile curled Harry Farrel's lips. 'Yer a clever bastard,' he said, thumping his hand down on the arm of the chair in admiration. 'Keepin' the old girl sweet – while cuttin' the fuckin' ground out from under 'er the whole time.' He got up and went to the table, pouring himself another measure. 'I'll tell yer, Vince, boy – you pull this off, an' I see big things fer us. Big things. That cunt, Archie?' He spat on to the carpet. 'Yer couldn't deal with 'im. 'E'd 'old a grudge till fuckin' judgement day – same goes fer Con. But with *you* running things up west? Ah, well, then all things are possible, ain't they?' He moved back to the chair, looking almost paternally at Eastman. 'But it ain't all plain sailin' yet. Con still 'as a lot of support – though fuck knows why – so yer goin' to 'ave to take it slow an' easy – an' that's where *I* can 'elp yer.'

*

Martha Tabram had been having a good evening until that moment. Now she grew red in the face. 'Watch where yer goin' yer silly bitch!' she screamed, coming to a halt in front of the Ten Bells.

On her way toward the Britannia, Kate glanced over her shoulder and gave a cheery wave. 'Sorry old cock,' she called, stepping from the pavement to thread her way through the evening traffic.

'I'll give you *old cock*!'

With her arms around two drunken soldiers, Pearly Poll watched as Martha lurched across the pavement. ''Ere, where yer goin? You ain't leavin' me with these two, are yer?'

'I'm just goin' to give that cheeky cow a bit of my mind – an' the toe of m' boot up 'er arse!'

Poll shrieked with laughter. 'You go to it, girl – an' be sure to give 'er one fer me, eh?' She hauled the two bemused soldiers after her. 'We'll be in the pub when yer've finished.'

With her eyes fixed firmly on Kate, Martha stepped off the pavement and straight into the path of a coster's donkey, causing it to rear up, spilling the contents of its overladen cart into the road.

'You blind or somethin'?' yelled the man. 'Look what yer've bleedin' done!'

'Fuck off!' Martha started across the street once more, but the man caught hold of her arm.

''Ere, you ain't goin' nowhere till yer've picked up all this stuff.'

'I *said* fuck off!' She aimed a kick at him, yanking her arm free.

'What about my stuff?'

'Shove it up yer arse!' She looked angrily about at the small crowd that had formed. 'An' what the fuck are you lookin' at? Go on, piss off!' The crowd moved back a little, with the exception of the three men who had just stepped from the Ten Bells, one of whom began to laugh loudly.

'Fuck me,' roared Harry Farrel. 'The bank 'oliday monkey parade ain't finished yet.'

Martha's already crimson face took on a darker, more purplish hue. 'Enjoyin' yerself, are yer? Yer great tub of piss an' wind!'

She stormed toward Farrel, and Baines made to put himself between them, but Harry elbowed him aside. 'What the fuck did you call me?'

Despite her drunken fury, Martha sensed danger. 'You 'eard,' she said defiantly, holding her ground, but advancing no further.

Eastman gave Farrel an amused glance. 'A bit of local colour?'

Instantly Martha rounded on him, seeing in his refined features a less dangerous outlet for her wrath. 'I'll give yer fuckin' *local colour*, yer stuck-up little ponce!' She drew the phlegm from the back of her throat with a rattling hiss, and spat into Eastman's face.

The muscle in Eastman's jaw twitched, unnoticed in the darkened street, but otherwise he remained impassive.

'Like yer say, Vince,' Farrel studied him with interest, watching for a reaction. '*A bit of local colour*.'

*

'I can't stand it, Kate. I've got to do something to get away.'

'Yer've been sayin' that for months. For Chris' sake just leave the silly bugger.'

Annie Chapman looked unhappily toward the bar. 'Can't we go over to the Bells?'

'It's cheaper 'ere, Darlin'.'

'Maybe t'is – but it's a bit more jollifyin' over there. It's puttin' me right off my rum, sittin' 'ere lookin' at old Wally's miserable mug.'

Kate chuckled, motioning with her eyes toward Mary. 'Well, thank yer lucky stars yer don't 'ave to go 'ome to one, eh?'

On the far side of the table Lizzie Albrook watched engrossed as Mary dipped her finger into a pool of spilled beer and began absent-mindedly drawing on the polished wooden top. 'That's really good,' she said in admiration. 'Really clever that is.'

Kate leaned across to look. 'She's right. 'Ere, why don't yer try doin' them there pictures yer get in the papers? I 'ear yer get a lot of money for doin' them.'

Mary shook her head. 'I'm not good enough.'

'Well, I don't know about that,' said Kate. 'It's better than I could do.' She looked up, searching for a face amongst the drinkers at the bar. 'Oi, Tickets. Come over 'ere an' take a look at this for me, will yer darlin'?'

The old man shuffled over. 'Vot you vont, Katie?' He shrugged his bony shoulders. 'I ain't got no money.'

'That's alright,' laughed Kate. 'What I've got to show these days ain't worth payin' for anyway.'

He smiled. 'So – vot can I do for you?'

'You're a bit of an artist. What d'yer reckon to this 'ere?'

'Is good,' he said, looking over the already disappearing drawing.

'D'yer reckon she could make money from it?'

'Maybe.' He shrugged again. 'Vhy not?'

Mary looked up at him. His face had the quality of a tired old blood-hound, and his clothes and greying moustache were equally bedraggled, but there remained the tiniest sparkle in his rheumy eyes. 'You're an artist?' she asked.

'Once, maybe. Now I only paint tickets for shop vindows – *Fourpence a Pound. Best Prices. Buy now.*' He shrugged again, then almost as an after-thought he reached into the pocket of his coat and took out a dog-eared book, offering it to her. 'Sometimes I still draw – just for me.'

Mary opened it to find page after page of exquisitely drawn street scenes, peopled with figures so filled with life and movement that she was torn between admiration and envy. 'They're *really* lovely,' she said at last, handing it back to him.

He pushed the book back into the depths of his pocket. 'Vell, I vish you good luck.'

'There you are,' said Kate. 'Why don't yer give the drawin' lark a go?'

Mary watched the old man shuffle back to the bar, his frayed trouser cuffs flapping around his down-at-heel boots. 'What would be the point?'

'He said you was good, didn't he?' asked Lizzie, as though doubting her own ears.

'He was just being kind. And anyway – just look at him.' Angrily she smeared her hand over the remnants of her drawing. 'And *I* couldn't do anything half as good as he has in that book.'

Annie stared at the blank patch of table, wearing an equally blank expression on her face. 'It's a puzzler, ain't it?' she said – then with far more feeling as she looked up, 'Oh, bugger!'

Following her gaze, Kate turned in her seat. 'Bloody 'ell. Your Joe's just come in.'

Mary sagged in her chair. 'I've got to get away,' she said, worrying at her lip. 'I've just *got to*. If I don't …' With a sudden determination she leaned forward, gripping Kate's arm. 'Will you come with me tomorrow?' she whispered urgently. 'Will you come with me to Knightsbridge?'

*

Murray Baines was thankful for his unseasonable topcoat. A few hours earlier he'd cursed it as he'd sweated in the heat of the Ten Bells bar, the ulster's heavy drag made worse by the bayonet that lay ready against trouble, hidden inside the deep poacher's pocket. But now, in the early hours, and with the temperature dropping, he was grateful for its warmth.

'Aren't you cold?' he asked under his breath.

Eastman remained quite still, watching the entrance to the buildings. 'I've been warmer.'

Since taking their leave of Farrel, they had followed the foul-mouthed Martha from one public house to another, until finally her soldier companion had demanded his dues and she had led him into the inky blackness of George Yard Buildings to conclude the transaction.

'How much longer are we going to wait?' persisted Baines. 'We should have taught her some manners there and then, in front of Mr Farrel. He must think we're a right pair of …'

'Is that what *you* would have done? Brawl with her in full view?' Keeping his eyes firmly fixed on the far side of the street, Eastman gave a gentle sigh. Minutes passed in silence, then he said, 'But since we're talking of Mr Farrel – does he know about you and Gussie?'

Baines shot him a look. 'What do you mean?'

'I mean, is he aware that you regularly plant yourself between the thighs of his most adored daughter, and poke away at …' he lifted an eyebrow, '*her indubitable charms*? Does Harry Farrel know about *that*?'

The blood rushed to Baines's cheeks. 'There's nothing for him to know, because I don't.'

'I'm not a fool, Murray – so please don't take me for one. And I only ask because, well, I *would* hate to see you ending up like Archie.'

'I told you, there's nothing between me and Gus … and Miss Farrel.'

Eastman shrugged. 'I see. Well, in a way it's rather a shame.' He breathed deeply, his breath misting in the night air. 'I *was* rather hoping to learn whether her cunny reeks differently to any other Whitechapel whore's.' Beside him in the darkness, Baines bristled, betraying his anger – and his lie – and Eastman gave the ghost of a smile.

Chapter Fifty

Standing by the park railings, Kate peered across the road at the house lying a little way down from the corner of Gloucester Gardens. 'If I end up in quad over this, then yer'd better be sure to come a-visitin' – *an'* with yer pockets fair bulgin', right?' She pulled some of Annie's crochet work from inside of her coat. 'So who 'ave I got to pretend to sell this stuff to?'

Mary glanced nervously about. 'Ask for Madame Bennaire. Tell whoever answers the door that you've been given her name by Sister Ignatius at Providence Row.'

'Oh, so I'm a bleedin' charity case now, am I?'

'If you manage to see Madame alone, then tell her Emma Black wants to see her, and to be by the bandstand at four o'clock today. But if there's anyone else there – anyone at all – then just ask her to buy your work and come away. Have you got that?'

'Dunno why yer can't just go an' talk to 'er yerself.'

'I've already told you. There might be someone watching. Someone who'd recognise me.'

With a sigh, Kate started off in the direction of the house. 'Alright, ducklin', but this better not be a bleedin' joke.'

'It's not. I promise.' She watched Kate go, then looked about, trying to appear casual. Living in Whitechapel she had become accustomed to people loitering on street corners, but here they were noticeable by their absence, and she suddenly realised how very conspicuous she was.

She was still fretting over it when, from out of the park, a policeman came into view, and immediately her heart began to pound. Without thinking she started to walk away, glancing over her shoulder in the hope he would go off in the opposite direction – but he didn't. After a moment's pause, he followed after her, walking at a slow and steady pace – and she began to panic. She was still within sight of the house when she saw the little shoe-black.

'Do you have any matches?'

Perched astride his blacking box, the boy looked up at her. 'Don't sell matches – try the tobacconist's down the road.'

'Shoe laces, then?'

'Ain't got them, neither.'

Mary sneaked a glance back along the road. The policeman was within ten yards and heading straight for her. 'Well … how much for a shine?'

The boy laughed at the ridiculousness of the idea. 'What? You goin' to put yer foot up on my box? Just like some gent?' Then he suddenly stood up, pointing away from the approaching constable. 'So, if yer go down there about half a mile or so, you'll come to a big old monument. Take the first on the left, then go about … oh, let's see, I should say about another half a mile ought to do it …'

The policeman passed without a word or a look.

'… then you'll see a …' The boy waited until the policeman was out of earshot. '… the back end of a big, fat-arsed copper.' He gave Mary a wink. 'It *was* him you was hidin' from, weren't it?'

Mary looked at him. He was about twelve years old, and when she'd lived in Gloucester Gardens she'd passed him nearly every day. He'd always tipped his cap respectfully, and she'd always smiled and sometimes given him money. Now he made no sign of knowing her, and the realisation of how much she must have changed made her feel sad, yet comfortingly safe. 'Yes,' she said.

'Thought so. What did yer do?' Then he looked across at the big houses. 'Or maybe it's somethin' yer plannin' to do?'

'What you don't know can't hurt you,' she said, feeling her courage returning. 'But here's a couple more coppers for your trouble.'

He looked down at the pennies she'd pressed into his hand. 'Ain't very much for keepin' the pair of you out of clink.' He caught her look. 'Oh, I've got eyes in my head,' he said, motioning to where Kate was running between the carts and carriages to join them.

'Good news an' bad news, ducklin',' she gasped, mounting the pavement. 'Your lady friend ain't there no more. But we'll 'ave us a right jollification in Ringer's tonight, 'cos the lady what lives there now – bein' a right charitable sort – only went an' gave me a bleedin' sovereign for Annie's bits of old crochet!'

*

The knife sliced upwards, opening the belly in a single sweep, the white flesh parting to expose the dull, glutinous mass of internal organs.

'So when are you an' Mary goin' to get married?'

'Get m-married?' Joe chewed at the ends of his moustache. 'All in good time, eh?'

'Well, I wouldn't 'ang about.' Daniel Barnett reached inside the fish, gutting it with practised ease and flinging the entrails into the wooden crate. 'She's a bit of a catch, your Mary, an' if you don't make an 'onest woman of 'er soon, then someone else will, sure as eggs is eggs.'

Joe heaved a large cod on to the bench and sliced it open. 'We're very comfortable as we are.'

'My arse!'

'M-My …?' Joe sputtered. 'I don't think there's any need for that sort of talk.'

'There's every need as I see it.' Daniel put down his knife and looked across at his brother. 'I don't know what you see when you look at Mary, but I see a girl who ain't 'appy – an' no bleedin' wonder at it. What the 'ell are you doin', Joe? You've moved lodgin's more times than I can remember – an' now you're livin' in …' He shook his head in despair. 'You earn the same as me – so why on earth are you livin' in that … that *shit-'ouse*?'

Joe made a mumbling sound, choking back the word. 'We've had a b-bit of b-bad luck, that's all.'

'What sort of bad luck?'

'*B-Bad luck.* I don't see any need for further discussion.'

Daniel eyed him suspiciously. 'It's not the old trouble?'

'Old trouble? No, of course not.'

*

The room above the Princess Alice was in darkness but for the glow from the coals and the light from the single lamp by which Eastman had been reading. He looked up from his chair. 'You're quite certain it was her?'

'Yes, sir.' The boy stood awkwardly to attention. 'She looked different, right enough, but it was her alright.'

'Did she recognise you?'

'I don't know, sir, but I pretended not to know her – just like you said.'

'So where did they go?'

'I … I don't know, sir.'

'You didn't follow them?'

'I couldn't, sir. I couldn't just leave my stuff.'

'Couldn't you?' Eastman closed the book and laid it down.

'I had to find someone to mind it, Mr Eastman – I mean, *sir* – but …'

'But by that time they had disappeared, hmm?'

'Yes, sir. I went lookin' for them, but they weren't nowhere to be seen.'

'They weren't *anywhere* to be seen.'

The boy swallowed hard. 'They … they weren't *anywhere* to be seen, sir.'

'I see.' Eastman got slowly to his feet, standing in silence for a moment. 'Now, tell me again. What time was it you encountered our Miss Black?'

'About a quarter after midday, sir.'

'Yes.' Eastman placed a pensive finger to his lips. 'Do you see the clock on the mantelpiece?'

'Yes, sir.'

'What time does it show?' He watched the boy strain to read the face. 'Please. Do step a little closer.'

Timidly the boy crossed to the fireplace. 'It's nearly ten o'clock, sir.'

'Yes – rather a long time has elapsed, don't you think?'

'I was goin' to come earlier, but ...'

'Of course.' Eastman smiled. 'No. No, please do stay where you are. I'm sure you must be cold after being out all day.' He moved closer, ruffling the boy's hair, then trailed a finger across his cheek. 'So, you have no idea where she might have gone, hmm?'

'No, sir.'

'She said nothing?'

'N-No, sir. Why would she?'

'I have no idea – I am merely clutching at straws.' The boy was standing with his back to the fire, and Eastman rested a paternal hand upon his shoulder. 'You're quite certain she gave you no clue?'

'No, sir. She didn't say nothin' ... I mean *anything*.'

Reaching for the poker, Eastman stirred the coals into flame, then gently guided the boy back until his heels were against the grate. 'Perhaps you'd like to think about it?'

'Sir ... I *don't* know where they went.'

Eastman cupped the boy's chin, his thumb stroking the downy cheek.

'Mr Eastman, I ... I'm *burning*.'

'Yes.'

The room began to fill with the stench of charred corduroy as the boy struggled to remain in position, his knees shaking violently, tears squeezing through his tightly shut eyelids. 'I'm sorry, sir ... *please* ...'

'What *exactly* did she say to you?'

'Nothin'. She asked for matches ... shoe laces ... but she didn't want them ... she was hidin' from the policeman ... *please* ...'

'The *policeman*?'

'Yes, I ... I don't know why. Maybe because of the other one?'

'Tell me about her.'

'She was older ... she sold somethin' ...'

'What? What did she sell?'

'I don't know. I can't remember ...' Blisters were forming on the backs of his legs, and he began to make a high-pitched whining sound, the prelude to a fully-fledged scream. 'Needlework! Some crochet ... *Please ... please, sir.*'

'Tell me about this *crochet*.'

'I don't know. Oh, please, God, I don't know, sir. They were goin' somewhere … I don't know where … for a good time, she said.'

Bright little points of light began to creep around the edges of the boy's trouser legs, the charred material curling in their wake, and unable to stand the pain any longer he made to throw himself from the fire, but Eastman stamped down hard across both his feet, pinning them in place while his hand seized the boy's collar, thrusting him hard up against the mantelpiece. 'Where? Where were they going to have this *good time?*'

The boy was screaming now. 'I don't know. I don't know … somewhere … I can't remember …' Blood dribbled from between his chewed lips. 'It was … it was … *Ringer's* … somewhere called … *Ringer's.*'

*

Lizzie Albrook's eyes were wide as saucers as Mary opened the door to her the following morning.

'Have you heard, Mary? There's been another one!'

'Another what?'

'Another horrible murder – over at George Yard Buildin's!' She looked about nervously. 'Can I come in? Only there's no one in at my place, and I don't fancy bein' on my own.'

'Yes, of course,' Rubbing the sleep from her eyes, Mary closed the door behind her. 'When was this?'

'Yesterday, but I only found out about it this mornin' – and a good job, too, or I wouldn't have got a wink o' sleep all night. I just knows I wouldn't.' She flitted excitably about the room. 'Old Indian Harry was readin' all about it when I went into work this mornin'. He told me this poor woman was stabbed hundreds and hundreds of times – *and* in places as he shouldn't like to mention – and that the blood was a-pourin' down the stairs like a bloomin' waterfall! Can you imagine? I tell you, I'm that frightened, Mary!'

'Do they know who she was?'

'Well, they printed her name – Martha Tabram or some strange name like that – but old Harry, he says she always called herself Emma when he knew her.' She paused, looking anxiously across the room. 'Here, Mary, you alright? Only you've gone a dreadful pale colour.'

*

'But Mrs Rees-Morgan was always most insistent, sir.'

'My mother is always most insistent – but since she is in Switzerland, I think we might take the small liberty of letting the boy out of the house, just this once, without swaddling him, don't you, Miss Reeves?'

The nanny looked extremely doubtful. 'Very well, sir. I'm sure you know best,' she said, unbuttoning the thick coat in which she had just encased Owen. 'Should I not accompany you, sir? Children can be rather …'

'I'm sure we'll be quite alright, Nanny.'

The morning had been wet, but now the sun was shining, and as they came down the steps from the house, Evan breathed deeply, enjoying the warmth on his face and the bright, freshly washed feel of the streets. 'You're sure you're warm enough?' he asked as soon as they were out of Miss Reeves hearing.

'Yes, sir.'

Evan looked down at the boy, choosing his words carefully. 'There's really no need to call me sir, you know.' He forced a laugh. 'As a matter of fact, it makes me feel damned old. Or rather …' he said, quickly correcting himself, '*very* old.'

Owen looked thoughtful. 'Is damned a *very* bad word?'

'Some people might say it is.'

'Grandmamma says it is.'

Evan laughed. 'You'd think she'd have grown used to it after all these …' Again he heard the niggling voice inside him. 'But, yes. I'm sure she's right. It's not a good word for children – and now that I come to think of it, it would probably be better if I didn't use it either.'

They walked on in awkward silence.

'So, what would you like to do today?' Evan asked as they passed through the tall park gates.

'We could feed the ducks.'

'I'm amazed those ducks can still float after all the bread we've given them.' But the joke was lost on the boy, and Evan fixed a smile upon his face. 'Yes, why don't we do that. I think I should like to very much. Here you are.' He took some change from his pocket. 'You run on ahead and see what you can buy for them, eh?'

*

Mary stared down at the spare dress and scattering of other clothes that lay on the bed, realising just how pitifully few were her possessions, then she bundled them together and thrust them into the sheet of brown paper that Lizzie had found for her, tying it up with string. With the parcel resting by her feet, she sat down at the table with a scrap of paper and a pencil. *Dear Joe*, she wrote, *I have to leave. I'm very sorry.*

She went to sign her name, but paused, biting her lip as she read the two stark lines. Finally she put the pencil to the paper once more. *There are so many things I haven't told you – and now there isn't the time, but I'm frightened, Joe. I did something a long time ago – and it has caught up with me. I must leave before it is too late. I can only hope you will understand.* She hesitated again, then gripping the pencil more firmly still, she wrote: *With all my heart, Mary.*

The pencil was still shaking in her hand when there came an urgent hammering at the door. She thrust the note into the pocket of her apron. 'W-Who is it?' she called, snatching up the parcel of clothing and shoving it out of sight beneath the bed.

'It's Maria. Open up, Mary, for God's sake!'

Mary unbolted the door to find the breathless figure of Maria Garbey propped against the wall. 'It's your Joe,' she said between gasps. 'You'd better come. *We think he's dead.*'

*

With the last of the bread gone, the ducks returned to the water, leaving Evan and Owen alone with a few opportunistic pigeons that continued to mill about in search of crumbs.

It was growing hot, and Evan found himself becoming drowsy as they sat on the bench overlooking the dark green lake. 'It is pleasant just sitting here,' he said, watching through half closed eyes as a group of young women passed, dazzling in their white dresses, their parasols raised to protect the delicate ivory of their features.

Owen swung his legs. 'I could go and buy some more bread, if you'd like me to?'

'Is that what you want to do?'

The boy shrugged. 'We could.'

'Yes, we certainly could.' Evan stretched his arm along the back of the bench, his hand falling upon Owen's shoulder, giving it a gentle squeeze. '*Or* we could do something different.'

'What sort of *different*?'

The corners of Evan's mouth lifted into a mischievous smile. 'Just something *different.*'

*

'Dead?' Daniel Barnett looked down to where Joe was sprawled on the cobbles. 'Dead drunk is all 'e is.' He knelt down, slapping his brother's pallid cheeks, but there was no response. 'Get up you daft sod. You 'ear me?'

Holding on to Mary's arm, Maria Garbey looked down in disgust. 'You mean I run all that way for nothin'?'

Daniel stood up, shaking his head. 'It's no good. I can't rouse 'im. Tell you what – you stay 'ere an' make sure no one runs over the silly bugger, an' I'll see about gettin' a barrow from the market so we can wheel 'im 'ome.'

*

Nanny Reeves was half way down the stairs when the front door burst open and Owen came running in, his face flushed and a grey smudge across his nose and cheek.

406

'Master Owen! What *do* you think you're doing?' she asked sharply as he came bounding toward her.

'You'll never guess,' he panted, 'You'll never guess how we came home!'

Evan appeared in the doorway, and she affected the semblance of a smile. 'Well, from the look of you, I should say you ran all the way.'

'Wrong! You're completely wrong! But you can try again if you like.'

'I can't possibly imagine. So why don't you just tell me.'

'On a bus!'

She looked at Evan, aghast. 'Surely not? They're a breeding ground for all manner of diseases. I'm sure Mrs Rees-Morgan would never …'

'No need for concern on that score,' Evan grinned. 'We travelled *outside.*'

'*Outside?*'

Owen was dancing with delight. 'You should try it, Nanny. It's wonderful! I shouldn't think Grandmamma would like it one bit because it's terrifically high, but it's quite safe really – though, if I were you, I should wait for Old Tom's bus. He's the driver – we sat next to him the whole way. He's had the ribbons in his hands these forty years, you know! Ever since he was not much more than a *nipper*! And never had an accident because he's the safest driver on the whole damned road!'

Miss Reeves' eyes widened in horror.

'Owen?' called Evan, quietly, 'I do believe we had an understanding about a certain word?'

'But I wasn't saying it for me – I was just saying what Old Tom said.'

'Even so.' He gave the boy a wink. 'Now, I should think you'll probably want to go and wash your face – at the very least?'

'I'll take him straight up, sir,' said Miss Reeves, protectively drawing Owen to her side.

He took her hand, and they began to climb the stairs. 'So, what would you like to hear about next, Nanny?' he asked excitedly. 'The ice-cream – or tossing for pies with the pie-man?'

*

Daniel dropped Joe on to the bed, then straightened up. 'I think 'e's wet 'imself,' he said, sounding embarrassed.

Maria came closer, looking down at the crumpled figure. 'You want to rub 'is bleedin' nose in it. That's what I used to do with my old man when 'e was too drunk to notice. Used to give 'im a bloody good kickin', too.'

'Well, thank you for fetching me, Maria.' Mary went to the door, opening it.

'Oh, that's alright. That's what friends are for. See you later, eh?' Maria pulled her shawl about her, then leaned closer. 'You take my advice and knock seven pounds of shit out of the bugger while you've got the chance

– 'e won't remember it when 'e sobers up.' She gave a little laugh. 'I used to tell my old man 'e'd got the bruises fallin' down the stairs.'

With Maria gone, Daniel remained ill at ease. 'She's an 'ard-faced cow,' he said, forcing a laugh.

'I don't know why she thinks we're friends,' said Mary, absently, coming to the bed and looking down at Joe's grey and clammy face.

'Well, anyway, I suppose I should be goin', too, eh?'

'How did he get like this, Danny?'

'You mean you 'aven't 'eard?'

'Heard what?'

He shuffled uncomfortably. 'It's not really my place to say, Mary. It's Joe should be the one to tell you … but …' he sighed. 'The fact is, 'e's gone an' lost 'is porter's licence.'

'Lost his licence? *Why*?'

'For stealin'.'

Mary stared at him. 'Stealing? Stealing what? *Fish*?'

'Money. Seems 'e's been at it for months. They set a trap for 'im, an' the silly bugger walked right into it. 'E's lucky they didn't send for the police.'

'No, it must be a mistake. He can't have been taking money.' She looked about the squalid little room. 'What would he have done with it?'

On the bed, Joe shifted restlessly, his breathing becoming laboured for a few seconds before he fell back into unconsciousness.

''E gambles,' said Danny, casting a despairing eye at his younger brother. 'Always 'as done. I'd sort of 'oped that perhaps … when you an' 'im got together …' He looked embarrassed. 'But I've already said more than I should 'ave. Will you be alright lookin' after 'im?'

Mary nodded.

'Then I'd better get back to work.' He went to the door, but on the threshold he paused. 'I just wanted to say … well, I'm right glad 'e's got you, Mary.'

Chapter Fifty-One

'Oh, my God, listen to that!' Lizzie Albrook craned forward in wide-eyed surprise. 'They're havin' a right old go, ain't they.'

Annie Chapman began to chuckle, then gave a rattling cough, spitting a mouthful of phlegm on to the flagstones.

The two women were standing by the lavatories at the far end of the court, and Mary's voice carried easily to them on the early evening air.

'Serves 'im bloody well right,' said Maria, from behind one of the cracked and battered doors.

'You know she goes out on the streets,' said Lizzie in an awed voice.

'You're a gormless 'a'p'orth, Lizzie.'

'She does! Kate told me. *Black Mary* they calls her.'

'Well, p'raps yer want to follow 'er example,' said Annie. 'Make yerself a bit o' money while yer still young, 'stead of scrubbin' doss'ouse floors for old McCarthy.'

'No, you wouldn't catch me doin' nothin' like that. Disgustin', I reckon.'

'Well you don't know nothin' about it, do you,' called Maria.

From the other end of the court came the sound of breaking glass.

'Oops,' said Annie as an orange came rolling towards them. 'There goes the window.'

Inside number thirteen the faint odour of vomit still lurked beneath the smell of carbolic soap.

'Now look what you've done,' said Joe.

'But I'm *not* done. I'm not done by a long way! How could you be so bloody, *bloody* stupid?'

'Stupid?' He put his hand to his temple as his headache worsened. 'Well, m-maybe I was a b-bit …'

'There's no *maybe* about it. We've both had a bit too much to drink at times – but if Danny hadn't found you in the street you could have died!'

'Died? I know, b-but …'

'But nothing! Two days you've been in that bed – and sick as a dog for most of it! Then the minute I turn my back you sneak off – to see your damned gambling friends again, I suppose?'

Surprised, Joe looked at her through red-rimmed eyes. 'You know about it?'

'Danny told me – and just as well, because you wouldn't have, would you!'

He crumpled on to the chair. 'M-Mary, I'm so ashamed.'

'I was sick with worry.'

'Worry? Yes. Yes, b-but you don't understand, M-Mary. I *had* to go out.'

'Why? To buy me that bloody orange?'

Joe shook his head. 'I owe some m-money,' he said, swallowing hard. '*A lot of m-money.*'

'How much?'

He raised his eyes, but unable to meet her gaze he lowered them again. 'Twenty-five pounds.'

'*Twenty-five pounds!*' She slumped back against the mantelpiece, running her hand through her hair. 'Oh, Joe.'

'I've been paying it b-back, week b-by week, b-but now they won't give m-me any m-more time.'

'Well, they'll just have to. Tell them you've lost your job, and that we'll pay it back when we can.'

'When we can?' He shook his head again. 'You don't understand. I've *got* to get that m-money, M-Mary. I've got to get it *now*. If I don't, they're going to cut m-me up.'

She looked at him. 'You're not serious?'

'Serious?' With trembling hands he picked at the splinters of broken glass littering the tabletop. 'I've never b-been m-more serious.'

'Then we have to leave here – the two of us.' She went to the table, sitting opposite him and gripping his hand. 'We'll get away from London.'

'Away from London? What with? We haven't got any m-money.'

'I've got …' Mary looked down guiltily. 'I've got some savings. Not much – but enough. Come with me to Wales. We'll be safe there.'

'Safe? You don't know these people. They'll never stop chasing us, *never*. I've seen it b-before.' He pulled his hand away, chewing at his fingernails. 'It's the way they are – it's how they live. It's not just the m-money – it's the principal. If they let the likes of us get away with it then …'

'But they won't find us.'

'They won't find us? How can we b-be sure? We'll always b-be looking over our shoulder, M-Mary. And anyway, what about Danny? What about the rest of m-my family?'

'But it's nothing to do with them.'

Joe looked across the table at her. 'No,' he said very deliberately. 'No, it isn't – b-but that won't m-make any difference to the likes of Harry Farrel.'

*

That afternoon I went to the bank and withdrew my twenty pounds – my 'Going Home Money'.

*

Gwyneth was washing the breakfast things at the sink when she became aware of the man standing by her front gate. It was a fine summer morning, but he was dressed in a heavy coat and muffler, with a hat pulled down over his white hair, partially obscuring his face. For several minutes he stood there, catching his breath, then instead of moving on he unfastened the latch and started up the path. It was only then she recognised the frail figure of Mr Abrahams.

'It's good to see you again, sir,' she said as she brought him into the cosy little kitchen.

'It's good to see you, too, Gwyneth.' He gave her a tremulous smile. 'Would it be alright if I sat down?'

'Yes, of course,' Gwyneth wiped her hands on her apron. 'Would you like some tea?'

'That would be very nice, thank you.' He looked about the kitchen, noting the welcoming little touches. 'You've made a fine home here.'

'I've had a lot of practice.'

'Yes, I suppose so.'

'So, how are you, sir? You're looking very well.' She half turned from filling the kettle. 'I heard about your … your bad luck.'

He sighed ruefully. 'Yes, my situation was looking rather bleak for a while, but fortunately for me the world is still not without its share of honourable men.' He saw Gwyneth's puzzled look, and he continued, 'I was contacted by one of the directors of the investment company to which I had entrusted my money. It seems there was a degree of negligence that contributed, at least in part, to my losses, and he was moved to return a portion of my original investment from his own personal funds. The very fact that I am not in the workhouse today is wholly due to the conscience and charity of this one man.'

'That's wonderful.'

Abrahams nodded. 'I've never been very religious, but …' He looked up, embarrassed. 'But what about yourself?'

'Me?' Gwyneth toyed with the lid of the tea caddy. Finally she said, 'You know I have a child?'

'Yes, I'd heard. But not your own?'

'I'm not her real mother, if that's what you mean. But in every other sense she's mine.'

'Gwyneth,' he said quietly, hearing the defensive tone of her voice. 'I'm not here to pass judgement.'

'You wouldn't be the first. You must have heard the talk.'

'There will always be gossip, especially in such small towns – but I think what you've done is very compassionate.'

She turned from him, fussing with the cups and saucers. 'So,' she said with exaggerated brightness. 'How is everyone else?' She searched for names, but none would come.

'I was rather hoping you could tell me.'

'Oh, I don't see too many people these days.'

Abrahams shifted in his seat. 'You remember Mrs Cartwright?'

'Yes.'

He saw the slight stiffening of her shoulders. 'She came to see me yesterday. She's going back to London.'

'Is she?'

'Gwyneth, I can tell by your voice you know what I'm about to ask – but I have to ask it. Have you *any* idea where Mary might be?'

Gwyneth turned around. 'It's *always* about Mary, isn't it? The whole world revolves around Mary.'

'Mrs Cartwright is worried – and so am I. Neither of us has heard from her for a long time.'

'So what makes you think I'd know anything?'

'We just thought …'

'I don't know where she is – and what's more, I don't care.' She waited for his protestations, but he made none, and she began to move agitatedly about the small kitchen. 'She cares for no one but herself, so why should *I* care about *her*? Tell me! *Why*?'

'I can't answer you, Gwyneth. I have no answer.'

'I *hate* her.'

With a sigh, Abrahams got slowly to his feet. 'I understand,' he said softly. 'But I don't believe you.'

'Then you don't understand at all.'

'Perhaps.' He made to leave. 'All I know is, Mary stayed by your brother, and, but for that one brief moment when she followed her heart, she would have stayed by him forever. Can you really stand in such terrible judgement over her?'

Gwyneth's lips compressed into a thin line. 'I can, and I have – and I find her more than guilty – but if you think she's so innocent …' She went to the dresser and took out the unopened letter, throwing it on to the tabletop. 'Here, take it!'

'Thank you, Gwyneth,' he said, putting the letter into his pocket.

Gwyneth looked at him. 'For what?'

He made to answer but she turned away, crossing to the sink and washing her hands.

*

The small brown and white mongrel was barely more than a puppy, just a soft round ball of exuberant affection playing at Harry Farrel's feet as he strolled about the empty boxing ring.

'Cute, ain't she.'

Michael Kidney smiled nervously. 'Yeah. She's alright.'

'You like dogs, Mickey?'

''Course.'

'Good – 'cos it's a bitch o' yours I wanted to talk to yer about.'

Kidney wiped his damp palms down the sides of his jacket. 'If you're meaning Liz …'

'Got it in one, old son. Yer know, that's what I like about you, Mickey – you're sharp.' He tugged at one of the thick ropes forming the ring, testing the tautness. 'See, I'm an easy-goin' sort of bloke, but when I 'ear that I'm bein' called all manner of stuff by some mouthy cow – well, naturally I gets a bit upset.'

'I know what you mean, Harry.'

'Do yer?'

'Yeah, 'course. But I've taken care of her. She'll be watching what she says in future.'

'Given 'er a bit of a bashin', 'ave yer?'

Kidney smiled, flexing his shoulders. 'You could say that.'

'Good boy.' Farrel gave the rope an extra hard pull then let it go so that it thrummed in the air. 'An' was that before or after she split yer 'ead open with that quart pot?' He watched Kidney blanche. 'You're a cunt, Mickey. A complete fuckin' …'

There was a movement near the door, and Farrel snapped his head round, glaring into the darkness, his face relaxing into a smile as he identified the reluctant visitor. 'Joe,' he called, as if greeting an old friend, then with a note of concern. 'Fer fuck's sake tell me *you're* bringin' good news.'

Joe came forward to stand awkwardly just outside the ring. 'News? Yes. I …' he took a deep breath, steadying his nerves. 'I've got the m-money.'

''Ear that, M-M-Mickey?' Farrel chuckled. ''E' says 'e's got the fuckin' m-m-m-money.'

Momentarily off the hook, Kidney affected an ingratiating laugh. 'He m-m-must think we're a p-p-pair of c-c-cunts.'

The humour left Farrel's eyes. 'Well, 'e's dead right about one of us!' He turned back to Joe. 'So, yer goin' to pay up then, Joe? That's funny that, 'cos I'd 'eard you'd 'ad a bit o' bad luck.' He cocked his head to one side. 'Yer wouldn't be takin' me fer some kind of mug?'

'A m-mug? No. No, I've got the m-money now.'

'All of it?'

'Not *all* of it.'

'Well, there's a fuckin' surprise! So 'ow much *'ave* yer got?'

'Got? Twenty pounds.'

Farrel sucked at his teeth in grudging respect. 'That *ain't* too bad,' he said, taking the money. The puppy was still playing at his feet and he scooped it up. 'You know about dogs, Joe?' He grinned. 'Nah, I don't suppose yer would. Not too keen on *proper* sports, are yer? Cards an' dice is more your thing, eh? Well, this 'ere is what we call a *taste dog*. Yer see, when yer raisin' a good fightin' dog – *bringin' it on,* as it were – well, yer need somethin' fer it to practise on – to give it the taste fer blood. So yer find it somethin' a bit soft. Somethin' that ain't goin to put up too much of fight while it's gettin' ripped apart.'

Joe looked in horror at the trusting little bundle of fur in Farrel's hands.

'I only tell yer this, Joe, so as yer'll understand. I'm goin' to give yer a little more time to find the other five pounds. Let's say a couple of months, eh? You find the money an' everythin'll be sweet as sarsaparilla. But you let me down, an' I'll throw yer to a young gentleman I've taken under my wing. Someone I'm *bringin' on*. I'll make *you* 'is taste dog.'

*

Mary stirred restlessly. Somewhere in the distance a woman was scream-ing, but it was the much closer rustling of clothes that had wakened her. She half turned in the bed. 'What are you doing?'

'Doing? Nothing. I can't sleep.'

A curtain made from an old coat hung across the broken window, and the lamplight creeping around the edges flickered as Joe moved back and forth in the darkness. 'The clock's just struck four. I thought I'd try the m-markets. I m-might get a day's work.' He came to her, touching her arm. 'You go b-back to sleep. I'll put m-my hand through the window and refasten the b-bolt.'

His lips brushed at her hair, and she rolled away from him, putting her face to the wall, listening to his footsteps as he withdrew, the soft click of the door, followed by the rustle of the coat over the window and the scrape of metal.

She lay for a while in that drowsy state between sleeping and waking until she was roused by the sound of the bolt being drawn and the door opening. 'No luck, Joe?' she asked sleepily. It was still very dark, but she heard the soft creak of the floor, and sensed him standing behind her. 'What time is it now?' she asked.

There was no answer, and suddenly the hairs on the back of her neck began to rise. 'Joe?' she asked anxiously, fully awake now but too frightened to turn around. 'Is … is that you, Joe?'

For what seemed an age she lay there, trembling, feeling the presence in the room pressing upon her like a ghastly touch – then as quietly and as suddenly as it had descended, so it lifted.

When she finally summoned the courage to look, she was quite alone.

*

'Joe?' Mary wandered over to where he was down on his hands and knees, peering into the crack between the wall and floorboards. 'Did you come back last night?'

'Last night?' He poked a finger into the hole, feeling about. 'I think it's down here, I can definitely feel something.'

'You didn't forget something and come back?'

'Come b-back? What time?'

'I don't know – what does it matter? Either you came back or you didn't. You must know.'

Joe turned his head to look at her. 'No, I didn't, now that you come to m-mention it. What's all this about?'

'I don't know. It's nothing.' She went to the bed and sat down, fretting with her hair. 'I must have dreamed it.'

'I had a dream the other night. Funny one it was.'

Mary watched his backside wriggling where it was shoved into the air. 'What *are* you doing?'

'Doing? I told you. I can't find the key – It's fallen down this hole.'

'It can't have. It's too big. You must have put it somewhere else.'

'Somewhere else? No. I always leave it up here on the m-mantelpiece. You know I do. I tell you, it's fallen down this hole.' He got up, rubbing his knees. 'I'll have to b-borrow some tools. In the m-meantime you'll just have to use the b-bolt like I do.'

'I don't suppose it matters. It's not as if we've got anything to steal.'

There was a note of despondency in her voice that brought Joe to her side. 'I'll get your m-money b-back, M-Mary. I promise.'

'It doesn't matter.' She lay down, curling into a foetal position on the grubby counterpane.

'I m-made two shillings today – and I've b-been promised m-more work tomorrow. We could treat ourselves this evening.'

'We'll need it all for the rent.'

'The rent? Yes, you're right, of course. Got to pay the rent.' He got up, going back to the fireplace. 'It will b-be alright, you know. Everything *will* b-be alright.'

'Yes.' She sighed heavily, pulling herself into an even tighter ball. 'I'll go along Whitechapel Road later on. Kate says there are some cleaning jobs going. It's only a few pence an hour, but it's better than nothing.'

'B-Better than nothing? Well, m-maybe that would b-be b-best – just for a short while, eh? Till we get b-back on our feet again?' He stood awkwardly for a few moments, chewing at the ends of his moustache. 'You look tired.'

'I didn't sleep very well.'

'That funny dream, eh?' he said, trying for a lighter note. 'I had a funny dream the other night ...' He saw her tense, and let his voice tail away. 'Well, never m-mind that. Look, why don't you leave looking for that job till tomorrow. Have yourself forty winks, and I'll take m-myself off for a stroll, get out of your way for a b-bit. That'd b-be nice, eh?'

'Yes,' she said. 'It would.'

*

It was the last day of August, and the annual meeting of the Loyal Company of Hop Pickers was gathered about a table in the corner of Ringers.

'That's a right old shiner she's given you.' Maria Garbey leaned down to touch the purple bruise under Annie Chapman's eye.

Annie pulled her head away. 'I ain't some freak show to be poked an' prodded, yer know.'

'I never said you was. Anyway, it's not that much. I've had ten times worse when I was livin' with my old man. I remember one time ...'

Kate sighed impatiently. 'If yer don't mind? We're tryin' to 'ave a meetin' 'ere this mornin'.' She waited until Maria had wandered a little way off, then she squared her shoulders, adopting a more business-like tone. 'Right, so who's comin' 'oppin'?'

'You're too late,' called Maria, leaning against the wall. 'Everywhere'll be full up by the time you get there.'

'Do us a favour will yer, darlin'? *Piss off.*'

Mary toyed lethargically with a strand of hair. 'I'll have a word with Joe.'

'Right – so we'll take that as a *no* shall we?'

'I'll come if I can borrow some better boots,' said Annie.

Kate eyed her with concern. 'It's a long ol' walk, darlin', – an' you ain't been that well lately. What if yer was to 'ave one of yer funny turns on the way?'

'Then yer can leave me by the side o' the road. I don't care. I reckon I'd be better off out of it.'

'I'm serious, Annie.'

'So am I.'

'So what about you?' asked Kate, turning to Lizzie Albrook.

'What about me?'

416

'Are yer comin' 'oppin'?'

''Course not! I already got a job, ain't I?' said Lizzie indignantly.

'Then what the bloody 'ell are yer doin' 'ere, then?'

'I dunno. I just come 'cos Mary did.'

Exasperated, Kate got to her feet. 'Well, it's been a pleasure doin' business with you ladies – but I've got to go an' meet my Jack. We've preparations to make for our *grand tour*. Anyone what wants to come can meet us at the corner of Flowery Dean tomorrow mornin' at eight o'clock sharp – otherwise you'll 'ave missed the bloomin' boat!'

'You goin' by boat?' asked Lizzie in surprise.

Kate looked pityingly at her. 'Gawd, Lizzie, I don't know 'ow yer make it through each day, 'onest I don't.' She'd begun to edge her way out from behind the table when the door burst open and Jack came rushing in.

'There's been another one!' he called, bringing the babble of bar-room conversations to a halt.

Walter Ringer continued polishing the glass he was holding. 'Another what?'

'Another murder – over at Bucks Row. There's a big crowd gatherin'.'

Drinks were hastily finished, and with a scraping of chairs and rattling of glasses the bar quickly emptied.

Continuing to polish his glass, the landlord looked gloomily around his almost empty pub. 'Thanks, Jack.'

Kate sat back down again. 'Come on, Jacky m'darlin', yer can buy us another round.'

'You lot not going to take a look?' asked Walter.

Kate shook her head. 'No point in goin' lookin' for misery, Wally. It comes to find yer soon enough.'

Chapter Fifty-Two

John McCarthy's shop was rather like its owner, neat and tidy, but with an air of having known better days. He sucked on his teeth. 'So when *do* you think you'll be able to pay?'

'Next week.'

'I wish I had a shilling for every time I've heard that.'

'Definitely next week. I've found a job and …'

He looked up from the ledger. 'Oh? What sort of job's that, then?'

'Tailoring,' said Mary, holding his gaze.

'Well, that should pay alright, I suppose.' He sucked at his teeth again, running his finger down the neat columns of figures. 'You're two weeks in arrears. That's nine bob, you know?'

She nodded. 'We can start paying it off next week. I promise.'

'Promises are like pie crusts – particularly around here – but alright, I'll trust you.' He looked her straight in the eyes. 'Now, what about the window?'

'Oh – yes, I was going mention that.'

'I've never been one to kick a person when they're down – anyone around here will tell you that – but I won't be taken for a ride, either. So it's up to you to get it mended. I can send my man round to do it if you want. It'll cost you two bob – but you won't get it done any cheaper.'

'Two shillings?' Mary hesitated. 'Can we leave it for now? Joe says he can mend it.'

'Suit yourself. As long as it's done – and done proper, I don't care who does it.' The bell above the shop door tinkled, and he shifted his gaze toward the sound, his eyebrows drawing into a frown. 'Morning, Annie,' he said wearily. 'Bit early in the day to be drunk, isn't it?'

'I'm not, Mr McCarthy. I swear it.'

Mary looked at her with concern. 'Are you alright? You look terrible.'

'I don't know what's the matter with me.' Annie swayed a little so that

Mary had to catch hold of her arm. 'I've just come from the 'ospital. I was on my way to Stratford, to borrow some boots, but I must have fainted right there on the 'ospital steps.' With trembling hands she reached into the pocket of her coat and took out a small cardboard box. 'They give me these 'ere pills to take – but my mouth's that dry, they stick in my throat an' I can't swallow 'em.'

'That's a new one,' said McCarthy, closing the ledger.

'It's God's own truth. I never could abide pills.' She swayed perilously again. 'They stick in my gullet.'

Mary steadied her. 'Come home with me. I'll make you some tea. Have you had anything to eat today?'

Annie shook her head.

'Then I'll get you something.' Apologetically, she turned to McCarthy. 'Could you let me have an ounce of tea – and perhaps half a loaf?'

McCarthy sighed, and opened the ledger once more.

With the kettle boiled and the tea brewing, Mary came to sit with Annie at the table. 'How are you feeling now?'

'Better.' She nibbled at the thinly buttered bread, swallowing painfully.

'Leave it until the tea's ready. It'll go down easier then.'

Annie managed a weak smile, putting the uneaten morsel back on the plate. 'I should eat, but I've just got no stomach for it.'

'But you must try.'

'I know. Thanks for carin', my love.' Then, feeling awkward, she nodded toward the broken window. 'Reckon you'll 'ave to improve yer aim a bit,' she said in a quavering voice.

Mary gave her a smile and picked up the jug that served as a teapot, pouring the dark brown liquid into a cup. 'There's no milk or sugar, I'm afraid.'

'That's alright. But what's this – ain't you 'avin' none?'

'I should be getting to work. I'm late already.'

'Why didn't yer say?' Annie fumbled for her pills, 'An' 'ere's me 'oldin' you up.'

'No, it's alright, you don't need to hurry.' Mary rose and took her shawl from the back of the door. 'Stay and finish your breakfast. Just reach through the window and bolt the door when you leave.'

Annie took a gulp of tea, then pushed a pill between her lips, screwing up her face as she chewed it. 'It's alright,' she said shuddering as she swallowed. 'I ought to be goin' anyway.'

'But you shouldn't go out in that state.'

'I can't give in to it – an' anyway, I've got my bed money to find.'

Mary looked at her. 'Be careful, Annie.'

'What – of this 'ere *Leather-Apron*, chap?' She rose unsteadily to her feet, her broad knuckles whitening as she gripped the table for support. 'Truth is I should welcome the meetin'. Ain't nothin' in this life for me that I'd fight to keep – so if 'e wants to serve me the same as them other women 'e's killed – well, I reckon I'd thank 'im for it.'

Mary frowned anxiously. 'Look, why don't you stay here. Get a few hours sleep. I shan't be back till this evening, and I don't suppose Joe will.'

'Oh, Mary,' Annie eyed the bed with undisguised longing, 'yer don't know 'ow tired I am. But I can't give way. *I daren't.*'

'It's not giving way – it's only being sensible. Come on.' She went to tidy the counterpane and plump up the thin pillow. 'Come and lie down. If you feel more like eating when you wake up, you can finish off the bread and make yourself some more tea.'

'Well … maybe just an hour or two?'

'Stay as long as you want.' Mary went to the door, lifting the latch. 'See you later, eh?'

*

Joe was already home when Mary returned, tired and hungry. He was sitting at the table, the evening paper spread out before him and his pipe jutting from between tightly compressed lips. 'You're b-back, then,' he said not looking up.

Without answering she hung her shawl behind the door, then went to the fire, poking at the embers. 'How did you get on today?'

'Today? Oh, I got on very well today – until I came b-back here, that is, and found that … that Chapman woman snoring away on the b-bed.'

'It's alright, I said she could.'

'Said she could, did you? Yes, well, that's what she told m-me – b-but that doesn't m-make it alright!'

Mary sighed wearily. 'Look, can we talk about this later, Joe? I haven't had anything to eat all day, and I'm worn out.'

'Worn out? What do you think I am? I'm down at the m-market at five o'clock every m-morning, going cap in hand for jobs a b-boy would likely turn his nose up at!'

'And whose fault is that?' Instantly regretting the words, she gave a small moan, putting her fingers to her temple. 'I'm sorry. I didn't mean it. I've had a bloody awful day. There's this horrible woman I work with …'

But Joe was not to be placated. 'Awful day or not …'

'So what was I to do? Annie was ill!'

'Ill? Then she should go to the infirmary.'

'She just needed somewhere to stay and rest for a while – just like I did once, remember?'

He nodded. 'Remember? Of course I do, b-but it's not the same.'

420

'Why? Because she's old and lost her looks?'

'Her looks?'

'Or is it just because you don't like *any* of my friends?'

'Friends?' He gave a dismissive snort. 'I shouldn't care to call such people *friends*. And you're right – I *don't* like them. You know I don't. They're a b-bad influence on you – b-but even if you don't care about that, for God's sake, M-Mary. *She smells.*'

'Of course she does. Who doesn't around here?' She drew her fingers through the damp patch at the armpit of her dress, holding it out in front of her. '*I* smell – and so do you. You haven't been to Billingsgate in weeks, but this place *still* stinks of fish!'

Joe rammed the pipe back in his mouth, then immediately took it out again. 'All I'm saying is, when I come home I *need* a few hours sleep. That's not too m-much to ask is it?' He looked pointedly at her. 'It's not as if I get to use the b-bed at any other time!'

'Then use it now. Go on! I'm not stopping you.'

He lowered his eyes, glowering. 'You know what I m-mean.'

'Yes, I know.' She too looked away. 'But that was *never* a part of our arrangement.'

'Part of our arrangement? I don't remember there ever b-being any *arrangement*. B-But I reckon that after all this time, a m-man m-might reasonably have an *expectation*.'

*

Slumped on a settle in the kitchen of Crossingham's lodging house, Annie swallowed the last of the baked potato she'd been forcing herself to eat. 'It's well past midnight. Can't yer let me just sit down 'ere?'

'I'm sorry, Annie, but you know the rules. If you 'aven't got your bed money, I've got to turn you out.'

With difficulty she struggled to her feet. 'Alright, I'll get it. Yer won't let my bed?'

'If someone wants it and they've got the money.' He gave a helpless shrug.

'Don't, Tim, *please*. I'll be back soon.'

*

'I *will* pay you b-back – all of it.'

The voice came from the darkened floor beyond the bed, and Mary turned away from it. 'Of course you won't. How could you? But it doesn't matter.'

There was a long pause, then he said. 'Did you talk to M-McCarthy?'

'Yes.'

'What did he say?'

'He's given us till next week.'

'Next week?' There was a frightened note to Joe's voice. 'B-But we can't – and what will we do then?'

'I don't know. Maybe we can pay him something – a few shillings?'

'A few shillings? No, I've *got* to get that five pounds.'

'I know. But we've got some time yet. Try not to worry about it.'

He fell silent, but then he said, 'M-Mary … can I ask you …?'

'Joe, I'm really tired, and I daren't be late for work again tomorrow.'

'Tomorrow? Yes, yes of course …'

She closed her eyes, lying quite still, trying to shut out the distant noise from the street and the occasional tramp of boots passing the door. At the far end of the court a dog barked, a man shouted, and the barking turned to a yelp. Somewhere else a door banged, once, twice, and she found herself waiting for a third that never came. She sighed and opened her eyes. 'What was it, Joe?'

'I just wanted to ask …' There was another long pause before he said, 'Do you … do you ever wish you'd never m-met m-me?'

All around her the darkness pressed in, stale, suffocating and despairingly black, and for a moment she couldn't bring herself to answer. 'No … no, of course not.' There was no reply, and she half turned. 'Why?'

'Why? Oh, nothing. It's just that lying here in the dark … well, I get sort of *frightened*.'

She rolled over. The fire had gone out, and she stared blindly toward the sound of his voice. 'You're frightened of the dark?'

'The dark? No.'

'Then what?'

'What?' He pondered it. 'The uncertainty, I suppose.'

'Joe, I don't understand what you're talking about. What uncertainty?'

He lay still for a long time, then he said, 'The uncertainty that, perhaps, one m-morning I'll wake up – and you won't b-be here.'

*

Dorset Street was almost deserted as Annie came from the brightly lit doorway of Crossingham's and made her way across the road to pause by the entrance to Miller's Court.

Someone had been sick just inside the covered archway, and her stomach heaved, forcing her to draw back to a safe distance from where she peered into the court, trying to discern a light under Mary's door – but all was in darkness.

She turned back. 'See Tim keeps the bed for me, Brummy,' she called to the night watchman who had come out to smoke a pipe in the fresh night air. 'I won't be long.'

*

'And she was just *gone*?' Mary's voice was little more than a whisper. 'How old were you?'

'Twelve.'

'And what about your da?'

'Da?' he said wistfully, the word sounding strange. 'Well, I don't really remember him. He died when I was about five or six.'

'And you've never seen your mam since?'

'Since? No. I've got no nice stories like you have, M-Mary. She said goodnight to us – just like she always did – b-but when we woke up in the m-morning she wasn't there. It's funny, you know? I can still b-bring to m-mind the smell of the soap on her cheek.' He fell silent for a moment. 'That's why I always like to get up early, I suppose – to m-make sure every-thing's still here.'

Mary made no answer, but stayed very still, looking into the cold and lonely darkness where he lay curled upon the floor, then she reached out to him. 'Come on, Joe,' she said softly, lifting the counterpane. 'Why don't you come to bed.'

*

Dawn was breaking as Annie Chapman made her way slowly up Brick Lane. She had been walking for the best part of the night and still the bed money eluded her – but then it so often did, for whatever charms she might once have possessed had long since been eroded by years of cling-ing to the marginal existence that was her life, and now, on top of every-thing, her illness was beginning to overwhelm her.

At the corner of Hanbury Street she paused, leaning her hand against a shop-front as a small group of men made their way toward her. Fighting the pain, she tried her best to give them a winsome smile, but they only laughed and crossed the road, avoiding her as if she carried the plague.

She shuffled on, turning the corner and making her way back towards Commercial Street. The pains were growing worse: sharp, shooting pains that cleaved through her, making her wince with every step, until halfway along Hanbury Street she had to stop, pressing herself against the wall as a wave of sickness washed over her.

'You alright, darlin'?' A man in a battered deerstalker cap came to a halt in front of her.

Annie forced open her eyes. 'Tuppence?' she said desperately. 'I'll do it for tuppence.'

'Oh, will yer?' He gave a chuckle. 'Yes, well, I'll think on it, eh?' he said, moving on.

She shivered, clutching her stomach with clawed hands, tears blurring her vision. 'Oh, sweet Jesus, 'elp me.' She pushed herself from the wall, staggering a few more steps before stopping again. It was then she saw the familiar figure walking briskly toward her, and a smile of relief quivered on her lips. 'Oh, thank God it's you. Please, you've got to 'elp me.'

*

Whitechapel Road was teeming with people, horses, vehicles of every shape and size, and in the midst of it all a Salvation Army band from which the faint strains of a hymn rose into the early evening air.

'Excuse me, could you let me through?'

Drawn less by the music than the prospect of hearing the lurid details already appearing in the papers, a large and mainly illiterate crowd had formed, spreading across the pavement, blocking Mary's way, their faces lifted to where a man's head poked above the throng, his gaunt features made even more pallid by the black suit he wore. The man raised one finger in the air. '*And now, before we sing again, I should like us to reflect for a few moments upon this most recent and terrible murder ...*'

Mary breathed heavily, pushing her way through the mass of bodies, the coarse, antagonistic sniping of the fat seamstress she worked with still ringing in her ears.

All about her people were listening intently, a few heckling, while others called to them crossly, telling them to be quiet. Mary continued to push her way through, grinding her teeth in anger. 'Excuse me. I just want to get through. Excuse me ...'

'*... a murder which has taken place only this morning – and not more than a few minutes walk from this very spot. Now, let me ask you ...*'

Around the perimeter of the crowd, uniformed men and women were handing out leaflets, but Mary ignored them, declining their tracts as she finally broke through to the other side and started away toward home.

'*... can it be any coincidence that the happenings of these past weeks ...*'

'Mary?'

It was a common enough name, and at first she paid no attention, but then hearing it called again she stopped and turned, searching in vain for a familiar face.

'*... that these butcheries have fallen upon women who themselves have fallen?*'

From out of the crowd a young woman in a black bonnet and uniform came slowly forward, stopping a few yards away. 'Is it really you, Mary?'

Confused, Mary started to shake her head, but then, looking more closely, she stopped – and the blood drained from her face. '*Julia?*' she asked in a whisper.

Chapter Fifty-Three

'They crucified me. There was this huge ceiling beam, and they used it as a cross.' Julia stroked her palms as she sat opposite Mary in the Temperance Tea Rooms. 'They couldn't find nails, so they used rope and hooks. But it still hurt, Mary. It hurt so much. You have no idea how Jesus must have suffered. I would have happily died – even before they started cutting me.'

'Your poor face.' Mary was still shaking as she reached out, her fingers hovering in the space between them.

Julia put a hand to the scars beneath her eyes. 'These? They're nothing. Just their little joke. When they couldn't make me cry tears, they made me cry blood.' A smile trembled for a moment on her lips. 'Quite amusing, don't you think?'

'Oh, Julia …'

'But I didn't tell them anything, Mary. Not a thing. I always said I'd keep you safe – and I did.' Mary's eyes were glistening, and Julia leaned forward, taking her hands and pressing them between her own. 'Oh, come on now. Don't go getting weepy. It's over – ancient history. And besides,' the old, familiar smile lit up her face, 'it was nothing compared to the pain of having all those roses tattooed on my thigh.'

'I've missed you *so* much. Elspeth said you were dead.'

'I very nearly was – and I would have been if those two kids hadn't chanced by.' She gave a small shrug. 'But then it wasn't really chance.'

'Wasn't it?'

'Everything is for a purpose, Mary.' She grinned, 'Even that dress you're wearing, I expect.'

Suddenly self-conscious, Mary tried to hide her frayed cuffs.

'What's happened to you, Mary? I barely recognised you back there.'

'I could say the same about you.' Mary looked at the uniform. 'Have you really joined them?'

'No, I'm just on my way to a fancy dress ball,' Julia laughed. 'Yes, of course I have. But I want to hear about you. What are you doing these days?'

'I'm working.'

'Where?'

'At a small tailoring shop in the Mile End Road.'

'Tailoring? I didn't know you could sew.'

Mary lowered her eyes. 'I can't. I scrub the floors.'

Julia chuckled. 'Still the same old Mary. So what do you *really* do?'

'That *is* what I really do.'

*

'They do it so much better in Paris,' said Spencer, looking around the Haymarket restaurant.

Evan folded his napkin and placed it on the table. 'You know, for some-one who professes to care so little for London, you seem to be spending a good deal of time here.'

'Not through choice, I assure you, though I have to admit Paris is a little dull now that both you *and* Gaston have chosen to desert me.'

'Gaston? I never realised he was a particular friend of yours.'

'He wasn't – but for pure amusement value he was worth a dozen acquaintances. I should dearly love to hear his ideas about this Leather-Apron chap.'

'So should I.' Evan smiled briefly. 'But it really isn't a laughing matter. Four women have been murdered in the past five months, and there's no reason to suspect he won't continue until he's caught.'

'Well, that surely can't take very long. According to some journalist friends of mine, he's apparently half man, half baboon, very short with an extremely thick neck – or possibly no neck, depending on which paper you read. Then there are the small, glittering eyes and the repulsive smile, not to mention this most peculiar running sort of walk that appears to perform the magical trick of making absolutely no noise. Good Lord, the man is a veritable freak show! How can the police fail to find him?'

'I don't know, but they appear to be doing so.' Evan reached for his pocket watch. 'Seven o'clock,' he said. 'I should be leaving. Owen will be going to bed soon.'

'You have a nanny, surely?'

'Of course.'

'Then let the poor woman do her work.' He saw Evan's uncertainty. 'Just a few weeks ago you were complaining of how your mother had molly-coddled him. Now you're doing exactly the same. And much as I appreciate knowing exactly what your son is doing every hour of the day, I have to say that as a topic of conversation it leaves a lot to be desired.'

426

Evan placed his hands flat upon the table, smiling guiltily. 'Then let us change the subject entirely. Coffee?'

'No, not for me, old boy.' Spencer took out his cigarette case. 'When in London, I do as the intelligent foreigner does – and stick to brandy.'

*

'And so I went into hiding,' said Mary. 'Then those two women were killed – first Emma Smith, and then Martha Tabram, except people knew her as *Emma*.'

Julia's voice grew anxious. 'You think they might have been mistaken for you?'

'I don't know. I don't know what to think. At first I thought so, but then came this latest murder, Mary Ann Nichols – she went by the name of Polly. So perhaps the first two were just a coincidence.'

'I'm sure they were. You're safe, Mary.' Julia squeezed her hand. 'We both are. These murders are nothing to do with us.'

'Joe thinks this Leather-Apron is just …'

'Joe? Who's Joe?'

'He's … he's the man I live with.'

'You're married?'

Mary glanced uncomfortably at the bonnet lying on the table. 'No. I just live with him.'

'Well, that's alright, then,' said Julia with a sigh.

'You don't mind?'

'Mind? Of course not. But I should certainly have minded if I'd missed your wedding.' She looked out into the darkened street. 'So, where do you live?'

'Not far.'

'Wonderful. Then I'll walk you home. I don't think Mr Leather-Apron will bother us as long as I've my bonnet on – he seems more interested in quite another type of lady – and when we get there, you can introduce me to Joe.'

*

'Surgeon-in-Chief?' Spencer looked impressed. 'Your stock is obviously rising, old boy. And in New York? Quite an adventure.'

Evan swirled the brandy about the glass. 'But I can't possibly go. Owen has just started school.'

'There *are* schools in America. They even speak English there, I believe.'

'But it wouldn't be fair to the boy. He's just experienced one upheaval. He needs time to settle again, to gain some confidence.'

'Yes, well, that is indeed a very laudable *excuse*.' Spencer drew on the cheroot. 'Come on, old man, don't look at me like that. You know as well as I do it *is* only an excuse. It's his mother that stops you from going. You've never gotten over her, have you?'

Evan looked down at his fingertips as they tapped the edge of the table. 'No. No, I haven't.'

'Well, they say time is a great healer.'

'Or maybe it's a great educator.'

'Oh? So you have become wise, have you?'

'No, but I think I may have become less of a *pious little prig* – as my father once called me.'

Spencer chuckled. 'I should like to meet your father. I admire people with such perception.'

'Have I really been *that* insufferable these past years?'

'Quite. You do know Gaston deduced the cause lay in the fact that your mother had rejected you due to your father's indiscretions with, shall we say, *unfortunates* – from whom he had contracted a rather unpleasant disease?'

'Did he? And his logic was?'

'Oh, God knows. I can't remember now – but it made perfect sense at the time.' He picked up the bottle. 'More brandy?'

Evan shook his head. 'I should have gone back for her – talked to her. Had more faith.'

'But you caught her in the act.'

'There may have been another explanation. We've both listened to Gaston give seemingly irrefutable evidence for a deduction, but he's still been completely wrong.'

'You're clutching at straws. Just accept the fact she's a whore.'

'Is that what you think?'

'Most certainly.'

Evan frowned. 'So what are you saying? That I should forget her?'

'No point in asking me, old man. I have the moral integrity of an alley cat.' He blew out a cloud of smoke, watching it drift up toward the ceiling. '*But*, I do remember when we first roomed together – before all that business with abandoned babies and lecherous artist chappies – when we would sit up late at night, talking. Do you remember?'

'Yes.'

'Well, I have to tell you – back then you were as insufferably boring about this woman as you currently are about your son.'

'I see.' Evan picked up his glass. 'Is that it – the sum total of your insight? I understand now why you so admire people with perception.'

'Oh, I'm not finished.' Spencer took another draw on the cheroot. 'No, indeed. Tedious though it was to listen to the endless litany of her virtues, I cannot deny being deeply envious – and should *I* ever be fortunate enough to encounter such a girl, you can take my word on it that I would take her on face value and wouldn't care whether she was also the whore of Babylon or even the sister of our freakish friend, Leather-Apron.'

Evan looked at him across the top of his brandy. 'I'm glad,' he said, 'because I've come to realise that I feel exactly the same way.'

*

'This is almost our old stomping ground,' said Julia with delight as they came to the corner of Commercial Street. 'So which way now?'

Mary looked uneasily about. 'It's getting late – I'm not even sure Joe will be in. Perhaps you should go home, and we'll meet another day?'

'Nonsense. We must be nearly there, and besides, no one is going to attack me.' She patted her chest, laughing. 'I'm wearing God's armour, aren't I? Now which way?'

Mary hesitated, then turned reluctantly toward home. 'Down here. It's about a quarter of a mile.'

'Near Spitalfields? We have a refuge not far from there. Angel Alley. Do you know it?'

Mary nodded.

'I stayed there when I came back from France.' Julia stopped, taking hold of Mary's arm, her casual tone falling away. 'I *did* look for you, you know. I looked all over London, everywhere I could think of.' She shook her head. 'And you were just around the corner the whole time. We must have passed each other a dozen times without realising.' Her eye fell upon the draggled tail of Mary's skirt. 'Still, perhaps that's not *so* surprising. We both look a little different these days.'

Mary sighed, but made no reply, and they walked on a little way. 'Are you really serious about all this?' she asked finally.

'About all what?'

'About finding God – or whatever it is you've done.'

'Yes, of course. Why?'

'It's just that …' She struggled to find the right words. 'Well, you don't seem very different. I would have thought you'd have become …'

'A vinegary-faced old crow?' Julia laughed. 'We're not all like that, you know. You should come and see for yourself.'

'I don't think it's really my cup of tea.'

'But then would you have ever imagined it was *mine?*'

Mary shook her head. 'No,' she said, starting to laugh. 'Never in a million years.'

'Well, then.' She linked her arm with Mary's. 'We've organised a special public meeting for next week. Why don't you come? It can't do any harm – and who knows, you might like it enough to join us.' Catching Mary's look, she laughed. 'Well, think about it, at least, eh?' She flashed a grin. 'After all, black always did suit you so very well.'

By Spitalfields church a mob had gathered, blocking the pavement despite the efforts of a handful of constables to disperse the increasingly vociferous crowd.

Mary drew to a halt. 'What do you think is going on?'

'It's about this latest murder, I expect.'

'The murder? Yes, I'd forgotten. Do they know who was killed?'

'I don't know, but there have been angry crowds gathering all day. There's going to be trouble if the police don't catch the killer soon. Come on, let's cross the road, just in case.'

They reached the other side and were just a short distance from the Britannia when Mary stopped again. 'Look, before we go any further, there's something I have to tell you.' Her jaw tightened defensively. 'You remember Dorset Street?'

'Doss-it Street?' laughed Julia. 'How could anyone ever forget that place. Do you remember when ...' She paused, the laugh dying on her lips as she looked searchingly at Mary. 'That's where you live, isn't it?'

'Yes ... well, in a court just off of it.' She turned her head, looking back along the road to avoid meeting Julia's eyes. 'It's a hovel, Julia – and the truth is, I don't want you to come any further.'

'Mary ...'

'*Please*, just go home.'

'You don't understand, Mary. Dorset Street? It couldn't be better.'

Mary stared at her.

'Oh, Mary. Believe me, it's perfect. Just absolutely *perfect*.'

*

'Come on, my love.'

'I can't.'

''Course yer can.'

'It's too soon.'

'No it ain't.' Gussie Farrel reached down, fingers splayed, running her hands over Murray Baines's bare behind as he lay between her thighs, his softening manhood still within her. She dug her nails into the clenched muscles, pulling him closer. 'Once ain't enough.' She nibbled at his ear, working at the soft lobe with tongue, teeth and lips. 'Not with you, it ain't, my sweet. I want more.'

Baines clenched his buttocks, willing the blood back into his member as he arched back, trying to drive into her, but it was no good, and he collapsed with a sigh, his cheek against hers, her damp ringlets brushing his nose and mouth.

'Not givin' up, are yer?' cooed Gussie, raking his softened flanks.

'I just need a minute.'

She slid her hands up over his back to stroke at his neck, then her eye fell upon the half-finished glass of wine standing on the table by the bed, the dark red liquid gleaming like a ruby in the candlelight. ''Ere,' she said, giggling seductively as she picked up the glass. 'I've got a little idea. Why don't yer just take yer weight off me fer a minute? No – don't let 'im fall out – I just need a little bit o' room, alright?' She looked up at him as he raised himself above her, then very deliberately she tilted the glass, letting a few drops trickle on to her left breast. 'Ooh, now what does that look like?' she purred. She spilled some more, the wine dribbling on to her nipple and running over the plump white flesh in thin rivulets. 'Oh dear. What 'ave you done?' Her tongue flicked out, moistening her lips as she felt him harden within her. '*What 'ave you done?*'

*

Joe sat by the light of a single candle, anxiety deepening the lines in his face and making him appear far older than his years. 'Where have you b-been? I've b-been worried about you. I didn't know ...' he stopped, suddenly aware of the unfamiliar figure standing just behind Mary. 'Oh, I ... er ...'

Mary looked about the bleak little room, as if seeing its true awfulness for the first time. 'Oh, Joe. Couldn't you have at least lit the fire?' She went to the hearth where some pieces of broken packing case lay ready for kindling, picking up a few and pushing them into the empty grate.

'The fire? There didn't seem m-much point. I didn't know where you were, and b-besides, there's no ...' He stopped short and pulled self-consciously at his clothes, straightening his collar and adjusting his waist-coat. 'Anyway, M-Mary,' he said, adopting a more formal tone. 'Surely you're going to introduce m-me to our guest?'

Without waiting for an introduction, Julia stepped into the room. 'You must be Joe,' she said, putting out her hand. 'Mary's told me so much about you. My name's Julia – Julia Jones.' She caught Mary's look of surprise, and smiled. 'For a short while I went under the name of Devereaux, but now I'm back to being plain old Jones.'

'Plain old Jones? Oh, I see,' said Joe, taking the proffered hand. 'Something in the nature of a *gnome de plume*, was it?'

She smiled. 'Exactly so.'

'Exactly so?' Joe brightened. 'Well, it's very nice to m-meet you, I'm sure – and to welcome you into our little *gnome.*'

'Joe!' The word hissed like a whip, and Mary dropped her eyes guiltily. 'Could you go and get some coal, please. I'm sure we could all do with some tea.'

'Tea? I should say so.' He took his jacket from the back of his chair. 'Right, well I'll b-be b-back with some Old King in just a jiffy.'

'Don't go to McCarthy's. Try the shop round the corner.'

'Round the corner? Yes, well, see you in a m-moment, M-Miss Jones.'

Mary waited until he had gone, then moved about the room in a futile attempt to make it more presentable. 'Well, *you* seem to have made an impression, at least.'

'Isn't he a darling.'

'Don't, Julia, please. Don't make fun of us.'

'I'm not.'

Mary looked at her. 'Then what?'

'Then nothing. I like him.'

'And I suppose you think that this ...' she gestured about the room, 'is *quite charming*?'

'No.' Julia thought for a moment, taking in the broken window and faded wallpaper. 'No, actually I think it's just about the worst place I've ever been in.' There was an impish glee in her eyes, and despite herself Mary began to laugh.

'So?' continued Julia, 'Now that we've addressed that matter, if you'd care to pass me a heavy object, I'll open another window – or would you prefer I drew the coat to make it a little more cosy?'

'You'd better draw the coat. If the neighbours see you in here dressed like that, they'll never speak to me again.'

Julia went to the window and pulled the old overcoat across it. 'One does realise, of course, this style of sleeve is terribly unfashionable for one's curtains these days?'

'One does realise,' said Mary with a half-hearted smile, 'that if one continues to poke fun, one will get a sharp kick up one's bottom?'

'One should just like to see one try,' chuckled Julia. She looked across to where Mary was kneeling by the hearth, putting a match to the small pile of wood and paper she'd laid. 'It's wonderful to find you again, Mary. It ... It feels just like old times.'

'Hardly.'

'Why? Because of this place? It's nothing – just bricks and mortar. It doesn't matter.'

'It does to me.'

'Well, it doesn't to me. The only thing that matters is I've found you again. I've missed you so much – you can't begin to imagine.'

The wood began to burn, and Mary watched it, keeping her face turned. 'I hope Joe hurries up. This wood will be gone through in no time.'

'Mary ...?' Julia came forward, putting a hand on Mary's shoulder. 'I mean it. I ...' The door opened, banging against the washstand, and she turned to find Joe, a metal pail in his hand. 'Ah, the arrival of Old King Cole,' she said cheerily.

'Old King Cole?' beamed Joe. 'Yes. Yes, that's it exactly. M-My b-but she's a sharp one, isn't she, M-Mary? As sharp as a ...' His face dropped.

'I nearly forgot,' he said, slowly putting down the pail. 'That's why I was looking for you, M-Mary. There's b-been another m-murder.'

'I know. They were talking about it at work – and we saw the crowds on the way home. Have they discovered her name?'

'Her name? Yes.' He swallowed hard. 'Yes, they have.'

There was something in his voice that made her suddenly very afraid. 'It ... It wasn't ... *Emma*?'

'Emma? No, not Emma. It was Annie.'

A wave of relief passed over Mary's face. 'Oh, thank God.'

Joe swallowed again. 'You don't understand,' he said very slowly and carefully. 'It was *Annie*. Annie Chapman.'

*

Gussie lay back, her thighs still parted, one hand cradling her head, the other toying with the remains of the wine on her white belly. 'Don't go.'

'Got to.' Baines finished knotting his tie. 'Bit of business to attend to.'

'An' what about *this* bit of business? You ain't goin' to leave me like this are yer?' She threw him a coy look. 'An' there was me thinkin' you'd become quite the gentleman, these days. S'pose it takes more than new clothes, eh?'

Grinning, he pulled on his jacket, brushing at the lapels. 'So what do you want me to do? Bath you?'

'Ooh, now there's an idea.'

'Haven't got the time.'

'Vince can wait, can't 'e?'

'What makes you think I'm meeting Vince?'

''Cos yer always with 'im. Yer even startin' to look like 'im.'

'Nothing wrong with looking smart.'

'No, nothin' at all. Just don't yer go gettin' to be too much of 'is *right-'and man*,' she laughed, making an obscene gesture.

Baines chuckled. 'No, I save that one for you.' He leaned down, running his hand up the inside of her thigh. 'Just for you.'

'Well, just to make sure yer do ...' Gussie removed her ring, a plain gold band adorned with a single diamond, and slipped it on to his little finger. 'There,' she said with a smile. 'Now it'll always be mine.'

*

'You knew her?' asked Julia. 'You knew the woman who was murdered this morning? Oh, Mary, I'm so sorry.'

'Don't be. There's no need.' For a brief moment Mary had gone a deathly white, but now the colour was returning to her cheeks. She went to the door and opened it, standing with her back to the room, breathing in the night air. 'It's funny,' she murmured. 'Practically the last thing Annie said to me was how she'd welcome it. Can you imagine? She said she'd actually welcome being killed.'

'Welcome b-being killed?' Joe went to her. 'Come b-back inside and sit down, M-Mary. You don't know what you're saying.'

'Yes I do.' She looked up at the tiny patch of night sky, a ragged tear in the loom of roofs and chimney pots. 'And I'm alright – really.'

*

I wasn't sad for Annie's death, though I would have spared her the means of her passing. I was sad for her life – for the pitiable waste and futility of it. From the little she had told me, I knew her to be no saint, but then who could be in such circumstances? Her life had been no life, merely an existence – a long wasting illness, to be endured, and eased, when money permitted, with the laudanum of the alehouse.

But worst of all, it was an unexceptional life – no different to thousands of others, and – as I looked into the future – no different to mine.

Chapter Fifty-four

'*Because thou sufferest that woman Jezebel to teach and to seduce my servants to commit fornication!*'

The speaker was slight of build but huge of forehead, beneath which his clear blue eyes flared as if limelight burned deep within.

'*I gave her space to repent of her fornication – and she repented not!*'

He glared about the hall, his eyes falling upon the congregation, not in condemnation but in collusion, as if he himself were God and they so many ragged angels, summoned to sit in belated judgement.

'*And he said: Behold, I will cast her into a bed, and them that commit adultery with her into great tribulation, except they repent of their deeds. And I will kill her children with death; and all the churches shall know that I am he which searcheth the reins and hearts.*'

Standing next to Joe at the back of the hall, Mary watched the speaker lift a finger as he spoke again, more quietly now. 'Wickedness walks in the world, now just as in bygone days – and God looks down and despairs. Yes, *despairs* – at the vileness of his creatures – us, whom He made in His image.' The finger began to tremble as it roved over the crowd, following the path of his accusing stare, for now the ragged angels had become sinners, and they trembled under his gaze.

'A fiend walks the streets of Whitechapel – isn't that what they say?' He drew himself up, his mouth forming a solemn curve as he slowly shook his head. 'A fiend? No! Not *a* fiend – but *fiends!*'

An excited murmuring broke out. 'I always said there 'ad to be more than one murderer,' said an old man sitting just in front of Mary. 'Stands to reason, don't it?'

The speaker held up his hands, and the room fell silent once more. 'Yes, *fiends* walk the streets of Whitechapel. Fiends whose names are known to me, just as they are known to the police – who have done nothing to prevent these foul crimes!'

The crowd erupted again, and scattered about the hall the handful of bored reporters scrabbled for their notebooks and pencils.

The speaker remained absolutely still, waiting until the last voice had died away, then he gripped the edges of the lectern. 'Well, this conspiracy of silence has gone on long enough – and tonight it is my intention to name the vile creatures whose crimes have caused God to weep at the wickedness of His world.'

A man near the front leaped to his feet. 'Tell us and we'll soon put a stop to 'em!'

'Their names? They are well known to you all. But lest there be any mistake …' The speaker paused, the iridescent eyes sweeping the expectant faces. 'The perpetrators of these crimes are – Emma Smith. Martha Tabram. Mary Ann Nichols. Annie Chapman – *Prostitutes!*' There was a deathly hush, and he lowered his voice, speaking with chilling gravitas. 'These are the names of just a few of the fiends who, night after night, prey on …'

'How dare you?' Mary flung herself from the wall. 'How *dare* you?'

The speaker regarded her patiently. 'I dare because someone must.'

Joe took hold of her arm. 'M-Mary, for goodness sake. Everybody's looking.'

'Then let them look.' She jerked her arm free, moving away from him and closer to the small stage. 'Those women are dead – murdered. What gives you the right to stand up there and talk about them like that? As if *they* were the criminals?'

'Criminals? You think their crimes can be equated to petty thievery and fraud? These women are worse than criminals. They have perverted God's design.' He looked deeply into her eyes. 'Tell me,' he said with a quiet intensity. 'Do you believe in love? The love between a man and a woman?'

'Of course!'

'That is God's love. His gift when he created Adam and took from him a rib to make Eve, that she might comfort him, that she might love him, give herself to him freely, in the true spirit of that gift, asking no reward other than to fulfil God's holy plan.' He breathed deeply and ominously. 'Jesus himself used violence in throwing the money-lenders from the temple – yet what was their crime in comparison to the sin of these women? Nothing! Is it then so surprising that such terrible violence should be visited upon those who would defile the most fundamental intention of our Lord?'

In the silence that followed, Mary could only shake her head, her lips working silently as she struggled to find the right words, but the words would not come. Then Joe was at her side once more.

'Come on, M-Mary,' he said quietly. 'I think we should go home.'

*

The strains of a waltz drifted from the ballroom to where Gaston stood, his imposing bulk dwarfing his fellow guest.

'Our professor was a remarkable man. As students, we were fascinated by his observations, and a great many of us would attempt to emulate his methods.' Dr Cosmo Gaston lifted his glass, drinking with relish, then dabbing at his lips with his handkerchief. 'But I believe I am the only one to *fully* develop them into a science.'

His listener, an older man, scratched doubtfully at his grey, mutton-chop whiskers. 'A *science* you say?'

'Of course.' Gaston turned toward the room, regarding the other guests with a clinical gaze. 'Once one has become conversant with the science of deduction, then one may understand *everything*. But perhaps, by way of an example, I might relate the case of a young lady I had cause to assist some while ago. She had fainted on the concourse of Gare du Nord, in Paris.'

'I should be greatly interested to hear it.'

Gaston smiled indulgently. 'Her clothes,' he said with the air of a con-jurer about to pull a rabbit from a hat, 'were far too warm for the Parisian weather. From this I easily deduced she had arrived from England that very morning. The question then was …' He broke off as his eye fell upon a familiar figure. 'Excuse me one moment, Dr Phillips,' he said, waddling away and returning moments later with his hand on the shoulder of a tall young man. 'Well, here is a delightful surprise. Do you know Dr Rees-Morgan?'

'I don't believe I do.' The older man put out his hand. 'George Bagster Phillips.'

'Evan Rees-Morgan,' said Evan.

'I've just been hearing of this *science of deduction*,' said Phillips.

Evan laughed. 'I don't doubt it.' He turned to Gaston. 'I'd heard you were in London.'

'Indeed,' said Gaston proudly. 'I am in Harley Street.'

'Though, I deduce, not at this very moment.'

Gaston looked puzzled, then let out a laugh, his great florid sack of a chin shaking with mirth.

'So, you are familiar with this *science*?' asked Phillips.

Evan smiled. 'Gaston has entertained us with his observations on many an evening.' He cast a thoughtful glance at the older man. 'Bagster Phillips? I recall that name. Aren't you the doctor who attended the Chapman woman murdered in Hanbury Street?'

Phillips nodded. 'Terrible business. You've been following the case?'

'I've read the reports in the papers. Are the police any nearer catching the man?'

'Not that I'm aware of. Been a lot of hysteria over this Leather-Apron chap, but it seems to have come to nothing.'

'You still believe the killer might be a doctor?'

'I shudder to think it, but the nature of the mutilations certainly point to someone with surgical knowledge.'

Gaston tutted loudly. 'The clues are all there and only need to be read. If the police cannot see them, then they are blind fools.'

'You have a theory?' asked Phillips, dubiously.

'Just look at the evidence,' said Gaston. 'We have two murders …'

Evan raised an eyebrow. 'Four, surely?'

'Smith and Tabram were murdered by a very different hand.' Gaston looked to Phillips. 'I'm sure you will agree?'

'There are *some* grounds to suspect that may be the case.'

'Come, come,' said Gaston. 'We are all professionals here. I can assure you any confidences will be respected.'

Phillips looked uncomfortable. 'Well, no one will testify, of course, but it's fairly certain Smith and Tabram were victims of a local gang.'

'So,' said Gaston triumphantly. 'As I said, we have two unattributable murders – the Nichols woman in Bucks Row, and now Chapman in the back-yard of a house in Hanbury Street.' He raised a finger. 'And we must ask ourselves, what have these two women in common?'

Phillips thought carefully. 'Well, they were both prostitutes, between forty and fifty years of age …'

'Yes!' Gaston broke in. 'We need no more! Now, let us concentrate on the murder method. The women were strangled, is that correct?'

'Yes,' said Phillips with some deliberation. 'That is, I believe strangulation to have been used initially, though, in my opinion, actual death may have come from the cutting of the throat.'

'But the women were first rendered unconscious by strangulation?'

'That is my belief.'

'It would take a man of some considerable strength,' said Evan. 'Strangulation is not instantaneous. Even if the women were old and sick, their natural reaction would be to struggle, yet neither of them appear to have done so.'

'Just so. Just so!' Gaston's eyes glinted with delight. 'You have hit upon it *exactly*, my friend.'

Phillips scratched at his whiskers in confusion. 'So you are saying the murderer is a very strong man?'

'No, not at all,' said Gaston. 'You are not thinking this through. But let us not get ahead of ourselves, we still have a number of deductions we must make.' He took a fresh glass of champagne from the tray of a passing maid, before shooing her away like a naughty child. 'Now,' he began as soon as she was out of earshot. 'Let us move on to the mutilations.'

'Must we?' asked Phillips, looking about the candlelit room. 'I hardly think this is the time and place.'

'Of course we must!' protested Gaston. 'The murderer is within our grasp if we will only exercise our powers …' he tapped a podgy forefinger to his temple, '*methodically!*'

Evan glanced over his shoulder, returning the smiles of two ladies who had come in from the dancing to stand sipping champagne a few feet away, then he turned back to Gaston. 'If that is the case, then might I suggest we exercise those powers whilst taking a stroll around the square?'

*

It was nearing midnight, and the night-shift warder was irritable.

For most of the day a barking dog had kept him awake. Now, as well as being tired, his trousers were soaked from carrying the heavy pails of ice up from the cellar, and he'd cut his hand where a piece of trim had come away from the galvanised tub to leave a sharp edge. Contemptuously he spat into the freezing water, then sucking at his injured palm he made his way back along the landing to the open cell door. 'Everything's ready, ma'am.'

The woman nodded. 'Well, Connie,' she said, taking a step toward the wild-eyed old woman standing naked and trembling between two burly warders. 'Bath-time. Are you going to be a good girl for us?' She took off her glove, drawing the mutilated remains of her thumb across Connie's cheek, hollowed and sunken where every one of her teeth had been extracted. 'I don't suppose so – but at least there'll be no more biting, hmmm?'

*

'On both occasions the throat had been cut. But in the case of Chapman,' Phillips shook his head in disbelief, 'I think the killer may have been attempting to decapitate her.'

Gaston spread like a huge inkblot across the bench on which he reclined. The suggested turn about the square had progressed no further than the first corner before the corpulent doctor had begged a halt, so that they now stood, or sat, in the dark just beyond the spill of light from the street lamp. 'Please go on,' he said, wheezing for breath.

Reluctantly, Phillips continued. 'Her abdomen had been laid completely open and the intestines lifted out and placed on her shoulder. The uterus, the upper portion of the vagina, and two thirds of the bladder had been removed and appear to have been taken away.'

'And the first victim – I understand her mutilations were also centred upon the genital area. You see where this is leading us, gentleman?'

Evan perched himself on the arm of the bench. 'You believe the killer is motivated by lust?'

'No, no! Far from it! You completely miss the point. If the objective was sadistic pleasure, then why strangle the poor wretches into a state of unconsciousness first?'

'Well, to keep them quiet, of course,' said Phillips. 'Nichols was killed in the street and Chapman in a place only slightly less public. In both cases, people were sleeping only a few yards away.'

'Exactly! If perverted lust were the motive, the murderer would surely have chosen younger, more attractive victims – lured them to some out-of-the-way place, where, by the simple application of a gag and some restraints, he might have performed his gruesome work while the poor women were fully conscious – a much more pleasing prospect to the sadistic mind, surely?'

Phillips stared at him aghast. 'I think, sir,' he said coldly, 'that you would be better advised to save such *sensationalist* ideas for the yellow press.'

'I'm sorry if I offend.' Gaston reached into the pocket of his evening suit and withdrew a cigarette case. 'But the idea of our killer being a sadist is complete poppycock.' He offered the opened case to Phillips. 'Will you join me?'

Half-heartedly, Phillips took a cigarette.

'You still abstain, Rees-Morgan?'

Evan nodded.

'So,' continued Gaston, striking a match. 'Where does this leave us in our quest?' He saw the irritation on Phillips's face as he leaned to the flame, and he continued quickly. 'If we dismiss the idea of lust as a motive – as we must surely do – then what have we left?'

'Well, what do we have left?' asked Phillips, drawing on the cigarette.

'Love, gentlemen.'

Phillips choked on the smoke. '*Love?*'

'Of course. Our murderer has no desire to hurt his victims. He could easily despatch them with the knife, yet he goes out of his way to render them senseless first – wanting to spare them the painful touch of the steel.'

'And then he *lovingly* hacks them open?' asked Evan.

'Well put, Rees-Morgan!' Phillips blew smoke into the air.

Gaston shrugged. 'Why not? The woman is dead. From that point on he does nothing that we do not do every time we enter the dissecting room.'

'There's no comparison,' protested Phillips. 'None at all!'

'There could be,' suggested Evan, 'if the killer felt he had a greater purpose?'

'Exactly so!' exclaimed Gaston. 'Our man is making a point. He kills in the open, leaving his victims arranged, on display. He is saying to us *behold – and take heed.*'

440

Evan looked doubtful. 'But that sounds more like vengeance than love.'

'No. His purpose is to save others, to turn them away from prostitution. His victims are sacrificial lambs – and he chooses them carefully. Both the murdered women were destitute – prostitutes of the very lowest kind. Chapman was already near to death through disease. I believe our man considers it a kindness to shorten their unhappy lives.'

Phillips shook his head. 'That's all very well – but it won't do! You haven't seen the mutilations to the genitals. The motive has to be sexual.'

'Not at all. Is it so long ago that we would cut off the hand of a thief? In the case of a prostitute, what better example can our man make than to mutilate the offending body part? Our man neither lusts after, nor hates women – far from it. They trust him because he cares for them. He feels an affinity with them – and they with him – so much so that we are undoubtedly looking for a man with a certain *effeminacy*.'

'Then surely we have come full circle?' protested Phillips. 'Because how on earth does such a man manage to keep the woman from struggling during strangulation?'

'An effeminate nature does not preclude great physical power. I have seen women possessed of enormous strength.' He turned to Evan. 'Then there is the strength born of madness or great emotional distress which I know you have witnessed. But our man requires none of these to subdue his victims.'

Phillips took the cigarette from his mouth. 'Then how the devil …?'

'Quite simple,' beamed Gaston, producing the metaphorical rabbit once more. 'You remember the bruises to her face? They are produced when he lowers her to the ground. One hand just so,' he placed his hand beneath his own jaw. 'The marks of fingers and thumb – just as you see here. The other hand cradles the nape of her neck, his forearm against her back, taking some of the weight. Don't you see? – Even in her unconscious state, he lowers her gently. Once she is safely down, he strangles her, for he is unable to contemplate the brutality of the knife until he feels sure she is dead.'

'He uses chloroform?' asked Evan.

Gaston shook his head. 'Pressing the pad to her face would cause any bruising to be higher.'

'Then how does he render her unconscious?' asked Phillips, tossing the half-finished cigarette into the gutter.

Gaston leaned back with a flourish. 'Hypnotism,' he said.

*

'Mary, I'm so, so sorry. I had no idea.' Julia laid her bonnet on the table. 'Are you very upset?'

'No, I'm bloody angry. I didn't know those other women, but Annie was a friend of mine. And yes, she was a prostitute – when she needed to be – but how else was she supposed to live?'

'How was she supposed to live?' asked Joe. 'Well, she could have found a job.'

'What, like me?' Angrily, Mary thrust her red and calloused hands toward him. 'Look at them! All for eighteen pence a day.'

'Eighteen pence a day, it m-may b-be! B-but at least it's *honest* work.'

'No. No, it's stupid work for stupid people like me!' She knew she should stop, but the blood was pounding at her temples and she couldn't. 'So what if Annie went on the streets? What's so bad about that?'

'What's so b-bad about that? Now you're just b-being silly.'

'What if *I'd* been a prostitute?'

'A prostitute? You?' He glanced uncomfortably at Julia, then back at Mary. 'No, you'd never do that.'

'But I have!' She saw his eyes widen. 'You have no idea, do you? I'll tell you something. When I was in Cardiff I earned *two shillings* – more than I earn now for a whole bloody day – just like that.' She clicked her fingers. 'Two shillings for something I only half remember. That's a lot of money for just a few minutes work – at least I thought so – but then I came to London.' She turned on Julia. 'Go on, tell him how much we earned at Gloucester Gardens – and for what.'

Julia looked embarrassed. 'Mary, there's no need for this.'

'Yes there is. I've just had to listen to that man going on about God's great design.' She strode to the door, throwing it back on its hinges. 'Is that it out there? Well, is it? Because if that's the best He can do, He should be bloody ashamed of himself.' She slammed the door shut again. 'Remember when we used to come down here from Knightsbridge – and what a laugh it was? Well, we should have come late at night, when it's cold and wet. We should have come without food in our bellies or money in our pockets – with nowhere to sleep and preferably too ill to put one foot in front of the other. That's when the best laughs are to be had. That's when you really see God's *great design*. And yet it goes on and on, and no one cares.' She shook her head. 'But let some poor, pathetic old woman earn her bed money by giving someone a few minutes pleasure, and God gets so upset, she has to be ripped apart!'

'That's not what he meant,' said Julia.

'Isn't it? It's what it sounded like. Perhaps you should listen a bit more closely. How dare he talk about Annie like that? Making her out to be a … what was it? A *fiend*?'

'His methods may be a little unconventional, but Mary, what she did *was* a sin. The bible tells us so.'

'Then the bible is wrong! Most of us sell ourselves every day. My husband, Thomas, sold every muscle in his body – and eventually his life

442

– just to put bread on the table. Now I sell myself to the owner of a bloody sweatshop. Annie sold the only bit of her that anyone might want. Christ, Julia, you once made the same argument yourself.'

'And I was wrong. What we did back then – it was very, very wrong. I know that now – and so do you. In fact you've known it all along.'

Mary looked at her.

'Well, haven't you?' Julia took a step closer. 'I remember you telling me the real story about that two shillings – *and* how you wouldn't take it. Even at Gloucester Gardens, you were never like the rest of us.'

Joe was looking confused. 'The rest of us? What is all this, M-Mary?'

'I was a whore, Joe. Just like Annie.'

'She wasn't. Don't listen to her.'

'Yes I was. The only difference is that I did for guineas what Annie did for pence.'

'With who?' Julia fixed her gaze upon her. 'Name someone.'

'The stockbroker, Fanshawe.'

'Is that the best you can do? Pluck out the first name that comes to mind?' Julia shook her head sadly. 'You were never a whore. It takes one to know one, so I'm a pretty good judge. You were an actress, a model, but *not* a whore.' She reached for Mary's hand. 'You're pure, Mary – and God loves you.'

Mary's eyes were unnaturally moist, but the bitterness still raged within her. 'Well I don't love Him!'

Chapter Fifty-Five

Holding a prayer book to his right breast, his fingers hooked into the folds of his black gown, the Headmaster strode along, boys parting on every side like the waves before Moses.

'It's about young Rees-Morgan.' The nervous young Form Master followed in the old man's wake, side-stepping those waves who found it sufficient to let only Moses pass.

'Oh yes? Settling in alright, is he?'

'Well, actually, I'm a little concerned.'

'Are you?' Above them the bell for morning assembly died away, and the Headmaster stopped and took out his watch, glaring accusingly at it before tucking it away again and striding on.

'I was saying, sir … about the Rees-Morgan boy?'

'Oh, yes? Getting on well, is he?'

'I've noticed some bruises on him.'

'Good. Good. Nothing like a bit of rough and tumble to knock the edges off a boy.' He stopped abruptly as a pupil came sprinting down the corridor. 'You boy. Yes, you, whatever your name is. Where does a gentleman run, sir?'

The boy skidded to a halt. 'Er, on the playing field, sir?'

'Yes, indeed, sir. And where *else*, sir?'

'I … I don't know, sir.'

'Nowhere else, sir! That's where a gentleman runs, sir! He runs nowhere else – and certainly not in my passageways!' He strode on.

'I'm worried the boy is being bullied,' persisted the Form Master.

The Headmaster pursed his lips. 'Don't like bullying. Don't like it at all! Do we know who?'

'Several boys, apparently, but the ringleader would appear to be Stebbings.'

'Stebbings? Yes, of course. Well, we must give young Rees-Morgan every

444

opportunity to deal with it without our intervention.' He stopped again, glaring across the corridor. 'Ah, Mr. Ponsonby, a word in your ear about the First Eleven, if you please.'

*

'Oh, I'm sorry, were you just going fishing?' asked Julia, standing in the doorway.

Joe stared at her, then down at the length of string he was holding, a piece of bent wire tied to one end. 'Fishing? Oh, yes, I see.' He gave a little laugh. 'I m-must remember that one.' Clumsily, he gathered up the line. 'I'm sorry, I didn't m-mean to stare like that just now. It's just that I didn't quite recognise you in your clothes.' He blushed. 'That is, I m-mean …'

'I know what you mean,' she smiled. 'I remembered what Mary said about the neighbours, and thought it better to come in civilian dress.' She waited expectantly, but when Joe made no sign of moving she asked. 'Is Mary in?'

'M-Mary in? No, she's not. She's still at work.' He bundled the string into his pocket. 'B-But do come in. Dear m-me, I don't know where my m-manners are today. Perhaps I could offer you a little Q.R.S?'

'T? Yes, I should love a cup of tea.'

'Tea, that's right,' he grinned. 'M-My, b-but you *are* a sharp one. I said to M-Mary only yesterday …' He paused, picking up the tea caddy. 'Oh, now there's a thing. We don't seem to have any. I could go to the shop?'

'No, please don't trouble.'

'Trouble? It's no trouble, b-but …' With transparent relief, Joe moved across to the table. 'Well, alright, if you insist, eh? Will you take a seat at least?'

'No, thank you. I have some of my own.'

For a moment he looked puzzled. 'Oh – oh, yes. I see,' he chuckled. 'I shall have to remember that one, too – or should that b-be *three, four*, eh?' He gave his little laugh. 'Do you get it? One, too – *three, four*?'

Smiling, Julia seated herself at the table. 'I can see why you've captured Mary's heart.'

He sat opposite her. 'Well …' he began, breaking off and looking away. 'Well, anyway, she'll b-be sorry to have m-missed you.'

'She won't be home soon?'

'Soon? No, not for a few hours yet.'

'Oh, I see. Well, then I'll come back another day. I wouldn't like you to miss a big one on my account.' She watched the furrow appear between his eyebrows. '*Your fishing*?'

'Fishing? Oh, yes,' he laughed apologetically. 'I dare say you m-must have thought that a b-bit strange. It's the key, you see. It's m-managed to get itself under the floor b-boards, and I was just trying to fish it out.'

Julia smiled. 'So, the key's a little too low for you?'

'Low? Well … yes. It's under the floor b-boards, you see?'

'Yes – of course.' She gave a little cough, clearing her throat. 'Have you tried a magnet?'

'A m-magnet?' He considered the idea. 'That would certainly do it, alright. Yes, I think you've hit upon it there. I'll see about b-borrowing one this evening.'

She started to rise, then changed her mind. 'Joe?' she asked quietly. 'Would you think it terribly forward of me if I asked you something? Something rather personal?'

'Personal?' He shifted uncomfortably. 'Well, I shouldn't like to promise you an answer … b-but, alright, ask away.'

'You *do* love Mary, don't you?'

He looked even more uncomfortable, and she said. 'It's alright, Joe. You don't need to answer. I can see you do, and I think that's wonderful.'

'Wonderful? Do you?' He reached for his pipe. It was empty, but it occupied his hands. 'I only wish M-Mary thought so.'

'You don't think she loves you?'

'Loves m-me?' He shook his head.

'I think you're wrong, Joe. I think she loves you very much. I've known Mary a long time, and I can tell – but something's not quite right. She's changed.'

'Changed? Yes, well, it's those friends of hers. When she's away from them we seem to rub along well enough, b-but …' There was a snap as the stem of his pipe broke, and he pushed the pieces to one side. 'I've told her I won't have them here – that I won't have common prostitutes m-making themselves at home in m-my … well … in *m-my home*! It's not right. I know I'm not b-blameless – and I've done things I shouldn't have, b-but …' He looked up guiltily. 'I'm sorry –I don't know what you m-must think of m-me – going on like this.'

'It's alright, Joe. I understand.'

He sighed and looked out of the window. 'It's just that I don't feel very charitable at the m-moment.'

'You're worried for Mary – about the people she's mixing with – and I share your concern.'

'Concern?' He pondered the word. 'Yes. Yes, I *am* concerned. I know things would b-be different with us if I could just stop her going out drinking.'

'You've got to be strong with her, Joe. She's very lost at the moment, and you've got to be the one to guide her.'

'Guide her? M-Me?'

'Who else?' Catching his look, she shook her head. 'I think the world of Mary. I'd die for her. But I'm not here with her every day – you are.

You're the only one who can keep her from these bad influences. You're the only one who can save her from herself. It won't be easy, I know that. But, ultimately, she will love you for it.' Julia got up. 'Now I really should be going. I've taken up quite enough of your time – and you've still to find your key.'

'Key? Oh, yes.' He too got to his feet. 'I'll tell M-Mary you called. I know she'll b-be sorry to have m-missed you.'

Julia looked thoughtful. 'I wouldn't like her to think I've been meddling.'

'M-Meddling? No, don't you worry about that. I shan't m-mention our little chat.'

*

Alone in the hospital laboratory, Evan looked up from the microscope, stretching and rubbing his eyes before moving a little further along the bench to where a glass jar of clear, bubbling liquid stood upon a tripod.

'Rees-Morgan?' The man in the doorway peered into the room, 'Is that you?'

'Dr Phillips?'

George Bagster Phillips looked a little embarrassed. 'Yes. I called earlier, but they told me you were lecturing.'

'Well, what can I do for you, Dr Phillips?'

'Not disturbing your work, I hope?' Phillips's eyes fell on the liquid steaming in the jar. 'An experiment?'

Evan turned off the gas burner. 'Tea,' he said with a smile. 'Might I offer you a cup?'

'Yes …' said Phillips, looking uncomfortable, 'that would be very nice, thank you.' He ran his fingers through his hair, contemplating the rows of specimen jars. 'The thing is,' he said, 'and I feel a complete fool for even asking, but do you think your friend Gaston may actually have something with this bizarre theory of his?'

Evan gave an amused smile. 'I doubt it. Gaston *is* very talented, but I'm afraid more as an *entertainer* than as a detective.'

'Well, I must say I originally considered the whole idea quite ridiculous – but you know, the more I think about it, the more I see it as a very logical argument.'

'Gaston's deductions are always extremely logical. I recall an occasion last summer when he visited me in my rooms. He observed the scorch marks on the soles of my new patent leather slippers, deduced that, despite the warm weather, I had been sitting with my feet to the fire – something no healthy person would do – concluded I had recently been ill, and complimented me on my quick recovery. I hadn't the heart to tell him that I'd bought the slippers that very day, and at a very good price, from a stall selling fire damaged stock.'

Phillips chuckled briefly. 'Yes. Yes, I'm sure you're right. You must forgive me for wasting your time with this nonsense. I suppose we can only hope and pray that we've heard the last of this Whitechapel murderer.'

'Other than of his arrest?'

There was a moment's silence. 'For myself,' said Phillips, gravely, 'I would just as soon we *never* heard of him again.' He caught Evan's look. 'As Police Surgeon, one naturally hears things, and – confidentially, just between ourselves – I can tell you that the police are at a complete loss over this case. Their only possible chance would seem to lie in catching the man in the act. But, having seen his butchery at first hand, I would sooner he gave up his murderous work and escaped scot-free, rather than have another woman mutilated in such a way.'

'Have they no clues?'

Phillips shook his head. 'They are clutching at straws – very much as I am doing in coming to see you, I'm afraid.'

Evan thought for a moment. 'Well, if they have nothing else to go on, perhaps we should not be too quick to discount my dear colleague's deductions. In my experience, his conclusions are invariably wrong, but there is no denying his powers of observation.'

'In which case there may be a grain of truth in this *effeminate hypnotist* theory, after all?'

'I don't know. It seems far-fetched.'

'But it would explain so much of the conflicting evidence,' said Phillips. 'And if he's right, and our killer really does have a point to make, then I fear these murders are going to continue – and with increasing savagery.'

Chapter Fifty-Six

Liz Stride had been pretty. As a young woman in Sweden she had been called *The Fair One*, and though the charms that once beguiled Gothenburg had faded, spoiled by disease and a propensity for violence with unwisely chosen adversaries, there remained more than a trace of that original beauty.

Idly, she ran her finger along her teeth. 'Jesus, my breath stinks.'

'I can't smell it.'

'You couldn't smell shit if your nose was stuck halfway up your arse, Mickey.'

Michael Kidney looked about the tiny bar room. It was early evening, and with the place half-empty, Liz's voice carried easily to the dozen or so drinkers. 'Just shut up, you silly cow, an' listen to what I'm saying.'

'Oh, bollocks to you.' She got up, taking from her pocket the small bag of breath-sweetening cachous, and popping one into her mouth.

'Liz. Sit down.'

'I haven't got time to sit around listening to your pathetic whining.'

'You've got to listen. Harry Farrel says ...'

'Oh, fuck him – and fuck you, too.' She raised her eyes to the man returning from his trip to the back yard. 'And fuck you as well, while I'm at it.'

The man regarded her stoically, watching along with the other drinkers as she tottered out into the street. 'Sorted it, then, Mickey?' he asked, sitting down at the table. He saw Kidney's embarrassment, and shook his head. 'Harry's right – you are a cunt.'

'So what am I supposed to do? She won't listen to reason.'

'You're still sweet on her, aren't you.'

'No. No, 'course not.'

'I wouldn't blame you if you were. She's still got her figure and ...'

'I tell you, I'm not sweet on her.'

'Then what's the problem?'

'There ain't no problem.'

'But there is.' The man glanced around the room. 'How long do you think it'll be before what she just said gets back to Harry?'

'I'll deal with it.'

'Of course you will.'

Kidney's eyes flickered nervously. 'I *will*.'

'I believe you, Mickey – because I'm going to help you.'

*

'Can I have a word?' John McCarthy stood blocking the entrance to the narrow passageway that led into the court.

Wearily Mary rubbed her hand across her face, pushing back her hair. 'I know we haven't paid much recently …'

'You haven't paid anything at all – and on top of that, I hear that when you do have any money you go to the shop round the corner. I don't think that's very fair, do you?'

'No, I know, but …'

'*And* the window's still broken. I've let it go all this summer, but it's almost October. Winter's just round the corner, and that window's got to be fixed.'

'We can't. We just can't.'

There was hopelessness in her voice that made him look more closely at her, noticing the dark circles about her eyes – and more alarmingly, the purple bruise on her cheek. 'I don't want to turn you out. It's no good for me, and it's certainly no good for you and Joe – but I shall have to cut my losses if I don't start getting paid soon. Now, I can see things are a bit rough for you just at the minute, so I'm going to give you one more chance. It's Saturday today. If I don't get at least a week's rent by next Friday …' He gave a resigned shrug. 'And one more thing. I don't care what sort of debt you run up round the corner, but I expect you to bring your ready cash to *my* shop.'

*

The smell of fried bacon filled the kitchen of Cooney's Common Lodging house, briefly masking the malodorous miasma that normally pervaded the dimly-lit room.

'They 'ad a pipe-smokin' oyster.'

Jack laughed. 'Get off with yer.'

'I'm tellin' yer they did.' Kate shoved a greasy rasher into her mouth, chewing with relish. 'Me an' my Tom, we 'ooked up with this 'ere travellin' fairground for a while, an' they 'ad a freak show with a pipe-smokin' oyster.'

On the other side of the room, the deputy leaned back, filling his own pipe. 'So what did it smoke? Herrings I suppose?'

'I don't know. I never saw it.'

'Then how d'yer know they had one?' asked Jack, dipping his bread into the still warm fat.

''Cos it was written on the side of the van – in between the fur-covered monkey-boy an' the five-legged donkey.'

'You sure it wasn't just an *excited* donkey?' laughed the deputy.

Jack thought for a moment. 'I can't see how an oyster could smoke a pipe. No. No, yer know what I reckon?' He gave a wink. 'I reckon they got a whelk to do it – an' just dressed it up to look like an oyster.'

'So, who's Tom, then?' asked the deputy, once he'd stopped laughing.

'Tom Conway? 'E was my first 'usband – well, sort of. We never was married, not proper, like. We used to sell these pamphlets an' things what 'e'd written. We'd 'oof it all over the place, sellin' 'em.' She gave a little chuckle. 'The bloomin' tricks we used to get up to.'

'So, Conway ain't your real name, then?'

'No, but it's as good as any.' She finished the last mouthful of breakfast and sat back, cradling her mug of tea. 'Well, that's your best boots gone, Jack. Now what we goin' to do for money? I ain't got nothin' worth pawnin'.'

'Hopping wasn't no good then?' asked the deputy.

Jack shook his head. 'Got there too late, didn't we.' He looked across at Kate. 'Maybe I'll go for a walk round the markets, see if I can pick up a couple of hours work.'

'Alright. I'll see yer back 'ere later. If all else fails I'll go an' find my little ducklin' – see if she can't 'elp us out.'

*

''Ere! You come away from there. What d'yer think yer doin'?'

Guiltily, the shambling figure of Joseph Fleming came away from the window. 'I weren't doing nothing.'

Kate put her hands on her hips. 'Well, don't do it 'ere. What d'yer want, anyway?'

'I come to see Mary.'

'What? Through the window?'

He grew red. 'No. No, not like that. Not like what you mean. I know not to do that.'

'Well, that's a start, I suppose.' She saw the wide, innocent eyes, and she softened her voice. 'So what's the matter. Ain't she in?'

'Yes, she's in there. I saw her.'

'Then why don't yer just knock?'

'I was going to – but she was crying.' He shook his head. 'I don't like it when she cries. I don't like it when anyone cries. I don't like it …'

'Yes, yes, alright. I've got the picture.' She gave him an encouraging smile. 'Look, why don't yer nip off an' leave it to me. I'm good with people what's down in the dumps.'

'Are you her friend?'

'I'm 'er *best* friend,' said Kate.

He looked at her, the agony of indecision puckering his usually smooth face. 'Alright then,' he said at last. 'You'll give her this for me? I got it for her, see?'

'Ooh, that's nice,' smiled Kate, taking the two shillings. 'You can come an' see *me* sometime if yer like.'

'No. No, I couldn't do that. It wouldn't be right.'

'Oh, wouldn't it? Oh, well, yer'd better run along, then, eh?'

She watched him amble out into the street, then quickly ran round to the window, peering in. 'Oi, Mary.'

'Go away.'

'What's the matter?'

'Nothing.'

With a deep sigh, Kate reached in through the broken pane, slipped the bolt, then went round and opened the door.

'What's up, ducklin'?'

Curled on the bed, Mary kept her face to the wall. 'I told you – nothing.'

Kate heard the catch in her voice, and came to sit down by her side. 'Bad old day?'

'Bad old day. Bad old year.' She sobbed. '*Bad old life.*'

'Yes, I know.' Kate rubbed the coin between her fingers. 'But what's so 'specially bad about today?'

Mary slowly turned, showing the bruise on her face.

'Did Joe do that?'

Mary shook her head. 'I got into a fight – with that woman where I work.'

'Did yer win?' smiled Kate.

'I lost my job.'

'So get another one.'

'And McCarthy's going to throw us out at the end of the week unless we start paying the rent.'

'*That's* a bit more tricky.'

'And Joe still has to find five …' She broke off, turning back to the wall. 'Well … he still has to find a job.'

'Gawd, sounds like yer need some serious jollifyin' before tacklin' that little lot. Come on. You come with me.' She held up the two-shilling coin. 'Aunty Kate's got just the thing.'

*

452

'So the 'op pickin' wasn't any good?' asked Maria Garbey

Kate shrugged. 'Got there too late, didn't we.'

'I told you, didn't I?'

'Did yer? I can't remember.'

'It was in 'ere – the day before you left. I said …'

'Yes, alright. No need to go on.' Kate finished her gin. 'So where's old ear ache?'

Mary put down her glass. 'Don't call him that.'

'Oh, so yer know who I'm talkin' about, then.' She gave her a nudge. ''Ere, yer know – the more I think about it, the more it wouldn't surprise me if 'e wasn't this 'ere Whitechapel murderer.'

'Who?' said Lizzie Albrook in fright.

'Joe.'

Already a little tipsy, Mary looked at her askance. 'My Joe?'

'That's daft, that is,' said Lizzie.

'Oh, is it?' said Kate, rolling her eyes. 'Well, *you'd* know all about that, wouldn't yer.'

'Anyway,' said Lizzie. 'I heard that this Leather-Apron, he ain't nothin' like Joe, see. I heard as how …' She leaned forward, lowering her voice in awe. 'Well, as how he's half man – *half balloon.*'

'Go on with yer?' said Kate, affecting a look of astonishment. ''Ere, d'yer reckon that's 'ow 'e makes 'is escape – 'e just sort of floats off over the 'ouses?'

Maria Garbey took a swig at her gin. 'Your mum must have been well pleased to see the back of you, Lizzie.'

'I'm just tellin' you what I heard.'

'It would make sense though, wouldn't it?' said Kate. 'About it bein' Joe? I mean, yer've got to ask yerself 'ow it is this bloke can come at yer with a bloody big knife, an' yer ain't goin' to put up any sort of a fight.'

'So?' asked Maria.

'Well, yer remember when Joe was in 'ere that night, before me an' Jack went off? An' 'ow 'e was goin' on an' on about 'ow many tons of 'orse shit 'ad to be cleared out of London every day – or some such nonsense?'

'I should say so. I bloody well nearly nodded off.'

'Exactly,' said Kate. 'I reckon 'e bores 'em so much – that when 'e pulls out 'is knife it's a blessed relief.' She started to laugh, but catching the look on Mary's face she stopped. 'What's up, ducklin'? We're only 'avin' a bit o' fun.'

'I don't think we should be laughing about it. This man, whoever he is, did kill Annie, you know.'

'I know. So what are we goin' to do – sit around all day with long faces?'

'I just don't think we should be laughing about it.'

'Listen, ducklin'. I knew Annie Chapman longer than any of you lot, an' she used to like a good laugh 'erself back then. Now, I can't say I wasn't sad to 'ear the news, but I also know that winter's comin' on, an' she wasn't likely to make it through – not this time. Well, she ain't got to worry about that no more, 'as she? So what I say is, let's 'ave a little drink to 'er – an' while we're at it, maybe ask 'er to put in a good word with them upstairs for those of us what *does* 'ave to go through the bloody freezin' cold an' wet.' She stood up. 'So – same again, is it?'

*

It was a damp evening, and the smell of cooking hung about the court as Julia knocked at the door of number thirteen.

'I'm sorry to come round in uniform,' she said as Joe appeared in the doorway, 'but I'm just on my way to a meeting, and I thought I'd call in.' She saw his uncertain look. 'But I won't stay if you're having dinner.'

'Dinner? No, we're not having dinner. Come inside, won't you.' He stepped aside to allow her to enter. 'Truth is, I'm a b-bit worried. I don't know where M-Mary is. She went out this afternoon – left a note saying she'd only b-be an hour – and I haven't seen her since.'

'Well, Mary always could look after herself. She'll be back soon. You'll tell her I called?'

'Called? Yes, yes of course.'

'Come on, cheer up, Joe. She'll be alright, honestly.' She smiled encouragingly. 'So, how did you get on with the magnet?'

'M-Magnet? Oh, I haven't b-been able to b-borrow one.'

'Then I'll see what I can do. We can't have any old Tom, Dick or Harry wandering in, can we?'

He gave a weak smile, looking up expectantly as the door opened, but it was only Maria Garbey, and his face fell once more. 'She's not in,' he said sourly.

'Well I know that, don't I. 'Cos if she was, then she wouldn't be up Aldgate 'igh Street with that there Kate Conway, both of them dead drunk and staggerin' about.'

'Aldgate High Street? You're sure it was her?'

'She's a friend of mine, ain't she? I tried to get her to come 'ome before the police run the pair of them in, but she wouldn't have none of it. Told me to piss off, if you please!' Suddenly aware of Julia's presence she pulled herself more erect. 'But it's just the drink talkin', so I forgive her.'

Joe reached for his jacket. 'I'd b-better go and fetch her.' He turned to Julia. 'Will you come with m-me?'

'I can't. I have to be at the meeting in a few minutes – and anyway,' she glanced down at herself. 'I don't think Mary would appreciate me going like this, do you?'

Joe gave a small nod. 'Well, I'd b-better go.'

'Yes, go on.' She went to the door. 'I'll come back tomorrow – and Joe?' She waited until Maria was out of earshot. 'You need to be firm with her about this.'

*

'Roll up, roll up. This way to see the pipe-smokin' oyster, the over-excited donkey – an' a very worried lookin' monkey boy!'

'You should be ashamed of yourself,' said Mary sternly, her stony expression dissolving into one of drunken merriment as she clung to Kate.

Propped in a doorway, Kate continued to harangue the passers-by. 'Who'll give me a penny? A penny a peep.' She jiggled her skirts. 'Come on, ladies an' gen'lemen. Pop inside the tent. It looks like an oyster, it smells like an oyster …'

'Shhhsshhh,' urged Mary, between fits of laughter, but Kate was enjoying herself too much. ''Ere, you!' she called to a strait-laced couple crossing the road to avoid her. 'Did yer know the average 'orse shits the weight o' London every day?' She stopped, frowned, then waved her hand frantically. 'No, no wait. That ain't right. No. I'll tell yer what it is. The average 'orse 'as to be carted out o' London on a pile o' shit …' She stopped again. 'Oh, bugger it, who cares anyway.'

'You want to go home and sleep it off,' called the woman.

'You want to go 'ome an' 'ave it off,' called back Kate. 'Might cheer yer up a bit, yer miserable old sod.'

With an outraged look the woman moved on, quickening her pace. 'I'll report you. You see if I don't.'

'Come on,' said Mary, giggling as she pushed away from the wall. 'We'd better go.'

'What? An' lose our pitch?' Kate began to do a little dance up and down the pavement, singing loudly,

> Tiddle-iddle-um-pum. Tiddle-iddle-um-pum.
> Tiddle-iddle-um-pum. *Pum-pum.*
> My ol' mum she said to me,
> Don't let young men be quite so free.
> Keep 'em well below the knee.
> But she spoke too late, my *Mo—ther.*

She held out an unsteady hand. 'Come on, ducklin'. I'm goin' to need a bit of 'elp in the chorus if we're goin' to earn some more beer money.'

Mary began to sing, clapping an accompaniment as Kate kicked up her heels. 'Tiddle-iddle-um-pum. Tiddle-iddle …'

'M-Mary!'

Mary turned sharply, staggering a little.

'What do you think you're doing?' Joe looked about, all too conscious of the eyes of the street upon him. 'Come away – come away *now*!'

'Leave 'er alone, can't yer?' giggled Kate. 'Can't yer see we're puttin' on a music 'all act?'

He ignored her. 'I said come home this m-minute.'

'I said come home this m-m-minute,' mimicked Kate.

Released from Kate's grip, Mary fell back into the doorway. 'Come and have a drink with us, Joe,' she said, leaning against the door. 'Come on – you can tell us all about … about …' she clamped her teeth down hard on her lip, trying to maintain a serious expression, but the effort was too great, and she broke into a fit of giggles. '… about shovelling horse shit.'

'An' while yer at it,' Kate screamed with laughter, 'shove yer pipe in yer mouth an' prove I ain't a bloomin' liar!'

Joe grabbed hold of Mary's wrist and started to pull her away.

'Leave me alone!' With her free hand she began to beat at him. 'Leave me alone. I want to stay here.'

A crowd had gathered, and there were knowing grins and a sprinkling of applause as Joe dragged her along the road, but he paid no attention, keeping his head lowered to hide his shame.

'Oooh,' Kate cried after them. 'You're in for a warm time, ducklin' – a right warm time.' Giggling, she began running up and down, ringing an imaginary bell and shouting, 'Ding-a-ling-ling. Arse on fire! Arse on fire!' until, by Aldgate Pump, she collapsed with laughter. But with Mary gone the merriment didn't last, and by the time Constable Robinson appeared on the scene she was fast asleep on the pavement.

*

'We'll just give her a bit of a beating, eh?'

The man walking at Michael Kidney's side looked straight ahead. 'Of course.'

'I mean … she ain't so bad really … an' I do *sort of* like her.'

'That's your trouble, Mickey.'

'So we'll just knock her about a bit?'

'Let's just play it by ear, eh?'

*

'I shall get a bloody good 'idin' when I get 'ome.'

'Serves you right for getting drunk.' The police constable yawned as he escorted Kate up from the cell where she'd been put to sleep it off. 'Still, at least it's stopped raining, so that's something, eh? Now you get yourself off to bed.' He went to warm himself by the fire. 'And be sure to close the door behind you.'

456

Kate flashed him an impish grin. 'Alright. Good night, old cock.' She left the police station with a jaunty step, but was no sooner outside and out of sight than she fell back against the dirty brickwork, the false bravado falling from her as she put her hand to her head. She felt sick, with a splitting headache that throbbed at her temples, and a dry, bitter taste in her mouth.

It was just after one o'clock in the morning and the pubs were closed, but across the road the lights of Liverpool Street Station gleamed invitingly. She'd half made up her mind to go there when she caught sight of the uniformed figure standing watching her from the far pavement, and instead she pushed herself from the wall, walking unsteadily toward Houndsditch.

The fire station was just a little way down the road, and she came to a halt before the wide open doors, fixing the cocky grin to her face once more. 'Wotcha, Tom.'

From the shadows behind the engine, a stocky figure came forward, a pail in his hand and his great bushy beard thrust out belligerently as he strained to identify the caller, then he chuckled. 'Should have known it was you.'

'Quiet night?'

'Mostly.'

'You should 'ave been with us earlier on. I was makin' a lovely little fire-engine.' She gave him a cheeky wink, 'But I didn't 'ave no big, 'andsome fireman to ride me.'

'Oh, that was you up Aldgate High Street, was it? I heard there was a bit of a commotion.'

She looked past him, into the wide, gas-lit room. 'Not 'avin a brew up, I suppose, are yer? I could kill for a cup o' tea.'

'As a matter of fact, I am.' He put down the pail. 'But that's *all* I can offer you.'

'Just a cup o' tea would be lovely.'

'Alright, you wait outside, just in case we get any unexpected visits, and I'll fetch us a couple of mugs.'

*

'Oh, God …' Sitting on the bed, Mary jerked forward, vomiting into the bowl on her lap.

'It's alright. Don't worry.'

'I'm sorry, Joe.'

'Sorry? No need to b-be sorry.' He stroked her back. 'I'm not b-blaming you, M-Mary. It's not your fault.'

*

'See yer around then, Tom. An' thanks for the tea.' Kate managed a grin despite the pounding in her head. 'Reckon yer've saved my life.'

'You take care.' He watched her walk away. 'Here, you're going the wrong way, aren't you?'

'Not goin' 'ome just yet. Thought I might take a walk down by the river. Clear my 'ead a bit.'

He chuckled. 'Better than smelling salts, that bloody river is. Well, you just be careful, they haven't caught this Leather-Apron yet.'

''E won't bother me. I know who he is.'

'Don't joke about it, Kate.'

'Alright, old cock.' She gave a weak laugh. 'You just tell your missus to watch out if someone starts tellin' 'er 'ow much shit the average 'orse makes each day.'

*

The single candle was beginning to gutter as Joe took the bowl from the bed and went out into the court to empty the foul-smelling contents. He breathed deeply, filling his lungs with the night air.

Inside, Mary was asleep, lying fully dressed across both sides of the bed, but it didn't matter, he was too wide awake, his head was too full of thoughts. He needed to walk and to think.

Carefully he rested the bowl against the wall, allowing it to drain, then he reached in through the broken window and slid the bolt home.

A cat appeared, briefly rubbing against his legs before carrying on through the narrow archway and into Dorset Street. Joe stood and watched it, then, feeling in his pocket for his pipe, he followed after.

*

Kate closed her eyes. Her head was pounding fit to burst, and the tea she had so recently drunk was splattered all over the pavement in front of her. She wiped her mouth, walking unsteadily from the shadow of the building and continuing on toward Aldgate and the river, paying scant attention to the few passers-by – but at the entrance to Church Passage, a man stood smoking, and she stopped in surprise.

'Wotcha, Joe,' she said. 'What you doin' 'ere?'

He looked equally startled. 'Doing here? Just thinking.' He took the pipe from his mouth. 'I hope you're proud of yourself. M-Mary's b-been sick all night.'

'Me, too.' She smiled guiltily. 'Still, we'll both be alright tomorrow.'

'Tomorrow? No, not tomorrow. Not any day. I want you to stay away from her.'

'Joe …' They were standing very close, and she put her hand to his chest. 'Me an' Mary are friends. I'm sorry about this evenin', but I can't just …'

458

Joe's voice was low, barely more than a whisper. 'I'm not asking you – I'm telling you. You stay away from her – or there'll b-be trouble.' He turned to go. 'Just stay away from the b-both of us.'

Kate watched him walk away, and was about to go after him when she was suddenly filled with the urgent need to urinate. Looking furtively about, she walked quickly into the passageway leading to Mitre Square. With its three exits and deep, dark corners the square was used for all manner of illicit purposes, and she hiked up her clothes, squatting over the gutter, letting the warm stream splash on to the cobbles – but the relief was short lived. A movement caught her eye, and she stood up, dropping her skirts.

'Oh, bloody 'ell!' she said.

Chapter Fifty-Seven

'Kate's dead.' Mary went to the window, looking out into the court, her eyes swollen from crying.

'Dead … yes, I know.' Joe stood awkwardly. 'I heard about it down at the m-market. I'm sorry.'

'My poor Kate.' Mary dragged her sleeve across her cheek. 'She saved me. Did you know that? I wouldn't be alive if it weren't for her – and now because of …' She broke off. 'I've got to leave, Joe. I've *got* to get away from here.'

'From here? B-but where will you go?'

'I don't know … but I've got to get away.'

Visibly shaking, he worried at the ends of his straggling moustache. 'What about … *m-me*?'

She looked out to where two small girls were trying to pet a reluctant cat, chasing it up and down the court until finally the animal turned on them, spitting and hissing. 'You'll be better off without me.'

'Without you? No!'

'You will. There are some things … things I've never told you.'

'Told m-me? Then tell m-me now.'

Slowly she shook her head. 'It's better you don't know. But I'm frightened, Joe. I'm *so* frightened.'

'Frightened? You? M-Mary, you're not m-making any sense. Just tell m-me what's b-bothering you.'

'I wish I could – it's been so hard not being able to tell anyone.'

'Then tell *m-me – please.*'

'Oh, Joe.' She put her hand to her face, looking at him uncertainly. 'I … I think Kate was killed because somebody thought she was me.' She saw his look of disbelief, and she went to him, taking his hand and sitting with him on the edge of the bed. 'It all started long before I met you. Julia and I went to Paris, to meet a client of Julia's. He was some kind of criminal, and somehow I ended up alone with him in his room. We'd both had too much to drink. He got violent – I thought he was going to kill me, so I locked myself in the bathroom. When I woke up, he was dead.'

Joe looked at her aghast.

'I didn't know what to do – so I ran away. I've been running ever since.'

'Ever since? The police think *you* killed him?'

'I don't know. But his friends do. They caught Julia and tortured her.'

He held her, feeling her tremble. 'And you think they're still after you?'

'You said yourself these people never give up – and Archie …'

'*Archie*? Not Archie B-Bull?'

Mary looked up in surprise. 'You knew him?'

'Knew him? No – b-but I've heard of him.' He put his hand to his mouth. 'Christ,' he said softly. 'If they think you killed him …'

*

The young woman lying on the bed wore only the filthy shreds of a shift that gaped to reveal her cancerous breast.

'Don't just stand there, Mary,' chided Julia. 'Pass me that bowl of water.'

Mary handed it to her, and Julia wetted a clean piece of flannel, wiping the face of the comatose woman. 'We found her this morning. Living in a cellar – with six young children, all of them naked as monkeys and as black as Newgate's knocker. Can you imagine?'

'Julia, I need to talk to you.'

Taking a pair of scissors, Julia cut away the remains of the shift. 'Her husband was there. Dead for about a week from the look of him. Not a pretty sight.' She looked down at the emaciated figure, the bones protruding, stretching the thin, yellowish skin. 'Poor cow. I don't suppose she's any older than us.'

'Julia … it's important!'

For a moment, Julia continued her ministrations, then she half-turned. 'This woman is *dying*, Mary. What could be more important than that?'

Chastened, Mary looked about, avoiding Julia's reproving glance. The refuge was well ordered and well scrubbed, but in every other respect it was little different to the slum dwellings it stood shoulder to shoulder with in the cramped, narrow passage known as Angel Alley. 'She shouldn't be here,' she said at last. 'She ought to be in the hospital, or the infirmary.'

'To what purpose? She has such a short time.' Julia slowly shook her head. 'No, she's better here. We'll care for her.' She gave Mary a meaningful look. 'And I do mean *we*. Why don't you put your experience in Cardiff to good use – you can start by washing her feet.'

Mary took the square of flannel Julia handed her, then laid it on the bed. 'I can't. I haven't time. I came to find you because … I'm going away – and I want you to come with me.'

'I can't leave. I have a duty here.'

'But we're in danger, Julia.'

'Why?'

'You know why.' They were alone in the room, but still Mary lowered her voice. 'The *murders*. Annie – then Kate. That can't be a coincidence. It just *can't*.'

Julia looked at her in amazement. 'Those women were old – worn out. You don't honestly believe they were mistaken for us?'

'Well … then, perhaps they were tortured. Annie and Kate both knew where I live.' Mary began to pace about in agitation. 'That must be it. They were tortured – just like you.'

'In the open street? And why the Nichols woman? You said yourself you didn't even know her.'

'Maybe I did know her – and I just don't remember …'

'Stop it, Mary. You're becoming hysterical.'

'But it's possible! Joe and I have lived in half-a-dozen different places over the last eighteen months. What if I *did* know this Polly Nichols? Then it would all make sense wouldn't it? *Well, wouldn't it?*'

Mary's voice had risen to a feverish pitch, causing the woman on the bed to stir.

'No! No, it wouldn't!' said Julia, jumping to her feet. 'And I want you to stop this nonsense right now.'

'We've got to get away, Julia – or we'll be next, *I know* it.'

'You don't know anything.' She seized Mary by the shoulders. 'Now just calm down.'

'Then why, Julia?' Mary's eyes glistened. 'Why would anyone want to kill Kate?'

'I don't know. But I'm certain it has nothing to do with Archie.' She stepped closer, taking Mary in her arms. 'You're safe, Mary. Trust me. We're both quite, quite safe.'

*

'Double fuckin' event!' Farrel threw the newspaper across the room. 'I'll give you double fuckin' event! What did yer kill 'er for? Did I say kill 'er? *Did I?*' He glared contemptuously at Kidney. 'Just what I needed, that is!'

'It wasn't my fault. I …'

Farrel came closer, poking Kidney in the chest. 'I was stopped twice on the way 'ere today. Me! Stopped in the fuckin' street like some ordinary cunt!' His face grew purple with indignation. 'First by one of these extra fuckin' coppers they're pullin' in from all over the place – cunt didn't even know who the fuck I was – then by a bloody reporter wantin' to know what I thought about 'em puttin' in more fuckin' street lightin'! *Street lightin'*! As if I give a fuck!'

462

White-faced and trembling, Michael Kidney summoned his most ingratiating smile. 'I … I know what you mean, Harry. There was these two toffs the other day, asked me all sorts of questions – one of 'em wanted to know if I knew where Ireland was. I told him I thought it must be within walking distance – on account of how many bloody Irishmen you get around here …'

Farrel's eyes bored into him with chilling ferocity. 'Are you takin' the fuckin' piss?'

'No, honest … I …'

'I don't give a fuck what yer said, you little turd. I've got this Jack-the-fuckin'-what's'it keepin' a lot of my girls off the streets. I've got the police an' the newspapers an' a whole bunch of do-gooders crawlin' all over the place – so that I can't even take a shit without someone reportin' it. An' on top of all that, I've got the pair of you cuttin' that mouthy bitch's throat. I just wanted 'er cut, yer dozy cunt – maybe crippled – but I wanted 'er *alive*. I wanted 'er walkin' about, lookin' like that elephant geezer's ugly fuckin' sister, showin' everyone what 'appens to people who don't show enough respect to 'Arry Farrel! But what 'ave I got instead? Just another fuckin' murder by this 'ere Jack the …' He glared at Kidney. 'What the fuck are they callin' 'im now?'

'Jack the Ripper.'

'Jack the Fuckin' Nuisance'd be more like it!'

*

'You appear to be doing well for yourself, Gaston,' said Evan, looking about the Harley Street rooms.

Without rising from his armchair, Gaston accepted the compliment.

'You remember Dr Phillips, of course?' asked Evan.

'Of course.' Gaston beamed. 'It is good to see you again, my dear sir. I had no sooner heard the news of this *so-called* double murder, than I began to wonder if I shouldn't have the pleasure of a visit from one or the other of you two gentlemen.'

Phillips looked uncomfortable. 'So you've been following recent events?'

'Most closely. But please, do sit down.'

'We were wondering if you'd had any further thoughts on the matter,' said Evan, taking the sofa whilst Phillips settled himself into the second armchair.

'Thoughts?' The corpulent doctor spread his hands in mute appeal. 'Of course – it's a *most* fascinating case. But I should welcome the opportunity of asking you a few questions first, if I may?'

Phillips shifted in his seat. 'Well, I shall answer if I can – but please understand that I'm here unofficially, and that any information I give *must* remain between the three of us.'

'Naturally.' A box of assorted bon-bons lay on the table by Gaston's elbow, and without taking his eyes from Phillips, he reached in and took one. 'Hmmm,' he said, chewing with surprise and delight. 'Nougat! How delicious. I can't tell you how much I had been missing such little treats, but then I found this most delightful shop ...' He paused, looking apologetic. 'But you have not come here to talk of confectionery.'

'No,' said Phillips.

Gaston wiped his lips. 'So, what of this Elizabeth Stride? I see they are attributing her death to the Whitechapel murderer – or *Jack the Ripper*, as he's begun calling himself in the letter and postcard he sent to the news-papers. You surely don't believe she was a victim of our correspondent friend?'

'I believe there is cause for doubt.'

'There is no doubt about it.'

Evan leaned forward. 'Just a moment. Are you saying you believe the letter and postcard to be genuine?'

'I am convinced of it.'

'But he claims on the postcard to have killed both women.'

'Of course.'

'But ...?' Evan shook his head in resignation, then sat back, smiling. 'I really should know better by now, shouldn't I?' He waved a hand toward Gaston. 'Please, do go on. I know we shall get there eventually.'

'Well, I don't understand at all,' said Phillips.

Gaston surveyed them both with the air of a long-suffering father. 'Our man is undoubtedly a showman. Publicity is both his business, and his goal. These letters were sent, not directly to the police, nor to any one newspaper, but to the Central News Agency. Who but a reporter or some-one well used to the publicising of events would possibly think to do that?'

'Then, if the letters are genuine, he must have killed Stride.'

'No, quite impossible. The weapon was different, the method was different, and the audacity required, quite superhuman.' Gaston shook his head, his voluminous chins wobbling. 'To be interrupted in the murder of one woman, then walk directly to Mitre Square and immediately kill and mutilate another, during the quietest hours of the early morning, and in the midst of a hue and cry, would be the act of a lunatic – and I do not believe our Mr Ripper to be *that* sort of lunatic. No, our man didn't kill Elizabeth Stride, but neither could he resist the temptation to take the credit for such audacity – and it is in this he reveals his theatrical conceit. But there is something far more important. You see gentlemen, I believe that, whatever his original motive, a note of animosity has now crept into the plot.'

'A note of *animosity*?' said Phillips, incredulously.

'Indeed. Just look at the mutilations suffered by this Catherine Conway

– or *Eddowes* as I believe she should more properly be known. But perhaps you would like to give us a summary, you were at the post mortem, I believe, and I doubt *everything* has been reported in the papers.'

Phillips looked across at Evan, then back at Gaston. 'Well,' he said at last. 'To begin with it appeared nothing more than butchery. She had been opened with a jagged cut stretching from the breast-bone to the pubes, with the intestines drawn out and laid over the shoulder in much the same fashion as in the Chapman case – though with Eddowes, a two foot section had been cut away and placed by her side. The liver had been stabbed several times, and the pubic region considerably more so.'

'And there were organs missing?' asked Gaston.

'The left kidney had been cut out and taken away along with the majority of the womb and some of the ligaments.'

'Interesting, don't you think? This progression from the fairly simple mutilation of Nichols, to Chapman where we first have body parts taken, and then to this new escalation with Eddowes? What do you think he does with these items he takes away?'

'I have no idea. What do *you* think he does with them?'

Gaston considered the question. 'I'm not sure – though I'm in no doubt as to *why* he takes them. However, I have interrupted you. Perhaps you would continue with your summary? I understand her face to have been quite disfigured?'

'Barbarous hacking – but of no anatomical significance.'

'But of great significance none-the-less.' Gaston spread his hands. '*Please?*'

Phillips sighed. 'Very well, if you insist. The tip of her nose was sliced off, and there was a deep cut across the bridge, running down to the jaw. There were other cuts to the nose, eyes, mouth and ears. But I really can't see the relevance …'

'But it's as plain as the nose on your own face, Dr Phillips. Can you not see that a personal note has entered the equation? With Nichols and Chapman, the genitalia and reproductive organs were the main focus. Our man made his statement, and left us to contemplate the lesson he intended us to learn. But with Eddowes, the face has also been furiously and savagely attacked. Why? Because the face holds such significance, especially for the fairer sex. It is my belief he hated this woman – and for the first time a personal motive has taken precedence over his greater plan.'

'A jilted lover?' asked Phillips.

Gaston shrugged. 'That remains to be seen.'

'So what of your original deduction?' asked Evan. 'The effeminate mesmerist? Do you still hold to that?'

'Nothing is more certain. And I deduce this will be no quack medical practitioner of the art, but most certainly a man who, if not still working the theatrical stage, will have done so in the past.'

Evan looked sceptical. 'It's an interesting idea, but there seems precious little evidence.'

'Little evidence? *Little evidence?*' Gaston shook his head in disbelief. 'The whole affair reeks of grease-paint and limelight, surely? The ritual disembowelling – complete with artistic flourishes?'

'That's one way of describing it, I suppose.'

'It is the only way to describe it. Come, come, how else is one to view the bizarre draping of the intestines, the removal of random body parts, not to mention the penchant for arranging the victims possessions around the body – unless it is designed purely to mystify and intrigue? I tell you, gentlemen. This affair has more to do with smoke and mirrors than sadistic butchery.'

'But it *wasn't* mere butchery,' insisted Phillips. 'To find and remove a kidney requires medical knowledge. He has to be a medical man.'

'You think so? Well, you are entitled to your opinion.' Gaston's eyes wandered toward the box of bon-bons, and he picked it up. 'Oh, but where are my manners? May I offer you one? They're all very nice, but do try the nougat.'

Phillips reached for the box.

'And, please,' said Gaston, 'just to humour me, find it without looking.'

'How on earth am I supposed to do that?'

'I just did.'

'But you weren't trying to. It was pure chance.'

'Exactly,' said Gaston.

*

Scritch. Scritch. Scritch. The sound was soft, inaudible beyond the confines of the cell, but its steady rhythm was compelling, making Connie rock back and forth as she sat naked upon the plank bed.

Scritch. Scritch. Scritch. It made her think of insects. *No, not insects*, she shook her head, her eyes two bright little points gleaming in the darkness beneath the tangle of unkempt hair. *Not insects.* Insects were no good. *But snakes? Yes! Snakes!* Immediately the sound lengthened, becoming an ominous hiss. *You need to be a snake to kill a snake. To kill that black snake.* Her lips drew back, forming into a snarl. *Black by name, black by nature. Well, I've poison enough for you, my girl. More than enough. And I've a fang, too. A nice sharp fang.* The rasping hiss stopped, and she held up the slender four-inch length of steel – the missing piece of the bathtub – letting the moonlight play along its sharpened edge. *Sharp enough for a Miss Emma, Black snake … and one or two others along the way.*

*

Joe came to the front door, peering into the thick yellow fog. 'M-Marie?'

Mary gritted her teeth. He'd taken to calling her Marie-Jeanette ever since she'd told him about Paris, and the more he continued with it, the more she hated it.

'M-Marie?'

'I'm just here, Joe.'

His vague outline appeared. 'What are you doing?'

'The washing.'

'The washing?' He began to cough as the sulphurous air got into his lungs. 'B-but you can b-barely see out here.'

'I can see the bowl. And anyway, it's been like this for three days now – I can't wait forever for it to clear.'

'Right old pea-souper, ain't it?' said Lizzie Albrook, materializing with two aprons and a grubby shift in her arms.

Joe ignored her. 'Come b-back in, M-Mary. The washing can wait.'

'I'm nearly done.'

'Done? B-But this fog will m-make it just as dirty …'

'Then I'll wash it again!' she snapped.

Lizzie took a nervous step back. 'I can bring these things another day?'

'No, it's alright.' Mary put a hand to her face, rubbing at her sore eyes. 'I'm sorry, Joe. I didn't mean to shout. Look, why don't you put the kettle on? I'll be finished in a minute, and we'll have a nice cup of tea.'

'Tea? Yes … well, alright.' He disappeared back inside.

'So what have you got?' asked Mary, wringing out the last of her linen.

Lizzie came cautiously forward. 'Just a few bits, that's all.'

'Well, put them on the back of the chair. But I haven't got the room to dry them, so you'll have to hang them up in your own place.'

'Alright. Thanks Mary.'

'I'll bring them down to you in a minute.' She picked up the first of the aprons and was about to plunge it into the water when her fingers encountered something. 'Lizzie?'

'Yes?' Lizzie's reply came from only a few yards away, though she was already invisible.

'You've left something in your apron pocket.' Mary brought out the letter, bringing it close to her face, her heart missing a beat as she read her own name in Peggy Cartwright's familiar hand.

'What is it?' asked Lizzie emerging from the fog.

'It's a letter, Lizzie. Addressed to *me*.'

Lizzie's eyes widened, and her hands flew to cover her open mouth. 'Oh, Mary. I'm sorry. It came last week while you were out. I forgot all about it.'

Chapter Fifty-Eight

The unassuming terraced house lay amongst a warren of back streets that spread like roots from the broad trunk of the Old Kent Road.

'Well, I feel a bit queer, I must say,' said Charlie, his ruddy features creasing into laughter while his eyes hovered on a point slightly to the left of Mary's shoulder. 'I mean, us sitting out here in the kitchen when there's the best room lying empty as a parson's promise.' He tightened his grip on Peggy's hand. 'Fine way to treat visitors. Still, I suppose you ladies know best, eh?'

'An' you suppose quite right,' said Peggy, her stern note undermined by the twinkle in her eye and the way she covered his hand with her own.

'I prefer it here,' smiled Mary. 'It's cosy – and anyway, we've had some of our best times sitting in the kitchen, haven't we, Peg?'

Peggy laughed. 'We 'ave that.'

'Well, then at least pour the girl another cup of tea.' He lifted his head, sniffing the air. 'And I reckon that cake's about ready, if I'm not mistaken.'

'Will yer listen to 'im? 'E thought the oven was for dryin' 'is socks till I come back t' teach 'im different.'

Charlie's face settled into a contented smile. 'She's right, you know.' He sighed. 'When I think of all them wasted years. I was such a daft bugger.'

Mary swallowed against the lump in her throat. 'Well, it's wonderful to meet you at last, Charlie. I've heard so much about you.'

'Used to tell you about me, did she?'

Peggy got up from her chair. 'Yes, I did. I used t' tell 'er what a cheeky devil you was.'

'Oh, I was that, alright. Used to try it on, didn't I, Peg. I was a bit of a rascal back then, you see, Mary.' He leaned forward. 'To be honest, I don't know what she ever saw in me. Sometimes, when we was out together, I used to have to pinch myself – just to make sure I wasn't dreaming. Used to come home with bruises the size of half-crowns.'

Peggy chuckled. 'If yer did, then yer got 'em from me – slappin' yer 'ands away from where they shouldn't 'ave been.'

'Well, you couldn't blame me, could you? My, but you was a handsome young thing.'

''Andsome?' said Peggy, 'Blimey, yer must have been as blind then as you are now.'

'Don't you take no notice of her, Mary. She was handsome, right enough. I don't mean *pretty*. Pretty you can get ten-a-penny – if that's what you want. No, my Peg was *handsome*.' Peggy came to stand behind him, her hand resting on his shoulder, and he reached up, patting it. 'But it wouldn't have mattered to me what she looked like. That's not what it's really about. I can't see her at all now – but I still know she's the only one for me.'

''E never did get married,' explained Peggy. 'Not t' the girl in the corner shop, nor no one else, neither. The great soft turnip stopped writin' t' me after 'is accident, 'cos 'e thought I wouldn't want 'im if 'e was blind.' She squeezed his shoulder. 'As if that would've made any difference t' me.'

'I was a fool, I know that now.'

'Well,' Peggy looked down at the gold ring on her finger. 'Better late than never, my ol' dad used to say.'

*

'Nanny's boy.'

Pressed against the playground wall, Owen kept his eyes lowered as faces filled with feral excitement crowded in on him.

'Go on,' said Stebbings. 'Say it.' He made a fist, the middle finger raised to make a hard, pointed knuckle, and punched Owen in the muscle of the upper arm. 'Say it!' He punched again. 'Say *I'm nanny's little pissy-drawers*.'

'I'm … I'm nanny's little pissy-drawers.'

The crowd of boys cackled with glee.

'Again,' grinned Stebbings. 'Only louder this time.'

'Yes, louder, *pissy-drawers*,' called another boy, giving Owen's shin a sharp kick.

'I'm nanny's little …'

'Watch out, it's the old man!'

All heads turned toward the school building, and in the next instant the crowd had dispersed to leave only Owen and Stebbings.

As the Headmaster sailed by, Stebbings reached out to ruffle Owen's hair in a show of friendliness. 'See you after school, eh?' he smiled.

*

'I'll just wash these things up,' said Charlie, starting to collect the cups and plates.'

'You leave 'em where they are. Mary an' me can do 'em.'

'But she's a guest.'

''Course she ain't.' Peggy looked across the table at Mary and smiled. 'She's *family*.'

'Better to be a guest, then,' he laughed, pushing himself from the chair. 'But, if you insist, I'll leave you ladies to it and go fetch some more coal to make up the fire, then we'll be all cosy for the evening, eh?'

Mary watched him feel his way along the edge of the table. 'I'll bring it,' she said, getting to her feet.

'No, no. I'll have it done in two shakes of a lamb's tail. You go and enjoy yourself with the washing up, eh.'

''E's still a cheeky devil,' said Peggy as soon as they were alone.

Gathering up the crockery, Mary took it through into the scullery. 'I think he's lovely. I'm so happy for you, Peg.'

'Funny what surprises life 'olds for yer.' Peggy took the kettle from the range and came to join her. 'Who'd 'ave thought it? After all these years?'

Mary felt an ache of envy in her heart. 'So, what happened? What made him write to you after such a long time?'

'Silly ol' devil thought 'e was dyin' an' wanted t' set the record straight afore 'e went. Turned out 'e didn't 'ave nothin' more than a touch of the gripe – but 'e'd already sent the letter by then. Mind you, 'e's lucky *I* didn't kill 'im when I found out why 'e'd stopped writin' all them years ago.' She gave Mary a sideways glance. 'It's odd the way life turns out. Nothin's 'ardly ever what it seems.'

'Yes … I suppose so.'

The forlorn quality to Mary's voice made Peggy want to hold her, but instead she turned back to the sink, taking up a plate and scrubbing it mercilessly. 'Anyways,' she said, clearing her throat, 'I meant what I said just now – about you bein' family. Yer know I've always looked on yer like a daughter.' Mary made no answer, and Peggy went on quickly. 'Well, whether yer did or yer didn't – yer do now.' She turned away, pouring the contents of the kettle over the dishes. 'So, that bein' the case, I'm supposin' yer won't take it the wrong way if I ask yer when was the last time them clothes o' yours 'ad a decent brushin'?'

'Today.'

'Oh, really? Then maybe yer need a new brush?' She glanced over her shoulder. 'An' perhaps another for yer boots – an' maybe one for yer 'air?'

Mary pushed guiltily at the loose strands about her ears. 'What do you mean? What's wrong?'

'I dunno.' Peggy turned to her again. 'Why don't *you* tell *me*? 'Cos I can tell somethin' is.'

'There isn't. Things have been a bit … *difficult* just lately, but that's all.'
'Difficult?'

'It doesn't matter.' She met Peggy's eyes. 'I'm twenty-five years old, Peg. I can't keep running to you every time I …'

Peggy frowned. ''Course yer can. Gawd, Mary. If yer've got troubles, then tell me. Maybe I can 'elp, maybe I can't – but at least I ain't so deaf as I can't listen.'

Mary sighed. 'I just wish I'd never been born.'

'Oh, do yer now? Life ain't easy, Mary – an' if yer believe all them bloomin' gospel grinders, it ain't supposed to be. But I'll tell yer now, *I'm* very glad you was born – an' I'll tell yer somethin' else, too. If you *'ad* been my own flesh an' blood, yer couldn't 'ave made me more proud.'

'Proud?' Mary shook her head. 'You don't know the things I've done.'

'Don't I? I know more than yer think – an' what I don't know, I can 'ave a good guess at – but it don't make me no less proud of yer. Remember what I said t' yer – back when you was leavin' for Cardiff? *Yer do what yer 'ave t' do.* Sometimes that means gettin' yer 'ands dirty, but in my book it depends on what yer accomplish as t' whether it was worth the candle.'

'Well, it wasn't worth it.' Mary leaned dejectedly against the wall. 'I'm back where I started, Peg – no, I'm even worse off than that. I've nothing to show for *any* of it, and …'

'That's a lot o' nonsense an' you know it. There was the money yer sent t' your Mr Abrahams for a start.'

Mary's eyes widened. 'How did you know about that?' Then, with concern, 'Does he know?'

'No, yer secret's safe enough. But it wasn't 'ard t' put two an' two together once I 'eard the name of 'is mysterious benefactor. Blimey, Mary, we've 'ad enough laughs over it in the past, 'aven't we?'

A smile struggled to lift the corners of Mary's mouth. 'How is he – Mr Abrahams?'

'Alright, last I 'eard. But 'e wouldn't 'ave been if it 'adn't been for you. From what I can gather, 'e was pretty near t' ruin when this 'ere Mr *Lafite* 'ad an attack of conscience an' began repayin' 'is investment – so whatever yer was doin' t' earn that money, I won't stand by an' see yer condemned for it.'

Mary's smile strengthened a little. 'Thank you, Peggy.'

'So?' said Peggy, making a show of returning to the washing up. 'Are yer goin' t' tell me what all this present trouble is, or ain't yer?'

'It's nothing, Peg. Honestly.'

'Well, if yer say so.' Peggy gave her a sideways glance. 'But just you remember – yer've always got a place t' come to.'

There was a rattling of the door handle, and the next moment Charlie was standing in the doorway, a full scuttle of coal in his hand and a black smudge across his cheek. 'Is that another cup of tea I smell?' he asked optimistically.

Peggy went to him. 'We're a bit behind with the dishes,' she said, wiping the coal dust from his face. 'The fire's alright for the minute, so why don't yer sit yerself down, an' keep Mary company – an' I'll put the kettle on t' boil again.'

'Life of Reilly, this is,' he laughed, sitting down at the table. 'Come on, Mary, why don't you come and tell me a few secrets about our Peg. Sounds like she's already told you enough about me.' He grinned mischievously as a thought struck him. 'Here, did she ever tell you about how I used to always be on at her to let me up to her room – so's I could look at the lights?'

'Yes, I did,' Peggy called from the scullery. 'So don't go thinkin' she don't know what a sly young devil you was.' She came back into the kitchen, setting the kettle to boil. 'An' I've also told 'er that you ain't changed – not one tiny little bit.'

*

Nanny Reeves dipped her fingers into the bath water, then stood up, her hands on her hips. 'Not undressed yet? We are a slow-coach today.' She came to where Owen was toying with the buttons of his shirt, gently but firmly moving his hands away and unfastening them herself.

'I think I'm old enough to bath myself now, Nanny.'

'Oh, are you indeed? And I suppose you're old enough to go without a bedtime story, hmmm? And perhaps sleep without a night-light?' Owen made no reply, and she continued to undress him, pulling out his shirt-tails before moving on to his cuffs, undoing them with a brisk efficiency. 'You have to realise, Owen, that you aren't as strong and healthy as other boys your age – and your Grandmother and I would never forgive ourselves if anything should happen to you.' She pulled off his shirt. 'And besides …' She broke off, staring at the bruises on his arms. 'Oh, my goodness! Whatever's happened to you?'

*

Peggy could hardly speak for laughing. 'So the 'otel's full o' guests. Mrs Llewellyn's taken to 'er bed with a fever. Me an' Mary are tryin' t' serve dinner – only she's gone an' dropped the shoulder o' mutton on the floor – an' Mr Llewellyn, 'e's runnin' up an' down the stairs like somethin' demented, tryin' t' look after the missus an' the guests, both at the same time.'

'Funny sort of hotel that only has a maid and a cook,' said Charlie.

'It weren't really an 'otel – more of a guest 'ouse – though yer daren't let the Llewellyns 'ear yer say so. Mind you, they were that tight-fisted I reckon they'd 'ave tried to run the Metropole with just the two of us. Ain't that right, Mary?'

Mary smiled, but her thoughts were with the flames flickering up the chimney.

'Well, sounds like you had good times together,' said Charlie, breaking the silence.

The room was growing dark, and Peggy studied Mary's profile, noting the small frown lines highlighted by the fire's glow. 'Yes, I s'pose we did,' she said, then looking at the clock on the mantelpiece. 'Lord! Is that the time?' She turned to Charlie. ''Ere's me natterin' on, an' you champin' at the bit t' get off down the pub with yer friends. Well, you go on. Mary an' me won't mind.'

Charlie turned his face in her direction. 'The pub, eh? Yes – well if you won't think it rude?'

'Not a bit, will we, Mary, m'love?'

Mary stirred from her reverie. 'No, of course not – and anyway, it's getting late. I should be going home.'

'It ain't *that* late,' said Peggy, getting to her feet. 'An' yer can't go yet, I'm just goin' t' put the kettle on. Yer'll be wantin' another cup o' tea an' a bit o' cake afore yer go, won't yer?'

Charlie was already pulling on his coat. 'Will you still be here when I get back, Mary?'

''Course she will. You're never gone much more than an hour, are yer?'

'No. No, I suppose not, now you mention it,' he grinned, going to the door. 'Well, see you later on, eh?'

Peggy filled the kettle and set it to boil, then fussed about the small kitchen. Only when she heard the front door close did she come to sit down by Mary's side. 'Thinkin' of old times?'

Mary nodded.

'They weren't so bad, I s'pose.'

'I wish I could go back, Peg. Have everything be just as it was.' She broke off guiltily. 'No. No, of course I don't – that wouldn't be fair to you. I think Charlie's wonderful – and I'm so happy for you both.'

'Never mind me an' Charlie,' said Peggy, sternly. 'I've been thinkin' about that conversation we 'ad this afternoon – an' it ain't goin' t' do, Mary. It ain't goin' t' do at all! An' I've got to ask this – whether yer like it or not. What's 'appened t' yer? Yer can tell me about that there bruise on yer face, for a start.'

Mary put her fingers to her cheek. 'It's nothing. I fell.'

'Fell? Gawd, the times I've 'eard that one! Someone's been 'ittin' yer, 'aven't they? Well, 'aven't they?'

'No. I told you I *fell.*'

'Oh, you've fallen alright.'

'Please, Peg, don't do this …'

'An' what about that dress? Charlie might be blind, but I ain't. Is that really the best yer could find t' come a-visitin' in? Well is it?'

'Yes! Yes, it is, if you must know! I don't own anything better – and if I did it would be in the pawnshop – to pay the rent on the hovel I live in! There! Are you satisfied, now?'

'No, I ain't,' goaded Peggy. 'Bein' poor is one thing. Bein' poor 'cos yer waste yer money on drink is another. Yer think I couldn't smell the gin on yer breath the minute yer walked in 'ere this mornin'?'

'I had one, that's all. Just one.'

'That's one too many when yer can't afford t' dress yerself.'

'What do you know about it?' Mary looked angrily about the room. 'You've got all this – a proper home – the man you love. I've got nothing, Peg! *Nothing*! My life's empty!'

'Oh, an' a drop o' gin fills it?'

'I needed the courage.'

'What, t' come 'ere?'

'Yes, to come here. Do you think I don't know how I look?' She plucked contemptuously at her dress, then at her hair. 'That I don't see my mother looking back at me every time I look in the mirror? That I wanted you, of all people, to know I've come to this? I nearly turned back a dozen times – but I so wanted to see you, Peggy. To see you and to feel safe again – just for one day.' Her eyes shone wetly, and she put her fist to her mouth, her teeth pressed hard against the knuckle to stem the tears.

'Mary, m'love,' Peggy took hold of her hand, coaxing it from her face, all pretence of anger gone. 'I don't care about yer clothes. I only care about you. So now we're finally 'avin' a proper talk, why don't yer start at the beginnin' an' tell me all about it?'

*

'*Well, mop it up, or you'll have your jacket spoilt. And you have got a nasty eye, Scud – you'd better go and bathe it well in cold water.*'

'*Cheap enough too, if we've done with our old friend Flashey,*' said East as they made off upstairs to bathe their wounds.

A good fire crackled in the grate as Evan closed the book. 'An excellent place to finish for tonight, I think, don't you?'

Dressed in his nightshirt and wrapped in a thick dressing gown, Owen finished the last of his warm milk. 'I think Tom Brown is lucky to have a good friend like East,' he said, cradling the empty mug in his lap.

Evan leaned back in the armchair, trying to keep the concern from his voice. 'I expect you have a special friend at school?' he asked casually.

'Yes.'

It was an unconvincing lie, and it took all of Evan's self control to pretend he was unaware of it. 'Someone just like young Scud, eh? Someone to share the bruises?'

At the mention of the word, Owen dropped his gaze even lower. 'It really isn't anything,' he said.

'But Nanny says you're covered in them.'

'Not *covered*, exactly.'

'But bruised, all the same. Can you tell me how it happened?'

'It was ... it was just rough and tumble. A chap must expect a bruise or two ...' he let his voice tail away.

Evan leaned forward, lifting the boy's face to his own. 'You know, when I was at school they'd make fun of the way I spoke. *Taffy* they used to call me.'

'They call me *nanny's-boy*,' blurted Owen, instantly regretting it.

'Why *nanny's-boy*?'

'I don't know ... they think she makes a fuss of me – I *suppose*.'

'What about the other day boys? Surely they are brought to school by someone?'

Owen shook his head. 'They're all older than me.'

'I see.' He considered the problem for a moment. 'Do you think you could find your own way to and from school?'

'I ... I should think so.' Owen frowned a little, thinking for a moment. 'Yes. Yes, I'm sure I could.'

'And what if you should get lost. What would you do?'

'I suppose ... I might ask a policeman for directions?'

Evan smiled. 'I think that would be just the thing to do.' He put his hand on Owen's shoulder. 'Alright, why don't you go off to bed and leave me to discuss it with Nanny Reeves?'

*

'I've always been weak, Peggy – weak and frightened. Gwyneth was always the strong one. She could stand the truth no matter how painful it was – but I couldn't. That's why I'd make up stories – no, not stories – *lies*! And when they didn't work, I'd turn to Emma. Emma's always looked after me, fought my battles for me.'

Peggy saw the tears in Mary's eyes, and leaned closer, gently stroking her neck. 'We all 'ave different people inside us, Mary – if we didn't we couldn't manage all the trials an' tribulations that come our way durin' a lifetime. It's just that most of us don't go givin' 'em names.'

'No, Peggy. It's as if Emma's a completely different person.'

'Stuff an' nonsense. Blimey, Mary, I used t' envy you yer imagination, but now I'm beginnin' t' see it as somethin' of a curse. There ain't no one else inside yer – no brave *Emma* that pops out every now an' then t' save poor little Mary Kelly.'

'But there is.'

Peggy began to laugh. ''Course there ain't, yer great dumplin'. Your *Emma* is just yer brave face – just one o' the parts that makes yer who you are. We've all got an Emma inside us – an' other bits as well – bits that are kind an' good – just as there's other bits that ain't so nice, an' all of 'em jostlin' for position. It's up to us t' keep those good bits t' the fore – t' stop the mean, cowardly an' uncharitable bits from gettin' the upper 'and. Every now an' then somethin' 'appens an' maybe yer lose the battle for a while – some people lose it for a lifetime. But it's always up t' you – it's always your choice.'

'No. You don't understand.'

'Oh yes I do.' Peggy sighed deeply. 'Listen, when I was girl I thought my dad was the bravest man in the whole world. 'E weren't a fightin' man, not like some from 'round where we lived – but there weren't no man 'e'd back down from, neither. Anyway, I remember once, when some kids 'ad been callin' me names an' I'd come in cryin', 'e said to me, *Peggy, yer can't let 'em beat yer. Yer might be a-tremblin' in yer boots an' wantin' more than anythin' t' run away – but yer can't show it. Yer've got t' bring out yer brave face, screw it on tight, an' brazen it out.* Well, that's what I did. Though, I remember thinkin' t' myself it was easy for 'im t' be sayin' such things, seein' as 'ow 'e wasn't afraid of nothin'.'

'I thought the same for years, right up 'til just before 'e died. 'E'd been ill for a good long while, but 'e'd kept it from us, always smilin' an' jokin', an' I suppose we just thought 'e was gettin' old, an' that was why 'e was lookin' so thin. Then one day I come 'ome unexpected, an' there 'e was – all on 'is own, sittin' at the kitchen table – cryin' like a little kid. I didn't know why, an' truth was, I was so embarrassed to see 'im like that I didn't let on I was there, but turned right around an' went straight back t' my job. When I called back a week later 'e was 'is old self again – like 'e 'adn't a care in the world. He died the week after that.'

Mary lifted her head. 'Oh, Peg.'

'The thing is,' said Peggy, keeping her face half turned. 'We always see the worst in ourselves – an' I reckon my dad probably always considered 'imself a coward – a coward who was just puttin' on a brave face. But that ain't the truth of it – no more for 'im than for you. See, if 'e 'adn't been sick with fear inside, then I don't see as 'ow yer could really call 'im brave – no more than yer might call some Saturday night brawler, too drunk t' care what 'appens to 'im, brave. You can give yer brave face any name yer like – but that don't make a penn'orth o' difference t' the fact it's still you, Mary – *an' no one but you.* Pretendin' to be Emma, or pretendin' to be brave, it comes to one an' the same thing.'

Mary began to fret at her cuff. 'I don't know, Peg.'

'Well, I don't know 'ow to make it any plainer. All I know is, I've seen that person you call Emma lots of times. I've seen 'er down on 'er knees for hours on end, scrubbin' floors, 'er 'ands red raw, an' tears in 'er eyes – but refusin' t' give in. I've watched 'er pick 'erself up off the floor time an' time again after life 'ad knocked 'er flat. An' I've seen 'er makin' decisions lots o' folk would 'ave been too weak an' frightened to make. Only I don't call 'er Emma. I call 'er Mary – *My Mary* – an' I want 'er back. I want it t' be my Mary that walks out of this 'ouse tomorrow mornin', with her brave face screwed on tight an' darin' the world to shake it loose. That's all I want.'

*

Charlie returned just after nine o'clock, pausing in the kitchen doorway, his head cocked to one side, listening. 'She hasn't gone, has she?'

'No.' Peggy got slowly to her feet and came over to him. 'I persuaded 'er it was too late t' go traipsin' back 'ome – so I've put 'er t' bed.'

'Have you now?' He laughed. 'You'd have made a right good mum, you know, Peg.'

'Yer don't mind, do yer?'

''Course not. She's welcome to stay as long as she likes.' He felt her take his hand, and allowed himself to be lead to his chair by the fire. 'So did you find out what's wrong?'

'Some of it. There's some more she ain't tellin' me, but …' Peggy gave a resigned sigh. 'So 'ow was the pub?'

'Oh, same as usual.' He chuckled to himself. 'Blimey, *me* in a pub. Can you imagine – after all these years? Couldn't you think of anything more suitable than that? Lord knows what Mary must think.'

'She won't 'ave given it a thought. So where *did* yer go?'

'To visit a couple of my many lady friends.'

'Oh, is that so? Then yer won't be too anxious t' get t' bed, I suppose.'

'Well, I wouldn't say that.' She was standing close by and he reached out, taking hold of her ample hips and pulling her to him. 'Matter of fact, I was just thinking as how it was about time we turned in.' He lay his head against the softness of her belly, then pulled away a little as a thought struck him. 'Here, just a minute,' he said. 'We've only got the one bed.'

'Yer did just say yer didn't mind – an' I'm 'oldin' yer t' that.'

'You crafty old woman.'

She moved closer, coaxing his head back against her. 'Yer don't really mind, do yer? I can make us up somethin' on the floor just 'ere.'

'What, just like we used to do all them years ago?' he grinned. 'You remember? When you'd let me into the kitchen after they'd all gone to bed upstairs?'

''Course I do.'

'They were lovely times.'

Peggy held him closer. 'All we ever did was cuddle an' talk.'

'I know.'

'I wish … I wish I'd taken yer up t' see them lights, Charlie. I should 'ave done it. Yer don't get no second chances in this life.'

'Here, don't you go carrying on, now,' he said, hearing the thickening of her voice. 'We got *our* second chance, didn't we?'

She sniffed back the tears that threatened. 'Yes, but it's too late for yer t' see them lights.'

'Don't you believe it, Peg.' He reached for her cheek, stroking it with the backs of his fingers. 'Now I've got you back, I see them every night. *Every blooming night.*'

Chapter Fifty-Nine

Nanny Reeves was flitting to and fro like an agitated bee denied access to the delicate flower that was Owen. 'I really must urge you to reconsider, sir. He's barely six years old.'

'Old enough, I think, to make his own way to school.' Evan placed the scarf about the boy's neck. 'Don't you agree, Owen?'

In the cold light of morning, Owen felt less sure, but he attempted a confident nod.

'But what if he should become ill?'

Evan looked at her. 'He's starting a cold?'

'No, sir.' She returned his look. 'But what of his *chest*?'

Evan was aware of the recurrence of Owen's old problems since his arrival in London, and for a moment he hesitated, but then he remembered the bruising. 'How are you feeling?' he asked, going down on one knee in front of the boy. 'Are you ready for your adventure?'

Owen swallowed hard. 'I think so.'

'And if you should get lost?'

'I'll ask a policeman.'

Nanny Reeves stood in quivering restraint. 'And what if he can't remember where he lives? Then what?'

'Here,' said Evan, taking a visiting card from his jacket and slipping it into the breast pocket of Owen's coat. 'A magic talisman. Something that will ensure you can always find your way home.'

*

Peggy took the empty plate from in front of Mary. 'Why not let me do yer some more? I can do another couple o' rashers in no time – an' there's plenty of eggs.'

'I couldn't, Peg. I'm bursting at the seams as it is.' She looked longingly around the kitchen. 'You know, I haven't had a breakfast like that since …

well, since I can't remember when.'

'Yes, well that don't surprise me none. Yer never 'ad much meat on yer t' begin with – but now?' She shook her head in despair. ''Ow many times 'ave I told yer? *Always* start with a good breakfast. Skimp the rest o' the day if yer must, but …'

From his armchair by the fire, Charlie began to laugh. 'Leave the poor girl be, Peg. You haven't stopped preaching at her since the minute she walked through the front door. You carry on like that and she won't be wanting to come back.' He turned a little more. 'You *will* come back and visit again, won't you? Or better still, why don't you stay another night – go home tomorrow?'

'Yes, why don't yer?' said Peggy. 'Yer said yer 'aven't no job t' go to.'

'I wish I could … but I must get back. Joe will be worried. And besides, I wouldn't have stayed last night if I'd known it meant the two of you sleeping on the floor. You should have told me, Peggy.'

'You needed the bed more'n we did – an' anyway, we was alright down there, weren't we, Charlie?'

'Oh, right as ninepence,' he said with a broad grin. 'Matter of fact, I'm thinking of doing it again tonight. Get a *right* good view over London from down there, you do. So just you remember – there's always a place for you here if ever you need it.'

Peggy went to the mantelpiece. 'I've got a couple o' things for yer. This 'ere's from Mr Abrahams. 'E thought yer might like it for a keepsake.' She handed over the photograph. 'Bit foggy lookin' if yer ask me, but maybe it's just my eyes.'

A lump came to Mary's throat. The picture was the one he'd taken of her on the hill overlooking Nant-y-Pridd, and the image of herself as she had been, young, poised, and with all the confidence of youth, almost broke her heart. Silently, she slipped it into her pocket.

'An' 'ere's a couple of other things,' continued Peggy, pushing a small packet across the table. 'One of 'em yer may or may not want,' she caught Mary's puzzled look, and went on quickly, 'so I'd rather yer didn't open it till yer get 'ome. At least, that way, if I ain't done the right thing, I won't 'ave it on my conscience till the next time yer come.'

*

Peggy walked with me as far as the High Street, and for her sake I fixed on my brave face until the omnibus came in sight. We'd said so many goodbyes over the years, yet along with the sadness I'd always felt hope – a sense of moving on, of travelling toward that elusive happiness waiting just beyond the next rise – but not this time. Now the road back to Whitechapel lay straight and flat, with only misery waiting to embrace me.

Seated inside the bus, I didn't wait to read Peggy's letter, but tore it open the moment she'd disappeared from view, despising myself for the selfish hope it would contain money. It did. A half-sovereign wrapped in a square of newspaper slipped from the envelope along with a neatly folded sheet.

'My dearest Mary', she'd written, and I felt my chest tighten, for I knew the enormity of feeling that had wrenched from her those three simple words – and how thoroughly unworthy of them I'd become.

I couldn't read on, not there in front of everyone, so I pushed it into my pocket, and sitting inside the cramped bus I wept inwardly.

I wept for the girl in the photograph, the girl I'd somehow mislaid along the way and replaced with a weak and pathetic creature whose single, over-whelming desire was to run crying to Peggy, to let her take me in her arms and bear the enormous weight for me – just as I'd let Gwyneth do on the night of the fire – just as I'd let so many other people do.

I wanted to believe I might possess the qualities I so admired in Emma, that she really was me – but no matter how I tried, I couldn't. But, for the present, it didn't matter. Peggy had reminded me of one thing – that I could act the part – and with that reminder came the realisation I did have a choice.

*

The morning was bright, but a mist hung about the streets, the aban-doned child of the smothering fog that had only recently lifted, causing Evan concern as he watched Owen stop yet again, his hand going to cover his mouth as he coughed.

The boy was fifty yards ahead, on the far side of the road, unaware of his father following at a discreet distance, and Evan felt heartened by the stud-ied, almost comic resolution in his son's step – but the frequent coughing was becoming a worry. London was not agreeing with the boy, and the prospect of New York had begun to occupy Evan's thoughts more and more. It was uppermost in his mind as they came in sight of the school.

A small crowd of boys were gathered about the gates, and to Evan it seemed that Owen faltered a little as he approached, but then one of the taller boys came forward, ruffling Owen's hair and putting a hand on his shoulder in a friendly gesture, leading him into the school, and Evan gave a sigh of relief.

For a few minutes more he lingered on the street corner, looking across at the distant building, then, satisfied all was well, he went to the kerb and hailed a passing cab.

'The London Hospital,' he said, climbing in.

*

'Is not for you. Take it from me. Is not for you.'

Mary shook her head. 'It's the one I want.'

The little old man's face melted into the smile of a doting father. 'You pretty girl – and *I* know what pretty girls like. This,' he held up a simple blue dress, 'this is what I know you like. Sure. You listen – this dress is for you. I see you in this dress, turning all the young gentlemen's heads, eh?'

'How much is the black velvet?'

'Too much.' His features took on an expression of infinite patience. 'Take it from me, black is not your colour. I know these things. Black? For you? No.' He looked ruefully at the blue dress, 'You sure you don't like?' He tossed it aside. 'Well, maybe you are right. I think yellow suit you better. I have nice dress in back of shop. It belong to very clean lady who only buy it to go to parties – only she never go to no parties. But there you are, eh, what can you do? Her bad luck is your good luck. You wait right here, eh? I fetch it.'

'I want the black suit.'

With the dejected air of a man just sentenced to ten years, he came from behind the counter. 'Well, well. If you want so bad, then you must have.' Lovingly, almost reverentially, he stroked the lapel of the jacket then lifted the full skirt, nodding in silent appreciation of the seamstress's art. 'You are lady who knows quality.'

'How much is it?'

'Too cheap.'

'Just now it was too expensive.'

He shrugged. 'Who can say? If I ask fifteen pounds, I insult the person who make such a garment.'

Mary felt her stomach tighten. 'But how much is it?' she asked, trying to keep her voice steady.

He eyed her, taking in the patched, threadbare dress she was wearing. 'Let me show you something else.'

'*How much?*'

'Thirty shillings.'

The twist in her stomach gave an extra turn. 'But it's damaged,' she said, her fingers trembling as she picked at the suit. 'Look there's a burn in the skirt – and here, the trimming is coming away.'

'Is nothing. My wife mend in ten minutes.' He leaned back against a rail of tawdry looking blouses. 'Listen. I like you – so I give you my bottom price. Twenty-five shillings.' He watched her face. 'Alright, so how much you got?'

Mary felt for Peggy's half-sovereign. 'Not enough.'

'So tell me.'

'Ten shillings.'

There was a sadness in his eyes as he went back behind the counter, picking up the blue dress once more. 'Maybe you reconsider, eh?'

'Eighteen shillings.'

'But you only got ten.'

'I can get the rest – by tomorrow.'

He looked sadly at the suit. 'Is good quality,' he said. 'Very good. I know such things. And I know the lady who would make such a suit will likely turn in her grave – but ...' he sighed. 'Alright, I keep it for you – *till tomorrow.*'

*

'*M-Marie?*' Joe awoke with a start to find Mary sitting at the table, a bottle of ink and several expensive sheets of paper laid before her. 'Where on earth did you get to? I've b-been out all night looking for you.'

Mary continued to write. 'I stayed at Peggy's. There was no way of letting you know. I'm sorry.'

'Sorry?' He climbed, fully dressed, from the bed. 'I was worried about you. Julia came b-by about eight o'clock ...'

She looked up. 'This morning?'

'This m-morning? Yes.'

'Where is she now? At the refuge?'

'The refuge?'

'Joe, *please* – can't you stop doing that?'

'Doing that? Doing what?'

'Oh, never mind.' She crumpled the sheet on which she'd been writing and threw it into the grate. 'She'll lend me the money. I'm going round to see her now.'

'Now? B-But she's not there.' He scratched wearily at his unkempt hair. 'And what m-money?'

'What do you mean she's not there? Where has she gone?'

'Gone? Gone to Ramsgate ... or somewhere. Some m-meeting or other, I *think* she said. I'd just fallen asleep when she called.'

'How long has she gone for?'

He stared vacantly for a few moments, then gave a weak shrug. 'A day? ... no ... was it a week? ... I can't really remember.'

Mary drew a hand over her face. 'Now of all times. Damn it! *Damn it!*'

'M-Marie. There's no call for that sort of ...'

'My name's Mary, Joe. Not Marie. *Mary.*'

He looked hurt. 'It's just m-my little joke. You always used to like them.'

He seemed to shrink, and part of her wanted to go to him, to take his head on her shoulder and tell him she was sorry, but instead she sat down at the table and took up her pen. 'I'm going to get us out of here, Joe.'

It was a few seconds before he answered, and when he did there was a helpless note to his voice. 'How?'

'I'm going to get a job.'

'A job? Cleaning?'

'No, not *cleaning*. A good job. In an office – or perhaps teaching. I could teach art. What is it they say? *Those who can – do. Those who can't – teach.'*

'Teach? B-But you can't.'

'Why not?'

'Why not? B-Because … b-because *you can't*. You'd need qualifications, a character at the very least …'

'What do you think I'm doing?' Mary dipped her pen in the ink.

He got up from the bed and came to where she was sitting. 'There's someone who'll write you one?'

'No.'

'No?' He looked closer, his eyes widening as he read over her shoulder. 'M-Mary, you *can't*! That's *forgery*. They'll b-be sure to find you out.'

'Perhaps. But it's worth the risk.' Joe opened his mouth in protest, but she forestalled him. 'Look, you don't have to approve, Joe. But I can't stay *here* – in this horrible room – for the rest of my life. I just *can't*.'

He stared about him in despair. 'Well, what if … what if I found us somewhere else? Somewhere b-better?'

'*Joe*. We can't even afford *this*.'

'This? No … no, you're right.' He rubbed at his eyes. 'I'm tired. I'm not thinking properly.'

'Why don't you go back to bed. I'll be finished here in a minute, then I'll be going out …'

'Out? B-But you've only just come in.'

'I've got to attend to some things.'

'Things? What things?'

'Just *things*. You get some sleep. I'll be back later, and then I'll make us something to eat.'

Submissively, he turned back toward the bed, but then his eye fell upon the folded piece of paper lying on the mantelpiece. 'What's that?'

Mary glanced up. 'A letter, from Peggy.'

'Peggy? B-But you've just b-been there.'

She gave a shrug.

'Can I read it?'

'If you want to,' she said, bending to her writing once more.

Joe picked it up, reading the words that Peggy could never have spoken. 'A nice letter,' he said at last.

'Yes.'

He hesitated, the paper trembling in his hands as he looked at the Bloomsbury address that had been added as a postscript. 'Who …' he swallowed hard, 'who is Owen?'

'My son,' she said, continuing to write.

*

John McCarthy was laughing. What had begun as a small chuckle of disbelief had grown and grown until he was quite red in the face. 'Is this a joke?' he asked at last, dabbing at his eyes with his sleeve. Mary made to answer but he quickly stopped her. 'No. No, don't spoil it. I was going to give you and Joe notice to quit – but I haven't laughed like this in years, so if I were you I'd stop while you're ahead, and just turn around and go home before I change my mind.'

'I'm very serious, Mr McCarthy. I know we already owe you twenty-two shillings …'

'Twenty-three and sixpence, to be exact.'

'Alright, twenty-three and sixpence, but I need to borrow a pound – ten shillings at the very least.'

'I told you not to go spoiling it. There's nothing worse than a joke that goes on too long.'

'But if you'll lend it to me I'll be able to pay you back everything – the outstanding rent, the window repair, *everything*.'

'Magic trick, is it?' He closed the ledger. 'I like magic tricks – but not with my money. Now I'm giving you fair warning. I need something on account this week or I'm putting you out next Saturday.'

Mary looked pleadingly at him. 'Please, Mr McCarthy. I know we've let you down in the past – but things are different. I'm going to get a job, a good job, but I can't do it in these rags. Just ten shillings?'

'I've already let you run up a bigger debt than I should have, and I'm not going to throw good money after bad. It's not as if you even own anything. What am I supposed to take when you can't pay up? The clothes off your back?'

Mary began to finger her cuff, then let it go and drew herself up. 'I need that money. It's my one way out of here – and I'll do anything to get it.' She looked him straight in the eye. 'There must be *something* you want?'

He shook his head. 'Do you know how many offers of that nature I get? Every time a woman's short of the rent – or short of a drink?' Mary made no reply and he was about to turn away, but he found he could not. His mouth had become suddenly dry, and his eyes would not be hurried, lingering of their own accord over the lithe body beneath the shabby dress. For long seconds they stood watching each other. '*Just* for the loan of ten shillings?' he asked in a soft, almost incredulous voice.

As a trysting place, the back room of McCarthy's chandlery left everything to be desired – but, smelling of oil, soap, tea, the earthy scent of potatoes, candle wax, bright new metal and dusty old wood, it was a place of business – and so admirably accommodated the transaction about to take place.

John McCarthy came through from the shop. 'I've locked up,' he said pulling the door shut behind him. 'But we can't be too long. I never close during …' He stopped short. Mary had undressed to her white chemise, and he felt the pressing urgency of desire as he looked at her. 'I wasn't expecting you to …' He paused again, licking his dry lips. 'Aren't you cold?'

Mary shook her head, waiting for him in awkward silence. 'I've put down some sacks.'

McCarthy looked at the improvised bedding, then at her bare feet, then at her slender ankles and calves, and then up again, following the white cotton folds of the chemise until he found her face once more.

But still he made no move toward her, and after another long silence she said, 'I'm clean – if that's what's worrying you?'

The words jolted McCarthy from his reverie. 'I never supposed you wasn't,' he said looking hurt. 'Do you think I'd do this with …?' His eyes held hers, searching, then he pushed himself from the wall. 'Oh, to hell with it. What does it matter?' His arm went about her waist, pulling her closer while his other hand felt hungrily for her breast, feasting on the firm round flesh like a man starved of sensation. He could smell her – the warm, sensuous smell of youth – and he ached with yearning as he gorged himself on her body, his hands moving urgently, trying to cover every inch. He buried his face in her bosom, drinking in the intoxicating scent of warm, vibrant skin, then fell to his knees before her, his hands scrabbling at the hem of her chemise, lifting it up around her waist.

He groaned, a plaintive moan of passion and of guilt, as he pressed his cheek to her belly, his hands moving adoringly over her smooth round flanks, one moment cherishing, the next gripping firmly, pulling her close, smothering himself in the glory of firm flesh and soft, springy hair.

Standing over him, Mary let herself be drawn to his kisses, her hands upon his head, fingers entwined in his grey, wavy locks as she struggled with her own emotions. It was a business arrangement – nothing more – but his panting breath was hot and moist between her legs, and despite herself she arched back her head, her feet instinctively moving apart.

McCarthy felt the movement – a gentle rippling of flesh as her thighs parted, and he eased himself back, gazing with abject desire – then slowly, and with an almost overwhelming reluctance, he took his hands from her and stood up. 'No,' he said, trembling, breathing hard. 'No, this isn't right. Not for me – and not for you.'

Surprised and confused, Mary let her chemise fall back, embarrassment colouring her face. 'I … I don't understand.'

'We're making fools of ourselves,' he said.

McCarthy was busying himself re-arranging the window display when Mary emerged from the back room, and they eyed each other in uneasy silence.

'Would you really have done it?' he asked, as she crossed to the door.

She paused, her hand upon the latch. 'It doesn't matter now, does it?'

'I think it does.'

'Then, yes – yes, I would have. Why not?'

His mouth drew down, thoughtfully. 'You and Joe – you're not religious folk, are you? Not church-goers?' He saw the question forming between her brows, and he said. 'I'm not either. But Mrs McCarthy, she's a believer. Believes every word that's written in the bible – and a good deal more that aren't. It can make aspects of life *disappointing* once procreation's no longer your aim.'

'Then why …?'

'Not because I didn't want to. But what sort of a man is it who cannot govern himself?'

'Why should a man have to?'

McCarthy looked into her eyes. 'As long as he has the money to pay for it, eh?' A blush came to Mary's cheeks, and he smiled, sadly. 'Or is this a love affair? Is that what we're having? Because if it is, then it's a very different matter. A man might very easily fall in love with you. I know *I* could. And if we went back in there right now – then tomorrow I'd want you even more. But once you'd got your ten shillings, would you still want me?'

She didn't answer.

'I thought not,' he said. 'And so, afterwards, would we remember the pleasure – or just the guilt – and begin to despise each other – and then ourselves?' He crossed to the counter and took two half-sovereigns from the drawer, laying them on the scarred wooden top. 'You take these and get yourself far away from here, Mary Kelly. You don't belong – and you need to get away before that stops being the case.'

Chapter Sixty

The man removed his half-moon spectacles with a flourish and looked up from the sheet of paper. 'This is a most glowing character, Miss Kelly. *Most* glowing.' He glanced at the paper again. 'The Cardiff Academy of Art? I'm afraid I cannot own to having heard of it.'

Seated across the desk from him, Mary bestowed her most gracious smile. 'It would be nice to think one's work merited recognition, whether it be in the provinces, or here in London – but one must be realistic.'

He nodded. 'It embarrasses me to admit I am more conversant with the schools of Milan and Paris than those of our own provincial towns.'

She made no answer, but casually brushed some imaginary specks from her skirt, an elegant distraction she had learned in Knightsbridge, but one she instantly knew to be a mistake for it brought to his attention the small, round burn mark on the otherwise flawless velvet. 'A rather careless old gentleman who travelled with me from Wales last week,' she explained, smiling. 'I'd quite forgotten about it.'

'One would have hoped he was gentleman enough to offer recompense.'

Mary imitated Mme Bennaire's musical laugh. 'I'm quite sure neither of us noticed at the time. You see, we'd fallen into a rather passionate discussion regarding Mr Ruskin's exhibition of Turner drawings some years ago. You may remember it?'

'Yes, most certainly.'

She saw the gleam come to his eyes, and she smiled. 'I thought it quite wonderful, too – but my dear old gentleman was of a rather different opinion, which he argued *most* expressively. And much as I love the aroma of a good cigar …' she ran her fingers over the soft folds, '… it *can* play havoc with one's clothes.'

Entranced, the man swallowed, then gave a little cough. 'Yes,' he said, his voice suddenly high and thin. 'Yes, well … Mr Protheroe's academy – it was an establishment that admitted female students, you say?'

'Indeed yes. Mr Protheroe took great pains to promote the academy as a progressive institution.'

'I see. Excellent. *Excellent.*' He got to his feet. 'Well, I shall not detain you any longer today, Miss Kelly – but I am delighted to have made your acquaintance and feel certain we shall be able to offer you a teaching position once the usual formalities have been undertaken. Have you an address where you may be contacted?'

For the briefest moment, Mary faltered. 'An address? Why yes … yes, of course. You can write to me care of the Alexandra Hotel, Hyde Park Corner.'

'The Alexandra? Goodness, I know it well. In fact, it makes us almost neighbours.' He walked with her to the door. 'Perhaps you would permit me to call on you there one evening?'

'Oh, I should find that most agreeable, but …' she smiled apologetically, 'I'm afraid I leave this afternoon for the country, and will not return for at least a week. Old friends can be *so* demanding, can't they?'

*

The gardens had a forlorn feel to them, the almost bare trees clinging to the final vestiges of their foliage like skeletal beggars clutching their rags about them in preparation for a winter already making itself felt – and Mary shivered as she sat alone on the bench. She had come to Bloomsbury, to the address Peggy had given her, with no plan or design, no intention of making herself known, merely an overwhelming desire to catch a glimpse of her son, to see what he had become – to know she had made the right choice.

Lights began to appear in windows, the warm orange glow of lamps echoing the fading skyline, and she rose, feeling the cold which had seeped into her bones during the long wait – yet still she could not leave. It was as she lingered, her eyes barely moving from the distant front door, that she became aware of the small boy who had entered quietly by the furthermost gate.

'Is everything alright?'

Sitting in a secluded spot, his schoolbooks beside him, the boy glanced up. His eyes were red and his cheeks were streaked from crying, but still the likeness to Evan was remarkable, and Mary's heart leaped.

'Yes, thank you. I … I had something in my eye,' he lied, quickly lowering his face once more.

Mary wanted to touch him, to hug him – but it was an impossible notion, and instead she sought refuge in the commonplace, reaching for her handkerchief. 'I *could* take a look for you – if you'd like me to?'

Owen shook his head. 'It's gone now.'

'I see.' She took a tentative step closer. 'Well, would you mind if I sat with you? I'm waiting for someone, you see, and … well … it's rather cold and lonely sitting here by myself.'

He gave a small, despondent shrug. 'You can if you like, but I can't stay very long – and anyway, the man will be closing the gates soon. He always does when it starts to get dark.'

'Well …' She searched for something to say. There were a thousand things she wanted to ask, a thousand things she wanted to tell him, but that too was impossible. 'Well,' she said again, looking down at him, then across at the houses, her eyes misting.

From the gardener's hut, an old man appeared and slowly made his way toward them. 'I shall be locking up in a few minutes, miss,' he said apologetically as he passed.

Owen got to his feet, drawing his cuff across his cheeks. 'I'd better go in. Nanny will be waiting.'

She watched him walk away, and the longing seized in her chest. 'Owen,' she called desperately, but the word came only as a hoarse whisper, and he went out of the gardens without a backward glance.

*

The soft, tentative knock came the following morning, just as the kettle began to boil.

'I'll be there in a minute.' Grabbing a towel, Mary took the iron kettle from its hook and set it down on the hearth. 'If that's you, Joe, I haven't even started yet.'

The grey morning light edged around the makeshift curtains, and the fire gave off a dull red glow, but otherwise the room was in darkness, and it took her eyes a while to adjust to the daylight as she opened the door.

'Joseph?'

The giant frame of Joseph Fleming moved a step closer, filling the doorway. 'Hello, Mary. I come to see you – just like I promised.' He was silhouetted against the light, and his head hung down, his chin resting on his chest. 'I couldn't come again … not till now … but I got some more for you. Look.' He opened his fist to show the silver half-crown.

'Oh, Joseph.' Mary smiled and felt for his hand. 'Come on. Come inside and sit down.'

He let himself be drawn into the room, sitting awkwardly at the table while Mary drew back the coat, letting the light stream in.

'I was just about to have a wash.'

'You like washing, don't you. I remember you like to wash.' Then he looked uneasy. 'But I don't want to be in the way.'

'It's alright.' The innocent naivety brought a smile to her face. 'I'll wait until later. Would you like some tea? The kettle's just …' She caught her

490

first proper sight of his face. 'Joseph! What happened to you?'

He put his hand to his cheek. 'T'ain't nothing.'

'Let me see.' Gently she prised away the great ham fist. Both his eyes were blackened, the yellowing bruise continuing down one side of his face to where the normally delicate lips were swollen and crusted with scabs. 'Who did this?'

'It didn't hurt.'

'Was it Miriam?'

'She can't hurt me. And anyway, I don't care if she does. T'ain't right what she did – t'ain't right at all. And she won't make me stop, neither. *Not never.*' The look of childish cunning came to his eyes. 'I'm too clever for her, see? She can change her hiding place – but I can always find it.'

'Joseph, you *mustn't*. Kate told me about the money you gave her – and I should have come to find you straight away, and given it back, but …' She crouched down in front of him, looking up into his face. 'You mustn't steal from her. It's not right.'

'T'ain't stealing. It's taking back is what it is. She stole from you – and she stole from Aunt Buki.'

'When?' Mary felt all the old bitterness welling up inside her. 'When we had the stall in the market?'

He nodded.

'But how?'

'Bad days,' he said, screwing up his face as he tried to recall the exact words. 'Bad, *bad* days – *but only for some.*' Timidly he met her gaze. 'But don't you worry. I'll get it back for you – all of it.'

Mary got to her feet, her hands bunched into fists and trembling with fury, but then she looked at his poor battered face, and she bit back her anger. 'Now you listen to me, Joseph,' she said, keeping her voice calm and controlled. 'You've been kinder to me than anyone – but you've misunderstood. Miriam – your mam – she never stole from me.'

'But she told me …'

'It was just her little joke – a bit of fun. Your mam … well …' Mary gritted her teeth and swallowed hard to dislodge the words that threatened to stick in her throat. 'She was *kind* to me when I first came to Whitechapel. She lent me some money – and I was just paying her back. Do you see?'

Joseph looked uncertainly at the coin still lying in the palm of his hand, and she gently closed his fingers over it. 'Your mam doesn't owe me anything. So I want you to put that back before she notices it's gone. Will you do that for me, Joseph?'

Very slowly he stood up. 'I've been stupid, haven't I?'

'No. No, of course you haven't.' She took his hand, squeezing it. 'You're my Prince Charming – always there, ready to battle dragons.'

He brightened a little. 'Like in the stories?'

'Just like in the stories.'

'And you're the princess?'

Mary looked at him, a lump in her throat. 'Yes,' she said, 'yes, that's right.'

*

'I'm tellin' yer – that snotty-nosed whelp's a bloody loose cannon!' Harry Farrel tilted back his head, drawing the razor upwards toward the point of his chin. 'An' that's all I need right now – a fuckin' loose cannon!'

Illuminated by the pale morning sunlight, Sadie drew open her silk dressing gown, turning this way and that before the bedroom mirror. 'So what yer goin' to do?'

'Terminate the arrangement – an' quick. Things are workin' out better than I'd 'oped – so I can afford to float the sick bastard before 'e gives me any more grief. I never liked the devious cunt, anyway.' He scraped at his neck a final time, nicking himself in the process. 'Oh, bollocks! Now look what 'e's made me do.'

'Yer can't blame 'im for that.'

'Can't I? You just watch me.' He wiped the remains of the soap from his face. 'An' while we're about it – this idea of yours is a bit of a fuckin' loose cannon as well, ain't it?'

'I thought yer'd be pleased.'

'What, at gettin' all dressed up like a performin' monkey – so's a couple of reporters can come an' take our fuckin' picture? We're goin' to look a right bunch of cunts.'

'No we ain't. They do all the posh 'ouses up west. They did this 'ere famous artist last week.'

'What famous fuckin' artist?'

'I dunno, do I?'

'So why the fuck do they want to write about us, then?'

'Because of all this Jack the Ripper business. It's got everybody talkin' about the East End. This reporter bloke said people can't get enough of it these days'

'So why us?'

Sadie gave him a long-suffering look. 'Well, they want someone a bit respectable, don't they? Don't want no riff-raff givin' a bad impression.'

'We're goin' to look proper cunts.'

'No we ain't.'

'Yes we fuckin' are.'

Gussie came to the door, a picture of gentility in a brand new confection of white lace. 'Get a move on, they'll be 'ere in a minute.'

Sadie continued to stare critically at her large, pendulous breasts and increasingly heavy belly.

'*Mum!*'

'What?'

'Fer Chris' sakes!' Gussie motioned with her eyes toward the dark-eyed little girl who had been kneeling by the grate all the while, a brush and pan in her hands.

'Well, *what?*' repeated Sadie, turning to face the room, her hands on her hips, the gown spread like a pair of music hall curtains. 'Ain't nothin' she ain't seen before.' She advanced on the girl who watched her approach with sullen eyes. 'I said it ain't nothin' you ain't seen before, is it?' said Sadie, more loudly, as if talking to an imbecile.

The girl continued to stare.

''Ere, you little cow. What yer lookin' at me like that for?'

The dull, hollow eyes followed the upward sweep of Sadie's arm, but otherwise the girl remained quite still – until the force of the blow threw her sideways to fall in a heap upon the floor.

'What the fuck's the matter with you?' said Harry wiping the soap from his razor. 'I thought yer liked 'er.'

'Cheeky little cow.' Sadie examined the back of her hand. 'Gone an' grazed my knuckles, now. Just wait till this bloody reporter's gone an' I'll give 'er what for.'

'Just leave the kid alone. If yer don't want 'er no more, it ain't no problem.' He gave the razor a final polish then folded it and slipped it into his trouser pocket. 'Stick 'er down in the cellar till we're done with all this newspaper nonsense, then I'll put 'er back on the market – 'ave Mickey take 'er up west. 'Ow about that?' Sadie was still fuming, so he cocked his head to one side. 'Then I'll buy yer another one, eh? A real young 'un. One yer can pet an' dress up all nice? Yer'd like that, wouldn't yer?'

*

The front door wasn't bolted, and Joe opened it a few inches. 'M-Marie? Can I come in?'

There was no answer so he pushed it a little wider, putting his head through the gap. 'M-Marie? Have you finished your wash?'

There was still no answer, so he went in. The bowl had been emptied and put away, but damp patches on the bare boards showed where it had rested, and he stood looking at them, then across at the bed where her old, familiar dress lay like a discarded skin.

Reverently he went to it, picking it up and holding it to his face, smelling her presence in the threadbare cloth, a presence that was already fading, evaporating like the water on the floor, and he stood for a long time, clutching the dress to him and staring unhappily about the lonely little room.

*

493

The gardens were growing dark, and the damp air smelled of smoke, the sour reek from the chimney pots softened now and then by the sweeter, friendlier scent of a bonfire burning somewhere.

'But what if you haven't got a brave face?'

'Everybody has one.' Mary glanced down at the boy. 'As a matter of fact, I've heard it said that our brave face is who we really are.'

Sitting by her side on the bench, Owen considered it. 'But then we'd never be afraid – would we?'

'I don't know. Perhaps … perhaps what we really have is a frightened face, and when we let it show, it hides our bravery?'

He thought for a few seconds more, then glanced up with uncertainty. 'So, when you were small … did *you* have a frightened face?'

'Oh, yes. A huge one – I *still* have it.'

He looked at her in surprise. 'But you're grown up.'

'It's always there, no matter how old you are – the secret is to never let it show.'

In the street, just beyond the screen of misty trees and bushes, lights were springing into view as the lamplighter made his rounds, and Owen got to his feet. 'I should be going. I hope your friend comes soon.' He paused, hovering uncertainly. 'But, if he doesn't, well, perhaps you could come to tea with us, that is, if *you'd* like to?'

Mary felt her heart quicken, but she shook her head. 'I don't think your parents would approve of casual callers, do you?'

'Father never gets home before seven.'

'Your mother, then.'

'She isn't here, either. She's …' he paused for a heartbeat, 'she's away … writing a book. She's very famous, you see, and … well, she has to travel a good deal. But she'll be back very soon I expect … very soon, maybe in a week … or perhaps a month … and then you could come and meet her.'

'Oh … yes.' To Mary, the damp evening air seemed suddenly chill. 'You must be very proud of her.'

'I am. We all are. Father says … well, he says she's the cleverest and most beautiful woman in the whole of London. So I'm sure *you'd* like her.'

'I'm sure I would.' Keeping her face raised, Mary blinked a few times, trying to take the sting from her eyes. 'She … she sounds wonderful.'

Owen came back a little way. 'Are you alright?'

'Yes … just my frightened face starting to show, I expect.' She smiled quickly and got up. 'I should be getting along, too. I've a long way to go.'

'But what about your friend?'

'I think I've missed him.'

'But you will come again tomorrow?'

Mary brushed at her cheeks. 'If you'd like me to?'

'I should like it – if *you* would like it.'

'I should like it very much.'

'Well, then.' He put out his hand. 'I suppose we should be introduced. My name's Owen. Owen Rees-Morgan.'

Mary took his hand in hers, holding it tightly. 'I'm Mary,' she said. '*Just* Mary.'

'Have you *very* far to go?'

'A *very* long way.'

'But you will find your way back here?'

She smiled, reluctantly letting go of his hand. 'If I get lost, I'll ask a policeman.'

'Yes, that's exactly the right thing to do. But …' A gleam came to his eyes, and he felt in the pocket of his jacket, taking out a small white card. 'There,' he said scribbling on the back of it with a stub of pencil and handing it to her. 'Now you'll always be able to find us, won't you.'

Mary looked at it. On the front, printed plainly in black ink: *Evan Rees-Morgan. 23 Cardigan Terrace. Bloomsbury. London W.C.* On the back, in neat, if childish writing: *To Mary from your new friend Owen.*

*

A fire was burning in the grate at Miller's Court, making it stiflingly warm; a new, dark green cloth covered the table, and on the wall above the mantelpiece hung an engraving of a young woman looking desperately out to sea, both print and frame much reduced in circumstance.

Mary looked about her.

'Like it?' asked Joe. 'I thought it would m-make the place a b-bit m-more cosy. A b-bit m-more like home.'

'It's … nice.'

'Nice? Yes, well, I thought you'd like it. Anyway, I suppose you'd like a *nice* cup of Q.R.S, eh?' He swung the kettle toward the fire. 'So? Any luck today?'

'I called by the Alexandra, but there was nothing.'

'Nothing? Well, I'm not surprised. The people at the hotel m-must know you aren't staying there.'

'Of course they do. But they don't know I'm not *going* to be. People often have letters sent to hotels to await their arrival.'

Joe looked doubtful. 'Await their arrival, eh? Well, I wouldn't know about such things.' He turned away, but something inside him wouldn't let the matter rest, and he turned back. 'Still, I can't see as it m-matters m-much. Once they've written to this M-Mister Pothole …'

'*Protheroe.* His name is *Protheroe.* And they may not write to him.'

'Not write to him? Of course they will. Otherwise everyone would b-be forging characters, wouldn't they? I m-mean, if it was …' He bit back his words and bent to check on the kettle. 'Well … m-maybe you're right.'

Mary put the small package she was carrying on to the table, and took off her jacket. 'You shouldn't have bothered with such a big fire, Joe. It's a waste of money when the weather's so mild.'

'M-Mild? Yes, well, I suppose it is for the time of year. Still, it m-makes it cosy, eh?'

'Yes – I suppose.' Pulling the coat across the window, she began to unbutton her dress.

'Won't you leave it on?'

'I daren't. I can't risk spoiling it.'

Joe watched her undress, chewing at his moustache all the while. 'It's just that I don't get to see you very m-much these days – and not all dressed up like that. And well, you look so nice when you're all dressed up, that's all.' He shuffled a little. 'Still, I expect you m-must have quite enough of turning young gentlemen's heads when you're out and about all day, eh?'

She made no answer and continued undressing, carefully laying the suit over the back of the chair, along with the stiff white petticoats, until she was standing in nothing but her chemise. 'Pass me my old dress, will you?'

Joe picked up the sorry-looking garment. 'Well, you still turn *this* young gentleman's head.'

She smiled and reached for her clothing, but Joe put it behind his back.

'How about a kiss for your prince?' he grinned, motioning toward the picture on the wall. 'Prince – do you get it? *Prints*?'

'Yes.' She leaned forward, giving him a chaste peck. 'Now can I have my dress?'

Sullenly, he handed it to her. 'You don't like it, do you – the picture?'

'It's very nice, Joe. And it was a lovely thought – but we didn't *need* it.'

'Need it?'

'Yes, *need* it. This place is never going to be a home – not even if you fill it up with prints – and we can't afford to waste our money.'

He dropped dejectedly on to the bed. 'It was only a shilling for the whole lot.'

'You should have used it to pay off your debt.'

'Debt? What difference does a *shilling* m-make? I owe five pounds!'

In the act of pulling on her old dress, Mary stopped. 'What do you mean, five pounds? You've been paying them every spare penny we get, haven't you? Well? *Haven't you*?'

Joe averted his gaze, chewing even more agitatedly at his thin moustache. 'I knew we could never save enough – not in such a short time. I thought if I m-made a few good b-bets …'

'Oh, for Christ's sake, Joe! Don't you *ever* learn?'

'Learn?' He sprang up defensively. 'I should like to *learn* what gives you the right to lecture m-me! How m-much did those clothes cost, eh? That's what *I'd* like to learn. We could have used *that* m-money to pay off Farrel.'

'Yes. Yes, we could have. And a year from now – ten years from now – we'd still be living in this … this *hole* – and you'd *still* be in debt!'

'And where did you *get* that m-money?' demanded Joe, ignoring her. 'That's another thing I'd like to *learn*!'

Mary's eyes grew icy. 'Where do you think?'

'Think?' He drew himself up in righteous indignation. 'You don't want to ask what I think.'

'Good! Then I *won't* ask!'

He glared at her, his mouth working in frustration. 'B-But … b-but if you *was* to ask …'

'But I'm not!'

Again his lips performed their impotent dance, and he dashed across the room, seizing on the brown paper package. 'And I should like to learn what this is! If every shilling has to be accounted for then what …?'

'Put it down!'

'Put it down? *Put it down?*' In a frenzy he began tearing off the wrapping. 'I'll not b-be ordered about in m-my own house, M-Marie!' Inside the brown paper lay a book. 'It's a b-book,' he said in surprise.

Mary finished dressing, her fingers working angrily at the buttons. 'Satisfied?'

'*Treasure Island?*' murmured Joe. 'A present?' Feeling a little foolish, he lifted the cover, reading the dedication in Mary's handwriting: *The story of a brave boy – for another brave boy.* He looked up in confusion. 'I don't understand.'

'It's not for you,' she said, going to the door and opening it. 'It's for my son. A story about courage – about a young boy facing up to some pirates.' She paused, casting him a disdainful glance. 'So on second thoughts, maybe you *should* read it.'

*

Joe shifted restlessly. 'M-Mary? Are you awake?'

'Please, Joe. Not now.'

His hand lingered over the swell of her bottom, warm and inviting beneath the blankets, then he turned again, sighing.

'What's the matter?' she whispered, 'Can't you sleep?'

'Sleep? No, my head's too full of things.'

'What sort of things?'

'*Things.*'

Reluctantly she rolled to face him, her hand creeping on to his chest. 'We can if you want? If it will help?'

'Help?' He sighed again. 'No, it's not that.'

'Then what is it?'

He lay still for a short while, then he said, 'You're going to leave m-me, aren't you?'

'Why would you say that?'

With a forlorn groan, he rolled away from her, swinging his feet to the floor to sit hunched on the edge of the bed. 'You don't love m-me. I don't b-believe you even care for m-me very m-much.'

'Joe, that's not true.'

'Not true?' He turned back to her, seizing her hand, the words bursting from him. 'Then m-marry m-me. We could m-make it a real East End wedding – on Christmas Day – it's only two m-months away.' But he felt her tense, and he released his grip. 'No, it's alright,' he said with a quiet sadness. 'You don't need to answer.' He got slowly to his feet. 'M-Maybe I'll go for a b-bit of a walk. Have a little think.'

'Joe …'

'You get some sleep. I'll slip the b-bolt when I leave.'

Chapter Sixty-One

'And so I said to 'im. If you think someone's goin' to pay four shillin's a week for a flea pit like this, then I should bloody well like to see them! So then 'e says to me, well, you can – they're outside, ready and waitin' – and 'ere's their four shillin's – and if you think my place is that much of a flea pit, then you won't want to be stayin' a minute longer, will you! Well, I was *that* taken aback …' Maria Garbey put her head on one side, looking across the room. ''Ere, are you listenin'?'

With the note still in her hand, Mary looked up. 'I'm sorry … yes … yes, of course I was.'

'Well?' said Maria. 'So can I?'

'Can you what?'

'Can I stay 'ere – with you and Joe – just for a day or two? Just till I find somewhere else. I promise I won't get in the way.'

Mary stared blankly at her. 'Stay here? Well – yes, I suppose so.'

'Oh, thanks, Mary. That's a real weight off my mind – though I knew you'd be alright about it – what with us bein' such good friends and all.' Her smile faded just a little. 'But what about Joe? I don't want to be the cause of no trouble between you two.'

'Joe?' Mary looked back at the note. 'Joe doesn't live here anymore.'

'Left you, 'as 'e?' asked Maria, peering at the scrap of paper in Mary's hand, trying in vain to read the words. 'Well, I wouldn't 'ave said nothin', of course – that's not my way – 'specially with us bein' such good friends, like. But now 'e's gone I don't mind tellin' you, I reckon you're well rid of 'im. My 'usband was just the same. I can't begin to tell you 'ow I suffered with that man. The times I'd beat him black and blue, and 'e'd still …' She paused again, aware that Mary's attention had drifted back to the letter. 'Well, anyway, I'd better go fetch my stuff eh? I expect you'll be glad to 'ave a bit of friendly company.'

*

I went to find Joe that afternoon and asked him to come home. He'd moved into a lodging house in Bishopsgate – a place very much like the one from which he'd once saved me – and I hated the thought of him living there, but though we talked for a long time, and parted as friends, he wouldn't return.

In the week that followed, I continued to search for a job. I had barely any money left, and so I rose early each morning to walk into the West End, calling by the Alexandra Hotel before doing the rounds of agencies and interviews. Then, each afternoon, just before dusk, I would make my way to Bloomsbury, to spend those few precious minutes with my son.

*

Resentful of the intrusion, the waspish old woman looked down her long, thin nose. 'Can we help you?'

Mary cast about the refuge. 'I'm looking for Julia.'

'Perhaps you'd like to tell *me* what it is you want?'

From the back room a slightly younger woman appeared, an apron covering her black uniform. 'You're her friend, aren't you?'

'Yes. I was wondering if she was back yet?'

'Yes, just last night. She's in the yard. I'll tell her you're here.' She turned to go but the old woman stopped her.

'Leave her. She's far too busy.' Then to Mary. 'If this is a personal visit you should come another time.'

Mary smiled sweetly. 'I'll just go out to her. I promise I won't keep her long.'

'Well, just see you don't!' the old woman snapped after her. 'It's God's work you're interrupting, you know.'

Julia was standing in the small, paved yard, surrounded by pails and bowls, some washed and leaning against the wall to dry, others still bearing the crusted signs of recent use. 'The Sunday morning dregs,' she said, wiping her hands on her stained apron. 'Saturday night is always our busiest time – and it's poor little me who has to clean it all up.' She pouted. 'And all on my own, too. Isn't it about time you came to join us? Many hands make light work, you know.' She saw Mary's discomfort, and she grinned. 'Well, you will – but perhaps not *just* yet, eh?'

'I said I wouldn't stay long.'

Julia looked past her, toward the house. 'Oh,' she laughed. 'You've met Vinegar Vera, have you? I shouldn't take too much notice of her. Her bark's worse than her bite. She's actually quite an old dear. But never mind about her. Want to hear about my trip?'

Mary could contain herself no longer. 'Julia, I just had to tell you …' She came forward, then froze in her tracks as a large dog scrambled, growling and snarling, from a makeshift kennel.

'It's alright, Tishy.' Julia called to him soothingly. 'This is a friend.'

The dog regarded Mary for a moment, then limped back to its shelter.

'You mustn't mind Tish. We rescued him a while ago, and we keep him for protection – but he's another one whose bark is worse than his bite.' Julia gave a broad grin. 'So, what is it that you just had to tell me?'

'I'm seeing Owen.'

'Owen?' A frown creased Julia's brow.

'My son.'

'I know who it is! But ... what do you mean you're seeing him?'

'Peggy gave me his address. He's here – in London.' Mary began working excitedly at her cuff. 'I wasn't sure what to do. I know I promised Mrs Rees-Morgan – and I didn't really intend to go, but ... I couldn't stay away, Julia. I just couldn't ...'

'Mary!'

'I see him every afternoon.' Her eyes became misty. 'I *talk* to him, Julia.'

Julia's mouth drew into a thin line. 'Mary, how could you? You made a solemn promise. You promised his family you'd never try to contact him – and now you're telling me you broke that promise. Doesn't that mean anything to you?'

'But he's my son.'

'Not any more he isn't.'

'He'll *always* be my son.'

Julia cast about angrily. 'And what about ... what was his name? Evan? Have you tried to see him, too?'

'No!'

'Is that *no* – or *no, not yet?*'

'Why are you being like this, Julia? I thought you'd understand.'

'I understand that you're being selfish. What good can you think will come of this? The boy was just a baby when you left him. He can't possibly remember you – and why should he have to? He has a family. Hasn't he? A father – *and a mother*? Can't you leave well enough alone?'

'I just wanted to see him.'

'And hurt everyone in the process?'

'I haven't told him who I am. We just sit for a while in the gardens, exchanging a few words. So who am I hurting?'

'Who do you think?' Julia's eyes flared angrily for a moment. '*Joe*. Surely you can see he'd be worried – frightened you might ...'

'Joe's left me.'

Julia stared in surprise. 'When?'

'A few days ago. It was his decision.'

'Oh, Mary, I'm so sorry. Look, he listens to me, perhaps if I spoke to him?'

'He won't come back, I've tried – and besides, it was for the best. We were never suited.'

'But …' Julia pursed her lips. 'Look, Mary, even if it is all off with you and Joe, there are other people who will get hurt if you continue with this. I want you to promise me you won't try to see Owen again.'

'I can't do that, Julia.'

'Can't? *Or won't?*'

'Either.'

'I see.' Julia turned from her. 'Then there really isn't very much more for us to say, is there!'

Mary took a step forward, tentatively reaching for Julia's arm. 'I can't believe you'd break our friendship over this.'

'*I* wouldn't,' Julia shrugged her off. 'But it appears *you* would.'

*

'I shall be locking up in a few minutes, miss.'

Intent on watching for Owen, Mary hadn't noticed the park keeper's approach. 'Oh, yes,' she said, disappointment showing in her eyes.

He was a small man, but very erect, and as he looked at her, he tilted his head a little to one side in a very military fashion. 'Well, I suppose I could leave this gate till last. It would give you a little more time.'

'No. It's alright.' Reluctantly she got to her feet. 'But it's very kind of you.'

He walked with her toward the street. 'None of my business, of course,' he said, closing the gate behind her and turning the key in the lock. 'But your young gentleman isn't usually this late – so you could try going to meet him on his way home from school.'

She stared at him through the iron railings. 'You know where it is?'

Mary was within sight of the school when she saw a boy standing by the entrance to a narrow alleyway. He was smartly dressed, but a furtiveness in his manner caused her to pause. She could not see into the dark recess he was guarding, yet she instinctively knew Owen was there, and she waited, moving out of the light from the street lamp and into the shadows by the wall.

Minutes passed, and the boy kept to his lookout, but still no one emerged from the alley, and finally she could wait no longer.

Stebbings was enjoying himself hugely. 'Do you see that?' He twisted Owen's ear, forcing his face toward a trail of green slime that ran down the wall from a leaking gutter somewhere above. 'Know what that is?'

Owen shook his head.

'Here, smell it.' Stebbings pushed him closer. 'What? You still don't recognise it?' He cuffed him hard. 'That's whore's piss, you ignoramus!'

Owen's eyes widened. He had no idea what a whore might be, but knew it was something terrible.

'Oh yes, that's what that is,' gloated Stebbings. '*Stinking whore's piss.* See that window up there?' He pointed to a dark opening in the wall high above them. 'A dozen filthy old whores live up there – too full of disease to ever come out except at the dead of night – and when they piss it runs out of a hole and down this wall.'

In blind panic, Owen began to struggle, but Stebbings took a firmer grip, pressing Owen's face closer to the evil looking slime. 'The last boy we brought here *only touched it* – and he went raving mad and had to be locked away.' He cuffed Owen again. 'But you're going to *lick it.* You're going to *lick* the whore's piss!'

The lookout shoved his head into the alley. 'Someone's coming!'

Immediately Stebbings let go, and Owen, terrified, tore blindly into the street, running pell-mell toward home.

Mary watched him go, then turned her attention to the alley. The lookout had already fled his post and only Stebbings remained, trapped in the blind passageway. 'What is going on in here?' she asked, a pleasant tone masking her seething anger.

Stebbings came forward, a picture of innocence and politeness. 'Just playing, ma'am.'

'I see.' He reached no higher than her shoulder, so she leaned forward, beckoning him with an elegant crook of her finger.

Stebbings took a step nearer. 'Yes, ma'am?'

'I like to see boys at play.' Mary leaned closer still, her voice dropping into a menacing Whitechapel growl as she whispered, 'But if I ever catch you bullyin' anyone again, I'll cut yer bloody ears off – *an' 'ave 'em for my supper.*'

The colour drained from Stebbings's face and Mary straightened, the sweet smile returning along with the refined tone. 'Now you'd better run along, hadn't you – but just remember what I said.'

Although momentarily frightened, Stebbings was well versed in the ways of intimidation and he quickly recovered. 'Very funny.'

'Oh, you think so?' She looked him over. 'Then perhaps I should have them now? I have a gentleman friend who'll whip them off this very minute if you'll just wait there a moment.'

A flicker of doubt crossed Stebbings's face, but he brazened it out. 'Well, I haven't all day, you know.'

'I shall only be a minute – and there's no point in running away because now we've seen you, we'll be watching for you in future – and we *will* have you sooner or later – most probably when you least expect it.'

With a smug smile, Stebbings watched her walk away, shoving his hands into his pockets and leaning back against the wall. He felt sure she'd look back, expecting him to have run off, and he intended to show his contempt for such a cheap trick.

But she didn't look back, not immediately. Instead she went straight to a very rough and dirty looking man standing a little way off, talking to him in a low voice, then turning and pointing in Stebbings's direction – making the boy's stomach turn over as the villainous looking rough peered at him with head thrust forward, a dark and dangerous scowl upon his face.

The final shreds of Stebbings's nerve held only long enough for the man to start in his direction – then he ran like a thing possessed.

Mary was waiting by the entrance as the man emerged from his exploration of the alley, his face still fixed in the characteristic frown of the shortsighted. 'Well, my eyes ain't so good in the dark – but I can't see no sign of 'er,' he said. 'Are you sure she ran in there?'

'I'm not sure. I thought so, but, well ...' she gave a helpless little shrug. 'But you've been more than kind. Please accept this.'

He squinted down at the sixpence she'd pressed into his hand. 'Oh, that's werry nice o' you. An' don't you go worryin', miss. If I knows cats, she'll be waitin' for you when you get 'ome.'

*

Nanny Reeves was in the hall as Evan let himself in the front door, and she waited while he took off his overcoat. 'I should like to speak to you about Master Owen, sir.'

'Of course.' He looked expectantly toward the stairs. 'It's very quiet. Where is he?'

'I've put him to bed.'

Evan raised an eyebrow. 'But it's only seven o'clock.'

'I thought it best. He's been sick, and barely eaten any of his supper.'

'I see. Well, I'll go up to him. But I'm sure it's nothing to worry about.'

'And he came home with a graze on his cheek.'

'A graze?' Evan became more concerned. 'Did he say how it happened?'

'*Chaps stuff*,' she said disapprovingly. 'I think you're making a great mistake in allowing him to ...' Catching herself, she paused. 'He shouldn't be mixing with rough boys – learning their foul, disgusting language.'

'Foul language? I see. Well, I shall have a word with him.'

'It's not just his language. He's far too delicate, he always has been.'

'Miss Reeves ...'

'It was always our ... that is, *Mrs Rees-Morgan's* intention for him to have a private tutor, and if she were here now ...'

'Then you'd still be dressing him in petticoats.'

Miss Reeves eyed him frostily. 'I've only ever had Owen's best interests in mind, sir.'

'Yes, of course.' He sighed, putting a hand to his face, massaging his eyelids. 'I'm sorry. That was uncalled for. I apologise.'

She made no acknowledgement, but walked primly to the stairs leading down to the kitchen. 'Oh,' she said, coldly, pausing. 'A parcel arrived for you this morning. I shall have Sarah bring it up and put it in the drawing-room.'

Sarah was standing at the sink, rinsing out cups. 'Want a cup of tea?' she asked as Miss Reeves came down into the kitchen. 'It's freshly made.'

'Doctor Rees-Morgan has just come home. You can take the parcel up.'

Sarah gave a nod.

'*Now*, Sarah.'

'There's no rush. He won't mind if it's not done right this minute – just as long as it *gets* done.' She glanced over her shoulder, her rounded features breaking into a smile. 'I've never worked in a place as free and easy as this – I could get *very* used to it.'

'Well I *couldn't*. Now take that package up this instant.'

The smile faded from the maid's face. 'That's funny. I don't remember anyone putting *you* in charge.'

'That's because no one has.' Miss Reeves glared. 'But *someone* in this household has to maintain some standards.'

'Are you awake, Owen?' Evan called softly, easing open the bedroom door.

'Yes.'

The voice from inside held a sad, lack-lustre note that touched a distant memory with Evan. 'Not feeling too well, I understand.'

'I'm alright now.'

'Well, that's good to hear.' He perched himself on the edge of the bed. 'So, are you hungry?'

'Not really.'

'Sleepy?'

'No, not really.' Owen climbed from between the sheets, sitting upon his pillow, his legs drawn up, chin resting on his knees. 'Is saying *whore* worse than saying *damned*?'

In the darkness, silhouetted by the open door, Evan allowed himself the smallest smile. 'Is that why you've been sent to bed early?'

Owen gave a nod.

'Do you even know what it means?'

'No. But it can't be such a terrible thing, can it? Because Grandmamma sometimes says *whore*, but she would never say *damned*. Never ever.'

'I don't think she would say *whore*, either – and certainly never to you.'

'But she does … well, not to me, but …' Owen chewed guiltily at his lip. 'Sometimes she'd say it to Nanny when she thought I wasn't listening.' He looked up anxiously. 'She said my mother was a whore.'

The words pierced Evan, and for a moment he could not speak. When he finally found his voice, it was thick with emotion. 'She had no right to say that.'

'But *was* she?' Owen pleaded, close to tears.

'No, she wasn't.'

'Then tell me about her, please, because I don't remember her, and Grandmamma only ever says nasty things.'

'Owen …'

'She must be bad, mustn't she? Why else would she have left us? Is that why you never talk about her … because *you* think she's bad?'

'No.' Evan reached for the boy, pulling him close and hugging him. 'I think your mother was the most wonderful person I've ever known …'

*

Nanny Reeves wore an expression of respectful disapproval as she stood in the drawing-room the following morning. 'I really think he should spend the day in bed.'

'As punishment?'

'To *recover*, sir.'

Evan smiled diplomatically. 'It was only a graze.'

'With respect, sir, you weren't here when he came home from school yesterday. I've never seen him so ill – as white as a ghost and barely able to breathe. And as for that awful language!'

'You mean the word *whore*?' he asked quietly.

Miss Reeves' lips compressed into a thin line. 'Yes, sir – that *was* the word.'

'It is a perfectly valid word. Found in the most proper of dictionaries.' Despite his best intentions, Evan felt himself growing angry. 'A word I believe my mother has used on occasion?'

The faintest wash of vermilion coloured the woman's cheeks, but she quickly composed herself. 'I couldn't possibly say, sir. But in my opinion such language from a six year old boy is quite unacceptable – and if Owen were a normal boy, I would most certainly have whipped him.'

'But he is a *normal* boy – and I won't have him wrapped in cotton wool – and neither will I have him punished for simply asking questions.' He heard the harsh edge in his voice and took a moment before continuing. 'Miss Reeves, I appreciate that when you worked for my mother she might have given you to understand certain things about my son.' He saw the colour rise to her cheeks once more. 'About his *health*. But I believe she has somewhat overstated any inherent weakness he may possess.'

'Mrs Rees-Morgan was always …' She got no further, for Evan raised a silencing hand as Owen came tentatively to the drawing-room door.

'Ah, Owen,' he said smiling. 'All ready for school?'

The boy looked to the nanny, then back to Evan. 'Am I to go?'

'Is there any reason why you shouldn't?'

His eyes flicked again toward Nanny Reeves. 'I do still feel *a little* unwell.'

'Where do you feel unwell?' Evan beckoned him closer.

'Well ...' Owen, gestured vaguely toward his middle.

'A pain?'

'Well ... *not exactly*.'

'A sick feeling?'

'Yes ... I suppose.'

Nanny Reeves started toward the boy. 'I think it best if I take him straight back upstairs, sir,' she said, reaching for Owen's hand.

'Just a minute, *please*, Nanny,' said Evan, going down on one knee. 'Now, tell me – this sick feeling – has it made you be sick? Or is it, perhaps, a little like the feeling you had when we were about to climb up on top of that bus?'

Owen chewed at his lip. 'A *little* bit like that.'

'I see.' Evan gave an encouraging smile. 'Well, I don't believe there's anyone in the world who hasn't felt that at one time or another. The important thing is deciding what to do about it.'

'So ... what should I do?' Owen lowered his eyes, already fearful of the answer.

'I think it's a decision only you can make.'

Miss Reeves could contain herself no longer. 'With respect, sir. He's far too young to know what is best for him.'

'*Please*, Nanny. Let him answer.'

Owen's lip began to tremble. The security of the nursery called temptingly, but he bit down hard, quelling the tremors. 'Mother wouldn't have been afraid, would she?'

'Oh, I'm sure she would.'

'But she wouldn't have let it stop her?'

'No.'

Again Owen thought about it, standing in an welter of indecision, until finally he said, 'Then *I* won't either.'

Evan stood up, resting a hand on the boy's shoulder. 'Then it's settled. Now, before you go, I have a surprise for you.' He crossed to the table and picked up a square package wrapped in brown paper. 'It came yesterday, and I thought I'd save it for you to unwrap.'

Nanny Reeves squared her shoulders. 'I should be getting about my work, if you'll excuse me, sir.'

'Yes, of course, Nanny. And thank you.'

With a bristling look, she made to go, but Owen had already begun to open the package, and reluctantly curious, she lingered.

'It's a painting!' announced Owen, pulling the last vestiges of paper from the ornate gilt frame and staring at the portrait it contained.

'It's what they call an oil sketch,' said Evan. 'It's a study the artist makes before starting on a larger painting. But even so, it's a very good likeness.' His fingers tightened imperceptibly about Owen's shoulder. 'Can you guess who she might be?'

Owen looked up at him in surprise. 'Of course,' he said. 'It's the lady I talk to in the gardens.'

Chapter Sixty-Two

'It's your boots.' The park keeper crossed his hands over the top of his besom, taking up the pose of a soldier at ease. 'You see, your proper gentry might not notice – but you'd never slip past the servants, not with boots like that. When I was in service, we could always tell the genuine article by the state of their shoes.'

There was no hint of animosity in the old man's voice, just a casual pronouncement of fact, and Mary took no offence, though she found herself drawing her feet further under the bench on which she was sitting. 'But how did you know about …?' She paused, unsure of how to phrase the question.

'Your son?'

A frown creased her brow. 'How could you possibly know?'

'Oh, that was plain enough. I've noticed the youngster in here many a time – so when I saw you together, well, I saw the resemblance straight off.'

Mary shook her head. 'He's the image of his father.'

'That may be so, but you can't take the mother out of the son.' He glanced up at the darkening sky. 'So what were you before you were turned out? Not a servant, I'm thinking. A Governess?'

'It wasn't anything like that.'

'Well, it's none of my business.' Across the rooftops, the church clock struck a lonesome note, and he looked up at the sky once again. 'Half past three, and almost dark already. I'd better get on and finish my sweeping.'

Mary picked up the brown paper parcel lying on the bench beside her and got to her feet. 'I hope I didn't sound rude just now.'

'No, miss. I never took it that way – and I should have deserved it if you did. I'm far too inquisitive for my own good. Comes from reading too many of these detective stories, I expect. The wife and I are fair addicted to them.' He started away down the path. 'And don't worry about locking up time tonight. I've got so far behind this afternoon I shall be here long after five.'

'Thank you, but it's alright. I'm going to walk over to the school. I just wanted to …'

'Oh, I shouldn't trouble to go there, miss. Your gentleman's just arrived.'

Surprised, Mary took a step forward, looking past the keeper toward the far gate, searching for Owen, but the pathway was deserted. 'Where?' she began, then suddenly she felt a presence behind her – and she turned, her eyes widening. 'Evan,' she whispered.

It was quiet, with only the distant sound of the twig broom on the path breaking in on the two figures seated, slightly apart, on the bench – their bodies turned earnestly toward each other.

'I would never have given him up, Evan. Never. But I was desperate. I knew Owen would die if he stayed with me – and so I came to your house. That was when your mother told me you were married.'

Stunned, Evan slowly shook his head. 'Mary … I'm so sorry.'

'But she was lying. You weren't married – so why didn't you come to find me? You *couldn't* have believed I'd just abandon our child?'

He looked guiltily at her. 'I *did* come to find you. I came to Cardiff one evening, to the academy, and I saw you there – with Protheroe.'

A chill touched Mary's heart, and she looked away.

'Mary, I don't care about it. *I* made the mistake. I should have trusted my heart, but I didn't. I love you – and that's all that matters.'

She turned back, steeling herself as she met his eyes. 'What I did with Protheroe – that was innocent compared to some of the things I've done since. I've made choices I'm not proud of, Evan – but I can't apologise for them, because I didn't know how to do things differently. But those choices – they'll always be between us, waiting to spoil things.' She put out one foot, drawing back her skirt a little. 'Like down-at-heel boots beneath an expensive dress.'

'No, they won't. Nothing is ever going to come between us again.'

'Don't, Evan. Don't say that until you know the truth.'

'Then tell it to me,' he said.

Owen had his nose pressed to the nursery window. 'I think I can see them. Yes I'm *sure* I can.'

'Come away from there.'

'Look, Nanny, can you see? Just down there. That's *our* bench. They're sitting on *our* bench.'

'*Our bench*?' Miss Reeves came to the window, peering down into the darkened gardens. 'I don't seem to remember *we've* ever sat there.'

'Not us, Nanny. I don't mean *us*, I mean …'

510

'Then I'm sure I don't know what you mean,' she said, firmly drawing the curtains.

Around the square, windows glowed and street lamps glimmered, turning the gardens into an island of darkness.

Mary looked steadily at him. 'So, now you know, can you honestly say it doesn't matter?'

'No,' he said with barely suppressed anger, 'no, I can't …' his words tailing away as he leaned back against the bench to stare past the black silhouettes of trees.

Mary felt the icy touch once more – for despite her worst fears she had still dared to hope. Now, yet again, Griffiths's words haunted her. *Facts, Mary Kelly. Not damned fairytales.* Fighting back her tears, she made to rise, but he turned to her suddenly, and even in the darkness she saw that his eyes too held a tearful look.

'Mary, I'm so sorry. I had no idea. The things you've endured, all because of …' The words eluded him, and slowly he shook his head. 'I don't think I can ever forgive my mother for the lies she told …' he looked at her, half ashamed, '… or myself for believing them. You tell me about the choices you've made, but you had no choice.'

'We all have choices, Evan. Can you truthfully say you would have made the same ones?'

He glanced away, and for a moment he made no answer, then his eyes met hers once more, 'I honestly don't know. But … I should like to think I'd have the courage to.'

From nearby there came a discreet cough. 'I'm sorry, sir, miss, but I really must be locking up now – otherwise my wife will be out searching the streets for me.'

Evan stood up. 'Yes, of course – *and thank you.*' He turned back to Mary, and slowly held out his hand. 'Come home?' he said.

*

'Jim,' says he, 'rum'; and as he spoke, he reeled a little, and caught himself with one hand against the wall.

'Are you hurt?' cried I.

'Rum,' he repeated. 'I must get away from here. Rum! Rum!'

Sitting on the edge of the bed, Mary closed the book.

'Oh, just a little more? To the end of the chapter?' Owen looked pleadingly, first at Mary, then at his father. '*Please?*'

Evan got to his feet. 'Well, I can't deny I should like to hear more myself, but I'm sure your mother is weary – and I can see quite clearly that you are.'

'But I'm not at all weary.' He stretched his drooping eyelids wide. 'Not the tiniest bit.'

'Well, even if that is the case, I think such a good book should be savoured. And the less we read tonight – the longer it will last.' Without thinking, he bent to tuck the boy in, but then he paused, stepping back to make way for Mary. 'I have a feeling he'd much prefer *you* to do the honours.'

For a moment she hesitated; the fears she'd expressed to Julia so long ago feeling all the more relevant as she watched her son slide down beneath the sheet and blankets. *Before it's too late – and I can't go back.* But even as the words returned to her, she knew she'd long since passed that point. She bent to tuck him in, her lips lightly pressing against his cheek. 'Goodnight, Owen, my love.'

'Goodnight …' His lips began to form another word, but it remained unspoken. Then, as she drew away, he asked, 'Will you be here to read the rest of the book?'

Mary looked at him, and even had she possessed the answer, she could not have uttered it.

'Goodnight, Owen,' said Evan stepping in and breaking the awkward silence. He leaned down, touching his lips to the boy's cheek, lingering for the briefest moment by his ear. 'Yes, she will,' he whispered, 'if I have any say in it.'

*

On the far side of London, two men came out into the damp night air and stood looking out over the river.

'Another one? Or shall we call it a night?'

'Let's call it a night.'

James Spencer took out his cigarette case. 'I was hoping you were going to say that.'

The smaller, older man half smiled, his white bushy eyebrows lifting above a pair of twinkling eyes. 'Another two, full power tests tomorrow, and I think we can dispense with your services. You can be back in Paris by the weekend. Get back to some proper medicine, eh?'

'Bugger medicine.' Spencer put a cheroot between his lips and felt for a match. 'I want to get back to some decent living. I'm expecting Her Majesty's Government to be more than a little generous in rewarding me for my efforts – and I intend to be equally free in the spending of it. I think a few months in Nice might just take the fog out of my lungs.' On the point of lighting the cheroot he paused, listening. 'A quiet night.'

'This damned Ripper business.'

'Oh, yes, I'd forgotten.' The match flared into life. 'We haven't heard from him in a while, have we.'

*

Evan pulled the drawing-room door closed behind them. 'Would you like something? Wine? Or tea?'

'No, thank you.'

Alone with him once more, Mary felt strangely ill-at-ease, and turned her attention to the small painting Owen had proudly shown her.

'It's a good likeness,' said Evan coming to stand by her. 'Owen recognised you the moment he saw it.'

She gazed at the small canvas, memories flooding back. 'It was a study for a painting of Venus. Where on earth did you find it?'

'In Protheroe's studio.'

She looked at him in surprise. 'You went back there, and bought it – after everything you'd seen?'

'Not immediately.' He wanted to touch her, to hold her, but there remained an emotional distance between them, and unconsciously he honoured it, moving away and pouring himself a small brandy. 'I had some growing up to do first.'

Her eyes went back to the picture. 'It's strange, isn't it? We were looking at a painting of Venus when we first …' She broke off, embarrassed. 'Do you remember?'

'There's not a day I don't think about it.'

She looked at him. 'So, what happens now?'

'A happy ending.'

A sad smile lifted the corners of Mary's mouth. 'If only it were that easy.'

'Why isn't it? It's *our* story. Can't we choose how it turns out?'

Mary closed her eyes. 'Just tear out the previous chapters?'

'No. I want to keep those chapters – they've brought us to this point – the two of us together again – and I'd never risk changing that.' He toyed uncertainly with the glass, then glanced up. 'Unless … somehow, they've changed your feelings toward me?'

'No!' Mary turned to look pleadingly at him. 'Evan, I love you. I loved you back then and I still love you – more than you can possibly imagine.'

Putting down his glass, he came to her, his fingers lightly brushing her cheek. Then his lips were on hers, thrilling her with the urgency of his desire as his hands began to re-learn her body. 'And I love you.'

'I know,' she said, tears forming in her eyes. 'I know – but …'

He silenced her with a kiss, and she returned it, melting against him, but then, gradually, she pulled away. 'Are you really sure, Evan? *Really* sure? I couldn't stand it if …'

'I know what I want, Mary – and it's you. You're all I've ever wanted.'

*

'Well I think it's nice.' Sarah came to sit at the kitchen table. 'All sort of romantic – just like in a book.'

Miss Reeves contemplated her tea. 'Yes – a Penny Dreadful.'

'Oh, cheer up. It's nothing to do with us what them upstairs get up to.'

'*Them upstairs*? She's not *upstairs* – she's not even *downstairs*. She's just a …'

'Look, it's no good you getting all steamed up. It's no skin off my nose what she is. I just do my job, see?'

'Really? And I suppose you like waiting on …' Miss Reeves' thin lips worked fitfully as she struggled to find an acceptable word. 'Well, shall we be kind and say *an unfortunate*?'

'So what if she is?'

'What do you mean, *so what if she is*?'

'I mean – so what if she is?' Sarah shrugged, then she smiled, her eyes glowing in the lamplight. 'Here,' she said dreamily, cradling the teacup in her hands. 'Did you see his face whenever he looked at her – and hers when she looked at him?' She gave a little shiver of delight. 'Made me go all goosepimply, it did.'

'You wouldn't think it so romantic if …'

'Look, I told you, I don't care. This is the best job I've ever had – and I don't intend losing it through worrying about things that don't concern me. So, whatever she's done, I don't give a jot. And besides, I like her. Not all stuck up like some I've worked for.' She took a sip of tea. 'And anyway, how come you know so much about her?'

'When I worked for Mrs Rees-Morgan, she told me …' Miss Reeves stopped abruptly, shocked to hear herself about to indulge in such appalling indiscretion. 'Never mind!' she snapped, getting up. 'It's nothing to do with you. Now, if you'll excuse me, I'm going up to check on Master Owen – and then I'm going to bed.'

*

The bedroom was unlit but for the firelight that gleamed off the white porcelain hipbath and cast deep shadows into the reaches beyond.

'Should I light the lamps?' asked Evan.

Mary looked about her, then to the bath where wispy tendrils of steam drifted above the inviting water. 'No, this is perfect.'

Standing very close, he studied her, his eyes upon hers, seeing the bright little flames dancing there. 'Mary?' His hands opened in readiness, but then, slowly and reluctantly, his fingers curled inwards once more. 'Well, I should leave you to your bath.'

She reached up, touching his cheek. 'I don't *ever* want you to leave me again. Promise me that.'

'I promise.' He felt for her hand, pressing it to his face, then drew it to his lips, kissing her fingers.

She felt the electric touch, but gently pulled away, feeling for the buttons of her dress, unfastening them, her eyes holding his as she undressed, slowly shedding her clothes to stand naked before him.

Evan looked at her, love and desire mixing and growing together, filling his chest so that he could barely breathe. He made to speak, but fearing to spoil the beauty of the moment he stayed silent, watching as she crossed to the bath.

She stepped in, conscious of his eyes upon her, and warmed by them in a way far deeper and more sensual than by the heat from the fire or the enveloping warmth of the water as she sank down into it.

But the fire and the water held a power that spoke to a far older instinct – one of which Mary was barely conscious – and as she washed, the gleaming water running over her body like a lover's fingers, she felt truly cleansed.

Slowly, almost shyly, she looked up. Evan was standing, half in shadow, watching her, and she rose, gracefully, her wet skin aglow with firelight. '*Evan*,' she called softly, reaching out her hand.

*

In the hours that followed I realised I'd never truly made love before. Not with Thomas, not with Joe – not even with Evan that one, glorious night at the clinic, lying on a cabman's coat before the dying embers in the stove – for then there had still been guilt and uncertainty – and sorrow for the parting we both knew must come.

But in Evan's bed that night we made love, unconstrained and in perfect trust. Possessing and being possessed. Giving and receiving, with body, mind and soul, every sense entwined, until we became as one.

But intense though the pleasure was, there was something greater still – for at last I could look beyond the minute, the hour – and into a future safe and secure and filled with happiness.

I had come home – and I felt whole once more.

Chapter Sixty-Three

Mary had barely registered the soft knock at the door before Sarah's voice intruded upon her dreams.

'I've brought your breakfast, m'um. I thought perhaps you'd prefer to take it in bed?'

'Breakfast?' Mary rubbed a hand over her eyes, trying to clear away the sleep, then sat up, looking about for Evan, feeling just a little embarrassed at being found in his bed. 'Oh, yes – please.'

'Thank you, m'um. If there's anything else you want, well, you just let me know.' Laying the tray in front of Mary, Sarah crossed to the windows, drawing back the curtains, tutting. 'Another gloomy day. Hope it clears up for the show tomorrow.' She turned back toward the bed. 'I expect you'll be going?'

'The Lord Mayor's Show?'

'Yes.' Sarah grinned. 'We've been given the day off to go and see it. It'll be the first time I've been since I was girl. Well, if there's nothing else, m'um?'

'No, thank you.' Mary looked down at her breakfast, then at the empty space next to her in the bed. 'Look, I'm terribly sorry – I can't remember your name.'

'Sarah, m'um.'

'Yes, of course. I was just wondering, Sarah. Is Evan – Dr Rees-Morgan – is he downstairs?'

'Oh, no, m'um. He went to the hospital over an hour ago, but he told me to tell you he'd be back as early as he could – and that in the meantime he was sure you and Master Owen would find something to do.'

*

'But Nanny, I don't want to go for a walk.'

'Nonsense. If we aren't to go to school, then we need to get some fresh air. A walk in the park, I think, hmmm?'

'But …'

'Billy-goats butt – children do not!' Miss Reeves hurriedly wound the scarf about his neck, crossing the ends over his chest and buttoning his coat over them. 'We shall have a lovely day – quite like old times – you'd like that, wouldn't you?'

'Here, what are you doing?' whispered Sarah, coming down the stairs.

'What does it look like?' Miss Reeves fastened the last of Owen's buttons and reached for his cap, settling it on his head. 'We're going for a nice walk, aren't we, Owen? Perhaps even feed the ducks?'

Sarah came across the hall. 'You can't take him out. *Not today.*'

'And why ever not? It is, after all, what I'm employed to do.'

'You *know* what I mean.' Sarah lifted her eyes toward the ceiling and bedroom above. 'It's the whole reason he's been kept off school.'

Miss Reeves turned Owen about, giving him a gentle push toward the front door. 'Why don't you wait for me on the steps,' she said, waiting until he was out of earshot before fixing Sarah with a cold stare. 'You are mistaken. It is my belief he's been kept away from school because someone is *finally* taking my advice. Now, if you don't mind, I have my duties to perform – and I'm sure *you* have *yours.*'

*

It was a little after two o'clock that the first casualties arrived: horrific scalds and burns for the most part, but then, as those nearer to the explosion were found, men with arms and legs speared or even severed by jagged pieces of metal. For over an hour the plain covered carts arrived at the rear of the hospital – and on one of them came James Spencer.

The young nurse took a step back, her eyes wide and her face as white as the sheet on which Spencer lay. Then her hand went to her mouth, and she hunched forward, her shoulders jerking spasmodically a few times before her scattered wits rallied enough to send her flying from the room.

'Nurse Lang!' The matron's brows drew together thunderously.

'It's alright. Let her go.' Evan did not look up from the bloody mess of mangled flesh and exposed bone. 'She's no good to us at present.'

'But you'll need someone.'

'Yes.' His fingers moved to Spencer's neck, feeling for a pulse. 'But someone with experience.'

Matron nodded. 'I'll do what I can, but with so many casualties …' She saw Evan's fingers pause, making tiny adjustments of position. 'Is he alive?'

Evan straightened. 'Yes,' he said gravely. 'For the moment.'

*

The sound of the front door opening brought Mary running from the upstairs drawing-room and on to the landing, but her anxious look was greeted for the fourth time that day by an apologetic Sarah. 'Just a gentleman leaving his card, m'um,' she called up, dropping it on to the tray that stood on the hall table, before returning to the kitchen below.

Mary went back to the window, looking out into the deserted square and gardens. She had sat there so often she could tell without need of a clock that it was almost four, but still there was no sign of Miss Reeves and Owen. She went to the table and picked up the newspaper, then almost immediately put it down again.

The telegram from Evan lay open on the sofa, and she picked it up, reading it yet again. *My Darling. Unexpected emergency. Doubtful I shall return before late. Commence dinner and pirates without me. Love. Evan.*

'Excuse me, m'um. Is it alright if I light the lamps?'

The sudden appearance of the maid caused Mary to start. 'Yes, please.' She went back to the window, watching the lights appearing on the far side of the square. 'Does she normally keep him out this long?'

Sarah kept her eyes lowered, fixing her attention on lighting the lamp. 'Not normally, m'um.'

'Then …?' Mary paused, unsure of how to phrase the question. 'Is this because of *me*?'

'I really couldn't say, m'um.'

From below came the sound of the front door closing, and Mary made to go, but stopped herself.

'That'll be her now,' said Sarah. She looked uncertainly at Mary. 'Should I ask her to come up?'

Mary took a slow, deep breath, straightening her shoulders. 'Yes,' she said, trying to remain calm. 'If you would, please.'

*

The pimply-faced warder – barely more than a boy – grinned as he took his eye from the spy-hole. 'Told you, didn't I?'

Already ill-tempered, the officer in charge went to the door, pushing the cover aside to look in. 'Well, nobody's said anything to me about any new arrivals – not that I should be surprised by that.'

'Bit of alright, though, eh? Not like the last one.'

Inside the cell, lying on her back upon the plank bed, the naked woman had her face turned to the wall, but was otherwise making no effort to conceal the rest of her shapely body, and the older man felt himself stiffen as he took in the dense bush of hair between her gaping thighs.

'I shan't mind bathing her,' leered the youth. 'Give her a good old soaping down there, I will. Reckon she might enjoy it, too, by the look of her.'

'You just be sure to keep your mind on your job. It's always the quiet

518

ones you've got to watch out for.' He let the cover fall back in place. 'So where's that old bag Connie been moved to?'

'Don't know. I've only just come on duty m'self.'

The older man snorted and rolled his eyes. 'Bloody marvellous this place is. I've been in half an hour already, and *Her Highness* still hasn't handed over to me yet.'

'She's probably with the doctor, watching him spark the old girl.'

'Yes, more than likely.' He turned to go, but then he frowned and returned to the cell door, flicking up the cover. The woman was in the same position, one hand hanging casually over the edge of the bed, the other resting on her stomach, the fingers curled, almost hiding the scarred stump of her thumb.

'Oh, shit! Quick, open the door.' He watched the boy fumble with his keys, finally snatching them from his hand. 'I'll do it. You get down to the office and ring that bloody alarm!'

*

Miss Reeves was unrepentant. 'I couldn't possibly know you had plans to spend time with the boy.'

'He's my son.'

'And *I'm* his nanny – and it is customary in a household such as this …'

Mary caught the disdain in the woman's voice and fought to quell her anger. 'Well, now that you *are* home, perhaps you'd bring him to me.'

'I don't think that would be wise. We've had rather a full day and …'

'*Just bring him to me.*'

Miss Reeves remained motionless, and Mary made to push past her. 'Very well, then *I* shall go up to *him.*'

'No!'

Shocked, Mary took a step back. 'What?'

'Mrs Rees-Morgan entrusted me to look after Master Owen. Now I perform that same duty for Dr Rees-Morgan. In his absence, *I* determine what is best for the boy. *I* know what he requires.' A hard gleam came to Miss Reeves' eyes. 'And it most certainly isn't *you!*'

'I'm his *mother.*'

'Oh, really? So where were you all those nights when he'd wake up crying unable to breathe? Where were you that terrible night he almost died?' She thrust out her chin. 'You didn't even know about that, did you! *I* was there. *I* sat up with him, night after night! Me! *I* was there when he said his first word – and do you know what it was? *Nanna!* And now you think you can waltz back into his life and take him away from me?'

'He's mine.'

'No. You don't deserve him. You forfeited your rights the day you gave him up.'

'You think I wanted to?'

'I think you couldn't wait to be rid of him. Mrs Rees-Morgan saw through you straight away.' She mistook Mary's look of outrage for one of surprise. 'What? You think she didn't tell me? Oh, she told me all about it. How you dumped the boy on her the moment you realised you weren't going to get any money.'

'That's a lie. She's lied to you – just like she lied to me. She told me Evan was married.'

'Of course she did. It was the easiest way to get rid of you – to scrape you off her shoe.'

Even in her anger, Mary had felt a sympathy for the woman, but now her heart hardened, and with it came a cold detachment. 'Please, just get out of my way.'

Miss Reeves' lips trembled, but she pressed herself defiantly against the door. 'Why couldn't you just leave us alone?'

'Because I love Evan, and I love my son – and I won't be parted from them ever again. Now, let me pass!'

'No! I won't let you take him from me.' A look of desperation came into Miss Reeves' eyes, and she flung herself at Mary, clawing at her face. 'I won't let you *contaminate* him! You're just a whore! A bloody whore!'

It was a passionate, but pathetically amateurish attack, and Mary simply pushed her aside, sending her sprawling against the sofa. 'I'm sorry,' she said coldly, reaching for the handle of the door.

'Don't you dare touch him! *Don't!*'

Mary gave her one final, pitying glance, then turned and walked from the room. 'Sarah?'

Sarah was hovering in the hallway, and came to the foot of the stairs. 'Yes, m'um?'

'Would you call me a cab, please?'

'A cab, m'um?'

'Yes. I'm going out – and I'm taking Owen with me.'

*

The weather was dull, but dry, and the early evening traffic around Threadneedle Street seemed lighter for it, allowing the old growler to pass without too much trouble from the affluence of the city and into the outskirts of Whitechapel.

Inside the cab, his nose pressed to the window, Owen watched fascinated as the character of the buildings changed from lofty grandeur to a run-down hodgepodge, a hag's smile of broken and rotting stumps.

'Is this where you live?'

'Nearby.'

Owen glanced at her. 'I like Bloomsbury better.'

'So do I.' She reached out, stroking his hair. 'You're tired, aren't you?'

'Just a bit.'

'We shouldn't have come – I'm sorry.'

'No, I should like to see your house. Is it very far?'

'Not very. And we won't stay long. There's just something I need to collect.' She saw the question forming on his lips, and she smiled. 'Just a letter and a photograph.'

The cab trundled on, passing the church where once a man had cradled a dead child; the shop doorway where Joe had stood sheltering from the rain; the streets she'd walked with Kate, and a dozen other places that held memories, some of them happy, but most of them sad or unpleasant. 'Owen?' she said, feeling for his hand. 'I don't know what people have told you about me, or what they might tell you in the future, but I should like you to hear it from me – and to see with your own eyes – so that maybe you can …'

With a small lurch, the cab came to a halt. 'Spitalfields Church,' called the driver.

*

The knock at the half-open door was surprisingly soft and deferential for someone with hands more accustomed to hammering men into bloody unconsciousness.

'Mr Eastman?'

Standing by a small table, Vincent Eastman slipped the object he'd been polishing into his pocket and looked up. 'Yes, Thomas?'

Tom Suggett came a little way into the room. 'You was right, sir. She's just arrived.'

'Well, don't look so surprised. It was only a matter of time, wasn't it?' He smiled, then on the point of turning away, he paused. 'Oh, I thought you'd like to know. I received one other telegram this evening – this time from your father. He's doing very well for us in Paris. *Very* well indeed. I'm very proud of him. I'm proud of you both.'

The younger Suggett beamed. 'Thank you, sir. Actually I was thinking … it's been some time and, well, perhaps I could go over – on a visit, like?'

'A visit?' Looking thoughtful, Eastman came to the door, casting a shadow over Tom Suggett's broad features. 'I don't see why not.' He smiled. 'Perhaps I might even come with you. Would you like that, Thomas?'

Despite his broad shoulders and thick, muscular neck, Suggett appeared almost bashful. 'Yes, sir.'

'Then we shall have to see, hmm?' Eastman marginally increased his smile.

'So – should I send 'er up?'

'*Her*, Thomas. It begins with an H. *Her*.'

'Yes, sir, 'Course, sir.' He collected himself, 'So, should I send *her* up?'

'Of course. It would be rude of us to keep Mrs Bull waiting.'

*

Owen looked confused. 'Why didn't we have the cabman bring us all the way? That's what we normally do.'

'It would only have attracted attention.'

'Is that a bad thing?'

'People see and do things a little differently here.'

'I see.' He looked about the court, then back through the archway into Dorset Street. 'Well … not really.'

Mary smiled. 'Look, I'll show you another thing we do differently.' She went to the window and reached through to draw back the bolt. 'More fun than a boring old key, don't you think?'

'But can't people get in and steal things?'

Mary came back to the door. 'Well, they *could*,' she said, pushing it open. 'But they'd have to be extremely clever to find anything worth stealing.'

Standing just inside the doorway, Owen watched her go to the mantelpiece and light the candle, then he stared about the room, taking in the few sticks of furniture, overshadowed by the wooden framed bed. 'Is this your bedroom?'

'When I'm in bed, it is.'

'But what about when you aren't?'

'Then it has to be whatever I need it to be. You see, Owen, not everyone lives in a big house – some people …'

But Owen's eyes had become bright with excitement. 'So it's a magic room?'

Mary looked about the squalid four walls. '*Magic*?'

'A room you can make into anything you want?'

'Yes … I suppose you could look at it like that.'

'Will you show me?' He ran to the centre. 'Show me how you do it?'

'It's very easy,' she began, hesitantly at first, but quickly getting caught up in his enthusiasm. 'Which room would sir like to see first?'

Owen thought for a moment. 'I know! The drawing-room!'

'And a wise choice, sir, if I may say so.' She made an obsequious bow, then resting her hands on Owen's shoulders, turned him one quarter of a turn. 'And here we are. Sir will doubtless note the fine collection of paintings. This one – The Fisherman's Widow,' she waved a hand toward the framed print above the fireplace, 'is a particularly fine example of the Billingsgate school.'

'It is very fine,' said Owen, doing his best to drop his voice an octave.

'Ah, I see sir is a connoisseur, and so will undoubtedly also appreciate our rare and expensive curtains. I might say the very same style currently adorn a royal residence.' She placed a finger alongside her nose. 'I cannot say which, of course, for I'm sworn to secrecy – though I'm sure you recognise the arms?'

The joke was lost on Owen, but it didn't matter, he was immersed in the excitement and magic of it all. 'Now make it the … the … *the morning-room.*'

'Nothing could be easier.' The door stood slightly ajar and Mary went to it, pulling it open to allow the court lamp to shine in. 'And a bright, warm morning it is, don't you think?'

Owen was sunning himself in the dull yellow glow of the gas when Lizzie Albrook traipsed past. 'Evenin' Mary,' she called, barely turning her head as she carried on down the court. 'Evenin', Joe. Still stinks of piss under that arch, don't it.'

'Simple Lizzie, the milkmaid,' explained Mary sweetly, closing the door. 'A quaint soul.'

'Can we go and see her cows?'

'Oh, I expect they're all tucked up in their byres by now. But maybe tomorrow?'

'And then we could get some milk?'

'Yes, and …' She stopped as there came a knock at the door. 'Yes? What is it, Lizzie?'

For a moment there came no answer, then in a low voice, 'It's me … Julia.'

Chapter Sixty-Four

The drawing-room of the Princess Alice was not quite as Connie remembered it. The room was the same, as was much of the furniture and decoration, but an alien atmosphere had crept in, making her feel an unwelcome stranger in her own home.

'It's good to see you out of that place, Connie,' said Eastman, making no effort to leave the comfort of his armchair. 'You're looking well.'

She cast about the room, turning up her nose at some recent additions in the Japanese style, and caught sight of herself in the mirror. Her empty gums made her look like a witch, and caused her words to hiss, snake-like. 'Am I?'

'Will you take some wine – or there's brandy, if you prefer?'

'I see you've made yourself at home.' Connie turned back. '*Permanently* at home, by the look of it.'

'I had no way of knowing when you'd return.'

'Or *if* I'd return, eh? But as you can see – *I have.*' She picked up the decanter and poured herself a measure. 'So, how about *I* offer *you* a drink? No? Well you won't mind if I do. It's been a long while.' Lifting the glass to her pinched lips, she ran the spirit over her tongue, savouring it.

'It must have been unpleasant.'

'Unpleasant?' She poured another drink, slopping it into the glass. 'Do you know what they do to you in those places? All manner of little treats, there are. Electric shocks and the ice cold baths. I got to thinking as how getting sliced up would be a holiday compared to that little lot. But you know what really got to me? I mean *really* got to me? It was being locked up, in that tiny little cell, sometimes never seeing a soul – but for an eyeball looking at me through the spy-hole – for day after day, week after fucking week, with only the poison you'd poured in my ear to think about – and I did think about it, Vince, over and over. It gnawed at my brain, like a rat at a skirting board – just like you intended, eh?'

Eastman looked disinterestedly down at his toecaps. 'I take it you have come here for a purpose – and not just to play the raconteur?'

'All in good time, Vince. We've got some catching up to do, you and me.' A maternal smile lifted the corners of her mouth. 'You've been a clever boy, Vincent. I'll give you that. *Bloody* clever – but you made one very big mistake. You see, you should have stopped them letting me have visitors.' She caught his look. 'Oh, you thought no one else came? Oh, no, Vince. I had *lots* of visitors. See, when you're locked away, you get time to think. Sometimes you think so much your brain runs red hot, like one of them steam engines with a boiler that's about to blow. You bang your head on the walls, hurt yourself, do anything just to make it stop.' She drained her glass and placed it carefully on the table. 'But then there's other times – times when your thoughts are that smooth and clear … Well, that's when they used to come to me – all of them. Lanky Bill was the first.' She saw Eastman's mild surprise, and she chuckled. 'Yeah, who'd have thought, eh? Poor old Lanky. He come to me this one night – and you should have seen him. A fucking big slit in his throat and stinking of Thames water. *Why, Con?* he asks me, *Why'd'yer do it?* So I tell him straight. I says, *you was a traitor, Lanky – just like all the rest of them arse-wipes – all a load of fucking traitors!* Well, then they all came, didn't they. All of them, Vince. All the old gang – can you imagine? Hookey Alf, Pistols, and the rest, all crowding into that tiny little cell, all wanting to know why. And you know what? I couldn't answer them. *I couldn't fucking answer them.* I'm sitting there on the floor, shaking my head because I realise … *I don't fucking know.* But they just keep asking – coming back night after night, asking over and over, *Why did you have us killed, Con? Why?* Then one night I saw it – just like that – like a flash of lightning. You know what I saw? I saw telegrams, Vince. Loads and loads of telegrams, all from France – a hint here, a suggestion there – here a name, there a fucking name.' She stared at him. 'Oh, yes. You were clever alright. You had me get rid of just about every loyal friend I had, didn't you?'

'*Just about?*' The revolver appeared in Eastman's hand with the deftness of a magician. 'Well,' he said magnanimously, 'let's not fall out over numbers, hmm?'

Except for her fingers working nervously at the folds of her skirt, Connie remained as unmoving as a rock. 'A gun, Vince? Not quite your style, is it?'

'We live in modern times.' He gave a small smile. 'So, have you any more revelations from beyond the grave? Or shall we just sit quietly until our friends from the asylum arrive?'

'You've told them I'm here? Well, 'course you would. Telegram was it?'

'It's a most efficient service.'

'I'm not going back to that place.'

'Ah, well there, I'm afraid, we must disagree.'

She moved a little closer. 'Then tell me one thing first. It was you behind all that business in France, wasn't it? *You killed Archie.*'

Holding the gun steady, Eastman surveyed her through half closed lids, then shook his head.

'You're lying to me, Vince.'

'Why on earth would I bother?' He looked with amusement toward the gun. 'Believe me, I wish I *could* take credit for it, but I merely seized on the opportunity it presented. No, I'm very much afraid that, tawdry though it all is, Archie really did die at the hands of a disgruntled whore.'

The hawkish eyes studied him intently, boring into his, then in an instant they softened and Connie breathed deeply, her hands ceasing to worry at her skirt as she relinquished her grip on the long, razor sharp piece of steel that lay concealed within its folds. 'Then I still have unfinished business,' she said.

'I'm afraid not.'

'You listen to me, Vince. I'm coming back. I'm coming back to avenge my Archie – and if I have to fight you to do it, then I will. There are still people who owe me favours.'

Eastman lifted an eyebrow. 'Is that what all this is about? Finding the *elusive* Miss Black?' He studied her thoughtfully. 'And what if I were to bring her to you?'

'Then you can keep the lot – everything. I've no more need of it. I've seen what the future holds for me, Vince, and I've no intention of waiting around for it.'

'Another of the dear, departed Lanky's insights?'

She shook her head. 'No, from a long time ago. My mum's parting gift – the sight of her being dragged, screaming, into a hell hole like the one I've just come from.'

'I see.' Slowly he lowered the gun. 'Very well, then we have a deal. I shall fetch her tonight.'

Connie eyed him, first with suspicion, then with dawning realisation. 'You *bastard*. You knew where she was, right from the start, didn't you.'

'Not quite. Of course, I knew we were looking for a Mary Kelly rather than an Emma Black.' He smiled to himself, remembering Elspeth's whimpering confessions. 'But it was a long time before she ventured back into Knightsbridge. However, once she had, well …' He spread his hands.

'And you know where she is now?'

He went to the mantelpiece and took down a key. 'Of course. I had a feeling she might become an asset one day.'

*

'I came to apologise.' Julia glanced over Mary's shoulder, 'But I can see this isn't the time.' She made to leave, but Mary caught hold of her arm.

'No, don't go – *please*. There's someone I'd like you to meet. This is my son, Owen.'

Julia regarded him uncertainly. 'Well,' she said finally, with a hint of resignation. 'We meet at last. I've heard a lot about you, young man.'

Owen looked surprised. 'You have?'

'Oh, yes.'

'Owen,' said Mary, coming to stand by him. 'This is Julia – my *very best* friend.'

The words caused Julia to look up. 'Still?' she asked, searching Mary's face, then she flung her arms about Mary's neck, sobbing against her shoulder. 'Oh, Mary. I've been so miserable without you. I should never have said those things.'

'It doesn't matter. Honestly.'

'It does. I had no right … and … it's horrible when we're not friends. Forgive me?'

Mary put her arms around her. 'There's nothing to forgive. You were right. You were right about everything, and I suppose that was why I was angry, but …' She left the sentence unfinished, her hand going to stroke Julia's hair. 'But it doesn't matter now. Everything has worked out for the best. And no matter what, you'll *always* be my best friend, Julia. Always …' She felt the prickle of tears. 'No, *more* than a best friend – you'll always be *my sister*.'

In the dimly lit room they stood holding each other, until, slowly, Julia eased herself away, brushing at her cheeks. 'So?' she said, embarrassed but happy, a smile quivering on her lips as she searched for something light-hearted to say. 'This is the new suit, is it?' She took a step back, still dabbing at her eyes as she admired it, 'Quite the business woman.' Then to Owen, still with a catch in her voice, 'Black always suited your mother very well. I feel quite the old frump being in the same room with her. Thank goodness it's almost too dark to see in here.'

Owen grinned. 'We could open the door and let the sunlight in, couldn't we, mother?'

It was the first time he'd called her that, and the simple word almost stopped Mary's heart. She tried to speak, but for a moment she could not, and slowly she reached out, touching his cheek.

Julia watched, trembling with emotion. 'Or we could just light the fire,' she said with forced levity. 'And maybe a few more candles.'

The spell broken, Mary drew Owen to her, 'I haven't any more candles, but I can soon light the fire.'

'What?' smiled Julia. 'In those clothes? I should think not. Better leave it to those of us more suitably attired.' She crouched down by the hearth, stuffing paper and kindling into the grate. 'But you could fill the kettle. I'd kill for a cup of tea.'

'I could fill it for you,' offered Owen. 'If someone will show me how.' But his voice held a weary note, and as Mary looked at him she could see his eyelids were beginning to droop.

'We really should be going home.'

'*Home?*' Julia looked up. 'Oh, not yet? You've time for some tea, surely? And besides,' she motioned with her eyes toward the boy, 'you've got to tell me how all this came about.'

Mary looked uncertain.

'Look,' said Julia, turning to Owen. 'Why don't you lie on the bed and close your eyes – just for a bit.'

'I can't do that.'

'Why not?'

Owen chuckled sleepily. 'Because now we're in the kitchen – and you don't have beds in a kitchen, do you?'

'It's a game of ours,' explained Mary. She went to him, giving him another quarter turn. 'Now, which bedroom would sir prefer?'

'Is there more than one?'

'Oh, most certainly. Any number. You may choose whichever your heart desires.'

But Owen was fading fast. 'I don't know,' he said, rubbing his eyes. 'You choose for me?'

She helped him on to the bed, pulling the counterpane over him. 'Let me see? The Royal Suite? No, far too dull. Something more exciting. I know ... how about Jim Hawkins's room at the Admiral Benbow Inn?'

Owen closed his eyes. 'Yes,' he smiled, already drifting off into sleep. 'That's just what I would have thought of.'

*

> '*My old girl's got a wink'll make yer laugh.*
> *She won't go bendin' over, 'cos it causes lots of chaff.*
> *I said to her on Friday as she stepped into the bath.*
> *Don't go winkin' at me, darlin' – don't go win–kin'.*'

Standing in the glare of the footlights, the portly man in the baggy suit lifted his arms, conducting the music hall crowd as they joined him in belting out a repeat of the last line.

'Don't go winkin' at me, darlin' – Don't go win–kin',' sang Harry Farrel, chuckling as the performer broke into an ungainly little dance, his feet more or less accompanying the small orchestra that was rattling out the tune with more enthusiasm than skill.

'You like the music hall, Joe?'

Joe shifted nervously in his seat. The box was very small and crammed to overflowing with Sadie and Gussie, a man Joe didn't recognise, and a small child in a froth of frilly lace who, having nowhere to sit, had been placed precariously on the front ledge, her little legs dangling above the stalls twenty feet below.

'Nothin' like a night out to put a bloke in good salts.' Farrel half turned, his simian features suddenly very serious. 'So what about you, Joe? *You* in good salts?'

'Good salts?'

Harry looked questioningly at him. 'Do you do that to be fuckin' annoyin' – or what?'

Below them, the man had stopped dancing and was waving the orchestra into silence. '*Here,*' he said, coming to the edge of the stage. '*Did you hear about the woman that went to get her kitchen table back from the pawnbrokers?*'

Farrel returned to watching the performance, but remained leaning close to Joe. 'Yer've 'ad a couple of months like I promised – *so,* 'ave yer got my five pounds?'

'Five pounds? Well, I … I *can* get it.'

'Tonight?'

'*But she's lost the ticket. So she says surely you must remember me? Only he don't. So she tries jogging his memory. It had a warped leg, she says …*'

'Tonight?' Joe could feel the sweat prickling beneath his clothes. 'No, not tonight.'

'*… But the bloke shakes his head. The woman tries again. Scratched top? she says. But he still can't recall it …*'

'Come on, Joe. It ain't goin' to be any fuckin' night, is it? I think yer takin' me for a cunt.'

'A …' Joe choked back the word.

'*….Well, the poor woman's about to give up when she suddenly remembers one last thing …*'

'I ain't a cunt, Joe. But I ain't the most patient bloke in the world, neither. That's why I wanted you 'ere – 'cos I know that if I wasn't 'avin' a good time, I'd be cuttin' you open right now.'

Joe went a deathly white.

'*… No drawers? she says.*'

'An' I don't want to do that, Joe – 'cos I've got another idea. There's somethin' I need doin'. A little job.'

'*…. Oh, no drawers!' he says, giving her a wink. 'Now, I remember you!*'

The theatre erupted into laughter, but to Joe the roar seemed far removed and distant. 'A little job?'

'Nothin' very much …' Farrel began to lean closer, but the curtain behind him parted, and Mickey came in, whispering into the ear of the young man by Gussie's side.

'What you doin' 'ere Mickey?' demanded Farrel. 'What the fuck's goin' on?'

Baines stood up. 'It's Eastman,' he said. 'Seems he's found the woman that killed Archie Bull – and he's going after her tonight. I'd better get back to Villiers Street.'

*

'Be happy for me, Julia?' Mary reached across the table, clasping Julia's hands.

'I *am*. Of course I am.' She attempted a smile. 'Why wouldn't I be? It's a dream come true, isn't it – a fairy tale?' She broke off, pressing her lips together to stop them from trembling.

'Don't cry, please … or you'll make me start.'

Julia felt the grip on her hands tighten and returned the pressure, giving a reassuring squeeze. 'You're right,' she said, trying to laugh. 'We should be celebrating. What we need is some champagne.'

'Champagne? I thought you'd given up drinking?'

'I have – but tonight I'd make an exception.'

'Then let's do it tomorrow. I'll meet you.'

Julia looked across the table, her fragile smile falling away as tears rolled down her cheeks once again. 'Tomorrow's too late. Once you leave here, I'll never see you again.'

'Of course you will.'

'No, this is the end – I know it. After tonight, I'll never see you again.'

'Why would you think that?'

Julia sniffed. 'Another premonitiony-thing?'

Mary laughed.

'I'm serious.' She slipped her hand from Mary's grasp and felt for the small pink scars beneath her eyes. 'I wasn't so far wrong last time, was I?'

'Of course you were. You said you were going to be disfigured, cut to shreds like that woman in the cab. But you're not. Not in the least. You were wrong then – and you're wrong now.'

Julia looked away. 'No. This *is* our last night together. I sensed it before I walked in here – it's why I came. I thought it was because of the row we'd had, and that if we made it up, everything would be alright, but now I understand what it was trying to tell me.'

'You're just being silly.'

'No. I can't explain it. I just *know*, Mary – and I *am* happy for you. I really am. But you have no idea how much I'm going to miss you.' She began to sob again. 'And sitting here, with *a bloody cup of tea*, is no way to say goodbye.'

Mary looked into Julia's eyes, seeing the pain there. 'I'm really sorry, but

I can't – not tonight. I need to take Owen home.'

'He'll be alright here for half-an-hour.'

'No, it's out of the question. Besides, what if he were to wake up, and there was no one here?'

'There must be someone you can ask to come and watch him? Just half-an-hour, Mary, that's all I'm asking. We'll be back before he even knows we've gone.'

'Julia, I …'

'Please, Mary. *Please*, give me this one last thing?'

Mary got to her feet, fretting with her cuff. 'I'd like to … I really would, but there's no one around here I could ask.'

'What about Lizzie? I saw her just as I arrived.' She caught Mary's look. 'Alright, perhaps not Lizzie, but there must be *someone*?'

'No, not really. I …' She stopped, startled by the sudden movement of the coat hanging over the window. It moved again, inching aside to reveal a face peering through the broken glass.

'Oh, you're back then?' said Maria Garbey, looking surprised, then guilty. 'I've run out of coal and was thinkin' that I might just borrow a bit?'

Chapter Sixty-Five

'It's no good you carrying on and getting yourself all in a tizzy.' Sarah leaned against the door, listening to the sound of crying from inside. 'It's nearly nine o'clock. She's going to be back soon, and you're going to have to face her.' There was no reply, and she rested her head against the frame. 'Then, at least let me in. My feet are killing me, standing out here.'

'Just go away and leave me alone!'

'Well, I will if you like. I can't stand here all night.' She started down the stairs, but after a few steps she stopped, sighed, and returned to the door. 'Oh, come on, Fanny – open the door?'

The crying broke into a series of splutters interspersed with great sobs. 'Don't … don't you dare call me that!'

'Why not? It's your name isn't it?'

'Not … to you it isn't.'

'Look, this isn't helping, you know.' She put her cheek to the wooden panel, dropping her voice to a gentle coo. 'Come on. Come downstairs. I'll go and make us a nice cup of tea – and I'll see you in a minute, alright?'

*

The barman looked surprised. '*Champagne?*'

Julia toyed with the shawl hiding her uniform. 'Yes. You know – fizzy stuff? Comes in a bottle?'

'I know what it is.'

'Then I should like a bottle, please – and two glasses.'

'I'll have to send out for it. We don't normally get asked for champagne.'

'I see. And how long will that take?'

'Ten minutes if I send the boy.'

'Then send him.' She placed sixpence on the counter. 'And tell him he can have that if he runs all the way there and back. And in the meantime we'll have two ginger beers. You do have that, don't you?'

The bar room was reasonably full with a good-natured crowd enjoying the earnest protestations of a lanky young man who appeared to have had one drink too many.

'What's all that about?' asked Julia as she brought the two glasses of ginger beer over to where Mary was waiting.

'It's only George. He's claiming to have seen the Ripper.' She looked at the glass she'd been given. 'Funny looking champagne.'

'The bubbly will be here in a minute. Thought this would do us until then. It's only ginger beer – can't have you going back tipsy, can we.' She took a sip and pulled a face. 'Though maybe we should have waited. Can't imagine what they put in this stuff. It's no wonder Temperance isn't more popular.'

A little way off, the young man was getting red in the face. 'That's why they can't catch him, ain't it? Because they won't listen.'

'You know him?' asked Julia.

'Sort of. I met him when I went hopping. We had a dance.'

'Oh?' A mischievous glint came to Julia's eyes, and she called across the room. 'So what did he look like, George?'

George Hutchinson eyed her defensively. 'I gave a full description to the papers, didn't I?'

'Did you? Well, I never read it.'

'Yer wouldn't 'ave, darlin'.' said a phlegmatic old man standing nearby. ''Cos they know a thing or two at them there newspapers.' He touched a finger to his nose. 'So they know when someone's full of piss an' wind.'

'I saw him, alright!' Hutchinson grew even redder.

'So what did he look like?' persisted Julia.

'Well, he was … sort of average.'

'Oh,' said Julia. '*Sort of average*? That narrows it down a bit.'

'Well, when I say average, what I mean is …'

Mary had begun to laugh. 'Stop teasing him, Julia. He doesn't mean any harm.'

'Neither do I.' She gave Mary a wink. 'I just want us to have some fun this one last time.'

*

'And about bleedin' time!'

'B-Bleeding time?' Wild eyed, and panting for breath, Joe scanned the room. 'Where's M-Marie?'

'Marie? Who the bloody 'ell's …?'

'M-Mary. I m-mean, M-Mary!'

Maria Garbey pushed past him, looking along the court, then back out toward Dorset Street. 'That's what *I'd* like to know. 'Aven't *you* seen 'er?'

'Seen her? No. B-But I've got to find her. Do you know where she is?'

'If I knew that I wouldn't be sat 'ere would I? 'Alf-an-hour she said! 'Alf-a-soddin'-hour! And that must have been two hours ago, if it was a day! Well,' she pulled her shawl about her, ready to leave, 'a favour's a favour – and anyone around 'ere will tell you I'd do anythin' for a friend – but I've got better things to do than sit 'ere lookin' after some … Oi! Where are you goin'?' She lurched after him into the narrow passageway. 'You come back 'ere, Joe Barnett. You come back 'ere and look after this bloody kid, or so 'elp me I'll …'

*

Sarah looked at the cup of tea sitting cold and untouched on the kitchen table, then across at the empty chair. 'Oh, Fanny,' she murmured, getting to her feet. 'Don't be such a bloody fool.'

She was considering going up to try again when she heard footsteps upstairs in the hall, and she went to the kitchen door. 'Miss Reeves?' she called up cheerfully. 'You're just in time, I was just about to make a fresh pot.'

There was no answer.

'Miss Reeves?' Sarah started up the stairs. 'Are you coming down?' The sound of the front door closing echoed through the empty house, and she ran up the remaining stairs, emerging into the deserted hallway. 'Fanny?'

*

Julia pointed an admonishing finger, swaying visibly as she focused on the object of her admonishment. 'You …' she said haughtily, steadying herself, 'you … are a naughty, naughty boy, Daniel Barnett. That's what you are – oh yes. Don't think …' she hiccupped, '… don't think I don't know what you've been up to. And now I'm very much afraid I'm going to have to smack your bottom … you naughty, *naughty* boy!'

Danny ignored her. 'Mary? *Mary*?'

Slumped over the table, Mary jerked into drunken wakefulness. 'What?'

'Oh, back with us?' giggled Julia, giving her a playful push. 'Well, I'll tell you what it is! You see – *he's* been a naughty boy – that's what it is alright.'

'Don't you think you two 'ave 'ad enough?'

'Enough?' The admonishing finger wagged. 'More than enough … and … and …' Julia began to giggle again, '… and we know who's fault it is, don't we, *Mr Daniel Barnett*? We only came in for a little cebel … clebera … a little drop of bubbly – and it's my …' she hiccuped again, '… my *consider-eded* opinion that *someone's* put a little something in …'

'Look, why don't I see you both 'ome?'

534

'See us home?' She gave Mary a great, sprawling nudge. 'Heard that one before, haven't we.'

Mary looked about, bemused. 'What? Where's Joe? Where's my Joe?'

'Joe 'asn't been 'ere all night.' Danny looked at her with concern, but then hope softened his features, 'But I could go an' find 'im for you. Would you go 'ome with Joe?'

'Home?' The word seemed to stir some distant memory she couldn't quite grasp. 'Yes … yes, must go home.'

'Anyway, *you* can't see us home – you naughty boy. We're both married.' Julia picked up her empty champagne glass, draining it for the second time before setting it carefully back on the table. 'Well … that isn't strictly true. My best friend Mary's *very nearly* married – and *I'm* married to God.' She pulled the shawl from her shoulders to show her uniform. 'See?'

'Blimey,' laughed a man at a nearby table. 'We've only got one o' them Sally Annie's in 'ere – an' stewed as a newt!' Several heads turned to look, and he leaned confidentially across the gap, speaking to her in a stage whisper. 'Well, I reckon God'll have 'is belt off to yer when yer get back 'ome.'

Danny gave him a withering look and turned away. '*Mary?*' Mary's eyelids were drooping once again, and he took hold of her arm, shaking her. 'Mary, wake up, we need to get you 'ome – while you can still walk.'

'Oh, he's a naughty boy,' giggled Julia, to no one in particular.

'Not as naughty as *you* though, I bet?' asked the man, getting to his feet. ''Ere, friend, yer want some 'elp gettin' these two 'ome to bed?'

Danny had Mary half out of her seat. 'It's alright,' he said, struggling to get her arm about his neck. 'We can manage.'

'Oh, go on. Don't be a spoilsport. You can have that one – an' I'll take Sally Annie.' He winked. 'I've often thought about takin' the plunge into religion.'

'I *said* we can manage.'

'Alright, alright! What's the matter, can't yer take a joke?' Irritably the man sat down, watching as Danny steered Mary toward the door, followed by a very unsteady Julia. ''Ere, Sally?' he called

Julia turned, swaying dangerously. 'Yes – my good man?'

'Since you're married to God, just tell me one thing before yer go. On Saturdays, after 'e's been to the pub … does 'e just roll off yer an' go to sleep … or does 'e kiss yer good night first?'

*

'Shssssh!' Julia put a finger to her lips, then pointed unsteadily toward the bed.

The room was lit only by the light from the dwindling fire but it was enough for Danny to see the sleeping figure. 'You didn't leave 'im 'ere on 'is own? Not for all this time?'

''Course not.'

'Then …?' But he saw from the silly expression on her face he was wasting his time.

The door banged against the wash-stand, toppling an empty ginger-beer bottle and sending it rolling perilously toward the edge until Danny caught hold of it.

'Shssssssh!' said Julia, even more emphatically, as Mary and the thickset man who was half carrying her stumbled into the room.

'Goodnight,' she called merrily to someone out of sight in the court.

'Shssshhh!'

Mary began to giggle. 'Don't you shsssssh me.' Then louder, to the unseen figure. 'I think I'm going to have a sing.'

'Oh no you're not!' said Julia sternly, but then something in the tone of her voice amused her and she too began to giggle.

'Thanks for your 'elp, Carrots. I couldn't 'ave managed the two of 'em.' Danny put the empty bottle on the window-sill then pulled out a chair and between them they manoeuvred Mary on to it. 'Now you'd better get off 'ome. We'll be alright now.'

The man nodded. 'See you at work?'

'Yeah.'

Julia grinned stupidly and blew an exaggerated kiss. 'Bye, bye, Mr Carrots.'

He ignored her. 'They won't think it so funny in the mornin'.'

'No.' Danny closed the door behind him. 'Jesus,' he muttered, turning to look at them – Mary, unconscious once more, slumped over the table, Julia propped against the mantelpiece, the silly expression fast becoming sickly and contrite. 'Now what am I supposed to do? Just leave you to sleep it off, I suppose – but …' He glanced toward the sleeping boy.

Julia followed his gaze. 'He can't stay here.'

'I can't see where else 'e's goin' to go tonight. Not with the pair of you in that state.'

She leaned her head back against the wall, her eyes tight shut, her brow creasing as she struggled to organise her thoughts. 'She's going to be married – to a doctor.'

'I know. You've told me – 'alf-a-dozen times.'

'We've got to get her …' She drew a hand over her face, suddenly looking very ill.

'Go outside if you're goin' to be sick.'

Julia leaned back once more, her breathing laboured. 'It's alright … I'm … I'm alright.' She licked her lips. 'We've *got* to get her home.'

'An' 'ow do we do that?'

'Don't know.'

'An' more to the point – where is 'ome?'

Julia shook her head. 'Don't know … West End … somewhere.'

'Well, Mary's so far gone she don't even know what day it is – so I don't see she's got any option but to stay 'ere.'

'It'll ruin everything.'

'I can't 'elp that. Come on, 'elp me get 'er on to the bed. You'll 'ave to sleep on the floor.'

'No. You don't understand. She'll never forgive me …' She stopped, suddenly, rolling glazed eyes in his direction. 'The hospital! He's working late … at the hospital. She told me.'

'What 'ospital?'

'The London … in Whitechapel Road.'

'Well, 'e won't be there now, it's nearly midnight.'

'He might be … there was something … an emergency.' She took a steadying breath, her hand going to her forehead as she braced herself against the wall for support, 'But even if he's not, they'll know his home address. *Please, Danny … for Mary's sake?*'

'It'll be a wild goose chase. She'll just 'ave to wait till mornin'.'

Julia began to cry. 'You don't understand. It's all my fault. All my *stupid* fault. I've ruined everything. *Please*, Danny …' She fumbled in the pocket of her skirt, drawing out a handful of coins and thrusting them toward him. 'Look, you can take a cab. At least … at least *try* to find him and bring him here?'

He looked at the money in her trembling hand, then at the boy, then at Mary slumped over the table. 'Do you even know 'is name?' A look of despair crossed Julia's face, melting his heart. 'You must remember?' he said, becoming caught up in the urgency of the situation. 'Think!'

She lifted her face as if in prayer, eyes tight shut, lips working silently. 'I … I can't remember. I did know it but … but it's gone … I think it's … Mawden? No, no, it's not that … it's … it's *Morgan!*' She turned wide, red-rimmed eyes upon him. '*Evan Rees-Morgan!*'

Chapter Sixty-Six

Julia tilted back her head, letting it rest against the wall, listening to the sound of Danny's footsteps in the covered passageway, the scrape of his boot nails fading as he went out into Dorset Street. Then, very slowly she opened her eyes and gave a long, satisfied sigh.

She looked about the room, first at Owen asleep on the bed, then at Mary, slumped over the table, her head resting on her forearms. She too seemed asleep, but as Julia went to her, putting a hand on her shoulder, she stirred fitfully. 'It's alright. Everything's going to be alright,' Julia whispered, stroking her fingers over the fine hairs at the nape of Mary's neck. 'You rest. I'll get everything ready.'

Mary inched opened one bloodshot eye. 'Ready?'

Walking steadily now, Julia went to the fire, crouching down before it. 'We're going to do a tableau – just like in the old days.' She added some wood and coal to the meagre flames then stood up and crossed to the window, pulling the coat firmly across it. 'There, that's better. Paying customers only, eh?'

'What …?' Mary licked her dry lips, her voice heavy. 'What are you doing?'

Julia smiled, moving back to the fire, her fingers going to the buttons of her uniform. 'Oh, my poor love.' She paused, looking down with pity. 'I know how you must feel – but what else could I do? There wasn't any other way. But you'll be alright – the drug will begin to wear off in a few hours – and by tomorrow you'll be your old self.' She continued undressing. 'Then you'll see it was all worthwhile.' The black uniform dress fell about her ankles, and she stepped out of it, her hands going to the laces of her corset. 'There are *such* plans for us, Mary.'

'Plans?'

'No, my love, don't try to talk, you'll only tire yourself.' The corset fell away and Julia slipped out of her remaining underwear to stand in nothing but her long white chemise. 'So? What do you think?' She ran her hands thoughtfully over the thin cotton, tracing the swell of her hips. 'Well, it's going to have to do. My nudity days are well and truly over.'

Flames were starting to lick up over the coals, and she stood warming herself for a moment before coming to stand by Mary, gently rubbing her shoulders, then leaning forward to lightly kiss the back of her neck. 'Come on, your turn.' She slipped off Mary's jacket, then kissed her again, lingering a fraction longer. 'But you're top of the bill – so no chemise for you, I'm afraid.' Her hands reached round, feeling for the buttons at the front of Mary's dress. 'Still, you've never minded that, have you.'

The touch of Julia's hand upon her breast caused Mary to stir. 'What ... what are you doing?'

'I'm getting you ready for the scene,' whispered Julia, her fingers working nimbly at the black pearly buttons. 'It's one we haven't done before.'

'No ... don't ... don't do that. Leave me alone.' Mary forced herself a little way up from the table.

'There's my good girl.' Slipping her hands under Mary's arms, Julia helped her to sit up, turning her to face the room, propping her against the back of the chair. 'Now we'll soon have you undressed.' She came to stand in front of her, unfastening the remaining buttons and working the bodice off, first one shoulder, then the other. 'You aren't going to be sick, are you?' she asked, concerned, but then she smiled and reached out, stroking Mary's ashen cheek. 'Well, don't worry if you are – it'll just be a bit more stage dressing, won't it.'

'Why ... why are you ...?'

'I told you. It's a new tableau.' She knelt at Mary's feet, trying to drag the dress down over her hips, but the narrow waist stuck fast, and after struggling with it for a few minutes she stopped, breathing hard. 'Well,' she said, wiping the perspiration from her forehead. 'It looks as if we'll need to get you on your feet.'

A pain began to throb at Mary's temple as consciousness trickled back. 'Please ... you must fetch Evan.'

'Don't worry, he's on his way. But we've plenty of time yet – so why don't I describe this new scene – to help you get into your role?' She moved closer, settling herself comfortably. 'The location is a squalid little room. On the bed, lit only by the glow of the fire, our young heroine lies naked – *indelicately* naked – sprawled in a drunken stupor.' Julia grinned. 'Enough to warrant the price of admission already, don't you think? But there's more.' Excitedly she gripped Mary's knees, her voice rising theatrically. 'Stage right, the door is thrust open – and there stands our angry fiancé, his arm raised in horror, concealing the awful sight from his eyes – perhaps even ...?' A fresh sparkle came to her eyes. 'Yes – he's clutching his child to him, hiding the tearful boy's face in the folds of his coat – that he might not witness the vile depravity of his mother. Oh, a truly heart-rending touch!'

Mary began to shake her head. 'No …'

'Shsssssh!' Julia made a grab for her hands, pressing them together to keep her still. 'The best and cleverest bit is still to come! You see, this man, *her fiancé*, is shocked – no, not shocked – *horrified*. Yet he may still be able to forgive – and that wouldn't suit our plot at all. So, we need a sin that is unforgivable. But what? Ah …' The wide, bright eyes narrowed with feline cunning. 'She's not alone on the bed – another woman's head lies upon her breast – another woman's hand lies …' A wistful look came over Julia, and tenderly she lay her head in Mary's lap, her hand gently stroking the length of her thigh. 'You see, Mary? The truth is, our heroine has a lover – one far more constant and true than *he* could ever be. One who was meant for her.' She lifted her head, looking into Mary's eyes. 'You *do* know, don't you? How much I've always loved you?'

'Loved … me?'

'Mary, I've loved you forever – does that make sense to you? I'm not sure I even understand it myself – but it's as if I knew you were there, somewhere, and I only had to find you – and on that wonderful day in Knightsbridge, when I saw you in the lobby of the hotel – I did find you – and it was as if I'd known you all my life. I can't really explain but …' She thought for a moment, then gripped Mary's hand excitedly. 'Do you remember when you told me about your imaginary sister – and how you found her the day we met? Well, that was exactly how it was for me – only I never saw you as a *sister*. Sometimes, during a tableau, I'd touch you, touch your bare skin, and you'd tremble, and I'd be so certain that *that* would be the night – the night you'd come to me – but you never did.' She looked up, her eyes warm and bright. 'But now I'm glad you didn't. Because it would have been wrong, and because it makes our love even more pure – don't you see? We are pure and chaste – and we'll remain so.' A tiny frown appeared. 'Except for tonight – but that won't be real – just play-acting – a tableau – and you don't have to worry, because whatever happens, it won't be *your* sin, Mary. It will be *mine*. *My* gift to you, to protect you and keep you safe, just like that night in Paris when I …' She paused, sitting back on her heels and cocking her head to one side. 'Did you honestly never guess?'

Mary struggled to clear her mind. 'What … what are you talking about?'

'You really didn't, did you? You never guessed – *about Archie*? I was so sure you would – and it would become a wonderful secret between us, binding us. But you never guessed. How could you not have? It was *you* who showed me the book that day in the park, don't you remember? All that nonsense about Cronus castrating Uranus and …?' Seeing Mary's confusion, she paused. 'It was *me*, Mary. *I* killed Archie – for *you* – to stop your suffering.' She reached out, laying a hand on Mary's leg. 'And give birth to my very own Venus.'

'No. You … you couldn't …'

'But I *did*. And it was easier than you'd think. He was too drunk to know what was going on. Didn't even remember sending me away. So we started playing – and once he was tied to the bed …' She gave a small shrug.

'No … I don't believe you.'

'Mary, I had no choice.' She gave a wry smile. 'Well, of course I didn't – I understand that now. But I only knew then that he was going to hurt you, and I couldn't let that happen, could I? After all I'd promised?'

Mary's eyes widened in horror, and with enormous effort she thrust Julia's hand from her. '*You*? Everything … everything that's happened … was because of *you*?'

For a moment there was a look of pride on Julia's face, then it softened into one of humility. 'No, I'm only the instrument of *His* will. I didn't realise it then, but I was only doing *His* bidding.'

Mary gazed vacantly about the room. 'All because of *you*?'

'It was for a purpose, Mary. Everything is always for a purpose – we just never see it – we never think to look for the design.' She grabbed Mary's hand, holding it tightly. 'I was such a fool not to see it that night in Paris when you went off alone with Archie. I had no idea where he would take you, so I had the cab driver wait just around the corner and we followed you – through the middle of the city. First to that sleazy little restaurant, then back to his hotel. I could have lost you a million times in the traffic – *but I didn't*! Then at the hotel – I was standing right there in the lobby when you stopped to talk to his two men. I swear Archie looked straight at me before I had time to hide myself, but *he didn't see me*.' She leaned forward, looking earnestly into Mary's eyes. 'And it just continued. I followed you upstairs, saw which room you were in – but one of Archie's men, the one called Baines, got there first and sat guard outside the door. I knew you were in danger, but what could I do? So I waited – *and he fell asleep* – just like that. I couldn't believe my luck. But of course, it wasn't luck, was it. It was meant to be – and that was when I should have begun to see the beauty of the design – to see how it all falls into place – to see how every tiny thing, no matter how insignificant, has a purpose in that design – even the simple fact that Archie always carried his razor in his pocket.'

'You're mad.'

'No.' Compassion shone from Julia's eyes. 'You just don't understand. But you *will*. I didn't understand at first – not at all. When I had to leave you in Archie's hotel room that night, because I couldn't force open the bathroom door – and then later, when they caught me and took me to that farmhouse, everything seemed to be going horribly wrong. But then, in the months after, lying in that French hospital – that was when my eyes were truly opened.' She smiled at the recollection. 'They only had one book in English – The Bible. You can imagine my reaction to that. But I had to do something to relieve the boredom, so I started to read it.'

On the bed, Owen moved restlessly, and she rose and went to him. 'Go back to sleep,' she murmured, covering him over. 'Auntie Julia will wake you in good time to play your part.'

Still slumped in the chair, Mary turned to look, starting to feel nauseous as the anaesthetising effect of the narcotic began to wear off. 'Don't … don't you touch him.'

'It's alright. He won't wake up. He's not meant to, you see?' She came back to where Mary was sitting. 'But time *is* getting on and *we* should be getting you ready. Now, do you think you can stand up?'

'No …' Mary eyed her nervously. 'I can't.'

'Well, it doesn't matter. Though it would be a shame to spoil that dress.' She knelt down again, lifting Mary's skirt and petticoats and laying them over her knees. 'Maybe by the time we've got these boots off, hmmm?'

Adrenalin coursed through Mary, slowly dispersing the fog that enshrouded her brain, but she still felt groggy, and needed more time. 'So … what did it say?' she asked, weakly.

'The Bible?' Julia paused in unbuttoning the black, ankle length boots. 'You know, it's the strangest thing. They make you read it when you're a child – but you can't possibly understand it then. You need to have lived, to have experienced things, to give it context. Do you remember how they were always telling us Jesus died for our sins – that His blood washed them away – did you *ever* understand that? I never did. I mean, how could someone's blood, shed nearly two thousand years ago, wash away *my* sins – sins I hadn't even committed then?' She looked up, her whole face alight. 'But as I read it I realised – it means everything is pre-ordained. You see, our sins are there by *His* design, to fulfil His design – and so I'm absolved of them, just as those who crucified Christ were absolved. Just as those who crucified me are absolved.' She returned to unfastening Mary's boot, but her eyes were drawn to the stockinged calf and bare knee, and she traced a finger over it. 'You know, you have such beautiful legs, Mary. I've wanted to tell you that so many times, but then *you* are beautiful, all of you. It almost makes me wish …' With a sigh, she leaned forward, giving the knee a gentle kiss.

Mary felt her flesh crawl, but forced herself to remain still. 'Those men … who tortured you … are abs …?' She stumbled over the word.

'Absolved?' Julia sat back on her heels. 'Yes, of course. They were my teachers.' Unfastening the last button, she took hold of the boot, easing it from Mary's foot. 'Just think, they could have stabbed me, slit my throat, killed me in any number of ways, but they didn't. They *stripped* me and *crucified* me.' She paused, looking meaningfully into Mary's eyes. 'Then they cut me – over and over again – and left me to die. And I *did* want to die, Mary – both then – and later when I saw what they'd done to me. But I didn't – *I rose again*. Do you see?'

'No … No, I don't.'

Julia placed the boot beneath the chair, then lifting Mary's leg, drew the stocking down and off. 'It was my awakening, Mary. The moment I became aware of the role I'd been chosen to fulfil.' Lingering over the bare white foot, she looked up again. 'And I believe tonight is intended as *your* awakening – the moment when your eyes are to be opened, and you finally walk out on to the stage to join me.'

'Stage? No … I'm going to be with Evan.'

Smiling patiently, Julia shook her head. 'That was *never* meant to be. This whole business …' she motioned with her eyes toward Owen. 'It was all a *mistake*. There was never intended to be a man in your life, Mary. Do you think it was just by chance your husband Thomas died? No, it happened because *you* were wanted here. You have duties to perform, Mary – and they require you to be with me.'

Feeling was creeping back into Mary's limbs, but she remained slumped in the chair. 'Then … what about Joe? Why did you try to keep us together?'

Julia laughed. 'I knew from the moment I saw him that you could never love him – which was why he was so perfect. While you were with Joe, your heart was safe. There was no chance of you making …' again her eyes flickered toward Owen, '*another mistake*.'

Mary swallowed hard, fighting the sickness that threatened to spill up into her mouth. 'I'm not going with you, Julia. Not now … not ever. I love Evan, and … '

'No, Mary, please …'

'I love Evan and he …'

'No! You've *got* to let him go! Don't you understand? Your destiny is with *me*. You can't change that. If you won't give him up – then he'll have to die – just like Kate.'

'Kate?' A dreadful chill ran down Mary's spine.

'It's alright. She's safe now. Redeemed.'

'Tell me you didn't.' Mary began to push herself up from the chair, teetering unsteadily. '*Please* … tell me you didn't.'

'I had to. She wouldn't leave you alone. I thought I could get Joe to make her stop seeing you – but he was as useless as always. Kate was corrupting you. You were drinking, swearing … I was ashamed of you, Mary. But now look. Look how much you've changed since …'

Mary edged away, staggering against the wall. 'I don't believe you. You're making all this up.'

'It's not always bad to kill someone, Mary. Sometimes it's a kindness.

Polly Nichols was sick, terribly sick. She told me herself she wished she were dead. And Annie said much the same to you.'

'Annie? Oh, Jesus Christ.'

'I didn't know she was a friend of yours. But you said yourself you couldn't be sorry for her. That morning I found her in Hanbury Street, she was already half dead, haemorrhaging, barely able to walk. She begged me to take her somewhere private so she could clean herself, so I took her into that back yard. You wouldn't let a dog suffer like that, would you?' She saw the horror in Mary's eyes, and a gentle smile softened her lips as she slowly shook her head. 'They feel nothing, really they don't. There's a trick to it, you see? An old midwife's trick my mother taught me. You remember the woman in the smashed cab? That's how I stopped her struggling. You just find this little place at the side of the neck and …' She smiled, 'Well, I'll show you when you're ready, but believe me, they feel no pain … nothing. They fall into unconsciousness – then all it takes is a little pressure, just enough to stop the breathing. Long before the first drop of blood is spilled they've passed on to that better place.'

The room seemed to be spinning, and Mary pressed herself to the wall, her fingers splayed against the grimy paper to prevent herself from falling down. 'But you mutilated them!'

'Of course.' Julia looked at her incredulously. 'Mary, you're not thinking clearly. Can't you see what's happening? You only need look about you – in the streets. Have you ever seen such changes? It's a miracle, Mary. A *miracle*. If I'd been in any doubt before …' She left the sentence unfinished, opening her hands in mute appeal. 'A light has been focused on Whitechapel, exposing every dark, dirty, festering corner – and people are demanding that something be done. And things *are* being done. Slowly and surely the filth and the rot is being swept away. It will take a long time – but it *will* happen – just as long as that light continues to shine. That's our mission, Mary – to keep it shining.' She crossed the small space between them, taking hold of Mary's shoulders, looking deep into her eyes. 'You're starting to see it now, aren't you. I can tell. Oh, Mary with the two of us – working together – there's nothing we can't achieve.'

'With more murders?'

'They're acts of mercy.' She searched Mary's eyes, and a shadow of uncertainty crossed her face. 'I know what you're thinking – those horrible mutilations – and they *are* horrible. But they don't feel it – they're dead. They don't care, so why should we? And isn't it worth it? Just think what's been achieved so far – with just three poor souls. More than that die on the streets of London every day, and no one cares. But with Polly Nichols I sparked a flame. With Annie Chapman the flame became a torch – and with Kate Eddowes it became a searchlight. Just think, Mary – think what we can accomplish together.'

544

'No.'

'*Yes*. Come on, you're almost there. Try to see it – to see *His* design. *He's* made it all so perfect. Everything, right down to the last detail. Right down to the uniform – *black* – the *perfect* colour to hide blood.' She smiled. 'And with it we can go anywhere – at any time – even when the streets are crawling with people on the look-out for the Ripper – the police, the vigilance committees, reporters, private detectives, anyone – because who would think to stop *us*?'

'And God told you to do all this?'

'Yes. Oh yes. Not like you read about. He didn't come to me in a cloud or anything. That's not how He works. He guides you. It's as if you're in a maze, only you can never take a wrong turn because whenever you're about to, *He* puts something in your way. It can be as simple as a chance meeting – a man offering you his card with an address in Knightsbridge – or as big as a mine explosion – anything to divert you from the wrong path. And you think you are the one making the decisions, Mary, but you're not. Oh, I know it's hard to understand, but just think about all the little *somethings* that have brought us both here – all the way from Wales, to Whitechapel, to the worst street in the whole of London, to *this* room, on *this* night. It's not chance, Mary. We've been guided every step of the way. Didn't you once tell me how, just when things were going well, something would always happen to send you off in a new direction? And can't you see now that it wasn't a *new* direction – it was the *right* direction. That everything that's happened to you, to me, the good things, and the bad things, everything was to *lead us here* – because that's where *He* needed us.'

'You're mad … you're completely mad.'

For the briefest moment, anger flared in Julia's eyes, then she turned away, going to where her uniform dress lay in a heap. 'I forgive you, Mary. It's not your fault, it's mine, for trying to make you understand too soon. I shouldn't expect you to see in a few moments a truth it took me months to grasp.' She picked up the dress, feeling in the concealed pocket of the skirt and taking out the long, thin-bladed knife.

Mary saw it glint in the firelight, and her eyes widened in fear. 'W-What are you going to do?'

'Do?' Julia looked at her, puzzled, then down at the knife in her hand – then she laughed. 'Nothing, you silly goose. Just cut the seams of your dress.'

'No … No it's alright … stay there, I can do it now.' Bracing herself against the wall, Mary's fingers scrabbled at the last few buttons.

'We're running short of time, Mary.'

'It's alright. I *can* do it.'

Julia stared at her, then very deliberately she put down the knife. 'I wouldn't cut you, Mary. Surely you know that – *don't you*?' She stood watching the frantic fumbling of Mary's fingers. '*Mary*? Tell me you believe me.'

'I … I believe you.'

An awful look crossed Julia's face. 'But you don't, do you. You think I'd hurt you.'

'I don't know …' Shaking, half crying, Mary tugged impotently at the dress. 'I … I don't know what to think.'

'Why would I?' Julia came closer, reaching to stroke her cheek, seeing her flinch. 'Don't cry, Mary, please. It's alright. I'd never, ever hurt you. *I* know what it feels like to have a blade slicing into you, again and again – and it's terrible. The pain is almost …' She broke off, gently wiping away Mary's tears. 'But there was no other way. I *had* to suffer, to learn the lessons – but I learned them for both of us.' Smiling tenderly, she began unfastening the last few buttons of the black velvet dress. 'It was certainly an unconventional schooling – even by Knightsbridge standards. The one called Baines just wanted to rape me, then kill me – so the other one, the posh one, kept explaining how they must leave a message so truly awful that people had no choice but to take notice. You would have laughed to have seen it, really you would. There they were, having this discussion, and all the while cutting me to pieces. But of course, the lesson wasn't really for this man Baines. It was for *me*. That's why they were there. *He'd* sent them – just as he sent Judas to the garden.'

The dress finally dropped around Mary's ankles, and Julia knelt down, clearing it from about her feet, running her hands over it. 'I'm glad we didn't have to cut it after all. It's far too nice to …' She got no further. In the next instant something seemed to explode against her skull, and she fell forward, clutching her head.

Seconds passed, then, slowly, Julia raised herself up, a thin trickle of blood running from her hairline into her left eye. 'Mary? What … what happened?'

Standing over her, Mary tried to raise the thick glass bottle again, but the effort was too great.

'Mary?' Julia looked at her, stunned. '*Why, Mary*?' She got to her feet, gently but firmly taking the ginger beer bottle from Mary's hand. 'Why on earth would you do that?'

Mary was deathly white and breathing hard. 'You're mad. Get away from me.'

'Mary?'

'I mean it.'

'I love you.'

'I *hate* you.'

'No!' For a second Julia's eyes widened in surprise, then they narrowed.

'You *love* me! You told me that!' The trickle of blood ran like a tear down her cheek. 'You *do* love me. I *know* you do. You're just not feeling well. The drug is making you confused.'

'I know what I'm saying.'

'No, you don't – or you wouldn't say it.' Julia dabbed at the blood. 'You *do* love me. You *have* to – because … because it's how it's meant to be – the two of us together. We *have* to be together – I thought I'd explained.'

'Just get away from me.'

'I can't, Mary. I love you. I love you more than anything. That's why I *know* you love me – because if we weren't meant to be together, then why would *He* make me love you so much? It wouldn't make any sense, would it? Why would He …?' She paused, a look of horror crossing her face. 'Oh … oh no … please, no.'

'Julia … just … just let us go?'

But Julia wasn't listening. 'No, *please* … not that.' She put her hand to her mouth, biting down on her knuckle as she took a step back. 'I've done everything … *everything*.'

'Julia …'

For a moment Julia stood very still, then slowly she raised her head, looking across the small space that separated them, a strange new light in her eyes. 'Oh, Mary,' she whispered in awe. 'Now I see it – I see it *all*. I thought …' Her breathing became fast and shallow, and she swallowed hard. 'I thought I'd seen the whole design, but … but it was just one, tiny piece.' The knife lay on the table, and she picked it up.

'W-what are you doing?'

'That's why he made me love you. It's the ultimate test, Mary – the test of Abraham.' Tears came to Julia's eyes, mixing with the blood. 'I have to kill you.' She began to advance. 'I have to kill you because you're the one I love most in the whole world – *that's* why you were put here.'

Trembling, Mary pressed herself against the wall. 'Don't come near me, or I'll scream. I'll scream the bloody place down – and then you'll be caught and …'

'That's right.' Julia's voice was soft and calm. 'I fully understand now.' She took a step forward, the knife gripped in her hand. '*You* are to be the Ripper's last victim, Mary. And when you scream it will be the Judas kiss, do you see? You'll scream, and I'll be taken, and tried, and executed, just as Jesus was – and my light will be like his, shining forever. No more murders, Mary. No more mutilations. Our *blood* will wash everything clean …'

'You … you wouldn't kill me?'

'I have to, Mary. Everything has led to this moment. But don't worry – we'll be together again, very soon – sitting at *His* right hand.' She reached up, stroking Mary's cheek once more. 'I'm sorry I can't spare you the pain, Mary. I wish I could, but – I'll make it quick.'

The knife loomed into view, and Mary forced her head back against the wall, her eyes wide with terror. 'I *won't* scream.'

'*Yes*, you will.'

'No!' Mary swallowed hard, summoning her last reserves of strength. 'No, I won't. I *can't* – because I can't let you be taken … because *I love you*. I love you too much to let you hang.' She saw the point of the knife pause, and she went on quickly, 'You were right – you were absolutely right – I *did* tell you I loved you … and it was true. I meant every word. And I *did* want to come to you those nights … I wanted to so much … but I didn't dare. But now we *can* be together … can't we?'

Searching deep into Mary's eyes, Julia smiled a sad sweet smile, and brought the blade to within a whisker of the pale white neck. '*Soon*, my dear, sweet love, *soon*. When we sit at His right hand.'

'No, now! Why not now?'

Julia hesitated again.

'Why not now, Julia? We don't have to die – either of us. Abraham didn't kill his son – he didn't! I remember. God stopped him at the last moment. It was just a test of obedience.' She saw the uncertainty in Julia's eyes. 'We *can* be together – exactly as you said. If you stop now, then won't it mean that God has stopped you? That you passed the test?'

Indecision clouded Julia's face, then she lowered the knife and took a faltering step back. 'Oh, Mary, if you're right … if I …'

Mary launched herself from the wall, hitting Julia with all her might, sending her sprawling against the bed – but the effort took every last ounce of her strength and though the empty bottle stood just a few feet away, she could not follow up her attack, and could only stagger against the table, watching as Julia rose, her eyes burning with a terrible look. '*Jezebel*,' she hissed.

Jolted awake, Owen sat up, rubbing his eyes. 'Mother?'

Julia rounded on him savagely. 'Go back to sleep!'

'Don't … don't you dare touch him!'

'I've no interest in him!' Julia drew back the knife, moving forward, slowly and deliberately, her free hand going to Mary's neck, her thumb pressing upwards into her jaw, tilting her head backwards to expose the soft white throat.

'Mother?'

Too weak to fight, Mary gave a small whimper.

'I do forgive you, Mary. I do. We *shall* sit at His …'

Owen tore from the bed, grabbing hold of Julia's wrist as she made ready for the killing stroke.

'Get away!' she snarled, but he clung fast, and in an attempt to shake him off, she struck out.

The passage of the knife caused barely a whisper, a soft sibilance, and

Owen staggered back, looking uncertainly at the gaping crescent that had opened across the front of his shirt, then with growing horror as the blood began to spread out like ink on blotting paper. Julia barely glanced at it before raising the knife once more. But for Mary it was as if time had slowed. The hiss of the blade through Owen's flesh seemed to stretch into an elastic sound. She watched the first small poppy of crimson appear, spreading with an infinite slowness – and as it spread, so it seemed to spread through her, not as blood, but as liquid fire, igniting her muscles, filling them with an unimaginable strength. She saw Julia begin to turn, felt the pressure on her neck increase, saw the glint of the knife, but there was no longer any pain, or sickness, or fear – nothing but the terrible anger she felt for the stranger standing before her.

With one hand she gripped Julia's fingers, prising them from her neck, the other moving to block the arm wielding the knife, closing about the wrist with a force that made Julia's eyes widen in astonishment. For a moment they stared at each other, then Mary jerked her head forward, butting Julia savagely, knocking her back on her heels, sending her staggering backwards, the two of them crashing on to the bed.

Sprawled beneath Mary's weight, Julia's lips drew back into a snarl, the blood streaming from her nose giving her a fiendish look as she struggled to break Mary's grip, pushing upwards, twisting the knife, inching its point closer and closer to Mary's face until it trembled inches from her eye. 'You can't win, Mary – it isn't meant to be. I've always been stronger than you.' There was no reply, just a cold, hard glare of hatred, and Julia renewed her efforts, sweat breaking beneath her thin shift as she fought to drive the blade home – but Mary seemed suddenly possessed of an almost inhuman power, and slowly, inexorably, the wicked-looking point began to retreat. 'Mary?' Fear and confusion clouded Julia's eyes. She could feel her own strength beginning to fade, yet Mary's seemed to be growing. 'I … I don't understand. Is … is this how it's meant to end?' Again she tried to force the knife upwards, thrashing wildly in an attempt to break free, but Mary's grip was like steel, and suddenly a look of realisation came to Julia's eyes. 'Mary, tell me …' The blade trembled in the air between them. 'Tell me … you … you *did* love me.'

It was as if she had never spoken, as if no word had passed her lips, and Julia looked deep into Mary's eyes, searching desperately, but finding only emptiness. The blade still quivered between them, caught in a deadlock of straining sinew and muscle, then, slowly, as if with a will of its own, the razor-sharp edge turned toward Julia, the vicious point toward her throat. 'At *His* right hand, Mary …' Julia's lips drew back in what could have been a smile. '… I shall be waiting for you …' The blade quivered a brief moment more, then plunged down as her resistance melted away.

Chapter Sixty-Seven

The drizzle had become a heavy rain as Danny led Evan into the covered passageway. 'Not the sort of place you're accustomed to, sir, I dare say,' he mumbled, aware of the sharp, fetid smell that always hung there.

Inside the court all was quiet, and he went round the corner to reach through the broken window. 'They lost the key and …' With a howl of pain, he snatched back his arm, rubbing at his skinned knuckles. '*What the* …!'

'B-B-Bugger off!' The voice from inside was quavery, but unmistakeably Joe's. 'Go on … b-bugger off, if you don't want some m-more of the same.'

'You dozy sod, Joe. It's *me, Danny!*'

A white face appeared cautiously in the window, peering out. 'Danny?'

'What the soddin' 'ell are you playin' at? I'll bloody well murder you, you daft …'

'I-I didn't know it was you. Hold on, I'll open the door.' The face disappeared, but immediately reappeared. 'You'll have to give m-me a m-minute, I've got to m-move the table.'

'*The table?*' Danny glared angrily. 'I don't know what you're up to, Joe, but get a bloody move on. We're gettin' soaked out 'ere.'

*

Eastman leaned back in the armchair, stretching out his legs, letting the firelight play on the polished leather of his shoes.

It was long after closing time, with the bar-room of the Princess Alice almost in darkness, and as he sat there, watching Tom Suggett bend to the task of toasting bread, Eastman could easily imagine himself in the common room of one of the great public schools he had read so much about. It made him smile.

He was still smiling to himself when Baines came into the bar, shaking the rain from his overcoat. 'What perfect timing, Murray,' he said, barely looking up. 'I was beginning to think I'd have to take young Tom with me.'

'Just in time?' Baines feigned surprise. 'Just in time for what?'

'Oh, a little job.' Eastman took the buttered toast Suggett passed him. 'Would you care for some? It's going to be rather a long night.'

'No, it's alright, thanks.' He gave Suggett a dismissive glance. 'So what's this job, then? And why the bloody hell are you sitting down here in the dark?'

'We have a visitor.'

'A visitor? Who?'

'Mrs Bull has come calling. She's upstairs.'

Baines's surprise became genuine. 'She's come back?'

'A short visit, only. We're going to give her Archie's killer to play with – then she'll be on her way.'

'Archie's killer? How the fuck are we supposed to find her?'

Eastman studied the slice of toast. 'I've known where she is for some time. Information is a valuable commodity, Murray. You might try keeping that in mind.' He gave a small laugh. 'Do you know what I've just bought with this particular piece of information? The *entire* West End.'

'So … Connie's not come back to take over?'

'No.' Eastman spoke quietly and deliberately, as if to a child. 'No, she's not.'

Baines felt his hackles rise, but kept his voice steady. 'Well then? Are we going to fetch this bloody woman, or what?'

'All in good time. Connie is a cat who likes her mice alive, so I think the early hours, when most people are asleep, are best suited to our purposes, don't you? Now, are you sure you won't take some toast?'

*

Danny stared at the body on the bed, then at Mary, slumped against the wall, then back to the body. '*She* was the Ripper?'

'What are we going to do?' Joe's eyes were wide with fright. 'We've got to get away. They'll b-be coming for M-Mary any m-minute.'

Crouched by Mary's side, Evan replaced the makeshift bandage Joe had tied around Owen's chest. 'What we *mustn't* do is panic.' He tried to smile convincingly as he ruffled Owen's hair. 'Just a superficial cut. We'll soon have you patched up once we get you home.'

Mary hugged the boy tighter. 'I'm sorry, Evan … I'm so sorry. I didn't mean for any of this …'

'It's alright, Mary. But Joe's right, we need to get you away from here. Once you're out of danger, then we can contact the police.'

'The police?' Joe's eyes widened even more. 'You can't do that!'

Danny shuffled awkwardly. ''E's right, sir. If Mary says that Miss Julia was the Ripper, then I believe 'er – but I doubt anyone else will. It's not as if we've got any proof. No – you go callin' the police an' at least one of us'll swing for this.'

'But we can't just walk away.'

'We've got to. Even if they did believe us – what about Mary? She's not goin' to be able to 'ide, is she – not with all the police an' the reporters an' the like. An' if what Joe says is true, then the men who are lookin' to kill 'er won't stop till they do – no matter where she goes or what she does.'

Mary began to retch dryly, and Evan comforted her, taking her head against his breast, gently prising her arms from around Owen. 'Will you take him a moment, Joe?'

Tentatively, Joe took the boy's hand. 'You'd b-best come and sit over here with your uncle Joe. Your m-mum will be alright in a m-minute.'

'So what do we do?' asked Evan as Mary sagged weakly against him, her face ashen.

Danny shrugged. 'You an' Mary must make a run for it. Say nothin'. Pretend you were never 'ere.'

'And what about you and Joe?'

'We 'aven't got nowhere to run to. But we'll be okay. We weren't 'ere neither. I was at 'ome with the wife – an' Joe was playin' cards with some friends, ain't that right, Joe?'

'But you'll need someone to vouch for you.'

'Me an' Joe 'ave lived around these parts all our lives – an' people round 'ere tend to stick together, if you know what I mean?'

'B-But ...' Joe froze as there came the sound of footsteps in the arch-way, passing by the door and fading away down the court. 'We've *got* to get away from here!'

Evan glanced at him. 'There *are* three of us.'

'Three of us? You don't know these people. We can't take them on. They won't stop until ...' His eyes fell upon Owen, and he broke off. 'Well – *until.*'

'Alright,' Evan put his arm about Mary's waist. 'Can you stand up? We need to leave.'

'Yes ... Yes, I think so.' With Evan's help she got to her feet. 'My dress?'

The floor was strewn with Julia's clothing, but near the wall lay Mary's black velvet, and Danny picked it up, handing it to her.

'She ... she was my twin sister. I didn't want her to die ...'

Evan looked thoughtfully toward the bed. 'Mary, listen. These people who are after you – would they recognise you again? You said you only saw one man outside that hotel room.'

'Yes, just one. No, wait ... two ... there were two – in the lounge.'

'Had you met them before?'

She shook her head.

Danny followed Evan's gaze to where Julia lay dead. 'It won't work. They might be fooled for a while, but Mary's too well known around 'ere. There'll be no mistake when it comes to identifyin' the body.'

'What if her face were disfigured?'

Danny stared at him. 'You can't be serious?'

Standing close to the boy, Joe's hands crept round to cover Owen's ears. 'It … It m-might work. There was a lecture, over at the Working Lads Institute the other week, all about this m-man who …' He caught Danny's look. 'Well, anyway, it *could* work.'

Evan went over to the body. 'She's the same height and build. It wouldn't be too difficult to …' Julia was lying on the bed, her face turned to the wall, partially hiding the gash across her throat, but it was something on the bare expanse of thigh where her chemise had ridden up that caught his eye, and he leaned forward, inching the material higher, exposing the garter of tattooed roses. 'Damn!'

'Does it m-matter?' asked Joe. 'M-Mary m-might easily have had one just like it. Who would know other than …' He paused, embarrassed. 'Well … you know what I m-mean.'

Evan caught Mary's eye and saw the shame there. 'We can't take any chances. I'll have to get rid of it.'

'Get rid of it?' said Joe. 'B-But how?'

'It *can* be done.' Evan gave a discretionary glance toward Owen. 'Most people are expecting the next Ripper murder to be even worse than the last.'

Danny shook his head in disbelief. 'You mean …? You wouldn't … you couldn't?'

'Why not? It's just dissection – something I do every day.' Evan looked about him. 'I'll need some more light. Are there any more candles?'

'M-More candles? No, I don't think so. Just the one.'

'We could burn this.' Danny scooped up Julia's uniform. 'If we cut it up small.'

'Yes. Yes, in fact, burn all her clothes. There mustn't be anything left.' Evan looked again at the body. 'If I'm to do this I shall have to be quick. Joe, I know it's a lot to ask, but will you take Mary and Owen back to Bloomsbury for me?'

'B-Bloomsbury? Yes, b-but …?'

'Here's the address.' Evan took a card from his wallet. 'And here's money for a cab.' An anxious look crossed his face. 'Will you find one around here?'

'Around here? No. B-But over b-by the m-market. Some of the b-bigger traders from out of town, they come b-by …'

'Is it far?'

'Far? The m-market? No … five – m-maybe six m-minutes …'

'Alright. Mary, you need to go. Do you think you can walk with Joe as far as the market?'

'Yes.' Trembling, Mary finished buttoning her dress, and pulled on her jacket.

'And you, Owen? Are you up to it?'

Still in a state of shock, Owen pressed his lips together, nodding resolutely.

Joe came forward. 'I can carry him.'

'Good. Then you'd better go now, I'll follow on as soon as I can.'

With the uniform in shreds about his feet, Danny paused, the knife halfway through the petticoat he was holding. 'If anyone recognises 'er in the street, then the game's up.'

'She could wear this,' said Joe taking her shawl from its hook and putting it over Mary's head so that her face disappeared into shadow.

Evan opened the door and looked cautiously about. 'There's no one in sight.' He moved into the covered passageway, searching up and down Dorset Street. It was almost deserted, and he beckoned to Joe, standing aside as the huddled group of three made their way through the arch and out into the street.

Evan watched them turn the corner into Commercial Street, then went back down the narrow alley and closed the door behind him. 'You'd better get away, too, Danny.'

Danny fed more of the uniform into the fire. ''Ow long will it take you to do it?'

'Ten minutes – but you don't want to be here.'

'Guttin' fish is part of my job.'

'But this isn't a fish. It's a human being.'

'Is it? I don't know so much – I've read what she did to those other women, an' I can't feel too sorry for 'er.' The flames began to roar up the chimney and he moved back a little, away from the heat. 'Besides, if Joe's right, then we could be 'avin' visitors any time now.'

'It's not your fight.'

'Oh yes it is. If you don't pull this off, they'll come lookin' for Mary – an' their first port of call will be Joe.' He threw another wad of material into the flames and stood up. 'I'll go an' stand just outside in the street. If I see anyone suspicious, I'll come an' warn you – an' you'd better be able to climb 'cos there ain't no other way out of this court except up over the shit-'ouse roofs.'

Evan picked up the knife. 'Then you'd better keep a sharp eye out – and I'd better be damned quick.' He moved to the bed, throwing back the chemise to expose the lower half of Julia's body, and for a moment his mind wouldn't register what he saw. 'Good God!'

With his hand on the latch, Danny stopped, chilled by the exclamation. 'What? What is it?' He came back, looking down at the pale white thighs and the triangle of hair, above which, stretching from hip to hip, a mass of jagged scars made up the word *whore*. 'Christ!' He looked at Evan. 'Now what the 'ell do we do?'

'I don't know.' Evan drew a hand down over his face. 'But we have to do something.' He raised the chemise higher, then higher still, staring in disbelief.

'Bloody 'ell,' muttered Danny. 'She's covered in soddin' scars!'

Evan leaned closer, his fingers tracing the pale red furrows around the base of each breast. 'It's … It's as if someone tried to cut them off …'

'Jesus, fuckin' Christ!' Danny moved away from the bed. 'Well, there's nothin' we can do now but make a run for it.'

'No. We have to go through with this. You said yourself it was the only chance – for all of us.'

'Yes, but … it's impossible now – *ain't it?*'

'I don't know.' Evan studied the mass of scar tissue. 'I *can* do it. I can cut into the scars – cut them away, along with the tattoo – but it will be too obvious – too different to the other killings, and this *has* to look like another Ripper murder.'

'You'd have to be a bloody magician.'

Evan looked at him, then back at the body. 'Smoke and mirrors?' he said.

*

Dawn was still several hours away as the two men sat hunched beneath their ragged greatcoats and wide brimmed hats.

'This fucking coat stinks,' muttered the driver as the cart loaded with old tarpaulins rolled wearily on toward Whitechapel.

'*Must* you keep swearing? It really is most ungentlemanly.'

Murray Baines took a firmer grip on the reins, flicking irritably at the horses flanks. 'And driving *this* … this *shit cart,* isn't? Why the f …' He stopped himself, hunching down into the old coat. 'Why the *hell* couldn't we use the Victoria?'

'A carriage? To Whitechapel? With everyone on the look out for this *Ripper*? You don't think we might have drawn just a *modicum* of attention?'

Baines flicked at the horse again.

'Besides,' continued Eastman, 'I rather like this. It appeals to my theatrical streak.'

*

Sarah was in the hallway, on her way to the kitchen, as Evan let himself in the front door.

'Where's Mary? Is she in bed?' he asked.

'No, sir, she's in the drawing-room. She wouldn't go until you came home. I've just taken her some tea.' She took in his wet clothes and drawn expression. 'I'll put the kettle back on and make some more, sir.'

'No, don't trouble. It's late, and you should be in bed yourself.'

'Oh, it's no trouble, sir – and I don't think I could sleep anyway – not tonight.'

He pulled off his coat. 'How is Owen?'

'He's upstairs, sir. I looked in on him just a few minutes ago, and he was fast asleep.'

He sighed. 'I shall have to wake him. That cut needs cleaning and a fresh bandage.'

'I took the liberty of doing it, sir. I've had a little bit of experience of such things and … well, I hope you don't mind?'

'Mind?' He ran his hands through his hair, and gave a tired smile. 'No. And thank you, Sarah.' She blushed a little, and he quickly crossed the hall, pausing half way up the stairs. 'And perhaps, if it really isn't any trouble, I think I *could* do with some tea.'

'Of course, sir. I'll bring it up straight away.'

Mary was huddled in a corner of the sofa, a blanket about her shoulders. 'Evan. Oh, thank God.'

She made to rise, but he came to sit by her. 'You should be in bed. Come on, I'll help you upstairs.'

'I can't sleep – not yet.' She looked searchingly at him. 'Are we really safe?'

'I think so. I'm sure no one saw me leave, and I was careful to take a cab from Liverpool Street station – then walk the last half-mile home, just in case anyone should make enquiries.'

Mary looked horrified. 'We … we came straight here – right to the door – I never even thought to …'

'It's alright. The police will only be interested in the movements of solitary men – I doubt even my friend Gaston would consider the possibility of the Ripper being a family of three.' He tried to laugh, but his face was drawn and his expression strained, and finally he gave it up and reached for her hand. 'You're safe now, Mary. Completely safe. I'm certain of it.'

She began to cry, and he comforted her, feeling her tremble against him, and trembling in his turn for what he knew he must tell her. 'Mary? It's about Julia – I'm afraid I had to …'

Fresh tears coursed down her cheeks. 'I killed her, Evan. *I killed her.*'

'You had no choice. If you hadn't killed her, she would have killed you. She was mad – perhaps she always was.' He rubbed wearily at his eyes. 'Or maybe that awful business in Cardiff turned her mind.'

Mary looked up at him. 'What do you mean? You *knew* her?'

'Yes, of course.' He saw her eyes widen. 'Don't you remember? She came to the clinic. We were just getting ready to go home one evening when she came to the back door. You waited for me while I went with her.'

The memory of the haunted eyes looking at her from the darkened courtyard came back to Mary, and she stared in disbelief. '*That was Julia?*'

*

'Just here,' said Eastman, jumping down from his seat as the cart ground to a halt just past the entrance to the court. The mist had become a light drizzle again, and he stood for a moment, looking up and down the street, taking in and quickly dismissing the few figures huddled in doorways, then he went to the back of the cart and drew the pins on the tailgate.

Baines came to join him and started hauling out one of the wet, greasy tarpaulins. 'And these stink worst of all.'

'Cleopatra was brought to Caesar in a carpet,' Eastman raised his face, the light from the lodging house lamp briefly illuminating it. 'So what could be more fitting for the delivery of a whore?' He saw the uncomprehending look in Baines's eyes and sighed. 'Oh, just leave it here. You can fetch it once we have her safely secured.'

The houses inside the court were all in darkness, but the gas lamp threw its flickering light upon the door to number thirteen. Baines eyed the flimsy wood and flaking paint with contempt. 'Shall I kick it in?'

With strained patience, Eastman shook his head. 'Since I have what is probably the only key, I very much doubt it's locked,' he said quietly, then allowed himself a smile. Baines was rarely anything other than infuriatingly dull, but there was no denying the pleasure to be had from his continual expressions of bemused surprise. 'Why don't you just step around the corner. I expect you'll find the window is still broken. Just reach in and *quietly* pull back the bolt, hmmm?'

The door opened with the tiniest creak, and in a moment they were inside, searching the darkness, muscles tensed against attack, but all was silent except for the gentle crack of dying embers and the soft fall of ash in the grate. It was then the awful smell of butchery hit them.

Eastman remained unmoved, but Baines stepped forward, drawn by the grisly spectacle. 'What the fuck!'

On the bed lay the horribly mutilated remains of a woman, the bloody, unrecognisable mask that had once been her face, turned toward the door.

'Light the candle,' said Eastman with a nod toward the mantelpiece.

Baines crossed to it and picked up the broken wine glass holding the remains of the halfpenny candle, oblivious to the small white card that fluttered from behind it to land face up in the hearth.

By candlelight, the body presented an even more ghastly sight. The throat had been cut, the breasts completely removed, along with a great deal of the flesh from the belly and right thigh, the severed parts placed in a bizarre arrangement about the bed and upon the nearby washstand.

Murray Baines stared at it. 'What the fuck are we going to do now?'

'I'm not sure.' Eastman put a finger to his lips, tapping at them in agitation. 'Connie's not going to be pleased. I doubt this is quite the *final act* she had in mind. But I've not come this far to let a twopenny whore turn the whole thing into a pantomime …' He paused, a slow smile curling the corners of his mouth. 'But then again – why not? Take a look in the cupboard – see if you can find a bowl.'

'A fucking *bowl*?'

'Yes, a *fucking* bowl.'

*

Evan's gaze lay somewhere beyond the four walls of the drawing-room. 'Her mother was dying – the worst case of syphilis I've ever seen. The poor woman was demented, raving and violent. It would have been a kindness just to have …' He sighed. 'Julia begged me to put an end to her mother's misery – but I couldn't. I had such lofty ideals back then, such certainty about what was right and what was wrong. Everything plainly black or white.' He drew a hand down over his face. 'Now I see there are only infinite shades of grey.'

He fell silent, tightening his grip on Mary's hand, and she moved closer, trying to look into his eyes. 'What is it, Evan? What's the matter?'

He sighed again. 'That night Julia came for me. What if I'd simply done as she asked? One small injection, that's all it would have taken – but instead I notified the authorities – committing the old lady to the asylum – only when they came for her the next day she was dead. Her throat had been cut, and Julia was gone. There was a hue and cry, but Julia was never found, and I never saw her again – not until tonight. But if I *had* just …' He shook his head. 'Perhaps the road to hell really is paved with good intentions.'

*

Mud, foul and stinking, stretched from the foot of the stone steps to the black water lapping twenty feet away, and Connie halted, lifting her face toward the east. Far away, past the distant forest of masts and spars, and well beyond where the Thames emptied into the sea, the first tiny glimmer of dawn streaked the night sky.

'Are you here, Archie?'

Her fingers picked excitedly at the cloth covering the cheap, enamel bowl she was carrying, casting it aside.

'See, I got it for you, just like I promised.'

Lying in the bowl, in a pool of darkly congealed blood, was the heart Eastman had brought her, and she gazed at it in triumph, her lips drawing back over empty gums to form a grotesque snarl – then she looked up, searching the water. 'Are you pleased, Archie?'

A chill wind ruffled the funereal black river as she stepped from the slippery cobbles and on to the shore, her boots sinking ankle deep in the ooze. 'I'll bring it to you, don't you worry.'

She took another step, and then another, wading forward, her skirts dragging behind her, befouled and increasingly heavy, making her lurch and stagger like some monstrous creation. 'Archie?'

'Who's she talkin' to?' asked the small girl.

'No one. She's just some mad old woman.'

Standing together, huddled in the shadows at the top of the steps, the boy put his arm around the girl, pulling her close, taking her warmth and giving his own as they watched Connie disappear beneath the water. 'It's what 'appens to yer when yer stay 'round 'ere.' He felt her shiver. 'But don't you worry – we ain't goin' to end up like 'er. Me an' you? We're goin' to be rich one day – one way or another.'

Chapter Sixty-Eight

Sarah looked in surprise at the figure standing unsteadily in the kitchen doorway. 'Oh, I'm sorry, m'um. We wasn't expecting you to be up for hours yet. Dr Rees-Morgan went off early this morning, but he said not to wake you.' She wiped her hands on her apron as she crossed to the stove, putting the kettle on to boil. 'But now you're up I'll make you some breakfast.'

'No. Please don't bother. Just some tea?'

'Yes, m'um. If you're sure, m'um. Shall I bring it to you in the morning-room?'

Supporting herself against the doorframe, Mary looked around the warm and inviting little kitchen. 'Would you mind if I took it down here?'

Sarah gave her an uncertain glance. 'If you wish to, m'um.'

'But … you'd rather I didn't?'

Keeping her back turned, Sarah wiped an imaginary spot from the brightly polished kettle. 'It's not that, m'um. Truth is I should welcome the company, but … it's just that it never works, you see. Your place is upstairs, and mine's down here, and I've only ever seen trouble come from people confusing the two.' She turned, embarrassed. 'I hope I haven't spoken out of turn, m'um?'

'No.' Mary looked at her with tired, dark rimmed eyes. 'I understand. I'm sorry if I …' She turned to go. 'Well, perhaps then – in the morning-room?'

'Of course, m'um.' The easy smile came back to Sarah's face. 'I'll bring it up as soon as it's ready. Are you sure you wouldn't like me to make you some …?' She broke off, hurrying forward as Mary, almost fainting, steadied herself against the wall. 'Are you alright, m'um?'

'Yes … still just a little giddy.'

Sarah took her arm, helping her back into the kitchen. 'Well you'd best not go back up just yet. Why don't you come and have a little sit down?'

*

'So what happened – or must I wait to read about it in the papers?'

Spencer gave a weak laugh, going rigid as the pain shot through him. 'You won't …' He took a cautious breath. 'You won't be reading very much about this, I'm afraid.' With his one good eye he caught Evan's look. 'Come on, old man. You surely never imagined that I was spending all this time in England … purely for amusement?'

'Then what?'

For a moment Spencer held his gaze, then he said, 'I don't suppose you have a cigarette about you?'

Evan shook his head. 'You should give them up. They're bad for your health.'

Swaddled in bandages and unable to move, Spencer managed a tremulous, lopsided smile. 'But not half as bad as poorly conducted experiments.' He winced as pain lanced the eye socket lying empty beneath the wadding. 'Perhaps I should consider foregoing both.'

'Do you need more morphine?'

'Why not?' Spencer paused again, letting another spasm pass. 'One should always be on the lookout for new vices.'

'You *are* going to be alright, you know.'

'But no longer quite so pretty, eh?' He saw the truth in Evan's eyes and looked up at the ceiling with feigned indifference. 'So, since I am unable to explore for myself, you had better tell me the worst. I have the very devil of a pain in my right eye – and I know *that's* no longer there. So what other bits do I only *think* I can feel?'

*

Sitting at the kitchen table, Mary sipped at her tea, the hot sweet liquid working its reviving magic. 'You must be wondering …' she put the cup into the saucer, 'about last night?'

Sarah reached for the teapot. 'No, m'um. It's really none of my business, m'um. I just do my job.'

'You did far more than that last night, especially for my son.' Mary looked across the table. 'And I wanted to thank you.'

'Oh, that's alright.' She turned her attention to refilling Mary's cup. 'He's a brave little 'un. Didn't hardly murmur when Dr Rees-Morgan sewed him up before going off to the hospital this morning. That reminds me, I should just pop up and check on him.'

'I looked in before coming down here. He's still sleeping. He will be for some time, I expect.' Shame clouded Mary's eyes, and she took another sip of tea. 'I wasn't drunk, you know.'

'I know, m'um. But even if you was, it wouldn't matter …'

'It would matter to *me*.'

Sarah looked at her with growing warmth and respect. 'Yes, m'um. I can see that it would. But you don't have to worry none. That chap who came with you in the cab, well, while he was carrying young master Owen upstairs, he told me something of what had happened.' She hesitated. 'I didn't ask or nothing – he just told me.'

'He would.' Mary sighed heavily, her eyes going to the window and the grey drizzle beyond.

'I'm sure he was only being considerate, like. He just said as how someone put something into your drink. That was all. And as how it wasn't your fault and … Oh, and that reminds me.' She felt in the pocket of her apron. 'He told me to make sure you got this. Said it was best if he didn't keep it.'

It was a small white visiting card, exactly like the one Owen had given her, and Mary froze. 'Oh, no,' she said, her eyes growing wide with fright. 'Oh, God, no.'

'What is it? Whatever's the matter?'

Knocking over her chair, Mary lurched to her feet, grabbing hold of the table for support. 'What time is it?'

'A little before eight.'

'It might already be too late.' She looked about wild-eyed. 'Is there any money in the house?'

'Money, m'um?'

'Evan must keep some somewhere?'

'I wouldn't know, m'um.'

'I've got to go back. I've got to go back to Whitechapel.'

'Whitechapel?' Sarah shook her head. 'I really don't think you should go anywhere just yet, m'um. Look, why don't you wait until …?'

'It can't wait. If I don't go back now, then … then it's all finished.'

'I don't know what you're talking about, I'm sure, m'um. But it can't be that serious.'

'It's worse. I left something – a card – and if I don't get it back, then … then it will all have been for nothing.'

'Shouldn't we wait for Dr Rees-Morgan?'

'There's no time. I have to go back. But how?'

Sarah watched her move unsteadily about the room. 'Alright, I'll come with you. I've some money in my purse. We can …' She stopped abruptly. 'But what about Master Owen?'

'Miss Reeves will look after him.'

Guilt spread across Sarah's face. 'Miss Reeves isn't here. She left yesterday evening, after you and she … I'm sorry, m'um. I should have said something last night, but I thought maybe she might come back – after she'd had a bit of time to think. I'm *really* sorry, m'um.'

'It's alright. It doesn't matter. I'll just have to go on my own.'

'I could ask next door. I know the nanny there and …'

'No. We can't.' She looked anxiously at the maid. 'I can't explain, Sarah, not now.'

Sarah fetched her purse, and pushed it into Mary's hand. 'You don't have to tell me anything. I'll stay and look after Master Owen.' She looked worriedly into Mary's colourless face. 'But for God's sake – *be careful.*'

*

Murray Baines was drinking champagne. He'd recently acquired a taste for it, and this was exceptionally expensive and exceptionally good champagne, fitting to the occasion.

Standing close by, Harry Farrel smiled at him. 'Yer've done well, Murray, my old son. Yer've done *bloody well.*' He punched playfully at Baines's arm. 'I always knew you 'ad what it takes – an' you ain't proved me wrong. Yer've played that cunt Eastman like a fuckin' fiddle.'

Baines grinned and threw Gussie a glance and a wink. 'Couldn't let my future family down, could I?'

'Become Vince's right 'and man, ain't yer,' said Gussie proudly, then widening her eyes in mock innocence. 'An' now that old cow Connie's given 'im everythin' on a silver platter, well, just think – if anythin' was to 'appen to poor Vince, why, *you'd* be runnin' everythin', wouldn't yer.'

'An' the funny thing is,' laughed Farrel, 'I got a feelin' somethin' *is* goin' to 'appen to the stuck-up little ponce.' He became suddenly very serious. 'It's time, Murray. Time we made our final move.'

Baines nodded, contemplating the bubbles in his champagne. 'You're going to kill him?'

'Not me, old son – *you.* Yer've made a right fuckin' mug out of 'im – an' much as I'd love to see the look on 'is face when 'e finds out yer've been workin' fer me the whole fuckin' time, I reckon I owe it to yer to let yer finish the job. Yer'd like that, wouldn't yer?' He took a step closer. 'I've picked yer out a couple of good blokes to go along – just to make sure there ain't no trouble – so you enjoy yerself. You just get rid of the little turd an' the whole fuckin' West End's ours – just like we planned. Yer should be back 'ere in a couple of hours …' He leaned even closer, giving him a wink. 'An' I know my little Gussie'll be waitin' for yer.'

*

An anxious sickness gripped Mary as she stood at the corner of Dorset Street.

Not since the day that Kate first brought her there had the grimy grey canyon of crumbling shops and lodging houses filled her with such dread, and she shivered as she peered out from beneath her cloaking shawl.

A fine drizzle of smoky, sulphurous rain hung like a veil over the street, and the few who had ventured from the stinking communal kitchens passed quickly by, their heads lowered, uncaring of the solitary figure loitering at the corner.

She pulled her shawl tighter, took a deep breath, and walked briskly down to the entrance to Miller's Court, pausing just long enough to look through the covered passageway. Everything was quiet, and she went through, going to the window and reaching through the broken pane.

The bolt was already drawn, and the latch lifted easily, but the door wouldn't open. She tried again, pulling harder, but the door remained firmly shut, and she withdrew her arm, looking about in fear and confusion, her heart beating like a hammer.

Starting to panic, she went to the door, pushing at it, putting her whole weight against it, but still it wouldn't budge, and suddenly overwhelmed, she leaned her head against the flaking paint, her fists beating weakly against the wood. She wanted to cry in frustration, but there came the sound of footsteps from the street, the clump of heavy boots approaching the narrow entrance, and she hurried round to the window, pressing herself against the wall, not daring to breathe until the clatter of hob-nails continued along Dorset Street.

She began sucking in deep breaths, trying to calm herself, trying to think. The key was lost, so the door couldn't be locked. Something had to have become jammed behind it. If so, perhaps she could reach in and move it. Fresh hope sprung within her, and she bent down, pulling aside the makeshift curtain and peering in – but there was nothing there. Just the bare boards and the sliver of daylight beneath the door.

Desperately, she cast about the room, looking for some clue. The fire was out, but she could make out the washstand, and then the bed, and then ... She shrank back from the window, her eyes wide and her lips trembling, every hair on her body standing on end.

With the contents of her stomach rising into her throat, she ran from the court and into Dorset Street, hunching over the kerb to vomit into the gutter.

'Morning, Mary.'

The voice struck her like a dash of cold water. Keeping her head lowered, she looked out from beneath the shawl. 'Oh ... it's you, Carrie.'

Standing on the far pavement, Caroline Maxwell gave her a pitying look. 'It's a bit early, isn't it?'

'I'm ... I'm just feeling a bit ill.'

'Then perhaps you'd better go and have another one – that seems to be the usual remedy around here. Though if you take my advice, you'll give it up before you go ruining your life.'

Mary slowly straightened. It was over – she'd let herself be seen, and she looked bitterly across at the woman. 'It's too late,' she murmured. 'I just have.'

Mrs Maxwell lifted her nose in the air. 'I pity you,' she said, walking away.

*

Joe hadn't slept a wink. He'd stayed at the lodging house as long as he could, feigning sleep, fretting in the darkness and listening to the grunting and snoring all around him, then at first light he'd risen along with those fortunate enough to have work to go to, and had been walking the streets ever since.

The morning had been dry to begin with, but very soon the rain began again, and by chance, or perhaps unconscious design, he found himself in Commercial Street, in the same doorway where he'd sheltered that fateful morning.

Ringmaster? he thought to himself. *No – just a bloody clown.*

He left the doorway and walked on.

After he'd moved out of Miller's Court he'd kept a spark of hope alive, but now the hope was gone, and he knew he would never see her again – knew it with such certainty that, as he passed by the Britannia, he didn't immediately recognise the huddled figure who came hurrying toward him.

'*M-Mary?*'

Mary pulled him into the doorway, her face drawn and sickly grey. 'Did you find the key, Joe? Did you find it?'

'Find it?' He stared at her in alarm. 'What are you doing b-back here? You m-must b-be m-mad.'

'I've been looking all over for you. The door's locked! How can the door be locked?'

'Locked? I don't know. Look, you've got to get away from here. If anyone sees you …'

'It's too late for that – I've been seen. Carrie saw me. It's all over, Joe. I've no choice now but to take my chances on my own.'

'No!'

'I've got to, Joe. I killed Julia.'

'Julia? B-But … Look, we can go to the police. I'll come with you.'

'They won't believe us. Danny was right, we have no proof, and I won't drag you all down with me. That's why I've got to get back into the room. The card Owen gave me – I left it on the mantelpiece. I have to get it back before the police find it.'

Joe chewed anxiously at his moustache. 'B-Bloody hell. Are you sure the door's locked?'

'Yes, I tried and tried to get in.' She sunk her head into her hands. 'Oh, Joe, what am I going to do? I have to get that card.'

The streets were already bustling, and Joe drew her close to keep her hidden from prying eyes, the feel of her against him bringing back memories that made his heart ache. 'I suppose Danny m-might have found the key, and locked up to keep the b-body from b-being found? I can't think how else …'

'Then I've got to find him.'

'No.' He gripped her shoulders. 'You can't. Someone's b-bound to recognise you, and if you're seen with him it'll just m-make things worse. Go home, b-back to B-Bloomsbury. *I'll* find Danny.'

'I daren't go home. What if …?'

'What if, what? The b-body's not b-been discovered yet. If the door's locked, then it'll b-be a long time b-before it is. The safest place for you is at home. I'll see if Danny's got the key, if he hasn't, then I'll try forcing the door. B-But either way, I'll get you the card.'

She looked at him. 'Alright. But be careful, Joe.'

Tenderly he pulled the shawl further down over her face. 'Don't worry. I will b-be. You know m-me, M-Mary. I'm not the heroic type.'

*

The headstone was large, but tasteful – and incongruous amongst the other paupers' graves. Eastman had once considered having the body moved, but there was a part of him that enjoyed the pre-eminence his mother's last resting place enjoyed amongst the ranks of the disowned and forgotten.

He leaned forward, placing the wreath against the weathered stone. 'Alright, Mum?' he murmured, in a voice that few other than she would have recognised. 'Happy birthday.'

He'd been aware of the men who had come quietly into the empty churchyard, but had paid them no heed, even when they had gathered in a discreet semi-circle about him – but now he turned. 'Hello, Murray,' he said, slipping back into his polished accent. 'This is a surprise. Nice of you to remember my mother's birthday.' He glanced around at the other men. 'And you've brought some friends – but no flowers?'

'Don't play the cunt, Vince. It's over. Time to call it a day. You've served your purpose – though it was a masterstroke, I'll give you that.' Baines shook his head, chuckling. 'Getting rid of the old cow in that way, and sliding right into her shoes – *fucking genius.*'

'It's nice to be appreciated.'

'Oh, we appreciated it, alright.'

'*We?*'

Baines felt in his pocket and almost absent-mindedly took out his razor. 'Me and Harry. It was him that suggested I get close to you. We had a scheme for taking over Archie's little empire – but we had no idea how quick things were going to work out for us. The old boy getting his nuts hacked off – well, that put wheels in motion we hadn't even dreamed of.'

'It would make an interesting novel.'

'Maybe.' Baines opened the razor, letting the cold grey light play along the polished steel. 'But *you're* not going to write it.'

'And you think you can trust Farrel? You really think he's going to let *you* run the West End?'

'Who better than family.'

Eastman raised an eyebrow.

'Oh, it's a big day for me, Vince.' Baines began to laugh. 'A *very* big day. Not only do I take over at Villiers Street, but, long before they pull your bollockless body out of the Thames, Gussie'll have become Mrs Baines. I can't see Harry wanting anything but the best for his new son-in-law, can you?'

'So, I'm to go the same way as Archie?'

'Seems fitting, don't it?'

Eastman considered it. 'It sounds – *indulgent*.'

'Just mixing business with pleasure, Vince. You taught me that.'

'No, I didn't. You misread the lesson, Murray. And *that's* the problem.'

One of the men standing close by Baines's side reached into his inside pocket, withdrawing a short, heavy club – but Murray motioned for him to be still. 'No need for that.' He turned back to Eastman, grinning maliciously. 'After all – we don't want you missing any of the fun, do we, Vince.'

'No. No, indeed not,' said Eastman as the cosh cracked against Baines's skull, and he fell senseless across the grave.

*

Indian Harry Bowyer pressed his nose to the pane of glass, looking up at the leaden sky. 'Looks like it might brighten a bit for the show. Hope so. This cold gets right into my bloody bones.' He straightened, turning his head to look at the small woman standing by the counter. 'Beggin' yer pardon, Mrs Maxwell. You'll have to be excusin' my rough soldier's language.'

McCarthy rolled the half-dozen candles in a sheet of newspaper and pushed them across the counter toward her. 'That'll be thrupence. You going up to watch the procession, Carrie?'

She shook her head. 'I wish I could, like a bit of a show, I do – but I shall be too busy.'

'Pity a few more round here aren't. Still, I suppose the pubs will do well out of it – they usually do.' He rubbed thoughtfully at his ear. 'Here,

Harry, maybe you'd better do a quick run round. See if you can't get some rent money before it all gets spent – and start with Mary down at number thirteen.'

'Right you are, Guv'nor.'

Mrs Maxwell watched him go, then picked up her purchases, tucking them into the crook of her arm. 'I doubt you'll get much out of her.'

McCarthy raised an eyebrow.

'I saw her just a few hours ago, being sick as a dog right there in the street.' She tutted disapprovingly.

'Drunk?'

'Either that or she's got the morning sickness – but from the way she was trying to hide her face, I'd say she was drunk. Still, I suppose it's to her credit she's got the decency to be ashamed.'

'She might just be ill.'

'I wouldn't go wasting your sympathy, Mr McCarthy. If she was ill, I wouldn't have seen her in the doorway of Ringer's, just a half hour later, would I?'

McCarthy gave a heavy sigh. But whatever he was about to say died on his lips as the shop door flew open, and Indian Harry burst in, his normally dark features a ghostly white. 'Bloody hell, Guv'nor!' he said, trembling from head to toe. 'Bloody hell …'

Chapter Sixty-Nine

The excruciating pain in Baines's head reached down into his stomach, lifting its contents into his mouth. He tried to jerk forward, but he was lashed to a stout wooden chair, giving him no choice but to vomit into his lap. He retched again, then slumped against the backrest, his face as greasy and grey as putty.

'Nice of you to join us again, Murray. Did you have a pleasant nap?' Eastman crossed the dingy cellar, positioning himself against a packing case some little way off. 'You'll forgive me if I keep my distance?' he said, motioning with his eyes toward the foul-smelling mess.

'W-What's all this about, Vince?'

'Just wanted a little chat.'

Baines tried to stop himself trembling. 'Listen, you'd better let me go. If Harry finds out about this …'

'Harry?' Eastman gave his thin smile. 'Yes, good old Harry. That was clever of him – putting you into Villiers Street like that. I never suspected for a moment you might be *his* right hand man, rather than mine. It was very, *very* clever.'

'Untie me, and I'll go and talk to him. Make him see reason. It wasn't my idea to kill you, Vince. I never wanted that.'

'Of course you didn't. All that talk about cutting off my balls – just a bit of ragging, hmmm?'

Baines forced a laugh. 'Yeah, that's right. Look, we can sort all this out. Harry listens to me.'

'Really? That's interesting – considering Harry was the one who sent you to me.'

Surprise, then unease showed on Baines's sickly face, but he brazened it out. 'You're lying.'

'You're a loose cannon, Murray. Harry's exact words.' Eastman smiled again, spreading his hands, 'Well – a *fuckin'* loose cannon to be precise

– but let's not quarrel over a superfluous expletive. You see, the problem is, Harry is a professional. *I'm* a professional. But you, Murray? You're just a bloody amateur with a perverted taste for cutting women.'

Baines strained angrily at his bonds. 'You've got a fucking cheek calling me that – after some of the tricks you've pulled.'

Eastman shook his head sadly. 'You've never really understood, have you.' He picked up a long splinter of wood, toying with it. 'Never seen the distinction between a calculated act of brutality, and the capricious sadism of which you've become so fond. The difference between making an *example,* and going on a drunken spree that ends with you smashing a bottle inside the cunt of some insignificant whore.'

Baines writhed to free himself. 'It was just a fucking laugh, for Chris'sake. What does it matter? Who gives a fuck about her?'

'Emma Smith? No one.' Eastman looked pityingly at him. 'But it's *unprofessional* – and unprofessionalism leads to mistakes – like Liz Stride – and mistakes lead to the gallows.' A thought struck him, and he raised a querying eyebrow. 'Just for my own interest, you understand – these Ripper murders, they weren't your handiwork, by any chance?'

'Those old hags? What do you think I am?'

Eastman almost laughed. 'I *know* what you are, Murray. I saw it emerge in that French farmhouse. You enjoyed yourself with Archie's little tart, didn't you?'

'You wanted her cut.'

'Oh, I'm not complaining. You were very creative, and I was happy to indulge you. But as I said earlier, mixing business with pleasure is a dangerous road to take.'

'You've taken it often enough. What about those two froggies!'

Eastman's eyes flared dangerously. 'Don't dare compare yourself to me. What I do, I do for a purpose. It's just business – and my business is instilling fear. But you? You just like to cut – and you don't care who. *That* makes you a loose cannon. And *that* is why Harry has delivered you to me.'

'You're a fucking liar! If Harry wanted me dead, I'd have been floating in the Thames by now.'

Eastman looked pleased. 'Do you know, that's the first intelligent observation I can ever recall you making. Perhaps, after all, a silk purse might have been made from a sow's ear. Now, unfortunately, we'll never know.' From on top of a packing case he took a small axe, running his thumb along the sharpened edge. 'Harry was all for killing you days ago – and was *very* unhappy when I prevented him.'

Baines's eyes widened, taking on the look of a frightened horse. 'S-So what are you going to do?'

'I'm not going to kill you, Murray. I should, of course. You've let me down – been a traitor – and I should take you apart, very slowly, and put the pieces on spikes all over London as a warning. But I'm not going to. Instead I'm going to give you one final lesson in professionalism.' He came closer, weighing the hatchet in his hands. 'You see, Harry and I, we're about to embark on a new understanding – a partnership – only *I* intend to be the *senior* partner. Are you following me so far?'

Terrified, Baines nodded frantically.

'Harry wants you dead – so *I'm* going to let you live. He won't like that – but he'll have to live with it – and I'll have made my point.' Standing over Baines, he rested a hand on his shoulder. 'You're a lucky man, Murray.'

Sweat was standing out on Baines's forehead. 'So, y-you're going to let me go?'

Eastman smiled his thin smile. 'Most of you,' he said quietly.

*

George Bagster Phillips looked uncomfortable. 'I'm very sorry, Rees-Morgan. I telegraphed you at the hospital the moment they called me. But I had no idea we'd be kept waiting this long.'

Evan glanced about at the press of officials crammed into the dreary confines of Miller's Court. 'Well, at least it's no longer raining.'

Standing a little way off, Dr Bond glanced across, excused himself from the company of the two other doctors present, and wandered over. 'I've just heard that the bloodhounds aren't coming after all. Still, little matter, the police already have their man.'

Evan gave him a querying look.

'The fellow she'd been living with until recently,' explained Phillips.

Bond gave a self-satisfied chuckle. 'He arrived soon after us. Barratt, or some such name. Never seen a more shifty, nervous looking creature. He identified the body through the window – supposedly by the eyes and the ear, if you please!' He shook his head in disbelief, then smiled. 'Fish porter, so I hear. Rather knocks your ideas about the perpetrator having some medical skill, eh, Phillips.'

Evan tried to keep his tone casual. 'Where is he now?'

Bond eyed him as if for the first time. 'I don't believe we have been introduced.'

'This is Evan Rees-Morgan,' said Phillips. 'From the London Hospital. He's very kindly acting as my assistant.'

'Ah. Well, I'm pleased to meet you, Rees-Morgan.'

Evan took the proffered hand. 'Likewise, Dr Bond. I have heard much of you these past months.'

'Oh, no doubt. Our butchering friend has made celebrities of us all, eh, Phillips?'

Phillips gave an irritable grunt.

571

'So,' continued Evan. 'This chap – Barratt?'

'Half-way to the gallows, or I'm a Dutchman.'

'Not a shred of evidence,' said Phillips. 'And his name is *Barnett.*'

'Barratt or Barnett, the man's a gibbering idiot.' Bond took his watch from his waistcoat. 'They've had him in custody for over an hour, so we can expect an announcement imminently.'

'But what on earth was he doing here?' persisted Evan. 'Surely if he was the murderer …?'

'Precisely,' said Phillips. 'This would be the last place he'd return to if he was guilty.'

'As I said – the man's a gibbering idiot. Or he may have been forced into coming back.' Bond looked thoughtfully to where the window had been removed to allow a better view into the room. 'Do you know – I do believe that must be the case. There's something in that room, gentleman – some piece of evidence that will put the noose about our friend Barnett's neck. And as soon as they make up their minds to let us inside …'

From a little way off came a crash and the sound of splintering wood as the door was broken open.

'Dr Phillips?' The young constable looked nervous. 'You and the other gentlemen can go in now, sir.'

The room smelled of death. By firelight the scene had been nightmarish enough, but in the cold light of that November afternoon, Evan found himself recoiling from the sight of his own work, and wondering at the strength, or madness, that had allowed him to perform such an atrocity.

Phillips made his way directly to the body, edging past the table with its grisly remains, to stand by the foot of the bed. 'I should be obliged if you would take notes for me, Rees-Morgan,' he said quietly, looking solemnly down at the horror before him.

Evan came to join him, taking a notebook and pencil from his pocket.

'Butchery, plain and simple.' Dr Bond planted himself in front of the fireplace.

'Possibly.' Phillips leaned closer, inspecting the wounds, his brows knitting into a frown. 'Well, we'd better get on with it. Are we all ready?'

'Yes, yes,' said Bond, distractedly, looking about the room. 'Though I can't help wondering what our Mr Barnett was so keen to fetch that he'd walk right back into the middle of a murder enquiry.' He bent down, peering into the grate. 'Looks like a good deal of clothing has been burned here, and …' He paused as something caught his eye. 'Hullo, what's this?' In the hearth lay a small white card, and he picked it up, reading the printed front. 'Well, well! Here's something the police will be *more* than interested in, I should think!' With a contemptuous laugh he slipped it into Evan's waistcoat pocket. 'Do let us be more careful about dropping things, gentleman. This is, after all, a crime scene, and we should try our best not to contaminate it any more than is absolutely necessary.'

*

It was early evening when the cab came to a halt beneath the street lamp, depositing its solitary passenger before moving away, the sound of hooves echoing around the square.

Evan watched it go. He was tired, almost too tired to climb the few steps up to the front door, but as he turned toward the house, looking up at the inviting glow from the drawing-room window, he saw the faintest twitch at the curtain, and in the next moment the door opened and Mary stood looking at him, her hollow eyes filled with foreboding.

'Are you alone?' she whispered, searching the street behind him.

'Yes, of course.'

He came up the steps, reaching for her, but she backed away into the house. 'The card. The card Owen gave me. I left it back in my room.'

'It's alright, Mary,' He took the card from his pocket. 'I've got it.'

Mary stared at it, then slumped against the wall. 'Oh, thank God,' she said – then almost immediately, 'What about Joe? And Danny? Have you heard anything?'

'They're alright. Joe was questioned, but there was nothing to implicate him, so they let him go.' He came closer. 'Come on, come and sit down.'

'No, Evan. I can't stay with you.' She turned from him. 'I should have known it was all too good to be true.'

The deathly chill he'd felt that New Year's morning in Caerphilly, descended upon him once again. 'Why? What's changed?'

'I went back this morning – to get the card, and I was seen. By now they must know it's not me lying dead, and soon the police will come looking for me – if Archie's men don't find me first.'

'No one is going to find you here.'

'Of course they will. Sooner or later someone will recognise me in the street – just like this morning – and then they'll come for us both. I don't care about me anymore, Evan – they can do what they like with me – but *you, and Owen*?' She shook her head. 'I couldn't stand that.'

'Mary, I said goodbye to you that morning at the station because I had no say in the matter. But this time I have – and I won't say goodbye a second time. Whatever happens to us, it can't be as bad as living life without you.'

She let him take her in his arms. 'I can't stay here, Evan.'

He held her close, feeling her tremble. 'Then we'll leave,' he said.

*

Coals glimmered in the grate, but otherwise the bedroom was in darkness as they lay beneath the sheets, warm and drowsy, their bodies touching, bare skin against bare skin.

They had not made love, and the feel of her breasts, soft against his side, and her thigh draped over his as she clung to him, roused him, not to urgent passion, but to a serene, dreamy sensuality that lay somewhere between waking and sleeping.

'Evan?' she asked, almost timidly, as she nestled against him, her fingers moving in gentle circles over his chest. 'Are you alright?'

'Yes.' He turned to look at her. 'Why?'

'It's just that ... I saw Julia's body through the window – I saw what you had to do. I never realised it would have to be so horrible.' She raised her face to look into his eyes. 'And I'm worried for you. I can't imagine where you found the strength to do such a thing.'

He looked at her. 'I found it in you.' He turned on to his side, feeling for her hand. 'Do you remember, when we first worked together, I told you how, when I was a child, my father had me dissect a rabbit – and I made such a mess of it?' He paused, taking a moment. 'It was just a dead rabbit from the butcher's shop – but I wasn't much older than Owen, and I didn't want to do it. The very idea horrified me. But my father was insistent.' He paused again. 'Well, I cried and retched my way through the whole business, and ended up making a complete mess of it. Father was furious with me. Not for being squeamish, but for letting it prevent me doing what he considered needed to be done. So, he took me outside, down to the very bottom of the garden where my pet rabbits were kept. I loved them, Mary. They were the two most beautiful white rabbits ... and he took one of them ... and he killed it there in front of me. Then he led me back inside and made me cut it open ... and I knew I daren't make another mistake or he'd ...'

'Oh, Evan,' Mary kissed him tenderly. 'Oh, my poor sweet love.'

'I hated him that day, Mary. It seemed the cruellest, most unnecessary lesson imaginable. Yet, when I came to cut it up, I didn't cry another tear. Perhaps it was because I was too full of hate, but I think it was because I knew it *had* to be done if I was to save the one thing left to me in the world that I loved.'

574

Chapter Seventy

Breakfast in the Farrel household often took on the qualities of a poorly conceived comic opera, but on this damp and foggy morning a particularly dark and brooding atmosphere hung over the table.

'I told yer they'd make us look like cunts.' Harry tossed the paper across the table. 'Is that supposed to be me? *Well, is it?*'

Gussie looked at the line drawing accompanying the article. 'Your 'at looks nice,' she offered diplomatically.

'My fuckin' 'at? I don't give a fuck about my *fuckin'* 'at. They've made *me* look like a fuckin' monkey!'

'Don't go shoutin',' said Sadie, stroking the hair of the tiny girl by her side. 'Yer frightenin' the poor little thing. Anyway, I thought it was a good likeness.'

Harry's brows drew together like two thunderclouds. 'We'll be a fuckin' laughin' stock. Well, just let me catch someone 'avin' a chuckle over it an' I'll 'ang 'em out to fuckin' dry.'

'So, what did they write?' asked Sadie, looking at the neat rows of meaningless black type.

Harry snatched back the newspaper, squinting, and moving the sheet back and forth as he tried to find a distance from which he could focus on it. ''Ere's a couple of choice bits. *A family of the more prosperous coster class.* Coster class? Fuckin' cheek!' He scanned down several more lines. '*Occupyin' a modest an' largely undistinguished 'ouse, furnished an' decorated in a style not uncommon in the East End, but carried to 'itherto unimagined magnitude: a style of exquisite Philistine ostentation from which even the smallest tenet of good taste 'as been thoroughly expunged.*' His great thick hands began to shake in rage. 'I'll give 'em fuckin' *modest!*'

On the far side of the table the bundle of frills and lace that was the little girl began to wail, her freshly scrubbed face screwing into an expression of fearful misery.

'Now look what yer've done,' said Sadie crossly.

Harry fumed in silence, and was on the point of getting up when his eye fell upon a parcel that stood on the table by the window. 'What the fuck's that?'

Gussie turned her head, following his gaze. 'Oh, it's for you. Came this mornin'.'

'Well, give it 'ere.'

Tilting back her chair, she took hold of it, passing it across the table.

Harry tore off the wrapping and lifted the lid of the cardboard box that lay inside. 'It's full of fuckin' sawdust. This better not be some cunt's idea of a joke.'

Lying on the top, half submerged beneath the shavings, was a card, and he pulled it out. '*Render unto Caesar that which is Caesar's.*' He looked up, first at his wife, then at Gussie. 'What the fuck's that supposed to mean?'

Gussie shrugged. 'Is that all that's in there?'

'Don't know.' He dug deeper into the box, and coming across the unmistakeable feel of dead flesh he brushed away the top layer of sawdust to expose a severed right hand.

'What is it?' asked Gussie.

Harry began to chuckle. 'Looks like yer engagement's off,' he said, pushing the box toward her. "E's sent yer ring back.'

For a moment she looked at the grisly contents of the package, then casually reached in and took the gold band, with its solitary diamond, from the little finger.

'Yer did well, Gussie,' said Harry. 'I wouldn't never 'ave known about 'im an' 'is little shenanigans if you 'adn't led 'im on.'

Gussie slipped the ring back on her own hand, glowing with pride. 'It was your idea, dad.'

'I know. But yer carried it off a treat, an' I'm right proud of yer.'

*

'Spatulate fingers, Doyle? There can be only two possible explanations.'

'You're *quite* certain?'

Gaston gazed at him with an air of infinite patience.

'Yes ...' The younger man looked embarrassed. 'Yes, of course. Well, then I really should be going.'

Standing by the door, George Bagster Phillips put out his hand. 'It was nice to meet you Dr Doyle – however briefly.'

'And you too, sir. I've been following the Ripper case most carefully. Actually I have a theory ...'

'Yes, yes,' Gaston sighed, rolling his eyes. 'A man dressed as a *woman*.' He motioned him away with a waft of his podgy fingers. 'Off to your scribblings, Doyle. I'm sure your theory has great merit – if only in the fanciful realms you inhabit.' He waited until the young doctor had closed the door behind him, then leaned back, almost engulfing the armchair. 'Have you read any of our young friend's jottings?'

'No, I haven't,' said Phillips, looking about the plush Harley Street consulting room. 'What does he write?'

'Detective stories. He consults me on a regular basis. Apparently he has it in mind to base a character on myself.' Gaston frowned. 'Though I confess, I thought he had already done so with this Mr Holmes of his. Still,' he wafted his hands once more, 'I deduce you have not come hot-foot from Whitechapel to discuss Dr Doyle's novelette?'

'No.'

'Then, please. Take a seat.'

Phillips took off his overcoat and sank into the second armchair. 'You've read the newspaper reports on the latest victim?'

'I've read *everything* – *and* seen the police photographs.' He caught Phillips's look of surprise. 'You don't imagine you are the only one to consult me on this matter, surely?'

'I see. May I ask …?' But then he shook his head. 'No, of course not. Forgive me.'

Gaston regarded him with satisfaction. 'So? I take it you have no new information to impart?'

'No, not really – except that …' Phillips's brows drew into a frown. 'I'm not entirely sure we are dealing with the same murderer.'

'Indeed? And what brings you to consider this possibility?'

'The mutilations. There is something very odd about them. When we came to put the body back together – not all of it was there.'

'Yes, yes,' said Gaston. 'I know all about the missing heart. But why should you consider it odd? It has been our man's trademark to remove and take away pieces of the body, has it not? What could be more natural than he should progress from kidneys and pieces of uterus, to the heart?'

'It wasn't just the heart. Some small amounts of skin and flesh were missing. But the really mysterious aspect presented itself in those places where nothing seemed to have been taken – the edges of the cuts were not a perfect match … almost as if they had been trimmed.'

Gaston chuckled. 'Oh, delightful, quite delightful. You really should go to the theatre more often, my dear sir, and study first hand the art of creating mystery.' He frowned. 'But why have I heard nothing of these *anomalies*?'

Phillips considered him for a moment. 'Because I've mentioned them to no one but Rees-Morgan who was assisting me at the post mortem. He believes the information would be better held back, but …'

'And our young friend is quite correct. If similar caution had been shown over the reporting of the earlier murders, the police would not have gotten themselves into such a muddle over the authenticity of the letters mentioning the kidney. Still, it is all rather academic now.'

There was a finality about the words that caused Phillips to stare, and Gaston's features took on the patient look once again. 'What was your purpose in coming here today, Dr Phillips? To prevent more murders?'

'Of course.'

'Then you've wasted your time. He will not kill again.' From the table by his elbow, Gaston took a large envelope, passing it across. 'Look closely at the photographs.'

'I've seen them. I was there when they were taken.'

'But look closely.'

Reluctantly, Phillips withdrew the pictures. 'So what am I looking for?'

'Why, the very *perfection* of it.'

'The *perfection* of it? Are you serious?'

'Of course.' Gaston reached for a bon-bon. 'You will remember how I told you at our last meeting that our perpetrator was a showman – a showman, not only with a message to impart, but with a showman's instinctive understanding of the public's need for greater and greater spectacle. It was therefore quite obvious to me that each new murder would be accompanied by ever-increasing butchery – and as you can see, I have been proved correct. But more than that – far more – these photographs show a masterwork – a tour de force in sensationalist horror. With the butchery of the Kelly woman he has created his Magnum Opus, and in the process left himself with only four options. Two of them we can reasonably dismiss, as I'm sure you'll agree?'

Phillips stared blankly. 'I'm sorry, but I have no idea what you're talking about. What *options*?'

'The first option is to continue killing.' Gaston shook his head, his multiple chins swaying back and forth. 'Repeating his great triumph until it becomes a sad and jaded pastiche? No. That would serve neither his purpose nor his vanity. The second option? Why, to attempt to surpass the unsurpassable in the only way possible, by giving himself up – taking his bow, as it were – basking in the blaze of public interest and doubtless crying his message from that greatest stage of all – the dock of the Old Bailey. But as any showman knows, timing is everything – and a week has passed, and we have heard nothing from him.'

'But it's not too late,' said Phillips, suddenly hopeful.

'No, not too late, and anything is possible. But I deduce that we are now left with the only two real possibilities. Realising he has nowhere left to go, his madness will have lead him to the Thames – or to the asylum. Either way, I am quite certain we shall hear no more of Jack the Ripper.'

*

The police sergeant took up the sheet of paper. 'So, Mr Hutchinson, let me just check if I have it all. At two o'clock in the morning you were standing in the street when you saw the murdered woman in the company of a man ...'

'The Ripper.'

'A man who might *possibly* have been the Ripper.'

'I don't see as there's any doubt about it.'

'Well, be that as it may, if we might stick to the description?' He smiled patiently. 'Thank you, sir. Now, you say he was carrying a small parcel wrapped in American cloth. He was of Jewish appearance, aged about thirty-five ...'

'He might have been thirty-four.'

Taking up his pen, the sergeant amended the sheet. '*Or thirty-four*. With a pale complexion, dark hair *and eyelashes* – and with a slight moustache curled up at the ends.'

'Yes, I said so, didn't I?'

'Please Mr Hutchinson. I just need to be sure of the facts.' He gave the sheet a business like shake. 'Now, he was wearing a dark felt hat, turned down to cover his face, a long dark coat with astrakhan collar and cuffs, a dark jacket and trousers, and a light waistcoat?'

'Yes, that's right.'

'On his feet he wore button boots covered by gaiters – with white buttons. Now, is that the boots or the gaiters?'

'The gaiters, of course – little round white ones they were.'

'I see.' He amended the sheet once more. 'He also had on a linen collar, a black tie fixed with a horseshoe pin, and all topped off with a thick gold chain. Is that all correct?'

'Yes, that was him alright.'

'I suppose you didn't get his hat size by any chance?'

George Hutchinson grew red in the face. 'Look, do you want to catch this bloke or not? I didn't have to come here, you know!'

'I do know that, sir.' The sergeant gave a placating smile. 'And we're very glad you saw fit to do your civic duty. I shall be sure to pass this statement on to the investigating detectives.'

'Yes, well ... Just be sure you do. It *was* the Ripper alright. You've got my name, haven't you? Hutchinson? George Hutchinson?'

'Yes, sir, that I have. The constable will show you out the back way if you'd like to avoid the reporters?'

'No, that's alright.' Hutchinson drew himself up importantly. 'I don't mind talkin' to 'em.'

The constable waited until the door closed. 'What do you reckon, Sarge? Load of bollocks?'

''Course. Still, I'll send it along with the rest. It'll give someone a laugh.'

He added the sheet to the growing pile. 'Nothing like a murder to bring the glory seekers crawling out of the woodwork. So? Who have we got next?'

'An even better one.' The young constable struggled to keep a straight face. 'A Mrs Caroline Maxwell – claims she spoke to the Kelly woman in the street – six hours after she'd been killed.'

*

It was mid-November, cold and wet, yet the darkened East End streets were crowded as the cab made its way back to Spitalfields.

George Bagster Phillips sank deeper into his overcoat. 'Did you see how people were trying to touch the coffin?' He shook his head. 'Barely anyone had heard of this Kelly woman until ten days ago. Yet those scenes today were almost – *biblical*.'

Evan looked thoughtfully at the returning groups of people, some drunk, but many more quiet and even tearful.

Sitting opposite Evan in the old growler, Phillips gave a shrug. 'Well, one thing's for certain. Whitechapel hasn't seen such a turn out since the Jubilee.' He wiped at his reddened nose. 'Speaking of which, you know even *she's* been involved?'

'Who?'

'The Queen. Apparently a day doesn't pass when she's not pestering the Prime Minister with some new scheme for improving the area, or the detective force, or …' He gave another shrug.

'It would be a strange twist if some good came out of all this.'

Phillips dabbed again at his nose. 'Strange? That's one way of putting it, I suppose. For myself, I should prefer *disgraceful*.' He stared across the small space with rheumy eyes. 'If it's worthwhile to make these proposed improvements now, then why not long ago? Why must it always take blood and death to shake us from our complacency?'

The cab drew to a halt. 'Leman Street Police Station,' called down the cabbie.

Wearily, Phillips made to rise. 'Well, I wish you luck in America, Rees-Morgan. I shall miss you.' He pushed open the door. 'If you'll send me your new address I shall be happy to keep you informed of any developments in the case.'

Evan glanced at him. 'Isn't Gaston convinced the murders are over?'

'Yes, and I pray to God he's correct. Though I very much fear he isn't.'

'I've never known him to be right, but who knows – there's always a first time.'

Phillips stepped down on to the kerb and closed the cab door. 'Well, I shall endeavour to share your optimism, but I'm not convinced by his explanation – especially regarding the removal of the body parts. I think they hold a much greater significance.'

'Not just smoke and mirrors?'

Phillips looked to the driver sitting high above him. 'Bloomsbury,' he said, then to Evan as the cab drew away. 'I rather doubt it.'

On the far side of the road a canvas banner hung above a mission hall door, and Phillips's eyes wandered over the bold black print. *Tonight. The Whitechapel Murders and the New Jerusalem.* It was one of a dozen or so similar meetings being held that night, and he turned away, shaking his head.

'Because thou sufferest that woman Jezebel to teach and seduce my servants to commit fornication!' Inside the hall, the crowd was deathly silent, and the speaker paused, raising his eyes to the rafters. 'Oh, dear Lord, how many times?' he asked. 'How many more Mary Kellys must there be before Your holy word is heard? How many more harlots must perish before we take notice? The list is already long. Smith!' He raised one finger. 'Tabram!' A second finger. 'Nichols! Chapman! Stride! Eddowes! Kelly!' Each name accompanied by the thrusting up of a finger. 'Seven names. Seven! Oh, yes, the list is already long.' He looked in wonderment at his hands. 'But *only* seven?' His mouth curved solemnly, and he slowly shook his head. 'No, not seven. Not seven times seven. Not even seventy times seven!'

He drew himself up, glaring about the packed mission hall, his luminescent eyes falling upon the faithful in silent rebuke. 'It is a list, *thousands* upon *thousands* times seven. A list that goes back as far as Jezebel herself! And that list will go on – stretching into the future, *thousands* upon *thousands* times seven – until *His* will be done! For this is the word of the Lord, which He spake by His servant Elijah the Tishbite, saying: In the portion of Jezreel *shall dogs eat the flesh of Jezebel!*'

*

'Christmas at sea, eh? That should b-be something … *different*, I suppose.' Joe looked self-consciously about the cabin. 'And you always wanted to travel, didn't you, M-Mary.'

She touched his arm, running her hand down his sleeve to take his hand. 'It was *you* who always wanted to travel. To see the pyramids, remember?'

'Remember? Yes, well, I *shall* see them, I expect – one day. M-Maybe Caernarvon first, though? Since it's a b-bit closer. And b-besides, I should like to stand in that hotel of yours and look across at the leaning tower.'

Mary smiled. 'Then it would be better if you went to Caerphilly.'

'Caerphilly?' He looked down at his feet. 'I never get anything right.'

'That's not true, Joe. But for you I wouldn't be here.' He began to shake his head, and she gripped his hand tighter. 'I owe you so much.'

He chewed at the end of his moustache. 'If anyone owes anything ...' There was a commotion just outside the door, and he fell silent as Sarah swept in, a portmanteau in one hand and Owen's hand clutched in the other.

'Uncle Joe!' Owen called excitedly. 'Are you coming to America, too?'

'America?' Joe stopped himself and gave an embarrassed chuckle. 'Funny old Uncle Joe, eh?' he said, going down on one knee. 'Just like a b-blooming parrot.'

The echo of Kate's words brought a lump to Mary's throat, but Owen beamed with delight. 'Just like a b-blooming parrot!'

'Master Owen!' Sarah looked at him askance. 'Whatever will the gentleman think.'

Joe gave the boy a wink. 'It's alright. All healed up then?'

'I've got a *huge* scar! Do you want to see?'

'I should think Mr Barnett's seen *plenty* of scars before.'

'Not like this one, Nanny.' He looked up at Joe. 'It's ever so long – and in a big sort of curve. Mother says it looks like a smile. But ...'

'B-but you'd like something a b-bit b-bolder, m-more piratey?'

Owen looked at him in surprise. 'Have you read *Treasure Island*?'

'*Treasure Island*? Well, yes, a b-bit of it.' He glanced up at Mary, 'Someone once recommended it to m-me.'

Mary put her hand on his shoulder, her fingers pressing tenderly.

'Well,' said Sarah, seeing the look that passed between them. 'If you'll excuse us, m'um, I ought to be helping Dr Rees-Morgan bring down the last few things.' She took a firm grip on Owen's hand. 'Come on, young Mister Hawkins, you can give me some help – and then, if you like, we'll go hunting up on deck for any suspicious looking one-legged sailors.'

Joe waited until they'd gone, then slowly got to his feet. 'I should b-be going, too.'

'What will you do, Joe? Have you any plans?'

'Plans? Well, I don't know. I've b-been staying with m-my sister. She has this little place over near Leather Lane m-market. She keeps m-me out of trouble.'

'You are safe? The police haven't asked you any more questions?'

'Questions? No. Nobody's interested in m-me anymore. We're b-both safe now, M-Mary. You're dead – and I'm just an insignificant nobody.'

'And neither one is true.'

He shrugged. 'M-Maybe.'

'What about the money we owed?'

'*We* owed?' He smiled wryly. 'I paid it all b-back. It was very generous of you, M-Mary. M-Mr M-McCarthy seemed a b-bit surprised, b-but I told him I'd had a b-bit of good luck – and how I knew you'd not have wanted to die in debt. Funny thing – I never had him down as the sort to b-believe in an afterlife or anything like that, b-but he said to me, *Well, I wish her luck.*'

*

In the week before we sailed I visited Julia's grave. The headstone read, Marie Jeanette Kelly. It was Joe's idea. He told me he couldn't bring himself to use my real name, and though I'd always hated him calling me that, it seemed appropriate.

I stood there for a long time, trying to reconcile the Julia I'd loved with the murderer she had become. I couldn't forgive her – not for Polly, not for Annie, and especially not for Kate – but such affection as we'd shared cannot be torn from the heart and casually cast aside, and alone by the graveside I wept for her.

On the night we'd swum in the Serpentine she'd said she'd always protect me. In Paris, in her own deluded way, she had. Now, in death, in an ironic twist of fate, she protected me still.

I'd written three letters. Evan had cautioned against it, but I couldn't bear the thought of those I loved reading of my death. The ones to Peggy and to Mr Abrahams I sent straight away. The third, to Gwyneth, I put in my pocket, intending every day to post it – but always there was doubt. Though my heart ached for a single word of reconciliation, the letter remained unposted. When the time came to leave, it sailed with me. We were a day away from New York when I dropped it into the sea.

Our first sighting of America was just before dark. Standing on deck with Evan's arms about me, and Owen's hand clasped in mine, I shivered.

Nant-y-Pridd was so very far away, yet still that hill seemed to cast its cold shadow. As I looked across at the unknown shore, I felt I was that small child again, about to lose her footing on the steep and muddy sides.

But only for a moment.

Because while we live, we grow – and there had come a day when my feet were no longer small, when my arms and legs, grown strong from trying, took me up those treacherous slopes by ways hard learned – to stand at the top, feeling the stinging rain on my skin – knowing it wasn't for the last time that the rain would come – but certain in my heart that, come what may, I would always make the climb.

EPILOGUE

Maryland 1990

The rented car slowed, bumping off the asphalt road and coming to a halt on the dry earth at the edge of the field. 'I'm sorry, honey,' he said, stretching back in his seat, 'I know it's only another fifteen miles or so, but I've got to take a break.'

Beth Williams looked down at the two faded photographs she held in her lap. 'It's okay, the place has been there all this time, it's not going anywhere in the next few hours.' She reached behind him, stroking the hairs at the back of his neck. 'This isn't much of a holiday for you, is it.'

He smiled lazily, relaxing into her touch. 'Well, you keep doing that and I'll be just fine.'

'You got it,' she said, laughing.

An old truck rumbled by, raising dust in its wake, and he frowned, holding the expression long after the vehicle had disappeared. 'Beth,' he said at last, 'I know how much this means to you – and how much you believe in it – but what if …'

'If it's just another dead end?'

He looked at her with concern. 'Well, more than that. What if the whole thing turns out to be nothing more than a hoax?'

'No.'

'It's a possibility, Beth. You said yourself the old guy wasn't really with it that last day. Maybe he was confused? Maybe it's not really a journal at all. Maybe it was an idea for a film script?'

Beth shook her head. 'You've read it. Does it sound like a film script?'

'It could be.'

'But the photographs we found hidden inside the binding?' She held out the creased, sepia print – a portrait of a young Victorian woman, her face blurred against the brightness of the sky.

'I've seen it a thousand times, Beth. It's just an old photograph – not even a good one. A dime a dozen in any junk shop.'

'No, it's the one Mr Abrahams took that day on the hill. I'm sure it is. Look you can just see the edge of the pit wheel.'

'You can see *something*. It could be a branch, a stain on the film – who knows what – maybe even the tip of the photographer's thumb.'

'Well, what about the book?' She reached for her bag and took out the larger of the two volumes. 'Treasure Island. The first edition – published in 1883. Twice I read it to Jimmy. You can't imagine how much this book meant to him.' She opened the cover, tracing her fingers over the copper-plate inscription on the flyleaf. '*The story of a brave boy – for another brave boy.* Just as she mentions in the journal. Even the writing is the same.' She caught his look. 'Alright, I know that doesn't prove anything – certainly not that Jimmy was Mary Kelly's son, but what about the scar? Crescent shaped, right across his chest – exactly as it says in …'

'But didn't he tell you he got cut up while filming with Fairbanks?'

Beth sighed. 'Yes. But he never made a film with Fairbanks. You know that. We've checked and re-checked.'

'But that's just my point.' He reached for her hand. 'Isn't it possible he was just a confused old man – and this is all a wild goose chase?'

'I don't know, Richard. I just don't know.' She shook her head in despair. 'There's lots of it that doesn't add up, but … I wish you could have met him. There was something so special, so …' She turned away, looking out over the corn fields blurred by the afternoon heat. 'If only he'd lived just a little while longer – so I could have asked him.'

He reached across and took the second photograph from her lap, glancing briefly at the faces of the two elderly women who stood side by side, smiling into the lens, then flicked it over and read the simple inscription: Gwyneth. 1938. 'You *really* think this is a picture of the two of them?'

Beth continued staring out across the fields. 'I *know* it is.'

'Listen,' he said softly, brushing at her hair. 'I just want you to be prepared. I hate seeing you disappointed over and over again.'

'I know.' She smiled at him. 'If we don't find anything this time, then I'll give it up. I promise.'

*

The streets of the small, coastal town of Lewis were filled with summer visitors: cars jamming the roads, and the sidewalks crowded with people ranging from deeply tanned to lobster red.

'A world away from Whitechapel,' said Richard as they sat in the window of the coffee shop.

The waitress finished writing down their order. 'Anything else I can get you folks?'

'No, thank you,' said Beth.

The girl made to leave, but Richard called her back. 'Excuse me, miss,' he said, bringing out the black and white photograph. 'I wonder if you recognise anything in the background of this picture? A friend of ours thinks the church might be that old Swedish one.'

She peered closely at it. 'Gee, I don't know. It's awfully small. I guess it could be, but you'd really need to ask someone who lives here. I'm only down for the summer.' She shrugged apologetically, then flashed him a smile. 'I'll be right back with your coffee.'

Beth watched her go. 'Mary was never here,' she said, leaning heavily on the table. 'The place feels all wrong.'

'Oh, so you're turning psychic now?'

She gazed through the window, watching the passing tourists. 'Can you really see them coming to live here?'

'Sure I can. It's a great little place. I wouldn't mind living here myself. I could do a little fishing, maybe.'

'You know what I mean. In their day this would have been a backwater. Evan was used to living in London and Paris – he hated small town life.' She sighed. 'I'm beginning to think you might be right. Maybe it *is* all just a hoax. In all these years we've never found anything …'

He looked at her in surprise. 'Hey, now hold on. *I'm* supposed to be the sceptic on this team, remember? And anyway, what about the census records – they were all there, weren't they? The Llewellyns, The Rees-Morgans,' he gave a small laugh, 'and more than one or two Owen and Meg Davies'.'

'But not *our* Davies'. Not one single family with all the right names and ages – and what about Mary? Why isn't she and her family there either?'

He shrugged. 'Like the guy at the records office said, people get missed, or names get entered wrongly, it doesn't mean they didn't exist.'

'I don't know, Richard. It just doesn't make any sense.'

'Look, why not let someone take a look at the diary? Get some expert help. It wouldn't be cheap, but we could find the money.'

She shook her head. 'No. I've wasted enough of our savings on this already, and besides I couldn't. Jimmy kept this book a secret all his life – right up till a few hours before he passed away. He could have proved its authenticity and made a fortune from it, yet he died barely able to cover his hospital bills.'

'Maybe he gave it to you because he *wanted* you to publish it.'

'No. *Just for you*, he said. He trusted me, and I owe it to him to keep that trust.'

He felt for her hand, giving it a reassuring squeeze.

'Two coffees.' The girl placed the cups on the table. 'And two blueberry muffins. Enjoy.' She flashed them her carbon copy smile. 'Oh – and that photograph? I mentioned it to the guy who owns this place. He said you should talk to the old lady across the street because she's been here, like *forever.*

*

'I don't recognise the people, but that's Savannah Street, alright.' The old lady's hand trembled as she traced her finger over the photograph. 'Must be before the war because old man Murdoch had that shop on the corner pulled down around 1940 to put up a gas station.'

'It says 1938 on the back,' offered Beth.

'Yes, well, that would be about right.'

'I expect this place was a lot different back then?' smiled Richard.

She eyed him with gentle amusement. 'If you're expecting me to get all dewy-eyed about the good old days, you can forget it. Different? It surely was. It was dull as dishwater and twice as dirty! I'll take today every time, though I wouldn't mind being twenty again so I could enjoy it a little more.' She gave the photograph back. 'Sorry to be wiping the rosy tint from your glasses.'

Beth looked down at the faces in the picture. 'Do you remember there being a doctor here? A Dr Rees-Morgan?'

'Rees-Morgan?' She shook her head. 'You sure you don't mean Price? He was our doctor, right from when I was a kid.'

A thrill ran through Beth, and she glanced quickly at her husband. 'Price? Was he … that is … did he sound Welsh – or maybe English?'

'No.' The old woman laughed. 'His family was as Maryland as crab-cakes. My mamma told me they lived over by Pilot's Landing. Real poor folks – used to scratch a living in winter, and do odd jobs for the city folk who'd come down for the summer. His daddy died pretty early on, and his mother could barely keep a roof over their heads. People round here never could figure out how she found the money to send him off to study. But that was all before my time, of course. He was a good doctor, though. Saw us through a lot of bad times. He died back in the sixties. We've got a young man now, with a fancy office and shiny equipment, but it isn't the same …' She broke off, chuckling. 'What was I saying about not getting all dewy-eyed with nostalgia?'

Beth lowered the photograph. 'Are you sure you can't remember any-one else? Another doctor? Maybe earlier?'

'Well, I only go back as far as 1905, but no, I don't recall there being any other doctors in town back then. I'm sorry.'

'Well, thank you for your time.'

'Think nothing of it. It was nice talking to you folks. Wish I could have helped.'

Outside the sun was almost at its zenith, and the old woman remained in the shadow of the porch. 'It's going to be a hot one, alright,' she said, squinting out into the busy street. 'You'll forgive me if I say goodbye just here.'

'Of course.' Beth put out her hand. 'Goodbye, and thanks again.'

The old lady watched them descend the wooden steps and start across the road, raising her hand in response to Beth's final wave. 'Go safely,' she called after them, her voice lost in the roar of the traffic.

*

'Ruelon Smith. Inez Smith. Bradley Pope. Mary Davies ...' Richard paused. 'Mary Davies?' He looked more closely at the weathered headstone, then shook his head. 'False alarm. She was only two years old when she died.' He moved on, stepping carefully between the lines of graves. 'Another two Smiths. Annette Murphy. John Severn. Mary Ann Severn. Irena Badz. Peter Watts.' He looked up. 'That's it, Beth. The last one. They're not here.'

Standing a little way off, Beth looked about her in the gathering gloom. 'There are so many broken ones. What if it was one of these?'

He went to her, hunkering down by the broken stone she was studying and running his hand over the fragment of pitted granite. 'Then we'll never know. We've already looked at the ones they were able to salvage. If it was one of these ...' He left the sentence unfinished and raised his eyes to her. 'Are you ready to call it a day? I'll buy you dinner?'

'Sure,' she said without enthusiasm, continuing to stare at the jagged stump. 'You know, it must have been a huge tree to do so much damage.'

'Over a hundred feet, that old guy told me. Largest one in Lewis. Says they felt the shock of it way over on the other side of town.'

She looked again at the remains of the stone. 'This *could* be the one.'

'Come on, Beth. All that's left is the date. You're clutching at straws.'

'But it is the *right* date – if that really is a three on the end ...'

'Don't you think it's time we faced facts?' He picked absently at the grass sprouting around the base. 'I mean, even if they did come to America they might well have changed their names – and if they did that, then finding them becomes virtually impossible. We could be looking at their graves and never even know it. Besides, if they were living here in 1938, wouldn't that old lady have recognised them from the photograph?'

'She's old – and we are talking about over fifty years ago. And who knows, maybe they didn't actually *live* here. When I was a kid we spent every summer up at Lake Tahoe, but we didn't live there. Maybe they lived in Washington, or Delaware or even New York, and ...'

'And maybe they never left England, and what we have is a picture of some old girlfriends of Jimmy's who stopped here for half an hour to get a coffee and a doughnut, and to take a picture.' He tugged absently at the grass. 'I'm as disappointed as you are, Beth, but it's been *twenty years.*

Can't we give it up and get on with what's left of our lives? Have a vacation that doesn't involve trudging around one churchyard after another – or looking through reels of microfilm in some dusty old archive?'

Beth looked at him. 'Oh, Richard, I'm sorry. You've always been so supportive ... I should have realised ...' She turned away, close to tears. 'I've been selfish. And you're right, it *is* hopeless. A stupid, selfish, waste of time.'

'Beth?'

'I'll give it up. I promise ...'

'*Beth.*'

She turned back, anxiously twisting the wedding ring on her finger. 'I know I've promised before ... but this time I really mean it. Next year we'll go to Hawaii, just like you've always wanted ...' She broke off, staring down at him as he tore at the grass, tugging back the turf.

'Look, Beth! Oh, Jesus Christ, will you just look at this.'

She took a step forward, dropping down on to her knees, her lips moving silently as she read the words carved at the very base of the stone:

Ble'r ei di, fe af finnau – Where you go, I will go.

The Real Mary Kelly

Virtually nothing factual is known about Mary Jane Kelly. More than one hundred years after the 'Autumn of Terror', she remains an enigma. Even the fact of her death has a question mark over it – the mutilations making it impossible to identify the body, with only Joe Barnett's claim to recognise her by the eyes and the ear standing testimony to it being Mary at all.

The Seduction of Mary Kelly is a novel woven around the facts of the Ripper murders and the supposed facts of Mary's life. In some instances, situations have been given a different slant, and reported dialogue has been purposely altered, whilst retaining its essence, for who can ever remember exactly what was said days, or even weeks, after the event?

Certain locations have been invented: there is no coastal town of Lewis in Maryland, no Gloucester Gardens in Knightsbridge, no Cardigan Terrace in Bloomsbury, no Cutler Street in Cardiff, and no Welsh mining village called Nant-y-Pridd, though each has its real life counterpart.

Pendragon, the Cross Keys Hotel, the Princess Alice, and others are also fictional places. However, in all but one instance, the real names of areas, buildings, and people connected with the Ripper investigation have been used, as have the documented events of the murders – even when, as in the case of George Hutchinson's witness report, they seem too bizarre to be real.

The story you have just read is fiction – but there is no reason in the world why it might not also be very close to the truth.